Biographical Narratives

BABUR THE TIGER
OMAR, THE GREAT
TAMERLANE: The Life of Genghis Khan
CHARLEMAGNE: The Legend and the Man
THEODORA AND THE EMPEROR
SULEIMAN THE MAGNIFICENT
GENGHIS KHAN
THE CRUSADES
CYRUS THE GREAT
ALEXANDER OF MACEDON: The Journey to World's End

Novels

THE CURVED SABER
The Adventures of Khlit the Cossack (Short Stories)
CITIES AND MEN, KIRDY

Historical Narratives

CONSTANTINOPLE: Birth of an Empire
THE MARCH OF THE BARBARIANS
IRAN: Past and Present
THE MARCH OF MUSCOVY
A GARDEN TO THE EASTWARD
THE CRUSADES: Iron Men and Saints and The League of Islam
THE MARCH OF MOSCOW: From Clan to Empire
THE CITY AND THE MAN: Peter the Great

For Older Children

DURANDAL
WHITE FALCON
KIROV: THE LORD OF THE SAMURAI
GENGHIS KHAN AND THE MONGOL HORDE
CHIEF OF THE COSSACKS

BY HAROLD LAMB

Biographical Narratives

BABUR THE TIGER

CYRUS THE GREAT

HANNIBAL: *One Man Against Rome*

CHARLEMAGNE: *The Legend and the Man*

THEODORA AND THE EMPEROR

SULEIMAN THE MAGNIFICENT

GENGHIS KHAN

NUR MAHAL

OMAR KHAYYAM

ALEXANDER OF MACEDON: *The Journey to World's End*

Novel

THE CURVED SABER:
The Adventures of Khlit the Cossack (Short Stories)

A GARDEN TO THE EASTWARD

Historical Narratives

CONSTANTINOPLE: *Birth of an Empire*

NEW FOUND WORLD:
How North America Was Discovered and Explored

THE EARTH SHAKERS:
Tamerlane and the March of the Barbarians

THE CRUSADES: *Iron Men and Saints and the Flame of Islam*

THE MARCH OF MUSCOVY: *Ivan the Terrible*

THE CITY AND THE TSAR: *Peter the Great*

For Older Children

DURANDAL

WHITE FALCON

KIRDY: THE ROAD OUT OF THE WORLD

GENGHIS KHAN AND THE MONGOL HORDE

CHIEF OF THE COSSACKS

The Curved Saber

HAROLD LAMB

The

Curved Saber

THE ADVENTURES OF
KHLIT THE COSSACK

DOUBLEDAY & COMPANY, INC.

GARDEN CITY, NEW YORK

1964

CONTENTS

CONTENTS

ADVENTURE ONE

ALAMUT

IT WAS THE YEAR OF THE LION AT THE VERY END OF THE SIXTEENTH century when Khlit guided his horse into Astrakan. No sentries challenged him in the streets of Astrakan, for the Cossacks were masters here and no Cossack would dishonor himself by taking precautions against danger. There were many Mohammedans in the streets of Astrakan, but it was evening and the followers of Allah were repeating the last of their prayers, facing, as was the law, toward the city of Mecca.

Sitting his steppe pony carelessly, Khlit allowed the beast to take its own course. The night, in Midsummer, was warm and his heavy *svitza* was thrown back on his high shoulders. A woolen cap covered one side of his gray head, and his new pair of costly red Morocco boots were smudged with tar to show his contempt for appearances. Under his shaggy mustache a pipe glowed and by his side hung the strangely shaped saber which had earned the Cossack the name of "Khlit of the Curved Saber."

Khlit rode alone, as he had done since he left the Siech, where Cossack leaders had said that he was too old to march with the army of the Ukraine. He paid no attention to the sprawling, drunken figures of Cossacks that his horse stepped over in the street. Clouds of flies from fish houses, odorous along the river front, buzzed around him. Donkeys driven by naked Tatar urchins passed him in the shadows. Occasionally the glow from the open front of an Ispahan rug dealer's shop showed him cloaked Tatars who swaggered and swore at him.

Being weary Khlit paid no heed to these. A dusty armorer's shop under an archway promised a resting-place for the night, and here he dismounted. Pushing aside the rug that served as a door he cursed as he stumbled over the proprietor of the shop, a Syrian who was bowing a yellow face over a purple shawl in prayer.

"*Lailat el kadr,*" the Syrian muttered, casting a swift side glance at the tall Cossack.

Khlit did not know the words; but that night thousands of lips were repeating them—*lailat el kadr,* night of power. This was the night which was potent for the followers of the true faith, when the *dhinns* smiled upon Mohammed, and Marduk was hung by his heels in Babylon. It is so written in the book of Abulghazi, called by some Abulfarajii, historian of dynasties.

It was on such a night of power, say the annals of Abulghazi, that Hulagu Khan, nephew of Ghengis Khan and leader of the Golden Horde overcame the citadel of Alamut, the place of strange wickedness, by the river Shahrud, in the province of Rudbar. It was on that night the power of Hagen ben Sabbah was broken.

But the power of Hagen ben Sabbah was evil. Evil, says Abulghazi, is slow to die. The wickedness of Alamut lived, and around it clung the shadow of the power that had belonged to Hagen ben Sabbah— a power not of god or man—who was called by some sheik, by others the Old Man of the Mountain, and by himself the prophet of God.

It was also written in the book of Abulghazi that there was a prophecy that the waters of the Shahrud would be red with blood, and that the evil would be hunted through the hidden places of Alamut. A strange prophecy. And never had Khlit, the Cossack of the Curved Saber, shared in such a hunt. It was not of his own seeking—the hunt that disclosed the secret of Alamut. It was chance that made him a hunter, the chance that brought him to the shop of the Syrian armorer, seeking rest.

So it happened that Khlit saw the prophecy of Abulghazi, who was wise with an ancient wisdom, come to pass—saw the river stair flash with sword blades, and the banquet-place, and the treasure of Alamut under the paradise of the Shadna.

"*Lailat el kadr,*" chanted the Syrian, his eye on the curved blade of Khlit, "Allah is mighty and there is no god but he."

"Spawn of Islam," grunted Khlit who disliked prayer, "lift your bones and find for me a place to spend the night. And food."

The Cossack spoke in Tatar, with which language he was on familiar terms. The response was not slow in coming, although from an unexpected quarter. A cloaked figure rose from the shadows behind the one lamp which lighted the shop and confronted him. The cloak fell to the floor and disclosed a sturdy form clad in a fur-tipped tunic under which gleamed a coat of mail, heavy pantaloons, and a peaked helmet. A pair of slant, bloodshot eyes stared at Khlit from a round face.

Khlit recognized the newcomer as a Tatar warrior of rank, and noted that while the other was short, his shoulders were wide and arms long as his knees. Simultaneously Khlit's curved saber flashed into view, with the Tatar's scimiter.

As quickly, the Syrian merchant darted into a corner. Cossack and Tatar, enemies by instinct and choice, measured each other cautiously. Neither moved, waiting for the other to act. Khlit's pipe fell to the floor and he did not stoop to pick it up.

"Toctamish!"

It was a woman's voice, shrill and angry that broke the silence. Khlit did not shift his gaze. The Tatar scowled sullenly, and growled something beneath his breath.

"Toctamish! Fool watch dog! Is there no end to your quarreling? Do your fingers itch for a sword until you forget my orders?"

The curtains were pushed aside from a recess in the shop, and out of the corner of his eye Khlit saw a slender woman dart forward and seize the Tatar by his squat shoulders. Toctamish tried in vain to throw off the grip that pinned his arms to his side.

"One without understanding," the Tatar growled, "here is a dog of a Cossack who would rather slay than eat. This is the Khlit I told of, the one with the curved sword. Are you a child at play?"

"Nay, you are the child, Toctamish," shrilled the woman, "for you would fight when the Cossack would eat. He means no harm. Allah keep you further from the wine cask! Put up your sword. Have you forgotten you are man and I am mistress?"

To Khlit's amusement Toctamish, who whether by virtue of wine or his natural foolhardiness was eager to match swords, dropped his weapon to his side. Whereupon Khlit lowered his sword and confronted the woman.

Beside the square form of Toctamish, she looked scarcely bigger than a reed of the river. A pale-blue reed, with a flower-face of delicate olive. Above the blue garment which covered her from foot to throat, her black hair hung around a face which arrested Khlit's attention. Too narrow to be a Tatar, yet too dark for a Georgian, her head was poised gracefully on slender shoulders. Her mouth was small, and her cheeks tinted from olive to pink. The eyes were wide and dark. Under Khlit's gaze she scowled. Abruptly she stepped to his side and watched him with frank curiosity.

"Do you leave courtesy outside when you enter a dwelling, Cossack?" she demanded. "You come unbidden, with dirty boots, and you flourish your curved sword in front of Toctamish who would have killed you because he is crafty as a Kurdish *farsang*, and feared you. I do not fear you. You have a soiled coat and you carry a foul stick in your mouth."

Khlit grunted in distaste. He had small liking for women. This one was neither Tatar nor Circassian nor Georgian, yet she spoke fair Tatar.

"Devil take me," he said, "I had not come had I known you were here, oh, loud voiced one. I came for food and a place to sleep."

"You deserve neither," she retorted, following her own thoughts. "Is it true that you are Khlit, who fought with the Tatars of Tal Taulai Khan? Toctamish is the man of Kiragai Khan who follows the banners of Tal Taulai Khan and he has seen you before. It seems he does not like you. Yet you have gray hair."

The Cossack was not anxious to stay, yet he did not like to go, with Toctamish at his back. While he hesitated, the girl watched him, her lips curved in mockery.

"Is this the Wolf you told me of?" said she to Toctamish. "I do not think he is the one the Tatar fold fear. See, he blinks like an owl in the light. An old, gray owl."

Toctamish made no reply, eying Khlit sullenly. Khlit was fast recovering from his surprise at the daring of this woman, of a race he had not seen before, and very beautiful, who seemed without fear. The daughter of a chieftain, he meditated; surely she was one brought up among many slaves.

"Aye, daughter," he responded moodily. "Gray, and therefore forbidden to ride with the free Cossacks, my brothers of the Siech. Wherefore am I alone, and my sword at the service of one who asks it. I am no longer a Cossack of Cossacks but one alone."

"I have heard tales of you." The black-eyed woman stared at him boldly, head on one side. "Did you truly enter here in peace, seeking only food?"

"Aye," said Khlit.

"Wait, then," said she, "and the nameless one whose house this is will prepare it for you. Meanwhile, sheath the sword you are playing with. I shall not hurt you."

Motioning Toctamish to her side, the woman of the blue cloak withdrew into a corner of the curtained armorer's shop. The Cossack, who had keen eyes, noted that the Syrian was bending his black-capped head over a bowl of stew which he was stirring in another corner. No others, he decided, were in the shop.

Toctamish seemed to like his companion's words little. He muttered angrily, at which the girl retorted sharply. Khlit could not catch their words, but he guessed that an argument was taking place, at which the Tatar was faring ill. The argument seemed to be about himself. Also, he heard the name Berca repeated.

Although Khlit was not of a curious nature, the identity of the girl puzzled him. With the beauty of a high-priced slave, and the manner of a king's daughter, she went unveiled in a land where women covered their faces from men. Moreover she was young, being scarce eighteen, and of delicate stature.

Khlit bethought him, and it crossed his memory that he had heard of dark-haired and fair-skinned women of unsurpassed beauty whose land was at the far end of the Sea of Khozar, the inland, salt sea. They were Persians, of the province of Rudbar. Yet, fair as they were in the sight of men, none were bought as slaves. Berca, if that were her name, might well be one of these. If that was the case, what was she doing in Astrakan, alone save for one Tatar, who while he was a man of rank and courage, was not her equal?

II

The Cossack's meditation was interrupted by the girl, who motioned to the Syrian to set his stew before Khlit.

"Eat," she cried impatiently, pointing to the steaming bowl. "You are hungry, Father of Battles, and I would speak with you. A man speaks ill on an empty belly, although a woman needs not food nor wine to sharpen her wits. Eh, look at me and say, Father of Battles, is it not true I am beautiful, that men would die for me? It is given to few to look at me so closely."

She stepped near the Cossack, so the edge of her silk garment touched his shaggy face where he crouched over the bowl. Khlit sniffed, and with the odor of lamb stew he smelled, although he knew not its nature, the scent of rose leaves and aloes. He dipped his hand into the bowl and ate.

"Speak, Khlit, Cossack boor," shrilled the woman, shaking his shoulder impatiently, "and say whether it is in your mind I am beautiful. Other men are not slow to say that Berca of Rudbar and Kuhistan is shapely, and tinted as the rose."

Khlit's hand paused midway to his mouth.

"Toctamish has a handsome harlot," he said and swallowed.

The girl stepped back hastily.

"Clown!" she whispered softly. "Nameless one of a dog's breeding. You shall remember that word. It was in my mind to bid you come with me, and be companion to Toctamish——"

"Am I a man for a Tatar's wench?" Khlit was making rapid inroads into the stew.

"Nay, a boor of the steppe. Remember, your speech is not to be forgotten. I am a chief's daughter, with many horsemen."

Berca was watching the Cossack half-angrily, half-anxiously. Toctamish moved his bulk to the bowl, regarding the disappearing contents with regret.

"How can one man be courteous, Berca of Rudbar," he asked gruffly, "when the tribe is without breeding? It were better to cut the throat of this *caphar,* dog without faith, before he ate of our bread and salt."

"Nay, eat also of the food, Toctamish," said Berca, "and let me think."

The Tatar's brown face wrinkled in distaste.

"Am I to share bread with a *caphar?*" he snarled. "Truly, I promised to obey you, but not thus. Bid the Cossack be gone and I will eat. Otherwise he will be brother in arms, and his danger shall be my danger."

Berca stamped her slippered foot impatiently.

"Has Allah given me a donkey to follow me? Eat your share of the stew, Toctamish, and cease your braying. Is it not written in the Koran that the most disagreeable of voices is the voice of asses."

Toctamish remained sullenly silent. He was very hungry. Likewise, Khlit was an enemy of his blood.

"Eat, Flat-Face," chuckled Khlit, who was beginning to enjoy himself, "the stew is rarely made. But the bottom of the bowl is not far off."

The odor of the food tormented the Tatar. And Berca, for reason of her own, allowed him no chance to back away from the bowl. Finally, in desperation, he squatted opposite Khlit and dipped his hand into the stew.

"Remember the law, Flat-Face," guffawed Khlit, as the other ate greedily. "We have shared bread and salt together—I would give a hundred ducats for a mouthful of wine."

"It is not I who will forget, *caphar*," retorted Toctamish with dignity. Tugging at his girdle, he held out a small gourd. "Here is *arak*; drink heartily."

"Aye," said Khlit.

He had tasted the heady mares' milk of the Tatars before and he sucked his mustache appreciatively after the draft. Pulling pipe and tobacco from a pouch he proceeded to smoke.

"Observe," said Toctamish to Berca, to show that he was not softened by what had passed, "that the *caphar* dog is one who must have two weeds to live. He sucks the top of one and drinks the juice of the other."

"Still your tongue," said Berca sharply, "and let me think."

She had seated herself cross-legged by the bowl, and her bird-like glance strayed from Khlit to Toctamish. The Cossack, engrossed in his pipe, ignored her.

"Why did you name me a harlot?" she asked abruptly, a flush deepening the olive of her cheeks.

"Eh, I know not, Sparrow. Devil take it, a blind man would see you are not kin to Toctamish. He is not of your people. And there is no old woman at hand to keep you out of mischief. You have said you were a chief's daughter. If that is not a lie, then the chief is dead."

The girl's eyes widened, and Toctamish gaped.

"Have you a magician's sight, *caphar*?" she cried. "It is true that the sheik, my father is dead. But I did not tell you."

"Yet you are alone, Berca, across the Sea of Khozar, without attendants. A wise sheik will keep his girl at home, except when she is sent to be married. Is it not true that another sent you out of Rud-bar?"

Berca's dark eyes closed and she rested her chin quietly on her folded hands. One hand she thrust into the folds of her cloak at the throat and drew it out clasped around a small object which hung by a chain from her slender neck. Opening her fingers she disclosed a sapphire of splendid size and brilliancy, set in carved gold. The jewel was of value, and appeared to be from the work-shops of skilled jewelers of Tabriz. Khlit eyed it indifferently and waited.

"It is true that another sent me from Rudbar, Khlit," said Berca softly, "and it was to be married. The one who sent me sent also some slaves and an attendant. He swore that a certain chief, a khan of the Kallmarks had asked me for his wife, and I went, not desiring to stay in Rudbar after my father died."

"The Kallmarks?" Khlit frowned. "Why, you are a Persian, and the Kallmark Tatars make war on Persians as did their fathers. A marriage would be strange. Eh, who sent you?"

Berca lowered her voice further and glanced at the Persian armorer who was snoring in his corner.

"One it was who is better not named," she whispered. "He is neither sheik nor khan. Listen, Cossack. This is a jewel of rare value. It has no mate this side of Damascus. Would you like to own it?"

"Aye," said Khlit indifferently, "at what price?"

"Service."

"Do you want another Toctamish? Buy him in the streets of Astra-kan. Is a free Cossack to be bought?"

"Nay, Khlit," whispered Berca leaning close to him until her loose curls touched his eyes, "the service is for one who can use his sword. We heard in Tatary how you escaped from Tal Taulai Khan and his myriad horsemen. Men say that you are truly the father of battles. I have work for such a one. Listen! I was sent from Rudbar to Kiragai Khan, up the Sea of Khozar, and across the Jaick River, with one attendant and a box which the attendant said held jewels and gold bars for my dowry. I came to the court of Kiragai Khan——"

"Bah, Sparrow," Khlit yawned sleepily, "you are tiresome. I want sleep, not words. In the morning——"

"We will be gone from Astrakan." Berca held up the sapphire. "You must listen, Cossack. I told Kiragai Khan my mission, for there were no others to speak, and opened the box in the hands of the attendant. The jewels were poor pearls and no gold was in the box. Then Kiragai Khan, before whom I had unveiled my face, laughed and said that he had not sent for me. At first it came to my mind that it was because the jewels were worthless. But it was the truth."

"Aye," said Toctamish suddenly, "it was the truth."

"I went quickly from the country of Kiragai Khan, aided by Toctamish, who pitied me when others tried to sell me as a slave—of a race that are not slaves. At Astrakan we learned the whole truth, for here word came to us that the one who sent me in marriage had killed my father. I was sent to be out of the way, for it would not do to sell one of my blood as slave. Such is not the law. He who killed my father heeds no law, yet he is crafty."

"Then," inquired Khlit, "you would slay him? Give Toctamish a dagger and a dark night and it is done."

Berca shook her head scornfully.

"No dagger could come near this man," she said bitterly. "And he is beyond our reach. He has many thousand hidden daggers at his call. His empire is from Samarkand to Aleppo, and from Tatary to the Indian Sea. He is more feared than Tal Taulai Khan, of the Horde."

"Then he must be a great sheik," yawned Khlit.

"He is not a sheik," protested Berca, and her eyes widened. "And his stronghold is under the ground, not on it. Men say his power lies in his will to break all laws, for he has made his followers free from all law. What he wants, he takes from others. And he is glad when blood is shed. Do you know of him?"

"Aye," said Khlit, grinning, "the steppe fox."

"They call you the Wolf," pleaded Berca, "and I need your counsel and wisdom. This man I am seeking has a name no one makes a jest of—twice. He is called by some the arch prophet, by others the Old Man of the Mountain, and by others the *Shadna* of the Refik folk. He is the head of an empire that lays tribute on every city in Persia, Kurdistan, Khorassan, Syria and Anatolia. If Allah decreed that I should be his death I should be content."

"More likely dead," responded Khlit. "Truly, if these are not lies, your Old Man of the Mountain must be a good fighter and I would cross swords with him. Can you show him to me?"

"Aye, Khlit," said Berca eagerly, "if you come with me. There is the sapphire if you will come to Rudbar with me."

Khlit stretched his tall bulk lazily.

"One way is as good as the other to me, if there is fighting," he muttered sleepily. "Only talk not of rewards, for a Cossack takes his pay from the bodies of enemies. I will kill this Master of the Mountain for you. Let me sleep now, for your voice is shrill."

When Toctamish and Berca had left the shop of the armorer, the former to seek a shed outside, and the Persian girl to sleep in her recess, Khlit's snores matched those of the Syrian shopkeeper in volume. For a while only. Then it happened that the snores of the Syrian ceased.

Without disturbing Khlit who was stretched full length on the floor, the Syrian silently pushed past the hangings over the door. Once outside he broke into a trot, his slippers *pad-padding* the dark street. Nor did he soon slacken his pace.

III

Khlit and Toctamish did not make the best of bed-fellows. Berca, however, was careful to see that no serious quarrel broke out between the two. In a bark that went from Astrakan, the day after their meeting, to the south shore of the Sea of Khozar, the two warriors of different races occupied a small cupboard which adjoined the cabin of the sheik's daughter.

Khlit had embarked not altogether willingly. When the fumes of *arak* had cleared from his head the next morning, he had half-repented of his bargain. Curiosity to see the other side of the salt sea, which he had known as the Caspian, rather than the pleadings of Berca, finally brought him aboard the bark with his horse from which he refused to be separated.

The girl had bought their passage with the last of her pearls, and some gold of Toctamish's, and had remained in her cabin since, to which Toctamish brought food. The Cossack, after a survey of the small vessel which disclosed his fellow-voyagers as some few Syrian silk-merchants, with the Tatar crew, took possession of a nook in the high poop deck, and kept a keen lookout for the islands and other vessels they passed, and for *Bab-al-abuab*, the lofty gate of gates as the ship made its way southward. Toctamish, who had not set foot on a ship before, was very ill, to Khlit's silent satisfaction.

One day, when the wind was too high for comfort on deck, the

Cossack sought Toctamish in the cupboard where the latter lay, ill at ease on some skins.

"Hey, Flat-Face," Khlit greeted him, sitting opposite against the side of the dark recess, "you look as if the devil himself was chewing at your entrails. Can you speak as well as you grunt? I have a word for you. Where is the little Berca?"

"In her cabin, oh, dog without breeding," snarled the Tatar, who was less disposed to speak, even, than usual, "looking at silks of a Syrian robber. This sickness of the sea is a great sickness, for I am not accustomed."

"You will not die." Khlit stroked his saber thoughtfully across his boots. "Toctamish, gully-jackal, and dog of an unbelieving race, you have been a fool. Perhaps a greater one than I. How did it happen that you became the follower of the little Berca? Has she bewitched you with her smooth skin and dark eyes?"

"Nay, that is not so," Toctamish growled. "She has told you her story. It is true that Kiragai Khan, my master, did not know of her coming. Her attendant and slaves ran away and she felt great shame. Yet she did not lose courage. When her shame was the greatest she begged me to take her to Astrakan, saying that I should be head of her army. She did not say her army was beyond the Salt Sea. Then she made me promise to take her to her people. As you know, her tongue is golden."

"Aye," said Khlit. "Then you are even a greater fool than I had thought. Have you heard of this emperor she is taking us to?"

Toctamish rolled his eyes, and shook his head vaguely.

"His name is not known in our countries. Mongol Tatars say that their great-grandfathers who followed the banners of Hulagu Khan made war on one calling himself the Old Man of the Mountain and slew many thousands with much booty, beside burning the citadel of Alamut, which was his stronghold. They gave me a dagger which came from Alamut. It is a strange shape."

"If the power of the Old Man of the Mountain was broken in the time of Hulagu Khan," said Khlit idly, "how can it exist now? Have you the dagger?"

The Tatar motioned to his belt with a groan, and Khlit drew from it a long blade with heavy handle. The dagger was of tempered steel, curved like a tongue of fire. On it were inscribed some characters which were meaningless to Khlit. He balanced it curiously in his bony hand.

"I have seen the like, Flat-Face," he meditated idly. "It could strike a good blow. Hey, I remember where I have seen others like it. In the shop of the Syrian armorer, at Astrakan. Who brought you to the shop?"

"We came, dog of a Cossack. The Syrian bade us stay, charging nothing for our beds, only for food."

"Does he understand Tatar language?"

"Nay, Berca spoke with him in her own tongue."

"Aye. Did she speak with you of this Old Man of the Mountain?"

"Once. She said that her people had come under the power of the Old Man of the Mountain. Also that her home was near to Alamut." Toctamish hesitated. "One thing more she said."

"Well, God has given you a tongue to speak."

"She said that your curved sword was useless against him who is called the Old Man of the Mountain."

With this the Tatar rolled over in his skins and kept silence. Wearying of questioning him, Khlit rose and went to the door of Berca's cabin. Toctamish, he meditated, was not one who could invent answers to questions out of his own wit. Either he spoke the truth, or he had been carefully taught what to say. Khlit was half-satisfied that the girl's and the Tatar's story was true in all its details, strange as it seemed. Yet he was wise, with the wisdom of years, and certain things troubled him.

It was not customary for a Tatar of rank to follow the leadership of a woman. Also, it was not clear why Berca should have been so eager for the services of Khlit, the Wolf. Again, she had declared that the Old Man of the Mountain was not to be met with, yet, apparently, she sought him.

Pondering these things, Khlit tapped lightly on the door of the girl's cabin. There was no response and he listened. From within he could hear the quiet breathing of a person in sleep.

He had come to speak with Berca, and he was loath to turn back. Pushing open the door he was about to step inside, when he paused.

Full length on the floor lay Berca, on the blue cloak she always wore. Her black curls flowed over a silk pillow on which her head rested. Her eyes were closed and her face so white that Khlit wondered it had ever been pink.

What drew the Cossack's gaze were two objects on the floor beside her. Khlit saw, so close that some of the dark hairs were caught in them, two daggers sticking upright on either side of the girl's head. The daggers were curved, like a tongue of fire.

Khlit's glance, roaming quickly about the cabin, told him that no one else was there. Berca had not carried two weapons of such size. Another had placed them there. As he noticed the silk cushion, he remembered the Syrian silk-merchant who had been with Berca.

With a muttered curse of surprise, Khlit stepped forward, treading lightly in his heavy boots. Leaning over the girl he scanned her closely. Her breathing was quiet and regular, and her clothing undisturbed. Seeing that she was asleep, the Cossack turned his attention to the weapons.

Drawing the latter softly from the wood, he retreated to the door. Closing this, he climbed to the deck and scanned it for the Syrian merchant. Almost within reach he saw the one he sought, in a group of several ragged traders, squatting by the rail of the ship. No one noticed him, their black sheepskin hats bent together in earnest conversation.

With the daggers under his arm, Khlit swaggered over to the group, the men looking up silently at his approach.

"Hey, infidel dogs," he greeted them, "here is a pair of good daggers I found lying by the steps. Who owns them? Speak!"

His eye traveled swiftly over the brown faces. None of the group showed interest beyond a curl of the lips at his words. If he had expected the owner to claim his property, he was disappointed. The Syrians resumed their talk together.

"So be it," said Khlit loudly. "They are useless to me. Away with them."

Balancing the weapons, he hurled them along the deck. As he did so, he glanced at the traders. Their conversation was uninterrupted. Yet Khlit saw one of the group look hastily after the flying daggers. It was only a flash of white eyeballs in a lean face, but Khlit stared closer at the fellow, who avoided his eye.

Something in the man's face was familiar to the Cossack. Khlit searched his memory and smiled to himself. The man who had watched the fate of the daggers Khlit had seen in Astrakan. The man had changed his style of garments, but Khlit was reasonably sure that he was no other than the Syrian armorer who had offered his shop to Berca and Toctamish.

Fingering his sword, the Cossack hesitated. It was in his mind to ask at the sword's point what the other had been doing in Berca's cabin. Yet, if the fellow admitted he had left the daggers by the girl, and Khlit did not kill him, the Syrian would be free to work other mischief. And Khlit, careless as he was of life, could see no just reason for killing the Syrian. Better to let the man go, he thought, unaware that he was suspected, and watch.

As an afterthought, Khlit went to where the twisted daggers lay on the deck and threw them over the side.

IV

In the year of the lion, there was a drouth around the Sea of Khozar, and the salt fields of its south shore whitened in the sun. Where the caravan route from Samarkand to Bagdad crossed the salt fields, the watering-places were dry, all save a very few.

The sun was reflected in burning waves from the crusted salt, from which a rock cropped out occasionally, and the wind from the sea did not serve to cool the air. In the annals of Abulghazi, it is written that men and camels of the caravans thirsted in this year, the year in which the waters of Shahrud, by the citadel of Alamut, were to be red with blood.

At one of the few watering-places near the shore, Berca's party of three, with a pack-donkey came to a halt, at the same time that a caravan, coming from the east stopped to refresh the animals.

The Persian girl watched the Kurdish camel-drivers lead their beasts to kneel by the well silently. Khlit, beside her, gazed attentively, although with apparent indifference at the mixed throng of white-and-brown-robed traders with their escort of mounted Kurds. Many looked at Berca, who was heavily veiled, but kept their distance at sight of Khlit.

"It is written, *Abulfetah Harb Issa*, Father of Battles," spoke the girl softly, "that a man must be crafty and wise when peril is 'round his road; else is his labor vain, he follows a luck that flees. Truly there is no luck, for Allah has traced our lives in the divining sands, and we follow our paths as water follows its course. Are you as wise as the masters of evil, oh, Cossack?"

The words were mocking, and Khlit laughed.

"Little Sparrow," he said, "I have seen ever so much evil, and there was none that did not fade when a good sword was waved in front of it. Yet never have I followed a woman."

"You will not follow me much further, Cossack. I will leave you at the foothills to go among my people, the hillmen, where I shall be safe. You and Toctamish will go alone the rest of the way. My face is known to the people of Alamut, who suppose that I am dead or a slave. In time they shall see me, but not yet. Meanwhile it is my wish that you and Toctamish seek the citadel of Alamut, which lies a two-days' journey into the interior."

Khlit shaded his eyes with a lean hand and gazed inland. Above the plain of salt levels he could see a nest of barren foothills which surrounded mountains of great size and height.

"Where lies the path to this Alamut—" he had begun, when Berca shook his arm angrily.

"Not so loud, fool of the steppe! Do you think we are still by the Volga? We are already in the territory of the Old Man of the Mountain. Listen, to what I have already told Toctamish. Two days' travel to the south will bring you to the district of Rudbar. You will find yourself near the River Shahrud which flows from the mountains. There will be hillmen about who do not love the Old Man of the Mountain.

"So do not speak his name, until you come to a bend in the Shahrud where the river doubles on itself, so, like a twisted snake. Across the river will be a mountain of rock which will appear to be a dog kneeling, facing you. Remain there until armed men ride up and question you. Then say you are come to join the ranks of Sheik Halen ibn Shaddah, who is the Old Man of the Mountain."

Khlit shook his head and tapped his sword thoughtfully.

"Nay, little Berca," he said reproachfully, "you have told me lies. You said it was your wish to slay one who had slain your father. And because it was a just quarrel and I was hungry for sight of the world below the Salt Sea, I came to aid you. Are you one, oh, Sparrow, to fight alone against a powerful chief? Where are your men that you told Toctamish of. Devil take me, if I'll put my head in the stronghold of any sheik, as you call him."

Berca bent nearer, rising on tiptoe so her breath was warm in his ear.

"My men are hillmen who will not attack until they see an enemy flee. Also, they have seen men who opposed Halen ibn Shaddah set over a fire, with the skin of their feet torn off. The master of Alamut is all powerful here. Are you afraid, whom they call the Wolf?"

"Nay, little Sparrow, how should I be afraid of women's tales and a mysterious name? Tell me your plan, and I will consider it. How can this sheik be reached?"

"Halen ibn Shaddah is safe from the swords of his enemies. Yet there is a way to reach him, in Alamut. The time will come when you and Toctamish will find yourselves at the head of many swords. How can I tell you, who are a fool in our way of fighting, and know not Alamut, what is in my mind? I swear that soon Halen ibn Shaddah will be attacked. Do you believe my word?"

"Wherefore should I?"

Khlit tugged at his mustache moodily. He was accustomed to settle his quarrels alone, and he liked little to move in the dark. Yet the woman spoke as one having authority, and Toctamish believed in her blindly.

"If this Sheik Halen is powerful and crafty——"

"Still, I am a woman, and wronged by a great wrong. I was sent to offer myself unveiled to a man who had not sought me; and at the same time my father was murdered, so that the hillmen, of whom he was sheik, might come under the shadow of Alamut." The girl's voice was low, but the words trembled with passion and the dark eyes that peered at the Cossack over her veil were dry as with fever, and burning. "Halen ibn Shaddah shall pay for his evil; for he is cursed in the sight of Allah. Wicked—wicked beyond telling is Alamut and therefore cursed."

"Chirp shrilly, little Sparrow," laughed Khlit, "while your white throat is still unslit. This Sheik Halen has no love for you, for one of his men on the bark placed two daggers, one on each side of your black head. Devil take me, if I did not think you would never chirp again. It was the Syrian who took you in for so little pay at Astra-kan——"

"Fool! Stupid Cossack!" Berca's eyes suddenly swam with laughter, "did you think I was asleep when you tiptoed in like a bear treading nettles? Or that I did not see the dirty Syrian, who thought to catch me asleep? Look among the men of the caravan, and tell me if you see the Syrian?"

Cautiously, Khlit scanned the groups about the well. Among the Kurdish riders and Tatars who were brown with the dust of the desert trail from Samarkand, he recognized a bent figure in a long gray cloak and black *kollah*. As he watched the figure, it bent still further over a box of goods, and lifted some silks to view. It was the Syrian, without doubt. Khlit felt a thrill, as of one who is hunted and hears the cry of the chase. He stepped forward with an oath, when Berca's grasp tightened on his arm.

"That is a *fedavie* of Alamut," she whispered. "I saw the curved daggers, and they are the weapons of the Refik folk of Halen ibn Shaddah. He must have overheard us in his shop at Astrakan, and has followed to slay, as is the law of Alamut. Probably there are more of the *fedavie* among the men of the caravan."

"Then we must deal with the Syrian before he can speak to them," muttered Khlit, but again Berca tugged him back.

"Did I not say you were a fool among my people, oh, Wolf," she whispered. "Watch. The Syrian shall have his reward. Your folly is very great, yet I need a man who is blunt and brave and knows not my plans. It is written that none knows where his grave is dug, yet the Syrian's grave is here. Watch, and do not move."

Khlit waited. The *fedavie* had stooped over his box. One or two Kurds gathered to look at its contents. Among the group Khlit noticed Toctamish who had come up quietly. The Tatar pushed past the others, heedless of their muttered curses until he stood directly in front of the trader. The Syrian looked up, and, seeing Toctamish, was motionless.

Khlit saw the Kurds stare and draw back as if they sensed trouble. The Syrian, still watching Toctamish, rose with a swift, cat-like movement, his hand hidden in the silks. Toctamish grunted something and spat upon the silks.

"See," whispered Berca softly, "his grave is dug, and the nameless one sees it."

Toctamish thrust his yellow, scarred face near the Syrian's. Around him a crowd pressed, watching with attention. With a cry, the Syrian, who seemed to have found the suspense too much for him, drew a pistol from the silks in which it had been concealed.

Instantly two giant arms were flung 'round him. Toctamish was on him with a speed that baffled him, and the Tatar's huge bulk pressed the Syrian backward to the ground. Writhing impotently, the Syrian saw Toctamish draw a dagger from his girdle. And Khlit grunted as he noted that it was the one he had seen with blade like a curved flame. While he held the smaller man powerless with one arm, Toctamish lifted the dagger and thrust it carefully into his foe's body, into stomach and chest.

Then, rising, he wiped the curved dagger on a handful of the trader's silks. For a moment the arms and legs of the unhappy Syrian stirred on the ground. And Khlit saw a strange thing. For, before life had gone from the body, several men of the caravan, Khirghiz warriors by their dress, pushed through the throng with daggers like that of Toctamish and struck at the Syrian. Not until the body was still did they cease to strike.

Then the Khirghiz men looked around for Toctamish, but the stocky Tatar had disappeared in the throng. Khlit, who had missed nothing of what happened, thought to himself that it was well that the dagger had been in the hand of Toctamish, not of the Syrian. Plainly, he thought, the Khirghiz murderers had been fellows, without knowing, to the Syrian. And he wondered how men of many races came to be banded together, not knowing that he was to wonder soon, and very greatly, at other things.

V

Berca had disappeared; and when Khlit strode through the crowd of the caravan seeking her, his horse at his elbow, he met Toctamish. The Tatar was mounted and leading the pack-mule.

"Mount," he said gruffly, "and follow."

"And what of the girl?" queried Khlit, who was unwilling to take orders from Toctamish.

"She has told us to go on, as you know, *caphar*," snarled the Tatar, who disliked to talk. "Later, she will send word to us. Come."

"We are both fools. You, to be the slave of a painted girl, and I to seek for an empire which is not to be found, to slay a man who is hidden."

Khlit's words were silenced by a sudden uproar in the caravan. Men sprang to their feet and hauled at the camels who had kneeled in weariness. Traders who had been eating gave shouts of lamentation. Laden slaves ran together in confusion.

Toctamish stared at the uproar, until Khlit touched his shoulder.

"Look!" he said.

From the south, over the salt desert a cloud of dust was threading in and out among the rocks. It was advancing swiftly toward them, and the Cossack could see that it was made by mounted men riding very fast. He made out turbans and spearpoints in the dust. The horsemen were headed directly toward the caravan.

"Robbers," said Toctamish briefly; "there will be a fight."

"A poor one, it seems," growled Khlit. "The Kurds are leaving us as fast as their horses can take them and your countrymen like the looks of things little—they have not drawn sword or bow."

In truth, the Tatars who were acting as guard, sat their horses stolidly, while the dismayed traders added to the confusion by rushing about frantically, trying to assemble their goods. Khlit turned his attention in disgust to the oncoming horsemen, and counted a bare two score. In numbers, the caravan was three times as strong; yet no attempt at defense was made.

Instead the traders were anxiously spreading out their bales of goods, so that all were displayed. Camels and donkeys were stripped and their burden placed on the ground. In the meantime the horsemen who had come up were trampling recklessly through the confusion.

A fat Greek merchant held out an armful of rugs to one of the riders who stared at it insolently and pointed to the heavy packs behind the merchant. Other riders jerked out the contents of these packs, and ranged them in nine piles.

Khlit, watching them, saw that they were men of varied race. He guessed at Persian, Kurd, Circassian, Turk and others with whom he was not familiar—dark-skinned, and heavily-cloaked who sat their horses as a swallow rides the wind. Also, the Khirghiz men of the caravan had joined the newcomers.

The first rider flung some words at the Greek who was cowering on the ground and Khlit thought he caught the phrase "Alamut." Then the horsemen picked up three of the nine piles of goods, and flung them over pack-horses. Other riders who had been similarly occupied joined them. All the while the Tatar guardians of the caravan watched without interest, as men who had seen the like before.

It was not until the horsemen were well away over the salt plain that Khlit recovered from his astonishment at the sight of few robbing many.

"Better the mountain-folk than these," he growled, spitting in the direction of the merchants who were putting their goods away amid lamentations.

So it came to pass that a Cossack rode into the foothills of Rudbar where, in the words of the historian Abulghazi, none set foot who held Allah or Christ for their true God, and with him rode a Tatar who, under other circumstances would gladly have slain him.

They rode in silence, as rapidly as the pack animal could move, and by nightfall had gained the edge of the salt deposits that made that part of Persia like a frozen lake.

Each made camp after his fashion. And two fires were lighted instead of one. Khlit produced some barley cakes and wine and made a good meal. Toctamish took some raw meat from under his saddle where he had placed it for seasoning and washed it down with his favorite *arak*. Both kindled pipes and sat in silence in the darkness.

Toctamish's pipe went out first, and Khlit knew that the Tatar had swallowed the smoke until with the burning *arak* he had lost consciousness. The Cossack was soon asleep.

His sleep was unbroken, except that, near dawn, he thought he heard the trampling of many horses' feet, which sounded until the rays of the sun, slipping into his eyes, awoke him. He made out at some distance the track of a cavalcade in the dust, and considered that it might have been a caravan. Yet it was out of the path of caravans. Moreover, he was reasonably sure the track had not been there the night before. Toctamish, when wakened, yawned in bad spirits and told Khlit he was an old woman, of great fear and unmentionable descent.

When they resumed their path, it led upward through the foothills of Rudbar. A few date trees and some thorn bushes lined the way, but for the most part there was little foliage and many rocks. The grass, however, was good, and this was, perhaps, the reason why groups of horses were met with under the care of single, mounted horsemen who watched Khlit and his companion with curiosity.

They rode apart and silently, as before. Khlit's thoughts dwelt on Berca's last words. The girl had spoken as one having authority. She was no ordinary sheik's daughter, living out of sight of men, he thought. She was daring, and he wondered if she came from one of the hill-tribes where the women ride with men.

Berca had told him they were in the land of Halen ibn Shaddah, in the territory of the Refik folk, yet Khlit saw no signs of a town or city. He did see the tracks of multitudes of horses in the mountains where caravans were unknown. And the horses themselves puzzled him. For he could see nothing of their riders.

Toctamish, apparently, wasted no thought on his surroundings. He rode warily, but kept his thoughts to himself and pressed on-ward rapidly. Thus it was that the two came to a wide, shallow river, and followed the bank along a valley that seemed to sink further into the hills as they advanced.

Until sunset they rode, making detours to avoid waterfalls and fording the river where it curved—for it was very shallow—and then Khlit who was in the lead came to a halt as they rounded a bend.

"By the bones of Satan," he swore, "here is the place Berca told us of. Devil take me, if it does not look like a dog with his front paws in the river."

Like an arched bow the river curved, with the two riders standing at the end of the bow looking inward. Across from them rose a high point of rock, serried and overgrown with bushes, several hundred feet. No trees were on the summit of the rock. Instead, Khlit could make out masses of stones tumbling together and overgrown. A few pillars stood up through the débris.

Around the summit ran the semblance of a wall. So great was the waste of stone that it was hard to see any semblance of order in it, but Khlit judged that a citadel as big as a good-sized town had once crowned the dog-promontory. The rock jutted out to make the mas-sive head of the beast, and ridges suggested paws.

"Here is no Alamut, Toctamish," growled Khlit in disgust. "Truly, we are fools—the little sparrow, Berca, has made game of us."

"Wait, *caphar*," retorted Toctamish, dismounting. "She said we would find the dog sitting in the river, thus, and we have found it. We will wait here and see what happens."

"Well, we will wait," laughed Khlit, "and see if the dog will give birth to a tribe."

VI

Little Khlit suspected how true his chance word was to be. The sun had dropped behind the furthest mountain summit, and the night cold of the high elevation had wrapped around the two watchers when they saw a sight that made their blood stir.

The Cossack had stretched on the ground a little distance from Toctamish, who had subsided into snores. He watched the last light melt from the ruins on the summit of the cliff, and as he watched he thought he heard echoes from across the river, as from far off. Straining his ears, he could catch bursts of music and shouting. Remembering his experience with the horses the previous night, he wondered if the mountains were playing tricks with his ears.

The sounds would come in bursts as though a gate had been opened to let them out, followed by silence. Khlit was not at home in the hills, and he did not recognize the peculiar resonance of echoes. What he thought he heard were songs and shouts repeated from mouth to mouth, as by giants, in the heart of the rock opposite him.

Lighting his pipe and cursing himself for a dreaming fool, Khlit sat up and scanned the darkness over the river. As if to mock him, the burst of shouting became clearer. And then the skin moved along Khlit's back of its own accord and his jaw dropped. He shook his head angrily, to make sure he was still awake.

Out of the rock across the river a multitude of lights were flickering. The lights came toward him rapidly, and the shouting grew. There were torches, moving out on the river, and by their glare he could see a mass of moving men armed with spears and bows. Splashing through the water, they were fording the shallow river.

Khlit could see that they were men of varied race, turbaned and cloaked, armed for the most part with bow and arrows, much like those who had robbed the caravan. As the throng came nearer, he shook Toctamish and stood up.

"Loosen your sword, Father of Swine," he grunted, "here are men who are not triflers."

Several of the leaders, who had caught sight of the two, closed around them. The torchlight was thrown in their faces, and for a moment the shouting of the band was silenced as they surveyed Khlit and his companion. One, very lean and dark of face, dressed in a white coat bossed with gold, and wearing a tufted turban of the same colors, spoke in a tongue Khlit did not understand.

"Hey, brothers," swore Khlit genially, laughing, for the presence of danger pleased him, "have you any who speak like Christians? Khlit, called the Wolf, would speak with you."

After some delay, a dirty tribesman was thrust beside the man of white and gold.

"Wherefore are you here?" the tribesman, who seemed to be a Kurd, asked in broken Russian, "and what is your purpose? Be brief, for the *Dais* are impatient to march. Are you a Christian, Cossack?"

"Say that you are not," whispered Toctamish, who had caught what was said, "for none with a god can go into the mountain."

"A dog will give up his faith," snarled Khlit, "but a Cossack does not deny God and the Orthodox Church. Aye," he responded to the Kurd, "I am a Christian. I have come to Rudbar, or to Alamut, whatever you call the place, to seek him who is called the Old Man of the Mountain. What is your name and faith?"

A peculiar look of fear crossed the face of the Kurd.

"Seek you the Master of the Mountain, Sheik Halen ibn Shaddah, Cossack? My name is Iba Kabash, and I was once a Christian. What is your mission with the Lord of Alamut?"

"Tell the unbeliever we have come to join the Refik, where there is no law—" began Toctamish, but Khlit motioned him to silence.

"Take us to Sheik Halen ibn Shaddah, and we will tell him our mission, Iba Kabash," he retorted. "We are not men to parley with slaves."

The man of white and gold had grown impatient, and spoke a few angry words to Iba Kabash, who cringed. Several of the bowmen ranged themselves beside them, and the throng pushed past, leaving a single torch with the Kurd, who motioned to Khlit to follow him. Leaving their horses with an attendant, Khlit and Toctamish made their way after Iba Kabash to the river. The current was not overswift, and the water came barely to their knees.

"It is the wish of the *Dai*, Cossack, that you shall enter Alamut. What is your mission? Tell me and I shall be a true friend. I swear it. Surely you have a strong reason for your coming." The Kurd's greasy head was thrust close to the Cossack's. "Let me hear but a word."

"If the *Dai* named you guide, Iba Kabash, of the mangy beard, lead us, and talk not."

In his heart Khlit distrusted the offered friendship of the Kurd.
And he watched closely where they went, across the Shahrud, into
the shadows of the further bank. And he saw how it was the *Dai's*
followers had come from the mountain.

Concealed by the shadows, were grottoes, where the water had
eaten into the rock, grottoes which ran deep into the mountain.
The torch reflected from the dark surface of the water, as they
splashed forward, with the river becoming shallower. Presently they
stood on dry rock. Here they were in a cave, of which Khlit could
not see the top.

Iba Kabash pulled impatiently at his arm and they went forward,
and up. Khlit saw that now they were on rock which was the handiwork of man. They were ascending broad steps, each one a pace in
width, and so broad that the torch barely showed rows of stone
pillars on either side.

Khlit had counted fifty steps when Iba Kabash came to a halt,
grinning. Lifting the torch overhead, he pointed to a square stone, set
in the rocky roof of the stairs. On this rock were lines of writing
strange to Khlit, and blackened with age and the dampness of the
place.

"The gateway of Alamut, oh, Cossack," laughed the Kurd. "And
the writing of one who was as great as Mohammed, prophet of
Allah. And the message:

"With the help of God
The ruler of the world
Loosened the bands of the law,
Blessed be his name."

Khlit was silent. He had not expected to find himself in a cave in
the heart of a mountain. The darkness and damp, rising from the
river, chilled him. Glancing ahead, he saw a rocky passage, wide and
lofty. The passage had been made by the river, perhaps in a former
age, when it had risen to that level. But the hands of men had
widened it and smoothed the walls. Toctamish, he saw, was scru-
tinizing his surroundings, his slant eyes staring from a lined, yellow
face.

"Come," said Iba Kabash, who seemed to enjoy the silence of his
visitors, "this was not the gateway of Alamut always, in the days of

the first Master of the Mountain. And Alamut has changed. It has sunk into the mountain. Men say the old Alamut was destroyed."

"Aye," said Toctamish suddenly, "by Hulagu Khan."

The Kurd stared at him curiously.

"Come," he muttered, and led the way up the winding rock passage.

Khlit followed closely. Other passages joined the one they were in. At times, sounds came down these passages—distant rumblings, and strains of music. Occasionally a figure armed with a spear stepped from them and scanned the group. Always a wind whipped around them, cold, in spite of the heat of the air outside.

After a time, Khlit saw that they were no longer in the passage. The torch did not reveal walls, and the footing was regular, of stone slabs. They had entered a chamber of some kind. Other torches made their appearance suddenly. The sound of voices came to them clearly.

They approached a fire around which lay several armed men. Khlit guessed from their dress that they were Khirghiz men; furthermore, that they appeared drunk. Only one or two looked up, without interest. Iba Kabash led them past many fires and men until they came to narrow stone stairs which led away from the rock chambers. Here, a giant Turk spoke with Iba Kabash before letting them pass.

"We will speak with Rashideddin," whispered the Kurd, "the astrologer of Halen ibn Shaddah. Tell me now your mission? I can help you."

Toctamish would have spoken, fingering a money pouch at his belt on which the Kurd's gaze fastened greedily, but Khlit shook his head. With a sneer, their guide stepped on the stairway. Khlit climbed after him, and noted that the stairs wound up still further. He guessed that they had ascended several hundred feet since leaving the bed of the river.

Then, leaving the stair, he found himself in a round chamber, hung with tapestries and rugs of great beauty. Several oil lamps, suspended from the ceiling lighted the place. A warm breath of air caused him to look up. A circular opening formed the center of the ceiling, and through this he could see the stars and the velvet vault of the sky.

Two of the dark-faced men, strange to Khlit, like the *Dai* of white and gold, stood by the wall, wearing mail and resting on spears. A small ebony table was loaded with parchments and instruments which the Cossack had never seen before. In the center of the floor was a chessboard, and sitting on either side of the chessboard were two men.

One, Khlit recognized by his tufted turban and brilliant white coat, to be of the kind Iba Kabash had called *Dai*. The other wore a close-fitting skullcap and a gray cloak without a sash. He looked at Khlit and the latter saw a lean face, gray, almost as the cloak, with close-set black eyes, and a loose-lipped mouth, very pale.

"Oh, Rashideddin," said Iba Kabash, "here are the two who have just come, of whom I have sent word. The Cossack is a Christian and insolent. The other is altogether a fool."

VII

Rashideddin is mentioned in the annals of Abulghazi as a savant of the *khalifate* of Bagdad and Damascus. He was a Persian, trained in the arts of astrology and divination, who could recite from memory the works of Jelaleddin Rumi. He was acquainted with many languages including Russian and Tatar. It is believed that he possessed all the works of the Alamut library which escaped the destructive hands of Hulagu Khan.

Inscrutable, and gifted, Rashideddin made a mockery of the Koran. He kept his truly great wisdom to himself, except for certain poems which he sent to princes of Persia and Arabia, who gained no happiness thereby. So it was not strange that Rashideddin, the savant of dark knowledge came to a place of evil, of strange and very potent evil. So say the annals of Abulghazi.

Rashideddin did not look at his visitors. He lifted a piece with care and replaced it on the chessboard. The *Dai*, who Khlit observed, was drunk, as were the men around the fires, yet very pale, did likewise. Khlit, who had small liking for chess, watched the players rather than the board. Especially did he watch Rashideddin. The pale-lipped astrologer sat with half-closed eyes, intent and motionless. The gray cloak seemed not to move with his breathing. When he spoke, his deep and musical voice startled them.

"Have you a god, Cossack? Is your faith firm in the Christian cross you wear around your neck?"

Startled, Khlit moved his hand to his throat, where hung a small, gold cross. Iba Kabash was making hasty signs to him which he did not see.

"Aye, Rashideddin," said he gravely, "the *batko* has told me about the cross which I carry, and it is a talisman against evil. Hey, it has been good, that cross, because I have killed many and am still living."

"Evil?" said Rashideddin, and moved a jeweled chessman to another square. "The earth is evil. If a saint handles earth it becomes gold. Yet who has seen a saint? Do you seek to bring your cross into Alamut?"

"Not so, Rashideddin," vouchsafed Khlit, crossing his arms. "I bring a sword to Alamut, to Halen ibn Shaddah. The cross is my own. If you can see it through my *svitza* then you must have good eyes. I am outcast from my people of the Ukraine, and men told me there was work for swords with Halen ibn Shaddah."

"And you call yourself Khlit, the Wolf?" queried the astrologer. "How did you find the gate of Alamut?"

Khlit was bewildered at the astrologer's knowledge of his name until he remembered that he had told it to Iba Kabash.

"Aye. There was a caravan by the Sea of Khozar that a band from Alamut robbed. We," Khlit bethought him swiftly, "followed the riders to the mountains and waited by the gate."

Rashideddin considered the chessboard silently.

"You came over the Sea of Khozar," he murmured, "from Astrakan? That must have been the way. There is another way around by land that the caravans take. They are our prey. What the Kallmark Tatars leave the merchants, we share. Did you see a Syrian armorer in Astrakan?"

"Aye, a bearded fellow. We stayed at his house. He told us we might find use for our swords with Halen ibn Shaddah."

With a delicate movement, Rashideddin lifted one of his opponent's pieces from the board.

"And your companion?" he said.

"A Tatar horseman who has quarreled with his kin," spoke up Toctamish bluntly. "I'm tired of laws, noble sir, and I——"

"Laws are too complex, Tatar. If a man has an enemy, slay him. If a man desires a certain thing, take it. Are not these the only laws? In Alamut you are free from all laws except those of the *Refik*. You have an image of Natagai in your girdle, Tatar." Rashideddin had not looked at Toctamish since the first moment. "Take it and throw it on the floor."

Toctamish hesitated. He glanced irresolutely at Khlit; then drew out a small cloth figure, painted like a doll and tossed it on the stones. The Cossack saw that it was ragged and worn by much use. He had not suspected that his companion cherished any holy image.

"Spit on it," directed Rashideddin softly.

With a muttered curse Toctamish did so. His lined face was damp with perspiration, and Khlit saw that his hands were trembling. The shifting eyes of Iba Kabash gleamed mockingly.

"The armorer at Astrakan must have told you that Alamut is no place for one who has a god," went on Rashideddin. "There is one here who is greater than Mohammed. We are his servants. Yet our *akd* says that none go forth who are not of us. Think, Khlit, and decide. Meanwhile——"

The astrologer spoke to Iba Kabash in another tongue and the Kurd went to a corner of the room where a pile of rugs and cloths lay. Selecting a long, white cloth, he laid it in front of Khlit. This done, he stepped back, licking his thick lips softly.

"Tell the Cossack what you have done, Iba Kabash," said Rashideddin.

"This cloth," whispered the Kurd, "is a shroud, Khlit. The astrologer may call his men and lay you in it dead, unless you say you have no god. Do as your friend—remember I have given you good advice. You are in a place where your life is worth no more than a dagger-thrust. Your sword will be useless."

With a beating heart, Khlit glanced around the chamber. The two mailed Tatars were watching him silently. He thought he could see the dim forms of other men in recesses in the wall. And for all Rashideddin's unconcern, he felt that the astrologer was alive to every move he made. He felt as he had once when the Krim Tatars had bound his limbs, leaving him powerless.

"Aye," he said.

Without looking at Rashideddin, he moved to the pile of cloths and selected another shroud. This he brought back and placed beside the other. Iba Kabash watched him with staring eyes. The *Dai* frowned and fingered a dagger at his girdle. Khlit drew his curved sword and stood over the white cloths.

"Tell Rashideddin, Iba Kabash," he said, "what this other shroud is for."

"What—how do you mean?" muttered the Kurd.

"It is for the man who first tries to kill me, dog," snarled Khlit.

The astrologer bent over the chessboard impassively. Apparently he was blind to what passed in the room and to the words of Iba Kabash. The others watched him, and there was silence. Until Rashideddin raised his head suddenly and compressed his pale lips.

"You fool," he smiled, "blunderer of the steppes! This is not Russia. Here there is one law, and punishment; murder! See!"

He pointed a white hand at one of the mailed Tatars. The man started forward, and drew back shivering.

"Kill thyself, fellow," said Rashideddin quietly.

The Tatar stared at him and cast a helpless glance around the room. Khlit saw his right hand go to his girdle and tremble convulsively.

"*Fedavie!*" the astrologer's voice was gentle, "show the Russian our law. By the oath of the *Refik*, kill thyself!"

With a grunt of sheer terror the man dropped his spear. His right hand rose from the girdle, gripping a dagger curved like a flame, rose, and sank it into his throat. With the hilt of the dagger wedged under his chin, the Tatar sagged to the floor, quivered and was still. One bloodstained hand had fallen among the chessmen.

There was silence in the room for a moment, broken by Toctamish. The Tatar stepped to Khlit's side.

"You and I are brothers, Cossack," he growled, "and your danger is my danger."

Rashideddin, who had given a sigh of pleasure at the death of the attendant, studied the disordered chessmen impassively. The *Dai* sprang to his feet with an oath. For several heart-beats no one moved. Iba Kabash stared in fascination at a red pool which had formed under the dead Tatar's head.

VIII

The astrologer, apparently giving up as hopeless the attempt to replace the chessmen, stood up. And Khlit, who was watching, wondered at his figure. The man was bent so that his back was in the form of a bow. His head stuck forward, pale as a fish's belly, topped by the red skullcap. His gray cloak came to the ground. Yet when he moved, it was with a soft quickness.

"You see," he said, as if nothing had happened, "the oath of Alamut—obedience, and——"

He stirred the shroud contemptuously with his foot. Then, as if arriving at a decision, he turned to Iba Kabash.

"Take these clowns to the banquet-place, and give them food. See that they are not harmed."

With that he motioned to the *Dai* and retreated through one of the recesses. Toctamish wiped his brow on which the perspiration had gathered and touched the dead man with his foot.

"The good Rashideddin will not kill you," chanted the Kurd eagerly. "It must be a miracle, for you are both fools. You have me to thank for your safety. I have given good advice, have I not?"

Toctamish eyed him dubiously. He did not feel oversure of safety. Khlit, however, whispered to him. Rashideddin was not the man to play with them if he desired their death. It might be that the astrologer's words were in good faith—Khlit learned later that the latter never troubled to lie—and if so they would gain nothing and lose much by staying where they were.

So it happened that both warriors sheathed their swords with apparent good grace and followed Iba Kabash who led them through empty rooms until they came out on a balcony overlooking the banquet-place of Alamut. And Khlit was little prepared for what he saw now.

The warm wind touched their faces again. Iba Kabash pointed up. In the center of the lofty ceiling of the place a square opening let in the starlight. A crescent moon added to the light which threw a silver sheen over the great floor of the hall. Toctamish grunted in surprise.

At first it seemed as if they were looking on the camp of an army from a hillside. Dozens of fires smoldered on the floor below them, and a hundred oil lamps sprinkled the intervening space. About the lamps men were lying, around small tables on which fruit, wine and dishes massed. A buzz of voices echoed down the hall, and Khlit was reminded of bees stirring about the surface of a hive.

The sound of eating and drinking drowned the noise of voices. Along the stone balcony where they stood other tables were placed with lamps. Numerous dark figures carried food and drink to these and carried away the refuse left at other tables.

"Slaves," said the Kurd, "captives of the *Refik*. Let us find a table and eat. It is a lucky night that I met you, for I shall go into the paradise of Alamut."

Khlit paid little attention to the last phrase. Later, he was to remember it. Being very hungry he sat down with Toctamish at a convenient table and took some of the bread and roasted meat which he found there. Toctamish was less restrained, and gulped down everything with zest.

As he ate Khlit considered his companions, and the banquet-place. All of them, he noticed, seemed drowsy, as if drunk, or very gay. In the lamplight their faces showed white. They lay in heaps about the tables, sometimes one on the other.

To the Cossack drunkenness was no sin, yet there was something about the white faces and limp figures of the men that stirred his blood. And the smell of the place was unpleasant, a damp, musky odor seemed to rise from the hall under them, as of beasts. Piles of fruit lay rotting about the floor.

"It is time," chattered the Kurd, who was sipping at a goblet of wine, "Halen ibn Shaddah showed himself. He comes to the banquet-place every night, and we drink to him. Drink, Khlit—are not Cossacks born with a grape in their mouths? You are lucky to be alive, for Rashideddin is a viper without mercy."

"Who is this Rashideddin?" asked Khlit, setting down the wine, for it was not to his liking.

"Oh, he is the wise man of the arch-prophet—the master of Alamut. He knows more magic than all the Greeks and dervishes put together. He reads the stars, and tells our master when it is time to send out expeditions. They say he has servants in every city of the world. But I think he learns everything from the magic sands." Iba Kabash's tongue was outstripping his wit. "There is nothing that goes on in Persia and Tatary that he does not see. How did he know you wore a cross?"

"He saw the chain at my neck, fool," retorted Khlit.

He began to feel strangely elated. He had had only a little wine, but his head was whirling and he had a curious languor in his limbs. The trouble extended to his eyes, for as he looked at the banquet-place, it seemed to have grown wider and lighter. He could see that Toctamish was half-unconscious.

Thus it was that Khlit, the Wolf, in the banquet-place of Alamut came under the influence of the strange evil that gripped the place. And came to know of the great wickedness, which set Alamut apart from the world, as with a curse.

Khlit, turning the situation over in his mind, saw that it was best to play the part he had taken on himself. He doubted if it were possible to escape past the guards by the river stairway, even if he could free himself from the guardianship of Iba Kabash. Rashideddin, he felt, had not left his visitors unwatched. Also, he was curious to see further of the strange world of Alamut, which was a riddle of which he had not found the key. He had seen a Tatar kill himself at a word from the astrologer, and Iba Kabash who was a man without honor, speak with awe of the master of Alamut. Who was Halen ibn Shaddah? And what was his power over the men of Alamut?

As it happened, it was not long before Khlit saw the man he was seeking, and whom he was sworn to kill. There came a pause in the murmur of talk and Iba Kabash clutched his shoulder.

"Look!" he whispered. "Here is Sheik Halen ibn Shaddah, who will choose those to go into paradise tonight. You are newcomers in Alamut and he may choose you, whereon I shall follow behind without being seen. Pray that his eye may fall on us, for few go to paradise."

Across the banquet-place, on the stone balcony, Khlit saw a group of torches. The bearers were *Dais*. In the center of the torches stood a tall man, dressed as the *Dais* except that he wore no turban, a cloak covering his head, drawn down so that nothing could be seen of his face. The sheik's shoulders were very broad and the hands that rested on his girdle were heavy.

As Khlit watched, Halen ibn Shaddah moved along the balcony among the eaters. On the banquet floor a murmur grew into a shout—

"Blessed be he that has unmade all laws; who is master of the *akd*; chief of chiefs, prophet of prophets, sheik of sheiks; who holds the keys of the gate of paradise."

Iba Kabash shouted as if in ecstasy, rising on his knees and beating his palms together, as the group of the sheik came nearer them. Once or twice Khlit saw Halen ibn Shaddah beckon to a man who rose hastily and followed the *Dais*. Iba Kabash, he thought, was drunk, yet not in a fashion known to Cossacks. Khlit himself felt drowsy, although clear in mind. He saw that the noise had wakened Toctamish who was swaying on his haunches and muttering.

Halen ibn Shaddah stood over them, and Khlit thought that one of the *Dais* whispered to him. The Cossack had fastened his gaze greedily on the cloaked face, for he wished to see the face of the master of Alamut. He could make out only a round, dark countenance, and eyes that showed much white. Vaguely he remembered that he had seen others who had faces like that, but he could not think who they were. The sight of Halen ibn Shaddah affected him like the foul smell of the banquet-place and the rat-eyes of Iba Kabash. Halen ibn Shaddah beckoned to him and Toctamish.

Khlit supported his companion to his feet, but found that the wine had taken away all his own strength. Hands belonging, he suspected, to slaves, helped him after the white figures of the *Dais*. They passed from the banquet-place through passages that he could see only dimly. The torchlight vanished, and there came a silence, which was broken by music, very sweet. Khlit's head was swimming strangely, and he felt himself moving forward through darkness. Darkness in which the music echoed, being repeated softly as he had heard the voices repeated when they first came into the passages of Alamut.

IX

If it was a dream, Khlit asked himself, why should he be able to taste the red wine that trinkled down his throat? Yet if it were not a dream, why should a torrent of the red wine issue from a rock? And sunlight burn on the red current, when Khlit was in the passages of Alamut, under the ground?

Truly, it must be a dream, he thought. It seemed that he was lying on his side near the flowing wine, with the sun warm on his face. Whenever he wanted to drink, he did not need to sit up, for he raised his hand and a girl with flowers around her head and breast came, and filled some vessel which she held out to him. Khlit was very thirsty and the wine was good.

The girl, he felt, sat by him, and her finger-nails and the soles of her bare feet were red. He had never seen such a maiden, for her hair also was red, and the sun glinted through it as she drew it across his face. Her hair must be perfumed, he thought, like the harlots of Samarkand, for it smelled very good.

The music came to his ears from time to time, and he snorted, for Khlit was no lover of soft sounds. Neither did he fully relish the wine, which was oversweet. He was well content to be in the sun, and too drowsy to wonder how it happened.

The dream, if it was that, changed, and Khlit was in a boat lying on some rugs. The boat was drifting along a canal. From time to time it would pass under a porcelain *kiosk*, tasselled and inlaid with ivory. From these *kiosks* girls laughed down at him and threw flowers. One of the tinted faces was like Berca's, and Khlit thought then it was surely a dream.

One other thing he remembered. It was in a grove of date trees where young boys ran, shouting, and pelted each other with fruit. In spite of the warmth and pleasantness, Khlit felt very tired. He was in the shade of one of the date trees with his sword across his knees. The music was very faint here, for which he was glad. He seemed very wakeful. The air was clear, and looking up he could see the sky, between jagged walls of stone. He had seen other walls of stone like these. That was when he and Toctamish had stood at the Shahrud looking up at the dog rock that was Alamut.

Even in the dream, Khlit felt ill. He saw the damsel of the red hair and flowers and beckoned to her, for he was thirsty. She ran away, probably at the sight of his sword. Khlit felt angry, for she had given him drink for what seemed many years.

Then he saw the gray-cloaked figure of Rashideddin, the astrologer of Alamut, beside him, and the white face stared at him until Khlit fidgeted. He heard Rashideddin speak, very faintly.

"Where art thou?"

Khlit was too tired to answer at first.

"I know not," he said finally.

"Thou art in paradise, and by favor of Halen ibn Shaddah. Do not forget."

Truly, Khlit had not forgotten. There were other things he remembered. Vistas of blue pools where dark-skinned men bathed, and date groves where bright-colored birds walked, dragging their tails on the ground. He saw girls pass, hand in hand, singing. And the music did not cease.

If it had been a dream, Khlit said to himself, how could the taste of the strange wine stick to his palate? Or the warmth of the sun be still burning on his skin? Nay, surely it must have been a dream. And the waking was disagreeable.

The place where he found himself on waking was dark, wet and smelled strongly of wine dregs. Khlit rose to his knees cautiously and felt about him with his hand. He could feel the outline of something round and moist on all sides except overhead. Also he came upon the body of a man lying by him, which he identified by its fur tunic and peaked helmet as Toctamish. The Tatar was snoring heavily.

"Wake, Flat-Face and son of an unclean animal," he growled, shaking him. "We are no longer in paradise. Devil take me, if it ain't a wine cask."

Toctamish roused at length and sat up reluctantly.

"Is it you, *caphar?*" he asked, stretching himself. "Many times have I been drunk as an ox, but never such as this. May the devil bite me, if there was ever such wine! Let us find some more."

"Then you have been dreaming, also," meditated Khlit. "Did you imagine that you saw Berca?"

"Berca? Nay, but she said that she would visit us here. That was no dream, *caphar*, for there was sunlight, and much feasting. Did Rashideddin tell you it was paradise? I met other Tatars there. They told me what it was."

"Were they also men who dishonored their god at Rashideddin's bidding? What said they concerning this paradise of yours?"

Toctamish snarled in anger, at the memory of the scene by the chessboard.

"You are one without brains, Cossack, and it is well that we are here alive. My companions said this: that all who came to Alamut were admitted to the paradise by Halen ibn Shaddah, if they were worthy. Then, if they were killed in the ranks of the *Refik* their souls returned to the paradise. That was a lie, for how can there be a soul in a man?"

Khlit said nothing. But he thought that he had found the key to the riddle. Halen ibn Shaddah's power lay in the lusts of his men. They looked on him, even so shrewd a man as Iba Kabash, as one who held the secret of paradise. And, although he did not know it, Khlit's thought had come near to the evil of Alamut, which was a plague spot on the face of the world.

X

In the next few days the two warriors, bound together by mutual
interest, although cordially hating each other, made frequent ex-
plorations of the chambers of Alamut. In the daytime sunlight filtered in at the banquet-place, the round chamber of Rashideddin
and other places, but at night the only light was from lamps or
torches. The chambers were large enough to hold a hundred men
in each and there were many. Khlit, who had keen eyes, learned
several things, including the place of the *Refik* treasure.

First, a certain area was guarded against intrusion by picked Tatars and Arabs. Into the guarded chambers he had seen *Dais* and
other higher dignitaries called *Dailkebirs* go, and he guessed they
were occupied by Halen ibn Shaddah and his court, where was
kept the gold that flowed into Alamut as tribute money.

Also, there was no exit from the chambers of Alamut save by way
of the stairway and the river, which was guarded. Frequently armed
bands went in and out, also messengers of many races, but all were
closely watched. Moreover, few except old residents of the place, like
Iba Kabash, the Kurd, knew the way to the river stairway.

The slaves, he learned, brought food not from the river stairway,
but another source. Also wood for the fires. The warriors of Alamut,
fedavie, as they were called, lived as they chose, under the eyes of
the *Dais,* ornamenting their quarters with spoil taken in raids or
from caravans. Each man was richly decked in whatever suited his
fancy, of silks or jewels. The *Dais* who commanded them took interest in them only when it was time to take an expedition out of
Alamut.

So much Khlit saw, and more he learned from the talkative Iba
Kabash, who had won some gold at dice from Toctamish, and was
inclined to be friendly. The slaves, he said, brought the food from
the side of Alamut away from the river, where they drew it up in
baskets to the summit of a wall that barred all egress from the citadel.

Iba Kabash had not been beyond the walls of Alamut since his
entry. Yet he had heard much of the empire of the *Refik* that
stretched its power from Samarkand to Aleppo and from Astrakan
to Basra. The murderers of the *Refik* were feared so greatly, he explained, that tribute was paid by the cities to Alamut. Questioned

by Khlit, he admitted that in numbers any of the califates were superior to Alamut. The power of Halen ibn Shaddah lay in the daggers of his men. No enemy escaped assassination once he was marked. And many were marked.

"Then there is no way to leave save by the river stair?" asked Khlit, who had listened attentively.

Iba Kabash stared and shook his head.

"Where is the fool who would escape, Khlit?" he responded. "Thrice lucky are we who are here. There was a calif who marched against us with horsemen from Irak. We rained down stones and baked clay on his men; then sallied forth, and the Shadrud was red with blood."

"Aye," said Toctamish sullenly. "There are no better fighters than those of Irak. Remember Hulaga Khan and his horsemen."

"Nay, I knew them not."

Iba Kabash glanced at the Tatar curiously, and Khlit laughed to distract his mind, for he did not trust the Kurd.

"There was another who opposed us," continued Iba Kabash. "That was a sheik of the hillmen in the mountains around Alamut. Him we killed by tearing out his belly and bowels. He had a daughter, who was a spit-fire. Rashideddin dealt with her."

"How?" asked Khlit carelessly, recognizing the description as Berca.

"Cleverly, very cleverly," chuckled the Kurd, rubbing his hands together. "He had Halen ibn Shaddah order her off to marry some Tatar chief who knew her not. It was when she had gone that we slew the old chief slowly, and scattered his tribe."

"Truly a shrewd trick." Khlit gave Toctamish a warning blow in the ribs that made the stocky warrior grunt. "How fared the chief's daughter at the hands of the Tatar? Your knowledge is greater than that of others, Iba Kabash. Can you tell me that?"

"Nay, that is a hard one," laughed the Kurd. "I have heard, from a slave that the chief's daughter, Berca, was seen in Astrakan. Also that she was taken as a slave by some caravan not far from here. I know not."

"Was the one who told you a slave in Alamut?" demanded Toctamish, who was becoming restive.

"Where else, offspring of a donkey?" muttered Iba Kabash. "I suppose you will also ask how he came to hear of the girl."

"Nay," interrupted Khlit. "Toctamish wondered at the power of Alamut. He is a clown. You and I, Iba Kabash, are men of wisdom."

So it happened that Khlit was not astonished when, as he came from the floor of the banquet-place one night, his head hazy with the fumes of the strange wine, a girl slave leaned close to him and whispered briefly.

"By the far corner of the balcony," she repeated, "in an hour."

He looked thoughtfully at an object the slave had thrust into his hand. It was the sapphire which Berca had once offered him.

He did not tell Toctamish of the message. And he was at some pains to get rid of Iba Kabash before the time appointed in the message. So he was alone when he went slowly along the stone balcony to a dark corner. The slaves had retired from the banquet-place and the *fedavie* were watching for Halen ibn Shaddah to come from his quarters. Standing so that he could not be seen by those below, Khlit waited. Waited until the torches came, with the *Dais* and the huge figure of Halen ibn Shaddah. He felt a touch on his coat, and turned.

"Follow," whispered the soft voice of the Persian, "and do not tread clumsily."

Khlit found that this was not so easy. Berca carried no light. He could barely see her cloaked form by the reflection of an occasional candle as she passed swiftly through chambers and rock passages. His head was light from the wine, although his mind was clear.

Berca kept to passages where there were few persons, and these Khlit saw to be slaves. She was taking him through the slave quarters where he had not been before. Through corridors that narrowed until he had to turn sideways to pass; by sunken walls which smelled evilly. Through a corridor that led out of the chambers of Alamut into the paradise of Halen ibn Shaddah.

Khlit paused in amazement and felt of his head which was throbbing. A half-moon glimmered down at him, and a cool night wind played in his hair. The branches of date trees stirred lazily. Under his feet he could feel grass, and he saw one of the strange birds that dragged its tail come from the shadow of the date trees.

Berca shook him angrily by the arm.

"One without sense, eater of swine flesh!" she hissed. "Are you a clown to gape at strange things?"

A fountain threw its spray on the wind into Khlit's face, with a scent like the roses of Ispahan. Below the fountain was a canal, which Khlit remembered vaguely, with a boat attached to the shore. In the water he could see the reflection of the moon gleaming at him. And he was dizzy.

"This is the paradise of Halen ibn Shaddah," he muttered unsteadily, "where I came by his favor. So Rashideddin told me."

Berca peered up at him silently. Her cloak fell back and Khlit saw the dark masses of hair which fell on either shoulder, and the white throat under the curved dark mouth that was twisted in scorn.

"A weak fool," she stormed, shaking him. "Toctamish is a better man than you."

"Toctamish is drunk. Nay, little Sparrow, it is my head. It will be better presently. This is no dream. How did you come to Alamut, little Berca?"

For answer the girl drew Khlit, who was fighting the dizziness in his head, to the canal, and into the boat. Pushing it from the shore, she paddled in the water until it floated into the shadows. Not content with this Berca urged the craft along the bank quietly, and Khlit who was flat on his back saw the shadow of a bridge fall over them.

"Nay," he said drowsily, "the stars are good. It is good to see them again. Where are we now? How did you bring me here?"

Berca came and sat by Khlit's head, feeling his hot forehead with a small hand. She wrapped her thin cloak tightly about her and rested her chin on her two hands, gazing at the round moon in the water.

"A man must be crafty and wise," she repeated softly, "yet, lo, it is a weak girl, a creature of the false prophet's paradise, who leads him. They told me you were very shrewd, oh, my Abulfetlah Harb Issa, gray Father of Battles. Soon there will be a great battle and the waters of Shahrud will be red again. Have you ever seen wolves of the steppe tear jackals of the mountains into bits, foam-flecked? Have you ever run with the pack of wolves, oh, one called the Wolf? Nay, they have clipped your fangs."

"That is a lie, Sparrow," growled Khlit surlily, "give me a horse and freedom to swing a sword, and I shall trounce some of these evil *fedavies* for you. Bah, it is a hotbed of sin, a reeking plague-house. Show me the way out of Alamut."

"And your promise," queried Berca, "to cut off the head of Halen ibn Shaddah?"

Khlit was silent. True, he had promised, and was in honor bound to Berca.

"Likewise, Berca," he said moodily, "you said that there was a plan. Why do you keep the plan hidden in your mind, if there is one? Better be in good faith with me. Say how Halen ibn Shaddah can be killed."

"How should I kill so strong a man?" she laughed softly. "The Koran reads that Allah weakens the stratagems of misbelievers. Also that they who store up evil shall taste what they store up. Such are the words of wisdom, despised by Rashideddin. Nay, destruction shall come upon Alamut like the storm from a cloud, quick as poison from a serpent's fang, and Halen ibn Shaddah——"

"Halen ibn Shaddah," chuckled Khlit, "is not easily to be found."

Abruptly, he gripped the girl's wrist. Beside the round orb of the moon in the water he saw the reflection of a turbaned man. It was a stout man, carrying a sword as broad as a horse's neck, or the reflection lied. Khlit rose on one elbow fingering his saber. At the same time the boat moved backward silently under impulse of the girl's paddling and passed from the bridge along the canal under date trees.

"A *eunuch*, one of the tribe who guard the creatures of the paradise," Berca whispered. "I have seen them often, because I am, also, a celestial houri—while it pleases me. I saw you when you came here a few days ago. Listen—" her voice changed—"for you must serve me, and the time is near."

Khlit nodded. The fresh night air had cleared some of the poison from his brain.

"I shall take you back to the chambers of Alamut, Khlit, by way of the slaves' quarters. We are on the top of Alamut, now, where Halen ibn Shaddah, whom may Allah lay in the dust, has built an evil paradise on the ruins of the old citadel to beguile his men. Verily what they have made—he and Rashideddin—is a magician's trick. The men who come here are drugged with a strange poison that I know not. I have tasted it in the wine—may Allah grant me mercy —and it is evil."

Khlit grunted in assent.

"It is some secret of Rashideddin's," she resumed. "The *fedavie*

are foul with it, until they lose fear of death. This drug chains them
to Halen ibn Shaddah. That and their lusts. And they have chained
others by fear of the *Refik*. Yet their doom is near. It is coming from
there—" pointing in the direction which Khlit thought to be north
—"and it is swift as the hunting falcon on the wing."

"Another riddle, Berca," muttered Khlit. "Where have you seen a
falcon?"

"Where you have seen them, Cossack," she laughed, "and Toctamish has hunted with them. Where swords are sharpened for the
cutting down of the *fedavie*. In the land of the Kallmark Tatars,
north of the Salt Sea. Oh, the doom of Alamut will be very great,
and Munkir and Nakir, the dark angels that flay dead men in their
graves will grow big with power."

"Another riddle, little Berca. It is many generations since Tatar
horsemen rode into Persia for conquest."

"The answer is under your blind eyes, Father of Battles. Am I not
beautiful as the rose garden of Tiflis in Spring? Is not my hair dark
as the mantle of Melik, and my skin white as aloes under the dew?"
Berca moved her perfumed head close to Khlit, and the Cossack drew
away. "Nay, others have eyes; so, Allah has willed that my honor
shall be cleared and the doom of Alamut shall come."

"The Tatars are marching on Alamut?" Khlit bit his mustache in
glee. "Devil take me, that is good news——"

"Hush, fool." Berca drew in her breath eagerly. "Twenty thousand
horsemen are riding along the Salt Sea toward Alamut. They will
not stop to plunder or gather spoil. Oh, it will be a good battle. My
father shall see it from the footstool of Mohammed. Aye, it will
gladden his eyes. I shall open the gate of Alamut to twenty thousand
Kallmark horsemen. The gate that leads to the banquet-place, where
I bring food every night with the slaves. Here is what you must do,
Father of Battles——"

She listened intently for a moment. The paradise of Halen ibn
Shaddah was still, and only the birds with long tails moved.

"On the third night, Father of Battles," she whispered, "the *Dai*
who is in command at the river stair, will change his sentries at the
second watch. Do you and Toctamish get among the sentries of the
river gate. I have seen you with Iba Kabash who is one without
honor. Pay him and it may be done. Two sentries are as is the custom, in the river, outside the gate. On the third night, those two

must be you and Toctamish, none other. That is your task. Then will you have a horse to ride, you and Toctamish. Meanwhile, keep out of sight of Rashideddin——"

"Aye," said Khlit, pondering, "Rashideddin."

XI

It is written in the annals of Abulghazi that as the year of the lion drew to its close, very great riches came to the treasury of Halen ibn Shaddah from the cities which lived in the shadow of fear. Save from the north, by the Salt Sea, where the tithes came not. Nor any riders. And in the north, said Abulghazi, a storm was gathering, swift as wind, rolling up all in its path. Yet no murmur of the storm came to Alamut, to the man who named himself prophet of God, to the banquet-place of the *fedavie*, to the man of wisdom, Rashideddin.

It was the second day after the visit of Berca that Khlit, who had been thinking deeply, sought out Iba Kabash where the Kurd lay sleeping on the floor of the banquet-place and roused him from his stupor.

"I have news for the ear of Halen ibn Shaddah himself," he said, squatting and lighting his pipe, "none other. He will surely reward me."

Iba Kabash ceased yawning and into his lined face came the look of a crafty fox.

"Halen ibn Shaddah will not see you, Khlit. He will see nobody except a few old fellows of Alamut, of whom I am one. Verily, I have the ear of the master of Alamut. Tell me your message and I will give it, for you are a man of brains. You, Khlit, are of the chosen. The others are ones without understanding."

Khlit knew that Iba Kabash lied, for the most part. He considered his pipe gravely and shook his head.

"My news is not to be repeated. Halen ibn Shaddah would pay a good price. How can you get such a good price for it as I?"

"Nay," remonstrated the Kurd, "I shall get a better price. For I know well the value of news. Tell me and we shall both profit, you and I."

Khlit grinned under his mustache. For a while he played, with the skill of one who understood the game well, with the growing inquisitiveness of his companion. Iba Kabash steadily raised the reward he assured Khlit, as he sensed the interest of the Cossack.

"Then," stated Khlit slowly, "you will do this. You will go direct to the master of Alamut and tell him my news. To no other. For here, a man takes what credit he can. And as the price of the good you will get for the telling, you will aid me in the plan I have. The plan concerns a girl that Halen ibn Shaddah would give a finger of his left hand to see brought before him."

"I swear it," said the Kurd readily, "on my *ahd*, the oath of a *fedavie*. Now tell me the news, and it shall go to Halen ibn Shaddah as you have said."

Khlit nodded. That much the Kurd would do, he was sure. Whether Iba Kabash would tell the source of his message was dubious. Khlit felt in his heart that if the news was important Iba Kabash would keep the credit for himself. Which was what Khlit wanted.

"Tell Halen ibn Shaddah this," he said slowly, "that Khlit, the Cossack, called the Wolf, has learned that Berca, the Persian girl who was sent from Rudbar by Rashideddin has returned, and is in Alamut. He will be very curious. Say no more, for you and I, Iba Kabash, can find the girl and take her to him. If you help me, it can be managed. That is my message."

Khlit watched the Kurd depart nimbly. Iba Kabash had sensed the importance of the Cossack's words. It would be a rare tale to pour into the ears of the master of Alamut. And, nimbly as the Kurd took his way from the banquet-place, Khlit was as quick to follow, keeping in the shadows of the passages, but well within sight of the other.

So it happened that Iba Kabash did not see Khlit when he turned into the winding stair that led to the room of Rashideddin, but the Cossack saw him and waited by the outer chamber. If Iba Kabash had looked behind, he might not have gone where he did. Yet he did not look behind, and Khlit waited patiently.

Presently one of the Khirghiz men came from the winding stair, walking idly, and Khlit halted him, asking if the Khirghiz had seen aught of a certain Kurd called Iba Kabash.

The man had seen him. Iba Kabash had come to the astrologer's chamber. Of a certainty, he had spoken to Rashideddin. Why else had he come? Was the astrologer one to stare at? They had talked together, and he had not heard what was said, although he listened carefully, for it was in another tongue.

Rashideddin, swore Khlit, was a man to be feared. Doubtless he was the one that spoke most often to Halen ibn Shaddah, the holy prophet. Nay, he surely had the ear of Halen ibn Shaddah, who held the keys to the blessed paradise.

The Khirghiz swore even more fluently. It was a lie that Rashideddin spoke with Halen ibn Shaddah more than others. Rashideddin was favored by the dark powers, for he read books. The Khirghiz knew that, for he was one of the chosen *fedavie* of the astrologer.

Khlit turned, at a step on the stair. Instead of Rashideddin, he saw the stout figure of Iba Kabash who halted in surprise.

"Listen, Cossack," the Kurd whispered, with a glance around the chamber. "I have not yet delivered your message, for Rashideddin stopped me on my way to Halen ibn Shaddah, and ordered me to bring you to him. But do not tell Rashideddin what you know. I shall see that you get a good reward, I swear it. We must try to get the girl. If you know a way tell me, and it shall be done. Remember, say nothing to Rashideddin."

Khlit weighed the words of the Kurd for their gist of truth and found very little. He little liked to face the astrologer, but he ascended the stair at once, swaggering, and stamping his boots.

In the round chamber of the astrologer he halted. It was night and candles were lighted around the tapestried walls. Rashideddin was crouched over rolls of parchment and instruments the like of which Khlit had not seen. In a cleared space on the floor in front of him the wise man of Alamut had ranged a number of images, silver and cleverly wrought, of stars.

The stars formed a circle and in the circle was a bag. Rashideddin sat quietly, arms crossed on knees, staring in front of him. Around the walls of the chamber silk hangings had been placed, on which were woven pictures of scenes which Khlit recognized as belonging to the paradise of Halen ibn Shaddah.

"Seat yourself, Cossack," said Rashideddin, in his slow, deep voice, "in front of me, and watch."

The astrologer's eyes were half-closed. Looking into them, Khlit could see nothing. The room was still and deserted except for the two. Khlit wished that others had been there. He felt ill at ease, and sucked at his pipe loudly.

"In the place of darkness, of the spirit Munkir," said Rashideddin, "there are no stars. Yet when men are alive they can look on the stars. Few can read them. From Alamut I have seen them, and learned many things. Do they read the stars in your country, Cossack?"

"Nay," said Khlit, "we know them not."

Rashideddin contemplated his circle thoughtfully. His hands, yellow and very clean, took up a pair of dividers with which he measured the distance between the silver stars.

"In the heart of Alamut, we have burned the law books of the Persians and the code books of the Medes. They were very old; yet is the dust of age a sacrament? What is there about an old law that makes it graven as on stone in the minds of men? One prophet has said that he who takes a tooth for a tooth is lawful; another has said that he who injures another for his own sake shall suffer greatly. Which is the truth?"

"Nay," answered Khlit, "I know not."

"It was written that when one man kills another the kin of that man shall kill the first. So I have seen many in the world outside Alamut kill each other without cause. Yet in Alamut, we kill only for a reason."

Khlit thought of the dead Tatar who had fallen where Rashideddin sat and was silent.

"Watch," said the astrologer. Putting aside his dividers, he took up the bag. Opening the top of this slightly he held it over the circle in both hands. Tipping it to one side, he allowed a thin stream of sand to fall in the space enclosed by the stars. The sand heaped itself in mounds, which Rashideddin considered carefully, setting down the bag.

"There are laws in the stars, Cossack," he repeated, tracing idly in the sand with his dividers. "And I have read them. Is it not true that when a man has found the sum of wisdom, he has none? The poet has said that no beauty is in the world save that of power over other men. The stars watch the evil and idleness of men. One who reads them learns many things. I shall tell you what I learned of you, Cossack."

"Aye," said Khlit grimly, "tell."

Under the cover of his bushy eyebrows he studied his companion.

Rashideddin was a magician, and in Khlit's mind a magician was not to be trusted. Was the astrologer playing with him, using him as a chess-player moves a piece on the board? What had Iba Kabash told Rashideddin? Khlit waited, paying no attention to the stars or the sand, watching only the eyes of the other.

"From the land of Ukraine you came, Khlit," said the astrologer. "Alone, and met Toctamish in Astrakan. When the wolf runs with the jackal over the steppe, the stars have a riddle to solve. Perhaps the wolf is hungry. And the jackal is useful."

"Aye," said Khlit, "Iba Kabash."

Rashideddin's expression did not change as he stirred the sands with his dividers. "At Astrakan there was a *fedavie* who is dead. You and the jackal Toctamish were under his roof. You came with him to a ship. And the *fedavie* was slain. Aye, the wolf was hungered. Much have I learned from the stars. There was a girl with you on the ship. She did not come with you to Alamut."

Khlit made no response, and Rashideddin continued to stir the sands.

"The girl was not one easy to forget. You have not forgotten her. The jackal is drunk. But you have an ear for wisdom. The girl might be found in Alamut. Aye, by one who knows her, in the thousands of slaves."

Khlit shook the ashes from his pipe. Out of the corner of his eye he saw the hangings move behind him. Well he knew the chamber of Rashideddin was pregnant with danger. The pallid astrologer toyed with men's lives as he did with the magic sands. He made no move, waiting for what was to come.

It came in a blinding flash. A burst of flame, and the sands leaped upward. Smoke and a wrenching smell filled Khlit's eyes and throat. The skin of his face burned hotly. Blinking and gasping, he rocked back on his haunches.

"The wolf is wise in the ways of the steppe," purred the astrologer. "Yet he came to Alamut, the vulture's nest. It is a pity. The girl, too, is missing. Perhaps she can be found."

The face of Rashideddin stared at him through thinning clouds of powder smoke, and Khlit wiped the tears of pain from his eyes. Rapidly, he thought. Rashideddin wanted Berca. Halen ibn Shaddah would pay a high price for the girl, who was dangerous, being not as other girls.

"Aye," he muttered, coughing, for the flame had burned his face, "she may be found."

"Tomorrow there will be an audience by Halen ibn Shaddah for the *fedavie*. She will be there. I shall send for you before evening. Fail, and the *fedavie* will break your bones slowly, with stones, or tear the skin from your back."

Khlit rose to his feet without obeisance.

"Have the stars," he asked, "any other message for me?"

For a long moment Rashideddin studied him through narrowed lids. Idly, the dividers traced patterns in the powder ash in the circle of stars. And Khlit cursed himself softly. For in the eyes of the other was the look of one who measures swords. Once too often he had drawn the attention of the astrologer on himself.

Dismissed from the round chamber, Khlit sought out Iba Kabash, and secured the promise of the Kurd that he would be put with Toctamish among the sentries for the next night, for being admitted to the paradise of Alamut this was their privilege. To gain this point, it was necessary to assure the Kurd that Berca could be found. Once more, Iba Kabash swore Khlit would get a good price, whereupon Khlit had the thought that the other was too glib with a promise.

Then he found Toctamish, and told the Tatar enough of what had passed in the garden of Halen ibn Shaddah to keep him sober overnight. This done, Khlit seated himself in a corner of the banquetplace and took out his sword. Placing it across his knees he began to whet it with the stone he always carried. As he did so, men near him stared curiously, for Khlit was singing to himself in a voice without music.

And Rashideddin sat over the circle of silver stars, tracing and retracing patterns in the ashes of powder, with the look of one in whose soul there is no peace.

XII

Came the time of the *divan*, the assembly of the *Refik*, and closed gates that guarded the apartments of Halen ibn Shaddah in the cellars of Alamut swung open. In poured the followers of the *Refik*; *fedavie*, hillmen of Persia, men of the Khirghiz steppe, *janissaries* of Yussouf, prince of princes. Scattered in the crowd were magicians of Rashideddin in white tunics and red girdles, in company with white and gold *Dais.* Also came Khlit with the Khirghiz chief who had seen fit to keep at his side.

The throng moved in silence, and Khlit waxed curious at this, until he questioned the Khirghiz. For reply, he received a hard blow in the ribs.

"You are surely a fool, Cossack," growled the other, "to bray at what is strange. We are walking through the talking chambers of the *Shadna,* built by Ala-eddin. Harken." He lifted his voice in a shrill syllable. "Aie!"

Instantly the sound was taken up and repeated through the corridors. A hundred echoes caught the word and flung it back. Shrilly, gruffly, it rang further into the caverns. Men near them stared and cursed. Khlit observed that the corridors were lofty and vaulted, with pillars of stone.

"It is said," whispered the Khirghiz, gratified by the effect of his experiment, "that before the time of Rashideddin, when the *Refik* prayed to Allah, these were the chambers of prayer. A man could pray a thousand times with one word."

"And now?"

"We do not pray."

Pushing a way through the crowd recklessly with his elbows, the Khirghiz gained a place where he and Khlit could see the array of the *divan.* In the center of a cleared space in one of the larger chambers stood Halen ibn Shaddah, easily marked by his great height and the cloak that shadowed his face. Around him were grouped certain men in heavy turbans and green embroidered coats. These Khlit recognized as *Daikebirs,* emissaries of the master of Alamut. At his side was the bent figure of Rashideddin.

These were talking in a tongue that Khlit did not know, not loudly, for fear of disturbing the echoes. His eye wandered over the throng. Wandered and halted. A woman's figure stood out from the crowd and he swore under his breath. Arm's length from Rashideddin among the *Dais,* her blue cloak closely wrapped on her slender form, stood Berca. Her black curls were pushed under a fold of the cloak; her brown eyes, darting from under fringed lashes, swept about the gathered *Refik* and passed Khlit by in unconcern. Yet he felt that she had seen him.

No other woman was present. Khlit saw that the eyes of many searched her, and he touched the Khirghiz on the shoulder.

"Is there talk about the woman?" he asked softly. "Tell me."

The chief listened, tolerantly, for a space.

"Aye," he said, "there is idle talk. The woman is the daughter of a hill sheik. She was sent to be the wife of Kiragai Khan. That is a good jest, for Kiragai Khan loves not the *Refik*. She has said that she was sent without a dowry. So, the painted flower has come to one who tramples on flowers, to ask that the dowry be given her."

"And will it be done?"

"Will the tiger give up its slain victim? Nay, you are without understanding, Cossack. Halen ibn Shaddah does not play with such. The sheik's daughter will find a place among the slaves, not otherwise."

"Such is not the law."

"There is no law in Alamut but one—the word of Halen ibn Shaddah. And the law that the curved dagger must avenge a wrong."

Khlit made no reply, considering carefully what had been said. Rashideddin, then, had found Berca as he had declared he would. Was it Berca's purpose to come before Halen ibn Shaddah? Had she forgotten the cunning and cruelty of the man who had dishonored her? Perhaps the girl's pride had impelled her to appeal for justice and a wedding dowry to give the khan to whom she had offered herself. Yet Berca had not forgotten the manner of her father's death, of that Khlit was sure. Wise in the ways of men, the heart of the sheik's daughter was a closed book to him. He looked around for Toctamish. The Tatar was not to be seen.

Meanwhile, Rashideddin had been speaking to the girl.

"What said the astrologer?" asked Khlit.

"The old one is crafty," grunted the Khirghiz. "Aye, he has learned the secrets of magic where Marduk hangs by his heels in the hell of Babylon. He asked why a girl so fair in face and form should bear a gift in offering herself in marriage."

Berca, who seemed to ignore her peril, lifted her dark head and answered quickly in tones that stirred the echoes.

"Hah, the painted flower has a sharp tongue," grunted the chieftain. "She says that her beauty has moved the heart of Kiragai Khan as wind stirs fire. The khan, who desires her, would have taken her for his favorite wife. Yet would she not, being ashamed for reason of the trick Halen ibn Shaddah played her. So she has come back to ask a dowry from the hand of the master of Alamut, who is her lawful ruler now that her father is dead."

The giant form of Halen ibn Shaddah turned on Berca, and a peculiarly shrill voice reached the ears of Khlit. Once more he wondered what kind of man was the master of Alamut, of the giant figure and shrill voice.

"Halen ibn Shaddah says," whispered the other, "that Berca belongs to Alamut. She has returned to Alamut and here she must stay."

Khlit thought of the paradise of the master of evil, and understood why the eyes of the *fedavie* in the throng burned as they stared at the girl's slender figure outlined in the blue cloak.

"She asked for justice—" he began.

"Nay," interrupted the Khirghiz carelessly, "her father was slain by Halen ibn Shaddah. How is she then to be trusted?"

Khlit did not answer. For the gaze of Berca had met his. In it he read anxiety, and a warning. Slowly her glance crept to Rashideddin and back. Again. And Khlit saw the astrologer turn to leave the chamber.

Truly, he considered, the sheik's daughter was daring and proud. And, obeying her look, he followed Rashideddin, slipping away from the Khirghiz.

So it happened that when the astrologer left the *divan*, Khlit did likewise. Rashideddin made his way quickly and alone down one of the corridors without waiting for a light. Khlit followed him, keeping as close as he could without being seen. Presently both halted.

A voice called through the corridor clearly, and seemingly very near.

"A man must be crafty and wise," the voice of Berca came to their ears, "when danger is 'round his path, else is his labor vain."

Khlit crossed himself in astonishment. For a moment he had forgotten the echoes of the corridors of Ala-eddin.

XIII

Rashideddin went straight to the winding stairs that led to his own apartment. At the foot of these stairs Khlit, who had traced the astrologer closely, paused. It would not be easy to go farther without being seen. And this Khlit wanted to avoid. He believed that Rashideddin was having him watched, and that the Khirghiz had attended him to the *divan* under orders. And at all costs he must be free to act that night.

Rashideddin, thought Khlit, sensed something impending. In some way the magician of Alamut kept himself informed of what went on in the citadel. His spies were everywhere. And on the night when Berca planned to admit the enemies of the *Refik*, both were under watch. Where was Toctamish?

Khlit wasted no time by the foot of the winding stair. There were other entrances to the circular chamber where Rashideddin kept his henchmen, and the Cossack cast about until he came to one of these. A passage led upward, unlighted in the direction he sought and this Khlit followed until he came to a curtain which he suspected divided it from the chamber of the astrologer. Beyond the curtain he could hear voices.

Lifting one edge of the hanging, Khlit looked out cautiously. Candle-light in the chamber dazzled him for a moment. He made out a dozen figures, Rashideddin not among them, dressed in the red and white of the magicians' cult. They were grouped around a man prone on the floor. This man was Toctamish.

The Tatar's coat and shirt had been removed. Two *fedavie* held each of his arms outstretched on the floor. His thick chest was strangely red, and he gasped as if in pain, not once or twice, but long, broken gasps that shook his body.

As Khlit watched, startled, one of the *fedavie*, a gaunt Tatar with a pocked face, placed some brown dust on the chest of the prostrate man. Khlit recognized the dust. It was the same that had singed his face when he sat opposite Rashideddin.

Thrusting aside the hanging, Khlit stepped into the room. The *fedavie* took no notice of him, believing that he was one of Rashideddin's henchmen stationed in the passage. Toctamish, however, lifted his eyes, which gleamed as they fell on the Cossack. Khlit saw that his brow was covered with sweat, and that blood ran from his mouth.

The man of the pitted face lifted some brown powder and sifted it on the chest of his victim. Another pushed a torch into his hand. Khlit realized then how his companion was being tortured. The smell of burning in the air came from singed flesh. And Toctamish was feeling the angry hand of Rashideddin.

Khlit stepped to the side of the *fedavie* with the torch, and peered closely at Toctamish. He saw then what made the Tatar's chest red, of a strange shade. Strips of skin had been torn off over the lungs, and here the powder was laid. Khlit swore and his hand strayed to his sword. And fell to his side. The *fedavie* numbered a full dozen, armed, and able-bodied. To draw his sword would be to bring ten whirling around him.

Khlit had no love for Toctamish. Yet in this room the other had stood with his sword drawn beside him. And they had shared bread and salt. Toctamish was standing the torture with the stark courage which was his creed. The lips of the sufferer moved and Khlit bent closer.

"Kiragai Khan—Khan of the Horde," the cracked lips gasped, "tell him. Blood for blood. We have shared bread—and salt, and *arak*. Tell him."

The Cossack nodded. Toctamish was asking him to report how he had endured torture to Kiragai Khan who was advancing on Alamut at the head of his men, and claiming vengeance. He was weak, and seemed to have no hope of living.

"What said the dog?" muttered the *fedavie* with the torch who had been trying to catch what Toctamish whispered. He spoke in a bastard Tatar with a strange lisping. "He will not speak and Rashideddin has said that he must or we will hang by the heels."

"He is out of his mind," answered Khlit carelessly. "What must he tell?"

"He stuck a dagger into a *fedavie*, a Syrian, on the shore of the Salt Sea. A girl, Berca, the sheik's daughter, was there also. This yellow-faced fool must tell if the girl ordered him to do it. Bah! His skin is tough as oxen hide, and his flesh is senseless as swine."

"And he has not spoken?"

"Nay. Rashideddin was here and questioned him, but the Tatar cursed him."

Khlit scanned the face of Toctamish. The yellow skin was dark and moist with sweat. The eyes were bloodshot and half-closed. The mouth lifted in a snarl, disclosing teeth pointed as an animal's. He felt that Toctamish would not yield to the torture. And great love for the man whose courage was proof against pain rose in the heart of Khlit whose own courage was such that men called him the "Wolf."

"Aye," he growled, "blood for blood. That is the law of Alamut. And Kiragai Khan shall know."

He saw by a quick opening of the eyes that Toctamish caught his words.

"What say you?" queried the *fedavie*. "Kiragai Khan?"

Toctamish's knotted figure writhed under the hands of his captors. He spat, blood and foam combined, at the other.

"Aye," he groaned, "Kiragai Khan—lord of fifty thousand spears—chief of a hundred ensigns—master of Alamut."

"He speaks," interpreted Khlit swiftly, "of one Hulagu Khan who conquered Alamut. Tell Rashideddin. And cease the torture, for the man has nothing to confess."

The *fedavie* stared at Khlit suspiciously.

"Nay," he snarled, "shall we hang by the heels?"

He thrust the torch near the powder. There was a hissing flash, a smell of burning flesh. Toctamish's body quivered spasmodically and sank back. The eyes closed.

Under cover of the flare and smoke Khlit slipped back through the circle and sought the stair. Gaining this he did not pause until he had reached the inner gate of the underground citadel where a *Dai* was assembling his men to guard the outer gate by the river.

When Khlit, who was nursing in his brain the sight he had just left, went down the river stairs to his post in the River Shahrud, he found that his companion was the bearded Khirghiz chieftain.

The outer post of the guard around the citadel of Alamut was in a small nest of rocks several hundred paces from the entrance, and midway in the stream. So shallow was the river that they could wade out to the rocks. The Khirghiz led the way.

It was not yet the middle of the night, and a bright moon lighted the winding ribbon of the Shahrud that twisted between the rocky heights of Rudbar. The mass of Alamut showed dark, giving no sign of the evil world it concealed. A wind from the heights brushed Khlit's face and he breathed it in deeply, for he was nauseated by the stench of the caverns.

"You and I, Cossack," said the Khirghiz, seating himself unsteadily on a ledge of the rocks, for he had been drinking, "will keep the outer post."

"Aye," said Khlit, "you and I."

He stared out into the moonlight haze that hung over the river.

Berca had said that he and Toctamish were to hold the outer post. From some quarter the horsemen of Kiragai Khan were nearing the gate of Alamut. Khlit realized that unless the attack came as a surprise the citadel was impregnable. A surprise might carry the Tatar horde into the entrance. Berca had said there was a way. And this was it. Yet, if a surprise was to succeed the Khirghiz must be disposed of. He had been drinking, but he was still watchful. No movement of the Cossack escaped him.

Quietly Khlit drew out a small vial. From this he poured a few grains of a white powder into his hand. Lifting his hand he made as if to take the powder into his mouth. The Khirghiz bent forward, and his face lighted with evil desire.

"Have you—" he began.

"Come, Brother," whispered Khlit genially, "we will be comfortable on the rocks. Is not the bread of the *Refik* the vintage of the Shadna to be eaten? Come."

The Khirghiz swore softly and held out his hand. In wine and food, the vintage of the Shadna was often in the hands of the *Refik* men. But not, except on expeditions of the Master of Alamut, or by costly bribery of the *Dais* was the pure powder of *hashish* to be had, the *hashish* that brought bright dreams of paradise and lulled the mind with pleasures, that hardened the souls of the men of Alamut, and steeled their hands to the dagger.

Khlit, who had discovered the secret of the drug through the babblings of Iba Kabash, quietly dropped his portion back into the vial. Later, he knew, the Khirghiz would want more and he had but a little.

XIV

It was not long before Khlit was alone. The Khirghiz lay at his side on the rocks, muttering to himself with enough *hashish* inside him to make an imbecile of an ordinary man. Khlit sat by his side, saber across his knees, and watched the moonlit sides of the heights that frowned down on him. On the slopes he could make out the shadowy outlines of droves of horses, and he wondered if the *Dais* were planning an expedition that night.

Usually, Khlit was not given to forebodings. Yet the black mass of Alamut rising at his back gave him the feeling of approaching danger, and when he scanned the shadows along the river they moved as if filled with the bands of drug-crazed *fedavie*. Especially, Khlit wondered if the spies of Rashideddin were watching him. Rashideddin had learned of the murder of the Syrian, had connected Berca with it, and Toctamish with Berca. Toctamish, at his order, had been tortured with such devilish cruelty that even the Tatar's fortitude might break down.

How much did the astrologer know of Berca's secret? Once the alarm was raised in Alamut a thousand swords would block the stairs at the river gate and the rope hoists of the slaves at the rear would be drawn up. There were no signs of activity that Khlit could see, but few ever saw the movements of the *fedavie*. Accustomed as he was to war on the steppe, he was skeptical of horsemen taking such a stronghold as Alamut.

Once the Tatar horde forced the entrance there would be a battle such as Khlit had never seen before. Himself a Cossack, he cared little whether *Refik* or Khan were the victor—except that he had sworn an oath, a double oath, that the life of the Master of Alamut, Halen ibn Shaddah, would fall to his sword. Wherefore, he waited patiently, eyes searching the road by the river where the invaders might come.

Berca had told him that twenty thousand Tatars were riding through the hills to Alamut. Yet the road was narrow and the way twisted. It would be hard to move quickly. And there were the horse-tenders on the hills who would give the alarm. Khlit had come to grant a grudging admiration to the sheik's daughter who had defied Halen ibn Shaddah. But she was in Rashideddin's hands, and the astrologer was the man Khlit had marked as most dangerous of the *Refik*.

Rising suddenly, Khlit drew in his breath sharply. Outlined against the summit of a hill he saw a horse and rider moving very swiftly. The man was bent low in his saddle and Khlit thought he saw the long cloak of the *fedavie* before the rider came over the brow of the hill. Half-way down the descent the horse stumbled and fell.

Khlit saw a dark object shoot from the rolling horse and lie passive, clear in the moonlight. The messenger, if such it was, of the *fedavie* would not reach his destination. And at the same time Khlit saw something else. Before his eyes as if by magic he beheld Kiragai Khan and thousands of his horsemen.

Then Khlit, surnamed the Wolf, buckled tight his belt and drew on his sheepskin hat firmly. There was to be a battle that would redden the waters of the Shahrud and, among the swords of the *fedavie* Halen ibn Shaddah was to be found.

Apparently there was nothing stirring on the mountain slopes of Rudbar except the shapes of the horse droves that drew down to the river as was their custom, awaiting the bands of the *Dais* which came out for mounts. Tonight there were no men issuing from Alamut. And it was only when one of the herds moved across the face of the moon that Khlit saw the tips of Tatar helmets moving among the horses, and understood why the horses seemed more numerous than before.

Even as Berca had promised, the Tatar horde was approaching the gate of Alamut. One of the herds reached the river's edge and pressed on, in the shadow of the hillside. Khlit could see the faces of men peering at him, and catch the glint of their spears. He gave a hasty glance at his companion. The man was sleeping heavily.

Familiar with the ways of the Tatars, the Cossack could guess how their whirlwind rush into Rudbar had cut off all news being sent to the citadel, and how, after dark, the *Refik* horse-tenders on the pastures had been singled out and cut down. One had broken away with the news that was to carry the doom of Alamut, only to fall by the river.

The foremost warriors had reached him, clingling closely to the sides of their horses. A low voice called out to him cautiously.

"You are the Cossack who will guide us?"

"Aye," said Khlit, "but the moon is bright here and there are others within the caverns. Are you ready to rush forward at once?"

"Lead," said the voice, "and we will follow. Lead us to the gate of Alamut and we will purge the devil's hole of its filth."

Khlit cast a quick glance at the hillsides. Other bodies were moving down. Some were nearly at the river. Thousands were coming over the hillcrest. More were coming by the river road. On the far flanks detachments were moving to the rear of Alamut.

Drawing his sword, he sprang down into the river and splashed toward the shore. Dark forms closed in beside him, and the welcome stench of sweat and leather filled his nose. The river was full of moving forms, and horses that dashed, riderless, to either side. Khlit's heart leaped, and his clasp tightened on his sword. One of the fore-

most caught him roughly by the arm. Khlit had a quick glimpse of a
dark, lined face and flashing eyes.

"I am Kiragai Khan, Cossack. Where is Toctamish? He was to stay
by the side of Berca!"

"She sent him to watch with me. Yet, very likely he is dead by
now."

The other swore, as they gained the shelter of the caverns.

"Take me to her, then," he snarled.

So it happened that before the light of day touched the date trees
on the summit of Alamut, citadel of the *Refik*, and place of plague
and evil, the first of the horde that had ridden from the shores of the
Salt Sea entered the river gate, overcoming a few guards, forced
their way up the stair, and spread through the passages of Alamut,
making no sound but silently, as tigers seeking their prey.

XV

In the annals of Abulghazi it is written how, in the year of the lion,
came the doom of Alamut. The *Refik* folk were cornered in the cellars of the citadel, and taken by surprise. The swords of the Kallmark Tatars flashed in the passages, and their sharp arrows sped
through the corridors. And, as the prophecy said, the waters of the
Shadrud were red.

Yet in the book of Abulghazi and the annals of the Persian dynasties there is nothing said of the fate of Halen ibn Shaddah who
was the last leader of the *Refik*. The followers of Kiragai Khan
sought through Alamut from the wine chambers to the gardens
among the ruins on the summit, and they did not find Halen ibn
Shaddah.

The battle was not over for many hours. Separate bands of
mounted Tatars had surrounded the height on which Alamut stood,
and when throngs of slaves, and the eunuchs with the houris of the
gardens swept out from hidden tunnels and were lowered over
the wall, they were cut down. They were not spared, for that was the
word of Kiragai Khan. The *fedavie*, cornered, and led by their *Dais*,
rallied and attacked the columns of invaders which were penetrating
to the heart of Alamut.

The Tatars without their horses and fighting in the gloom of the
caverns were at a disadvantage, which was offset by greater num-

bers and the leadership of Kiragai Khan. For the *fedavie* had no
leader. Messengers who sought through the tapestried apartments
of the Shadna for Halen ibn Shaddah found none but panic-struck
Daikebirs. The tide of battle flung the *fedavie* back to the banquet-
place, and to the treasure-house beyond. If there had been a leader
they might have held the dark passages until the Tatars were sickened by the slaughter of their men.

Such was the doom of Alamut. Torches flaring through chambers
hung with gold cloth and littered with jeweled statuary from Tre-
bizond, with silk rugs of Ispahan. Swords flashing in dark tunnels,
where naught was heard but the gasping of men bitten by steel and
the sound of bodies falling to the earth. Wailing and lamentation
in the gardens under the date trees which were the evil paradise of
Halen ibn Shaddah, and the splash of stricken women in the canals.
Dark-faced, squat men in mail and fur cloaks trampling through
treasure-rooms where the riches of a thousand caravans and a hundred cities stood.

Never had the followers of Kiragai Khan taken spoil so rich. Pearls
from Damascus, golden fish from Che-ting, emeralds and sapphires
from Tabriz, urns of gold shekels from the merchants of Samarkand
and ornaments from the califate of Bagdad that would grace the
court of a Mongol emperor. Slant eyes of the Kallmark horsemen
widened, and they urged their dogs into the rivers of wine in the
gardens, ripping into shreds rugs and hangings, splintering porcelain
kiosks with rocks, and trampling on the bodies of the dead. Few
lived.

And still the Master of Alamut was not found. Once Iba Kabash,
who had attached himself to the winning side, and was spared because he brought Berca safe to Kiragai Khan, paused beside the body
of a very large man, cloaked and jeweled. But he spurned it with
his foot when he turned it over, for the giant face was that of a black
eunuch.

Yet there was one who said he had found Halen ibn Shaddah.
Iba Kabash, who was eager to find favor with his new lord, offered,
trembling, to take him to the circular chamber of Rashideddin. Berca
came with them, for she was not one to leave the side of Kiragai
Khan in battle, being the daughter of a hill sheik and not a Tatar
woman.

They climbed the winding stairs escorted by the renegade with torch-bearers and armed Kallmarks. In the circular chamber of the astrologer they saw a strange sight. The room had been dark. By the flare of their torches they made out three men, two dead, and the third sitting on the floor. Kiragai Khan paused for a moment by the body of Toctamish, burned and bloody, for the man had been one of his lieutenants, and very brave.

"He died under torture, lord and Celestial Master," gibbered Iba Kabash, pointing. "For he would not tell of the queenly Berca, or the coming of the noble Tatars."

Kiragai Khan said nothing, passing to the next body, and pressing the hand of Berca when the girl cried out. This one was Rashideddin, his gray robe stained with red, and his lean face convulsed. His arms flung wide, and sightless, leering eyes staring upward through the opening to the stars, the astrologer had died in the grip of anger. Berca, leaning over him, watched vainly for a breath to stir the gray cloak. Seated beside Rashideddin she saw Khlit, wiping his sword calmly with a corner of the dead man's cloak.

"Have you seen Halen ibn Shaddah?" demanded Iba Kabash officiously. "The noble Kiragai Khan has missed you, since he came into the entrance of Alamut. Was it you that killed Rashideddin?"

"Aye," answered Khlit, looking up indifferently. "Have the Kallmarks or the *Refik* the upper hand? I have seen Halen ibn Shaddah."

"The battle is over, Khlit," exclaimed Berca pressing forward, but keeping the hand of the Tatar leader. Her eyes were shining, and she held her head proudly. "The doom of Alamut has come, as I swore it would. It was my will that it should, mine and my lord's. For I came to him without a gift and was ashamed. Yet did he marry me in spite of that. And I swore to him that if he would avenge my father such a gift should be his as no other bride could bring. Alamut would be his, with the treasure of the *Refik*. And now he has seen that the gift is rich. All that Halen ibn Shaddah had."

Khlit's glance sought that of the Tatar leader, and they measured each other silently.

"The way is long from Tatary," went on Berca, tossing her head, "but I am very beautiful in the sight of my lord, and he consented to my plan—to come to open the gate to him—saying only that Toctamish should come. I picked you, Cossack, as my father of battles. Yet I am grieved. You swore that you would slay for me Halen ibn Shaddah——"

"Have you seen," broke in Kiragai Khan gruffly, "the one who is called Master of Alamut?"

"Aye, he was here."

"Which way did he go? Speak."

"He did not go."

The khan looked around the chamber. It was empty except for the two bodies. A sudden blast of air from the opening overhead made the flame of the torches whirl, and cast a gleam on the face of Rashideddin as if the dead man had moved. Berca drew back with a smothered cry.

"The man who was called Halen ibn Shaddah," said Khlit, "was a eunuch of great size. The real Master of Alamut was another. He concealed his identity to avoid the daggers of those who would slay him. Yet is he slain. And I have kept my oath, Berca, princess."

The eyes of the others strayed to the body of Rashideddin, and rested on the red stains that garnished the gray cloak with the red ribbons of death. The blind eyes of Halen ibn Shaddah were fixed on the stars visible through the opening in the ceiling. And Khlit, seeing this, knew that he would be very glad to turn his horse again toward the steppe and away from Alamut.

ADVENTURE TWO

THE MIGHTY MANSLAYER

The Wealth-Bearers are heavily burdened. Their burden is more precious than gold gleaming under enamel. The Wealth-Bearers are strong. Their burden is finer than the seven precious substances.

The faces of the Onon Muren are turned toward the mountains of Khantai Khan. The white faces of the Onon Muren are still. There is fear in the shadows of Khantai Khan. Yet the fear does not touch the Wealth-Bearers.

The five sons of Alan Goa have dried their blood in the earth. But the fear is still in the forests of Khantai Khan. Can another hand lift what One hand held? Nay, the fear is too great!

From the book of Chakar Noyon, the gylong of the Uhoten Lamasery.

CHAKAR NOYON WAS DEAD, LONG BEFORE THE END OF THE SIXTEENTH century, when Khlit, the Cossack called the "Wolf," he of the Curved Saber, rode into Samarkand. Yet the book of Chakar Noyon, who was very wise, was owned by Mir Turek, the merchant; and in the bazaars of Samarkand Khlit met with Mir Turek.

Truly, there are many books that are not to be believed. Yet did Mir Turek believe the book of Chakar Noyon, and Mir Turek was not only a shrewd merchant, but a scholar. And he thirsted for gold. Likewise there was the tale of the Leo Tung astrologer. The astrologer did not see the Bearers of Wealth, but he saw the white faces of the Onon Muren and he told of the terror of Khantai Khan.

Khlit could not read, not even the gold inscription on his famous curved sword. He was sick of the hot sands of Persia and the ruined towns of Turkestan. His dress had changed since he became an exile from the Cossack camps—he wore green leather pantaloons, topped by a wide purple sash, with a flowing cloak of crimson silk. He still had his sheepskin hat, and his burned pipe. As he rode through the sun-baked bazaars of Samarkand his eye fell on the booth of Mir Turek, and on the elephant in the booth.

It was a small elephant, or rather a pair of them, of ivory and gold. Khlit had never seen such a creature before, and the sight delighted him. He dismounted and sauntered slowly to the bazaar of the merchant, lest the latter suspect that he was anxious to buy.

Mir Turek was a stout man, with a broad nose and slant, bleared eyes. He was dressed in the white robe of a scholar, and he put down a parchment he was reading as the Cossack seated himself crosslegged on the rug before him. Mir Turek watched the stars with the astrologers, and the month was one when his star was ascendent. The ivory elephants, he said, in bastard Usbek which Khlit understood, were not to be sold. They were a talisman of good fortune.

Khlit took from his wallet the last of the gold coins left from the sack of Alamut and laid them on the rug before the merchant. Likewise he drew his sword from its sheath and laid it across his knees. The sun, gleaming on the bright blade with its curious lettering, threw a pallid glow over the yellow face of Mir Turek.

The merchant glanced curiously from the sword to Khlit. His eyes widened as he scanned the inscription on the weapon. Long and steadfastly he looked at its owner. Truly, thought Mir Turek, his star was ascendent.

"Offspring of the devil's jackal!" growled Khlit. "Scouring of a beggar's pot! Where is there a merchant who will not sell his goods? Sell me the images or I will slit your fat belly for you."

Mir Turek turned a shade grayer and his eyes watered. Still, he could not tear his eyes from the inscription. He pointed to the sword.

"Is that, like the gold pieces, from Persia?" he asked.

"Nay, one without honor," replied Khlit carelessly, "a Cossack does not buy or steal his sword. It was my father's and his father's. I will take the images."

"Nay, lord," hastily broke in the merchant, "they are a talisman. I dare not sell." He glanced swiftly to each side down the bazaars. "But come to my house tonight—the house of Mir Turek, the merchant—in the alley at the south corner of the Registan, and we will talk concerning them, you and I."

When Khlit had gone Mir Turek drew together the silk curtains in front of his booth. Yet he did not leave the stall. He sat motionless, in thought. He fingered the parchment as one caresses a treasure. Carefully he read over a portion of the book and drew in his breath with a grateful sigh. Without doubt, his star was watching over him, as the astrologer had said. And the elephants were truly a potent talisman.

In the mind of Mir Turek was a picture. The picture was of a host of fighting men following their banners over the steppe. Also, of the oak trees of Khantai Khan where few men ventured. In the back of Mir Turek's mind, like the reflection in a pool of water, was a fear, an old fear, that had been his father's and his father's before him.

Khlit was weary of Samarkand and homesick for the wide plains of the steppe. Wherefore he drank much that night, many bowls of Esbek wine, that stirred his memories of the Ukraine and the Tatar land, but did not affect his head or the firmness of his step. He remembered that Mir Turek had invited him to come to his house. So Khlit sought and found the door of the merchant's home on the Registan, and, although he could not read, he came to know somewhat of the book of Chakar Noyon.

The door of Mir Turek opened at his touch and the Cossack swaggered through the antechamber and walked uninvited to a room in the rear. It was a chamber hung with yellow silk of a strange kind, and filled with ivory images of elephants and small pagodas. A girl who had been sleeping curled up on some rugs in one corner sprang to her feet and would have fled swiftly, but Khlit checked her.

She was a child of fourteen, slender and delicate of face with a mass of dark hair that descended over her shoulders. The small, olive face that turned up at the Cossack was frightened. So it was that Khlit met the girl Kerula, child of Mir Turek, whose mother, a Kallmark slave, was dead.

"Eh, little sparrow," chuckled Khlit, patting the girl's hair, "I will not hurt you. Tell your master, Mir Turek, the shrewd merchant, that Khlit, called the Wolf, is come to his house."

He seated himself on the rugs the girl had left. No sooner had he done so than she approached shyly and began to tug at one of his heavy boots.

"Truly, lord," she said softly, "when a lord is drunk it is hard to take off his high shoes. Yet I would show honor to the one who comes to buy me. Such is the will of my master, Mir Turek, who can cheat better than any other merchant of Samarkand."

"In the house of a stranger, little daughter, they must slay me before my boots can be taken off, or my sword from my side." Khlit threw back his shaggy, white-haired head, with a roar of laughter that startled the girl. "So, I have come to buy you? Nay, devil take it, I have come for some ivory trinkets."

"I did not know, lord," the girl drew back and Khlit saw that she was trembling. "Mir Turek said that he would sell me, and that I should comb my hair, for men would come to look at me and feel my limbs. They have never seen my face in the streets of Samarkand, yet Mir Turek told Fogan Ultai, chief of the servants, that I would bring the price of two good horses. Fogan Ultai doubted, and for that Mir Turek beat me. Then Fogan Ultai struck me on the ears to ease his honor——"

A sound of shuffling steps caused the child to break off in alarm. Mir Turek stood before them, scowling.

"Chatterer! Slanderer of your master! Be off to the slaves' quarters. This is a Cossack lord, not a buyer of slaves, Kerula. Leave us."

The girl slipped from the room, and a smile replaced the scowl on the merchant's face as he seated himself by Khlit. The Cossack considered him in silence. He had never seen a man who resembled Mir Turek. The man's eyes slanted even more than those of a Turkoman; his black hair was straight, instead of curly, and his hands were long and carefully kept. The merchant proffered a cup of wine from an ebony stand, but Khlit shook his head.

"The Turkomans say," said Khlit grimly, "that when a sword is drawn, no excuse is needed. I have come for the trinkets, not wine."

"Yet I am no Turkoman," smiled Mir Turek, and his voice purred. "See, it is written that he who drinks from the cup need have no care. Can you read the words on the cup? The language is like that on your sword."

"Nay, it looks as if a dog had scratched it," responded the Cossack idly.

He could not read in books, but he was wise in the language of men's faces and he knew that Mir Turek had more in his mind than he spoke.

"Here is the money, I will take the trinkets."

He nodded at where the elephants stood on an ebony cabinet, but Mir Turek held up one hand.

"The men of Samarkand are fools—Usbeks—and are fit only to be slaves. The chief of my slaves, Fogan Ultai, has told me that there is a story in the bazaars that you are Khlit, the Cossack who outwitted Tal Taulai Khan, leader of the Golden Horde, and that your sword is as much to be feared as that of Kaidu, the warrior of the Tatars. Truly, I see that you are a man of valor. I have need of such a man."

"Aye, I am Khlit. Men call me the Wolf. Say what is on your mind, Mir Turek. The short word is best, if it is the truth."

Mir Turek's eyes half-closed. Through the narrowed lids they rested on Khlit's sword.

"Before the star Ortu descends from its zenith," he said slowly, "I am going from Samarkand to Karakorum, in the land of the Tatars far to the north. The journey will be over the mountains that these fools call the Roof of the World, past Kashgar, to the Great Desert of Gobi. There is no one in Samarkand who will go with me, yet the journey is not difficult, for my grandfather's father came over the route from Karakorum to Samarkand."

"Aye," said Khlit.

"I need a man who will lead the Turkomans who go with me as guard," pursued the other. "There are robbers in the Roof of the World and by the borders of the Great Desert the Tatar tribes fight among themselves, for Tal Taulai Khan is dead and the Jun-gar fight with the Kallmarks and the Boron-gar with both.

"The home of my family is in Altur Haiten, by the mountains of Khantai Khan. But the journey to the north is perilous, and I need a leader of fighting men. I am learned in the knowledge of books and trade, but I can not wield a sword. The name of Khlit, the Wolf, will protect my caravan."

"Aye," said Khlit. Something in his tone caused Mir Turek to glance at him sharply.

"Will you come to Karakorum, lord?" he asked. "Name what price you ask. It will be paid. As a pledge, take, without payment the twin elephants."

"I will come," said Khlit, "when your tongue has learned to speak the truth, Mir Turek. Truly, I am not a fool, like these of Samarkand. An Usbek chief could lead your men, and for little pay. My name is not known north of the Roof of the World. Cease these lies, Mir Turek—I like them little."

The slant eyes of the merchant closed, and he folded his arms into his long sleeves. He was silent for a space as if listening, and as he listened a change came over his face. Khlit heard the sound, too, a low murmur in an adjoining room. Mir Turek got to his feet without noise and vanished in the direction of the sound. Khlit waited watchfully, but in a moment the merchant reappeared, dragging Kerula by the arm. The girl's brown eyes were filled with tears.

"Busybody! One without honor!" He flung the slender form of the slave girl on the rugs, and planted his slippered toes in her ribs. "Blessed is the day when I can sell you and be bothered no longer by tears. Did I not say the lord was not a buyer of women? Fogan Ultai shall reward you for listening."

The girl sobbed quietly, rolling over to escape the assault of Mir Turek's broad feet. Khlit watched in silence. She was the merchant's property, and he was entitled to do with her as he chose. Still, the sight was not pleasant. Mir Turek continued his imprecations, mingled with promises that Kerula would be sold without fail, on the morrow. Khlit touched the girl's hair as if admiring its fine texture.

"Harken, Kerula," he said. "Is there no young Turkoman who looks upon you with favor and who would please you for a master?"

"Nay, lord," sobbed the girl, withdrawing beyond the merchant's reach, "why should I like a Turkoman? Without doubt, they are shaggy as mountain sheep."

"She can not come to Karakorum," put in Mir Turek. "The journey through the mountains is too hard, and she would die, without profit to me."

Khlit regarded his black pipe thoughtfully. It was long since he had seen the fresh face and clear eyes of a child. He reached into his wallet and drew out the coins he had offered for the elephants. These he laid before Mir Turek.

"You have named a price for the girl, Mir Turek," he said, "the price of two horses. Here it is. I will buy the child."

The merchant's slant eyes gleamed at sight of the gold, but he shook his head dubiously.

"I could get a better price in the bazaars. What do you want with the girl, Cossack? She can not come on the journey."

Khlit's beard wrinkled in a snarl.

"Take the money for the girl, Mir Turek. I will take Kerula. Nay, she will not come with us, one-without-understanding!" Turning to the slave, Khlit's tone softened. "Tomorrow, Kerula, you can beat the back of Fogan Ultai with a stick, for I will watch. Go where you will in Samarkand, for you are free. I have bought you of Mir Turek. And I say to go where you will."

The girl gazed at him wide-eyed. As if to convince herself she had heard aright she put out her hand and touched the Cossack's coat. The latter, however, took no more notice of her.

II

Khlit had said that Mir Turek lied. It was then that the merchant told Khlit the true cause of his journey to Karakorum. And this tale was strange, strange beyond belief. It was the fruit of Mir Turek's reading, and the tale of the Leo Tung astrologer who had gone, with Mir Turek's grandfather's father, to the mountains of Khantai Khan, to the tomb of Genghis Khan.

Yet in spite of the strangeness of the tale, Khlit did not say this time that Mir Turek lied. In Khlit's veins was the blood of the Cossack Tatar folk who had ruled the empire of the steppe, and taken treasure from their enemies. He wondered, but did not speak his thoughts.

It was a tale that began with the death of Genghis Khan, called the "Master of the Earth," and ended with the death of Mir Turek's ancestor and the Leo Tung man from the vapor that lay among the trees of Khantai Khan. It was about a treasure such as Khlit had not thought existed in the world, the treasure of Genghis Khan.

There came a time, said Mir Turek, when the "Mighty Man-slayer" paused in his conquest of the world. The beast Kotwan appeared to Genghis Khan in a vision and the ruler of the Tatar horde which had subjugated the world from Khorassan to Zipangu, and from Lake Baikal to the furthest city of Persia, returned home to die.

Genghis Khan was wiser than all other rulers. Knowing that he was dying, he gave orders that peace be made with his worthiest foes, the Chinese of Tangut and Sung, and that his death should not be disclosed. When his body was carried to the tomb in the mountains of Khantai, twenty thousand persons were slain to keep him company to the shades of the Teneri, among them those who built the tomb. So said the astrologer of Leo Tung. Thus none could say they had seen the spot where the Master of the Earth lay in the grip of the Angel of Death.

Twenty thousand souls accompanied Genghis Khan on his journey to the Teneri, and the treasure, spoils of a thousand cities, was placed in his tomb. This tomb was unmolested by the Tatars, until the coming of Leo Tung, who was a Chinaman and dared to look on the dead face of the leader of the Horde. Leo Tung had found the spot in the forests of Khantai Khan, with Mir Turek's ancestor. They had passed the gate of the Kukukon River; they had passed the Onon Muren; they had seen the starlight gleam on the Bearers of Wealth.

They had seen the treasure of Genghis Khan, said Mir Turek, his eyes gleaming as with fever, but the mists of Khantai Khan had closed around them. Mir Turek did not know just why they had left the tomb. He knew that a great fear came on them and they fled. The Leo Tung man had died very quickly, and the other went from the Khantai Khan region to Samarkand.

Before he died he had told his son the way to the tomb of Genghis Khan. And so the tale had come to Mir Turek. The merchant of Samarkand knew that a change had taken place in the Tatar people. Their power had been broken by the Chinese, shortly after the death of Genghis Khan. With the assistance of Khlit, he might enter the tomb and find the treasure of Genghis Khan, Master of the Earth and leader of the Golden Horde.

Aye, said Mir Turek softly, he was a scholar, but he had searched in books for the wealth of Genghis Khan. There was the tale of Chakar Noyon, *gylong,* which told of the tomb. Chakar Noyon, being a priest, had said that the Onon Muren or spirits of the slain twenty thousand guarded the tomb; that was an idle story. Mir Turek did not believe it.

Nevertheless, when the other had finished, Khlit asked himself why the fathers of Mir Turek had not sought for the tomb of Genghis Khan. He found the answer in the fever that burned in the other's eyes and the restless movements of the white hands. Mir Turek felt in his heart a great fear of what he was to do, and this fear had been his fathers'.

Khlit was not the man to shrink from seizing gold. Even the gold of the tomb of Genghis Khan. Yet, with his desire for gold was mingled delight at the thought of returning to the steppe that had been his home, even in another part of the world.

III

Thus it happened that Khlit began the journey which was to take him over the mountains called the Roof of the World, above Ladak, or Tibet, north of Kashgar, past Issyuk Kul and Son Kul, the twin lakes of the clouds to the desert of Gobi.

Concerning this journey and its ending there are few who believe the story of Khlit. Yet the Cossack was not the man to say what was not so, for love of the telling. And there is the book of Chakar Noyon, to be found in one of the Samarkand mosques, and the annals of the chronicler of Hang-Hi, the great general of the Son of Heaven. Truly, belief is, after all, the fancy of the hearer and only the fool is proud of his ignorance.

When the sun gilded the top of the ruins of Bibi Khanum, the followers of Mir Turek had pitched their felt tents on the slope of Chupan Ata, on the way to the Syr River. Already the heat of the Samarkand valley had been replaced by the cool winds of the mountains and Khlit was glad to don his old sheepskin coat. He looked around with some satisfaction at the camp.

Mir Turek's following consisted of a dozen Turkomans and Fogan Ultai, master of the slaves. These had placed their small tents in a circle beside the donkeys, the pack-animals of the expedition.

Khlit's leadership had already instilled discipline into the sturdy but independent followers. Two stood as sentries near the caravan path. The Turkomans had tried rebellion against the Cossack, and had learned why he was called the Wolf. Fogan Ultai, however, as the servant of Mir Turek, was not under Khlit's orders. Twice during the day the leader of the slaves had refused obedience and Mir Turek had upheld him.

Fogan Ultai was a small man, pale in face, with dark hair like his master's, and the same slant eyes. Khlit did not like the man, who was watchful and silent, speaking occasionally to Mir Turek in a tongue the Cossack did not understand. As long as Fogan Ultai did not interfere with his authority over the Turkomans, Khlit was willing to leave the other in peace.

It was after the evening meal, and Khlit was smoking his pipe in front of the tent he had pitched for himself. He sat with his back to the tent, his sword over his knees, watchful of what went on. In the twilight gloom he could make out the figures of the men throwing dice by a fire.

Suddenly Khlit took his pipe from his mouth. He made no other movement, but his tall figure stiffened to alertness and his keen eyes searched the gloom. A shadow had appeared, slipping from tent to tent, making no sound. And the sentries had not given warning.

The shadow paused in front of him, and Khlit's hand went to his sword. The form approached him, and a small figure cast itself at his feet. A pair of white hands clasped his boots.

"Lord, you are my master—be merciful," the voice of Kerula came out of the darkness. "Lord, do not kick me, because I followed after you on a donkey that was lame, so it was not taken with the others, and slipped past the men who are watching. I followed because you would have sent me back if I had come sooner. But my hunger is very great now, and I am cold."

Khlit reached out his rough hand and took the girl by the shoulder. Kerula's white face looked up into his. He could feel the girl's warm breath against his cheek.

"I said you could not come, Kerula," he replied gruffly. "Why do you seek the hardship of the journey? It is no path for a girl. There are gallants in Samarkand who would buy you flowers and slaves——"

"Nay, lord. I am afraid of the men of Samarkand. I have no master but you, Khlit, lord. The others would bring shame on me, the women say. I will follow after the caravan, truly, on the lame donkey, and you will not know I am there. Perhaps I can prepare your food, or clean the mud from your boots. Do not let them send me to Samarkand."

Khlit shook his head, and the child gave a soft wail of distress.

"The way is too hard," he said. "The men will give you food, but tomorrow——"

The girl rose from her knees, with bowed head.

"You are my lord, and you send me to the bazaars of Samarkand. I have no home. If you would let me follow, I would sleep with your horse, and bring your wine cups, until we reach the land where Genghis Khan rules. My mother, before she died, told me of the land."

Khlit raised his head in surprise at the girl's speech. Before he could answer a shadow appeared beside Kerula, and Fogan Ultai's soft voice spoke.

"Get back where you came from, Kerula, or your palms will be well whipped! You have heard the word of the Cossack lord. Our master, Mir Turek, would let you off less easily if he knew you were here."

The master of the slaves caught the child roughly and shook her. She clasped his hand and sank her teeth into it viciously. Fogan Ultai gave a cry of pain. As he lifted his free hand to strike the girl she sprang free defiantly.

"Mir Turek shall know of this, offspring of the low-born," hissed the servant. "You say you have had no food for a day. Good! You will pray to me for food before you shall leave the camp."

"Who gave you authority, Fogan Ultai," said Khlit, "to give orders in the camp? If I say the child shall eat, you will bring her food."

"I?" Fogan Ultai shivered as if with cold. "I am no slave, and my caste——" he broke off—"nay, I heard you say she was to go, Khlit."

"I said that the men would give her food. You have keen ears, Fogan Ultai. Since you have come, like a dog at the scent of a carcass, you may bring the food to Kerula. She is hungry."

"Mir Turek would not allow that to come to pass, Khlit," the other's voice was smooth and sibilant. "He knows it is not for such as I to bring food, or for a Cossack to give me orders——"

Fogan Ultai's speech ended in a strangling gasp. Khlit had risen from his sitting posture, and as he rose his heavy fist crashed into the other's face. Fogan Ultai lay on the ground, his arms moving slowly, half-stunned. Slowly he got to his feet, staggering. The girl drew in her breath sharply and shrank back.

"Cossack," Fogan Ultai mumbled, for blood was in his mouth,

"the girl is yours and if it is your wish—she shall eat. But a man is a fool who seeks an enemy. Let another bring the food."

"I said you, Fogan Ultai, not another."

The attendant was silent for a moment. He felt his injured face tenderly. Khlit waited for the flash of a dagger or the hiss of an imprecation but Fogan Ultai was silent. Surely, Khlit thought, he was a strange man.

"The food shall be brought, Cossack, if it is still your wish. Yet it would be well to say otherwise."

Receiving no response from Khlit, the man turned and disappeared into the darkness. Khlit turned to the girl roughly, for he knew that he had earned an enemy.

"Sit in my tent, Kerula," he said shortly. "The wind is cold. After you have eaten, roll yourself in my woolen robe. I shall sleep with my horse."

The next day saw Kerula mounted on her lame donkey riding behind Khlit and Mir Turek. The latter said nothing concerning the appearance of the girl, and Khlit thought that he had spoken with Fogan Ultai. The difficulty of the way grew, and cold gripped the riders. The Turkoman horses, wrapped in their felt layers, with their high-peaked wooden saddles seemed indifferent to the change in climate, but the donkeys shivered, and Mir Turek wrapped himself in a costly fur robe. Khlit saw to it that the girl had a sheepskin cloak that had been carried in the baggage.

The moon which had been bright at the start of the journey had vanished to a circlet of silver when the riders, under guidance of one of the Turkomans, passed the blue waters of the mountain lakes, Issyuk Kul and Son Kul, and reached the passes of the Thian Shan Hills. Here the Turkoman guide gave up the leadership, but Fogan Ultai declared that he could find his way among the passes with the aid of the merchantman's maps and the stars.

Khlit, who saw everything as he rode, noted that Mir Turek had fallen silent, and that the merchant spent much time in talk with Fogan Ultai in the *yurtas* in the evenings. So far, however, the master of the slaves had been content to keep out of Khlit's way. The Cossack paid no further attention to Fogan Ultai, other than to see to the loading and priming of the brace of Turkish pistols he carried in his belt. These were the only firearms of the expedition.

Mir Turek broke his silence, one day when the sunlight lay on the rock slopes of the mountains without warming the faces of the riders, to speak of Genghis Khan. It was through these passes, said the merchant, that the slaves of the Mighty Manslayer carried the wealth that had been taken from the cities of Damascus and Herat to Karakorum.

The fever burned in the man's eyes as he spoke. The wealth of Genghis Khan had been so great that his minister had never counted it. From the four corners of Asia slaves brought it to the Master of the Earth. Genghis Khan had kept a hoard of gold, the book of Chakar Noyon said, at his palace. One minister had given away jewels to his wives, until Genghis Khan had learned of it, when the minister had cut his own throat to avoid the wrath of the conqueror.

Khlit listened while Mir Turek told of the campaigns of Genghis Khan, and how victories had come to the standard of the Horde, the standard of yaks' tails that had traveled from Karakorum to Herat.

The merchant halted his words as the advance rider of the party came to them. The Turkoman, who had been some hundred paces in front of Khlit and Mir Turek, brought with him a slender man, in a long robe who carried a pack. The man, Khlit saw, was clean-shaven, with the hair of his forehead cut to the skin.

The stranger spoke with Mir Turek, who shook his head to show that he did not understand. At the merchant's gesture Fogan Ultai rode up and addressed the newcomer. The two fell back among the attendants where Kerula was. But Mir Turek did not resume his conversation. He seemed impatient to halt, when before he had been eager to push on. As his reason, he gave the rising wind which seemed to promise snow. The star Ortu, said Mir Turek, was no longer above them, and they could not count on its protection.

Khlit accordingly called a halt. The felt tents were pitched, the *yurta* formed. Kerula was accustomed to see to the erecting of the Cossack's shelter, which was beside her own, and Khlit rode into the twilight to see to the posting of the sentries. Before he returned he saw a strange sight. For the Turkomans on watch had kneeled to the ground and laid their ears against the path.

Khlit brought the men to their feet with a hearty imprecation. The Turkomans were sullen, saying that they listened for signs of approaching danger. What this danger was, they would not say. But one, the less sullen of the two, muttered that danger might be met along the path that could be heard, and could not be seen.

Impatient of the men's superstition, Khlit returned to his tent where Kerula sat with his evening meal. Around the fire which blazed very brightly, the others of the party were gathered. And Khlit frowned as he watched. The stranger they had met that day stood in front of the fire, throwing grease from a pot upon it.

As the man with the shaven head did this, he read aloud from a small book he held. The words meant nothing to Khlit, but Mir Turek and Fogan Ultai listened intently. Truly, Khlit thought, Mir Turek was a man of double meanings. For the merchant had declared that the newcomer was a beggar. Khlit had never known a beggar who could read. As he turned this over in his mind, Kerula, who had crept near him spoke.

"Khlit, lord," she whispered, her eyes bright in the firelight, and all save her eyes covered by the fur cloak for the cold, "last night I dreamed a strange dream. It was that a falcon flew down on my wrist, and it held the sun and a star in its talons. The falcon had flown far, and was weary, but it held the sun. And I was glad."

"You have many dreams, little sparrow," smiled Khlit.

When he smiled, the bitterness faded from his hard face. Kerula loved to see him smile. More often of late she had coaxed him to do so.

"Am I a conjuror, to tell you what they mean?"

"Nay, Khlit, lord," she chattered, "you are too tall and big for a conjuror. See, the man who is reading prayers by the fire is such a one. I heard Fogan Ultai say he was a *gylong*, servant of the great lamas, and a man of wisdom."

Fogan Ultai had called the stranger a man of wisdom. Mir Turek had said he was a beggar. One had lied, and Khlit suspected it was Mir Turek.

"Did Fogan Ultai say more than that, Kerula?" he asked carelessly, watching the group by the fire.

"Aye, Khlit, lord. I heard him say to Mir Turek the man was a conjuror. Then he said to the man with the long robe that he was clever, he could conjure the two pistols away from you, and he— Fogan Ultai—would give him a donkey and some gold."

"Hey, little Kerula, he would have to be a very wise man to do that," chuckled Khlit. "Are you sure you did not dream that, too?"

"Nay, Khlit, lord," the girl looked at him strangely, "but I dreamed that we met an evil, two-headed snake, and that you buried it. After that, the snake was no longer evil."

Khlit said no more, but long after Kerula had crept into her tent, and the group around the fire had scattered, he sat in thought, his curved sword across his knees. What had prompted the Turkomans to turn sullen and lay their ears to the ground? Why had Mir Turek, who trusted him, lied that evening about the *gylong*? And why did Fogan Ultai desire his pistols?

IV

In a dream the beast Kotwan with the head of a horse and a horn in its forehead, that speaks all languages, came to Genghis Khan, the Mighty Manslayer. The beast Kotwan spoke as follows: "It is time for the Master to return to his own land." Whereupon Genghis Khan turned homeward. And when he reached his home he died.

From the book of Chakar Noyon, gylong.

Concerning the events that came to pass when the party of Mir Turek crossed the desert of Gobi, Khlit is the only one who will tell. It is true that the narrative of the Hang-Hi chronicler mentions the sights and sounds which Khlit and Kerula heard in the night. But the Chinese historian ascribes the sounds to wind in the sand and the imagination of the Tatar travelers whose minds were filled with stories of Genghis Khan. Fools, said the Chinaman, walk unreflecting. Yet Khlit was not the man to be led astray by sounds that he imagined.

As for Kerula, Khlit found that the girl's tongue was eager to repeat stories of Genghis Khan that she heard from Mir Turek. The child had listened while the scholar read from his books. The books were all she knew, and so she supposed that Genghis Khan and his Tatar Horde were still alive, and might be met with on the sands of the Great Desert.

Khlit humored her in her fancies, and smiled at the dreams she repeated. He knew that the "dreams" of Kerula were her way of telling things that she thought he might not believe. The Cossack did not laugh at the girl for her fancies, because he was always ready to hear more of Genghis Khan, a conqueror more powerful than any Khlit had known. Even Tal Taulai Khan seemed a *mirza* beside the figure of the man who was called the Mighty Manslayer.

Mir Turek had ceased to talk with Khlit concerning their journey, and the tomb in the forest of Khantai Khan. The merchant and Fogan Ultai rode with the *gylong*. Neither interfered with his leadership, which was all Khlit asked. He was aware that since the coming of the *gylong*, a change had taken place in the party. The Turkomans became more sullen and had to be driven forward. And Mir Turek grew silent, seemingly waiting for something. Khlit took care to keep Kerula with him as much as possible. He had heard the Turkomans talking about her.

"Fogan Ultai says," he had heard them say, "that the girl Kerula has the ears of a skunk and the eyes of an ermine."

When the party descended the slope of the Thian Shan Hills and entered the desert, the Turkomans murmured further. This was natural, however, in face of the difficulties in front of them.

The desert, the first that Khlit had seen, was an ocean of sand, with wind ridges and gullies. In order to keep to a straight course by the sun, it was necessary to cut across the ridges, which varied from eight to some twenty feet in height. There were few springs to be met with, and the party was forced to keep an outlook for the coming of wind, which meant a halt and hurried preparation against sand-storms.

Although the country was new to Khlit, he did not give up his leadership of the party. On the advice of the *gylong*, Khlit exchanged their donkeys at a village on the edge of the desert, for a smaller number of camels. He kept his own horse, but the others gave up theirs. Thus the *gylong* gained a camel for his donkey.

After a rest at the village, Khlit ordered an advance into the desert, when the moon was again full. Mir Turek was content, as the star he regarded as his protection was now high in the heavens. Khlit rode at the rear of the little caravan where he could watch the Turkomans and where there was no one at his back.

The party had gone far into the desert and the Thian Shan summits had vanished on the horizon when the first of the strange events came to pass.

Khlit had been sleeping soundly in his felt tent, when he was awakened by Kerula crawling through the flap in early daylight. The girl's hair hung loose around her face, and Khlit saw that her eyes were wide and fixed. He had grasped his sword when the flaps of the tent moved, but now he released it, and sat up, wide awake on the instant. The girl crept close to him, shivering, yet it was not from cold of the night.

"I am frightened, Khlit, lord," she whispered. "For I have had a dream in the night. It was that an animal crawled around my tent, crying my name. I heard it sniffing, and clawing at the tent. How could an animal call my name? I am afraid."

"A dream will not hurt you, little sparrow," answered Khlit cheerfully. "And the sun has come up to chase it away."

The girl however, did not smile.

"When I came from my tent," she said softly, "I saw the marks of the beast. It had gone away. But how could it speak? I heard it calling, calling 'Kerula.' Animals can not speak, can they, unless——"

Khlit, to distract her, bade her gruffly prepare his morning meal. Later, however, when he left his shelter he took care to look at the ground around Kerula's tent which was beside his. He saw that there were actually marks on the ground.

Carefully, Khlit scanned them. They were marks of hoofs, and ran completely around the tent, clearly visible in the sand. When he tried to follow them away from the place he lost them in the tracks of the party. The hoof-marks, he saw, were smaller than those of a horse. He had heard that there were antelopes in the desert. Yet the tracks were larger than antelope hoofs. He said nothing of what he had seen to the girl.

The day's journey was short, and Mir Turek halted early, fearing a sand-storm, for the sun had gone behind clouds. The Turkomans gathered about the fire at dusk, and Khlit was obliged to drive one from the *yurta* to watch from a sand ridge. For his own satisfaction he placed a pointed stake firmly in the ground by his tent, indicating the direction they were to take in the morning. He had learned by experience that the ridges were often changed in appearance overnight.

As he sat over his evening meal with Kerula pensive beside him, the figure of Fogan Ultai detached itself from the group by the fire and approached him.

"Health to you, Khlit," said the master of the slaves with a bow. "The Turkomans have asked that I come as spokesman. It is not well to force a man to do what his habits forbid. They are murmuring against standing sentry during the night. The Turkomans have heard stories of the desert in the village we left. They think evil things may come to the sentries. You and I are wise—we know they are fools. Still, it is best to let a man do as he is accustomed."

"Does a sheep hide his head when the tiger hunts, Fogan Ultai?"

said Khlit. "Shall the camp be blind during the night when there may be danger? Nay, a beast came last night and passed around Kerula's shelter."

Fogan Ultai shook his head, smiling.

"There are no beasts in the desert, Khlit. The evils the Turkomans fear are not to be seen. Let them sleep in their tents. It is not well," the man's voice dropped, "to tie the knot of hatred."

"Then, Fogan Ultai, you and I are wise. We do not fear the stories of evil. We two will watch, each taking half the night."

For a long moment Fogan Ultai's slant eyes gleamed into Khlit's. Then he turned away indifferently.

"Let the Turkomans stand watch. They are low-born."

Yet the Turkomans could not have watched well that night. Before dawn Kerula burst into Khlit's shelter and clung to him sobbing. The same animal, she said, had come close to her tent. She had not been asleep this time, and she had heard its claws on the felt. Its breath had smelled of musk, so strong that it sickened her.

When the beast had been on the other side of the tent, the girl had slipped out on the side nearest Khlit and had dashed into his shelter. She was shaken with sobs, pressing her hands against her face.

"It is the beast, Kotwan," she sobbed. "He has come to take me with him. Oh, do not let him take me, Khlit, lord. I am afraid of Kotwan, who smells of musk. He called my name and he wants me to follow him to the shades of the Teneri, up into the air over the desert."

Khlit tried to quiet the girl, saying that he heard nothing, but when he made a move to leave the shelter, she clung to him tearfully. It was long before she dropped off to sleep, wrapped in some of his furs. Khlit listened, without moving for fear of disturbing her, and heard nothing more. Yet he fancied that an odor of musk filled the shelter.

V

The next day the girl had recovered somewhat from her fright. She refused to leave Khlit's side during the march over the shifting sands. Sleep overtook her at times on the camel, and she swayed in the cords that kept her in place. Each time this happened, she awoke with a start, and cried out for Khlit.

The Cossack did not like the look in the girl's face. She was pale and the lack of sleep added to the fatigue of the journey was beginning to tell on her. Khlit did not mention her experience of the night, for he found that she believed the strange beast Kotwan had come to her tent. The girl's brain was filled with idle fancies. His heart was heavy, however, at the look of dread in her eyes, for Kerula had endeared herself to him, as much as another person could win the affection of a man who counted his enemies by the thousand, and thirsted for fighting.

That night Kerula begged to be allowed to sleep in his tent, but the Cossack sternly ordered her to her own, and she went reluctantly. Contrary to his custom, he did not post a sentry, but retired early to his shelter, and his snores soon kept accompaniment to the monotonous reading of the *gylong* by the fire.

Before midnight, however, when the camp was quiet, Khlit's snores ceased. The flap of his tent was lifted cautiously and the Cossack crawled out on all fours. Noiselessly he made his way from his tent to the edge of the camp.

The *yurta* had been placed in a gully. Khlit, surveying his surroundings in the starlight, saw that the camels and the Turkoman shelters were some paces distant from the tents of the leaders.

Crawling down the gully, Khlit sought a depression where he could see the tent of Kerula against the skyline, within bowshot. He scooped out a seat for himself in the sand, with his back against the wind. Drawing his sheepskin *svitza* close about him, for the night was cold, he settled himself to watch, denying himself the comfort of a pipe. If an animal visited the tents between then and dawn, he was determined to have a look at it.

Khlit did not attach significance to the fears of the girl about the mythical animal she called Kotwan. He had seen, however, the tracks around the tent which were too large for an antelope, and he had caught the scent of musk, which Kerula declared came from the visitant of the night. No animal that Khlit knew smelled of musk, and had sharp hoofs. As far as he knew Fogan Ultai was right when he said there were no beasts in the desert, for the party had not met any since leaving the foothills of the Thian Shan. Wherefore Khlit was curious.

The Cossack was accustomed to watching, and he did not nod as he sat in the sand depression, with his scrutiny fixed on the horizon

near the tents. The stars gleamed at him, and an occasional puff of
wind stirred the sand about him. He must have watched for some
hours, and the stars were not paler when he sat erect, gazing closely
at the tents.

Something had moved near Kerula's shelter. The light was indis-
tinct and Khlit could not make it out. He had heard nothing. Presently he felt that the thing was moving away from the tent and nearer
him.

Khlit softly removed one of the pistols from his belt and got to his
knees. Crouching low over the sand he could make out a dark object
passing across the stars moving down the gully toward him. For the
first time he heard a sound, a low hiss that he could not place.

Then Khlit stiffened alertly. The wind had brought him the odor
of musk. The scent clung to his nostrils and ascended to his brain.
He felt the hair at the back of his neck stir, and a chill puff of wind
sent tingles down his spine.

The black object was within a few paces, and he saw that it was
something moving on all fours. Carefully he leveled the pistol, taking
the best aim he could in the dark.

And then Khlit let the pistol fall to his side. The odor of musk
that came to him so strongly was surely from the windward side.
Yet the dark object came toward him from the *yurta* which was
away from the wind. Khlit drew a deep breath and his eyes strained
toward the moving form. His heart gave a leap as he recognized it.
It was Kerula, moving over the sand on her hands and knees.

The child had crept from her tent out into the night that she
feared. He could hear her labored breathing as she passed him
slowly. The scent of musk could not have come from the girl. It had
come from the windward side. Khlit turned quickly and searched
the darkness with anxious glance.

On the further side of the gully, some distance in front of the girl
was a larger object, defined against the sand. It moved in the same
direction, away from the camp. Khlit heard a hissing sound come
from it, and understood why he had smelled the musk. Watching
the girl, he had not seen the other thing pass him. He made it out
as an animal of powerful build, with horns, that seemed to drag its
hind legs.

Quickly Khlit raised his pistol. Sighting it at the beast's head he
pulled the trigger. The weapon clicked dully and he thrust it into

his belt with a curse. The sand must have choked its flint and powder.

With a hasty glance at the moving forms, Khlit rose to his feet. Bending low, he trotted over the sand ridge at his side into the gully that ran beside the one he had been in. For some distance he ran, following the winding of the gully.

Fearful of losing trace of the girl and the animal, he turned back to the ridge, to find that he was running through an opening into the other gully. His heavy boots made no sound in the sand, and Khlit did not see that he was heading straight for the creeping animal until he heard a sharp hiss, and saw the object rise up before him.

He caught a brief glimpse of horns and long ears outlined against the sky, and felt a hot breath on his face. His hand leaped to his sword, and the curved blade was pulled from its sheath.

As Khlit's arm swept upward with the sword, it moved outward. The blade struck the beast where it was aimed, under the head. Khlit saw it stagger back and slashed it twice across the head as it fell to the sand. Moving back from the struggling object he called to the girl.

"Kerula! Here is Khlit, do not be afraid."

A moment more and Kerula was beside him, clinging to his coat, her head buried in his sleeve.

"It was the beast Kotwan," she cried, "calling me outside my tent. I heard it calling me and I came. Oh, it smelled of musk, and it kept calling. My legs would not hold me up and I crawled—where is the beast Kotwan?"

"Nay, little Kerula," laughed Khlit, "the beast Kotwan is a strange beast. But it will not come for you again. See!"

Drawing the girl after him, the Cossack stepped to the side of the dark object on the sand. He felt of it cautiously. It did not move. And when Khlit drew up his hand it held a beast's hide and horns. The hide seemed to be that of an antelope. The girl had bent over the figure that lay at their feet, fearfully. She tugged at Khlit's arm excitedly.

"Khlit, lord," she whispered, "it is the *gylong*. You have slain the *gylong*."

"Aye," said Khlit shortly. "The conjuror will conjure no more. I thought it was a strange animal that stood up on two legs when it saw you."

He felt in the sand and lifted two objects. One was a pony's hoof, cut off above the fetlock and dried. The other was a long dagger. He showed them to the girl.

"There is Kotwan's hoof, little Kerula. And the hide stinks of musk."

Khlit said nothing to Kerula, but he remembered the words of Fogan Ultai, and he guessed it was not wantonness, but the promise of a reward that had led the conjuror to terrify the girl and lure her into the desert. Also he began to understand why Fogan Ultai had coveted his pistols. Yet much was not clear to Khlit. He knew that Fogan Ultai hated Kerula because Khlit had made him demean himself in bringing her food. Still, this did not seem a sufficient reason for the girl's death.

Khlit's détour into the other gullies had confused him as to the direction of the camp. Unwilling to run the risk of going further from the *yurta* in trying to find it, he took the girl a short distance from the dead man and sat down to wait for dawn, sheltering her with his *svitza*. Kerula, relieved of her fear, soon became sleepy.

"How is it, Kerula," he asked thoughtfully, "that this fellow Fogan Ultai is so trusted by Mir Turek. Hey, your father fears him—as he feared the *gylong*."

"I do not know, Khlit, lord," Kerula responded sleepily. "Mir Turek will not give orders to Fogan Ultai. When the master of the slaves came to Samarkand he showed Mir Turek a gold disk he wore. They thought I was sleeping, but I looked out at them, and the gold disk was made like a sun, with rays, with writing in the center. That was not long ago—and soon Mir Turek began to speak of the tomb of Genghis Khan to himself when he read the books."

The voice of the girl trailed off and she was soon sleeping. Khlit waited patiently for dawn. The stars had begun to fade and the fresh wind sprang up.

Khlit's thoughts were busy and he was not aware that he slept. Surely, he felt the wind on his face and heard the girl's calm breathing. They were sitting near the top of one of the ridges, and he could make out the nearest waves of sand.

The moon was high above him, and there was a faint line of scarlet to the east. No, Khlit could not have been asleep. He did not remember dozing, nor did he waken. And yet, as a mist comes from the mountains, the mystery of the desert of Gobi came from the dark wastes of sand and gathered around the Cossack, the girl, and the still figure that had been the *gylong*.

It came without warning, and gradually. Khlit thought at first that the camels were stirring. He listened and he heard the wave of sound come from the east and close around him. This time he did not feel the fear that had gripped him for a space when he saw the strange beast in the dark.

Awe came upon Khlit as he listened. He strained his eyes, yet he could see nothing. With the wind the sounds swelled, and swept over him. Khlit marveled, as he listened, not moving. And something deep in him stirred at the sounds. He felt a swift exultation that rose with the sounds and left him when they had gone.

Out of the desert came the murmur of many horses' feet in the sand—the feet of thousands of horses that galloped with a clashing of harness. Surely, there were riders on the horses, for a chant rose from the sands, from thousands of throats, a low, wild chant that gripped Khlit's heart.

Came the creak of laden carts from the darkness. Carts that were drawn by oxen laboring under the *kang*. With them sounded the *pad-pad* of camels' feet. The chant of the riders died and swelled. When it swelled, it drowned the other sounds.

With it echoed the clash of arms, myriad of scabbards beating against the sides of horses. Another sound that Khlit knew was the flapping of standards came to his ears. In the darkness beside him a cavalcade was passing. No cavalcade, a host of mounted warriors. The chant was the song of the warriors and Khlit's throat trembled to answer it.

Mingling with the chant came a heavy tread that was strange to Khlit. The sands trembled under the tread. The sound neared Khlit and passed, not by him but over him. This was no tread of horses.

Khlit peered into the darkness, but the sand ridges were desolate. The stars were not obscured, and the line of crimson grew in the east. Louder swelled the chant of the horsemen, and the heavy tread of giant feet.

The clash of cymbals echoed faintly and with it the sound of distant trumpets. Then came the sound of a mighty trumpeting, not of horns, but of animals. The trumpeting drowned the chant of the riders. It ceased and silence descended suddenly on the desert.

Kerula stirred in his arms, and Khlit stood up to look over the sand ocean.

"Nay, Khlit, lord," the girl whispered, "you will not see them. I am not asleep. I am awake, and I heard it also. The passing of the *tumans*, with their standards of yaks' tails. I heard the wagons, and their oxen. And the creaking of the leather castles on the Bearers of Wealth. It was just as Mir Turek told me it would be. The chant of the mounted men was loudest of all, until the Bearers of Wealth gave the greeting of Dawn to the Master of the Earth."

Khlit rubbed his hand across his forehead and gazed at the dead *gylong*.

"I heard some sounds as of horsemen passing—" he began doubtfully.

"Aye, Khlit, lord. It was the army of Genghis Khan crossing the desert."

Then Khlit wondered if he had truly slept. The chant of the riders was still in his ears. But the rising sun showed the sands empty, and the camp at a little distance.

"Nay, little Kerula," he said finally, "you have dreamed another dream."

Yet when Khlit and Kerula returned to the *yurta*, they found only Mir Turek and Fogan Ultai with three camels. The Turkomans had gone, late in the night with the greater number of camels and most of the food. Fogan Ultai said that he had not been able to stop them, for they had heard sounds in the desert, and they were afraid.

VI

If a man despoils the tomb of a wise and just ruler he loses his virtue. Evil follows him and his sons. He is like a sal tree with a creeper o'ergrown.

Yen Lui Kiang, chronicler of Hang-Hi.

It was the beginning of Winter when Mir Turek and his companions left the desert of Gobi and reached a small village of mud huts to the north in the Tatar country of Karakorum, near the mountains of Khantai Khan.

The desert had taken its toll from the travelers. The Turkomans had not been seen after their departure. The *gylong* lay where he had fallen, covered by the shifting sands. Mir Turek believed the conjuror had gone with the attendants. Fogan Ultai said nothing, and Khlit wondered what the master of the slaves knew of the death of the *gylong*. Fogan Ultai had an uncanny way of getting information for himself. Before the party reached the village, the master of the slaves joined them with the tidings that all the surrounding country had been vacated by the Tatars.

From a herdsman, he said, he had learned that the Tatars were gathered within the walls of Altur Haiten where they had been besieged by the Chinese for a year. Altur Haiten was one of the strongholds of Tatary, to which the retreating hordes had been driven by Hang-Hi, the general of Wanleh, Emperor of China. Thus Mir Turek's prophecy that they would find the way to the mountains of Khantai Khan clear, was verified. Yet Khlit, wearied by the months of hardship in the desert, saw that if the way was clear, it was also barren of food and the supplies they needed.

They had come from the desert on the two surviving camels. Kerula and the remaining stock of grain and dates had been placed on the stronger of the beasts, and the three men took turns in riding the other. Khlit saw to it that Mir Turek and Fogan Ultai never rode on the other camel together. Since the affair of the *gylong* he had been wary of the two. Yet he had noticed two things.

One—Mir Turek feared Fogan Ultai more than at the start of the expedition. Two—Mir Turek was unwilling to part with Khlit, owing for some reason to his ownership of the curved sword. This, Kerula had told him, and Khlit had asked the girl if she could read the lettering on the sword. She could not do so, as the inscription was neither Chinese nor Usbek Tatar.

The girl had borne the journey bravely, yet she was very weak when they came to the village of mud huts. She was disappointed, too, because she had imagined that when they neared Karakorum they would find the Tatar country alive and flourishing as it had been in the days of Genghis Khan. Truly, thought Khlit, this was strange; for Kerula had learned of the old Tatars from Mir Turek, and she believed she lived in the land of the Master of the Earth. Khlit placed her in one of the mud huts of the empty village, and gave her fruit and water that he found near by.

He would not have left the girl if it had not been for Mir Turek. The merchant had been in a fever of excitement since he saw the summits of Khantai Khan. His fat figure was wasted by hardships, and his frame was hot with fever. He would not rest until he had left the girl with Fogan Ultai and set out, with Khlit and the two camels for the mountains.

"The girl will be safe, Khlit," he declared, "for Fogan Ultai can not leave the village without the camels. Come, we will go to the Kukulon gate, and the tomb of Genghis Khan while the way is open."

Khlit went reluctantly. He did not like to leave the girl with Fogan Ultai in the village. He liked even less the deserted appearance of the country. He knew what Mir Turek chose to forget, that they were at the end of their supplies, and must have food.

Yet he was not less eager than Mir Turek to go to the tomb of Genghis Khan. They were near a treasure which Mir Turek said was without equal in the world. Khlit had seen the treasure of the Turks, but he knew this would be greater, for the Tatars had despoiled the cities of the Turks. Lust of the gold gripped him.

The two set out at daybreak in the absence of Fogan Ultai and rode toward the mountains at the best pace of the camels. And as the slopes of Khantai Khan rose above them, Mir Turek's fever grew on him. He fastened his slant eyes greedily on the hills, and when they came in sight of a blue sheet of water, he gave a hoarse cry of triumph.

"The Lake Kukulon," he whispered. "The books told the truth. A river runs to the lake from the mountains. Aye, here we will find the Kukulon gate where my ancestor saw the Onon Muren."

But Khlit looked beyond the lake, and saw that where a river made its way down the slopes, the earth was a yellow and grayish color. He saw for the first time the forest of Khantai Khan. The trees, instead of the green verdure of pine and the brown foliage of oak, were bare of leaves. The forest of Khantai Khan was a dead forest. And Khlit's forebodings grew on him as he urged his camel after Mir Turek.

VII

Mir Turek skirted the edge of the lake, which was small, and followed an invisible path through the foothills, evidently finding his way by the instructions he had received from the man who had been there before. He headed toward a ravine that formed the valley between two crests of Khantai Khan. In this valley he could catch glimpses of the River Kukulon.

The merchant was gripped by the fever of gold. But Khlit kept his presence of mind, and watched carefully where they went. The Cossack was not superstitious; still, what he saw gave him misgivings. The ground they passed over was a dull gray in color, and the trees seemed withered as if by flames. The camels went ahead unwillingly. If he had been alone, Khlit might have gone no further. It was not fear of the mythical Onon Muren that oppressed him, or the fate of the others who had preceded them. A warning instinct, bred of the dead forests, that held them back.

At the edge of the River Kukulon they dismounted from the camels, fastening the beasts to a blasted tree-trunk, and went forward on foot, Mir Turek keeping to the bank of the stream which now descended from the gorge in the valley. Mir Turek went more slowly, scanning his surroundings, especially the river. The din of the waters drowned conversation, but the merchant signified by a gesture that he was sure of the way. Above them the gorge changed to a rocky ravine, down which the Kukulon boiled, a succession of waterfalls and pools.

The sun was at its highest point when Khlit saw the first sign of what had struck the attention of their predecessors. He halted above a large pool and caught Mir Turek's shoulder, pointing down into the blue water. The sun struck through to the bottom of the pool.

Among the rocks which formed the bottom Khlit had made out a series of white objects. Round, and white, polished by the water and gravel, he saw dozens of human skulls, and the tracework of skeletons.

"Hey, Mir Turek," he shouted grimly, "here are the Onon Muren come to greet us. Did your ancestor say we would see them?"

The merchant gazed down into the pool, and stared at the skulls with watery eyes.

"Aye, Khlit," he cried, "these are the Onon Muren. Did not the books say that twenty thousand had been slain at the tomb? It is proof we are on the right path."

"That may be, Mir Turek," replied Khlit without stirring, "yet the books said the Onon Muren guarded the tomb. Are they not a warning to go back?"

Mir Turek laughed eagerly, but his hand was shaking as he pointed up the gorge.

"There is the Kukulon gate," he cried, "you and I are wise, Khlit. We do not fear the bones of dead men. The star Ortu is again high in its orbit, and you, Cossack, have the curved sword of——"

He broke off, and stumbled forward, raising a gray cloud of dust that choked Khlit. The latter followed, muttering. The curved sword, he grumbled, would not cut the throats of spirits. Why did Mir Turek remind him so often of his sword? Khlit wondered why there were no bones visible on the ground. He thought that they had been covered by the gray dust. In that, Khlit was right. Yet, with all his wise knowledge, he did not guess the nature of the gray dust. If he had done so, he would not have followed Mir Turek further.

Khlit saw no gate, yet when they reached a pool larger than the others, at the bottom of a waterfall that fell between two pinnacles of rock, Mir Turek declared that they had come to the Kukulon gate. Here Khlit made his last protest, as Mir Turek informed him that the Kukulon gate was not to be seen. It lay, the merchant said, behind the waterfall, under the column of water. Khlit pointed to the skulls which gleamed at them again from the pool.

"In Samarkand," he said, "I swore that I would go with you, Mir Turek, to the tomb of Genghis Khan. If you go, I will go also. Yet I heard strange things in the desert of Gobi. The forest of Khantai Khan is not to my liking. I have a foreboding, Mir Turek. Men call me Wolf not because I have the courage of a fool. It would be well to turn back here."

Mir Turek thrust his lined face close to Khlit, and his smooth lips curled in a snarl, as of an animal that finds itself at bay.

"Do men truly call you Wolf, Khlit, or are you a jackal that whimpers at danger?"

"Nay, Mir Turek," said Khlit angrily, "you are a fool not to know fear from wisdom. Come!"

With this the Cossack jumped waist-deep into the pool. His heavy boots slipping and sliding over the skulls on the rocks, he crouched low and made his way along the rock at the rear of the waterfall. The force of the current carried the stream a yard out from the rock and Khlit was able to advance under the fall. Keeping his footing with difficulty he pressed forward in the semidarkness of the place. He was wet through with the spray which rose from the rocks.

Feeling the rock's surface carefully, he found that at a point it gave way. He could see a dark fissure where the rocks divided to the height of a man. Planting his feet cautiously he turned into the opening. For several yards he made his way forward until free of the spray from the waterfall.

"We are in the caverns now," the voice of Mir Turek echoed in his ear excitedly. "The books said that those who built the tomb changed the course of the Kukulon to cover the gate."

The gate of Kukulon! Beyond it lay the treasure of Genghis Khan. Mir Turek had spoken truly, Khlit thought as he sniffed the damp air of the cavern. And as he did so Khlit smelled danger as a hound smells a fox. A thin, strong odor came to him, not from the river but from the cavern. Was it dust from the gray earth?

"See," repeated Mir Turek, "there is the place where the sun comes in. The cavern leads to there. Come."

As Mir Turek ran stumbling ahead Khlit saw for the first time a circle of gray light, at some distance. Toward this the other headed, as fast as his weakened legs could carry him. The footing seemed smooth, as though prepared by men. As the gray light grew stronger Khlit saw that the cavern was littered with rusted arms and Tatar helmets. Here and there the skulls of the Onon Muren lay. Strange, thought Khlit, that the Tatars had been slain at the threshold of the tomb of Genghis Khan.

When he caught up with Mir Turek the other was standing at the end of the cavern, looking down into a chasm. Khlit glanced up and saw that the illumination was daylight, coming from an opening in the roof of the chasm. The opening was round, and as far as he could see, the chasm was round, descending straight into the heart of the mountain.

They stood at the entrance of the tunnel. The path, however, did not end here. A bridge of rock stretched across to the further side of the chasm. It was narrow and rose slightly, like a bent bow. Surely, thought Khlit, the hands of men had made this. He smelled the strange odor more strongly.

He saw also, why the light was dimmed. Up from the chasm thin streams of vapor rose, twining around the rock bridge. These streams of vapor did not eddy, as there was no wind. They wound upward in dense columns through which the further side of the gorge could be seen.

Mir Turek caught his arm and pointed to the further side.

"The Bearers of Wealth!" he screamed. "See, the Bearers of Wealth, and their burden. The tomb of Genghis Khan. We have found the tomb of Genghis Khan!"

The shout echoed wildly up the cavern, and Khlit thought that he heard a rumbling in the depths of the cavern in answer. He looked where Mir Turek pointed. At first he saw only the veil of smoke. Then he made out a plateau of rock jutting out from the further side. On this plateau, abreast of them, and at the other end of the rock bridge gigantic shapes loomed through the vapor. Twin forms of mammoth size reared themselves, and Khlit thought that they moved, with the movement of the vapor. These forms were not men but beasts that stood side by side. Between them they supported a square object which hung as if suspended in the air.

As he looked he saw that the twin shapes did not move—that it was the smoke which had deceived him. They faced him, tranquil and monstrous, and Khlit's heart quivered at the sight. He had seen similar beasts once before. His mind leaped back to the bazaars of Samarkand. Of giant size, the twin forms across the chasm were like the two elephants he had sought to buy from Mir Turek.

"The Bearers of Wealth!" chanted the merchant, stretching out both hands. "The golden elephants. All the treasure of Genghis Khan is melted into the Bearers of Wealth. So the books said and they did not lie. Akh, the star Ortu is truly a blessed omen. The followers of the dead Genghis Khan brought the treasure into the caverns of Khantai Khan. There they molded it into the elephant-forms and hung the casket of Genghis Khan between them. Yet none left the mountain alive."

Khlit stared across the chasm in wonder. If the forms of the Bearers of Wealth were gold, there must be tons of it. Even if jewels were not melted in the gold, the wealth was beyond measure. Lust of the gold surged over him, and at the same time another feeling.

Far below him the rumbling sounded in the mountain, and brought a fleeting thought of the rumbling he had heard on the desert of Gobi—the tread of the Bearers of Wealth. For the second time a sense of coming danger gripped him. Nothing moved in the chasm, and the rumbling might well be stones dropping in the depths. Khlit peered down and could not see the bottom.

"Aye," he said grimly, "it is the tomb of a hero."

As he spoke he caught the scent of the vapors and staggered back. "The wealth of Genghis Khan," screamed Mir Turek, trembling. "I have found it and it is mine. Blessings to the *Teneri* and the great Buddha!"

With that he started across the rock bridge. Khlit ran after him.

The rumblings echoed in the depths below them, and the vapors twined around the form of Mir Turek. Khlit felt them close around him, with a warm touch. Mir Turek stumbled and threw up his arms with a choking cry.

"*Akh! Akh!* The Onon Muren—at my throat——"

Khlit leaped forward, dizzy with the stifling vapors. He caught Mir Turek as the merchant was falling to the rock bridge. For an instant both were poised over the side of the bridge, half-way across to the tomb of Genghis Khan.

With all the force of his powerful muscles, Khlit dragged Mir Turek back, and hauled the senseless form of the other to safety in the cavern where they had stood a moment before. His head was swimming and his throat burned with the touch of the vapors. He sat down on a rock near the suffering Mir Turek and tore open the fastenings of his coat, at the throat. It was many moments before his head cleared and he was able to see the gray forms of the Wealth-Bearers across the chasm.

Truly, thought Khlit, the Onon Muren watched over the tomb of Genghis Khan. And those who invaded the tomb must have earned the wrath of the Onon Muren.

As soon as his strength had returned, Khlit lifted the form of the merchant to his shoulder and made his way back to the Kukulon gate, under the waterfall, to the hills of Khantai Khan.

VIII

Mir Turek had partly recovered when the two reached the village that night, but he was weak, and badly shaken by the experience in the chasm of the Wealth-Bearers. They found, however, that food was running low, and Khlit was anxious that Kerula should have medicines, for the girl was still suffering from her trip across the desert. She greeted Khlit joyfully, however, as he descended stiffly from his camel.

"Fogan Ultai has returned, Khlit, lord," she said, "and he has a plan. He has been to the edge of the Chinese camp around Altur Haiten, and he says that we can get to the city at night. The Tatars come through the Chinese lines. Then we can see the great Tatar warriors who are fighting there, and we can get plenty of food in the city."

Khlit considered this.

"Aye," he said, "it might be done. Yet you had better stay here with Mir Turek, Kerula."

"Nay, I would be frightened!" she exclaimed quickly. "Fogan Ultai says we can all go. And I do not want to be away from you, my lord, with the curved sword that every one fears. I dreamed last night that the two-headed snake you met and buried was not really buried, but it pursued me."

So it happened that when Mir Turek had recovered strength sufficiently, the four went with the camels to the outskirts of the Chinese camp, waiting there until darkness permitted a passage to the city. Khlit had agreed to this, after talking with Fogan Ultai. He did not trust the master of the slaves, who was sullen because Khlit and Mir Turek had gone to the mountains of Khantai Khan without him, yet he calculated that where his own safety was at stake, Fogan Ultai would act with them. The country around was stripped of provisions by the cavalry of the Chinese, and Fogan Ultai had promised that he knew a way to the city.

Mir Turek was eager to gain Altur Haiten, being shaken by his trip to the tomb of Genghis Khan. The merchant remained feverish, talking to himself often and startled by the slightest sound. While the party were waiting for darkness at the edge of a wood within sight of the tents and pavilions of the Chinese camp and the brown walls of the besieged city, Mir Turek laid a cloth on the ground and prayed earnestly. Kerula was in high spirits.

"Now we shall see the men of Genghis Khan," she sang, "the men of the Golden Horde. They will welcome us because Mir Turek is a man of wisdom and Khlit, lord, is a chieftain."

So Khlit went to the Chinese camp, not suspecting. With Kerula's hand in his he followed Fogan Ultai. In the darkness they followed ravines, keeping clear of the camp-fires. Seldom had Khlit, the Wolf, been trapped. Yet how should he suspect?

He heard Mir Turek murmuring prayers behind him, and turned to curse the merchant, with Kerula's hand still in his. For an instant the strange words of the other caused him suspicion. What language was the merchant speaking? Why had Mir Turek been so curious about his sword? And why had he given up thought of the treasure of Genghis Khan? The suspicion came too late.

They were threading a ravine within bowshot of the Chinese sentinels. Suddenly Khlit heard a quick cry from Kerula. His hand went to his sword. But the same instant a heavy blow fell across the back of his neck.

Khlit sank to his knees. Before he could rise, hands closed on him. The darkness seemed to give birth to forms that sprang at him. His arms were pinned, and bound to his sides. A cloth was thrown over his head, and he was picked up bodily by many men and borne off.

IX

One evening, early in the Winter which marked the first year of the siege of Altur Haiten, as related by Yen Kui Kiang, chronicler of Hang-Hi, the general of the Imperial forces sat in the Hall of Judgment in his pavilion. The pavilion was distant from the walls of Altur Haiten, but the sound of the cannon, and the roar of flame could be heard distinctly.

Hang-Hi, mandarin of a high order, master of literature, and favorite general of Wanleh, Son of Heaven, had been listening to Yen Kui Kiang, in company with his councillors and mandarins of the tribunal of ceremonies, as the chronicler read from the books of Confucius. Always, said Yen Kui Kiang, in his chronicles, Hang-Hi listened to words of the great Confucius before undertaking to judge cases that came to him for trial, in order that his mind might be open and just.

The man who commanded a Chinese army to the number of two hundred thousand was tall, with a portly figure, imposing in his robe of blue-and-gold silk embroidered with a miniature dragon and the likeness of Kwan-Ti, god of war. His eyes were dark and brilliant, and his arms crossed on his breast were the arms of a wrestler.

The ebony and lacquer Hall of Judgment was occupied only by Hang-Hi's advisors and lieutenants, seated in order of rank on each side of the carpet that ran up the center of the hall to the dais on which the viceroy of the Son of Heaven sat.

At Hang-Hi's side sat Chan Kieh Shi, old and wizened, a veteran of a hundred battles, who had no equal at chess play. It was Chan Kieh Shi who had brought the heavy cannon from Persia that were battering down the walls of Altur Haiten, and who had sworn an oath on his ancestral tablets to bury the last of the Khans of Tatary, the hereditary enemies of the Son of Heaven, before he died.

This evening, Yen Kui Kiang relates, only one case was brought to judgment. That was the case of a stranger, Khlit, called the Wolf, and Mir Turek, a resident of Samarkand whose great-grandfather had been a mandarin.

When the attendant of the Hall of Judgment brought in the two prisoners, the eyes of the Chinese council surveyed them impassively. Behind the slant eyes lurked the cruelty of a conquering race and the craft of the wisest men in Asia. Not once during the startling events of the evening, did the slant eyes open wide or the breath come faster in the thin lips.

They noted silently that while one prisoner, the man called Mir Turek, prostrated himself before the dais, the other, called Khlit, stood erect with folded arms, although heavily chained. Especially did Chan Kieh Shi watch Khlit, while the Chinaman's fan moved slowly before his face. The fan was inscribed with the battles he had won.

When the attendant had brought a curved sword to the dais and laid it at Hang-Hi's feet, Yen Kui Kiang bowed before Hang-Hi.

"Gracious Excellency," the secretary said softly, "the man at your feet is one called Mir Turek, although he has a Chinese name. He was found in Samarkand by one of our agents. Many times he has sworn that he would aid the cause of the Son of Heaven and remain true to the faith of his ancestors. The man called Mir Turek says that he has news for you, such news as will earn him absolution from his neglect. He swears that he has been working for Wanleh, and that he is ready to show the fruits of his work."

"And the other, Yen Kui Kiang," put in Chan Kieh Shi abruptly, "who is he?"

"I do not know, Excellency," the secretary said, "he was taken a few nights ago with Mir Turek, and he has twice tried to break free."

"Oh, gracious Excellency," said Mir Turek, eagerly, "give your servant leave to speak his news, and you shall know of this man."

Receiving a nod of assent from the general, the merchant hurried on, his voice trembling.

"This man, called Khlit, the Wolf, a Russian Cossack, came to my house in Samarkand. I was curious, for he speaks as one having high authority, yet he had no rank or wealth. When he showed me his sword I saw the answer. Knowing how valuable the man's secret would be to your Excellency, I hastened to bring him, unknowing, to the army before Altur Haiten. Truly, Khlit's secret is written on his sword. He can not read. And he can not understand what we are saying."

As one, the eyes of the council turned to Khlit. The Cossack stood erect without noticing them, gazing moodily at his curved sword which lay at the feet of Hang-Hi. It had been taken from him the night of his capture, and for the first time since he had received it from his father other hands had held the blade. And, Kerula, in spite of her prayers to be allowed to share his prison tent had been taken away, he knew not where.

Khlit had made two efforts to escape, without result other than the heavy chains he wore on wrists and ankles. He had shared his tent with Mir Turek. Fogan Ultai had disappeared. Khlit had not been slow to lay his seizure on Fogan Ultai and he had sworn an oath that the other should repent it. Now, he waited, proudly for what was to come.

"Gracious Excellency," Mir Turek went on, bowing, "I saw that the man's face resembled a Russian Tatar, and the message of the sword showed that I was right. Lo, I am a student of learned books, a humble follower in the path of Hang-Hi and his men of wisdom. The sword, Khlit said, had been handed down from father to son for many generations, and in truth the inscription is ancient.

"It says on the sword," Mir Turek pointed to the blade, "that it was the sword of Kaidu, great khan of the Kallmark Tatars, and descendant of Genghis Khan. Khlit, although he does not know it, is one of the few who are of the royal blood of the grand khans of Tatary."

The fan of Chan Kieh Shi paused for a second and resumed its sweep. Hang-Hi glanced impassively from Khlit to Mir Turek and bent over the sword, studying the inscription. It was the first time he had had a sword of the grand khans at his feet.

"Wherefore, Excellency," hastened Mir Turek, "I brought Khlit, called the Wolf, to the mountains of Khantai Khan on a pretense of finding treasure, hoping to yield him prisoner to your Graciousness, and atone for my absence from the empire, and perhaps earn a place among your men of wisdom."

Mir Turek bowed anxiously and stepped back at a sign from the attendant. His face was bathed in sweat but his eyes were gleaming with a feverish hope.

"Is this all you have to tell?" asked Hang-Hi.

"That is all, Excellency," responded Mir Turek.

But his eyes fell. For he thought of the mountains of Khantai Khan and the tomb of untold riches.

"Call the agent from Samarkand, who has taken the name of Fogan Ultai," said Hang-Hi.

Mir Turek's eyes swept the assembly in sudden fear. He had known of the mission of Fogan Ultai, but he had hoped he would not be confronted with the secret agent of all-powerful Wanleh. Fogan Ultai was very crafty.

Khlit stirred for the first time when he saw Fogan Ultai enter the tribunal. The erstwhile master of the slaves was dressed in the silken robe of a mandarin of caste. Around his neck was suspended a gold disk wrought in the likeness of a sun. The councillors who were of lesser rank than Fogan Ultai, rose and bowed. The agent advanced to the dais, bowing low three times, and touched his forehead. Khlit's arms strained at the chains, then dropped to his side. The attendant was beside him with drawn sword, and he waited.

"Tell the one called Khlit," suggested Chan Kieh Shi softly, "the truth of his descent. Then he will suffer more greatly under our punishment."

Thus it was that Khlit, the Cossack named the Wolf, came to know in the tribunal of Hang-Hi, that he was descended from the grand khans, hereditary rulers of Tatary and enemies of China. No name was hated by the Chinese like the name of Tatar.

He listened to Fogan Ultai's words without change of countenance. His people had been of the same race as the Tatars. And he had won the respect of Tal Taulai Khan, his brother in blood, and of the Kallmarks. Khlit's only allegiance in life had been to his sword. He exulted in the knowledge that he had come of a royal line. It did not surprise him that the fact had not been known before. In the bloody warfare of Cossack and Tatar the man was lucky who could name his race beyond his grandfather. At the same time he was aware of the danger he stood from the Chinese.

"Ask him," said Hang-Hi curiously, "what he would say to us, now that he is our prisoner?"

Fogan Ultai spoke with Khlit and turned to the general thoughtfully.

"Excellency," he said slowly, "this man is no common man. He has the wisdom of a fox and the courage of a wounded wolf. He asks which should be honored, a royal prisoner or the man who betrayed him?"

X

Khlit's next act was to ask for Kerula. He had sought for information of the girl, but no one had told him where she was. Fogan Ultai bared his teeth as he answered, for he remembered how Khlit had made him, a mandarin of high caste, bring food to the girl.

Kerula, he told Khlit, had been offered the choice of two things, when she had come before him. She had been taken to the Chinese camp with the two others. And Fogan Ultai had given her the choice of becoming a slave with the captives who labored at the siege work, or of joining the household of Hang-Hi. The child, he said, was fair of face and body. She had chosen to become one of the women of the household when she was told that Khlit was a captive and his sword taken from him.

Khlit became silent at this, and moody. He could not blame the girl for her choice. She had chosen life instead of hardships and death. And she was young. Fogan Ultai turned to Hang-Hi with a low bow.

"Excellency, Almighty Commander of the Ming host, the man, Mir Turek, lied when he said he had told you all he knew. He knows a secret of great importance. This secret is what first took me to Samarkand, for I had heard that a scholar of that city had said that he knew the hiding-place of the treasure of Genghis Khan."

Mir Turek started and would have thrown himself prostrate before Hang-Hi, but the attendant restrained him.

"In Samarkand," went on Fogan Ultai, "I joined the household of Mir Turek, showing him, in order to avoid menial service, the gold-rayed sun which he recognized. I was not able to learn his secret, for Mir Turek was crafty and he suspected me. When he joined company with the Tatar, Khlit, descendant of Kaidu, I came with them across the desert to the mountains of Khantai Khan. From what I overheard and the words of the girl of Mir Turek, Kerula, I knew that they had come to find the tomb of Genghis Khan.

"One day Mir Turek and his companion visited the mountains in my absence, and it is certain they went to the place of the treasure. Knowing that Mir Turek planned to deliver Khlit a prisoner to you, I waited until they had come within our lines, when I took them with some men I had posted for that purpose. Thus Mir Turek lied, for he kept from you the secret of the treasure which is very great."

Fogan Ultai folded his arms into his silken sleeves and waited with bent head. Mir Turek's agonized gaze went from face to face that was turned to him and he tried to speak but could not.

"Your plan was excellent, Fogan Ultai," said Hang-Hi at length. Turning to his favorite general the commander asked: "What is your word concerning Mir Turek, Chan Kieh Shi?"

Chan Kieh Shi shrugged his bent shoulders slightly. He was the advisor of Hang-Hi. Sometimes he thought that the latter asked too often for his advice. He wondered what the famous commander would do without him.

"Pour molten silver into the ears of Mir Turek until he tells us the place of the treasure. Then we shall have the Tatar hoard of wealth, at the same time that we slay the Jun-gar khans in Altur Haiten, and your Excellency's wars will be over."

Mir Turek stretched out his arms imploringly.

"Oh, Gracious One—Viceroy of the Son of Heaven, harken. Truly I planned to take you to the place of the treasure of Genghis Khan. Yet is the place perilous. The Onon Muren watch over it—the gods allow no one to come there——"

"Even the gods," said Hang-Hi ominously, "pay homage to the victor in the conflict. So it says in the sacred book."

He lifted his hand to the attendant who stood beside the trembling merchant with bared sword.

"Strike once," he said, "and sever the sinews of the traitor behind the knees. Thus will he learn to kneel to me. Strike again and slit his mouth wide into both cheeks. Thus he may learn to speak the truth."

A shriek from the unhappy Mir Turek was silenced as the armed attendant swung his short sword, without hesitation, against the back of the man's legs. Mir Turek fell to his knees. Khlit, looking around in surprise, saw the man in armor take the face of Mir Turek in the hollow of his arm. In spite of the merchant's struggles, the other twice drew the sharp edge of his weapon against Mir Turek's mouth. A choking form, prostrate on the floor, hands pressed against his bleeding mouth, was all that remained of Mir Turek.

Khlit took a deep breath and his eyes sought Hang-Hi's. The commander bent over Mir Turek.

"You will not die until you have shown us the way to the tomb of Genghis Khan, Mir Turek," he said softly. "How am I to trust a man without honor?"

At a sign from him Khlit and the moaning Mir Turek were conducted to their tent. By signs the guard indicated that the crippled man was to remain in the tent, while Khlit must take his turn at labor with the other captives.

For several days while the merchant lay tossing on the floor of the tent, Khlit went out at night under guard to the siege works of the Chinese engineers. With other Tatar captives he hauled heavy stones for the Persian cannon, and dug earthworks opposite the walls of Altur Haiten under the arrows of the Tatar defenders.

Never had Khlit seen a battle like this, and his interest grew each night that he worked. The Chinese had pushed a network of earthen mounds, backed by leather and timbers to within a few feet of the crumbling walls where they planned to deliver their final assault. Beyond bowshot of the walls the giant Persian cannon were ranged which steadily enlarged the breaches in the brick ramparts to the east.

The Chinese were not content to demolish the walls which were breached at several points. A fire from a few muskets was kept up at the Tatars who sought to man the ramparts. Mangonels, formed of giant beams, cast buckets of unquenchable fire, prepared by the special fire-makers of Hang-Hi over the walls. Into the city beyond, iron chests were dropped by the mangonels. These chests held powder, lighted by a fuse which exploded after they had fallen in the houses.

Against the Chinese the Tatars made only feeble efforts. Being naturally mounted fighters, accustomed to warfare on the plains, the defenders were at a disadvantage which was heightened by their lack of firearms. Arrows did little damage against the earthworks of the besiegers which lined the eastern side.

The Tatars, numbering about seventy thousand fighting men, Khlit discovered from the captives, had given up assaults against the Chinese. They still had their horses which subsisted on the fields between the walls and the city proper, but each sortie from the gates had been greeted by heavy musketry fire, and the terrible flames of the fire-makers.

Khlit saw that the plight of the defenders was near desperate. They awaited the day, with the fortitude of their race, when Hang-Hi should storm the walls. The Jun-gar khans, he heard, quarreled and drank their time away.

Khlit helped feed the cannon, toiling half-naked at the giant stones. He became silent, and made no effort to resent the whips of the Chinese overseers that scorched his back when he rested. Much he thought over the words of Fogan Ultai. His identity as a descendant of the grand khans, he knew, would earn him death with the fall of the city, or later at the court of Wanleh. The thought of dying a captive was bitter.

Kerula had gone from his existence. Khlit had not had many companions, but the girl had touched his heart—perhaps with her tales of the Tatar warriors. He took a grim satisfaction in the sufferings of Mir Turek. He had no hope of escape, chained and under guard. Yet Khlit counted the blows of the Chinese overseers and remembered them.

XI

It was one night when he was stumbling with fatigue, and had lost thought of everything except the stones he was hauling and the count of the blows he received that Khlit heard from Kerula. That night hope came to him again, and all his old craft.

One of his guards halted him abruptly by the cannon, and urged him back toward the tent. The guards habitually vented their fear of the followers of Genghis Khan on the prisoners.

"Come, Tatar," he said in broken Usbek, "there is a woman of the royal household that asks for you among the prisoners. Why does she want to see a dog? We must do her bidding, for she wears the clothes of a favorite."

The tent of the two prisoners was lighted by the glow from the fire caldrons near by. Khlit's heart leaped as he saw a cloaked, slender form standing beside the couch of Mir Turek. He had guessed who it was, before the girl had pushed the guards from the tent and closed the flap.

The cloak fell back from her face and Khlit stared. It was Kerula, but her cheeks were red with henna, and her eyebrows blackened and arched. Her long hair was tied in a close knot, and its scent came to his nostrils.

She gave a low cry as she saw the half-naked figure of Khlit, his body blackened with powder and dirt. She pointed inquiringly to where Mir Turek gazed at them helplessly from his couch.

"Tell me, Khlit, lord," Kerula whispered, her face close to his, tinged with the red of the flames outside, "will Mir Turek live? He told me how grievously he suffered. What have they done to you? I searched for two days and nights before I found you. Did you think I would forget you, Khlit, lord?"

Khlit crossed his powerful arms on his chest.

"The thought was mine, Kerula," he said quietly. "Yet I believed that you were the one to feel pain, not I. As for Mir Turek, he is dying of his hurts."

The girl raised her head proudly, although her cheeks flamed.

"Aye," she said, "I have suffered. I am your slave. It was my will to serve you. So I chose to go to the pavilion of Hang-Hi instead of the siege works."

"I do not understand," Khlit shook his head. "The household of the Chinese general will give you comforts and you will have honor —of a kind."

"Nay, Khlit, lord, it was for you."

The girl smiled at him eagerly. With a glance at Mir Turek she stepped closer.

"I saw them take your sword from you. Your curved sword. And my heart was heavy. Tell me, will not the noble Tatar khans come from Altur Haiten and break the power of Hang-Hi? I told them so at the pavilion, but they laughed, saying that Genghis Khan was dead."

"The noble khans," said Khlit bitterly, "will not attack."

"They will, they must. And you must join them, Khlit, lord, when they do so. See, this is why I went to the household of Hang-Hi. They watched it carefully, but I was too clever for them. I took it from them to give to you. See——"

The girl felt under her silk cloak and drew out a weapon which she pressed into Khlit's hand. He stared at it dumbly.

"It is your curved sword, Khlit, the sword that makes men afraid of you. As soon as I had taken it I came to find you."

Khlit took his sword in his hand and touched it lovingly. He eyed the inscription curiously. Surely, Kerula had been faithful to him.

"If no one suspects you, Kerula," he said gruffly, for he was moved, "go whence you have come. The tent is dangerous, for Fogan Ultai is coming at dawn and he must not find you."

"I have made you glad," said the girl softly, "and my heart is light. I do not want to leave you, but if they found me they would suspect. Now that you have your curved sword they will not keep you prisoner, will they? Harken, Khlit, lord." She drew off a slender silken girdle that confined her cloak. "When one Tatar and another are true friends they become *andas*. Each helps and protects the other. Give me your girdle."

Puzzled, Khlit lifted his sash from the pile of his discarded clothing. At a sign from the girl he bound it around her slim waist under the cloak. She touched his hand shyly as he did so. Then she tied her own girdle around him.

"Now we are comrades, Khlit, lord, although I am still a slave. Truly the honor is great and I am happy. When two persons become *andas* both have one life; neither abandons the other, and each guards the life of his *anda*. Thus we strengthen our *anda* anew and refresh it."

"Aye," said Khlit gruffly, "I will protect you, little sparrow."

At a warning sound from the guards outside the tent Kerula slipped away, with a glance at Mir Turek, who turned his mutilated face away. No one else entered and Khlit seated himself in a corner of the tent. He took his sheepskin coat and tied the sword deftly in the lining. The coat he placed over his shoulders. Until the gray light of dawn lightened the tent he remained motionless. He did not sleep, nor did Mir Turek who lay moaning and gasping for breath. The fire that stood in a caldron by Mir Turek's bed was smoldering to embers when Khlit arose, casting aside his coat and came to the bed of the other.

"Mir Turek," he said softly, "Hang-Hi has made you a cripple. Fogan Ultai is coming to get you to show the way to the tomb of

Genghis Khan. Yet you will not do it. Do you fear greatly? I have no fear."

The merchant raised himself on his elbow and his ghastly face peered at Khlit.

"Mir Turek, Fogan Ultai would throw you down the chasm to the Muren, when you have shown him the path. You have bled much, and your heart is weakening until death stands near tonight. We two, Mir Turek, know of the tomb of Genghis Khan. You will not live to take him there at dawn."

A hoarse sound came from the throat of Mir Turek and his eyes sought Khlit's feverishly.

"Man, born to life is deathless, Mir Turek," resumed Khlit slowly. "He must go hence without home, without resting-place. So said the great Genghis Khan. A few days ago I saved your life. But now you are dying and I can not save you."

Mir Turek sank back upon his couch, shuddering. Khlit looked at him not angrily, but sadly, as at one who was no longer a man. Death, he thought, would be a good friend to Mir Turek. And he would watch until it had come, freeing him from his pain.

XII

The sentries were dozing on their spears outside the door of the tent in the early dawn when they were awakened by the crackle of flames. There was a crash as of the lacquer sides of the tent falling in and a burst of flames swirled up behind their backs.

The door of the tent was thrust open and Khlit staggered out, his garments smoking. Inside the door they could see a wall of flame that caught at the woodwork and hangings of the structure. The sentry who spoke Usbek shook Khlit by the shoulder.

"Where is the other?" he shouted, stepping back from the heat of the fire.

Khlit drew his long coat closer about him, so that the hidden sword could not be seen. "Go and bring him forth, dog!" he snarled. "How can a man in chains carry another?"

But he knew that no man could go into the flames. He had waited until the last moment before coming out, so that the flames might get to the remains of Mir Turek. Thus he had seen to it that the body was not dishonored. And now no one but Khlit knew the way to the tomb of Genghis Khan.

An angry shout caused them to turn. Several men had ridden up on camels, and Fogan Ultai dismounted. The agent of Wanleh caught the chief sentry by the throat furiously.

The unhappy man pointed to the burning tent and Fogan Ultai released him with a curse. He scanned the flames for a moment. Then he faced Khlit and the Cossack saw that his slant eyes were cold and hard as those of a snake.

"This is your doing, Khlit," he snarled. "Once before, in the desert you slew a man of mine. You have taken the life of Mir Turek. Your turn will not wait. The torture will be finer, and longer, for this."

"Aye, Khlit," said the voice of Chan Kieh Shi behind him, "you will see if the blood of Kaidu is truly in you. We will take your life slowly, so you will not die for three days."

Khlit threw back his head and laughed, and the sentries wondered.

"When you are dead," resumed Fogan Ultai with relish, "your head will be cast over the ramparts of Altur Haiten, and the Tatar dogs will know we have slain one of their breed."

"Nay," said Khlit grimly, "it is not I that am a dog! Was it I that made Mir Turek a beast that crawled to death? Did I send the *gylong* to murder a child in the desert? Men have not named me dog but Wolf. And the wolf knows well the ways of the dog."

"When Hang-Hi rides into the city of Altur Haiten," growled Chan Kieh Shi, pointing a withered finger at Khlit, "you shall bear him company, tied to his horse's tail. Thus will the Tatars know their kind."

"Truly, Fogan Ultai," said Khlit, "a man who is feared is greatly honored. You do me honor in spite of yourselves."

"Is this honor?" The agent struck him viciously across the face with his whip. "Or this?"

"Aye," laughed Khlit, "for the overseer has done me greater homage. He had struck me twenty-eight times."

Fogan Ultai fingered his sword longingly, but Chan Kieh Shi made a warning gesture.

"Then you can count the days until your death, which will be when Altur Haiten is sacked."

"Nay," replied Khlit, "I shall not die."

"Dog!" Fogan Ultai spat in his direction. "Hang-Hi has promised it me."

Khlit stepped to the camel's side.

"Fool!" he snarled, "blind jackal! If you kill me there will be no one to show you the way to the tomb of Genghis Khan. Mir Turek knew the secret, but he is dead."

Fogan Ultai's expression did not change but his eyes consulted Chan Kieh Shi. The old general stared long at Khlit. He spoke quickly to Fogan Ultai, and then turned to Khlit.

"We shall find the way to the tomb," he said. "The torture will make you take us there."

Khlit appeared to consider this.

"Will Hang-Hi give me my freedom if I take you to the tomb?"

"If you show us the treasure of Genghis Khan—" Fogan Ultai's slant eyes closed cunningly—"Hang-Hi may give you freedom."

"Aye," added Chan Kieh Shi, "he may do so."

Again, Khlit seemed to ponder their words. He raised several objections which Fogan Ultai met shortly. Finally he raised his manacled hands.

"How can I climb the mountains of Khantai Khan in chains?" he asked.

At a sign from Chan Kieh Shi the sentries unlocked Khlit's chains around his arms, and at his request from his feet. He was led to a camel and mounted, thrusting his arms into the sleeves of his coat and wrapping it about him. He hugged his sword fastened to the inside of his coat, over his chest, close to him as they started. Khlit rode in the center, with Fogan Ultai and Chan Kieh Shi one on either side and two spearmen to the rear. Khlit smiled grimly as he noted that they had given him the clumsiest camel.

He did not put trust in the promise of Fogan Ultai. More than once he caught the agent looking at him contemptuously, sidelong. But he said nothing.

They passed out of the Chinese encampment and gained the plain. Khlit headed toward the Kukulon Lake. The group rode without speaking, Khlit busied with his thoughts. There was no hope of breaking free from his guards, he saw, and he did not intend to try.

Khlit had been playmate with death for many years. He had never, however, planned to come so close to death as at the cavern of Khantai Khan, by the Onon Muren. He circled the lake in the path Mir

Turek had taken. He thought of the dead merchant, and it occurred to him that he was the only survivor of the four who had ventured into the tomb of Genghis Khan. Verily, he marveled, the Onon Muren watched over the treasure well.

He noted grimly how his companions stared at the skeletons in the lake. But he did not pause when they dismounted from the camels, pressing onward over the gray soil, among the blasted trees. Fogan Ultai had fallen silent, and more than once the agent stopped and stared about him curiously as Khlit had done. Chan Kieh Shi, however, pushed ahead as fast as his bent legs could carry him.

At the Kukulon gate Khlit paused to explain to his companions how they must go under the waterfall. They followed him without hesitation, first the mandarins, then the guards. Khlit stood again in the cavern under the falls and smelled the strange odor that came from the chasm. Here he noted that Fogan Ultai spoke with Chan Kieh Shi but the old man replied impatiently and pushed on.

Still Khlit had not spoken. They felt their way to the light that came down the corridor, Chan Kieh Shi turning over with his foot the Tatar forms that lined the way. They came out into the light and stood on the ledge by the rock bridge.

Khlit pointed silently to the giant forms outlined in the vapor on the other side of the bridge. The Chinese stared curiously about them, at the gray vault overhead and the chasm.

For the second time Khlit stood before the tomb of his ancestor. He raised his hand as if in greeting to the casket that hung between the golden elephants. Then he drew his belt closer about him, and spoke for the first time.

"There is the tomb," he said, "come!"

Fogan Ultai stepped back cautiously, motioning for him to go ahead. As he advanced the Chinese followed closely, their eyes straining on the dim forms across the chasm through the mist.

Khlit bent his head low on his chest and raised the sleeve of his coat against his mouth and nose. He broke into a run as he stepped on the rock bridge. He felt the vapors warm his face and heard the rumbling below. On he ran, without looking back. He heard a sound that was not the rumbling of the mountain.

His brain was dizzy as the stifling fumes gripped him. Staggering forward he fell to his knees and crawled onward. Biting his lips to keep from breathing the poison he gained the further end of the bridge and the clearer air of the plateau. A cold breeze from some cavern drove the vapors back. Khlit had crossed the rock bridge in safety.

He climbed to his feet, supporting himself by one of the legs of the elephants. His hand touched a long pole, and he glanced at it. The pole supported a crest of horns hung with a hundred yaks' tails. Khlit knew that he held the standard of Genghis Khan.

Leaning on the standard for support he looked back the way he had come. On the rock bridge one man was crawling, choking and gasping. Khlit saw that it was one of the guards, the last to venture on the bridge. He watched the man draw himself forward. The Chinese, blinded and strangling, slipped to the side of the rock bridge. Vainly he tried to gain his balance, clutching at the smooth rock. His hold slipped, Khlit heard a hoarse cry, and a white figure dropped into the depths of the chasm, after the others.

Khlit was alone in the tomb of Genghis Khan.

The Cossack seated himself against the form of the Bearer of Wealth. His eyes wandered idly over the standard, gray with dust, above him. Then he stretched out at full length on the rock, and in a little while was asleep.

XIII

In times which are gone thou didst swoop like a falcon before us; today a car bears thee as it rumbles, advancing,

Oh thou, my Khan.

Hast thou left us; hast thou left wife and children, and the *kurultai* of thy nation?

Oh thou, my Khan.

Sweeping forward in pride, as sweeps forward an eagle, thou didst lead us aforetime,

Oh thou, my Khan.

Thou didst bring triumph and joy to thy people for sixty and six years; art thou leaving them now?

Oh thou, my Khan.

Death chant of Genghis Khan.

The night sentries were dozing at the door of the *kurultai* hall where the Tatar chieftains of the Jun-gar were assembled. In the hall, where the sound of the Chinese cannon echoed at intervals, were the nine khans that ruled what was left of the Tatar race on the borderland of China. Here was the leader of the Kalkas horde, from Karakorum, the chief of the Chakars, whose people had been between the Great Wall and the desert of Gobi, the commander of the Eleuts, and others.

The ranks of the commanders of the Tatars were thinned. A Kall-mark khan had left Altur Haiten with his followers when they deserted the ill-fated city. The leaders of the Hoshot and Torgot hordes had fallen in unsuccessful sallies. Evil was the plight of the chiefs of the Jun-gar, and they drank deeply, to forget.

They lay on benches around the long table of the *kurultai* council, swords and spears stacked against the walls, waiting for word of the expected attack of the army of Hang-Hi. For a year they had been directing the defense of the walls, leaders of horsemen penned in a citadel. They were veteran fighters, but they were weary and there had been many quarrels over the wine goblets.

They had been drinking deeply, these lords of Tatary, and few looked up when a man entered the hall. Yet these few did not again lay their heads upon the table. They stared in amazement and rose to their feet, feeling for swords.

The man who had come in was tall, with gray mustaches hanging to his broad shoulders. His face was scarred, and his eyes alert. His heavy boots were covered with gray dust, as was his *svitza*.

High was the ceiling of the hall, yet the standard of yaks' tails, which the man carried reached nearly to the ceiling. It was a standard like those of the Jun-gar, but of a different pattern. It bore a gold image of the sun and moon, tarnished by age.

Without speaking the man stood in the doorway and looked at the chiefs of the Jun-gar. Leaning on the stout pole of the standard, he watched them and his mouth curled in a snarl.

"Who are you, warrior, and what do you seek?" asked a khan whose head was clearer than the others. "What standard do you bring to the *kurultai?*"

One by one the sleepy warriors awakened, and fixed their eyes on the newcomer. A veteran, chief of the Chakars, gave a hoarse cry as he saw the standard of yaks' tails and rose dizzily fighting the wine fumes in his brain.

"Who are you, Standard-Bearer?" he asked.

Still the stranger did not speak. He leaned on the pole, and watched them until the last of the chieftains had risen.

"Evil is the day," he said in broken Tatar, "when the Jun-gar khans put aside their swords for the wine cup."

"Who is it that speaks thus to the Jun-gar chiefs?" asked the Chakar veteran. "These are not the words of a common man."

"My name is Khlit," said the newcomer, gazing at the circle of watchers, "and I am the Standard-Bearer of Genghis Khan. I have come from the tomb of the Master of the Earth with the banner of the sun and moon, because there will be a great battle, aye, such a battle as has not been for many years—since the Grand Khans were dead."

In the silence that followed the chieftains consulted each other with their eyes. The man who had appeared in the hall had startled them, and the Jun-gar khans felt a quick dread. The words of Khlit did not reassure them. The old Chakar leader stepped close to the standard and ran his eye over each detail of the design and emblems. He faced Khlit and his face was stern.

"Whence came this warrior?" he spoke in his gruff tones. "Answer truly, for a lie will earn death. The banner of Genghis Khan was like this, yet it has been buried for generations in the hills of Khantai Khan."

"From the tomb in the hills of Khantai Khan came this," said Khlit grimly. "From where the Onon Muren watch, by the Kukulon gate. I have slept at the tomb of Genghis Khan, among the twenty thousand slain. Have the chieftains of the Jun-gar forgotten the standard of a thousand battles?"

"Nay," said the old man, "it is truly the banner of Genghis Khan. For here, by the sun and moon are the emblems of the old hordes, the wolf of the Kallmarks, the doe of the Chakars——"

The other chieftains crowded around the two, and their slant eyes gleamed at Khlit. In the eyes he read amazement, suspicion, and uncertainty. Khlit saw that they but half-believed the words of the elder. He raised his hand for attention.

"Harken, lords of the Jun-gar," he said slowly. "You ask who I am. I am a fighter of the steppes and I follow the paths of battles. I found the road to the tomb of Genghis Khan, looking for treasure. Yet while I slept in the tomb a thought and a plan came to me. Genghis Khan is dead. Yet the thought came to me. It was to carry the standard that stood in the tomb to the chiefs of the Jun-gar, through the Chinese lines, so that they might have new heart for battle. If you truly believe this to be the standard of the Mighty Manslayer, I will tell you the plan, for words of wisdom should not fall on dead ears. Speak, do you believe?"

The chieftains looked at each other with bleared eyes. Then the Chakar lord raised both hands and bowed his head.

"Said I not this was the banner? Aye, it is an omen."

One by one the Jun-gar chiefs raised their hands and bowed. In their hearts was the dread of the name of the Mighty Manslayer. One of their number stepped forward.

"Aye," he said slowly, "this is the standard that was buried. But it belongs to the grave of the One. The man who brought it from the grave will die, for it is written that none shall come from the tomb of Genghis Khan and live. Shall we keep the standard for the men of Hang-Hi to carry to Liang Yang? Altur Haiten and all in it are doomed. How may we keep the standard, when it can not serve us, except to fall into the hands of the enemies of Genghis Khan and make their triumph greater?"

"Not so," said Khlit, "for there will be a great battle. And the standard of the dead Khan should be with the men who are the remnants of his power. There is fear in the hearts of the Chinese at the name of Genghis Khan."

He saw, however, that the Tatars had been impressed with the speech of their companion. Even the Chakar khan nodded his head in agreement to what the other had said.

"The battle," continued the khan, "will be the assault of the city. How can we prevent it? Hang-Hi has a quarter million men. We have a scant sixty-five thousand horsemen. The Chinese have driven us from the Wall of Shensi and across the desert to Altur Haiten. Many Tatars died in the desert. Those in Altur Haiten are deserting by night to go to their homes. The engines of the Chinese are breaching the walls. We have only spears and arrows to fight against gunpowder. Our food supplies are running out, and the men fight among themselves for what is left. We are shut in on four sides. The men are losing their strength from lack of food."

A murmur of assent went up. Khlit found no encouragement in the yellow faces that were lined with weariness and drunkenness.

"If we were in the plains," said the Chakar chief, "there might be hope. But our sallies have been repulsed. We are penned in the city. Truly, Hang-Hi is too great a general to outwit."

"Fools!" Khlit's lips curled in scorn. "Would Genghis Khan fear such a man as Hang-Hi? I have seen him, and he is like a fat woman. I have seen the fortifications of the Chinese and the cannon. They can be taken."

"The earthworks keep us from attacking on the east," returned the Chakar leader, "and the walls are breached so that an army can march through." He laid his hand on the pole. "What is the word of the *kurultai*, noble lords; shall we lay the standard of Genghis Khan in the flames, so that it will not be taken by the enemy? This man must not have it, for no low-born hand should touch it. Such is the law."

An assenting shout went up. Instantly Khlit snatched his sword from its sheath. The Chakar khan was quick, or his hand would have been severed from his arm. As it was, Khlit's sword slit the skin of his fingers which dripped blood. The others reached for their weapons angrily. Khlit raised his sword as they closed about him.

"Aye," he said gruffly, "no low-born hand shall touch the standard. I will keep it, for I am of the blood of the Grand Khans. My sword which was my father's and his before him bears witness. Read the writings, dogs!"

Several of the Tatars scanned the inscription and wonder replaced the rage in their slant eyes. The Chakar chief broke the silence.

"I bear no grudge," he said, "for this man is of the royal blood. How otherwise could he come from the tomb and live? It is so written. Yet shall he burn the standard rather than let it fall into the hands of the Chinese."

"If I am the keeper of the standard," growled Khlit, "shall I burn what it is my duty to protect?"

He leaned on the pole and watched the Jun-gar chiefs. Khlit had brought the standard from the tomb with him with much difficulty, into Altur Haiten because he saw an opportunity to throw in his lot with the defeated Tatars. He counted on the banner restoring their spirit. He had not counted on the reception he met, but all his cunning was aroused to make the Jun-gar chiefs believe in the standard of the dead conqueror as an omen of victory.

He planned to place all his cunning, with the talisman of Genghis Khan, to the aid of the weakening chieftains. He understood the plan of the Chinese camp, thanks to his experience as a prisoner. And he was burning to seek revenge for the twenty-nine blows that had been given him. Kerula had named him her *anda*. The girl had sacrificed herself for him, and Khlit was determined to win her back alive or take payment for her death. And the prospect of the coming battle intoxicated him.

Already he had won the Jun-gar to acknowledgment of the standard and of his right to advise them. But he proceeded warily.

"As one of the royal blood, oh Khan," said the man shrewdly who had first objected, "you will take the command from us? We will yield you the command, for since Tal Taulai Khan died we have had no one of the blood of Kaidu on the frontier."

"As one of the royal blood, Chief," responded Khlit dryly, for he saw jealousy flame in the faces of the others, "I shall carry the standard of Genghis Khan. Is not that the greatest honor? You and your companions will lead the hordes, for I have come only to bring the banner, and to tell you the plan that came to me in the tomb of Genghis Khan. Do not insult my ears further by saying that the standard should be burned, however."

He saw understanding come into the faces of the Jun-gar, and they sheathed their swords.

"Did the spirit of Genghis Khan suggest this plan to you?" asked the Chakar.

But Khlit was not to be trapped.

"As I slept in the tomb the plan came to me," he said. "Who am I to say whence it came? I am not a man of wisdom, but a fighter.

"Harken, men of the Jun-gar," he went on, raising his voice, "you say that your men are deserting? Will they desert if the banner of Genghis Khan leads them? You say that the Chinese engines are breaching the walls. Are we prisoners, to stay behind walls? You say that your men are horsemen. Let them fight, then as horsemen."

The Chakar khan bowed low. This time he kneeled and the others followed his example.

"Speak, warrior," he said, "for we will listen. Tell us your plan and our ears will not be dead. We, also, are fighters, not men of wisdom."

XIV

The day set for the capture of Altur Haiten by Hang-Hi dawned fair upon the activity of the Chinese camp. A pavilion of silk, supported by bamboo poles and hung with banners was erected for the general of Wanleh on a rise fronting the eastern walls of the city which had been breached for the assault.

Hang-Hi's lieutenants had made final preparations for the attack the night before. Junks, moored at the river bank had brought extra powder and supplies from China. Scaling ladders had been assembled in the earthworks. The ditch around the city had been filled in long ago by Chinese engineers. The cannon were loaded and primed for the salvo that was to start the attack.

Early in the day Hang-Hi took his station in the pavilion where he could see the eastern walls. Past the pavilion marched streams of bannermen with picked footmen and regiments in complete armor. Hang-Hi's advisors assembled by his chair. But the general wore a frown.

"Has no trace been found," he asked Yen Kui Kiang, impatiently, "of Chan Kieh Shi?"

The secretary bowed low and crossed his arms in his sleeves.

"Gracious Excellency," he explained, "riders have searched the surrounding country. They have been to the mountains of Khantai Khan. Chan Kieh Shi went with the agent, Fogan Ultai to find the tomb of Genghis Khan, and since that day we have found no sign——"

"Fool!" Hang-Hi struck his ivory wand against his knee. "Tell me not what I know already. Have you learned that Chan Kieh Shi lives?"

"Nay, Excellency," muttered the secretary, "we know not."

"There are volcanos in the mountains of Khantai Khan," mused Hang-Hi, "and our men have been troubled by the sulfur fumes, which the Tatars fear, not knowing their nature. It is possible——"

He broke off, for some of his men were staring at him curiously. Hang-Hi did not desire to let them know how much he felt the loss of the wisest of the Chinese generals. Still, there was nothing to fear. The Tatars, his spies had reported, were weak with hunger and torn by divided leadership. Their number was small. And his preparations for the attack were flawless. It could not fail.

"Excellency," ventured Yen Kui Kiang, "new reports from spies have come in. They say that the people of Altur Haiten are talking much of Genghis Khan. Our spies heard mention of his tomb. It may be that they hope for a miracle to save them."

"There are no miracles, Yen Kui Kiang," said Hang-Hi softly, "and Genghis Khan is dead. Why should I fear a dead man? Yet the tomb —Mir Turek said that was where the treasure of the Tatars was hidden. It may be that one of them found the tomb——"

"Send me the girl Kerula, who was taken with Mir Turek," he said after a moment. "She may know something of the treasure. Still, the Tatar dogs can not eat gold, nor can they melt it into swords."

He waited when one of the mandarins of the court of ceremonies read to him the annals of the court, until the girl was brought.

Kerula, pale but erect stood at the foot of Hang-Hi's chair, and the Chinese general surveyed her impassively. Women, he thought, were a toy, fashioned for the pleasure of men, unschooled in the higher virtues.

Yen Kui Kiang interpreted the questions of Hang-Hi. Then he turned to the general humbly.

"Oh, right hand of Wanleh, Son of Heaven, harken. The girl Kerula says that she has no knowledge of the tomb of Genghis Khan. She was a slave of Mir Turek, and he guarded his secret from her. She says that men who have gone to the tomb died within a short time. And she has a strange thought——"

"Speak, Yen Kui Kiang," urged the general as he hesitated. "It is written that Heaven sometimes puts wise thoughts into the heads of children."

"It is strange, Excellency. The girl says that Genghis Khan still rides over Tatary. That he and his army are to be heard in the night."

Kerula caught the meaning of what the secretary was saying, and raised her head eagerly. Her eyes were swollen from weeping, and her thin hands were clasped over the splendor of her gold-embroidered garment.

"Aye, lord," she said quickly, "I have heard the army. It was in the desert. We heard the *tumans*, Khlit and I, and they were many. The Tatar horsemen sang their chant for us, and we heard the greeting to Dawn, by the elephants."

"Child's fancies," murmured Hang-Hi when the other interpreted. "Our travelers have reported that the Tatar herdsmen believe these tales of the desert. If a grown man believes, why should not a child?"

"She says further," added Yen Kui Kiang after a moment, "that what she heard was true. For Chinese sentries have reported armed men moving over the plains. The child thinks this is the army of Genghis Khan, coming to slay the Chinese. Then she says that last night she heard again the chant of the Tatar horsemen."

Hang-Hi smiled impassively. Well he knew that the Tatars Kerula had heard of were deserters slipping out from the doomed city at night. Many thousands had made their way past the sentries by the west walls, who had orders not to see them—for Hang-Hi wished to allow the number of defenders to dwindle. Since the loss of Chan Kieh Shi he had grown cautious.

"What was the chant Kerula heard?" he asked indifferently. "Perchance it was the dogs fighting among themselves. Although, so fast do they desert in the night, there are few to quarrel."

The cheeks of the girl flushed under the paint. All her fancies had been wound around the Tatar warriors and the great Genghis Khan. Even the beleaguered city and the imprisonment of Khlit had failed to convince the child that she did not live in the time of the Tatar conquerors. So much had the books of Mir Turek done.

She sang softly, her eyes half-closed:

"Oh lion of the Teneri, wilt thou come? The devotion of thy people, thy golden palace, the great Hordes of thy nation—all these are awaiting thee.

"Thy chiefs, thy commanders, thy great kinsfolk, all these are awaiting thy coming in the birth-land which is thy stronghold.

"Thy standard of yaks' tails, thy drums and trumpets in the hands of thy warriors of the Kalkas, the Torgots, the Jun-gar—all are awaiting thee.

"That is the chant," she said proudly, "I heard it over the walls last night when the cannon did not growl. It was the same that the riders sang in the desert."

Hang-Hi stared at her and shook his head. He looked inquiringly at Yen Kui Kiang.

"There was some revelry and shouting in the town, Excellency," declared the secretary. "Assuredly, the child has strange fancies."

"It was not fancy, Yen Kui Kiang," observed Hang-Hi thoughtfully, "when Kerula said that no men returned from the tomb of Genghis Khan. Take her back to the women's quarters and watch her. She may be useful as hostage."

He held up his hand for silence as a blast of trumpets sounded from the walls of Altur Haiten.

"Wait: our enemies sound a parley. Go, Yen Kui Kiang and bring us their message. It may be the surrender of the city."

Hang-Hi and his councillors watched while the eastern gate in front of them swung back to allow the exit of a Tatar party. Yen Kui Kiang with some Chinese officers met them just outside the walls. After the brief conference the Chinese party returned to the silk pavilion, while the Tatars waited.

The secretary bowed very low before Hang-Hi and his face was troubled with the message he was to deliver.

"The Tatar dogs are mad, Excellency," he muttered, "truly their madness is great. They say that they will give us terms. If we yield all our prisoners, and the wealth our army has taken, with our arms and banners, they will allow us to return in safety to the Great Wall. They ask hostages, of half our generals. On these terms the Tatars, in their madness, say we can return safely. Otherwise they will give battle."

Hang-Hi rose from his throne, and his heavy face flamed in anger. He had not expected this.

"Hunger must have maddened them, Excellency," repeated Yen Kui Kiang, prostrating himself, "for they say Genghis Khan has taken command of their army. Their terms, they say, are the terms of Genghis Khan to his enemies——"

A joyous cry from Kerula interrupted him. The girl was looking eagerly toward the walls of the city, her pale face alight. Hang-Hi motioned her aside, and some soldiers grasped her, thrusting her back into the pavilion.

"This is our answer," cried Hang-Hi. He lifted his ivory wand. "Sound the assault. Our cannon will answer them."

"But, Excellency," remonstrated Yen Kui Kiang, who was a just man, "the envoys——"

He was interrupted by the blast of a hundred cannon. The walls of Altur Haiten shook under the impact of giant rocks, which had undermined their base. A volley of musketry followed, and few of the envoys reached the gateway in safety before the iron doors closed.

Trumpets rang out through the Chinese camp. The regiments of assault were set in motion toward the walls, led by men in armor with scaling ladders, and mercenaries with muskets. The attack on Altur Haiten had begun.

XV

Hang-Hi sank back in his chair and watched. Yen Kui Kiang took his place at the general's side. The chronicler of the Chinese saw all that took place that day. And the sight was strange. Never had a battle begun as this one did.

Hang-Hi saw the Chinese ranks advance in good order beyond the breastworks to the filled-in moat. Then, for the first time, he began to wonder. The walls of Altur Haiten, shattered by cannon, were barren of defenders. No arrows or rocks greeted the attackers who climbed to the breaches and planted their scaling ladders without opposition.

At a signal from one of the generals, rows of men in armor began to mount the scaling ladders. The columns that faced the breaches made their way slowly over the débris. Hang-Hi wondered if the defenders had lost heart. Truly, there could be few in the city, for his sentries had counted many thousand who fled from the place during the last few nights on horseback.

The Chinese forces mounted scaling ladders to the top of the walls without opposition. Not a shot had been fired. No one had fallen wounded. The men in the breaches were slower, for the Tatars had erected barricades.

A frown appeared on the smooth brow of Hang-Hi. It seemed as if the city was in his grasp. Yet he wondered at the silence. Suddenly he arose. Men on the walls were shouting and running about. The ranks under the walls swayed in confusion. Were the shouts an omen of victory?

Hang-Hi gripped his ivory wand quickly. His councillors stared, wide-eyed. Slowly, before their eyes the walls of Altur Haiten began to crumple and fall. They fell not inward, but outward.

The eastern wall, a section at a time, fell with a sonorous crash. Fell upon the ranks of the attackers, with the men who had gained the top. Hang-Hi saw men leaping desperately into space. The men under the walls crowded back in disorder. A moan sounded with the crash of bricks, the cry of thousands of men in pain. Then the space where the walls had been was covered by a rising cloud of dust and pulverized clay.

Through this smoke, Hang-Hi could make out giant beams thrusting. He guessed at the means which had toppled the walls on the attackers, after the Chinese cannon had undermined them.

The moans of the wounded gave place to a shrill battle-cry from behind the dust curtain. Hang-Hi saw ranks of Tatars with bared weapons surging forward. As the battle-cry mounted the oncoming ranks met the retreating attackers and the blended roar of a mêlée drowned all other sounds.

Hang-Hi glanced over the scene of conflict. Only a portion of the east walls facing him had fallen. The rest stood. But the sally of the Tatars carried them forward into the breastworks of the Chinese. There the disordered regiments of assault rallied, only to be pushed back further, among the guns and machines. In the dense mass of fighting men it was useless to fire a musket, and the cannon were silent.

Hang-Hi turned to his aides and began to give orders swiftly. Mounted couriers were sent to the other quarters of the camp for reinforcements. Reserve regiments were brought up and thrown into the mêlée. Chosen men of Leo Tung and the Sung commanders advanced from the junks in the river. The rush of the Tatars was stemmed in the rear of the cannon.

Then Hang-Hi addressed his generals. It was a stroke of fortune from heaven, he said, that levelled the walls. The Tatars were few and already they were retreating to the city, fighting desperately. The Chinese would be victorious, he said, for there was no longer any obstacle to their capture of Altur Haiten. Surely, the Tatars had become mad. Why otherwise should they speak of Genghis Khan, who was dead?

When the sun was high at mid-day Hang-Hi's meal was served in the pavilion and he ate and drank heartily. Messengers had informed him of all that was taking place. The Tatars, they said, were fighting with a courage which they had not previously shown. They had spiked the cannon, and thinned the ranks of the musketmen.

On the other hand, the sally had been by a few thousand, who had retired behind the mounds of brick and clay where the walls had been. A second assault by the Chinese, ordered for the afternoon, could not fail of success.

In the midst of Hang-Hi's meal, came a mounted courier from the west quarter of the camp.

"Oh, Excellency," he cried, bowing to the floor of the pavilion, "we have been attacked by mounted Tatars from the plains. They came suddenly, and many were killed. They came, many thousands, from the woods."

Other messengers confirmed this. Unexpectedly a strong force of mounted Tatars had appeared and defeated the weakened regiments who were stationed on the west side. These had retreated in confusion to the north and south.

"Dogs!" snarled the general of Wanleh. "Are you women to run from a few riders? Order the forces on the south and north to hold their ground. My men will be in Altur Haiten in a few hours. Whence came these new foemen?"

Yen Kui Kiang advanced and bowed.

"Favored of Heaven," he said, "they must be some of the deserters returned. They are fighting fiercely, but their number can not be great. Without doubt they can be easily checked during our assault."

But the secretary had not reckoned on the mobility and prowess of the Horde, fighting in their favorite manner, maneuvering on horseback against infantry. Before the assault could be ordered, Hang-Hi learned that a second column of the enemy, stronger than the first had struck the rear of the Chinese camp to the north and broken the ranks of the besiegers. Yen Kui Kiang declared that the latter were falling back in orderly manner on the masses of troops to the east, but the quick eyes of Hang-Hi saw crowds of his men pouring from the north side in rout.

By mid-afternoon the situation of the Chinese had not improved. They held two of the four sides of the city—the east and south. More than sixty thousand men had fallen in the destruction of the walls, and the defeat by the cavalry. Hang-Hi found that the river at his rear which had served as a means of communication from China, hindered movements of his troops and menaced him if he should retreat further.

Assembling his generals, Hang-Hi ordered the veteran Leo Tung men to take the first ranks on the east, facing the cavalry, between the town and the river, and the legions of the Sung generals to hold the southern camp. The other troops he had drawn up for the assault of the city he ordered to the breastworks facing the demolished walls.

The southern camp which had escaped attack, he ordered to be watchful. This portion of his troops faced both the city and the plains, without the support of the river. Hang-Hi was thankful in his heart that the Tatar cavalry had drawn off in the afternoon. His men feared the Tatars on horseback.

He wished vainly for Chan Kieh Shi. As evening fell he heard the chant of the defenders inside the walls. Whence had come the army of mounted men? They seemed to have sprung from the plains —Chakars and Tchoros, and even Kallmarks from the horde which had deserted early in the siege. And messengers brought him word that they had seen the standard of Genghis Khan among the Kall-marks.

The signal for the final assault of Altur Haiten was never given.

XVI

Kerula had taken refuge soon after the battle began in the household pagoda of Hang-Hi with the other women. Here she took her place at one of the windows looking toward the south, listening with all her ears to the reports that were brought to the pagoda.

Night had fallen and she could not see the flare of the flame cal-drons, or the flash of cannon. The camp of the Chinese seemed thronged with soldiers in confusion who passed hither and thither with torches, and red lanterns. Mounted men fought to get through the throngs, trampling the infantry. Moaning of the wounded could be heard. Kerula's thoughts were busy as she watched.

She had heard of the Tatar army that attacked from the plains. The Chinese had told wild tales of the fierceness and daring of the riders. Kerula pressed her hands together and trembled with joy. She had no doubt that this army was the Horde of Genghis Khan that she had heard in the desert. Did not the messengers say they had seen the yaks'-tails banner and heard the name of the Mighty Man-slayer shouted? She had told this to the women and they had cried out in fear, leaving her alone as one accursed. Kerula was glad of this.

She listened intently at the window. She had caught the distant roar of battle in the dark. This time, however, it came from the south, in a new quarter. The sounds came nearer instead of receding. Kerula leaned far out and listened.

Truly, a great battle was being fought, unknown to the girl. Scarcely had nightfall come when the Chinese regiments to the south had been struck in the rear by successive phalanxes of Tatar horsemen that broke their ranks and threw them into confusion. For the second time the army of the plains had appeared, led by the banner of yaks' tails, and chanting their war-song. These were not the warriors who had waited for a year behind the walls of Altur Haiten. Who were they and whence had they come?

Messages began to reach the women's quarters. A rumor said that the Sung generals had been captured or killed with most of their men. Another reported that a myriad Tatars were attacking in the dark. Genghis Khan had been seen riding at the head of his men, aided by demons who gave no quarter.

The confusion in the streets below Kerula grew worse. Men shouted that Altur Haiten was empty of defenders—that the Tatars were all in the plains. Reinforcements hurrying to the south lost their way in the dark and were scattered by fugitive regiments.

A mandarin in a torn robe ran into the hall of the pagoda and ordered the women to get ready to take refuge in the junks.

"A million devils have come out of the plains," he cried, "and our doctors are pronouncing incantations to ward them off. Hang-Hi has ordered all his household to the boats."

A wail greeted this, which grew as the women surged toward the doors in a panic. Kerula was caught in the crowd and thrust through the gate of the pagoda into the street.

She could see her way now, for buildings in the camp were in flames some distance away. Beside the women hurried soldiers without arms. She saw one or two of the helmeted Leo Tung warriors strive to push back the mob.

"Fools and dogs!" growled one sturdy warrior. "Hang-Hi holds the southern camp with one hundred thousand men. The bannermen of Leo Tung are coming to aid him. There is no battle, save on the south. Blind, and without courage!"

But the women pushed past him, screaming and calling:

"The junks! We were told to go to the junks. There we will be safe!"

As often happens, the confusion of the Chinese camp was heightened by the frantic women, and their outcry caused further panic at a time when the Leo Tung warriors who were trying to win through the mob of routed soldiers, prisoners, camp-followers and women, might have restored order. It was an evil hour for Hang-Hi that he left his pavilion to go to the front, with great bravery. In his absence the terror of the unknown gripped the camp.

"The junks!" a fleeing soldier shouted. "We shall be safe there."

The spear of a Leo Tung pierced his chest but other voices took up the cry:

"The junks! The camp is lost."

The cry spread through the camp, and the crowds began to push toward the river front, carrying with them many of the Leo Tung men.

Kerula cast about for a shelter, for she did not wish to be carried to the river. Rather she hoped to be picked up by some of the Tatars who she knew were coming. An open archway invited her and she slipped inside, to find herself in the empty Hall of Judgment.

Lanterns of many colors were lighted along the walls of the hall, and banners of victory hung around the vacant chair of Hang-Hi. The Chinese general had planned to sit there that night with his councillors, after the fall of Altur Haiten.

Kerula ran up the silken carpet to the dais and crouched in some of the hangings where she was safe from observation.

"The junks!" she heard continually. "Hang-Hi is defeated. His men are running back from the south. To the river!"

Gradually the shouting diminished, and Kerula guessed that that part of the camp was deserted. She was about to venture out from her hiding-place for a look into the street when she heard the sound of horses' feet outside.

Her heart leaped, for she thought that the men of Genghis Khan had come. Surely, she felt, the horsemen must be Tatars, for the Chinese had no cavalry. She heard voices at the archway and listened. Her heart sank as she heard Hang-Hi's voice.

"Go to the Leo Tung men, Yen Kui Kiang, and order them to hold the other side of the river. Put the junks in motion and take the survivors of the Sung forces with my own Guard back along this side of the river. The flames of the camp will light the way. Go! The battle is lost, for those we let pass as deserters were not deserters, but an army, few at a time."

"Nay, Excellency," Yen Kui Kiang remonstrated, "my place is with you. Shall the viceroy of the Son of Heaven go unattended?"

"Does the viceroy of the Son of Heaven need the help of men?" Hang-Hi answered. "I give you this as a duty. Go!"

A brief silence followed, when the horses' hoofs sounded again down the street. A murmur of voices, and Kerula heard the doors of the Hall of Judgment close. She looked out from her hiding-place. Hang-Hi, gorgeous in his silken and gold robe, was walking up the carpet toward his seat.

XVII

Kerula did not move. It was too late to hide behind the hangings. A movement would have attracted the attention of the general, who advanced quietly to the dais. The girl wondered, for the appearance of the commander was not that of a conquered man.

He seated himself on his throne and spread his robe on his knee. Kerula watching him, saw the wide, yellow face bend over his robe thoughtfully. He was writing on the cloth with a brush dipped in gilt.

Hang-Hi's stately head turned and the slant eyes fastened on her. Kerula did not shrink back. Her eyes met the general's proudly, and the man smiled at her. Again Kerula marveled. Was this the man who had been defeated by Genghis Khan?

"Little captive," said the Chinese slowly, and she understood, for she had learned the language quickly, "why are you not with the other women? Have you come to die with your master, as an honorable woman should?"

"Nay, Hang-Hi, lord," Kerula answered proudly, "I am waiting for my *anda*—a warrior to protect me. He has promised. He is a great warrior—Khlit, the Wolf. He has been to the tomb of Genghis Khan."

Hang-Hi had finished his writing, and laid down his brush. He took a stout silk cord from the breast of his robe and fingered it curiously.

"Khlit said that the banner of Genghis Khan was at the tomb," added the girl. "He will come, for he has promised."

Hang-Hi lifted his head and pointed to the writing on the robe.

"This is an ode," he said slowly, "and it means that it is better to lose one's life than to lose honor by saving it. Little captive, you also will lose yours. We shall know the secrets of life and death, you and I. The banner of Genghis Khan?" His brow darkened moodily. "Could it have been brought from the tomb to the Tatars? If Chan Kieh Shi were here he could answer my question."

He listened, as a roar and crackling that was not of a mob came to his ears. He passed his hand over his forehead, seeming to forget the girl.

"Fools!" he murmured. "How could they believe—Tatars and Chinese—that Genghis Khan was alive? He is dead, and the dead can not live. Yet the name of Genghis Khan was on the lips of the Tatars, and my men feared. Fools! Their folly was their undoing."

The roar and crackling came nearer and Kerula thought she smelled smoke. She gazed in fascination at the silken cord.

"Nay," he said grimly, catching her glance, "the cord is for me, little captive. It is easier than the flames. The flames are near us, for I ordered my men to set fire to the Hall. Listen——"

Kerula heard a crackling that soared overhead. Smoke dimmed the banners along the wall. She saw Hang-Hi lift his hands to his throat. Once they fell to his lap, and rose again with the silken cord. With a cry she sped down the aisle.

The heavy teak door at the further end was closed. She beat on it with her fists helplessly, and wrenched at the fastenings. Behind her the hall glowed with a new light.

She pulled at the door with all her strength and it gave a little. She squeezed through the opening, and ran under the archway into the street.

As she did so she threw up her hands with a cry. Rank upon rank of dark horsemen were passing. Their cloaked figures and helmets were not Chinese. She was struck by one of the horses and fell to the ground. Dimly she was aware that the horse which struck her had turned. Then the black mantle of night seemed to fall on her and her eyes closed.

When she opened her eyes again and looked around her she was in a very different place. She lay on a pallet, covered with straw, in a small hut. The sun was streaming into it from a window over her head.

Kerula turned her head. She felt weak. The darkness that had closed on her was very near, but the sun's rays heartened her. The hut was empty save for one man. She looked at him, and her pulse quickened.

Khlit was seated on a stool, watching her, his black pipe between his teeth, and his curved sword over one knee. His clothing was covered with dust, but his eyes were keen and alert. She put out one hand and touched the sword over his knee.

"Khlit, lord," she said happily, "you came to me as you promised you would. I told Hang-Hi you would come. But——"

A frown crossed her face as if she was striving to remember something.

"I dreamed such a dream, Khlit, lord. It seemed as if I was being carried on a horse by a warrior. I saw flames, and then darkness of the plains. Then I saw that he carried the standard of Genghis Khan that Hang-Hi feared. The standard of yaks' tails flapped over me as we went to the tomb in the mountains, and I cried with happiness. I dreamed it was Genghis Khan that carried me."

"It was a good battle," Khlit growled, "it was a battle such as I have never seen. Nay, little Kerula, was your dream anything but a dream?"

"Aye, Khlit, lord. But then the standard of Genghis Khan. Surely that was real, for the men of Hang-Hi saw it."

Khlit touched the lettering on his sword.

"Nay, Kerula," he said slowly, "the standard of Genghis Khan lies in his tomb where the Onon Muren watch. No man will go there. For the standard, and what is in the tomb belong to Genghis Khan."

In his eyes as he spoke was the look of a man who has looked upon forbidden things, unafraid. Yet when men asked him if he knew the way to the tomb where the treasure was he said that surely no man could find his way to the dead. And when Kerula told him again that her memory of the ride was real, he laughed and told her that it was a dream, among dreams.

CHANGA NOR

Older than the five sons of Alan Toa; older than the god Natagai or the sword of the hero Afrasiab is the hunting-ground of the Dead World.

Skillful must the hunter be—wary, and mindful of the guiding star—or he will not come back from the Dead World.

Aye, he will join the thing that he hunts. And the game he seeks has been dead for ten thousand moons.

WHEN THE RISING SUN SHONE ON THE BLUE WATERS OF CHANGA NOR, in the year of our Lord sixteen hundred and seven, Gurd the hunter set forth on his Summer hunt. He left the castle of Changa in a small boat which took him to the shore of the lake. On the shore he found his reindeer waiting.

By Gurd's reckoning it was the year of the lion according to the Tatar calendar. Although the summits of the Khantai Khan mountains around Lake Nor were capped with snow, the sun still held its Midsummer warmth, and Gurd knew that the way to the Dead World, above Lake Baikal, was open.

Gurd was clean-limbed and massive of shoulder. He had the black hair, high cheek-bones and sparkling black eyes of the Siberian Buriate Tatar. His head was shaved in front, allowing a long tress to fall back over one shoulder. His clear eyes, somewhat slant, and white teeth bespoke youth.

He wore a reindeer jerkin, girded about the waist, with a quiver at his side. His baggy trousers of nankeen were tucked into horse-hide boots. Although Gurd was young he looked to the saddling of his reindeer with the skill of an old hunter. His hands, veined and corded, revealed great physical strength. Without these two qualities Gurd could not have gone as he had done for the past five years into the Northern hunting-ground, and returned alive.

Gurd was not a hunter of sables or ermine. Nor did he follow the reindeer herds of the Baikal region. He was one of the few hardy spirits that went after the treasure of the Dead World, up the bank of the Lena to the Frozen Sea.

Taking a firm grasp on his staff, the brown-faced Tatar sprang nimbly into the saddle on the shoulders of one of the reindeer. At once the beast was in motion, the pack-reindeer following. The cloven hoofs of the animals made a clattering sound as they trotted with their peculiar swinging motion over the hard ground up the trail into the mountains.

When he had reached the pass where he had a last view of Changa and the lake, Gurd halted his mount and looked back. He caught the white flutter of a scarf waving from the battlements. A soft light came into his shrewd black eyes as he lifted his hand in answer before taking up his journey.

Gurd did not delay. He knew that he was late in starting on his hunt. The barriers of frost and snow would descend on the entrance to the Dead World within two months, and before that time he must be on his way home. By the time the sun had climbed the mountain summits he had vanished into the passes leading to the North.

But if he could have looked back at Changa he would have seen the white scarf still waving at intervals to speed him on his way.

II

The setting sun that day lighted the encampment of the Jun-gar Tatars by the Tula River, not far from Lake Baikal. Sunset was the signal for gathering the *kurultai* council. But no *nacars* were needed to summon the khans. For the encampment was small, and the council consisted of a scant half-dozen of the lords of Tatary—a remnant of the warriors who had held dominion over China, Tibet, Sogdiana and Persia for centuries.

The council assembled in the pavilion of the Kha Khan, or White Khan, of the Jun-gar. This was a felt-covered tent, erected on a large wagon. As the warriors entered they seated themselves, after greeting the Kha Khan, on bearskins ranged around the fire. Behind them the walls of the pavilion were hung with weapons and trophies of their recent victory—the last of its kind—over the Chinese at Shan-kiang.

Opposite the entrance to the tent sat the Kha Khan, a white-haired Cossack, keen-eyed and scarred of face, known to his enemies as the Wolf. Over Khlit's knees lay the curved sword of Kaidu which had earned him his right to leadership of the khans.

On Khlit's left sat Chepé Buga, a swarthy veteran of fifty battles, and a man quick of wit with tongue or sword.

On the right of the Kha Khan was Berang, the young khan of the Ordu horde. The khans of the Hoshot and Torgot tribes completed the circle. Opposite Khlit sat Lhon Otai, a *shaman* and leader of the priest-conjurers. By the entrance lounged the giant figure of Chagan, swordbearer of the Kha Khan.

Grim men they were, hard riders and fighters. With the Kallmarks, their powerful neighbors, they formed the last of the race of Ghenghis Khan, conqueror of Asia. But today their faces were sullen and downcast. Chepé Buga puffed silently at his pipe, while Berang fumbled uneasily with his sword.

"We are like a herd of horned cattle, Khlit, lord," spoke Chepé Buga at length, twisting his mustache, "with flocks of sheep pressing in on our pasture on all sides. Hey, soon there will not be room on the Tatar steppe for our horses' dung!"

"Aye, that is true," nodded Berang. "The tidings we have received today is that the Kallmarks are driving their herds over our southwest boundaries, near Khamil. And there are many horsemen in the Kallmark horde. Now they are quarrelsome, being more numerous than we are."

"The Mings and Manchus," added another khan, "have driven us from the *dorok* graves of our fathers by the great desert of Kobi, to the river Kerulon and the Khantai Khan Mountains. They have killed many of us."

"We can go no further north, Khlit, lord," agreed Chepé Buga moodily, "for the frozen rivers of Baikal are near us, and the cattle can not graze in the snow."

Khlit smoked his black pipe silently, scanning the faces of his companions shrewdly. He understood their anger. The Tatar of the steppe must have freedom to rove, without tie of home or god; no

intruder can take their lands. They looked to him for protection of
their boundaries. He had aided them twice to defeat Chinese invaders of the steppe. But since then the strength of the khans had
been diminished by the loss of the powerful Kallmark horde.

"Our lands," he said slowly, "the lands of the Jun-gar which
stretch from the desert of Kobi to Muscovy and from the white regions of the North to the Thian Shan Mountains are the richest in
the world for grazing, and for hunting. I know, for I have seen the
steppe of Russia, the fertile valleys of Persia, and the hinterland of
Cathay. So long as we keep these lands we shall have large herds
and plenty of food."

"That may be, Khlit, lord," spoke Berang respectfully. "But how
shall we keep them, when the Keraits are driving their sheep over
our boundary to the south, and the Muscovy soldiers and traders are
at Tomsk? By the god Meik who watches over the forests we must
give these Kallmark men a taste of sharp swords."

"Aye," growled another khan approvingly, "we will take their
herds that have come over the boundary, and their widows will seek
new husbands."

"Our swords grow rusty, O Kha Khan," broke in the mighty
Chagan from the door. "Come, let us whet them up a bit with bones
and blood."

Khlit made no answer. He knew better than his companions the
strength of the Kallmarks whose territory was the heart of Asia.
Furthermore they were allied to the men of Muscovy who were as
numerous as the sands of the great desert. War with the Kallmarks
must be avoided at all cost. But how was he to keep the lands of the
Jun-gar from invasion?

To gain time to think, he addressed Lhon Otai the *shaman* who
had not yet spoken.

"What is your word, Lhon Otai?" he asked. "Do you also counsel
war?"

The *shaman's* shrewd eyes swept the circle. He was an old man
and stout. The khans declared that he had the craft to coax a fish
from a river. He was a leader of the *shamans* who played the double
rôle of physician and priest to the tribes of central Asia.

"A *shaman* does not counsel war or peace, Khlit, lord," he responded with a bow. "Truly we can heal the sick, or drive out un-

clean spirits by the aid of the god Natagai, as our fathers have done, or prophesy events that will come to pass——"

"Prophesy then, Lhon Otai," demanded Chepé Buga who was lacking in reverence, "how we may be rid of this plague of invaders. Come, give us a good prophecy!"

The khans muttered agreement. A frown passed swiftly over the *shaman's* smooth brow. He stood up by the fire in his long fur robe ornamented with rabbits' ears and walrus teeth.

"A prophecy!" chorused the khans, with the exception of Khlit. "Read us the future, O wise shepherd of the spirits."

Lhon Otai made no response. He doffed his fur coat. Advancing to the half-circle of chiefs, he drew a long cord from his girdle. One end of this he gave to a khan. Then he passed the cord in a loop around his neck under the chin.

For a moment Lhon Otai stared mutely at the ridgepole of the tent. While the khans watched intently, he lay down full length on the ground. The remaining end of the cord which was still around his neck, he tossed to Chagan who took it gingerly. Lhon Otai now lay on his back, both arms extended wide.

Berang, who had witnessed many manifestations of the *shaman*, took the fur coat and laid it over the prostrate figure which was now concealed except for the extended hands. The khans fell silent. The heavy breathing of Lhon Otai raised and lowered the coat. The exposed hands clenched as if in suffering.

"See," whispered Berang to Khlit, "the *shaman* is visiting the forest of Meik in spirit, where he learns wisdom of the king of the ravens. That is why his face is hidden—that we may not read his thoughts, whether good or ill. The ancient raven knows all that has happened, or will happen."

The hands of Lhon Otai dug themselves into the rugs on the floor of the tent, and the *shaman* groaned. Chepé Buga watched proceedings with a half-smile hidden under his black mustache, but the smile faded at a groan from the conjurer.

"That is the signal!" cried Berang. "Pull on the cord."

Chagan and the khan who held the other end both tugged quickly on the cord. The rope appeared from under the coat, taut and whole.

A sigh of amazement came from Berang, for the hands of the

conjurer had not been lost to sight. The young khan rose and drew off the fur coat. Lhon Otai lay as if asleep, and his yellow face was pale.

"Presently," whispered Berang again, "he will return from the spirit forest and will tell us the wisdom he has learned. Truly, he must have been among the spirits in the radiance of *Begli* the moon, for the cord cut through his neck."

Khlit made no response and before long Lhon Otai sat erect, his eyes half closed.

"I have heard the words of the raven," he chanted, "by the pine-trees of Meik. The raven that has talked with Ghenghis Khan, of the Golden Horde, and with the five sons of Alan Goa. I have heard the sacred magpie fluttering in the trees by the tomb of Ghenghis Khan, the conqueror of the world. I bring a wisdom from the spirit world of *Begli* to the living paladins of Tatary. This is the wisdom."

Lhon Otai paused, while the khans bent closer, and Chagan stared from the *shaman* to the cord.

"The land of the khans," resumed Lhon Otai, "has been entered by strangers. But there is a way to drive them from the land of the Jun-gar. A day's ride to the south from Lake Baikal, from the three gods of Dianda, is the lake of Changa Nor. In the castle which stands in the middle of the lake there is a treasure. The khans must seize the castle, with its treasure. Then they can pay the Kallmarks to leave the land of the bowmen, and their boundaries shall be as before."

Silence greeted the words of the *shaman,* broken by Berang.

"Aye, Lhon Otai," he said respectfully, "there is a ruined castle that stands on some rocks in the waters of Changa Nor. I have heard it belongs to an ivory-hunter. But I heard nothing of a treasure therein."

"That may be," broke in Chepé Buga, "for I have heard a similar tale. My father told it. There was a powerful kingdom to the south, ruled by a rich Gur-Khan in the time of Ghenghis Khan. The Gur-Khan was slain in a battle. But his treasure was not found. He had kept it in one of the castles. Speak, O gossiper with magpies and ravens, is this the treasure you would have us seek?"

Lhon Otai scowled, for Chepé Buga, who was one of the most powerful of the Tatars, treated him with scant reverence.

"You have seen, Chepé Buga, how true are the words of wisdom.

Aye, this is the hoard of the Gur-Khan, watched over by a hunter named Gurd who is a solitary fellow of dark pursuits. He has gone on a hunt to the North and Changa castle may be easily seized. But the wisdom told me that it was guarded by evil spirits."

"No doubt," retorted Chepé Buga grimly, "it is well guarded or you would have had your claws in it before now."

Lhon Otai pulled his fur robe about him and rose to his feet. The khans drew back at the dark glance he threw Chepé Buga. He bowed before Khlit.

"Go to Changa Nor, O Kha Khan," he said firmly. "There you will find the aid you seek."

Khlit, who was stroking the sword on his knees, did not look up.

"They are evil folk, I hear," put in Berang. Unbuckling his gold-chased girdle, the khan tossed it to Lhon Otai. "Take this, *Shaman*. There will be other rewards, of jewels when we find the treasure."

"Aye," muttered Chepé Buga, rising and stretching like a dog, "and there will be split bamboos for the soles of your fat feet, if we do not find it, *Shaman*."

With that the *kurultai* broke up. But Khlit remained in his tent in thought. The words of the *shaman* had touched a chord of memory. In his Cossack days he had heard of a kingdom like that of the Gur-Khan and a treasure. There had been tales of a rich monarch in Asia, whose wealth had escaped search. But he could recall neither name nor place.

Khlit dismissed the matter from his mind with a grunt, resolved that Changa Nor should tell him the truth, if there were truth, in the tale.

III

The second sun was high when Khlit, followed by Chagan and the khans with two hundred picked horsemen from the encampment reached the summit of the hills around Changa Nor. Lhon Otai, at Chepé Buga's request, had accompanied them.

They saw a blue lake, a scant half-mile in width, with a castle a short distance from the opposite shore. The castle, a square, massive structure, stood upon a stone foundation which rose a few feet above the surface of the lake sheer with the walls. There was no sign of a gateway, although narrow slits pierced the walls and the single tower.

A small boat was moored beside the castle, showing how the occupants gained the shore. But there was no sign of life about the place. The battlements of the keep and tower were in ruins, although the walls seemed solid enough.

"Hey, here is a fair stronghold to which you have brought us, Lhon Otai," growled Chepé Buga. "Methinks it would take an army of sea serpents to seize it, or a regiment of harpies. Did the ancient raven croak to you how we were to take it, if perchance its people refuse surrender?"

"Nay, that is your business, not mine," muttered the *shaman*. "Said I not, it was guarded by evil spirits?"

As the riders surveyed the scene its desolation impressed them. The snow-capped mountains in the background cast their reflection into the still waters of the lake. The shores were a wooded wilderness. The boat was the only indication of human beings about the place.

"It will take more than spirits, evil or otherwise," retorted the Tatar, "to keep me out, if I choose to enter. By the same token, only a devil's brood would infest such a place, where there are no horses or pastures."

When they had gained the shore nearest the castle Khlit directed Berang to swim his horse out the short distance to the castle and demand that the place be opened to them and the boat sent ashore.

The young khan carried out his orders eagerly. He spurred his mount into the water and steered him toward the black bulk of the castle. The watchers saw him linger under the walls for a moment, his face turned up to the openings overhead. Then Berang slid from his saddle and swam alongside his horse back to shore.

The khan swaggered up to the group of horsemen, happy in the display he had made of his mount.

"Strange folk are those, Khlit, lord," he made report. "I told them your word, but they answered that the castle would not yield. Then I swore that we would storm it, and the voice within cried that many who had tried to do that had died."

"We have warned them," said Khlit, "now we will take the castle."

Berang cast a doubtful glance at the lake. He had seen no foothold in the smooth walls, slippery with moss, nor any door. Cannon would batter the place into submission, but the khans had no cannon. The walls were within long bow-shot. Yet there were no defenders visible to shoot at.

Khlit, however, soon showed how he meant to set about the attack. Under his direction the Tatars were divided into two parties. One, commanded by Chepé Buga, set about cutting down large pine-trees with the axes they always carried at their saddles. The other party trimmed the fallen trees and rolled them to the water's edge.

In a short time a sufficient number of pine trunks were assembled to bind together with strong vines and fibers into a raft, twenty paces square.

Not content with this, Khlit saw to it that certain trunks, tall and slender, were fastened in pairs and laid on the raft. The sun was low by the time this was done, so the Cossack ordered his followers to make camp for the night.

The men were veterans at warfare and lost no time in picketing their horses for the night. Fires were lighted and the warriors were soon toasting pieces of meat they had brought in their saddle bags at the flames, and sampling *arak* in high good humor at the prospect of an engagement on the morrow. Khlit meanwhile took Chepé Buga and Berang aside and gave them instructions.

Seventy picked men, he said, were to go on the raft at dawn and paddle to the castle, using branches as oars. The trimmed pines on the raft they were to raise against the battlements after the manner of storming ladders. Berang would have command of the raft.

The best archers under Chepé Buga were to line the heights along the shore and direct a flight of arrows against the battlements while the makeshift ladders were raised and the attackers swarmed up them.

The plan promised well, and fell in with the Tatars' mood. They were awake before daybreak, armed and ready for the onset. The walls of the castle showed dark. Even when the raft was pushed out from shore and steered toward the castle there were no signs of life among the defenders.

Silently the raft was propelled nearer its object. It reached the rock foundation of the castle. Still there had been no sound from the walls. Khlit with his bowmen on the shore scanned the dark bulk of the keep against the crimson of sunrise but saw nothing at which to direct their arrows. For the first time Khlit felt a pang of foreboding;

he would have been better pleased if the walls had been manned with defenders.

Khlit was a Christian after the manner of the Cossacks and he had not been inclined to credit the *shaman's* talk of evil spirits, or the warning from the castle of Changa. But he frowned as he watched the raft come to rest under the menacing walls, and the tree trunks raised against the battlements. Another moment and the Tatars would have been swarming up the improvised ladders. And then he saw a glint of light in one of the slits in the walls.

At the same instant a shout came from the men on the raft. The point of light grew to a strange flare. The watchers on the shore saw a weird thing. From the slit in the wall a curtain of fire descended on the raft. Flame and smoke cascaded down the raised tree trunks and ran along the surface of the raft.

The shout changed to a wild yell of pain. Khlit saw figures of men leaping from the raft into the water, and the tree trunks falling back into the lake. In a moment the raft was empty, save for the flickering flames and curling smoke.

At Khlit's command a volley of arrows sped against the castle, only to rattle from the wall harmlessly. The flame torrent from the slit ceased, and he saw his men swimming toward shore. Using the tree trunks to keep them afloat, they were making their way slowly toward him. The walls of Changa showed dark and silent as before.

"Nay, Khlit, lord," Berang stood before him, armor and clothing drenched, "it was death to stay on the raft. The flames caught even on green wood and leather garment. By the white falcon of Kaidu, we were near death! Some were burned but saved their lives by leaping in the lake. If it had not been for the tree trunks, we in armor would not have lived."

"You did right to come back, Berang," said Khlit, seeing the young khan's shame at his retreat. "You could not guard against flames."

Lhon Otai, the *shaman,* approached them with a triumphant smile.

"Said I not the place was infested with evil spirits, Khlit, lord?" he bowed. "The words of the raven were true."

"Nay, Lhon Otai," growled Chepé Buga, who had been watching the proceedings closely, "that was not demon-work, but fire. The stuff is made by Chinese fire-makers. I have seen it used before, in siege work."

"Nevertheless," retorted the *shaman,* "my prophecy was true. And you have not yet taken Changa Nor, in spite of your loud-tongued boasting."

"Peace!" growled Khlit, seeing Chepé Buga flush dangerously. "Before we act further, we must know if there be truly a treasure in this hold."

Chepé Buga stroked his mustache thoughtfully.

"Last night, O Kha Khan," he said gruffly, "the old fellows among my men told me more of the tale of the Gur-Khan. When they heard we were to attack Changa Nor they were eager for the onset, because of the story of treasure. Many minstrels have sung of the Gur-Khan on their *dombras*—the Gur-Khan who was the friend of Ghenghis Khan."

Berang and his dripping warriors crowded close about the khans as Chepé Buga spoke, forgetful of their wet garments.

"The Gur-Khan," resumed the veteran chief, "was a follower of a strange faith. He did not pour libations to Natagai or Meik of the forest, nor did he pray in the temple of Fo. So runs the tale. His daughter who was also of his faith, married a strong warrior who kept the treasure safe. This treasure they cherished because it belonged to their god."

"An evil demon," amended Lhon Otai.

"Evil or not, the treasure was great. The grandfather of one of my minstrels has seen robes set with jewels of Persia, pearls and sapphires. And crowns of heavy gold with rubies. And the tale tells of a scepter of pure emeralds as large as a small sword. The empire of the Gur-Khan has been scattered as the dust before the wind. But the treasure has been kept by his children."

"The grandfather of my minstrel," continued Chepé Buga carelessly, "swears that the treasure was last seen in the hands of the sixth in descent from the Gur-Khan, at a place which is called the Lake of Stones, by the Sea of Sand, north of the Thian Shan Mountains."

"There is the lake!" cried Berang, pointing to the blue waters of Changa.

"And the Sea of Sand must be the great desert which lies not far from here," added another warrior eagerly.

"It may be," nodded Chepé Buga. "The minstrels tell of strange animals belonging to the Gur-Khan, of tame stags and gerfalcons that needed no training to bring down herons for their masters. Also of beasts of the forest that once guarded the treasure.

"I care not for such tales; but here is wind of a goodly treasure. Moreover, there is Gurd, the hunter who brings sledloads of costly ivory to trade at Irkutsk, on Lake Baikal. Gurd lives at Changa Nor. Where does he get the ivory? Aye, by Afrasiab's sword, I have a mind to see the vaults of Chang! I scent plunder here."

"Nay, we have great need of such treasure," put in Berang seriously. "For we must ransom our lands from the Kallmarks, with their Kerait and Muscovy rascals. We must take Changa Nor."

"A hard lair to crack open!" Chepé Buga stroked his scarred chin thoughtfully. "We must assemble not one but four rafts, light smoke fires against the walls to blind the defenders and attack with all our strength."

Khlit shook his shaggy head.

"That would cost us many lives—needlessly," he objected. "Changa Nor may be taken in another way."

The khans watched him expectantly. They had seen Khlit overthrow two Chinese generals by strategy, and they had firm confidence in the craft of the veteran Cossack.

"In two months it will be the time of frost and snow," explained Khlit. "And the waters of Changa will be frozen. When the ice is thick enough to bear our men we can attack unseen in the dark or in a snowstorm and take the castle by surprise. We have too few horsemen to waste lives."

Berang and Chepé Buga nodded in understanding. Truly, Khlit was a wise leader.

"But the Kallmarks," objected Berang. "They will be advancing into our choicest grazing lands."

"We will send an envoy to them, asking them to go back to the boundaries in peace. If they refuse, we will assemble our horsemen from the Jun-gar hordes. We will meet—all of our tribes—by the shore of Baikal. Then we will march south, taking Changa by surprise on the way, for the lake will then be frozen."

"Ha, a good word, O Kha Khan," grunted Chepé Buga, tapping his sword. "And the treasure of Changa Nor——"

A shout of approval greeted this, in which Berang joined heartily. The two magic words of treasure and battle spread through the assembled ranks of horsemen and made them forget their mishap of the morning. Once again Khlit had wrought a change of heart through his leadership.

But Khlit did not smile. He had little hope that the powerful Kallmarks would accept his offer of peace.

For the second time the memory of the Gur-Khan story troubled him. In Russia he had heard the tale of a treasure guarded by animals, belonging to a monarch who was a priest. Almost he recalled the name of the king—the words "Prester John" rose in his mind. He felt, however, that Lhon Otai, who knew the secrets of central Asia from the wide-spread *shaman* cult, could supply him with the name he sought.

Lhon Otai pushed through the throng.

"Wisely have you spoken, O Kha Khan," he bowed, a smile on his thick lips. "But would it not be well to capture the hunter Gurd? He knows the secret of Changa Nor. Two days ago I have heard he left here for the North. He must pass through Irkutsk, and he may be followed from there to the Dead World where he can be traced in the snow."

"I will go after him," ventured Berang quickly.

"Nay, Berang," Khlit looked fondly on his youngest khan. "You must assemble the men of the Ordus for me."

"Then I will bring you the demon hunter," offered Chepé Buga, "bound and trussed to the reindeer they say he rides, like a sack of meal to a camel."

A chorus of voices announced the willingness of the other horsemen to go in quest of the hunter who had a dark name in Tatary. But Khlit waved them aside.

"I have heard," he said grimly, "that the hunter Gurd is in league with the powers of evil. You and I, men of the Jun-gar, do not fear the *Rakchas* or the demons of the icy caves of the dead. But we will send after Gurd a man who can meet his wiles with enchantments. This man shall pick a score of fleet horsemen. Lhon Otai will go."

The *shaman* started and the glance he threw at Khlit was far from kindly. He protested that he was not a warrior, that his bulk would break the back of a horse. Berang and some of the Tatars objected that the *shaman* must remain with them. But Khlit was not to be moved. Lhon Otai and no other, he declared, must go after Gurd.

Chepé Buga, who was well pleased with the plight of the revered *shaman*, added his word to that of Khlit. So, when the khans left the shore of Changa Nor, they went in two parties. One returned to their encampment; the other, headed by Lhon Otai, wound into the passes leading to the North, in the tracks of Gurd, the hunter.

But as they entered the mountains one of the riders selected by Lhon Otai turned off, unseen by the others, to the south.

IV

For the second time in one day Gurd the hunter was puzzled. Halting his little cavalcade of reindeer at the summit of a pass, he looked back the way he had come. He saw no one, heard no one. The rocky waste of the tundras of the Dead World lay behind him and on all sides. Barren hills thrust their summits through the scarred plain. But a mile behind him some rooks were circling over the pass he had taken. Not so long before, he had startled the rooks into flight. They had settled down again in the firs after his departure. Now they were again in flight.

There was nothing unusual in the flight of rooks. Save early that morning Gurd had looked back and seen some mountain goats bounding from their rocks an hour after he had passed. It was not likely that other hunters were passing that way, for it was near the bank of the Lena where few sables and lynxes were to be found.

Gurd cast a speculative glance at the tracks his reindeer made. The splay-footed beasts left clear prints in the moss and dirt. A clever hunter might easily follow such tracks. But why should any one follow him?

A week before Gurd had left the three Dianda rocks on Lake Baikal and struck into the tundras which would lead him to the Lena. Already the silence and chill of the Dead World had closed around him. Until today he had thought he was alone in the near-by tundras. He urged on his reindeer thoughtfully. From time to time he stopped to change his saddle to another beast, to make better speed. And as he did so, he looked back. He saw nothing save the fir clumps and moss valleys of the waste land. By nightfall he was convinced that he had been mistaken in thinking others were near him.

Gurd was afoot an hour before sunrise. The sky to the north was aflicker with the reflection of the Northern Lights, the sparks from the anvil of the *Cheooki* gods, as the Yakut fur-hunters had told him.

The cold stirred Gurd's appetite but he contented himself with chewing a handful of cheese and drawn beef which he drew from his saddle bags. For the cold reminded him that he was still two days' travel from his hunting-ground and Autumn with its heavy snowfall was at hand. Already the messengers of frost were in the air.

Before noon that day the waters of the Lena appeared before him. Without hesitation Gurd drove the reindeer into the icy river, steeling himself against the chill of the water which came to his waist. Some seals which were sporting about the film of ice on the further bank dived into the water at his approach.

"Live well, brothers," Gurd called to them gaily as he left the river. "It is not your pelts I seek."

Humming to himself he sought the farther edge of the firs. Before plunging into the tundras again he looked back. He drew in his breath sharply.

Swimming the Lena at the point where he had crossed he saw a score of horsemen. From their caps he made out that they were Tatars, not Yakuts. He waited to see if they would attempt to kill the tempting seals which were swimming near. They paid no attention to the animals.

Gurd's keen black eyes scanned them as they disappeared into the firs. Here were Tatars who had not the bearing of hunters. Moreover they seemed to be following in his tracks.

After a moment's deliberation, Gurd turned the head of his reindeer aside into the firs and took up another course. His impassive olive face betrayed no surprise at what he had seen. A life of battling with cold and hunger, with the relentless forces of the Dead World, and with the hatred of men had steeled him to hardship and tempered his courage.

On the summit of a hillock some distance on, he looked back. The riders had come to the point where he turned aside. After a moment's delay, he saw them take the course he had followed. He knew now that they were after him.

Gurd wasted no time in wondering why he was pursued. All his life the hand of other Tatars had been against him. Against him and the others of Changa Nor.

He urged his reindeer to greater speed, at the same time realizing how hard it would be to outdistance the horsemen. The reindeer could go no faster than their swinging trot, and the pack-animals must be whipped on continually.

At the edge of a clearing he looked back and saw that his pursuers were a scant half-mile behind. Moreover they had sighted him now, and were heading straight for him. But Gurd saw that the shadows were lengthening and the Northern night was at hand.

He drew his reindeer farther into the firs where the ground showed tracks less easily, and where he was lost to sight. He could hear the horsemen crashing through the underbrush and guessed that they had divided in seeking him.

Gurd was now in his own hunting-ground, which was familiar to him, and he was able to dodge the riders until twilight had veiled his tracks. The sound of pursuit lessened and he guessed that the others had assembled. He led the reindeer a short distance further to avoid the chance of being found by accident in the night, and tied them fast. Then he sat down and made a hearty meal—not before he had seen that his beasts were fed and their packs removed. With a grunt of satisfaction he caught sight of a gleam of fire back in the woods.

When the Northern Lights began flickering in the sky Gurd left his reindeer and advanced cautiously in the direction of the fire. Slipping from fir to fir silently he soon arrived outside the circle of firelight.

Here he crouched and watched. He saw a dozen Tatars stretched out asleep in their cloaks. Others were sitting by the blaze drinking *arak* and tossing dice. Apart from the rest was a fat man in a costly fur robe adorned with bears' claws. Him Gurd scanned thoughtfully.

The Tatars paid no heed to him, and he could have shot arrows into the group from the bow at his back with impunity. But such was not Gurd's plan. He waited until others of the men had dropped off to sleep.

Placing his hands to his mouth Gurd made a peculiar croaking sound. A second time he did this. One of the men raised his head sleepily.

"Go yonder, Lhon Otai," the Tatar chuckled, "your brother the raven calls you into the forest. Perhaps he will tell you where the rascal Gurd is hiding."

The *shaman* made no response. But again came the croaking summons from the forest. Lhon Otai turned his heavy head and scanned the trees from slant eyes. He saw nothing. At a third summons, he got to his feet with a sigh and made his way into the wood.

Gurd watched his coming intently. Drawing a heavy knife from his girdle he crept into the path of the *shaman* and waited. Lhon Otai halted and he repeated the raven's croak very softly. Lhon Otai stepped forward.

As he did so a dark figure rose up before him. He felt himself gripped by the shoulders and something cold pressed against his sleek throat under the chin. His squeal of alarm ended in a gurgle.

"Be silent, *Shaman*," a voice hissed in his ear, "and come with me. If you make a sound, my brothers the wolves will feast well from your carcass."

The *shaman* shivered. He threw a longing glance in the direction of the fire. Then, impelled by whisper and dagger's prick, he stepped forward feeling his way slowly through the pines in the direction Gurd indicated.

When they came to the reindeer, the hunter released Lhon Otai for a moment. He returned with a stout cord. With this he bound the *shaman* to a tree trunk.

"Harken, *Shaman*," he whispered, "you came to find a raven and you found a man who has no love for you or your kind. You are afraid of me now. Presently you shall fear more. Watch."

Gurd crouched beside his prisoner. Placing his hands to his mouth he uttered a shrill wail. He repeated the call and waited. Lhon Otai watched him as well as he could by the flickering lights in the sky. Then Lhon Otai grunted with terror.

A pair of green eyes gleamed from the darkness in front of him. The eyes stared at him, unblinkingly. He heard the reindeer scuffling in fright. Gurd laughed.

"That is my cousin, the lynx, Lhon Otai," he whispered. "He has learned to come to me for meat. He would find rare picking in your fat carcass."

The *shaman* shivered, and strained against his bonds. But Gurd laughed softly and tossed a piece of meat from his bags toward the eyes. There was a soft pad-pad of feet in the darkness and the lynx disappeared.

"You are crafty, Lhon Otai," cautioned the hunter, "but loosen not your cords. Or my cousin yonder will be upon your back."

The *shaman* needed no further warning to remain passive, even after Gurd had vanished in the shadows. He did not doubt that Gurd held power over the beasts of the tundras. He had heard tales of the hunter of the Dead World, who rode upon reindeer. He cursed the drunkenness of his men, and Khlit, who had sent him on this quest.

It was near daybreak when Gurd returned. Lhon Otai heard the trampling of a large beast accompanying the hunter and he shivered anew. But Gurd's speech relieved him.

"Here is a horse for you to ride, *Shaman*," he grunted. "You would break the back of my reindeer. I will tie you to the saddle. Hey, if you try to flee I will bury the feathers of an arrow in your kidneys. Come!"

When the *shaman* was mounted, and the hunter had loosened his reindeer the two set off in the half-light of dawn through the forest. Lhon Otai cast a vengeful glance in the direction of the Tatar encampment.

"Your fellows will not follow us, *Shaman*," laughed Gurd who had caught the glance. "For their horses are well on the way to the Lena, and they can not catch us, afoot. I have seen to it."

Lhon Otai smothered a curse. Truly this hunter was in league with the evil spirits of the forest, if not with Meik himself. For, single-handed and armed only with a bow and knife, he had outwitted a score of horsemen of the khans.

V

"And now, Lhon Otai—if that be your name—you can tell me whence you and your men come, and why you follow me into the Dead World."

As Gurd spoke, his clear black eyes scanned the *shaman* thoughtfully. They were camped for the night well beyond reach of the dismounted Tatars, in a grotto by a small stream in the waste country. Around them reared a nest of rocky hillocks, barren even of firs. The cold wind of the North searched the ravine where they were, and fanned the fire Gurd had lighted. The hunter, however, seemed to know his way. He had led them without hesitation to the grotto. Lhon Otai bethought him swiftly.

"We came, I and my men," he explained, "from the khans of

the Jun-gar. Khlit, the Kha Khan, ordered that you be brought to him. He has heard tales of your hunting."

Gurd, busy toasting meat on a wooden spit, made no response.

"I did as the Kha Khan bade me," went on Lhon Otai. "We learned the course you had taken from the hamlet of Irkutsk. Then hunters told us you had been seen heading for the Lena. Before long my men found the trail of your reindeer."

Still Gurd was silent.

"We heard you had left Changa Nor," the *shaman* said uneasily. "But we meant not to harm you."

Gurd bared his teeth, but he did not laugh.

"My cousin the lynx, O *Shaman*," he said softly, "has followed us, unseen by you. He is near by, in the rocks, sniffing at the roasting meat. Shall I call him? Or will you tell me truth instead of lies. In a month I would return to Irkutsk with ivory. The Kha Khan could have found me then. Why did he send after me to the North? What were you doing near Changa Nor?"

The *shaman* threw a fearful look at the rocks behind him.

"What do I know of the will of the khans?" he whined. "Did I come willingly to the North? Nay, Khlit has a mind to Changa Nor and what it hides. He has been there with his horsemen——"

A change came over the impassive face of the hunter. His eyes narrowed in anger, and his heavy hand clutched the spit.

"Who brought the khans to Changa Nor?" he cried. "Come, speak——"

"They attacked the castle, Gurd," ventured Lhon Otai shrewdly, "and because of the accursed fires that drove them away, Khlit set a price on your head. Aye, and he bade me seek you, thinking that I might die thereby."

"The fires," quoth Gurd with a laugh, "guard well Changa castle and what is within. Truly then, this Khlit loves you not, Lhon Otai?"

The *shaman's* thick lips twisted in a snarl. Memory of the long feud between himself and the Cossack rankled. In his anger he spoke what he had long kept secret. Yet he spoke not unknowingly, for he was shrewd and Gurd might serve him.

"Aye," he responded, "the Kha Khan is my foe. Once I saw the gold cross he carried on a chain about his neck. The khans know it not, but he is a *caphar*, a Christian. He is hated of the god Natagai whose priest I am."

"A Christian?" Gurd surveyed his companion thoughtfully. "You know it?"

"Aye. But so great is Khlit's skill in war that the blind fools of the Jun-gar hold him in awe."

Gurd turned his spit slowly, while Lhon Otai watched.

"Men have told me, Lhon Otai, that Khlit is a paladin among warriors. Yet he did not come to Changa Nor to sport with fire. Why, therefore?"

The *shaman* leaned closer.

"Khlit has wind of the treasure of Changa Nor, Gurd—such a treasure as Tatary knows not. He has heard the old tale of the Gur-Khan. I, too have heard the tale, through my priests. Harken, hunter. You know what truth there is in the story. Tell me what you know. I can reward you."

Gurd's level brow darkened, and he ceased turning the spit.

"Open the door of Changa castle to me," pursued Lhon Otai, "when I come with my friends, and you will not lack for jewels, hunter. It is better that I should have the treasure than the *caphar*, Khlit."

"So you have friends, Lhon Otai?" Gurd asked softly. "Berang and Chepé Buga? The khan of the dark face is second to Khlit in power."

"Nay, Chepé Buga's wit lies in his sword. He is an honest dolt——"

The *shaman* broke off. Gurd had shown no liking for his words. He strove in vain to read the expressionless face of the hunter. But Gurd kept silence while they ate. Afterward, he bound Lhon Otai.

"Tomorrow, Lhon Otai," the hunter said, "you will see a hunt in the Dead World."

Again, Lhon Otai wondered. What manner of hunt was this, in the waste of tundras? He slept little that night. When he looked beyond the circle of fire he saw green eyes staring at him unblinkingly, and remembered that Gurd's cousin had had no meat that night.

Gurd set out early the next day afoot, leading the three pack-reindeer. Lhon Otai followed him curiously. The hunter had his bow slung over his back, and he walked carelessly, looking about him as if seeking for landmarks. Never had Lhon Otai seen a hunt begin as this one.

The place, too, was barren of game. A keen-eyed falcon could not have spied a rabbit or wild mountain sheep. It was desolate of vegetation, save for stunted larches and the dry moss that the reindeer fed upon. Lhon Otai panted as he stumbled over the rocks, but Gurd walked swiftly ahead, casting anxious glances at the overcast sky which foretold snowfall.

As they advanced Lhon Otai became aware of a peculiar odor. Dry and stringent, it resembled the smell of dead things. Gurd paid no heed to it, but pressed on. The odor grew, and Lhon Otai shivered, for he liked it not.

At the side of a nest of rocks Gurd paused and tied the reindeer. He pointed beyond the rocks.

"Here is the hunting-ground of the Dead World, Lhon Otai," he said grimly. "And the game of ten thousand moons."

Urged by his curiosity the *shaman* advanced beyond the rocks. Then he halted in amazement.

Before him stretched a plain. It was void of vegetation. But in the ground were heaps of white bones. And the bones were gigantic. He made out skulls measuring the height of a man in width.

The strange odor assailed him more strongly. It went up his nostrils to his brain, and Lhon Otai shivered. For the bones he saw were not those of ordinary animals. They were many times the size of a horse. A single jaw-bone at his feet was too heavy for him to lift. Tusks projected from the half-buried skulls to twice the height of a man.

"The bones of elephants!" he cried to Gurd, who was watching him.

The hunter shook his head.

"Nay, saw you elephants with tusks like those? These beasts belong to another time. I heard the story in Irkutsk of giant tusks along the frozen rivers and years ago I found this spot. Here is ivory without end. It is yellow with age. But it is choice, and more valuable than that of the Asia elephants. See."

He advanced to a near-by skeleton. With the heavy hatchet he carried he cut at the socket of one of the tusks. A few moments' wielding of the ax loosened the tusk, and Gurd brought it back to the *shaman*. It was seared with age, but of massive ivory, and weighty.

"These are the *manuts*, Lhon Otai," said Gurd gravely. "The beasts that lived before the time of Ghenghis Khan, or the Christian prophets. A herd of them must have died here, perhaps frozen to death in the ice."

Lhon Otai touched the tusk gingerly, muttering a charm as he did so against evil spirits. He knew now where Gurd got his ivory that he sold at Irkutsk. But his fear of the hunter was not diminished. Here was a man who entered unafraid the burial-place of the past, and held communion with beasts of the forest. Surely he must be guided by evil spirits, or he would be afraid.

Gurd wasted no more time in talk. By hard work he had enough of the tusks to load the three pack-reindeer by noon. A cold wind had sprung up and scattering flakes of snow were falling. Knowing the danger of being caught in these regions by the Autumn snow, Lhon Otai helped the hunter break camp and take up the journey to the south. More than once, however, he cast uneasy glances at the giant tusks which he held to be things of ill omen and hateful to Meik, the deity of the forests.

The next day they were well on their way back to the Lena's bank. The first snowfall had whitened the ground, but the day was clear. So clear that Lhon Otai made out a score of dark figures crossing a plain in front of them, heading not toward the south, but west. These, he knew, were his late companions, now seeking their way homeward afoot.

Gurd halted his reindeer when he sighted them.

"They have lost their way," cried Lhon Otai, with a swift glance at Gurd. "If they follow their course they will go further into the Dead World and perish at the hands of the *Cheooki* gods. Warn them to turn south."

"How may that be done?" Gurd's black eyes held no sympathy. "They would send an arrow through my jerkin if I came near enough to speak to them. And the sun will guide them."

"Nay, Gurd," objected Lhon Otai, "the sun is veiled by the clouds. The cold grows daily. The wolf packs will begin to hunt soon. They will die if you do not warn them to go back and follow the river south."

Gurd hesitated.

"You will be safe on the reindeer," urged the *shaman*. "And they will not dare to shoot at you for fear of hitting me."

Gurd set the reindeer in motion toward the men reluctantly. The Tatars had seen them, and halted.

Unnoticed by Gurd the *shaman* drew his horse behind the mount of the hunter. The men were coming toward them eagerly. Gurd could see their faces, drawn with hunger. He halted a good distance away.

"This will do," he said. "Do you call to them, and waste no breath."

The *shaman* waved his hand to attract the attention of the men, whom Gurd was watching keenly for signs of an arrow fitted to bow. Apparently without intent the *shaman* urged his horse beside the hunter.

Then, seizing a moment when Gurd was not watching him, Lhon Otai flung his great bulk from his horse upon Gurd. The weight of the *shaman* and Gurd's sudden twist in the saddle as he turned too late to avoid the other, sent the reindeer stumbling to its knees. Hunter and *shaman* rolled to the snow.

A shout went up from the Tatars who broke into a run when they saw what had happened. They were still some two hundred paces away, but Gurd was helpless under the weight of his foe. His bow had slipped from his back in the fall, and he was unable to reach his knife.

Abruptly, Lhon Otai felt Gurd go limp in his grasp. A shrill wail echoed from the hunter's lips. Lhon Otai had heard such a call before and in sudden alarm he glanced over his shoulder.

From some rocks a few feet away bounded the gray form of a lean lynx. Gurd's friend of the tundras had heard the call which meant food to him, and he had not eaten for three days. Lhon Otai shivered with terror, for the Tatars were still too far away to aid him. Loosening his grip of the hunter he sprang to his feet, grasping at the stirrup of his horse, which was dancing in terror.

At once Gurd was on his feet. A swift glance at the approaching men warned him of his peril. He leaped into the saddle of the reindeer which had recovered its balance while the two men were on the ground.

"That was an ill deed, Lhon Otai," he growled, "and I will not forget."

Wheeling his mount he bent low to avoid the arrows which the Tatars sped after him. The reindeer trotted swiftly out of range, but the pack-animals which tried to follow, fell under the arrows.

The gray lynx hesitated, snarling. Then it bounded after Gurd, and in a moment hunter, reindeer and lynx were lost to sight in the firs.

VI

What is the measure of a warrior?

Is it the strong sword, with finely jeweled hilt; or the well-balanced spear with gleaming point that can shear through silvered mail? Is it the war-horse that spurns the earth and pants in eagerness for battle?

Is it the chased armor, spoils from slain enemies, renowned in minstrel's song? Or the crafty brain, quick to devise stratagems of war?

Nay, it is the heart beneath the mail!

Tatar song.

Khlit, the Kha Khan, surnamed the Wolf, followed far the chase over the snow-covered ground. A pair of leopards with dragging leash sped before him, their black noses close over the tracks of a deer. Khlit had left the other horsemen behind and galloped close after the leopards, through the pine forest of Khantai Khan, near Changa Nor.

But the eyes of the Cossack were not on the trained leopards. The reins hung loose on the neck of his horse, which followed the beasts from habit. He paid no heed to an unhooded falcon which clutched the glove on his wrist and flapped encouragement to the leopards.

Khlit's mind was heavy with care. Nearly two months had passed since he had left Changa Nor after the unsuccessful assault. His envoy had returned from the invading Kallmarks with the reply he expected—an insolent refusal to leave the lands of the Jun-gar.

Chepé Buga and Berang had been exerting every effort to gather the fighting men of the hordes together. But they had been strangely unsuccessful. The warriors told them that the Winter season was at hand, when their flocks and herds must be guarded against the wandering wolf packs that came south in the track of the reindeer herds. The men of the Ordus and Chakars seemed to have lost heart for fighting. Khlit had never known them to hold back before when a battle was in the wind. Vainly his shrewd mind sought for the cause.

The encampment at Lake Baikal numbered fewer fighting men than in the Summer. And the Kallmarks were advancing, driving their herds and taking possession of the stores of hay and grain the Jun-gar Tatars had laid up for the Winter.

The *shamans* who held great power among the Tatars were loath to help Khlit assemble his regiments because he had sent Lhon Otai to the North, whence the leader of the conjurers had not yet returned.

Although the ice was forming over Changa Lake, Khlit had not dared to venture the assault of the castle until he had more men under his command. The few who had been held together by Chepé Buga, Berang, and the mighty Chagan had been filled with stories of the treasure they were to seize at Changa Nor. Khlit dared not fail of taking the castle. He dreaded to think that it might not hold the wealth they suspected. Yet evidence had been flowing in from all quarters of the treasure. Fishermen on Changa Lake had heard of it. Old men had seen caskets carried there.

Khlit was aroused from his reverie by a whimper of eagerness from the leopards. The lithe beasts had swung into a fast run that pressed his horse to keep up. Khlit, searching the tracks they were following, thought that he noticed a difference in them. The next moment he reined in his horse sharply.

From behind the trunks of two giant trees in front of him, a rider had stepped out. Khlit saw a tall man, closely wrapped in a *malitza* of lynx skin, with the hood drawn over his head. The face was veiled by the hood, but Khlit saw a firm mouth, and a pair of steady, dark eyes. He noted that the man carried no weapon save a large hunting-knife, and that he appeared careless of the leopards which had drawn back, snarling when they scented the man.

The stranger was mounted on a reindeer, and Khlit guessed swiftly that the leopards had been following the latter, having changed from the tracks of the deer to fresher scent. He uttered a sharp word of command to the crouching beasts, and walked his horse forward slowly, his hand on the hilt of his sword.

The brown-faced man raised a mittened hand, the fringe of his glove ornamented with reindeer ears. Khlit waited.

"My name is Gurd, the hunter," the stranger spoke in a deep voice.

"I am Khlit, called by my enemies the Wolf," answered the Kha Khan at once.

"Aye," said Gurd, "I saw you lead the hunt and crossed the tracks of your quarry, for you were alone."

Khlit's shrewd glance swept the near-forest for signs of a possible ambush and rested, reassured, on the hunter. The two men measured each other with frank curiosity. Gurd marked the rich, sable cloak of the Kha Khan, the copper and silver chasing of his saddle, and his deep-set eyes under tufted brows. He appreciated the ease with which the old Cossack sat his horse, the smooth play of his broad shoulders.

On his part Khlit scanned the frank face of the hunter, his simple attire, and noted the boldness of his bearing. Being armed, he had Gurd at his mercy. Silently he waited for the other to speak.

"I have come unarmed," began Gurd in his deep voice, "to take you to Changa Nor. There is one at Changa Nor who must see the Kha Khan of the Jun-gar. Your men have hunted me through the Dead World. Yet I have come unarmed to bear you this message."

Khlit's mustache twitched in a hard smile.

"Does a wolf put his head into the noose of a trap, hunter?"

"No harm will come to you, Khlit. Would I risk my life to speak to you, if the need were not great? Nay, if you do not come, your sorrow will be greater than that of one who has killed his father by mischance, or broken his sword in dishonor."

"Hey, that is strange!" Khlit regarded his companion curiously. "Who is the one who sent you?"

Gurd hesitated.

"The master of Changa Nor, O Kha Khan. By the token around your neck, he said that you would come."

Khlit put his hand to his throat. Under the *svitza* he felt the outline of the gold cross he always wore. Was this the token? There were few who knew Khlit was a Christian. Who was the master of Changa Nor? He was eager to know, and to see the inside of the lonely castle.

"Lead on, rider of stags," he laughed lightly. "To the devil himself——"

VII

At one of the embrasures of Changa Nor stood a young girl. She was slender and straight, with round, strong arms, and twin braids of red-gold hair bound at her forehead by a fillet of pearl. Her dark eyes were fixed on the shore. Her skin was olive, deepened by the sun's touch.

She leaned anxiously against the heavy stones of the embrasure, her delicate face thrust into the opening, peering out to the pines. At times she turned and glanced with a pretty, impatient frown at the sand clock in the chamber. Once a high voice from another room startled her. She listened a moment, and then, as if satisfied, returned to her watch.

The shadows were long from the pines on the shore when she made out two dark figures that rode down to the shore. Dismounting, the two men advanced out on the ice toward the castle. Pausing a moment to make sure that she was not mistaken in them, she left the embrasure and turned to the wall of the chamber.

Her fingers feeling deftly over the stone of the wall moved two sturdy iron bars from their rest with the ease of habit. These she laid aside. Clutching an iron lever that projected from the stone, she hung the weight of her slender body on this, moving it downward. At once two stone blocks to the height of a man swung inward, leaving space for a person to enter with difficulty.

The opening was blocked by a human form and in another moment Gurd the hunter stood within the chamber. He looked at her quickly and nodded as if in answer to an unspoken question. She flushed with pleasure and watched the tall figure of Khlit enter the room.

The Cossack glanced about him curiously, his hand on his sword. He looked only casually at the girl in spite of her beauty. She turned away at once, readjusted the stone blocks. The heavy bars, however, she did not replace, in her hurry to follow the men.

The three, led by Gurd, went from the chamber which acted as an anteroom into the long hall of the castle. An old servant in a faded leather jerkin bowed before them.

"Tell Atagon," commanded Gurd of the man, "that the Kha Khan is here."

Khlit glanced at the empty hall, with its faded tapestries and heavy furniture. The place had an air of antiquity, heightened by its silence. The hall stretched the entire length of the castle, and was lighted only by the narrow embrasures under which a gallery ran, as if for archers to stand, by the openings. The Cossack knew that the castle dated from many generations ago.

"A lonely place!" he grunted. "Where are the demons who tipped hell-fire on my men?"

Gurd smiled and pointed after the old servant.

"There is one of the demons, Gutchluk, the ancient," he said, "and here is the other—Chinsi, the grand-daughter of Atagon. When I am away from Changa Nor these two guard the castle, as you have seen."

Khlit glanced from Gurd to the slender, golden-haired girl.

"Devil take the place!" he swore. "A bed-ridden slave and a half-weaned girl! Nay, that can not be."

"It is so, lord," the girl's musical voice made answer. "Gurd has taught us to prepare and cast the Chinese fire from the window slits. Atagon brought the fire here for our protection, but he is too old——"

Gurd held up his hand for silence. He stepped to the side of the hall and drew back the tapestry that concealed another chamber.

"Here, O Kha Khan," he said slowly, "you shall learn the secret of Changa Nor. Truly, the secret belongs to you, as well as to us. Come."

Curiously, Khlit glanced from Gurd to Chinsi. The hunter's face was impassive, but the girl's eyes were alight with eagerness, and a kind of fear. Without hesitation Khlit stepped under the tapestry. He halted abruptly within the chamber.

It was a narrow room, scarcely illumined by the embrasure. A long table ran across the chamber in front of him. A single candle and a parchment were on the table.

By the candle Khlit saw the figure of an old man, in a long robe of white camel's-hair. The hood of the robe was thrown back, and he had a full view of the face of the man. He saw a high forehead, fringed with snowy hair, a pair of steadfast eyes, and a pale, lined countenance. A long beard, pure white in color, fell over the robe to the black girdle around the waist.

A rush of memory took Khlit back to the Cossack camp he had quitted many years ago. He had seen men like these, at the monastery of the Holy Spirit.

For a long moment the eyes of the Kha Khan and the man in the white robe challenged each other. The fierce gaze of the Cossack was fairly met by the mild light in Atagon's deep-set eyes.

"Welcome, Christian warrior—" Atagon raised a withered hand

in greeting—"to Changa Nor. Long has Atagon, of Changa, been waiting your coming. God, through his servant Gurd, has led you to our gate, in the time of our need."

Incredulity and belief struggled in Khlit's mind. Atagon had spoken as a priest, haltingly as if using a language long unfamiliar. And Khlit had not revealed the fact that he was a Christian. But his gesture was that of a *batko*, a father-priest of the Orthodox church.

"I am Atagon," the calm voice of the priest went on, "and so the Christians of my little flock call me. But I was baptized under the name of John, and I am presbyter of the church."

The two words stirred anew Khlit's memory. Presbyter John. Where had he heard that phrase before? The answer to his question came to him in a flash.

"Presbyter John!" he cried. "Prester John, of Asia. The king who was sought by missionaries! The guardian of hidden treasure, and the keeper of strange beasts——"

He had remembered the name of the king he had forgotten. The story of Prester John and the treasure had spread through Europe centuries ago. But the mythical king had never been seen. Was the aged Atagon the true descendant of Prester John? The monarch of the hidden treasure?

Atagon shook his head solemnly.

"Not Prester John, my son. But Presbyter. Your words are strange. I know nothing of treasure, or of beasts. I am the guardian of the Christian shrine of Cathay, beside the Sea of Sand."

Again Khlit was stirred. The Sea of Sand! Chepé Buga had mentioned that. And the Lake of Stones, which must be Changa Nor. Here was the place that the legend had named. Surely Atagon was Prester John!

"I see you are troubled with doubt, my son," smiled the patriarch. "Come, I will show you proof. You speak of treasure. There is no pagan gold on Changa Nor, but a treasure more precious. See."

Getting to his feet Atagon took up a staff which was fashioned like a shepherd's crook. He walked slowly to another door of the chamber which he pushed open, motioning for Khlit to follow. A light from the interior shone on his majestic face.

Khlit stepped beside the patriarch, and caught his breath in amazement. He stood in a shrine of the Christian church. In front of him candles glowed before an icon, a painting of Christ and the Virgin Mary; myriad gems sparkled from the frame of the icon. Below the painting stood a small cross. Khlit saw that it was a single stone, an emerald which shone with a soft light. He thought of the emerald scepter that the Tatars had said was in Changa Nor.

On a table in front of the icon were several jeweled caskets of lapis-lazuli set with rubies. The candle-sticks were gold, with jade blocks for their bases. Silk vestments hung from the walls, embroidered with gold and silver thread. Also a girdle with a clasp brilliant with diamonds.

The patriarch crossed himself. Khlit, in obedience to an old impulse, removed his fur cap.

"The treasure of the Gur-Khan," he muttered. "Aye, the legend was true."

VIII

A quick frown crossed Atagon's tranquil features.

"Nay, my son," he corrected, "the shrine of God in a pagan land. These riches are the offerings of the Gur-Khan to God, and their contents are the true treasures. The painting comes from Constantinople. The caskets shelter a portion of the garment of St. Paul, the wanderer, and a finger with a lock of hair of the blessed St. Thomas."

He motioned for Khlit to approach the shrine. The Cossack did so fearlessly. At the same time, his heart was heavy. Here was indeed a treasure, such as the khans were seeking. But it was a treasure of the church. And Khlit was a Christian.

"Harken, Kha Khan," spoke Gurd from the doorway, "said I not you must come to Changa Nor? The Tatars have wind of these riches and they plan to despoil the shrine of Atagon. They are pagans and care naught for the sacred relics, or for the holy cross. That was why I sought you, at the hunt. You can protect Changa Nor."

Khlit was silent, under the eyes of the three Christians. He had promised his men the treasure of Changa Nor. Khlit's life as a Cossack was past. He was now the leader of the khans. They had fought with him. His word was law in the horde. And he had promised them the riches of Changa Nor.

"Tell me," he said slowly, "is this truly the treasure of the Gur-Khan?"

Chinsi stepped forward.

"Father Atagon," she said, "knows the story of the treasure. But he does not know what the Tatars say of the legend. Gurd has told me. The Tatars say that centuries ago a Gur-Khan hid his treasure where it could not be found, by a sea of sand and a river of stones. They say it is guarded by fierce beasts."

"Aye," assented Khlit grimly, "that is what they told me."

The patriarch bowed his head in thought, stroking his beard gently.

"I will give you the answer you seek to your questions, my children," he observed at length. "Truly, I have heard the story of the beasts. The first presbyter told it to his successor. Considering it in the light of the holy word, I think it means that the beasts of the forest might, by the power of God, seek to guard the chosen ones of the true faith. Was it not so with Daniel and the lions?

"As to the story of the Gur-Khan," he went on, "it is true. The first Gur-Khan was converted by a presbyter from Europe—Olopan, who came from Judea. Obeying the mandates of a higher will, he turned his pagan treasures into offerings to God—as you see." He waved a white hand at the shrine and the table. "And so the treasure became hidden from the evil ones who sought it. The Gur-Khan was killed, and his empire broken up, in battle. But his daughter, who was a Christian, survived and hid in the castle of Changa Nor, with the treasure of the church, accompanied by the presbyter, and a few knights. Before the presbyter died, he ordained the most worthy of the knights to be his successor. And that patriarch in turn selected one to succeed him."

Atagon took the hand of the girl fondly.

"Behold, Kha Khan, the last princess of the line of the Gur-Khan, Chinsi, the golden-haired. And I, Atagon, am the last of the patriarchs. Truly my flock is small. For save Gurd, who ministers to our needs, there are only a few wandering Nestorians from Hsi'en-fu, in Shensi, who visit Changa Nor. It is they who spread the story of a treasure."

"Aye, Father," grunted Khlit, "your fame is great, although you know it not. For you are the one men have sought by the name of Prester John. But the Tatars of the Jun-gar do not bow to the name of God. Their *shamans* say that Gurd is a hunter guided by an evil spirit; and that Changa Nor is a refuge of the devil himself, with all his brimstone."

"Nay, Kha Khan," Gurd showed his white teeth in a smile. "That is because I fetch *mamut* tusks from the Dead World, where Tatar hunters go not. And the *shamans* call this a haunt of the devil, for they have tried for many years to take our treasure. Lhon Otai's palms itch for these jewels."

"That is not all, O Kha Khan," cried the girl defiantly. "Gurd who brings us candles and firewood with food and drink has fought for his life against the *shamans* more than once. He brought you here at peril of death for the Tatar warriors have been told he is a son of the were-wolves, an evil spirit."

"No matter, Chinsi," laughed Gurd lightly, "now that I have brought you a better protector. Khlit, the Kha Khan, will guard us for he is also a Christian."

The eyes of the patriarch sought Khlit shrewdly. Pride was in his glance, and hope, but also uncertainty. Khlit raised his head.

"Harken," he said; his keen ears had caught a sound without the castle.

Footsteps pattered to the door of the shrine. Gutchluk appeared.

"Riders are coming over the lake, Father," he cried. "They are coming very swiftly."

Chinsi gave a startled cry. Atagon and Gurd turned to her in surprise.

"The door!" she whispered. "I forgot to put up the bars. It can be opened from without."

Gurd sprang to the door. Then he halted. The sound of many boots echoed on the stone floor of the hall. The hunter glared at Khlit.

"What is this? You knew——"

"I know not," growled Khlit.

As he spoke he remembered that his companions must have followed in his tracks, seeking the end of the hunt. The footsteps grew louder without. A shout rang through the castle. Atagon took up his staff and stepped to the door. Gurd drew his knife and placed himself before the priest.

"Fool!" hissed Gurd to the trembling Gutchluk. "Why did you not see to the door? Hush! They may not find the entrance under the tapestry."

"I left it open, lord," muttered the servant. "How could men enter Changa Nor?"

A cry announced that the men without had found the opening into the adjoining chamber. There was a quick tread of feet. Khlit's hand went to his sword. Then it fell to his side.

In the entrance to the shrine appeared the giant form of a man in armor. Chagan the swordbearer entered, dragging back with all his strength at the leash which held the two straining leopards. Behind the hunting beasts appeared Chepé Buga's swarthy countenance. A *shaman* and a half-dozen warriors blocked the door behind the khan.

Chepé Buga threw a keen glance at the group in the shrine.

"Ha, Khlit, lord," he growled, "we followed the leopards which were by the horses at the edge of the lake to the wall of Changa. When we pushed against the stones where they smelt, the wall gave in, by cursed witchcraft. Glad am I to see you alive. We thought the devils of Changa had borne you off to Satan's bonfire."

Chagan gave a cry and pointed to the treasures of the shrine. Chepé Buga's eye lighted gleefully.

"By the mighty beard of Afrasiab!" he swore. "Here is a pretty sight. Nay, the Wolf has led us as he promised without bloodshed to the treasure of Changa Nor."

His glance fell on Gurd and Chinsi, and he gave a hearty laugh.

"What! Here is the devil-hunter, ripe for the torture, and a maid, for our sport. By Satan's cloven hoof, that was well done, Khlit, lord!"

Their eyes aflame with greed, the Tatars echoed their khan's words with a shout that rang through the castle of Changa, and caused the leopards to snarl.

IX

A poisonous vine hanging upon a strong cedar—such is a traitor at the gate of a king.

Chinese proverb.

Gurd had been reared in the forest, among animals quick to slay. He had had all men for his enemies, save the few at Changa Nor. So, while he possessed the patience of the animals he hunted, he had also their fierce anger. Chepé Buga's mocking words brought a flush to his brown cheeks, and before any one could move he had drawn the knife at his girdle.

The Tatar khan had no time to lift his sword. Gurd was upon him with gleaming knife, when Atagon, who had anticipated the hunter's movement, thrust his staff against the latter's chest. Held away from his enemy, Gurd glared at Chepé Buga with blazing eyes. The Tatar returned his gaze with cool insolence. Atagon placed his hand on his companion's shoulder.

"Peace, my son," he said quietly. "It is not fitting that blood should flow because of a hasty word. We must not quarrel in the shrine of God. Let me speak to this man."

Chepé Buga eyed the patriarch in astonishment, which deepened into disgust. The proud words of the priest had no effect on him.

"Who are you, Graybeard?" he growled. "And who is the girl?"

Khlit spoke for the first time.

"This is Atagon," he said, "master of Changa Nor. And the woman is Chinsi, daughter of a Gur-Khan."

Chepé Buga stared at the girl's delicate face and ruddy hair in open approval. Gurd ground his teeth as he caught the glance, but the hand of Atagon restrained him.

"Aye, she bears herself like a princess, Khlit, lord," assented the Tatar carelessly. "She is worthy of a better master than this thin-blooded priest, or yon scowling hunter. I will give up my share of the jewels for her. Hey, there is a pretty emerald!"

He walked to the cross and balanced it tentatively in his hand. Atagon lifted his hand in protest.

"Take the caskets," cried the *shaman* from the door; "they are priceless!"

"Nay," cried Atagon, "touch them not. They hold sacred relics."

Some of the Tatars drew back from the door at this. But Chepé Buga did not move.

"A curse upon your quaverings, dogs," he growled. "String the old man up by his thumbs, and take the knife from the hunter. He is overquick to use it."

"Nay," Atagon responded at once. "There is no charm, save the wrath of God upon the despoiler. But have a care what you do, Tatar. There is one whom you may offend."

"Where?" The khan glanced idly about the chamber. "I see him not, unless you mean yon Gurd of the scowling brow. He will make good eating for the leopards, Chagan."

"Not he," responded Atagon. The patriarch pointed to Khlit who was watching moodily. "The Kha Khan has not said that you may take these things. They belong not to me, but to God. Have a fear what you do, Khan, for your master knows the name of God."

All eyes were fixed on Khlit. Gurd folded his arms and glanced at the intruders blackly. He had not forgotten it was his doing that they came here, in Khlit's tracks. The girl clasped her hands in silent appeal.

Chepé Buga's face bore a look of sincere astonishment. He cared nothing for the deities of the *shamans,* or for others. It had not occurred to him that Khlit would hesitate to seize the treasure. Had the Kha Khan not promised he would do so?

"Speak, Khlit, lord," he cried, "and bid us close the mouth of this long-robed conjurer with a sword. Then he will trouble us no more."

But Khlit was silent. It had been long since he had seen a cross other than the one he wore around his neck, or the candles burning before an icon. He had been a wanderer, far from the church. Yet he knew that his faith was alive in his heart. To refuse Chepé Buga and his companions permission to take the treasure of Changa Nor would mean protest, discontent, a weakening of the small force of Tatars which was still at his command. It would be hard, even dangerous. He had given his word that the treasure of Changa Nor would be theirs before he knew its nature. How was he to do otherwise?

"Remember your promise, O Kha Khan," the voice of the *shaman* cried from the group at the door.

Khlit whipped out his sword on the instant.

"Bring me that knave!" he cried.

The Tatar warriors turned, but the *shaman* had slipped away into the shadows of the outer chamber. They returned empty-handed after a hurried search through the castle.

"Such words are spoken by cowards," said Khlit grimly. "I love not to be told to keep my word. Did I not keep my promise when I led the khans against Hang-Hi at Altai Haiten? Was not my word true when I brought you to the army of Li Jusong? Speak!"

"Aye, lord," cried Chagan's deep voice. "It was true."

"What I have sworn," said Khlit, "I will carry out."

He sheathed his sword. Stepping to Chepé Buga's side he replaced the emerald cross on the altar of the shrine. The Tatars watched him in silence. Atagon closed his eyes as if in prayer. Khlit faced his men, his back to the shrine. His shaggy brows were close knitted in thought.

"Harken, warriors of the Jun-gar," he growled. "What did I say to you by the shore of Changa Lake? I promised that the castle should be taken without bloodshed. Have we not done so? I said it would be ours when the lake was coated with ice. Is it not covered with ice today?"

"Aye, but you promised us the treasure, Khlit, lord," spoke one of the men respectfully.

Khlit's keen eye flashed, and he tapped his sword angrily.

"And is not the treasure ours?" he asked. Gurd made an angry movement, but Atagon motioned him back. "We have it in our hands. Nay, I will tell you more. It was decided in the *kurultai* that we would use the money to buy back our lands from the Kallmark invaders. That would not be wise. I thought so at the time, and now I will speak my reason. Who would buy back what is theirs—save a whipped slave? If we pay the treasure to the Kallmarks, they will be back next Summer for more."

"Aye, that is well said," nodded Chepé Buga.

"But what of the Kallmarks?" objected Chagan. "Riders have come to us in the last few days who say that the Kallmarks are riding north with two thousand men."

Khlit stroked the curved scabbard at his side thoughtfully. He knew as well as Chagan the numbers and strength of the Kallmarks who were bent on the destruction of the horde of the Jun-gar.

"Have the hearts of the Jun-gar turned weak as women?" he made reply. "Nay, it is the Kallmarks who will pay for their invasion. We will keep the treasure of Changa Nor."

"Then let us take it to the camp by Lake Baikal," broke in Chepé Buga, "where it will be in our hands."

"Is not the Kha Khan, Chepé Buga," growled Khlit, "the one to say what we will do with the treasure? Nay, where is there a better place or one more secure than Changa Nor?"

"We got into here," protested the khan stubbornly, "by good hap, and the scent of our leopards. It is a hard nut to crack, this castle. Who knows whether we can get in again?"

Khlit stroked his mustache and frowned. His purpose to safe-guard the treasure of Atagon was hard to carry out.

"We will leave a guard here over the treasure, Chepé Buga," he said at length. "Chagan will stay. Gurd will come with us, so that the swordbearer will have no foe within the castle. Then, when we return, we may decide about the treasure."

"And the pay for our horsemen?" cried one of the Tatars. "The money for powder and new weapons?"

"We will take spoil from the Kallmarks."

Chagan nodded heavily.

"But how may we turn them back? They are many, and strong!"

"With this." Khlit drew his sword with a quick motion and laid it on the table. "Aye, by the sword of Kaidu, the hero and guardian of the Jun-gar, we will drive back the Kallmarks, and take their herds."

The words and the act appealed to the war-like feelings of the Tatar throng. With one voice they gave a ringing shout of approval. Khlit smiled grimly. Without earning the ill-will of the khans he had achieved what he wanted—time, and the safety of the shrine of Changa Nor.

As he was about to pick up his sword, the group by the door parted. In strode the portly figure of the *shaman*, Lhon Otai, ac-companied by the man who had fled a few minutes before.

X

The slant eyes of Lhon Otai glinted shrewdly as he surveyed the men in the shrine. His words came smoothly and softly from his thick lips.

"Where are your wits, men of the Jun-gar?" he cried. "The evil spirits of Changa Nor have cast a spell over you. You are blinded by an unclean charm. It is well I came to save you from the dangers of this place."

The Tatars glanced uneasily at each other. The chief of the *shamans* knew well his power over them. He pointed angrily to Khlit.

"Aye, the evil priest of the *caphars* has bewitched you. Know you not this man who calls himself the Kha Khan is a Christian? He will not give you the treasure. He has deceived you with lying words."

Chagan stared at Khlit blankly.

"Nay, lord," he protested, "tell them this is not so. How can a Kha Khan of the Jun-gar be a Christian?"

A murmur of assent came from the warriors. Lhon Otai crossed his stout arms with a triumphant smile. His glance swept from Gurd to Khlit and back again.

"It is so," he said. "Your chief is a *caphar*, a brother in faith to yon dark hunter who is allied to evil spirits. The place here is accursed. I have come from the North, where I saw this hunter Gurd talk to a lynx of the forest as his brother, and summon ivory bones from the ground by a dark spell. By my power I overcame him and took the ivory. Then I hurried here to safeguard you against the *caphars*."

Gurd smiled scornfully, but the Tatars had eyes for no one but Khlit.

"Speak, lord," said Chagan again, "and tell us this is not true."

Khlit surveyed his followers moodily. He knew that they were superstitious, and under the influence of the *shamans*. He had only to deny his faith, and all would be well. Lhon Otai would be silenced.

The *shaman* had long been Khlit's enemy, for he was jealous of the Cossack's power. Khlit wondered if Lhon Otai had seen the gold cross he carried under his *svitza*. The conjurer and his followers had spies everywhere and there was little in central Asia that they did not know.

And Lhon Otai had chosen the moment well. Khlit had already risked his popularity with the khans by holding back the treasure of Changa Nor from their hands. Probably the *shamans* who accompanied Lhon Otai had told the latter what had passed in the shrine of Atagon. Khlit decided to make one more bid for favor with his followers.

"Nay, Chagan," he said slowly, "do you tell me this. Have I failed in my duty to the khans? Have the Jun-gar ever gone to defeat under my leadership? Let the *kurultai* of the Jun-gar decide. I will abide by their word. If they say that I have done ill, I will give over my command to Chepé Buga."

"He speaks with a double tongue!" cried Lhon Otai, seizing his advantage cleverly. "For he has kept the treasure of Changa Nor for himself and the *caphar* priest. This treasure would buy your lands from the Kallmarks. He sent me to the Dead World, where the hunter Gurd tried to slay me——"

"A lie!" cried Gurd. "I knew not the Kha Khan. It was Lhon Otai who followed me, and slew my reindeer by treachery."

"Nay, then," put in the other *shaman* swiftly, "if Khlit knew you not, how comes he here, with the *caphars,* unknown to the khans?"

Chepé Buga waved his heavy hand for silence.

"Say one word, Khlit, lord," he bellowed, "and we will boil this conjurer's tongue in oil."

Khlit glanced wearily from under shaggy brows at his comrade in arms. His pride was great, and he had no fear for himself, despite the hostility of Lhon Otai. But he feared for the shrine of Atagon.

"Nay, Chepé Buga," he said, "I am a Christian."

A stunned silence greeted this. A proud light shone in the eyes of Atagon. Lhon Otai was not slow to seize his advantage. His cunning was a match for Khlit's craft.

"Come!" he cried, raising both arms. "You have heard. This is a place of evil. We will drive out the dark spirits in the manner of our fathers and their fathers before them. Come! A sword-dance. We will purge the place."

He ran from the chamber, followed by the Tatar warriors and the other *shaman*. Chagan was next to go, dragging the two leopards with him. At a sign from Atagon, Gurd and the girl Chinsi accompanied the priest without. Khlit and Chepé Buga remained. The Cossack stretched out his hand to Chepé Buga.

"Speak, *anda,* brother in arms," he said gruffly, "what matters my faith to you? We have fought together and shared the same bed. Will you leave me for the fat conjurer?"

The Tatar's handsome face twisted in vexation.

"I swore to follow you, O Kha Khan," he said slowly, "to be at the front in every battle, to bring the horses and spoil we captured to you, to beat the wild beasts for your hunting, to give you to eat of the game I took in hunting, and to guard you from danger with my sword. Christian or not, I remember my oath. Yet, we have need of the treasure of Changa Nor. Bid us take the treasure, that we may know your heart is with us."

Khlit turned away from the appeal in his friend's eyes. He made as if to speak; then his head dropped on his chest. He was silent. He heard the Tatar leave the shrine.

When he looked up he saw that he was alone with the icon and the flickering candles on the altar.

XI

In the hall of Changa Nor, Lhon Otai mustered the Tatars for the sword-dance. Two tall candles gave the only light in the long chamber, for it had grown dark outside the castle. When Khlit entered the hall, he saw that Atagon and the Christians had taken their places in the balcony. The Tatars, who had drawn their swords, occupied the floor. Lhon Otai faced them at the farther end.

Even Chagan had taken his place with Chepé Buga in the ranks of the warriors, after tying his leopards fast to a pillar. The Tatars watched eagerly while Lhon Otai took from the pouch at his girdle a human skull fashioned into a drinking cup. Then he summoned the trembling Gutchluk to bring him wine. With this he filled the cup.

Lhon Otai bent nine times in homage to the west, where the sun had set. The Tatars lifted their swords with a single shout.

"Heigh!"

The *shaman's* heavy face was alight with triumph. He placed his girdle across his shoulders and poured out a little wine from the cup to the floor.

"Precious wine I pour to Natagai," he chanted, "I give the *tarasun* to the god Natagai."

The warriors swung their swords overhead.

"Heigh!"

Lhon Otai tipped the cup again.

"An offering I pour to Meik," he sang, "to Meik, guardian of the forest."

"Heigh!" cried the Tatars.

They bent their bodies, lowering their swords. Then they came erect, swinging their shining blades above their heads. Khlit knew the fascination the sword-dance held for them. Already they were breathing more quickly.

"Wine I pour to the *Cheooki* gods, to the *Cheooki* gods of the North who light the sky with their fire."

"Heigh!"

An echo of music sounded in the hall. The other *shaman* had drawn a *dombra* from under his cloak, and was striking upon it. As the sword-dance, led by Lhon Otai, continued, the Tatars became more excited. They bent their bodies and circled three times. Then they raised their blades with a shout.

"Heigh!"

Lhon Otai now stood erect, his face raised to the rafters, his eyes closed. When the Tatars saw this their shout changed.

"A wisdom!" they cried. "Our *shaman* sees the raven in the rafters. He is listening to the words of wisdom."

At this they ran to the sides of the hall, and returned, raising their swords in concert. To the strains of the *dombra* they circled, making their blades play about their heads. Sweat shone on their brows. Their teeth gleamed through their mustaches.

Khlit watched impassively. He saw that Lhon Otai was working the warriors to a pitch of excitement. It would be useless for him to interrupt the sword-dance. Yet his fear was not so much for himself as for the group watching silently from the balcony.

Then Lhon Otai raised his arms. The sound of the *dombra* ceased. The Tatars lowered their swords and waited, panting from their exertions.

"A wisdom!" cried Lhon Otai in a high voice, his eyes still closed.

"A wisdom!" echoed the warriors. "Tell us the word of the raven."

The *shaman* crossed his arms over his chest.

"Danger is near the horde of the Jun-gar," he chanted. "The soul of Ghenghis Khan mutters in his tomb, and the sun is darkened in night. The treasure of Changa Nor must be our safeguard. With it we will buy our homes and our pastures from the Kallmarks. We will send riders to the camp of the khan Berang by Lake Baikal and bid him disband the horde. Thus will the Kallmark chieftains know we mean friendship."

Khlit made a gesture of protest unheeded by the Tatars who were hanging on the words of the *shaman*.

"Evil omens are afoot," went on Lhon Otai. "Dead fish infest the ice of Baikal under the three Diandas. The great wolf pack of the North is hunting for its prey. Evil is the plight of the Jun-gar, owing to the false words of a Christian. Bind the arms of the Christian Kha Khan with stout ropes, that he may not harm us again. Him we must leave in Changa Nor. The *shamans* with the khan Chepé

Buga and the swordbearer Chagan must watch over the treasure, until the army at the Baikal camp can be disbanded."

Khlit thrust out his arms in grim silence, to be bound, while Chepé Buga watched. The khan glanced at him uneasily while they tied his hands but avoided meeting Khlit's eye. Only once Khlit spoke.

"These hands carried the standard of Ghenghis Khan," he growled. "Who will lead the Jun-gar if I am bound? Yon fat toad?"

Lhon Otai's broad face twisted in anger, and his eyes flew open. At a sign from him the *shaman* bound Khlit's arms close to his side.

"Harken, Tatars!"

The words, in a clear voice from the gallery made them look up. Gurd was leaning on the stone railing, his heavy hands clutching the barrier. His dark face was bent down. His eyes were glowing.

"You know the legend of Changa Nor, Lhon Otai," went on Gurd. "How is it that for ten lifetimes the treasure of Changa Nor has not been touched? Others have tried to take it. And they have died. No pagan has lived who put hand to the sanctuary of God, in Changa Nor. Nay, not one. Yet we have no swordsmen or archers here to defend the treasure. They have died from another cause."

"The Chinese fire!" cried the *shaman* contemptuously. "We can deal with such sorcery."

"Nay, it is not the fire, Lhon Otai. You know the legend. Changa Nor is guarded by a power greater than your swords. Death awaits you in the shadows of the castle. Tempt it not. I give you this warning. There is a curse upon the foe of Changa Nor, and upon his children and his herds. I have seen men die from this curse. Brave men."

"Kill me that rascal!" cried Lhon Otai to his followers.

With the exception of Chepé Buga and Chagan the Tatars rushed for the stairway leading to the gallery.

"I have seen you touch the treasure of the shrine," Gurd called to Chepé Buga. Pointing at Lhon Otai he added, heedless of the rush of his enemies, "And I can see the mark of death on your forehead."

Chepé Buga laughed lightly, while the *shaman* glared at Gurd vindictively. The Tatar warriors had gained the gallery. They cut down the old Gutchluk who stood in their way and rushed toward Gurd.

As their swords were lifted to strike him, the hunter sprang over the railing. Hanging by his hands an instant from the balcony, he leaped to the stone floor below. He landed lightly, for all his great size.

Chagan drew his two-handed sword and stepped toward Gurd. The latter crouched and dodged the sweep of the sword. Grappling with the mighty swordbearer he flung Chagan headlong to the floor. The Tatars were returning down the stairs, unwilling to take Gurd's daring leap from the gallery.

The hunter darted swiftly toward the chamber where the door opened to the lake. His pursuers were after him in a moment, but he had vanished in the darkness. Chagan stumbled to his feet.

"Back, fools!" he roared. "We will deal with the hunter as he deserves. He is unarmed. Watch."

While speaking, he loosed the two leopards. The beasts were infuriated by the excitement, and at Chagan's bidding they bounded after the man whom they had trailed earlier in the afternoon. The men in the hall listened, but no sound came from the lake without, where the trained leopards were already on Gurd's tracks.

"They will feed well tonight," laughed the swordbearer. "May Satan roast me, if yon *caphar* will live to curse you more, Lhon Otai."

"He spoke words like the point of a sharp sword," said Chepé Buga grimly, with a sidelong glance at where Chinsi crouched by Atagon in the gallery. "Nay, Lhon Otai, if the curse comes true I shall have good company. You and I will dance together in Satan's court. But until then, bethink yourself well, Conjurer, for I too am master here. Chagan obeys me."

As Lhon Otai was about to answer, his mouth fell open in sheer astonishment. His eyes widened, and he pointed to the door of the chamber whence Gurd had fled.

Four spots of green light showed where the leopards were returning in the gloom. The animals issued into the hall. But they came slowly, crawling along the floor, their bellies dragging on the stone, and their tails limp underfoot. Every movement of their lithe bodies bespoke fear.

When the Tatars had recovered from their surprise at the return of the leopards they searched the lake and the surrounding shore. They followed Gurd's tracks up one of the hills. But there tracks and hunter alike disappeared. Gurd had gone into the mountains, and with him he had taken his entire herd of reindeer.

XII

From the summit of the tower of Changa Nor Chinsi and Khlit looked out over the frozen lake and the snow-clad hills. A cold wind nipped at their cheeks and stirred the girl's gold plaits of hair. Khlit watched her curiously as she stared at the hills, her smooth chin resting pensively on a strong, round hand.

Two days they had been prisoners in Changa. All the Tatars except Chepé Buga and Chagan had left for the Baikal encampment, under Lhon Otai's orders. The *shaman* himself remained at Changa. The treasure, thanks to the vigilance of Chepé Buga and Chagan, was untouched.

Chinsi and Atagon had not been further molested. Since Gutchluk's death, Chagan had attended to their wants after a fashion. The patriarch, however, had kept himself shut up in the shrine where he passed most of the time in prayer. Chepé Buga roamed restlessly over the castle, inspecting the apparatus for defense and visiting the treasure where he spent hours in fingering the jewels, which he took good care Lhon Otai did not disturb.

Khlit touched the girl on the sleeve of her reindeer-skin parka.

"Tell me, little Sparrow," he observed, "what is this curse Gurd called down upon Lhon Otai?"

Chinsi glanced around to see if they were alone. It was some time before she answered.

"The curse is part of the legend of Prester John, father. The legend runs that there were beasts that watched over the treasure long ago. It must be merely a fable; for how could that be true? Yet one thing I have seen. It was when I was a child. A band of robbers came to Changa when the lake was frozen over. It was in the night. We would not let them in. They tried to climb over the walls. Presently I heard them screaming. They were crying out, as if in pain."

"The Chinese fire, Chinsi," suggested Khlit.

"Nay, we had not used the fire. Gurd was in the castle when they came. Then he left. In the morning I saw their bodies. The men were horribly torn and mangled. The snow was red with their blood. They lay as if they had fallen while running from the castle. But I saw other tracks in the snow."

"They might have been horses, little Sparrow," grunted Khlit.

"Nay, they were not horses' tracks. I was too young to know what they were. Gurd would not tell me. He has always watched over the castle."

Khlit puffed at his pipe in silence for a while.

"Gurd is a brave man," he said, "although he does not carry a sword as a warrior should. But I fear he can not avail against the men who hold Changa Nor today. Lhon Otai is shrewd."

"Aye," said the girl, tossing her curls proudly, "but Gurd is feared through all the Khantai Khan Mountains. Because his enemies can not kill him, they say he is allied to the beasts."

"Your tongue betrays its secret, Chinsi," smiled Khlit. "Devil take me, if you want not this stout fellow Gurd for a husband."

The girl flushed and lowered her gaze.

"It is Atagon's will," she said simply.

"Aye, and yours too," chuckled Khlit.

The girl made haste to speak of another subject.

"You spoke the name of Lhon Otai, father," she said quickly. "Before he leaped from the gallery, Gurd whispered something to me. He bade me tell you to beware of the *shaman*. Not until now have I had a chance to tell you."

"Nay, I need no warning, little Sparrow. Lhon Otai held power in the Jun-gar until I came. He has hated me since the day I joined the ranks of the khans. Not until now could he break my power in the Jun-gar. Yet Chepé Buga remains, who loves him not. Wherefore, I wonder that Lhon Otai bade the khan stay at Changa Nor. Nay, I fear not the conjuring dog. But your peril, little Chinsi, is greater."

"You were brave, father," said the girl softly, "to speak your faith as you did. Atagon has mentioned you in his prayers to God."

"Let him pray for himself," growled Khlit who was impatient of praise. "The *batko* stands near to death. I can do little more for him."

The girl was silent at this. Woman-like, she realized Khlit's rugged nature, that scorned weakness. At the same time she knew that the Cossack would defend the priest of his faith to the death. He craved no sympathy, and rebuked the advances of Atagon. He did not like to speak of his sacrifice for the patriarch. At the same time, she had seen him hold up his gold cross to be blessed by Atagon.

"That is not all Gurd told me," resumed the girl. "In the Northern forest when Lhon Otai was hunting him, he heard the *shaman* talk of his plans to the other Tatars. Lhon Otai said that they had sent one man south——"

A step sounded behind the girl, and she broke off. At Khlit's exclamation, she put her finger to her lips.

"Later, I will tell you, Khlit, father."

The lithe form of Chepé Buga appeared beside them. The khan, who had polished the metal ornaments of his costume and combed his black hair into sleek submission, stared at the slender girl with bold admiration.

"By the mighty beard of Afrasiab," he swore, "you are as hard to find as a live heron on a falcon's roost, Chinsi. The old priest guards you as he would his own life. May the devil mate with me but you are a likely girl!"

Chinsi stamped her booted foot angrily.

"Aye, I have heard you prowling through the castle, like a dog that fears to be seen. And Lhon Otai has stood and mocked Atagon at his prayer."

"Atagon has not much longer to pray, Chinsi," responded the khan idly. "Lhon Otai has told me that when his men come to the castle there will be another sword-dance and the blood of the old priest will be shed as an offering to Natagai."

The girl shivered. At this Chepé Buga stepped close to her, his dark eyes glowing. He caught her chin in a stalwart hand.

"Nay, Chinsi, I would taste of your golden sweetness. Come, a kiss!"

Khlit looked up. But at sight of the girl the Cossack paused. Chinsi's dark eyes were blazing with anger and her cheeks were scarlet.

"Dog!" she whispered. "You are brave when Gurd is not here."

Sheer astonishment showed in the khan's handsome face, and his hand dropped as if he had touched a burning brand.

"That swordless hunter!" He bared his teeth in a hard smile. "If your hero comes back to Changa I will tear out his throat for him with my hands—since he carries no weapon. Nay, Khlit, these be strange folk—never have I taken captives who were so stubborn. The old Atagon watches jealously when Lhon Otai fingers the jewels in the treasure-chamber, although the *shaman* cherishes them like a mare with her first colt. And now the girl prates to me of the hunter who rides reindeer and tames wolves."

He shrugged his shoulders in chagrin.

"I had forgotten the reason I sought you, Chinsi. I looked by chance into the arms chest where you kept the Chinese fire, and the iron flagons for preparing it. The chest was empty. Nay, you are beautiful as a Spring sunrise on the Kerulon, Chinsi, but I have no liking for a baptism of fire from your pretty hands some night when I walk under the gallery. Where have you put the contrivance?"

Khlit glanced at the girl quickly. But she returned their look frankly.

"I have not been near the chest," she said coldly.

Chepé Buga eyed her meditatively.

"Your words have the ring of truth. And I searched your sleeping-chamber before coming here. But Atagon?"

"He knows or cares nothing about the fire."

Chepé Buga glanced instinctively at Khlit. Then he looked away in shame.

"I meant not to doubt you, Khlit, lord," he said gravely. "Come, let me cut away those ropes. It is not fitting that the Kha Khan be bound."

"Nay, Khan," responded Khlit, "your *shaman* would put them back again. He has made us enemies, you and I, who fought together."

Before Chepé Buga could reply, a faint sound came to them over the hills.

"The howl of wolves," said Khlit.

"It is well we are behind walls," assented the khan. "I have seen some dark forms yonder in the pines, whether wolves or not."

The sound was heard by Chagan the swordbearer, seated in the hall of the castle. He raised his head hastily. As he did so he caught sight of a figure moving along the wall toward the chamber of Atagon.

Chagan half rose to his feet. Then he saw that it was Lhon Otai. The *shaman* paused when he perceived Chagan's glance on him, and retraced his steps, away from Atagon's door.

Chagan caught a gleam of steel in the other's hand. But he shook his shoulders indifferently. It was none of his affair what Lhon Otai did.

Again the howl of a wolf echoed through the castle. This time Lhon Otai turned toward the gallery. He looked long from a casement, over the hills. Then he slipped the dagger he carried back in

his girdle. And Chagan wondered, for a smile wreathed the broad
cheeks of the *shaman*.

XIII

If a warrior dies, how may his friend aid him?

*A man's life goes out like a candle in the wind. His limbs are empty
as the branches of a dead birch tree. But his friend may carry the body
from the field of battle. Aye, so it may not be eaten by beasts.*

Tatar saying.

From the window of her sleeping chamber Chinsi the golden-haired
looked out over the snow, where Gurd had disappeared. It was the
night after her talk with Khlit on the tower, and she had been crying. She still wore the reindeer coat for there were few fires in the
castle of Changa, and at present a keen wind was sweeping through
the rooms.

Chinsi drew her parka close over her shoulders, wondering where
the air could have entered the castle. The arrow slits were too small
to create a draft. But what she saw without the window held her
attention.

In the shadow of the pines on the shore of the lake she observed
a movement. A dark body passed from one tree trunk to another.
She saw another body follow it and another.

Her first thought was of Gurd. The hunter had been gone nearly
three days. There had been no sign of his presence around the lake,
although Chinsi had watched with the persistent hope of those who
are in danger. She wondered if the moving forms could be the hunter's reindeer. Then she thought with a shudder of the wolf pack
which passed that way from the North in the early Winter. Gurd
had taught her to watch for the beasts which were ferocious from
hunger, and bold by reason of the numbers of the huge pack.

What she saw among the pines made her press close to the window. She saw a man's figure, outlined against the snow, going from
the castle toward the shore. Presently the man disappeared under
the pines.

So intent was she that she did not hear a stealthy step in the chamber, as Chepé Buga entered, closing the door noiselessly behind him.
Before she had realized that another was in the room the Tatar had

gained her side and thrown his arms around her. The girl's slender form stiffened in fright. A startled cry was cut short by Chepé Buga's hand over her lips.

"The old Atagon is at his prayers, Chinsi, of the golden hair," the Tatar whispered. "You would not like to disturb him. Nay, I have taken the song-bird in her nest."

The girl twisted and turned in a vain struggle. The Tatar's powerful arms held her easily. He pressed his face against the sweet tangle of her hair.

Chinsi's heart was beating heavily. She remembered Chepé Buga's admiring glances, and the persistency with which the khan had followed her about the castle. She realized that it was hopeless to try to free herself from his hold.

A sudden thought came to her, and she ceased her struggles. Chepé Buga cautiously lifted his hand from her mouth. Seeing that she was silent he laughed.

"I am weary of waiting to slay your lover Gurd," he said. "You are the fairest woman of the Khantai Khan Mountains—nay, of Tatary."

His hand passed over her hair eagerly, but he did not give up his grasp of her shoulders. The blood rushed to the girl's face under his touch. Although she was passive, her mind worked quickly.

"You are fair as the pine flowers in Summer, Chinsi," his voice was deep with passion. "You have quickened my blood with love."

His hand grasped her chin. But this time the girl tore herself free.

"Look, Tatar," she cried, "there are wolves around the castle. I have seen them from the window."

Chepé Buga laughed softly.

"You are as full of words as the magpie of Lhon Otai, Chinsi. And as wayward as an unbroken horse. Nay——"

"Fool!" stormed the girl. "Am I so witless as to try to deceive you? While you are prating of love, the castle may be in danger. I saw a man run from Changa to the shore. Who it was, I know not. Look, and you can see for yourself."

Doubtfully, Chepé Buga dragged her to the arrow slit. He looked long and keenly at the shore and the dark figures outlined in the snow.

"Ha! Little Chinsi," he whispered, "these may be wolves, but they have two legs and those two legs are wrapped around the barrels of horses."

He released the girl, without taking his eyes from the scene outside. What he saw roused his warrior's instincts. The dark forms under the pines were in motion now and moving toward the castle. Already they were out on the lake.

"They do not bear themselves like true men," meditated Chepé Buga aloud. "Unless my eyes deceive me yon strangers mean evil."

A cold breath of air touched the girl's shoulders where the parka had been loosened by her struggles. She recalled that the wind was blowing strangely through the castle. On a sudden impulse she turned toward the door of her chamber.

"The wind!" she cried in quick alarm. "The outer door must be open."

Without waiting for Chepé Buga's response she darted from the room into the hall. A glance into the entrance chamber showed her that the door to the lake was open. A pale square of snow showed without.

Chinsi knew that the dark figures she had seen on the lake could not be Gurd or his allies. The sight of the open door, which she had seen closed and barred earlier in the day by Chagan, filled her with sudden terror.

She sprang to the wall and swung the heavy mass of stone back on its massive iron supports. Tugging with all her strength at the lever, she moved it slowly into place. Chepé Buga was beside her, fumbling in the dark for the iron bars.

As Chinsi drew the lever up to its full length, the Tatar dropped the bars into place. As the iron fell into its sockets with a clang a heavy blow resounded on the door. They heard a muffled clamor on the surface of the lake.

Chepé Buga sprang to the arrow slit. He stepped back immediately and Chinsi heard the clang of a steel weapon against the stone of the opening. A light appeared in the chamber behind them. Chagan stood in the room, bearing a torch in one hand and his sword in the other.

"We are attacked, Chagan," shouted the khan, above the tumult. "Come into the hall. The light betrays us here!"

In the hall they found Khlit. In a few words Chepé Buga told his leader what had happened.

"Are you sure it is not Berang with his men?" demanded Khlit, his keen eyes searching the three before him. "Who opened the door?"

"Nay, Khlit, lord," said Chepé Buga grimly, "would Berang give me a love pat with a spear point through the embrasure? We found the door open. Had Chinsi not been as quick as a fox to close it, we should have been taken like sheep in pasture."

"Father," spoke Chinsi, "I saw a man not long since run from the gate to the shore——"

"Where is Lhon Otai?" questioned Khlit.

"Asleep among the jewels of the treasure-chamber, without doubt," grunted the khan. "Nay, I wonder if that fellow Gurd has not been at work here."

"If he had come I would have known it," cried the girl angrily. "It was not Gurd."

"Then it must have been Satan himself or the long-bearded priest. Come, Khlit, lord, we will search the castle. Yon thick stones will keep out our visitors, I fancy. I suspect they knew something of Changa castle, for they came straight to the door, as a dog to his kennel."

"Lhon Otai is not in the treasure-chamber, lords," growled Chagan, who had left the group to investigate.

"I will go to his room," Chepé Buga ran to the stairs. "Do you waken the old priest, Khlit, if he is still here."

A moment served to show Khlit that Atagon was praying in his sleeping-chamber, ignorant or careless of what had happened. Chepé Buga, however, returned with more important news.

"The *shaman* is gone from his lair," he informed them grimly. "There is not so much as a smell of him in the castle. That is not all. Under his pallet where I thought the fat master of mysteries might have betaken himself in fright I found the remains of Chinsi's fire device. The instruments were broken, and the powder, by the traces, cast from the window. My nose tells me the *shaman* has been working us ill."

"Ill!" Khlit's brows knit in thought. "Then it was Lhon Otai that Chinsi saw. But then he must be with the men without, whether prisoner or not. Did he know of their coming?"

"Aye, lord," said Chagan suddenly, "I saw him listening at the embrasures."

"Yet he has not taken one of the jewels," put in Chepé Buga. "Hey, it is not like the fat toad to leave them untouched. He must think to gain them another way. I marked his eyes gleam upon them——"

"Pardon, sirs," Chinsi's musical voice broke in on them. The girl's eyes were bright and her breath came quickly. "On the tower, Father Khlit, I tried to tell you what I knew, but Chepé Buga came. Gurd warned me of what he heard during the hunt to the north. When he had Lhon Otai prisoner the *shaman* whispered to him that he should open the gate of Changa castle to the conjurers, not knowing that Gurd was a Christian. Nay more—before that, Gurd overheard Lhon Otai talking to his men by the fire at night where he thought he was safe from listeners in the woods. The *shaman* plans to leave the Kha Khan and Chepé Buga with the treasure of Changa Nor. But only so that he can take the two khans, who are his enemies, at the same time he seizes the treasure."

The Tatars exchanged glances. Chagan scowled blankly; but understanding dawned on Chepé Buga.

"By its coiling track a serpent is known," he said softly. "Lhon Otai saw to it that my horsemen who came here with me were sent to Baikal. And that the horde under Berang was dispersed. He has left us here with the gate open, like trussed fowls."

Khlit held out his bound hands in grim silence. In the excitement of the talk the others had not thought to cut loose the cords.

"Aye," he growled, "trussed. An evil day when the Jun-gar exchanged leaders. Being disowned I have not spoken what was in my mind. Nay, it was Lhon Otai who bound you also in his toils. He it was who destroyed the fire device that might guard Changa. And left open the gate tonight. Harken!"

Muffled blows resounded on the stones of the door. Chepé Buga flushed. Whipping out his sword he deftly severed the cords around Khlit's wrists.

"Such was not my doing, Khlit, lord," he muttered. "I have sworn an oath to guard you with my sword from danger. So be it. By the winged steed to Kaidu, it warms my blood that we are to fight together! We are your men, O Kha Khan, Chagan and I."

"Aye," roared the swordbearer, "I scent a battle."

Khlit's somber eyes lighted as he studied his comrades. Their scarred countenances were cast in shamed appeal.

"Say that we are one again, Khlit, lord," begged Chepé Buga.

A reckless smile twitched the Cossack's gray mustache. He placed his hands on the sword-hilts of the Tatars.

"We are three men, O brothers in arms, but our enemies will find we are one."

"That is a good word, lord," growled Chagan triumphantly.

Chepé Buga's eyes were eloquent of satisfaction. He cleared his throat gruffly. Lacking words, he caught Khlit's hand in a binding clasp.

"Nay," cried Chinsi, "Lhon Otai and the men with him will suffer, because they have lifted their hands against the altar of God, in Changa Nor."

The assurance of her speech made the warriors smile. They were men of direct thought and took little stock in the legend. As the three Tatars glanced at each other, each knew that one idea was in the minds of his companions.

It was Khlit who voiced this thought when the three stood on the tower of the castle at sunrise. The light showed them that the shores of the lake were filled with horsemen. Tents darkened the snow of the pine forests. Even beyond the forests, on the summits of the hills, the Tatars could see herds, and the *wagon-yurts* of a horde. Oxen and horses were tethered thickly throughout the encampment.

It was an army of hundreds, with their herds. And it made the circuit of Changa Lake.

"Lhon Otai," said Khlit, when he had surveyed the scene, "has brought the Kallmarks to Changa. Aye, his messenger, whom he sent to the south has brought them. And with the treasure, he has trapped the khans of the Jun-gar."

XIV

That same sunrise showed the inhabitants of the Khantai Khan Mountains to the west a strange sight.

By the headwaters of the Tunguska River, far from Changa Nor the men of Khantai Khan saw a herd of reindeer passing through the forest at a swinging trot. The beasts were lean with hunger, yet they did not stop to browse on patches of moss or on birch tips.

In the middle of the herd, mounted on a buck was the figure of a man. He was a tall man, wrapped in furs, with a dark face. As he rode he looked neither to right nor left. But the reindeer sniffed the wind as they paced along. Their muzzles were flecked with foam. Their eyes were starting from their sockets.

And the men of Khantai Khan wondered. For they knew it was fear that drove the reindeer past them without stopping.

XV

The morning brought a parley from the Kallmarks around Changa Nor. Several of their khans rode up to the castle with Lhon Otai. They offered to spare the lives of those in Changa Nor, if the castle and the treasure were given up.

Khlit's answer was brief.

"How can we trust one who has already betrayed us?"

To Chepé Buga and Chagan Khlit proposed that they take advantage of the Kallmarks' offer to gain safety. He would remain with Atagon to defend the Christian altar. Both Tatars replied with one voice that they would not leave him.

"Let the dogs come," growled Chagan, balancing his two-handed weapon, "they hunt in a large pack, but the killing will be easier for us. They will have a taste of our swords. Would that Berang knew of this!"

"Lhon Otai has taken good care that he does not," retorted Chepé Buga.

Khlit occupied the morning in making a survey of the defenses of the castle. What they saw encouraged them. Changa castle had been built long before the days of cannon, and its stone walls were two yards in thickness. Save for the concealed door there was no entrance in the walls.

There was no opening in the roof of the castle proper. In the round tower, at one corner of the structure, a small postern gave access to the roof. By gaining the roof, therefore, the Kallmarks would have no means of winning their way into the castle until they had forced the tower door.

The summit of the tower was too high to be reached by ladders, and it commanded the roof of the castle proper. Arrow embrasures in the tower would permit the defenders to make things warm for any of their foes who climbed to the roof. The stone door to the lake was stout.

Under Khlit's direction the Tatars, assisted by Chinsi, brought chests, heavy furniture and logs of firewood to the entrance chamber. These they arranged to form a barricade in a half-circle around the door. This done, they ransacked the place for arms.

The girl brought them many weapons which had belonged to old defenders of the castle. Sturdy bows, with sheaves of arrows, stiff but powerful; several long spears, rusted with age, one of which Chagan promptly appropriated. Khlit ordered the other spears left at the barricade behind the lake door. The arrows they carried to the tower summit.

Chagan disappeared and presently returned, grinning, clad in a suit of linked Turkish mail that had belonged to the old Gutchluk. Chinsi brought Khlit a similar coat of mail left in the castle by Gurd. These were welcome, for the khans had arrived at Changa in hunting costume, unarmed save for their swords.

Their preparations were nearly complete when they were startled by a footstep behind them. They saw the figure of a man in complete armor, hauberk, breastplate and greaves, engraved with costly gold. It was Atagon, his white beard hanging down over his mailed chest, and a light, triangular shield on which a cross was inscrolled, on his left arm. In his right he bore a long bow.

The sudden appearance of the patriarch in his costume of a century ago startled the khans. Chagan gaped as if he had seen a spirit, while Khlit crossed himself with an oath.

"I heard what has passed, my children," said the patriarch's calm voice, "and my prayers are ended. It is our custom when a battle is on, for the presbyter to be with his knights. Our arms shall be strengthened by God."

"Ha!" laughed Chepé Buga. "There is a priest to my liking. Harken, old man, if you see the fat Lhon Otai in the throng, speed an arrow into his gizzard for me. If the curse of Changa Nor on its spoilers rings true, the arrow will go straight."

A sudden tumult on the ice outside drew the defenders to the tower top. They found that the expected attack was under way. Khlit had taken all his small force with him, leaving Chinsi to watch the door and warn them if it showed signs of giving way.

A single glance showed the experienced warriors, veterans of fifty battles, the plan of their enemy. The tower was too high, and too far removed from the hills at the shore of the lake for effective arrow fire from that quarter. The dark-faced warriors of the Kallmarks tried a few shafts that rattled harmlessly against the stones, and gave it up.

While a few score men advanced on foot against the lake door, bearing the stripped trunk of a giant pine, a hundred others circled the castle on horseback, discharging arrows at the tower top.

This fire, however, was handicapped by the slippery footing of the snow-covered ice which caused the horses to flounder, and by the height of the tower. A few pistol shots, directed against the tower, went wide of the mark. Protected by the battlements, the defenders made good play with arrows. Atagon proved himself a master of the long bow, while Chepé Buga and Chagan shot more rapidly, although scarce less surely, with their short Tatar weapons.

Especially when the ranks of Kallmarks around the pine trunk reached the door the defenders did murderous execution. The tower was nearly over the door, and the arrows, speeding from a height went through furs, leather and armor with ease. The space around the door was soon black with bodies.

As fast as men fell, however, others took their places. Spurred on by trumpets on the shore, and by the multitude of watching Kallmarks, the attackers wielded the heavy trunk against the stones.

"Look, lord!" cried Chagan. "Here come more of the dogs."

Kallmark warriors were appearing over the side of the castle furthest from the tower. Unseen and unmolested by the defenders, they had placed tree trunks against the walls, and now they easily gained the roof of the castle.

Khlit and Chagan at once turned their bows on the newcomers, who were a bare twenty feet below them. The Kallmarks threw themselves vainly against the tower postern, while the arrows made play among them.

"They will soon find their new nest well feathered," chuckled Khlit, as he struck down a brown-coated spearman.

The Kallmarks, finding that there was no direct entrance from the roof into the castle, beat a retreat to their ladders, leaving a score of dead and wounded on the summit of Changa.

Khlit turned to find Chagan busily wielding one of the heavy spears against the battlements of the tower. Using the massive iron point as a crowbar, the swordbearer was prying loose one of the stone blocks. Khlit lent his aid to the task, and in a moment Chagan had freed the stone enough to lift it from its resting place.

Exerting all his strength, the giant swordbearer raised the heavy block over his head. A warning cry went up from below, but the stone hurtled down, crushing three of the men about the pine trunk to the ice.

With a cry of triumph Chagan looked around for another missile. His ambition was heightened by his success, and this time he sprang to the battlement where a solid block of granite, three yards square formed a base for some ancient engine of war. Probably in past generations a ballista had cast its stone from the foundation of the granite. The spear was helpless to budge this weight, but Chagan disappeared down the tower stairs, presently returning with a heavy log of firewood, twice his own height, and one of the andirons from the hall grate.

Working furiously, he wedged the haft of the andiron under the nearer side of the granite block, which was about a foot in thickness. Little by little he raised the massive block sufficiently to insert the end of the log under it. The granite flag stood on masonry which elevated it almost to the height of the battlement.

Putting his shoulder under the log, Chagan dropped to his knees. Rising slowly, the powerful swordbearer lifted the lever with him, his muscles bulging and quivering under the strain. Another second, and, with a grunt, he pushed granite and log over the battlement.

The Kallmarks sprang back as it flew down on them. But the stone achieved a result as unexpected to Chagan as it was to the attackers. As it crashed upon the ice there was an ominous crackle.

A series of sharp cracks followed and the men on the tower saw a section of the ice before the door give way, and vanish into dark water. Other sections caved in, once the surface of the lake had been broken, and the Kallmarks about the door, with their pine trunk, were soon floundering in icy water. Those in mail were pulled under by the weight of their clothing.

Others on the outskirts of the breaking ice scrambled to safety, numbed and stunned by their plunge. The horsemen drew back on all sides, giving the castle a clear berth, for the break in the ice had weakened the whole surface.

Chagan's stones had proved too much for the ice coating, already severely tried by the crowd of men bearing the heavy pine trunk.

The swordbearer eyed the destruction he had wrought with a surprised eye.

"Now by Meik and the winged steed of Kaidu!" he swore. "That was a mighty blow. No less than fifty are dead, at one stroke. Would that Berang and our comrades could have seen it."

The brown-coated horsemen now drew beyond bow-shot of Changa. The first attack on Changa had failed. But Khlit's face was grave. A careful inspection of the lake door had shown him that the hinges had fallen and the iron bars had been nearly wrenched from their sockets. A few more blows from the pine trunk and it must have fallen in. And their stock of arrows had been diminished by half.

XVI

Throughout the night Chinsi took her turn at watching and sleeping by the fire in the hall with the warriors. Chagan was in high spirits, because of the breaking of the ice. But Chepé Buga and Khlit were silent. Atagon was as calm as ever.

"You fought with the might of a Christian hero," said the patriarch to Chepé Buga, "and God is watching over his shrine, from the clouds of heaven."

"Nay, Priest," muttered the handsome khan scornfully, "say rather that you fought like a paladin of Tatary. I saw two arrows strike that helmet of yours but you heeded them not."

"The helmet has been worn by Christian knights," responded the patriarch. "Except for Chagan's wound where an arrow has slit his cheek, we are still whole. But before long the evil minds of the pagans will think to carry their ladders to the roof, where they can lay them against the tower."

"By Satan's cloven hoof," swore Chepé Buga, "a shrewd thought, that!"

Khlit glanced at Atagon curiously. The words as well as the attire of the old man were those of many years ago. Atagon seemed to be without fear. The Cossack felt that this was because Atagon believed in the legend of Changa Nor. But how could the castle be held? So far they had done so, yet they could not hope to much longer, against the numbers of their foe.

If they still cherished hope that the Jun-gar horde of Berang would learn of their danger and bring aid from Baikal, they soon saw their error. And they had new proof of the cunning of Lhon Otai. The next morning the Kallmarks came for a new parley. Khlit took their message from the tower and when he came to the hall his face was serious.

"Lhon Otai has tricked us again," he said grimly. "He sent one of his *shamans* to Lake Baikal with a message to Berang to hurry here alone. Not suspecting, the khan has done so. He is bound hand and foot, in the camp of the Kallmarks. They showed me his sword, as proof."

A gloomy silence greeted this. With the young Berang a prisoner their last hope of aid from the Jun-gar horde had vanished. A sally from the castle under cover of night was not to be thought of. Even if the Kallmark horde had not surrounded the lake, the snow outlined the castle too clearly for them to hope to escape the keen eyes of the watchers.

Late that afternoon Atagon who had been watching in the tower came down to the hall.

"The pagans are in motion on the shore," he said.

Khlit and his followers made their way to the tower. They saw that several of the *wagon-yurts* of the encampment were being drawn down to the shore of the lake by oxen. In puzzled silence they watched while the wheeled tents were dragged out on the ice. The *yurts* came half-way to the castle, within easy bow-shot, and then halted.

Kallmark horsemen drove the oxen back, leaving the heavy wagons on the ice. No signs of life were to be observed about the *yurts*. The mystery was solved in a moment, however. A flight of arrows sped from openings in the heavy tents toward the tower. The defenders ducked hastily as the missiles whistled past them.

Atagon drew his long bow and sent a shaft whizzing at the tents. It stuck fast in the covering. The Kallmarks had cleverly placed strong hides over the felt of the tents. The loose hides formed an effectual protection against anything short of a pistol shot. Through openings in the covering the Kallmark archers could shoot at the tower with safety.

In this way they overcame the handicap of the slippery ice, and the uneven balance of their horses' backs.

Realizing that it was useless to return the fire of the *yurts,* Khlit bade his companions lie under the shelter of the battlements, while Chinsi brought them fur robes as protection against the growing cold of evening. Atagon, who was shielded by his helmet, kept watch over the ramparts for signs of a renewal of the attack.

It came in the period of twilight between sunset and the beginning of the Northern Lights.

They heard a confused murmur on the farther side of the castle. Watching cautiously from the tower they saw dark forms moving along the battlements of the roof below them. The Kallmarks had placed their ladders again against the further side and had gained the roof.

They could see their foemen advancing slowly among the dead bodies, bearing what seemed to be the trunk of a tree. The Kallmarks as well as Atagon had seen the advantage of storming the tower from the summit of the castle, and they relied on darkness to cover their movements, after their costly repulse of yesterday.

Khlit rose to his feet, bow in hand. Instantly his shoulder stung sharply under the mail and he dropped to his knees. The arrows of the Kallmarks in the *yurts* were still flying over the tower which they could see after a fashion outlined against the sky.

Atagon stood erect, plying his arrows heedless of the peril, but Khlit drew Chagan to his knees.

"Their arrows will harm us here," he whispered. "Go you down the stairs leading up the tower. Beside the postern door I marked an embrasure giving on the castle roof. Take your spear——"

The experienced swordbearer needed no further advice. Taking up his heavy weapon he trundled down the stairs. Abreast the postern he peered from the embrasure. He was now on a level with the Kallmarks on the roof, and he could see their forms vaguely, as they raised the tree trunks they had fashioned into rough ladders against the tower.

Silently Chagan inserted the point of his spear in the opening and waited.

On the tower top Khlit heard the ladder scraping against the stone. Atagon had reeled back, struck by an arrow which clanged wickedly against his armor. The next moment the helmeted head of a Kallmark appeared cautiously over the battlements. Khlit and Chepé Buga rose to their feet gripping their swords. Then an angry shout rang out from below.

The men on the tower heard a groan. The head of the Kallmark disappeared. Looking over the side Khlit made out the dim bulk of the ladder falling sidewise. A cry of terror from the men clinging to it, and it crashed over the side of the castle, to the ice below.

"That was Chagan's spear," grunted Khlit, "the swordbearer has toppled over their ladder."

The remaining invaders had left the roof. The arrows from the *yurts* had ceased. Quiet reigned once more around Changa, while the Northern Lights began their play in the sky. But Atagon lay unconscious where he had fallen on the tower.

Chepé Buga lifted the patriarch on his back and made his way past Chagan on the tower steps. He bore his burden to the hall where Chinsi was waiting anxiously by the fire.

"The old hero has stopped one arrow too many, Chinsi," he muttered. "Nay, he is not dead. Help me take off his armor."

The girl with the Tatar's assistance removed Atagon's helmet and body armor, and unstrapped the shield from his arm. The arrow had struck in a joint of the armor at the priest's throat. Chinsi withdrew it tenderly and bound the wound with a strip of her under-garment. There was little bleeding but the stern face of the patriarch was pale. He had been sorely hurt.

Chepé Buga warmed himself at the fire, watching Chinsi as she tended the priest.

XVII

"The curse of Changa Nor upon its spoilers is slow in coming to pass, Chinsi of the golden hair," the khan observed. "I still live and Lhon Otai still is snug in his fat carcass. Your lover Gurd has disappeared, methinks."

The girl looked up from the priest. There was a line of weariness under her eyes, but the eyes were clear and fearless.

"Nay," she said, "Gurd will come. And we will be saved from our enemies."

"Satan himself could not get through the Kallmark camp. There is no man living who can aid us now."

"No man, perhaps, Chepé Buga," she said strangely, and was silent.

The khan's eyes dwelt lingeringly on her slender form. He was loath to think Chinsi would fall into the hands of the Kallmarks. Better that he should end the girl's life with his own sword. The next attack would be the end of them. He put scant trust in the legend of Changa Nor.

"Do you still hate me, little Chinsi?" questioned the khan. "My arrows have sped faster because of you. If we must die, say that you hate me not."

The girl returned his glance steadily.

"You are a bold man, Chepé Buga," she said slowly. "Nay, because you have carried Atagon from danger, I forgive you the evil you would have done me."

A sudden clamor over their heads startled both into silence. Chepé Buga leaped to his feet.

"They are attacking the tower," he cried. "Stay here, Chinsi, and I will come for you if things go ill. Aye——"

He broke off as the girl put her finger to her lips. Another sound came to their ears, a dull knocking. The pounding continued, nearly drowned by the tumult on the roof. Then came a loud crash. It was close to them, so close that it must be in one of the near-by rooms.

"The lake door!" cried Chepé Buga.

"Aye," Chinsi sprang to her feet in quick alarm, "the lake must have frozen over again during the night. The Kallmarks have beaten down the gate."

But Chepé Buga was already in the next chamber, where the barricade had been erected around the door. He saw dark figures blocking the open gate. Spears were thrusting down the barrier. With a shout he leaped to the barricade, swinging his blade over his head. The sword struck against a body and a groan echoed through the chamber.

There was scant light, yet the khan guessed that few of the Kallmarks had squeezed through the door. Protected by the bulwark of logs he swung his sword into the dark in front of him. He heard men cry out, and felt an arrow whiz past him.

Chepé Buga was a skilled swordsman, and he had the advantage of position. He leaped back and forth behind the barrier, slashing at his enemies, who were penned in the space between the gate and the barricade.

Another moment and he felt that he had cleared the space of the invaders. But others were coming through the door. He stumbled over the spear which Khlit had laid on the floor in readiness. Seizing it he thrust at the opening. A groan rewarded his effort.

He heard Chinsi beside him, and called over his shoulder.

"Go for Chagan. There are many more without."

The girl sped away and Chepé Buga devoted himself anew to his spear work. For a space the door was cleared. Then Chepé Buga felt his spear caught and held. He released the shaft and took up his sword.

Stepping quietly to one side of the opening, he struck down the first man who entered. As he did so he felt a sharp pain in the side of his head. One of the wounded who lay below had struck him. Dazed by the blow, the khan shifted his position.

He lost precious time by this movement. Two men had entered and his sword crashed against their weapons. In the darkness none of the three could see to strike surely. Chepé Buga sought for an opening cautiously, wearied by his efforts and the loss of blood. He listened anxiously for the coming of Chagan.

The next instant he reeled back. A spear had entered his armor, at the side. As he thrust weakly at his foe he caught the flash of a sword beside him. A groan came from one of his foemen.

"Ha, Chagan!" he panted.

The last of the invaders fell before a thrust of the sword that gleamed beside him in the light from the fire behind them. The chamber was now empty of foemen, and the door was blocked with bodies. Quiet was restored.

Weakly Chepé Buga staggered out into the hall. His companion closed the door behind him. Then the khan sank down beside Atagon. For the first time he saw his companion by the firelight. Even to his dimmed eyes the figure did not seem like Chagan's bulk. The firelight gleamed on the small shield of Atagon which the other carried.

Above the shield was a white, anxious face and a tangle of gold hair.

"Chinsi!" he gasped. "How——"

"Chagan could not leave the tower," she said softly, "they are hard beset. I took Atagon's sword and shield, to help you if I could."

The girl laid down her shield and knelt beside him.

"They have gone from the door," she said eagerly, "I heard them."

Her glance fell on the dark stain that covered the khan's mail, and she gave a cry of dismay.

Chepé Buga shook his head in mute protest as she tried to draw off his heavy mail.

"The spear," he whispered, "went deep. Your sword killed the man that did it. Brave Chinsi, the golden-haired!"

Chepé Buga's dark head sank back on the floor, and his sword fell from his fingers. The watching girl saw a gray hue steal into his stern face. Chepé Buga, she knew, was dying.

"Harken," she whispered, pointing to Atagon who lay beside them, conscious. "Let the presbyter bless you, Chepé Buga. The priest will save your soul, for heaven."

The Tatar moved his head weakly until he could see Atagon. Something like a smile touched his drawn lips. The girl bent her head close to his to hear what he was trying to say.

"Nay, Chinsi. Do you bless me. Heaven is—where you are."

Raising one hand, Chepé Buga caught a strand of the girl's hair which lay across his face. The girl, who had stretched out her hand to Atagon, sighed regretfully. Yet she did not move her head away.

Chepé Buga's hand was still fast in her hair. But its weight hung upon the strand, and the Tatar's eyes were closed when Khlit and Chagan ran from the tower stairs into the hall a moment later.

The two halted beside the form of Chepé Buga. A single glance told Khlit that the khan was dead. He placed his hand on the girl's shoulder.

"Harken, Chinsi," he said, "what do you hear?"

The girl strained her ears, but she could hear nothing. The hall was silent save for the heavy breathing of the two warriors. Yet the silence was ominous after the storm of the assault.

"What is it?" asked the girl, her heart beating heavily.

"It is the curse of Changa Nor," said Khlit grimly. "It has fallen on the Kallmarks."

The girl rose to her feet with a startled cry.

"Aye," said Chagan, leaning wearily on his bloodied spear, "it must be the curse, for Chepé Buga is dead."

XVIII

"Go to the tower, and you can see what has happened," Khlit directed. "Take Chagan with you, Chinsi, for some of the Kallmarks might think to take shelter in Changa castle. I will stay with Chepé Buga."

Khlit took his seat beside Atagon and the body of his comrade. The girl sought the tower, followed more slowly by the swordbearer.

As she climbed the steps she became conscious of a noise outside the castle. It was a distant tumult, unlike the clamor of the assault. As she gained the summit of the tower it grew to a roar that echoed between the walls of the tower and the hills.

The darkness was pierced by the Northern Lights. When Chinsi's eyes had become accustomed to the gloom she beheld a strange scene.

Across the surface of the lake horsemen were darting. In the camp itself on shore all was confusion. She heard the shrill neighing of horses, the bellowing of cattle in fear. The shouts of the Kallmarks resounded through the confusion. Fires had sprung up in a wide arc through the pine forest. She saw the dark bulk of the *yurts* hurrying along the shore of the lake.

Her first thought was that the forest was on fire. This could not be, however, in the snow. The fires were separate. And she could see men throwing branches on them. Above the tumult of the beasts and the crackling of fire she caught a hideous snarling and snapping. Then she saw for the first time that the woods beyond the camp were filled with masses of dark forms. In front of these masses riders were wheeling, swinging their swords. By the fires she saw animals trotting through the pines.

"Wolves!" she cried.

"Aye," assented Chagan, who had come up. "The great wolf pack of the North is yonder. It came on the Kallmarks when they were attacking the castle. They had no sentries out in the hills. The pack got among the herds before they knew it."

"The fires will keep the wolves away from the camp," cried Chinsi.

"Nay, they were built too late. The pack has tasted blood. The wolves are mingled in the herds now. The beasts are mad with fear. Harken!"

The shrill scream of a horse in pain came to the ears of the girl and she shuddered. She saw that the herds of cattle which had been placed in the hills beyond the camp were now mingled in the camp itself. In spite of the efforts of the horsemen, the animals were stampeding along the shore, rushing from one point to another. The fires excited them further. Even the oxen yoked to the *wagon-yurts* had caught the fever of fear. The contagion had spread to the horses, which were becoming unmanageable.

"If it were not for the animals, the plight of our friends yonder would not be so bad," continued Chagan who was watching events intently. "By lighting more fires, they might save themselves. But the herds are in the grip of fear. And the pack is among them, having tasted blood. Ha!"

He pointed to the further shore, where there were fewer fires. From this place groups of cattle and oxen were moving in the direction of the lake. Horsemen rode among them, powerless to check them because their mounts were beyond control. The tide of beasts swept down to the lake. By the lights in the sky Chinsi could see whips lifted, and the blades of swords flashing. Here and there a rider went down under the mass.

A group of Kallmarks had mustered at the edge of the lake and were endeavoring to turn the frantic animals to each side, along the shore. But the snarling of the wolves echoed in the rear of the herd and masses of the cattle ventured out on the frozen lake. A number of *yurts* drawn by oxen were in their midst. To the girl it seemed as if an invisible hand were driving the beasts to destruction. On the nearer side of the lake where the main body of Kallmarks was, the men were making headway in their fight against the wolves.

"They are out on the lake," she cried. "Oh——"

With a rending crackle whole surfaces of the ice gave way under the weight of the animals and the *yurts*. Horsemen, beasts and tents disappeared into the black water. The flickering glow of the sky showed her the horns of cattle swimming in the water. A frantic rumble sounded from the doomed beasts.

This catastrophe was fatal to the Kallmarks. The parts of the herd that had gone along the shore became panic-stricken and broke into a run. They merged with the horses, mad with the double fear of the wolves and the breaking ice. In a moment the whole mass was in motion in one direction. The leading beasts hesitated as they reached the fires and the men tending them, and then drove on, urged by the multitude behind.

Chinsi saw the men by the fires leap into passing *yurts* or on the backs of horses. By now the mass was flowing out into the woods, past the fires. On either side ran the wolf pack, pulling down beasts from the herd.

The Kallmarks were powerless to halt their animals. The horses went with the cattle, and the men went perforce with the horses, or crowded in the *yurts*.

By dawn the main body of the Kallmarks had passed from the lake. Isolated groups of horsemen rode after them, escorted by wolves. The fires in the forest were dying down. About fallen beasts the wolves gathered, snarling. In the path of the riders lay overturned *yurts*, and dark forms invisible under a slavering press of wolves.

XIX

When he had recovered from his wound Atagon, the aged presbyter of Changa Nor who was sometimes called by visiting Christians the last descendant of Prester John, prayed reverently before his shrine. In his prayers he gave heartfelt thanks to God for saving the altar of Changa Nor from the pagans. Surely, thought Atagon, it was the hand of God; for Lhon Otai, the *shaman* who desecrated the shrine, was found dead, mangled by the wolves; and since that night Kallmarks and Jun-gar alike respected Changa castle.

True, Atagon did not know that it was the command of Khlit, called the Wolf, that the shrine be unmolested by the Tatars. For Khlit's position as Kha Khan was unquestioned after the death of Lhon Otai, and the retreat of the Kallmarks to the border, following upon the defeat of their plans and the slaughter at Changa Nor.

And hearing the prayers of Atagon, Gurd, the hunter, did not find it in his heart to tell the presbyter the truth of what had happened. Only to Chinsi, as is the way of lovers, did Gurd reveal that, knowing the treachery of Lhon Otai and the coming of the Kallmarks, he had taken the desperate chance to drive the besiegers from Changa Nor. He had led his reindeer herd across the course of the great wolf pack of the North, which was on its annual migration southward along the shore of Lake Baikal. Then he had fled for the Kallmark camp, with the pack at his heels, striking down his reindeer until all but one had fallen to the wolves.

And so Chinsi laughed softly to herself when she heard the khan Berang tell how, from the door of a *wagon-yurt*, he had seen a man clad in the furs of animals and mounted on a stag lead the wolves into the Kallmark herds that night.

For Berang's face bore the look of one who has seen a miracle as great as the dance of the *Rakchas* by the three Diandas, or even the flaming anvils of the *Cheooki* gods in the skies.

ADVENTURE FOUR

ROOF OF THE WORLD

For three times a thousand years the camels and men have passed in their caravans by the Jallat Kum. Where Taklamaklan rises to the mountains, the caravans journey by the Jallat Kum.

The camels go and leave their dung to be food for the fires of those who come after. The men die and their bones dry in the sands. Under the star eyes of Jitti Karakchi are the Jallat Kum. And what is it that the stars have not seen? Nay, they have seen the men and camels of three thousand years ago come to the Jallat Kum again.

For the stars and the Jallat Kum and the spirits of the dead are as one.
From the book of Batur Madi, priest of the Kashgar lamasery.

IT WAS THE SPRING HUNT OF THE TATARS IN THE YEAR OF THE APE, AT the beginning of the seventeenth century. The Tatar riders had circled through the steppe by the blue waters of Kobdo Nor, at the southern boundary of their lands, and had made a good kill of antelope, wild sheep and yaks. And in their circle they came upon a Chutuktu lama of the Holy City of Lhassa with his followers.

And this, says the priest, Batur Madi, was the beginning of the strange events that brought Khlit, the Cossack of the Curved Saber, to Taklamaklan and trouble to the lamasery of Kashgar. A trouble which only ended with the death of many men at the Roof of the World.

The setting sun was casting its level rays across the steppe grass as the last of the beaters brought in their game on the backs of packhorses. The game was piled by the shore of the lake where Khlit, the Cossack of the Curved Saber, and Kha Khan of the Jun-gar

Tatars, had ordered the night's encampment. Through the ranks of the hunters spurred a powerful man with a scarred face, who reined his horse to a halt before the *kibitka* of Khlit.

"Our outriders, lord," he cried to the Cossack, who was standing before his tent, "have come upon one who says that he is from the Holy City. He wears the orange robe of a Chutuktu lama, and his name is Dongkor Gelong."

Khlit raised his gray head and scanned the messenger keenly. Although his costume of furred coat with wide sash and horse-hide boots was similar to those of his companions, the Cossack was taller. His hard gray eyes were not aslant like those of the Tatars. He had taken off his heavy woolen cap and his gray hair hung to his powerful, stooped shoulders. A veined hand tugged thoughtfully at his drooping, white mustache. The deep lines of his browned face alone showed his age.

"Dongkor Gelong," he said in his deep voice, "must be the envoy of the Dalai Lama whom we have come to meet. Take a hundred horsemen, Chagan, and bring him to my *kibitka* with all due honor. Tell the khans of the Jun-gar that he has come."

The rider wheeled his mount and spurred away, leaping the piles of game with the ease of a man who had been weaned on mare's milk. But the tidings had already spread through the encampment. The Tatar khans left the game they had taken and hurried to the Kha Khan's tent, before which the standard was planted. Ranging themselves in a semicircle, they watched for the coming of the envoy from the Holy City.

Khlit's searching gaze scrutinized the eager faces of the Tatars. They were grim men, these of the Jun-gar, descendants of Ghenghis Khan and the Golden Horde. The broad faces of many bore battle-scars. They had been more numerous when Khlit came to them, for they had been with him in many battles. His leadership over them rested on two things: his consummate skill as a warrior, bred of fighting from the Cossack Ukraine, Persia, Turkestan to the Tatar steppe, and his descent from Kaidu, the hero of the Tatars, whose curved sword he bore.

By sheer daring and shrewdness Khlit had held the Tatar clans together against their enemies. His craft had earned him the name of Wolf among men bred to war and conquest. And had earned him as well many enemies, chiefly among the priesthood, for Khlit alone of the Tatar khans carried the gold cross of a Christian about his neck under his tunic.

The throng of hunters parted and a cavalcade appeared, headed by Chagan, the sword-bearer, and a man in bright robes mounted on a white camel, who wore a crystal rosary on his chest. Two attendants in black and orange robes followed, an array of spearmen on camels trailing behind them.

As the white camel knelt, Khlit raised his right hand in greeting, carrying it to his mouth. He did not advance from his tent, and, seeing this, the lama remained by the head of his camel instead of coming forward. The gaze of the Tatars went eagerly from one to the other as they matched glances.

Dongkor Gelong was unlike the *shamans* and monks whom Khlit had seen on the steppe. He was a tall man, stout and richly robed in furs and Chinese silks; moreover, he had the carriage of one accustomed to command. He had the smooth olive skin of a Chinese and the broad frame of a Tibetan. He wore the close-fitting orange hat of a lama of the Gedum Dubpa monastery, the home of the Dalai Lama. It was evident that his stately appearance had already produced a strong effect on the Tatars, to whom the name of the Dalai Lama was an earnest of supernatural power.

"Welcome to the camp of the Jun-gar, Dongkor Gelong," observed Khlit gravely in Tatar, which the other understood readily. "We have had a good hunt, and choice meats will be prepared for you. Tonight we will summon a *kurultai* council of the khans, and hear the word of the Dalai Lama who has sent you."

Dongkor Gelong inclined his dark head courteously.

"It is well that you should hear the word of the almighty Tsong Khapa, O Kha Khan. Although it is many *li* from the Jun-gar steppe to the Holy City, the power of the Dalai Lama to safeguard his servants knows no limits of space."

Evening saw a bustling preparation of mutton and horseflesh in the camp by the lake. When the envoy and his attendants had been feasted, the expectant khans assembled around a circle of fires built in front of Khlit's *kibitka*. The Cossack and Dongkor Gelong sat together in the center of the circle. Behind Khlit, as was customary, loomed the stalwart form of the sword-bearer, Chagan, accompanied this time by the two Chubil Khans who had come with the envoy from Lhassa.

At the right and left of the two leaders were seated the khans of the Jun-gar, headed by Berang, of the Ordus, and the chieftains of the Hoshot, Torgot and Tchoros hordes. Behind these were ranged the lesser personages: cloaked *shamans* and tawny masters of the horse-herds, together with warriors of the rank of khans who were not leaders of a horde.

The *kurultai* of the Jun-gar was assembled.

II

Dongkor Gelong stepped into the semicircle of light. To the watchers it seemed as if his eyes were closed, but the lama had not failed to scrutinize his listeners shrewdly. He faced toward the south, where was Lhassa, and drew a parchment from the breast of his robe. This he pressed reverently to his forehead.

"To the Khans of the Jun-gar," he read aloud, "greeting from the almighty Tsong Khapa, Dalai Lama of the Gedun Dubpa and keeper of the sacred *Kandjur* books."

Khlit stroked the scabbard across his knees pensively. He noted, as did all the listeners, that the Dalai Lama had omitted mention of the Kha Khan in his greeting. This might have been, thought Khlit, because it was the council of khans and not himself who had appealed to the master of Lhassa.

"The messenger of the khans," went on the musical voice of Dongkor Gelong, "has brought to the Dalai Lama word of the trouble of the Jun-gar. The word that the Tatar hordes are threatened with doom and the loss of the lands which are their birthright. In their trouble they have rightly asked aid of the only one who can restore their power."

A murmur of agreement greeted this. Khlit chewed at his black pipe impassively. Still the lama had made no mention of him, treating the matter as one between the khans and the Dalai Lama. He did not look at Dongkor Gelong, watching instead the attentive faces of the Tatars.

"On the east the khans have complained," continued the lama, "that the Ming armies of China have forced them across the great desert of Kobi. To the south the Khirghiz clans have invaded the Jun-gar steppe where the children of the mighty Kha Khan, Ghenghis, were accustomed to graze their herds."

Another murmur, louder this time, greeted the mention of the great Tatar conqueror. Was it by chance that Dongkor Gelong spoke first of Ghenghis Khan, before the living Kha Khan of the Jun-gar? Had he meant to compare the two in the mind of his audience?

"To the west, by Tomsk and the Yenissei, the traders and soldiers of Muskovy are taking the lands of the Jun-gar. Many of the hordes have deserted the Jun-gar, taking with them their *tumens* of horsemen. Only on the north are there no enemies. And there is the land of ice—the Dead World beyond the frozen waters of Baikal. The power of the Jun-gar trembles like a reed when the wind blows. It is time they asked for aid from the glorious spiritual king whose name is heard with reverence from the Great Wall to the cities of the Moguls, from the Roof of the World to the sea."

Chagan, the sword-bearer, was a man of tranquil wits, but he stirred uneasily. Truly, he thought, Dongkor Gelong had the voice of a golden eagle, for he painted the evils that beset the Jun-gar with an all-seeing eye. Chagan did not perceive, as the envoy went on with his oration, how cleverly Dongkor Gelong played upon the name of Ghenghis Khan, and the power of the master of Lhassa.

But it was clear to Chagan that Dongkor Gelong was appealing to the khans and not to the Kha Khan, Khlit, called by them the Wolf. Many glances besides his own sought out the impassive Cossack. The allegiance of the khans to Khlit, Chagan knew, was strong by reason of the Kha Khan's leadership in battle. Khlit had broken the power of the *shaman* priesthood. But the *shamans*, with their conjuring tricks, were allied to the Dalai Lama as the fleas on the belly of a horse were kin to the horse.

So much Chagan was aware of. He, like Berang and the other khans, did not choose to realize that their present plight was the fault of the jealousy and waning power of the hordes, rather than any mistake in leadership by Khlit. Chagan leaned forward eagerly as Dongkor Gelong came to the end of his parchment and paused, one hand uplifted for his final word.

"Wisely have the khans of the Jun-gar," he cried, "appealed to the precept of the gods. It was well they asked for an oracle. The question has been put to the oracle in Gedun Dubpa. The sacred ashes have formed the answering words, which have been truly read by the clergy of the Yellow Cap. This is the answer."

A breathless silence greeted this. Khlit raised his keen eyes and scanned the lama. Dongkor Gelong turned and pointed at him.

"In this way may the Jun-gar restore their power and safeguard their lands from the Khirghiz. Like the sun and moon, the Lama and the Kha Khan should mount the sky together. The Kha Khan, by order of the Lama, must do this."

He swung his long-sleeved arm until it pointed to the south.

"In the fifth moon of the year of the Ape the Wolf of the Jun-gar must go to the citadel of Talas on the Jallat Kum, where the river Tarim goes to its grave in the sands of Taklamaklan Desert. There he will find aid for the Jun-gar. In this manner the oracle has spoken."

Profound silence reigned in the council. The dark faces of the khans showed blank surprize and a dawning hope. Dongkor Gelong regarded them gravely, with folded arms.

"Truly, lords of the Jun-gar," he said in a low voice, "this is little short of a miracle. For at Lhassa none save the gods knew that the Kha Khan Khlit was surnamed the Wolf. Since I have come, I have been told that is the case. Such is the wisdom of the gods. Now, to aid his people, the Kha Khan must choose those among you whom he can most trust and travel to Talas by the Taklamaklan Desert, beyond the Thian Shan, to the south."

There was an excited stir among the shamans at mention of the verification of the prophecy. From somewhere back in their ranks came a voice.

"We have heard the oracle of Lhassa. What is the answer of the Kha Khan?"

At this all eyes were turned to Khlit. The Cossack did not move to rise, for it was not his custom to speak hastily. Tugging at his mustache, he considered the message of Dongkor Gelong. The city of Talas he had never heard of, but it must lie a week's fast riding to the south, if it was beyond the Thian Shan Mountains. The Taklamaklan Desert, he had heard, was a portion of the great Kobi, at a high altitude. It should not be hard to find the river Tarim at the edge of the Taklamaklan and follow it to its end. So much was clear.

The message of the Dalai Lama was little less than a command. The master of Lhassa was head of the Buddhist priests in Mongolia, China and Central Asia. To disobey would be to risk the allegiance of his own people. And it was possible that the Dalai Lama knew of assistance that Khlit could gain at Talas. The Dalai Lama knew many things—from the eyes and ears of the Tsong Khapa, the priesthood of the lamas.

Khlit's shrewdness probed the words of Dongkor Gelong for their inner meaning. The Dalai Lama must have heard that Khlit was a Christian. As such, he would not be favored by the clergy of the Holy City. Did Dongkor Gelong hope that Khlit would refuse to undertake the mission proposed by the oracle? Or did he reason that, having gained aid through the Dalai Lama, the Cossack's prestige would suffer?

Khlit got to his feet and surveyed the ranks of the Tatars. Dongkor Gelong folded his arms and waited.

"Harken, Dongkor Gelong," spoke Khlit slowly. "Look into the sky and tell me what you see."

As one the eyes of the Tatars flew upward, the firelight glaring white on their eye-balls.

"O Kha Khan," responded the lama composedly, "I see the crescent moon and Jitti Karaktchi, the great bear among the stars. And it is the fifth moon of the year of the Ape. The Ice Pass that leads to the Jallat Kum will be open for your coming."

"Do you see the sun, O man of wisdom?" growled the Cossack.

"Nay; how could that be? The earth is in the dark, Erlik clouds of night."

"Truly have you spoken, Dongkor Gelong. Then tell me, how can it be that the sun and the moon mount the sky together? Or the Kha Khan and the Dalai Lama rule one people?"

III

The Chutuktu Lama smiled and turned to the assembled warriors. "Nay," he answered promptly, "when the moon steals into the light of day, her radiance dies because of the glory of the sun. Is not the almighty Tsong Khapa the father of many nations? In all the world there is not a king with a glory such as his. For the Dalai Lama knows the wisdom of former ages, being incarnate. The light of his wisdom points to the citadel of Talas as the salvation of the Jun-gar."

A murmur of agreement echoed this, in which the *shamans* joined the loudest. The more warlike khans stirred uneasily and looked at Khlit.

"The wisdom of the master of Lhassa is beyond my knowing, O envoy of the Yellow Hat," said Khlit slowly. "My skill is in arranging battles and the clash of armies on the steppe. Ask the Jun-gar where lies the host of Hang-Hi, general of the Son of Heaven. Or the banners of Li Jusong. They have fallen before the yak-tailed banner of Tatary. How has the Tsong Khapa thought, in his wisdom, that we may have aid from Talas? Who are the people of Talas? I know them not."

Dongkor Gelong bent one cotton-wrapped knee and bowed his head.

"I came as the bearer of words more precious than the seven substances, because they were inspired by the gods. Who am I to seek to explain them?"

From the ranks of listeners came the voice of the hidden *shaman*.

"Question not what is written, O Kha Khan."

Khlit stared at his followers moodily.

"You have sworn an oath, O Khans of the Jun-gar, that my word should be law in the *kurultai* of the Tatars. It is not in written words but in the fellowship of warriors that a khan may put his trust. Nay, tonight I will not ask the advice of the *kurultai*. Does a wolf seek the will of the pack when he makes a kill? I alone will choose my course."

In the deep silence that followed this, Dongkor Gelong raised his arms in alarmed surprize.

"Will you dare to disobey the Tsong Khapa?"

"I have chosen my path," responded Khlit shortly. "It lies to Talas. But I will go alone."

Cries of protest greeted this. The khans of the inner circle sprang to their feet, protesting. Berang of the Ordus declared that he would go with Khlit.

"Nay, Kha Khan," objected Dongkor Gelong. "It was the wish of the Dalai Lama himself that you should take followers whom you could trust. The journey will be through the lands of Iskander Khan and Bassanghor Khan of the Khirghiz who have violated your boundaries——"

"I have chosen," growled Khlit. "And I will go tonight."

The news spread swiftly through the encampment. The Tatar hunters gathered about the *kibitka* and watched silently while Khlit arranged a few things in his saddle-bags—some meat smoked until it was dry, milk curds hardened into cakes, a flask of kumiss, spare powder for his pistols—and selected a horse from several that Chagan brought him. Khlit had never forsaken his fondness for a horse in favor of the hardier camel.

Still in silence the khans watched him mount. Dongkor Gelong and Berang said a few words of farewell. Khlit thought that he caught a disappointed light in the lama's eyes. Was Dongkor Gelong sorry that he had agreed to go to Talas?

The stolid faces of his followers veiled strong feelings. Hope, disappointment, relief and uneasiness were in the glances they fixed on him. If he had not gone, to a man they would have turned against him—such was their faith in the word of the Dalai Lama. But, now that the old Kha Khan was leaving on his mission, some felt misgiving.

Khlit sprang from the ground into the saddle—a trick of his Cossack days—not sitting, but standing erect in the saddle. The horse wheeled and darted away from the *kibitka* through the tents. There was hardly a Tatar who could not have done as much. Yet the trick stirred their fancy and a hoarse shout of approval followed him as he vanished into the dark.

Once clear of the encampment, Khlit reined in his horse and seated himself in the saddle. He cast a shrewd eye up at the stars and struck off across the plain to the south. The steppe here was level as the surface of a lake. A warm breeze stirred the lush grass, and his horse sniffed heavily of the fragrant air. As he rode, Khlit struck flint and steel and lighted his long-stemmed pipe. Thus did Cossacks always ride.

The magic of the steppe warmed Khlit's blood. It was the same endless plain that stretched to the Ukraine, lighted by the same stars. It had been Khlit's home, and here he was always happy. He muttered to himself—he had never been known to sing—fragments of Cossack songs. And then he suddenly drew his mount to a halt.

His keen ears had caught the sound of riders behind him. He judged there were several and that they were coming at a rapid pace. Alert for possible danger, he turned toward the sound and drew one of the pistols he carried in his sash.

The patter of hoofs neared him and presently he made out a group of dark shadows. At first he guessed them to be riderless horses escaped from the encampment. Then he saw that one horse had a rider. The man saw him at the same moment and halted the small cavalcade he was leading.

"Chagan!" swore Khlit, peering at the other's bulk in the gloom. "Devil take the dog! Why do you follow me?"

The sword-bearer laughed uneasily.

"Lord," he growled, "you said before Dongkor Gelong that you would ride to Talas alone. Wherefore I slipped from the camp and followed with extra horses, so that none would see me. Almost, I lost you in the dark."

"I need but one horse, Chagan. Get back to the camp, where there is horseflesh to be eaten."

Chagan laid his heavy hand on Khlit's knee.

"Nay, lord," he said gruffly; "you have said that a fat hound hunts but ill. Since the time of Ghenghis, when did not the sword-bearer follow the Kha Khan in battle or hunt?"

"Yet I give you this as a duty—go back."

"Harken, lord." Chagan moved nearer. "I have a thought, that you had best make haste. I have listened at the camp——"

"Dolt, offspring of a wild ass! Speak not to me of your thoughts. Silence is sweeter than the bellow of an ass."

Khlit, knowing the uselessness of arguing with the sturdy sword-bearer, put spurs to his horse and sped away into the darkness. Chagan lost no time in following.

A streak of crimson showed to the east. The light of the stars paled overhead. From the occasional thickets that the riders passed, bird notes trilled. The crimson spread into yellow and violet. The rays of the morning sun shot up over the plain and showed Chagan with his led horses galloping a scant mile behind Khlit. By shifting, as he rode, from one mount to another, he had managed to keep within sight of the better-mettled steed of the Cossack.

Once Chagan sighted Khlit, he drew up rapidly. Seeing this, the Cossack stopped. His first words to the sword-bearer showed that his mood had altered.

"Devil roast me, Chagan, but this is a ride fit for an emperor. Hey, man, you would come to Talas? Ride then—ride! Let the horse leap between your knees. Light your pipe and feel the kiss of the harlot wind in your face. Ride to meet Erlik on his black steed of death. Hey, Tatar, come!"

Taking two of the horses from the sword-bearer, who echoed his words with an exultant shout, Khlit led the way to the south. Through the day they rode, after the manner of their kind, sleeping at intervals in the saddle and chewing on the dried meat when they were hungry.

In this manner Khlit, called the Wolf, and Chagan, the sword-bearer, made their way to the passes of the Thian Shan Mountains, swimming the river Ili, and crossing the Southern steppe, to the Ice Pass. To the sands of Taklamaklan and the Jallat Kum.

This was the route from Khamil south to Talas and the caravan track, as written in the annals of Batur Madi, who had inscribed after the words Jallat Kum a mark to ward off evil spirits. For Batur Madi declared that the bones of many men were drying in the Jallat Kum and that the caravans from the east went a week's journey to the north to avoid the Jallat Kum, where no men went willingly, unless they knew that their graves were dug there.

IV

Of the numerous passes leading through the Thian Shan Mountains to the south, Khlit chose the Ice Pass mentioned by Dongkor Gelong, for two reasons. It was well to the north of the Tarim, beneath the snow-crest of the mighty Khan Tengri, and rather beyond the territory of the Khirghiz chieftains. While the defiles of the pass might well be infested with mountaineers—who were, of course, robbers—there was less danger of their meeting their enemies the Khirghiz. And Chagan pointed out that it was the quickest way to the Tarim.

Indeed Chagan was unmistakably anxious to push on with all speed. The two riders found that their choice was justified. They gained the southern end of the defile with no greater loss than two of their horses, given as toll to a chieftain of the Khan Tengri who had not demanded more because he saw that the two Tatars were well-armed and disposed to use their weapons. The high altitude of the pass, where glaciers pressed the sides of the gorge and freshets flooded the gullies, hindered their progress.

Chagan gave an exclamation of satisfaction as they began the downward path to the south, their woolen coats drawn close against the chill winds that whistled down the pass at their backs. Khlit glanced at him curiously, for the sword-bearer, who had been urging haste, was not the man to be anxious about possible danger.

"Nay, lord," Chagan answered his blunt query, "the lamas say that spirits infest the mountain passes, and I saw no idols fastened to the trees by the way to ward them off. So——"

"So you lie like a Mussulman merchant of Samarkand. You have ridden the flesh from your horse's belly. I have watched you counting the days of our journey on your fingers as if a young maiden awaited your coming in a comfortable *yurt*. Speak from your mind what is true, Chagan, and save lies for thieves and *shamans*."

The sword-bearer's slant eyes widened guiltily, and he looked involuntarily back along the trail down which they had come. Khlit's glance followed his. The pass was empty of all save a hovering raven. Before this, Khlit had assured himself that they were not followed. Moreover, their speed had been such that none save a Tatar or Khirghiz on picked mounts could have kept near them. Why, then, had Chagan been uneasy?

"When the Dalai Lama commands, lord," muttered the other, "it is well to hasten."

Khlit laughed and shook his shoulders lightly.

"Aye. There is meat to that bone, Tatar. The words of the Dalai Lama are such as to blind the eyes of children or fools. But I am neither one nor the other. Truly the words of a magician are a veil. To read the truth you must tear the veil aside."

Chagan blinked and spat forcibly.

"The Dalai Lama is not a magician, lord. I have seen the lamas raise up a man who was dead. They know all that happens in the mountains. We must guard well our tongues, for this is their land."

"Lamas, *shamans*, or conjurers—they are all one, Chagan. Hey, their tricks are as many as the wiles of the steppe fox! Yet to one who knows they are but tricks there is no danger. Wherefore I would have come alone."

Chagan turned this over in his mind and shook his head dubiously.

"Nay, lord," he said, and hesitated. "You came by these mountains to Tatary, men say. Did you see the city of Talas?"

"Nay, nor heard of it. The Dalai Lama is fond of riddles, Chagan. When we see Talas we may know the meaning of this riddle. Not before."

From the foot-hills of the Thian Shan, called in the annals of

Batur Madi the Kok Shal Tau, Khlit and Chagan glimpsed in the distance the wide valley of the Tarim. Here was a country different from that they had come through. The level steppe gave way to broken, wooded ridges, through which the horses took their way slowly. The defiles gleamed brown with sandstone pinnacles of rock. Game was thick and Chagan succeeded in bringing down an *arkhan* —a species of mountain-sheep strange to them both, but eatable.

They came out abruptly from the poplars and willows of the forest to a wide sweep of sluggish water. Neither boats nor signs of habitations were visible, and the two took their course down-stream, noting that the forest thinned as they went.

The current also lost its force, and the footing became sandy. The poplars gave way to tamarisks. Khlit pushed ahead, anxious to see the end of the river, where Dongkor Gelong had promised that they would find Talas.

The silence of the place stilled Chagan's tongue. Khlit had never been fond of words. The Cossack surveyed their surroundings keenly as they advanced, looking back with a frown at the distant summits of the Thian Shan. Truly, this was a strange place. For on the Tarim they did not meet any horsemen. Even when they came to the end of the river at a willow thicket, there was no sign of habitation. Why had they been sent to such a spot?

Chagan pulled up his tired horse with an oath. Khlit pushed ahead to the summit of a sand-dune beyond the thicket. Then he halted and leaned forward curiously.

The slight elevation of the dune gave him a view over the surrounding landscape. He saw that they were on the edge of a desert, for the tamarisk trees became scattering and a series of dunes stretched before him like the summits of waves on an ocean. A few paces below him was a rough shepherd's *aul*—tree branches and thorns woven into a small enclosure in which were a score of sheep, a horse, a felt tent and a man in tattered woolen garments asleep.

Khlit trotted up to the enclosure and scanned the man. He lay flat on his face: a short, stocky figure, legs wrapped in soiled cloths and a dingy black *kollah* on his tousled head. A fire of sheep dung smoldered near him.

The rustle of branches, as the Cossack's horse nibbled at the fence, startled the fellow from his sleep, and he sprang to his feet grasping at a short spear. Khlit raised his right hand reassuringly, and after a careful inspection the man advanced gingerly toward him, holding the weapon poised. Chagan came up and grinned at sight of the scared shepherd.

"Here is a poor kind of city, lord," he grunted, "for aught but fleas. Can the man speak Tatar?"

It was soon apparent that the shepherd could not. But he showed a glimmer of understanding at the Uigur that Khlit spoke—a dialect much used by the traveling merchants of Central Asia and therefore widely known. The Cossack questioned him to the best of his ability and turned to Chagan.

"The rascal is slower of wit than of tongue, Chagan. He is a Dungan—a Chinese Mussulman—and he lives here because his father was here before him. Azim, as he calls himself, says that the main caravan track from China to Samarkand runs past here, a short distance out in the desert."

"What does he know of Talas?"

Khlit stroked the scabbard of his curved sword thoughtfully, his eyes on the swart face of Azim.

"He has heard the name of Talas. It lies a half-day's ride into the desert, away from the setting sun. He has sent men there before. They came, he says, for what is buried in Talas. And here they have stayed. What that is he does not know, or he will not tell."

"But Dongkor Gelong swore that it was at the end of the Tarim."

"Aye—and here Azim's words have a ring of truth. For he says that the Tarim formerly ran further into the desert. Our way lies along its river bed."

As the sun was still high, the two pressed on, leaving the shepherd staring at them stupidly over his *aul*. They found that Azim spoke the truth. They came upon a wide ravine in the sand-dunes where red sandstone cropped through the soil. Khlit chose a path along the bank of the river bed, wishing to see the nature of the country he entered.

The sun gleamed redly behind their backs when they came out upon a dune higher than the others, and Khlit pointed to the river bed. Chagan peered at it inquisitively. Here was in truth the end of the Tarim.

The smooth sand of the dry river bed formed an arena in the gully under them. A few tamarisks clung to the slope. But at the farther end of the arena a small stream of black water, which was all that remained of the Tarim, sank into the ground.

The sword-bearer was about to urge his horse down the slope into the basin when Khlit touched him on the arm.

The Cossack pointed to the sides of the arena. The sand-dunes here presented a strange appearance. Pillars of rock stood upright in the gullies; square blocks of sandstone were scattered about. Further on, walls of stone in the form of buildings were visible. But the structures had no roofs.

On the summit of the hillock at the end of the river was a mass of masonry that had once been a tower. Ruins, nearly hidden in the sand, stretched on every quarter. Khlit laughed softly to himself.

"Hey, what think you of the citadel of Talas, Chagan?"

The sword-bearer gaped at the ruins and muttered under his breath. Clearly there had once been a city of size and importance here. Now he saw only the wrecks of dwellings, unroofed and buried in the sand. Silence hung heavily over the place.

Khlit dismounted from his horse and inspected the nearest remnant of a house. To Chagan the sight of the place was unaccountable, bordering on the uncanny. The desolate city seemed to him ill-omened. But Khlit remembered that he had heard that the sands of the Taklamaklan had been advancing into the foot-hills of the mountains. The Cossack guessed shrewdly that the attack of the sand had driven the inhabitants from the place, perhaps several hundred years ago.

It was now clear to Khlit what Dongkor Gelong had meant. The lama had said there was a place where the sands of the Taklamaklan join the mountains. And where the river Tarim sank to its grave. They had come to the place.

But why had the Dalai Lama directed them here? Talas had been without inhabitants certainly for several generations. No living person was to be seen save the miserable shepherd Azim. Where was the Jallat Kum? The caravan path might run near them, but there was no caravanserai in the ruined city of Talas. No human being stirred along the sand-dunes except themselves.

Khlit had said to Chagan that Talas would solve the riddle of the Tsong Khapa's words. But here was a deeper riddle. Khlit shook his shaggy head moodily, watching one of the horses which was descending to the basin for the tamarisk foliage that it had sighted.

Chagan, too, eyed the horse. Suddenly both men stiffened alertly.

The animal had stepped out on the smooth, moist sand of the
arena. As it did so it gave a shrill scream of terror. The sound cut
the silence of the place sharply. Khlit swore.

The horse had sunk to its haunches in the sand. The surface of the
soil ebbed around the beast in a sinister fashion as the horse struggled to free itself. Half its trunk was now engulfed. Its head reared
frantically; then it sank down into the sand which closed over it
with a dull murmur. The surface of the basin was again level and
smooth.

Khlit whirled at the sound of a guttural laugh behind him. A
few paces away Azim sat on his bedraggled pony. The shepherd
pointed to the sand of the river bed grimly.

"Jallat Kum," he said.

V

If shadows are seen, there is danger if the owners of the shadows are
hidden. Aye, even though they come with open hands, for shadows have
no tongues with which to lie.

Khirghiz proverb.

Chagan yawned and stretched his limbs painfully. He pushed aside
his sheepskin robe and stood up, staring with bleared eyes at the rising sun which had wakened him and stamping circulation into his
booted legs. For the night on the Taklamaklan was cold.

The sword-bearer buckled his belt tight and looked around at the
ruins of Talas with disgust written large on his broad face. He
stiffened his muscles and shook his black tangle of hair like a dog.
He was not a tall man, but his shoulders were knitted to an ox's
neck, and his long arms were heavily thewed. Legs, bent to the shape
of a horse's barrel, supported an erect and massive trunk. Men who
had glanced only at his height and sleepy, pock-marked face had
learned to their cost that the sword-bearer's strength lay in muscles
invisible to the eye and in an inexorable, destructive energy when
aroused.

Chagan gave vent to his disgust to Khlit when he had prepared
some of the *arkhan* meat over a fire of tamarisk roots and added some

water from a goatskin purchased from Azim to their scanty stock of kumiss.

"An ill place to water at—this," he growled. "The Jallat Kum of the Tarim river bed swallows a horse as Azim would gulp a milk curd. Ha! Azim stayed not when the stars came out. He likes not the ruins. By signs he made plain to me that it is an unholy spot, which the caravans avoid. Twice in the night I heard wailing and sighing as if the desert spirits that hamstring straying travelers were about us. By the head of Ghenghis Khan, I like it not."

Khlit finished the last of the meat and drank his share of the mare's milk calmly. Then he leaned back on the sand and scrutinized Chagan.

"How long, dog, have you been a breeder of lies? Am I a whispering maiden to be beguiled by words such as these? Not so. You have a thought, Chagan, in your thick head. You are trying to paint the thought in another guise. Why were you in a hurry to reach Talas? And now you talk of going hence."

Chagan juggled the kumiss flask sullenly.

"Last night," he repeated, "I wakened and heard a voice like that of a woman crying—crying and then singing. It was not far away. This is a cursed spot, for there is no woman here."

"I heard it not." Khlit took a twig from the fire and idly traced figures in the sand. "Harken, Chagan, I am neither magician nor oracle, but I will unravel the meaning of a riddle. It is a riddle of the master of Lhassa, who is monarch of many khans and squadrons of cavalry. Why did he send the message by Dongkor Gelong that I should come here?"

Chagan started to speak; then he thought better of it. Khlit studied his tracings in the sand idly.

"When a hunter seeks one wolf from the pack, he does not follow the pack. He sets a bait, and, when the wolf comes, he can then slay it. The master of Lhassa is crafty; he has the wisdom of many *shamans*. Yet it is hard to hide the bait that covers the snare. Harken, Chagan. The Jun-gar are a power on the steppe, midway between the Kallmarks and the Chinese. The Khirghiz are their own masters, yet they are not hostile to the Dalai Lama. From the Kha Khans before me, tribute in sheep, horses and cloths was sent to Lhassa. I have not sent it. When this was known, the Dalai Lama persuaded the Khirghiz to cross our frontiers for plunder."

Chagan nodded. Most of this he had known.

"The clergy of the Yellow Hat," went on the Cossack slowly, "are actual rulers of Kashgaria, which reaches as far north as the Thian Shan, and in Tibet to the south of the Taklamaklan. Also of portions of China by the headwaters of the Yang-tze River. To the northwest of Kashgaria and the northeast of the Yang-tze the Tsong Khapa, I have heard, has pulled his magician's veil over the Khan of the Kallmarks, and the Emperor of the Chinese. They believe he is the envoy of the gods upon earth. Such is the blindness even of a ruler of millions."

Khlit stuck his twig upright in the center of the figures he had been tracing.

"In the heart of the Tatar steppe between the Kallmarks and China is the land of the bowmen, the Jun-gar. Like an eagle flying above the mountains, the Dalai Lama has marked Jungaria for his priests. Already the khans of the *kurultai* council are overawed by his magician's tricks and the wiles of the *shamans*."

"But you are his enemy, lord," objected Chagan bluntly.

"Aye, for he sent the Khirghiz against us when the tribute stopped. Now the Dalai Lama has marked me as one who must be removed. The enmity of priests is more dangerous than the sting of a serpent. And I will not be a tribute-payer of Lhassa. We can not make this a war, Chagan, for the Jun-gar will not take up arms against the Dalai Lama; and, if we did, the Khirghiz and Kallmarks together have thrice our number of horsemen."

"They are crafty fighters," grunted Chagan. "Yet, they are not slaves to do the will of the master of Lhassa——"

"Nay; that is truth. But they have the taste of our lands and herds in their mouth. While the plundering is good, they will invade our boundaries. The Jun-gar are too far from Lhassa to enjoy the care of the Dalai Lama, yet he desires their lands for the Khirghiz and for himself. So he sent Dongkor Gelong with all his mummery to fetch me and those that I trusted here to the desert. Why? He would remove the horns from the cattle he wishes to slaughter."

Khlit stood up and stretched himself.

"Aye, there is the veil of words that covered the trap. Chagan, I smell treachery. Long have I smelled danger; the wind whispers tidings of evil. Ha! We have come to the trap, you and I."

"Khlit, lord," said Chagan slowly, "I smelled the trap in the camp on the steppe. Likewise, when I bridled the horses, I heard the two Chubil Khans speaking together within a tent close by. They planned to set out in the night for the Thian Shan, to bear word of your departure to the Kashgar lamasery."

"And still you came with me? Nay, you are one without brains."

"I came, lord," Chagan straightened with rough dignity, "to bring the horses, that we might arrive here before the men of the Tsong Khapa expect us. Thus you might see the jaws of the trap before it was ready. Now you can ride back to the Thian Shan safely. There is no time to be lost. And there is nothing here that can fulfil the Dalai Lama's promise. Hasten; there is no time to be lost."

Khlit's mustache twitched in a hard smile.

"It is true that you are a fool, Chagan. Where am I to go? Back to the Jun-gar? Matters would be no better. And where else? Here we stay, Chagan, you and I, until we see what manner of thing the Yellow Hats have prepared for us."

Chagan swore blackly.

"Death is brewing for us here, lord. We will fare no better than the cursed horse that walked into the Jallat Kum."

"I will stay," repeated Khlit. "But you can choose a horse and go."

Something like fear flashed into the stolid face of the sword-bearer.

"Nay, lord," he cried anxiously. "I have ridden at your horse's tail in battle and hunt. I have eaten meat and salt with you. I have slept beside you and gained honor thereby. We two are one."

"So be it, then," said Khlit, turning away.

Chagan left him to his thoughts and sought out the horses. These he looked over carefully, picketing them so they would not wander on the quicksand and cutting some foliage for fodder. He then inspected their horn horseshoes and made sure that the saddles had not suffered from the hard riding of the last six days. He gave them a little water from the goatskin and departed in search of a possible spring in the ruins. For the stagnant pool in the river bed was well out on the quicksand beyond reach.

After a moment of this, Chagan paused and scratched his head. He had come upon a series of tracks in the sand, made by horses shod differently from his own. He followed out the winding trails and presently compared the marks with those of Azim's mount. They were the same.

It occurred to Chagan that the shepherd might have returned in the night. But the other had professed to be afraid of the ruins after sundown. Further inspection convinced the Tatar that the tracks were a day or two old. Azim, then, had been here before, not once but frequently in spite of his talk of evil spirits.

Tracing out the course of the tracks, Chagan found that they led to the mound of sand which rose at the end of the Tarim basin behind the place where the river had once sunk into the earth. This mound, Chagan noted, was different in shape from most of the sand-dunes. It was round instead of wave-shape, and it was a good sixty feet in height. Buttresses of stone projected through the sand at points.

Chagan made the half-circle of the place. Abruptly he halted, and his jaw dropped. The sound of singing came to his ears, faint but distinct. To his fancy, it was a woman's voice. And it seemed to issue from the mound of sand.

VI

The hair had not descended to its normal position on the back of Chagan's head when Khlit joined him. The Cossack had heard the voice. The two men gazed at the mound curiously.

"Said I not the place was rife with evil spirits?" growled the sword-bearer. "That is the song I heard in the night."

The voice dwindled and was silent. Khlit inspected the stone ruins which showed through the sand. Then he motioned to Chagan.

"Here is no sand-dune," he growled. "The sand has covered up a building, and one of size. Some parts of the walls show through the sand. If we look we will find a woman in the ruins."

"Nay, then she must eat rock and drink from the Jallat Kum," protested the Tatar. "If there was a house here, even a palace, the sand has filled it up——"

Nevertheless he followed Khlit as the Cossack climbed over the débris of rock that littered the sides of the mound. They went as far as they could, stopping at the edge of the basin which the mound adjoined. There was no sign of a person among the remnants of walls. But Khlit pointed to the tower on the summit of the mound.

Chagan objected that there were no footsteps to be seen leading to the ruined tower. Khlit, however, solved this difficulty by scrambling up the slope. The shifting sand, dislodged by his progress, fell into place again behind him, erasing all mark of his footsteps. He vanished into the pile of masonry. Presently he reappeared and directed Chagan to bind together a torch of dead tamarisk branches and to light it at their fire.

When the sword-bearer had done this, Khlit assisted him to the summit of the hillock. There he pointed to the stone tower. Its walls had crumbled into piles of stones, projecting from the sand no more than the height of a man, but in the center of the walls a black opening led downward.

Steps were visible through the aperture. Khlit took the torch and descended into the opening, followed by Chagan. The stairs had originally led to the tower summit, for they curved downward along the walls. As they climbed down, sand sifted in from occasional embrasures in the walls. Chagan guessed that they had descended to about the level of the desert plain without when the steps terminated in a pile of sand.

Throwing the light of the torch around them, Khlit saw that they were in a square chamber somewhat larger than the diameter of the tower. At one side a door showed, dark in the flickering light from the burning branches.

Through this doorway Khlit went, stooping under the lintel, for the sand had piled itself a foot or so on what must have been the flooring of the building. As they stood up in the chamber beyond the door, both halted in surprise.

A candle lighted the place—a small room with stone walls, the floor cleared of sand and carpeted with rugs. Some Turkish cushions were piled in one corner, and on the cushions a girl was seated. She was unveiled and the candle glinted on her startled face, delicate and olive-hued.

She was dressed in a dainty, fur-tipped *khalat* and baggy trousers of nankeen. She had the very slender figure of a dancer, with the customary veil penning her black hair behind turquoise ear-rings. What held the eyes of the two men was her face, fair for middle Asia, small-mouthed and proud. Not since he had left Persia had Khlit seen a woman of such loveliness; moreover, the girl stirred his interest, for she had the garb and henna-hued countenance of a dancer—yet there was authority in the erect carriage of her small head and in her quick movements.

Chagan sniffed at the elusive scent that filled the room, a faint odor of dried rose leaves tinged with musk.

"By the winged horse of Kaidu!" he swore. "If this be truly a woman and not a spirit, it is no wonder that Azim's horse left tracks around this place."

The girl frowned at his words, as if trying to grasp their meaning. She rose quickly to her feet with the gliding motion of the trained dancer. Her breath rose and fell tumultuously under the *khalat* with her startled breathing. Her brown eyes were wide and alert. Still the look she cast them was not so much fear as curiosity. Khlit, seeing that she did not understand the Tatar of Chagan, spoke to her in Uigur.

"How came you here, little sparrow?" he asked gruffly. "And what is this place?"

She held out her hand appealingly.

"Have you water, Khan? I have had no water for a day and a night, nor food."

For the first time Khlit noted that her olive cheeks were pinched and there were dark circles in the paint under her eyes. He took the flask of watered kumiss from the sword-bearer's belt and gave it to her. She caught it to her lips eagerly; then, remembering, she drank a swallow slowly, repeating the name of Allah after the fashion of Islam.

"The gully jackal who bears the name of Azim has not come, as he is wont, to bring me water and rice for the last day," she said angrily. "For that I will pull many hairs from his beard when he comes."

Khlit scanned her idly. He had little liking for women who were soft and quarrelsome. Yet this one spoke as if she was accustomed to give orders. By her speech he guessed her from the region of Samarkand.

"How can Azim pay such a handsome harlot?" Chagan growled, for his mind admitted of but one idea at a time.

The girl caught something of his meaning. Her slender hands clenched, and she stepped close to Khlit until her perfumed veil touched his mustache.

"What says the one without breeding? Eh, have I the manner of a slave? Azim is a dog who does my bidding. Since I came here, escaped from a caravan upon a camel, he has tended to my wants, thinking to sell me for a good price."

Khlit motioned around the chamber.

"Why did you come here?"

She scrutinized him, head on one side, with the bright curiosity of a bird.

"My name is Sheillil," she made answer, "and I am the dancer of Samarkand. There is a fat merchant of Kashgar who thought that he had bought me for five times a hundred gold shekels. Nay, men are fools. I left the caravan during a sandstorm and came where I knew none would follow. The camel stepped upon the Jallat Kum and is not. But Azim came and showed me this place."

Khlit said a word to Chagan, who left the tower and presently returned, grumbling, with a handful of meat he had warmed at the fire and dried milk curds. These the Cossack gave to the girl, for he saw that she was weak with hunger. When she had finished, he took up the candle, which was a large one and of good yellow wax. Sheillil took his hand and led him through a further door, into what seemed a hall of considerable size.

"Azim has fewer wits than a camel," she commented, "but he has heard the tale of this place from his father, who heard it from his father. It is a place of strange gods. Look!"

She pointed to the walls of the chamber. Khlit saw carved wooden columns with faded paintings on the walls between them. A balcony ran around the chamber, and there was a dais of jade at one end, as if the statue of a god had been removed from it. He saw why the place had not been filled by the sand which had risen over its roof.

Evidently the structure had been a temple, built to endure. For the walls were massive blocks of stone, and the embrasures were small. Under each opening was a waist-high pile of sand which had filtered through. A coating of sand covered the floor. Several carved ebony benches stood by the walls in a litter of rugs, bronze candlesticks and candles of the kind that Sheillil had appropriated.

"It is the temple of Talas," whispered the girl, a little awed by the gloom of the empty chamber. "When the sands drove the people from Talas, the other houses crumbled, but this was strongly made, being the home of a god, and it stood. For a while men came to plunder, and many of them were lost in the Jallat Kum. Now it is forgotten. There are other rooms. But the god has been taken away."

Abruptly she ceased speaking. Khlit and Chagan whirled involuntarily. The silence of the temple was disturbed by a muttering sound.

It stole in through the stone walls, echoing in the vaulted space. It was a sound that stirred their blood, vast, grumbling with a thunder-like note.

Sheillil looked from one to the other, her eyes mischievously alight.

"Eh, that is a rare music," pointing to the tower entrance; "it is the voice of the Jallat Kum when the sands are moving. Azim calls it the singing sand."

She touched Khlit lightly on the arm.

"Send your man up the tower. I would speak with you."

VII

Sheillil disposed herself comfortably on the cushions in the ante-chamber of the temple, with a catlike daintiness. Leaning on one slim arm, her eyes sought the Cossack's from under long lashes. He was conscious of the delicate perfume that came from the dancer's garments, of the scent of rose and aloes in her hair. He seated himself cross-legged on the stones, a little distance from her.

"I wonder," she began slowly, "how many daughters of khans have come to this temple, leaving their slippers outside, and prayed with rich offerings before the god who is no longer here? Yet behold, I am here, a woman of Islam, and you a *caphar*."

Khlit returned her gaze indifferently. He had seen many women and all were fond of talking. Sheillil puzzled him slightly, for she went unveiled and seemed without fear. He judged that she had been much with men, bought and sold in many bazaars. Still she could not be more than seventeen.

"It is written," she pursued, "that with Allah are the keys of the unseen. Can you read the future, Khlit, Khan——"

"The devil!" Khlit stared at her. "How knew you my name?"

Sheillil propped her chin on her two hands and smiled.

"I know many things, Khlit, Khan. Messages travel quickly across the steppe to the mountains where my home was. Nay, you wear the curved saber of Kaidu. Once you were in Samarkand. I have been there also, and men talk freely to me, for I am lovely as the dawn in the hill gardens of Kabul. Their blood is warmed as with wine when they look at me."

The Cossack felt that the girl was trying to catch his glance. He lit his pipe and smoked silently.

"In Kashgar," continued Sheillil, disappointed, "I heard it said that the horsemen of the Khirghiz were at war with the Tatars of the Jun-gar. Is that the truth?"

"The Khirghiz bands invaded our boundaries. They will come again with Summer. Why do you ask, little sparrow?"

"Because I would know, fool!" Sheillil's delicate brows met in a frown. "There is much talk in Kashgar among the clergy of the Yellow Hat and their followers, the Usbeks. They say the strength of the Jun-gar is gone, and that their lands will be spoil for the first comer before the next snow."

"In the cities," Khlit responded calmly, "men say what it pleases them to hear."

"Then it is true?" Sheillil waited for a response and, receiving none, rattled the bracelets on her round arms angrily. "The Khirghiz clans will take what land they need. I know, for I was born among them. My father was a khan. You are truly one without wit. I had the thought that the owner of the sword of Kaidu would be a wise man. Why are you not with the Jun-gar?"

Khlit's gray eyes peered at the girl from under shaggy brows, and her lips parted at the somber fire she beheld there.

"It was the word of the Dalai Lama that I could find aid here for the Jun-gar," he said. "So I have come to learn the meaning of the message. Truly it is a strange place——"

Sheillil threw back her dark head with a peal of shrill laughter. She lay back on the cushions and laughed, rocking her slender form in joyous mirth. Khlit regarded her impassively.

"A wise khan," she cried, "a true shepherd of his flock! Nay, tell me. What aid do you find here? A ruined city and a flea-ridden Azim. What think you now of the word of the Tsong Khapa?"

"I think," responded Khlit slowly, "that I may hear from the Dalai Lama at this spot."

Sheillil sat up, wiping the tears from her eyes.

"Truly," she responded, "you are a man of the steppe. It is not the way of the hillmen to wait for what is to come. Life is too short for that, and Allah has favor for the bold in heart."

A step sounded behind them, and Chagan made his appearance.

"Azim is without," he motioned up the steps. "He has come with two men from a passing caravan. One, who is a merchant, says that he may buy the girl Sheillil if she is fair."

The girl tossed her head proudly.

"Am I one to be sold by a shepherd? Nay, tell them to begone."

Khlit left the dancer in the chamber to ascend the tower with Chagan. He found the Dungan shepherd with two others, mounted and of important bearing. They had met Azim, they said, at the near-by watering-place on the caravan track, and the man had said he had a Uigur girl of beauty for sale.

Azim disappeared into the tower steps and presently returned, cursing and hauling at the girl, who was resisting vigorously. Sheillil had drawn her veil across her face, and, as they stumbled down the sand slope, she tore herself free from Azim and ran to Khlit.

"I am the daughter of a khan," she panted, "and women of my blood may not be bought and sold. Such is the law. Slay this scoundrel for me and bid the others go."

"Nay—it is not my affair," said Khlit shortly.

The merchants had reined their horses up to the girl, and, as she spoke, Azim seized her again, tearing the veil from her face. To Khlit's surprise she flushed crimson with shame and turned from the strangers. Chagan grinned at the sight. One of the merchants, a stout Dungan, leaned down and tried to draw the *khalat* from the shoulders of the struggling girl.

Sheillil, who was weeping with rage, twisted in Azim's grasp. Suddenly she freed one arm and snatched at the sword that hung from Chagan's belt. So quickly had she acted that the Tatar had no chance to prevent her. The weapon was a heavy one, made for Chagan's great strength, and the girl could barely lift it. At sight of the gleaming blade, however, Azim jumped nimbly back.

"Dolt!" cried Sheillil furiously. "Dirt, of a jackal's begetting! Am I one to be sold by your breed?"

"She is not ugly," said the Dungan merchant with a grin. "We will take her."

At a sign from Khlit, Chagan stepped forward and deftly took the sword from the unsuspecting girl. The Cossack eyed Sheillil doubtfully and caught the reproachful glance she threw at Chagan. A dancing woman of the bazaars she might be, but she had the manner of a girl of noble blood. It was no business of his whether Azim disposed of her to the merchants.

"She is worth much," put in Azim craftily. "And she can dance."

The girl faced the merchants proudly, her slender figure tense and her cheeks flushed. Khlit stepped forward between her and the others.

"Nay," he said gruffly. "She is not a slave. She comes from the hills, and she has the blood of a khan." He wheeled on Azim. "Are you her master?"

The shepherd muttered that he was free to do with the girl as he chose. The merchants glanced at each other. Sheillil was a beauty and would fetch a high price at one of the city bazaars. She was worth taking.

"Azim," said Khlit grimly, "when you have fought a battle and taken captives it will be time to speak of slaves. This woman has sought refuge here. She is not to be sold——"

"The caravan is moving on," broke in the Dungan merchant. "We have no time to haggle. The three of you can divide the money. Here; we can not wait——"

He fumbled in the money bag at his belt. The other merchant moved nearer to the girl, who stood close beside Chagan, watching all that went on eagerly. At a signal from the Dungan, the man spurred his horse forward, hoping to ride down the Tatar.

Chagan, however, was not to be caught unawares. The merchant had whipped out his sword, and, as Chagan sprang aside, he slashed at him. The sword-bearer warded the blow easily. The return sweep of his weapon caught the rider in the side. The man swayed and slid from his saddle to the sand.

The Tatar turned toward the Dungan. But the latter, with a startled glance at his fallen companion, wheeled his horse away. He hesitated for a moment, then he rode through the dunes in the direction he had come. The girl clapped her hands in delight.

"That was a good blow," she cried. "See, the man is cut half-way through!"

A glance told Chagan that she spoke the truth. Picking up the dying man by the belt the sword-bearer lugged him around the mound to the slope of the Jallat Kum. Khlit, who had followed, saw the Tatar toss the body down the slope. It rolled upon the damp sands, and in a moment was gone.

"Evil comes of such women, lord," muttered Chagan with a shake of the head. "Harken. You have said that the Tsong Khapa has laid a trap for us. The trap is rarely baited. How else comes the dancing girl here? She is no common slave escaped from a caravan."

Khlit made no response to this. He returned to the spot where they had left Azim, intending to question the shepherd. But Azim had vanished.

VIII

Late that afternoon Khlit sat with Sheillil on the summit of the temple mound, from which he had a good view of the ruins of Talas. The girl was humming softly to herself, cross-legged in the sand. Khlit, engrossed in his own thoughts, paid little attention to her.

Azim had not reappeared, and Chagan, making a cast into the desert, had learned that the caravan had gone on its way. The silence of the ruins irked Khlit, who had little liking for cities, living or dead. So far there had been no signs of envoys of the Dalai Lama. But Khlit reasoned shrewdly that they would seek him out, once they were aware that he had arrived. What did they want with him? What were the plans of the Tsong Khapa?

Khlit did not bother himself about what would happen at Talas. It was his policy when dealing with enemies more powerful than himself to enter their ranks, whatever the danger might be. A single man, he reasoned, was useless fighting against an overpowering force. But in the stronghold of his enemies that man might accomplish much. To learn the plans of his foe and to defeat them from within by a stroke of the coldest daring was possible only to one of Khlit's craft, and in a country where an alliance of tribes might be broken up in a night, or two chieftains come to blows over a word.

But in following his usual scheme of attack, Khlit now faced two considerable obstacles. He could not count on the aid of his own followers, who were under the influence for the time being of the Dalai Lama and were held at home by the fear of the coming Khirghiz invasion. And in pitting his strength against the master of Lhassa, Khlit knew that he was meeting a foeman of extraordinary keenness, whose intentions were a secret to him.

It was a desperate venture. Khlit had only two advantages in his lone struggle for the life of the Jun-gar. The clergy of Tibet, informed by Dongkor Gelong, would doubtless underestimate his own ability, as other enemies had done to their cost, aided by his simulation of blunt thickheadedness. And he was dealing with two enemies instead of one.

He glanced carelessly at the girl, who crooned to herself well-pleased with the event of the morning. Who was she? What was her mission in Talas? What master did she serve?

Sheillil yawned prettily and stretched herself.

"You are not good company, Khan," she said idly. "Go below with the big Tatar and sleep. I will watch if any come."

Khlit presently followed her advice. He found Chagan snoring on his back on the rugs of the anteroom. The Cossack had not intended to sleep, but he found that his head dropped on his shoulders. He had slept but a few hours of the last week, and the girl's singing soothed him. His mind drifted away, and Chagan's snores dwindled to silence.

He woke almost at once. Sheillil's song had stopped. He heard muffled voices, and presently a step sounded on the stairs. Khlit became wide-awake on the instant. There was not one step but several. He had only time to kick Chagan to consciousness when the light from the narrow doorway was blotted out.

Sheillil entered, and after her came a half-dozen men in a motley dress ranging from the sheepskin coat of the plainsman to the black hat and long robe of a Dungan spearman. The group parted, and a man wearing a familiar garb of orange and black stepped forward. It was one of the Chubil Khans who had attended Dongkor Gelong.

"See, O man of the Yellow Hat," cried Sheillil gleefully, "here be the two Tatars who came here yesterday taken drowsing like sheep in an *aul*. Take heed of the broad-shouldered one. He wields a sword like one possessed of Erlik."

Chagan, who had sprung to his feet, clutched at his weapon. But Khlit motioned him back. The tower without was filled with armed men. The Chubil Khan had come well escorted. Still, men seldom traveled alone in those days of ever-present danger.

"What seek you with me?" Khlit asked bluffly.

Sheillil made a deep and mocking salaam, hands outstretched over her dark head, forgetful or heedless of the fact that she had promised to warn the Tatars of the coming of strangers.

"It is a messenger, O Khlit, from one who is wiser than you, to command your attendance——"

"At the Kashgar lamasery, Kha Khan," put in the Chubil Khan, a crafty gleam in his narrow eyes. "The almighty Tsong Khapa, whom

Heaven has honored by divine reincarnation, has further tidings for you."

"I will hear them," said Khlit calmly. "But I did not know the Dalai Lama was at Kashgar."

The Chubil Khan spread both arms outward.

"I am but a lesser servant of the Tsong Khapa, Khan Tuvron; the Tsong Khapa is, like the light of the sun, everywhere among his people; yet none but the higher priesthood see his face—never strangers."

There was a bustle in the group of men, and the tattered figure of Azim pushed forward, falling on his knees before Tuvron. He clasped the bandaged feet of the envoy, speaking, to Khlit's surprise, the tongue of the lamas.

"O mighty Chubil Khan, do not forget your servant Azim, who tends the empty shrine of Talas and who sent you word by way of the Dungan caravan of the coming of the Tatars. I ask humbly but a single ray of light from the radiance of the beneficent Tsong Khapa —only a very tiny reward. Give your servant Azim the dancing girl Sheillil, who wandered here, for my comfort and enjoyment. Then, when I am through with her, she can be sold for a good price——"

Tuvron stared at the girl in surprise. Sheillil drew close to him and whispered. The man's expression changed, and he would have spoken. But the girl checked him. She placed her slippered foot on Azim's neck, pressing his head to the floor, and laughed delightedly.

"Your comfort, Azim!" she mocked. "Little comfort would Sheillil of Samarkand be to you. It is in my mind to throw you to the Jallat Kum, but one needs you who has use for even such a low-born thing as you. Pray to your departed god to bring you a mate—from the cattle herd."

With that she turned and ran up the tower steps. When Khlit and Chagan mounted camels and set out in the midst of the Tibetans, Sheillil rode ahead on Tuvron's white camel, which she had chosen for herself, singing to herself as she guided them to the caravan track that led to Kashgar, a two-days' journey to the west.

IX

There are many gods in the world, but no man shall have two gods lest evil come to his household.

Khirghiz saying.

A knock sounded on the heavy door of Chu'n Yuen, armorer of Kashgar. The proprietor rose, took up a lantern, and sought the door, his pot belly shaking under the silken curtain of its costly robe. Chu'n Yuen wore the black skull-cap of a Dungan. Otherwise his face and dress were those of a Chinaman, blessed with vast flesh and full years of prosperity.

Chu'n Yuen opened a narrow panel in the door at the height of his eyes and peered out cautiously. Only by consummate shrewdness had the Chinaman, who sold to the mountaineers arms brought from Damascus and Persia by caravan, been able to keep his wrinkled head whole on his plump body. By shrewdness and the fact that as a Dungan he was allied to none of the warring clans of Central Asia.

The armorer scrutinized the person who had knocked, through slant eyes. He had learned to discriminate carefully between the thin, bearded and turbaned face of an Usbek of Kashgar and the hard, round countenance, with the small, black eyes and drooping mustache, of a Khirghiz hillman. For the Usbek was keen to cheat him of his wares, while the Khirghiz would pay generously on one occasion and lay waste his shop on another.

But Chu'n Yuen saw the slender form of a veiled woman and opened the barred door readily. His visitor stepped inside with a quick flash of brown eyes around the shop and the curtained door beyond it. Chu'n Yuen barred the door again and set down the lantern with a silent chuckle. If a woman came alone to his shop at night, it could be but for one purpose. Indeed, as if reading his thoughts, she walked with a light, swaying step to the curtains and slipped into the inner chamber where the Chinaman was wont to dispense wine to those who desired.

His visitor quite clearly did not wish wine. She surveyed the greasy benches, the dingy couches and the wine casks with something like contempt. The shop was empty, save for two camel-drivers too drunk to sit upright. Chu'n Yuen stepped forward and inclined his massive shoulders politely.

"Here is a soft nest for those who seek good living," he murmured. "I am a kind master and the hillmen who come here pay well, especially for a dancer who is light on her feet——"

"For a woman who has danced in the palaces of Samarkand before the sultans?" The girl's voice sounded musically with a hint of laughter. "Nay, this does not look like a palace and you, Chu'n Yuen, have the face of one whose soul is rolled in fat."

The brown eyes flashed at the owner of the shop quizzically, and Chu'n Yuen drew his breath quickly, for he was not used to mockery from a woman.

"If you can dance, Strumpet-tongue, I will see that the great Khirghiz chieftains come to see it—although when they were last here they carried off my Turkish pistols without a silver coin in payment."

He grasped her hand, and made as if to pull off the veil. The girl slipped away deftly.

"Ho, you will need taming, I see. But you will not leave as easily as you entered yonder door."

His visitor seemed not to be listening.

"The Khirghiz are here—Iskander Khan and Bassanghor Khan? Are many Khirghiz with them? Or Kallmarks?"

"They came with a small following—a hundred hillmen. There are to be horse races and games, by request of the lamas, I have heard," said the Chinaman in surprise. "Still, that is no concern for your pretty head. Perhaps you want me to pay you silver, as a sign of good faith. If I could see your face——"

Again the girl avoided his clutch at the veil. Chu'n Yuen's pig eyes narrowed ominously. It had been in his mind to deal gently with the mysterious woman who came unmasked to his shop. Her figure suggested beauty, which was more than the women had who were brought here by Khirghiz or Tibetan raiding parties to be inmates of the vendor's shop. But if she flouted him, Chu'n Yuen was prepared to whip her into submission, for she would mean many shekels for him.

"Fool," said the girl mockingly, "and half-caste thief of a race without honor! What will the mollahs of Islam say when they hear that you traffic in wine! Have you forgotten the Koran?"

In spite of himself Chu'n Yuen gave back a step and lifted his fat hand as if to ward off a blow.

"There is no word in the Koran against selling wine," he responded sullenly, "and there is no mollah in Kashgar."

"Fool! To sell your honor for the gold of unbelievers. Dirt for each passer-by to spit upon, if he pays! Is there no word in the Koran against that——"

With a cry half of fear, half of rage, the shopkeeper lifted his fist to strike the girl. Quickly she thrust her arm in front of his scowling face. A gold bangle, glittering on her wrist, caught his eye. His hand fell to his side and his jaw dropped.

"A sign of the true faith!" he muttered. "Upon a woman's bracelet. Nay, I have heard—I meant no harm to a follower of Islam. But you came here alone and at night, honorable lady——"

"Oh, it is honorable lady now," she gibed. "How quickly your tongue twists! Nay, remember to treat Sheillil of Samarkand with courtesy. Or there are those who will stick a dagger between your fat ribs, Chu'n Yuen. Now take heed and tell me what I wish to know. Iskander Khan is here?"

Chu'n Yuen stared at the gold bracelet as if fascinated.

"He is here with his followers—whom may Allah curse with a lasting blight—in the caravanserai without the walls. Already there have been brawls between the Khirghiz hillmen and the Usbek people of the town. *Mo fi kalbi hir'allah*—there is nothing save Allah in my heart, honorable lady."

"Then," said Sheillil coolly, "Iskander Khan will rejoice to know there is a wine-bartering Mussulman here who has a goodly store of weapons. This shop will make rare picking for his hillmen, and Iskander Khan, they say, has turned his face more to Lhassa than to Mecca."

"May Allah—" Chu'n Yuen began and choked.

Verily this woman was a fiend incarnate! Sheillil read the blind fear in his quivering, fat face and judged it would not be wise to anger the shopkeeper too greatly, or he might kill her.

"Yet it may be, Chu'n Yuen," she added gravely, "that I shall whisper to Dongkor Gelong, who is head of the lamasery here, that he has a worthy servant, an armorer and a wine-dealer, who is a man of parts and may be relied on in need. Eh, what say you to that?

The star of the Dalai Lama is rising in Kashgaria and, as you know, the half-moon of Mecca is low on the horizon."

The Chinaman's eyes flickered shrewdly. The name of Dongkor Gelong was one to conjure with in Kashgar.

"For two days and nights," he whispered, with a glance around the room, "the Yellow Hats, whose ways are baneful as the coming of the star of ill-omen, have been passing into the city gates in numbers. They are not to be seen in the streets, for they have gone to the lamasery. And it is not the custom for Dongkor Gelong the all-powerful to celebrate games."

Sheillil watched the shopkeeper through half-closed eyes, a gaze which he tried to meet and could not.

"Eh, you are clever, O Mandarin," smiled the girl, and Chu'n Yuen held his head higher. "You have the eye of a steppe fox. We shall be friends, you and I. Is Dongkor Gelong in the town?"

"Alas, that can not be known. He goes and comes like a shadow."

"How many of the Yellow Hats are within the walls?"

"Very many. The Chubil Khans are assembling with the higher lamas. Of their followers perhaps a thousand are here—besides the Usbeks who are of their faith. They are waiting for the games, which will be the day after tomorrow."

"Aye, they are waiting," said Sheillil, half to herself. "Harken, Chu'n Yuen, give wine freely to the hillmen when they come. And say nothing to the Yellow Hats concerning my visit. I shall have need of you later—and you will be paid thrice over."

Chu'n Yuen bowed profoundly. Sheillil guessed shrewdly that he would obey the first part of her instructions, but would not still his wagging tongue concerning her. Which was what she wished. She slipped through the curtains and had unbarred the outer door before the Chinaman realized she was gone.

X

In his cell in the lamasery Dongkor Gelong sat beside a plain wooden table. It was a bare room, fitted with pallet, stools and a few books on the table, for, although Dongkor Gelong wore the high hat and ornate robe of a Chutuktu Lama, it was his pride to live simply and unostentatiously as when he was a monk.

A candle on the table cast its glint on the prominent forehead of the Tibetan, under which gleamed dark eyes in a white face—the face of an ascetic and a fanatic. He looked up as the door opened and Tuvron Khan entered with a bow. On a sign from his superior the Chubil Khan ushered in Khlit with an attendant of the lamasery and took his stand by the door.

The Cossack declined Dongkor Gelong's courteous offer of a seat and faced the lama across the table. For a long moment the two men studied each other, Dongkor Gelong's long, dark countenance wearing a slight smile, Khlit's lined face impassive.

"I think, O Kha Khan," began the lama slowly, "that I can read your thoughts. You are thinking that you have been tricked—brought here among enemies, because you obeyed the instructions of the Tsong Khapa. Yet it is not so. You see you are an honored guest. You still have your sword, which I have heard is one to be prized above many. And it is not the fault of the master of Lhassa that you are alone. He urged that you bring your followers."

Dongkor Gelong paused as if to hear what the Cossack would answer. But Khlit was silent.

"And you are wondering, perhaps, why the Dalai Lama should send a man of rank like yourself to such a place as Talas. It was no trickery. Nay, it had been our intention to welcome you fittingly at the spot but you traveled with such speed that you were there before us. It was not well to let the news get abroad on the steppe that you had come to Kashgar. So much the Dalai Lama in his wisdom foresaw. And he is ready to make good the words of the oracle."

"The wisdom of the Dalai Lama is beyond my understanding," returned Khlit calmly.

Dongkor Gelong bowed assent, although his eyes swept the Cossack's face keenly.

"It is well-spoken, O Kha Khan. You are not a fool like some of those from the steppe. Harken to the plan of the master of Lhassa. There are enemies you fear, who are planning to invade the lands of the Jun-gar. They are the Khirghiz, who are under the leadership of two khans, Iskander and Bassanghor. Both are formidable men in their way and, being of the hills, are independent of all authority, even that of the Tsong Khapa."

"Aye," said Khlit briefly.

Once again the Chutuktu Lama studied him and nodded as if satisfied.

"Iskander Khan and Bassanghor Khan are here in Kashgar," he went on slowly. "Without those two the Khirghiz are like a body without a head. They are the ones who planned the war against you. And the Tsong Khapa has noted with grief the injuries inflicted on you. We have made, the ones of the Yellow Hat, an opportunity for you to strike at them, swiftly and fatally, and to escape unharmed."

"To kill them?"

"Aye, both. It is for that we have brought you here. Harken, Kha Khan. We have given out the word that there will be games on the Kashgar plain in two days. The matter is easily disposed of. Both khans are reckless, and they are proud of their horsemanship. A dancer, one of the beauties of Samarkand, has come here at our bidding. A favorite game of the Khirghiz is called the Love Chase—a sport where a woman is set loose on a horse among several riders on a plain and falls to the possession of the one who can first secure her. Nay, you can see——"

"Chagan and I," Khlit broke in, "are among the riders. In the confusion of horsemen we could strike down the khans, saying afterward that it was a brawl. That is what you plan. But afterward——"

"The Khirghiz are few. My followers are numerous; they will surround you and Chagan before the Khirghiz understand what has happened, and you will be safe in the lamasery. Also, the Khirghiz have never seen you. They will not look for you here."

Khlit nodded.

"We will be escorted safely back to the Jun-gar boundary?"

Dongkor Gelong smiled and waved his hand amiably.

"Such is the will of the all-wise Tsong Khapa. There are other leaders of the Khirghiz who can be dealt with as they ride back to the Thian Shan passes. The pick of the hill chieftains are here in Kashgar. Unless I am mistaken, few will survive to carry on the war against the Jun-gar. And the Tsong Khapa will give you further aid through the Yellow Hats—when, of course, you show your gratitude for his help by continuing the tribute that the Jun-gar owes to Lhassa."

"And the Khirghiz?"

"The death of their leaders, who are overbearing ruffians without good-will or understanding, will strengthen the tie of the Yellow Hats to their lands. I speak bluntly, for I see you like short and truthful phrases."

"Aye, it is ill to lie, among true men," assented Khlit, tugging at his mustache.

Thereupon followed a silence of such length that the attendants of Dongkor Gelong stirred expectantly, watching the Cossack. Khlit's shaggy countenance was inscrutable, until he turned suddenly to Dongkor Gelong and, to their surprize, laughed heartily.

XI

"I have heard your wisdom, Chutuktu Lama," he grinned; "now you must listen to mine. Nay, I am no *shaman* or conjuring monk, but I can read what is hidden. I can tell you what is in your thoughts. Would you like to hear?"

"But you have already agreed to the plan of the Tsong Khapa," frowned Dongkor Gelong.

He studied the tall figure of the Cossack with the cold, blank stare of one who held the lash of fear over a multitude of slaves.

"Aye. That may be," admitted Khlit. "I have no love for the Khirghiz khans. Eh, I shall tell your thoughts. The Tsong Khapa has lost the control of his priests over the Khirghiz. And the Tatars of the Jun-gar do not love to pay tribute, especially as I—an unbeliever—have taught them the folly of doing so. Is it not so?"

"Obedience to the Tsong Khapa will reward you fully," objected the lama.

"Aye. The seed of evil will bear fruit. Am I a fledgling, to be fooled by the mummery of Lhassa?" Khlit's voice sank with a growl.

Dongkor Gelong half-rose in his seat; then he sat back, staring at the Cossack.

"Suppose I slay this Iskander Khan and the other. Then the ill-will between the Jun-gar and the Khirghiz will become a blood-feud. Do the hillmen ever forget the shedding of blood? Nay; the horde of the Thian Shan, the Kara Khirghiz, the Kazaks and some of the Kallmark clans who are allied to them will ride against the Jun-gar steppe and lay waste our villages. Then the wisdom of the Tsong Khapa will be fulfilled, because his enemies will have weakened each other. His cursed Yellow Hats will pour over the hills and the steppe, gaining lands and power where good men have died in a blood-feud. Is this not the truth?"

Dongkor Gelong had mastered his surprize. He held up his hand calmly, although his dark eyes had narrowed.

"Take heed, Kha Khan. The Tsong Khapa, in agreement with the sacred oracle which declared in the ashes of forthcoming truth that the Jun-gar should find salvation at Talas, has laid before you a plan. Do you decline?"

Khlit's mustache twitched in a smile which held no mirth.

"It may be. What if I do?"

"You speak like one without wits." Dongkor Gelong shrugged his shoulders contemptuously. "Harken, Kha Khan. If you set aside the word of Lhassa, the invisible forces which are at the disposal of the master of the Yellow Hats will claim you. Little you know how strong they are and how weak you are. The Jun-gar know that you came to Talas. It shall be told them how you defied the almighty Tsong Khapa—aye, your very words. And they will hear how your sinful conduct had its reward—for you will fall, by mischance, into the Jallat Kum."

Khlit shrank back as if in horror. The full force of the lama's trickery revealed itself to him. Also the emptiness of the pledge given by his master, the Dalai Lama. He knew that Kashgar was filled with the open and disguised followers of the Yellow Hats. He was powerless to escape from the walled city. He shivered in spite of himself, as he thought of the black sands of the Jallat Kum.

Dongkor Gelong surveyed him with a pallid smile. The Cossack, he thought, was not altogether to be deceived. But he had been taught a lesson.

"And Iskander Khan?" Khlit asked hoarsely.

"We will deal with him in another way. The girl Sheillil is fair, and she has been well-paid to serve the Dalai Lama. Iskander Khan will be a slave to her beauty."

Khlit stretched out his hand and saw that it was shivering. His thoughts would not tear themselves from the Jallat Kum. He recalled the unfortunate horse that had blundered into the sands. . . .

"Nay," he complained, "if I slay Iskander Khan, even if I live, there will be a war to the death between his people and mine. Now we may still make peace. It is not too late."

Dongkor Gelong's face hardened.

"You have your choice. The will of the Tsong Khapa must be carried out. I am but one of his many servants. And do not think to draw your sword in the lamasery. Even now there are two men within arm's-reach of your tall body. A move—and you go to the Jallat Kum. Azim has thrown many into the sands."

The sweat came to Khlit's forehead. Truly, it was asking greatly of him to face such a death for the Tatars, who, after all, were not of his faith. And, if he did die as Dongkor Gelong threatened, how would the Jun-gar be guarded against further stratagems of the Tsong Khapa?

"Not the Jallat Kum!" he cried and moistened his lips, finding them dry.

"That—or the death of the khans. Choose."

Then it was that the lama saw what brought the light of satisfaction to his eyes and a hidden sneer to his lips. He saw the lined face of the Cossack quiver as with dread and heard the harsh voice plead brokenly for mercy. Khlit's shoulders bowed, and he clutched the table for support. His eyes wavered about the room, wide with fear. Then he straightened with an effort at control.

"Nay, I am the Kha Khan of the Jun-gar. The strength of my people is in me. Am I to die like that, at price of the life of Iskander Khan? Nay, let the Khirghiz die. I will slay him, and Chagan the other, as you have planned."

Dongkor Gelong rose.

"Think not to fool us. You will be watched by those who have no mercy. You have chosen."

"Aye," mumbled Khlit. "I will take my place in the games. But you must have your followers at the place. And the doors of the lamasery must be open for me when I return, for I will ride here at once."

"It is well," agreed Dongkor Gelong.

At a sign from him the attendants led Khlit from the room. He walked slowly, as one who had been broken in spirit.

The eyes of the lama followed him from the chamber. Dongkor Gelong frowned, as if not altogether content with himself. Presently he took a small sandalwood box from the bosom of his gown.

Holding the box well above the table, the lama opened it suddenly. A flood of black wood ashes fell softly to the table. With ill-concealed eagerness the man held the candle close to the ashes. With his finger he tried to trace out diagrams in the black piles. His frown deepened.

When Tuvron returned at a late hour that night the Chutuktu Lama was still musing over the ashes.

XII

It was the twelfth night of the fifth moon, as related by Batur Madi, *gylong*, that the tribes assembled in the courtyard of the lamasery at Kashgar. The moon shed its cold light on the summits of the hills overlooking the town, leaving the valley, and the river in dense shadow. A deeper shadow revealed the mass of the lamasery, erected against the wall of the town.

Inhospitable it was, this monastery, with its massive walls of sandstone, its narrow gates and small embrasures. And it was symbolic in its gloomy secretiveness of the priests it housed. Tonight, however, the courtyard was bright. Lanterns hung from the sides of the wide court, and torch-bearers came and went. From the narrow street outside the place a throng of turbaned and cloaked figures elbowed each other with curses in many tongues for entrance at the gate guarded by armed Tibetans.

Dongkor Gelong had so far departed from the custom of the monastery as to invite the guests from the hills to witness dancing. It was the law that no woman should enter the doors of the monastery itself, so the visitors were not surprized that the festival was held in the court, or that the lamas themselves did not put in appearance. For rumor had it that one of the dancers of Samarkand, a girl from the sultan's courts, would share in the dance.

These tidings stirred the expectation of the restless Khirghiz. Before the first sound of drums was heard in the street, the hillmen were crowding into the court. With them came richly-dressed Jewish merchants of Bokhara, turbaned Usbeks of the town, tousled Dungan camel-drivers and Chinese travelers of the caravans. Among the throng, squatted in rows in the dirt or leaning against the walls, the hillmen made a small minority. Yet, as was their custom, they chose the best places, pushing Usbeks and Tibetans aside, reckless of clutched daggers and black looks.

Khlit and Chagan had selected a place against the monastery wall where they could see without being conspicuous. Apparently they were free to move where they wished, but they suspected that a watch was kept on them from the windows of the lamasery and that any attempt to push through the crowd to the courtyard gate would be prevented.

A space had been cleared in the center of the court, and here there were musicians with drums, tambourines and guitars. Some boy dancers of the Usbeks stepped into the open space and began their lively posturing, watched attentively by the throng. Khlit, after a brief glance, paid no further heed to these, knowing that the purpose of Dongkor Gelong was to show Sheillil to the visiting khans, that they could judge of her beauty before the events of the morrow.

Khlit's keen gaze swept the crowd, seeking for the two khans of the Khirghiz. He turned carelessly to a mild-looking *hafiz*—a reader of poems—in a threadbare *khalat*.

"I have heard," he said idly, lest the other suspect his interest, "that two khans from the hills, Iskander and Bassanghor, are here. Do you know the two, man of wisdom?"

The *hafiz* inclined his head and pointed to the farther side of the cleared space. Khlit made out two men who knelt in the first row of spectators. Their dark faces, lean and hawk-like, were fixed indifferently on the dancers; apparently they were waiting impatiently for the appearance of the girl. The Cossack noted that they were richly dressed, even for wealthy chieftains, in leather breeches, velvet outer robes embroidered with gold and jewels. Their sheepskin hoods were clasped at the throat with silver plates.

"The one with the scar is Iskander," declared the *hafiz*, pointing. "Allah grant that he and his riders take not to plundering. Truly, he is a man without faith, serving this god or that as he chooses, but chiefly himself."

"He looks like one who is more at ease in the hills than in a town. What does he here?"

The scholar turned his eyes to the moonlit heavens.

"Allah knows what is before and behind such as he. Nay, I have heard the lamas sent for him."

This agreed with what Khlit had learned from Dongkor Gelong, and he was silent. He saw a flash of eagerness on the face of Iskander Khan. At the same instant a murmur went through the crowd. Those who were in the rear pushed and elbowed for a better view as several figures advanced from the courtyard gate to the cleared space.

"Here is the harlot of the desert," growled Chagan.

Sheillil, cloaked and escorted by two sturdy Tibetans with drawn scimitars, stepped out beside the musicians. She had pushed her veil boldly back, and a sigh went through the crowd at sight of her loveliness. Iskander Khan sat back on his heels with an exclamation of satisfaction.

The muttering and cursing of the throng was silenced as the girl slipped forward into the enclosure, dropping her heavy cloak. The torchlight glinted on her long, dark hair and on the red veil which floated behind it. The satin trousers and tiny, jeweled slippers gleamed in a double light, for the moon was now shining into the courtyard over the dark towers of the lamasery.

Khlit had seen many women dancers of the bazaars, and he paid little heed to Sheillil at first. He was surprized to hear the music change from its shrill whimper to a low monotone of drums, threaded by the soft note of the flutes. Then he saw the *hafiz* standing motionless, pushing against the man in front of him.

"Look, lord," grunted Chagan. "Here is no woman, but a spirit."

Sheillil had grasped her floating veil in both hands. The drapery billowed about her as she moved softly, whirling the veil close to her or holding it wide as her slim form bent and swayed. Her hair tumbled around her shoulders, the moonlight gleamed whitely on bare throat and dainty feet.

This was no dance of the bazaars. It was freer in movement, more subtle in its intoxication. Khlit saw that the hillmen were bending forward, scarcely breathing as they watched.

The plaintive note of the flutes grew louder as the veil leaped and tossed about the girl's form. Her eyes were wide and calm, fixed on the sky. Her smile had become fainter, almost wistful.

Then a hoarse mutter of approval ran through the watchers. Two daggers appeared in Sheillil's hands. As she swayed, the twin blades glittered up and down her breast and about her head. Darting swiftly from man to man, Sheillil poised like a bird in flight. Before one she thrust the daggers, laughing as the man drew back, startled. To another she offered her lips swiftly—then slipped away with a glint of a dagger before the bearded face that leaned toward her.

Abruptly she whirled before Iskander Khan. The Khirghiz did not flinch at the knife that passed around his head. His slant eyes, half-closed, were fixed hungrily on the dancer, and his dark face was flushed. As she darted away, he tore the jeweled clasp from his throat and tossed it after her.

As quickly as the dance had begun, it was ended. Sheillil had disappeared among the Tibetan attendants and donned her cloak. The kneeling hillmen rose to their feet clamorously. But the drawn swords of the guards held them back. The dancer turned to make her way through the crowd.

"It is strange," murmured the *hafiz,* half to himself. "That was not like a dance of a sultan's woman. I have not seen the like in the towns. Yet it stirred the hillmen to the *hazzi shaitan*—the passion-spot in the heart. See; she is coming here!"

He stepped back as the girl tripped by, followed by her guards. She paused before Khlit mockingly.

"Here is a graybeard of the steppe!" she cried shrilly. "I like not such as he. Where is your felt tent and mangy pony? By Allah, the man has no wit to his tongue!"

"He has no words for a harlot," growled Chagan, on whom the events of the morrow weighed heavily and who had no fondness for the dancer whom he held responsible for their evil plight.

Sheillil did not understand or notice the speech. She touched Khlit's sword and peered into his face laughingly.

"Eh, it is a clown. Harken, Graybeard, if you will ride in the *kök bura* tomorrow, take care to sharpen that curved sword you wear. Many younger men will ride with me tomorrow. If you would guard your life, have the curved sword sharpened by Chu'n Yuen, the armorer of Kashgar. Aye, Chu'n Yuen will quicken your blood with wine in the morning."

She smiled in the Cossack's face, so close that he caught the subtle scent of roses that came from her garments.

"And will tell you of the Jun-gar," she added so softly that even Chagan, who was beside them, did not hear.

With that she was gone in the crowd.

The *hafiz* looked after her with a sigh.

"There will be good sport at the *kök bura,*" he murmured. "Chu'n Yuen, who hears the whispers of Kashgar, swears that the girl Sheillil was born in the hills, where she learned to ride like a goshawk upon the wind. It will take a shrewd horseman to catch her and hold her. Allah the generous has ordained that I should be too

poor to buy a horse. Yet it is well, for I have a thought there will be
shedding of blood. The woman is fair-faced and shapely."

"Aye, there will be blood, *hafiz*," growled Chagan.

Khlit made no answer. In his mind was running the phrase the
girl had whispered. "And will tell you of the Jun-gar." What did
Chu'n Yuen, or Sheillil, know of the Tatars? Had she news? Again
he asked himself the question that had perplexed him since the day
at Talas.

Who was Sheillil? What was her part in the web of intrigue woven
by the lamas at Kashgar? Dongkor Gelong had said that he had
bought her. If not the lama, what master did she serve?

XIII

Is there aught that goes faster than a loose-reined horse on the plains?
Or a well-sped arrow from the bow? Aye; it is the dark hand of death.

Tatar proverb.

Khlit had discovered that, so long as he kept to himself and in view
of the attendants of the monastery, he was free to go where he chose.
He had not seen Dongkor Gelong or Tuvron again. On the morning
after Sheillil's dance Chagan slept late. Khlit, however, had little
rest, and he was glad to leave the gloomy pile of the lamasery, with
its robed attendants, for the courtyard.

He had learned that Chu'n Yuen's shop lay in an alley on one
of the streets opening into the neighborhood of the monastery. He
decided to venture there, for he was curious to learn what Sheillil
had meant by her whispered speech.

Sauntering across the courtyard, he approached the guards at the
gate. The spearmen glanced at him keenly, but offered no opposition
when he walked through the gate into the street without. He saw,
however, that two men—a Tibetan soldier and a Chubil Khan—who
were loitering in the arena walked after him.

Khlit made no haste. He was aware that it would be useless to
attempt to escape from his new guardians. Kashgar was walled and
guarded. The men of the Yellow Hat in various garb were scattered
through the streets. Should a cry be raised after him, he could not
go far without being cornered.

He turned down the alley where he knew the armorer's shop was located. The heavy door of Chu'n Yuen stood open. Chu'n Yuen himself was ordering his slaves about shrilly as they served wine to the drunken Khirghiz who lay thick on the floor of the room and the outer shop. At sight of the Cossack, the proprietor halted and approached him respectfully.

"How can I serve you, noble sir?" Chu'n Yuen murmured. "Would the honorable khan, who condescends to dignify my shop with his presence, desire to see some rare scimitars newly brought from Damascus? Or to have his own blade sharpened to an edge that will sever a floating feather?"

Khlit's sidelong glance told him that the Tibetan soldier had followed him into the outer room. The Chubil Khan, being reluctant to enter a wine-shop, had remained in the street, he guessed. He drew his curved saber and balanced the blade in one hand. Chu'n Yuen stared at the rich chasing of the steel and the delicately wrought inscription with professional interest.

"Nay, am I a drunken fool like such—" Khlit kicked one of the insensible forms on the floor contemptuously—"to give up my sword to another? Fetch me a steel, and I will temper the edge to suit myself."

Chu'n Yuen bowed politely.

"It shall be as you wish, noble sir. In the room within a good couch and a cup of wine await you. If you will follow——"

He disappeared through the hangings. Khlit strode after without hesitation, but keeping the weapon poised in his hand. The Chinaman passed through the wine-shop, heavy with the stench of tobacco and stale wine, to the women's court in the rear of his establishment. Here a few female slaves were stretched out asleep on benches.

Chu'n Yuen opened a small door and led his visitor through the courtyard wall. Khlit saw that they were in a walled garden, shaded by poplars under which rugs were placed. It was empty except for themselves and the Tibetan, who had followed closely and was now squatted by the gate.

Khlit seated himself on a rug that the shopkeeper arranged for him, his back to a tree-trunk. He liked the aspect of the place little, or that of Chu'n Yuen, who bustled back into the shop with a glance at the Tibetan. The latter was in the shadow of the wall, apparently drowsing. Khlit wondered if it had been Sheillil's wish that he should give up his weapon. One place was as good as another, however, to the Cossack who was carefully watched by the men of the Yellow Hat.

Chu'n Yuen did not return. Presently the gate opened, and a figure that Khlit recognized immediately as Sheillil entered. The Cossack had half-expected to see the girl, and he did not look up a second time as the dancer knelt beside him and offered him a bowl of wine, laying at the same time a whet-stone at his knees.

Sheillil was veiled. She had changed her dancing costume for a fur-tipped *khalat*, boots and a sheepskin hood. In the shadow of the hood her dark eyes peered up at the Cossack. Khlit had taken up the whet-stone and was gently stroking the blade of the weapon across his knees.

"Have you news of the Jun-gar?" he asked finally, without looking up.

"Nay; how should I know aught of the Tatars?" the girl laughed softly, pleased at the involuntary disappointment she saw in the old chieftain's face.

Khlit did not speak again, which irked her.

"Do you put faith in the word of a woman?" she mocked, watching him brightly. "Or have you come to ask aid of a slave dancer, hired to the wiles of the Tsong Khapa and his crafty servant, Dongkor Gelong? Truly, the men of the Yellow Hats have stripped your strength from you, O Kha Khan, and hold you prisoner like a trussed boar. I have heard how you pleaded for mercy from Dongkor Gelong —you have not lost your voice."

The veins stood out on Khlit's forehead, and the hand holding the sword trembled. Seeing this, Sheillil smiled, well-pleased.

"The Tsong Khapa has a servant to attend you." She nodded at the Tibetan by the gate. "But the fellow speaks not Uigur; so we are free to talk together, you and I. Oh, they know at the lamasery that I am here, but Dongkor Gelong has agreed that I should see you —to arrange for what is to happen this noon. I am free to come and go as I choose."

She dropped her chin into her hands idly, watching Khlit's stroking of the sword.

"I shall have many suitors to ride after me today at the *kök bura*," she murmured, "for I am more beautiful than the flowers of the hills. Iskander Khan has sworn he will have me. He is a bold fellow. There will be scimitars drawn and blows struck. Dongkor Gelong has whispered to me that Iskander Khan will fall by your sword—from behind. Others, too, will die. It will be good sport. Have you truly sworn to kill the Khirghiz, O one without honor?"

The taunting words brought a grunt of anger from Khlit. The sword in his hand flew up. The edge of the blade drew swiftly across Sheillil's throat, pressing in the veil that hung from her cheeks.

The girl's eyes widened suddenly. Then she laughed musically. The veil hung by a few threads. It had been nearly severed in two under her chin. But there was not so much as a speck of blood on her throat to show where the curved sword had kissed the light veil. It had been a bold feat, by one who wielded a sword as deftly as Sheillil had whirled her tiny daggers in the dance of the night before.

Khlit was staring at her now, from deep-set eyes in which burned a sullen fire. She leaned closer to him, and the expression of her brown eyes changed.

"A shrewd blow!" she said softly. "But, if you slay the Khirghiz, it will be a curse upon your people, for there will be black war between the men from the Roof of the World and the Jun-gar. It will be the end of the power of the khans, Khirghiz and Jun-gar. The evil priesthood of the Yellow Hats will seize the citadels of the hills when the war has wasted the ranks of both sides. Oh, Dongkor Gelong is a man to be feared. He is reaching out from Kashgar for the mastery of the passes to the Roof of the World."

Khlit studied the girl attentively. Accustomed as he was to the moods of the dancer, he found that a new note had come into her voice. Her breath was quickened under the *khalat*.

"Fool," she said bitterly. "Do you think Dongkor Gelong will spare you when you have done what he desires? Your death is as needful as that of the bold Khirghiz."

"He has promised," responded Khlit gruffly, "that the gates of the lamasery shall be opened for me when I flee from the field of games."

Sheillil clasped the sleeve of the Cossack's coat.

"Men said that Khlit of the Curved Saber was crafty and wise in war. Have your wits fled? Are you stricken with fear of the Jallat Kum? Has Dongkor Gelong clouded your spirit so you can not see that the stroke that slays Iskander Khan will be the end of your people and mine?"

Khlit sheathed his weapon and took the girl's chin in a hand, lean but still powerful.

"Who are your people, Sheillil?" he asked.

XIV

The girl did not draw back, nor did her eyes waver. She pointed behind Khlit, upward. The Cossack, however, did not shift his gaze.

"Yonder, above the walls of Kashgar," Sheillil whispered, "are the hills of the Roof of the World. There are my people, although I have not lived among them since I was a child."

"Your face is not that of a Khirghiz," growled Khlit.

"Nay; that is true." Sheillil paused briefly. "I have heard that my people once lived in a city at the threshold of the hills. It was the city of Talas and my father's ancestors worshiped in the mosque of Talas. Came the sand, and they took refuge in the higher land of their kingdom, called by some the Thian Shan and by us the Roof of the World. From time to time those who were strongest in faith made pilgrimages to the mosque of Talas, which was a holy spot, beloved of Allah. Now, that the blight of the Tsong Khapa has reached up into the hills and taken the Jallat Kum for a burial-ground, few go there. Nevertheless, when Dongkor Gelong confided his plan to me before he went to the Jun-gar, I went to Talas to await your coming. I wished to see if you were a weakling, who would fall prey to the lama, or a strong man. When Tuvron came, I pretended to be well-pleased with your plight, so that he should not suspect."

"And then?"

"Before I was a woman," went on Sheillil softly, "a raiding party of Usbeks, servants of the Tsong Khapa, carried me into slavery at Samarkand. But I was beautiful, and I did not die, living instead in favor and buying my freedom with gold. Yet I returned not to the hills. For a woman to be the wife of a khan must have honor, and I was a dancer. The day will come when Allah will show his mercy and I may go back."

Khlit was silent, pondering on what she had said. The ways of women were strange to him, and Sheillil was one of many faces.

"What master do you serve?" he growled.

In a flash the girl's expression changed.

"Has the wind a master? Has the eagle of the mountain-tops one whom he obeys? Nay; I follow my own will——"

"Today," broke in Khlit, "you will be sought by many suitors. Which will you favor?"

Sheillil touched his hand appealingly.

"Iskander Khan," she whispered. "He is the chieftain of my people. His arms are strong as his sword is quick. Many times have I watched him from a distance in Kashgar. It may be his heart will be touched with love for Sheillil. Allah may will that he take me to his home—for Dongkor Gelong has promised that my tongue will be slit and I shall be given for the sport of the camel-drivers if I fail him."

"And so you have asked that I harm him not? That would be my death."

"Nay," put in the girl. "At Talas you slew a man for me. I have not forgotten. I have arranged with Chu'n Yuen, who is blind as an over-fed jackal, a plan by which you and the Tatar can escape. While the *kök bura* is in full play ride swiftly from the horsemen to the city—the games will be on a plain without—and come to the shop of Chu'n Yuen. Most of the followers of the Yellow Hat will be at the games. Leave your tired horses in the street. Run through the shop of the armorer to this garden. In the corner behind that tree is a gate."

Sheillil pointed to a barred door, half-concealed by bushes.

"The city wall is within a few paces, outside that gate. Chu'n Yuen is a fox with two doors to his burrow. One of the poplars overhangs the city wall—the largest tree of the group, ripped by lightning. On the farther side of the tree are nails, cleverly placed so that a man may climb to the summit of the wall. In the overhanging branch is a rope of Chu'n Yuen's. By this you may drop over the wall. A servant will be waiting there with fresh horses. Ride straight for the hills. You may meet a party of horsemen, but they will be friends. Do this, and you will be safe!"

The brown eyes sought Khlit's hard face pleadingly. The Cossack smiled grimly.

"Many tales have you told me, little sparrow. How do I know that this one is the truth? It has the smell of a trap. And Iskander Khan is my foe——"

"Would I take so much trouble to slay you?" Sheillil demanded.

"If Iskander Khan had been so minded, and I had spoken your name to him, you would not leave here alive."

"Nay, Sheillil," Khlit shook his head. "Then Dongkor Gelong would have disposed of your lover promptly. This is a city of lies. Go you with Iskander Khan. The Khirghiz is no weakling; he can guard himself and you."

"And you?"

Sheillil leaned forward breathlessly. Khlit stretched himself like one awakening from sleep.

"I, Sheillil? Chagan and I will ride from *kök bura* to the gates of the lamasery. Dongkor Gelong has promised that they will not be closed to us, for he will see to it himself, being kept by the law of his priesthood from attendance at the games."

With that he rose and left the garden. The Tibetan followed silently, with a glance at Sheillil. The girl knelt with hands clenched against her sides, the veil hiding her features, but her eyes dark with a woman's anger.

Then she sprang to her feet swiftly and unbarred the door in the bushes. When Chu'n Yuen returned, he found only the empty bowl of wine and the whet-stone lying on the rug.

XV

The *kök bura* of Kashgar in the fifth moon of that year, it is written in the annals of Batur Madi, was long remembered by those who saw it. And the riders told their children what they had seen in the Love Chase of Sheillil of Samarkand. As is usual with those who share in an event, the tale told by them grew until it magnified the number of men killed and the mysterious events which followed upon the ending of the *kök bura*.

According to Batur Madi, the Love Chase grew from the first form of the *kök bura,* in which a slain sheep was given to a rider. This man was pursued by his comrades until another had contrived to take the sheep. But, in the Love Chase of the Khirghiz, a girl who had it in her heart to yield to a husband, mounted a well-chosen horse and armed herself with a heavy whip. The spectators formed a circle about the girl and her suitors while the men tried to seize her as she eluded them. Thus, says Batur Madi, the strongest man and most skilful became the possessor of the girl, as was fitting, while those who failed had only the stinging scars of the whip-lash to heal their empty hearts.

But the *kök bura* of the fifth moon was such a one as had not been seen before. And in the annals of Batur Madi such a one is not recorded since that time.

Two things served to draw nearly the whole of the people of Kashgar out to the stretch of plain by the river bank on the side of the city farthest from the mountains. All, in fact, save a few drunken Khirghiz, some slaves and mendicants and Chu'n Yuen, who would not leave his shop, and Dongkor Gelong, who was never seen in public. First, rumor of weighty events that might come to pass had somehow spread among the Khirghiz and Usbeks, who rode fully armed and alert to the spot.

And Sheillil, the beauty of Samarkand and the dancer of the lamasery courtyard, was to be the object of the chase.

It was noted by the *hafiz*, who was among the first to arrive, that even the Chubil Khans were present, having come in a procession of state from the lamasery, preceded by *manshis* bearing the sacred pastils and basins wherein were glowing coals and sweet-scented roots. The lamas, mounted on silk-canopied horses and accompanied by the standards of their order, were joined by an array of the Yellow Hat soldiery.

Khlit, who was early upon the scene with Chagan and well-mounted by order of Dongkor Gelong, noted that Tuvron, who was in charge of the soldiery, arranged his followers in the form of a three-sided square with the fourth side nearest the city walls. The spectators of the caravans and the townspeople were afoot. But the Tibetans and Usbeks, who were very numerous, were mounted.

Thus the watchers formed a solid wall about a cleared stretch on the plain, perhaps five hundred paces square. The followers of the Khirghiz khans were grouped in a mass on the side of the enclosure farthest from the walls of Kashgar. Iskander Khan, with his companion, Bassanghor, and several other nobles of the hillmen, rode to the center, waiting for the arrival of Sheillil. They were joined by single riders from among the Usbeks and even a Dungan or two of rank.

Khlit and Chagan were the last to ride out from the crowd. Chagan's powerful figure drew instant attention from the group of horsemen, who noted his Tatar dress and the ease with which he sat his rangy mount. Khlit was the object of less attention, for he was gray-haired and the manner in which he held himself betokened little interest in what was to happen.

Keenly the contestants eyed each other and the horses. Khlit saw that Iskander Khan rode a small, dun-colored pony of vicious temper, but, as he guessed shrewdly, quick and active on its feet. Bassanghor was well-mounted—a mettlesome Persian horse which threaded in and out among the group at the pressure of his rider's knees, to the delight of the watchers who were keen judges of horseflesh.

Khlit's mustache twitched in a grim smile as he noted that all the contenders were armed—a fact which prophesied ill for some. Chagan had shaken off the gloom that had possessed him for the last two days and was taunting the Usbek youths in high good-humor. Action and the prospect of conflict roused him, and Khlit, who missed nothing, saw that the Khirghiz were equally gay.

A shout went up from the spectators, who saw Sheillil escorted by Tibetan guards come through the throng by the walls. The girl wore her costume of the morning, with a heavy, knotted whip in her hand. She rode a white Arabian horse of Dongkor Gelong's stables, sitting lightly in the small, wooden saddle. She went directly to one of the corners of the square, and Tuvron, who was acting as judge, motioned the riders back to the opposite corner.

Here they formed in a line, Khlit taking his place between Chagan and a trembling youth in Dungan garb. Tuvron shouted to the Tibetans. The watchers nearest the riders cried out at them shrilly, a word of praise for the Usbeks and a gibe for the Khirghiz. Some, however, were silent, for there was a tensity of suppressed excitement in the air.

Abruptly a rumble of drums sounded by Tuvron. Sheillil spurred her horse from her corner of the square. Khlit saw the line of riders dart forward. But he and Chagan held their impatient horses to a trot, keeping on one flank of the horsemen.

Sheillil had reined in her mount and was watching the oncoming group keenly. Whips waving in air, bent low on their saddles, the men were shortening the distance rapidly. As they came within fifty paces of her, Khlit saw the girl crouch and put spurs to her horse's side. The Arab leaped and was away swiftly, quartering across the course of the approaching men.

So well-timed had been Sheillil's move that the group swept past her almost within arm's-reach. Iskander Khan, however, on his active pony was about on the instant and after her. Khlit called to Chagan and galloped down toward her. He saw Sheillil glance at them fleetingly and urge her mount farther to the side away from them.

The spectators, who had greeted the girl's maneuver with a shout of approval, were silent for a moment. Then cries rang out. Bassanghor had approached close to Sheillil on the side away from Khlit when an Usbek rider blundered into him. A quick thrust of the shoulder of the Persian horse and the latter was on the ground, rider pinned beneath him. A Dungan coming behind was too close or too clumsy to turn out and fell headlong, lying quietly where he had rolled.

The girl smiled as she saw what had happened. Then another Usbek, angered at the fate of his countryman, rode at Bassanghor. Two swords flashed simultaneously. Bassanghor rode clear, but the other swayed in his saddle and turned his mount toward the spectators, blood streaming from the side of his neck.

The girl, who was watching her pursuers closely, was now near the point from which the men had started, Iskander Khan riding with furious swiftness close behind her, and the Cossack and Tatar holding aloof on her right hand.

Suddenly she swerved to the left, eluding a Khirghiz who grasped at her. This turn brought the riders together as they followed her, and Khlit saw another go down in the crush. The girl circled swiftly around the square, her Arab keeping easily ahead of the others. But, quickly as she maneuvered, Iskander Khan kept his place close to her horse's tail.

A Dungan, well-mounted, drew abreast of the Khirghiz leader. Instantly Iskander Khan had drawn his scimitar. The Dungan swerved away, but too late to save himself a slashed shoulder.

"Ha, lord," chuckled Chagan, "the blood is beginning to flow, even as I foretold."

"Keep close to the Khirghiz, fool!" growled the Cossack.

They were now in the lead of the remaining riders, who were watching each other warily with drawn weapons, and close to Iskander Khan. Sheillil threw them a swift glance, dashing the long hair from her flushed face. She was heading now straight for the side of the square nearest the walls, with the riders strung nearly across the field.

XVI

And then for the second time the watchers raised a delighted shout. Verily, this was a chase to be remembered! Seldom had such riding as that of the girl been seen by the men of Kashgar. For Sheillil had dodged once and then again to the other side. She whirled her horse on its haunches and darted back straight through the pursuers.

Iskander Khan cursed and wheeled his pony after her in time to see her lean to the side of her mount, avoiding the clutch of one rider, and strike another heavily in the face with the whip.

There were but four after her now, owing to the slain and injured and the fact that Khlit and Chagan waited, where she had turned, near the town side of the square. The two Khirghiz chieftains, one of their followers and a lone Usbek pressed her close.

"By the winged horse of Kaidu!" swore the sword-bearer. "She rides like one born of the winds. Ho! Yon Khirghiz had a taste of the whip. See; Iskander Khan has her *khalat*. Nay—may the devil roast me—she has shed the cloak. They come back to us now."

"Aye," growled Khlit. "Be ready."

Sheillil was flying toward them, the two khans and the Usbek after her. Khlit sat his horse silently, watching closely what happened. He saw that the girl was being penned in one of the corners. At the same time he noted that Bassanghor Khan had edged toward the Usbek. Another moment and the Persian horse had crossed the path of the Usbek, who pulled up with an oath. Seeing the Khirghiz's ready weapon, however, the other drew off.

"Ha! That was well done," commented Chagan. "Has our time come?"

"Come," said Khlit.

They wheeled toward the girl, who was near the corner. But Iskander Khan, coming up swiftly, was before them. The Khirghiz rose in his saddle as Sheillil leaned away from him. Then the girl reined in her horse. To Khlit it seemed that it was done purposely. A shout went up as Iskander Khan caught her bodily from the saddle and held her close.

The Khirghiz horsemen spurred toward their chief, for there were angry mutterings from the Usbeks. Then the voice of Tuvron rose above the confusion.

"Fools!" he stormed at his men, pointing. "Look yonder. After them!"

Two riders had broken through the spectators on the city side of the square and were speeding for the walls, bent low on their mounts. Khlit and Chagan, instead of following Iskander Khan, had wheeled through the square and were now nearing the gate of the almost deserted town.

Choosing the moment when the attention of spectators and riders was centered on the end of the *kök bura,* the Tatars had gained a good start on the horsemen who spurred after them, led by Tuvron in a black rage. Their course took them through the gate, which was unguarded, and straight to the lamasery courtyard.

Here a few servants gaped at them in surprise. As Dongkor Gelong had promised, the door of the monastery was ajar. Khlit and Chagan flung themselves from their horses and ran up the steps.

A half dozen Tibetan spearmen sprang up in the entrance, hearing the footsteps, but drew back on seeing who the two were. They had had orders to expect Khlit and Chagan and to allow them to pass. True, the Tibetans heard a confused shouting in the street outside; yet this also was to be anticipated, for they had been informed that the two Tatars might be pursued. As yet the courtyard wall concealed the pursuers from sight.

From the stairway the two crossed the main hall of the building, to the narrow flight of steps that led to the monks' cells above. Even Chagan was silent as Khlit paused for a second to listen to the clatter of hoofs in the courtyard. The sword-bearer's scarred face was tense and recklessly alight. The Cossack was breathing heavily from his run, but his eyes burned with a steady fire. He caught Chagan by the arm.

"Guard the stairs," he said quickly, "for a space. Then escape—if you can."

Chagan nodded understanding and drew his sword, the heavy, two-handed weapon that had earned him his surname.

"Nay, lord," he growled, "we may yet win free of this cursed place. I marked a window that gave on the courtyard wall——"

But Khlit had vanished in the shadows above him. There was a rush of feet across the hall, and a group of the Yellow Hats, following the directions of a startled monk, dashed at the stairs. They drew back at sight of Chagan's bulk in the dark stairway.

Tuvron's voice pierced the momentary silence while Tatar and soldiers stared at each other.

"There is but one here!" the Chubil Khan cried shrilly. "Cut him down——"

The men made a rush for the steps. Chagan had taken his stand several feet above the level of the wall. He had the advantage of being in semi-darkness while his foes were exposed to view. Moreover the space was narrow. Two rapid blows of his weapon knocked down the spears that menaced him, and the head of the leading Tibetan, still wearing its bright-hued hat, went spinning among them.

Chagan gave back a step or two shrewdly as they pressed him. His long sword made deadly play in the close mass of assailants whose shorter scimitars sought vainly to pierce his guard.

"Come to the feast, dogs," growled the Tatar with bared teeth, "the kites are waiting to pick at the eyes of the fallen, and the wolves scent carrion! Nay, this is a feast of the gods!"

He grunted as a spear scraped his leg and another tore the coat from his chest. Heaving his powerful body forward, he lashed viciously at his foes until the mass fell back with dead and torn bodies weighing on their shoulders. Chagan taunted them as he fought, revelling in the press of bodies and the shrieks of pain.

Then he saw that the hall was filled with lamas and their followers, come from the kök bura. Tuvron had vanished, however, and Chagan recalled that this was not the only stairway to the floor above. With a last shout he turned and dashed up the steps.

Through the deserted passages of the monastery he sped, his eyes strained anxiously for sight of Khlit. He met no one until he came to the door of Dongkor Gelong's cell. Here he halted in his tracks. Through the open door he saw the figure of a guard on the floor. Khlit was calmly wiping the bloodied blade of his sword upon the man's clothes.

At his table sat Dongkor Gelong, Chutuktu Lama of the Tsong Khapa. He was dressed in state robes. As if asleep, he rested his body and head on the table, both arms outstretched, his forehead pressed among the black wood ashes of divination beside the sandalwood box. A crimson rivulet issued from under his chin and traced its way across the table.

"Dongkor Gelong," said Khlit grimly, seeing the sword-bearer, "has found that we are men of our word, you and I. The carrion priest loved too well to see men tremble to know my fear of him was pretended. As we promised, we have come back to the lamasery."

XVII

The window that Chagan had mentioned was not far from the cell of the dead lama. It was lucky for them that this was so. A passageway leading from the cell enabled them to avoid the followers of Tuvron and gain the gallery which overlooked the courtyard.

As they ran, they heard the rush of footsteps through the corridors of the upper floor as the men of the Yellow Hat spread through the place looking for them. The stairs up which they had come were guarded, as was the lower door. But Chagan, with an eye to future necessity, had seen that the window to which they came was in a sheltered spot and was wide enough to admit the passage of even his bulky frame.

As they reached the window a startled shout proclaimed that the men of the Yellow Hat had found their dead leader. A hasty glance showed Khlit that the courtyard held a great number of horses, but few men, the greater part having pressed into the monastery. There was no time to weigh their chances. It was the courtyard wall or death at the hands of the Yellow Hats behind them.

Clinging to Chagan's hand, Khlit pushed himself through the aperture and dropped to the surface of the wall beneath them. Chagan followed at once with a leap that almost pitched him headlong to the stone pavement of the court. Their appearance was greeted with a cry by the men below.

Arrows whistled by Khlit as he ran along the flat top of the wall. The Usbeks and Yellow Hats in the courtyard were scrambling to their horses or running for the entrance. But their progress was hindered by the number of horses. Khlit and the Tatar gained the corner of the court before those within could reach the gate, some hundred paces distant.

Khlit noted that the alley leading to Chu'n Yuen's was opposite them and nearer than the gate of the courtyard. Without slackening

his pace, he leaped from the wall, landing heavily but without losing
his feet. Chagan, who was heavier, fell to his knees with a grunt,
for the wall was twice the height of a man.

Horsemen were issuing from the gate by now and heading down
the street toward them. From the embrasures of the monastery pistols
cracked. But the alley was near at hand.

Khlit heard Chagan pounding behind him and swearing. And the
clatter of hoofs sounded behind the sword-bearer. If the door of the
shop should be barred, they were lost. But Sheillil had promised that
it would be open.

The Cossack gained the door and thrust it open with his foot. He
jerked the panting Tatar inside as spear-points flashed past them
with a rush of horses. Slamming the heavy gate shut, he barred it
and ran through the shop. Chu'n Yuen was not to be seen.

A few men in the wine-shop started to their feet as the two ran
through the place and the women's court. The garden to the rear
was deserted.

They found the tree, as Sheillil had promised, and on the other
side of the city wall four horses were in waiting, held by a servant.
The man disappeared into the bushes as they mounted.

"By Satan's bones!" swore Chagan. "I am glad to let a horse's
legs do my running for me after that foot-race. Whither now, Khlit,
lord?"

Khlit led the way at a trot out of the thicket in the direction of the
hills which loomed not far away. As they came out in the open,
leading the spare horses by their tethers, he pointed to the plain
abreast of them.

In a cloud of dust an array of horsemen was headed in their direction at a furious pace. The leaders were Khirghiz, closely pressed by
Usbek riders. In the dust he saw scimitars rise and fall and the glint
of speeding arrows.

XVIII

In the annals of Batur Madi it is related how swords were drawn at
the ending of the *kök bura* and a battle ensued which lasted until
darkness. Around the person of Sheillil, the dancer of Samarkand,
says Batur Madi, the Khirghiz and Usbeks fought until the slain
hillmen littered the way to the mountains. Following this, the woman

disappeared from the towns of Kashgaria, and it was not known whether she was among the slain or not.

Yet this is not the whole truth.

When Sheillil was caught and held by Iskander Khan, the chieftain raised a shout of triumph and would have pressed her hot face to his bearded lips to seal his conquest. But the girl twisted in his grasp until she faced him and thrust her slim hand in his beard, holding him back.

"Fool! Blind of the blind!" she hissed. "See you not this is not your doing, but mine? Harken to me if you would save your life."

Sheer surprize held the khan silent. Surprize at her words and at hearing his own tongue spoken.

"Bend closer," whispered Sheillil; "you alone must hear this. Great is your peril, O Khan. Dongkor Gelong has laid a trap for you here. This game was his doing, and an assassin of his was to stab you in the back as you rode after me. Failing that, the Yellow Hats in the square around us will take care that you and your men do not leave the field. It was for this he brought you to Kashgar and had me dance before you. I was to be the bait. This is the truth."

Slowness of wit was not one of Iskander Khan's failings. His sharp eyes bored into the girl's flushed face as if he would strip her of her loveliness and sift the meaning of her words.

"Ha!" he growled. "Dongkor Gelong pledged our safety. Why do you say this?"

"Because I, too, am of the hills, and your people are mine." The girl tried to shake the sturdy form of the chieftain in her earnestness. "Nay, I could not speak before this, for you would not have left the gates of Kashgar alive. If the man who was to slay you had approached you, I would have ridden between. Allah has granted me this mercy, to open your eyes to this peril. Summon your men and ride for the hills. Look! See if it is not the truth."

The khan tore his eyes from the quivering face of the girl and glanced around what had been the square. He beheld Usbeks and Tibetans riding toward them with black looks. Groups of the Yellow Hats under the lamas were circling toward the town. The Chinese and Dungans were fleeing the field, sensing coming trouble. Iskander Khan, still holding the girl, rose in his saddle.

"Ho! Kara Khirghiz!" he bellowed. "Here is treachery. To me, men of the hills. To me!"

Bassanghor's shout answered him, and the Khirghiz closed their ranks, spurring to the side of their khan. The hillmen had scented conflict, and their dark faces were alight, for they loved well the giving and taking of blows. At Iskander's rapid command they formed into a group and galloped toward the town, riding down spearmen who tried to oppose them and fleeing townspeople indifferently.

Iskander Khan, from the center of his men, had seen that the Yellow Hats were fewer on this side, and he led his men in a circle of the walls to gain the side nearest the hills where was shelter. But the lamas' men outnumbered the Khirghiz, keeping pace closely and doing serious execution with their arrows.

Once clear of the town it became a running fight, with the Khirghiz, who were skilled at this form of warfare, making frequent stands to hold off their enemies. Yet their number became rapidly smaller. In their path two horsemen appeared, waiting their coming.

"What men are those, Sheillil?" demanded Iskander Khan.

"They are Tatars, lord," explained the girl, who had recognized Khlit and Chagan. "They are the ones, tricked by Dongkor Gelong, who were to have slain you or suffer death themselves. Yet they did not attempt it. One is the Cossack, Khlit, the Kha Khan of the Jun-gar. They are one with us in peril."

"Nay, they will get little but hard blows if they join us. Still, if they carry swords, they are welcome."

Khlit and Iskander Khan exchanged no greeting when they met, beyond a quick glance, but the Cossack offered the hard-pressed chieftain the two spare horses they led. Sheillil sprang to the back of one, the khan taking the other without slackening pace.

In the book of Batur Madi it is written how the Khirghiz band fought off the men of the Yellow Hats as they rode into the foothills toward the Roof of the World. How they swam a river and held it for a while against the men of the lamas. How Khlit and a dozen Khirghiz blocked a mountain pass while the others rode ahead. And how all but a few of the hillmen fell fighting before darkness closed down on the mountain defiles and the remnant of the Khirghiz vanished into the shadows of the forests.

The moon had risen and turned the snow-crests of the Thian Shan into white beacons and the mist in the valleys into a gray veil when the party of Iskander Khan came to a halt wearily. Only two horses were left them and Iskander Khan counted only nine of his hundred left alive.

Bassanghor Khan was not among the nine.

The Khirghiz chieftain leaned against the horse which Sheillil rode and sheathed his sword.

"By the bones of my grandsire," he said solemnly, "by the grave of my father and by the faith of a hillman of the Black Khirghiz, I swear an oath. Witness, Tatars. The passes of the hills and the caravan paths shall be closed to the breed of the Yellow Hats. Their enemies will be my friends. I and my men will bring death and dishonor upon Dongkor Gelong and those who have betrayed us and slain Bassanghor Khan."

Sheillil leaned toward him shyly, yet with a trace of her customary boldness. Her voice was light, in spite of weariness, for Iskander Khan, who was the chieftain of her people, had said that she would be his wife and have honor for the service she had done him at Kashgar.

"It was the plan of Dongkor Gelong," she said softly, "to make war between the Jun-gar and the Khirghiz. It was for that he summoned Khlit, the Kha Khan, and you to Kashgar. Your safety lies in an alliance. So much I learned in the towns, for men spoke freely before me. Why not have peace between the hillmen and the Tatars?"

Iskander Khan was silent in thought. Then he left Sheillil and went to where Khlit and Chagan were standing a little apart. He held up his hand.

"Treachery has made bad blood between your people and mine, Khlit," he said bluntly. "But the blood that was shed today has made that as naught. We have fought together, you and I, and my quarrel has been yours. Henceforth, if it is your will, the boundary between our lands shall be inviolate and there will be a welcome for you and the khans of the Jun-gar in my tent. I swear it."

Khlit nodded. By his tone Iskander Khan did not suspect how much the words he had spoken meant to the Cossack. From the time when the two from the Jun-gar had waited for the Khirghiz outside Kashgar, Khlit had hoped that they could come to an understanding.

"The boundary will be inviolate, Iskander Khan," he repeated gravely. "And I shall tell the *kurultai* of the Jun-gar there is peace. I give the pledge for myself and my people."

He went to his horse and loosened one of the saddle-bags on the beast's back. He took the bulky bag to Iskander Khan.

"Here is a gift," he observed briefly, "to seal our new peace."

Chagan watched silently. But as the moonlight faded some hours later and the first tinge of dawn colored the peaks at their backs, a thought came to the sword-bearer, and he turned to Khlit, who was sitting beside him, nursing his sword.

"Ho, lord," he muttered sleepily, rubbing his sore legs, "it was a good day's work. But when we ride back to the *kurultai* how will you explain the oracle of the Dalai Lama that sent you to Talas?"

Khlit laughed like one newly freed from care.

"We will tell the truth, Chagan. Has not the oracle come true! It was the word of the Dalai Lama that we should find aid for the Jun-gar in the fifth moon of the year of the Ape. Have we not found it?"

As Khlit said, so it proved. Iskander Khan kept his word. Some said this was because of the wisdom of his wife, Sheillil of Samarkand; others, because Khlit had been his companion in battle. But others, who were wise, whispered that it was because Iskander Khan found in the saddle-bag Khlit gave him the newly severed head of Dongkor Gelong.

THE STAR OF EVIL OMEN

When a man touches the thread of Fate, he is like the blind who feel
their way in darkness. His wisdom is less than the grain of sand in the
Great Desert.

When a warrior ventures into the unknown, he also is like to the blind.
If he is foolhardy, his grave is dug before the close of the first day's
journey.

Yet if a warrior is brave, he sees his path clearly. For even in the dark
there are stars, some of good omen, some of evil.

Chinese proverb.

AT THE MOUNTAIN-PASS ABOVE THE RIVER KERULON, KHLIT, THE COS-
sack, reined in his horse. It was the early seventeenth century when
the Kerulon marked the boundary between Chinese territory and
the land of the Tatars, the scene of many hard-fought battles.

In spite of his sixty-odd years, Khlit, known as the Cossack of the
Curved Saber to his enemies, was not accustomed to waste thought
upon his past. As he looked back, however, down the dark gorge to
the river and the level steppe beyond, still warm under the rays of
the setting sun, he rested his scarred hands on the peak of the saddle.

It was his last look at the steppe that had been his home for several
years. Such places were few in Khlit's life. Yet this Tatar steppe,
just south of the waters of Lake Baikal, was much like the plains
of his Cossack days, and therefore Khlit was meditative.

He had chosen. And, having chosen, he had no regret. Of his
own will he had given up the leadership, his place as Kha Khan, of

the Jun-gar Tatars, who were the last survivors, except for some
bandit tribes of the frontier, of the race of Ghenghis Khan.

To Khlit's mind that had been the only way. He was a Christian,
and the men of the Jun-gar were followers of Natagai or of the
Dalai Lama. He had made enemies among the priests and the other
khans. So long as there was fighting, his shrewdness, born of a dozen
campaigns, won him respect.

Now, he mused, the paladins of Tatary waxed fat as well-fed
hunting-dogs. They had horses and cattle in plenty. He had nothing.

"There will be a *kurultai*," Khlit had told the khans one evening,
"a council of the chiefs."

Because they were curious, the khans had come to his *kibitka* without exception. Khlit, during his rule as Kha Khan, had never called
a council unless an important event was forthcoming. So the khans
had come, grim fighters of a warlike race, who had found kinship
in the Cossack who had in his veins the blood of Ghenghis Khan
and who wore the sword of a dead Tatar hero.

He had done right. Khlit had no doubt about that. Once before
this he had been the victim of jealousy in the Cossack encampment,
and he had gone forth alone. Wandering, he had obeyed the call of
his race—of men born to the saddle, accustomed to roving.

Khlit's words to the Jun-gar chiefs had been few. He would not
be the leader, he said, of men who had it in their heart to choose
another. Let them select a younger man for Kha Khan.

He had given back to them the metal ornaments of rank—the
gold neckband and silver-chased belt and scabbard. They had taken
them. Khlit, they knew, was old. There were deep lines in his lean
face, although his back was straight when he sat in the saddle. The
flesh was spare on his sloping shoulders.

In Khlit's thoughts was the memory of those who had been his
close companions in the battles with Chinese and Kallmarks. But
Berang was the new Kha Khan. And burly Chagan, the sword-
bearer, was hereditary attendant of the Kha Khan of the Jun-gar.

Truly, he reasoned, it was well. He had ridden from the encampment that same night. Emotion and talk were for women. Yet
Chagan had filled the beakers of the khans with *tarasun*. They had
drunk with him the *tarasun*.

"He is of our blood," Berang swore, "and he has shared our meat and kumiss. Let him choose the best of our horses, men of Tatary, and riders to attend him."

Khlit had accepted no more than the one horse Chagan brought him—a mettled steppe pony. He was accustomed to go his way alone.

It did not escape him that Berang, flushed with his new dignity, had been silent when he left the Tatar *yurts*. And Chagan had been moodily drunk. Not too drunk to hold his stirrup and touch his knee to his own breast in farewell, after the manner of the Tatars. Then it was that Khlit made the speech that lingered in the mind of the khans.

"I have shared your bread and wine," he said, "and one tent has sheltered us both. I have become rich in the kinship of brave men. When snow comes to the steppe, you shall have a gift from me. Such a gift as shall honor our friendship."

Word of Khlit's promise passed through the encampment. For, thought the khans, how could he send to them a gift after he was gone from the steppe? He had taken neither men nor gold. How was a gift to be gleaned from the bandit tribes of the borderland, or the sands of the Great Desert?

The khans knew that Khlit was not given to idle words. And, with the coming of snow, they remembered what he had said.

Khlit, they supposed, would return to the territory of the Cossacks. He turned his horse, however, to the east—to the northern edge of the Great Desert which is called Kobi, beyond which is China. This was a new land, and he entered upon it with a light heart.

Khlit started, as he sat his horse, noting that the sun had left the distant steppe. The cold of night gripped the gorge, and the Cossack dismounted. Tethering his horse in a thicket, he gathered some brush for a fire. Wrapping himself in his sheepskin cloak and saddle-cloth, he sat by the fire, munching the dried beef that had been warmed against his horse's back under the saddle. This, with a drink of kumiss from the flask in his saddle-bags, completed his meal.

Truly, thought the Cossack dreamily, it was well to be afoot again. What other life was fit for a man than that with a horse's barrel between his knees, a pipe in his mouth and open plains before him! Slaves sat by the hearths in the *yurts*. Swine lay in their wallow. To be at large was best. In this manner he had gone from the steppe to the mountains and to another steppe.

Aye, it was good to feel the night wind in the face!

China, he mused drowsily, was the land of treasure. He had heard there were khans who numbered followers by the thousand. Here there would be fighting, the sharp clash of swords, the taking of rich spoil. Here were men of wisdom who played high stakes—life and fortune. Soon he would see, with his own eyes, the Dragon Emperor that travelers had described—the land of the hat and girdle. Of the Yellow Banners, where even the gongs were gold and warriors traced their blood a thousand years.

The way from Tatary to China lay along the hinterland of the desert of Kobi—a space peopled by wandering tribes of both races. Through this Khlit pushed as rapidly as possible, avoiding the caravan routes and keeping to the open steppe.

Thus it was that he came abreast of the Togra Nor and its ravines. The Togra Nor, a mist-shrouded lake, lay among the defiles overlooking the northern caravan route. From the defiles a convenient point was offered for the *barrancas*—raids—of the steppe clans. Khlit, guiding his horse straight to the east, found himself among the rocks of the Togra.

These were no ordinary rocks. Veiled in the customary blue haze of the Mongolian plains, they formed a waste of defiles, barren of the tufts of steppe grass, with occasional lakes in which were mirrored cold white mountain-peaks. Unwilling to turn back, Khlit kept to his course, wending deeper in the purple ridges in spite of the uneasiness of his horse.

It was the second day of his entrance into the Togra defiles that he saw the first human occupant of the place. On a rock peak a horseman stood outlined against the sky. A glance identified him to Khlit as one of the outlaw riders of the steppe. Khlit took no further notice of the man, who appeared not to have seen him, but reined in his horse at sight of smoke rising in a gorge near at hand.

It was Summer, but the Mongolian steppe is never warm, and the Togra was chilled by its rock heights. No game was to be seen, and the Cossack had had no opportunity to replenish his stock of smoke-dried meat by use of his pistols. His horse had sensed the presence of an encampment, indicated to Khlit by the smoke, and, where an encampment was, forage might be obtained.

Hence it was that Khlit trotted up the defile and came upon a *yurt* of rather more than the usual size. It was cleverly located in a bend in the ravine—some two dozen felt tents ranged in a clump of stunted larch. A woman, laying milk curds to dry upon a flat stone, ran to the tents at his approach.

Khlit noted that a large number of horses were grazing in a grassy stretch further along the defile—a number too large for the size of the *yurt*. The fact that they were watched by an armed rider tended to confirm his suspicion that the beasts had come to their present position not altogether lawfully. This, however, was a common matter on the steppe, where horses were wealth.

It was the appearance of the khan who stepped from the tent into which the woman had run that excited his interest. The man was of medium height but so broad that he seemed of unusual size. His heavy hands hung well to his booted knees. A black silk cap trimmed with fur and a red shawl around the waist of his horse-hide coat indicated that he was a plainsman of Khirghiz descent. His broad head had a lop-sided air, owing to a missing ear, probably carved off by an unlucky sword-stroke.

The khan's slant eyes were set wide apart, and his heavy features indicated mingled good-nature and dangerous temper. All this Khlit, who was wise in the ways of men, noted as the other came forward and took his stirrup. When he dismounted, the khan touched him courteously on the chest.

"Greeting, brother rider of the steppe," his voice rumbled forth in enormous volume. "Why have you come to the *yurt* of Dokadur Khan? Ha! May I feed the devil's swine, but you have a good horse. How came you past my sentries?"

His glance, good-natured and shrewd, swept Khlit. The Cossack had discarded his Tatar clothes for sheepskin coat, leather belt and horse-hide boots. Even the owl's feather denoting his descent from Ghenghis Khan he no longer wore. In the eyes of Dokadur Khan he might be a well-to-do horseman of Tatar speech but unknown descent. Wherefore the Khirghiz was curious. Khlit had heard of his companion, a bandit of the Togra.

"The sentries were drunk if they saw me not," he responded carelessly. "I wish to see the noted khan whom men call Dokadur. Hence I am here."

Other men had gathered around the two, with some women in

the background that Khlit guessed to be captives. The burly khan surveyed him agape.

"Ho!" he muttered loudly. "That is a good jest. For the fools of the caravans will travel a day's detour to keep from my *yurt*. Your name?"

"Matters not."

The khan's black eyes sparkled with curiosity.

"You came from Tatary, eh?" he hazarded clumsily. "Perchance you can find ripe picking in the caravans. Camels can be cut out by one rider, and the Manchu guards are fools."

"It may be. The Togra is not far from the China frontier?"

"Two days fast riding is the Liao River, and a hunting pavilion of the emperor. When the World Honored One—may his arrival in purgatory be speedy—hunts, there is rare spoil for the plucking."

Dokadur Khan ushered Khlit into his tent and seated his guest by the side of the fire, sunk in the center of the earth floor. At his side a woman poured out the *tarasun*—fermented mare's milk—from a barrel. The other warriors crowded the enclosure. But Khlit, familiar with the ways of the steppe, knew that he had nothing to fear as long as he was in the *yurt* of the khan. A guest by the fireside is inviolable.

"You like not the Dragon Emperor?" He tugged at his long mustache thoughtfully.

"Nay; how should I?" roared the other. "When his guards cut us down as if we were leper beggars by the highway."

"Yet your *yurt* is near the Liao."

"The Togra is a rare nest for the outlaws. Plundering is good. Nay, there is talk of a new hunt of the Lord of Ten Thousand Years —may he die without honor!" Dokadur Khan glanced sidewise at Khlit, as if to observe the effect of his speech, as he fondled a hooded falcon on a perch beside him. "I have sent the word to the outer districts of the Togra."

"Hey," laughed Khlit, for it was his custom to learn what others knew, "then your men wax fat on the slain game?"

"And on the hunters," chuckled his companion. "A plump mandarin adorns himself with more silks and jewels than a dozen merchants."

"Stripped of his clothing," added Khlit shrewdly, "the mandarin fetches a good ransom."

"Eh, that is true," grinned the khan.

The suspicion had faded from his eyes, which had become moist from the heady drink. Here was a meet soul to drink with, whatever his name. He ordered the kettle of mutton, which had been preparing, to be placed between himself and his guest. Around them grouped the listening warriors and behind them the women. The dirty urchins sought place as best they could, while the dogs whined expectantly against the tent felt.

It was the evening meal of the *yurt*.

Khlit was accustomed to observe his surroundings keenly.

Hence it was that he still lived in a time when few men survived middle age. His wits, sharpened by conflict with many races, had grown more alert with the years that weakened the vigor of his sword-arm.

So, before the boys who had brought water and cloths to cleanse their hands had departed, he had assured himself that the followers of Dokadur Khan were men above the average of the steppe bands, that the khan himself enjoyed complete mastery over them; that his rule embraced the entire Togra, and that, for all his protestations of enmity to the Chinese, his loyalty was for sale to whoever paid best.

From Khlit and the khan the mutton kettle had passed to the men and then to the women. By the time it reached the urchins, there was little but bones and sinew. Khlit noticed that one boy had armed himself with a bare thigh-bone and was fighting the dogs with it for the morsels they had ravished from the mess. On an impulse the Cossack tossed the child his half-consumed portion.

The boy caught it eagerly, laying about him sturdily to drive away the dogs, and vanished through the tent-flap with a surprized glance at his benefactor. Dokadur Khan grunted. But the act had caused Khlit's pistols to flash in the firelight.

"Those be good weapons," observed Dokadur Khan, scanning them enviously. "I will buy them."

"Nay," Khlit laughed. "I will not sell."

"There be two, of Turkish workmanship. I will give a horse for them."

The Cossack shook his head. He was not willing to part with the serviceable weapons—and still less willing to have them in the hands of the Khirghiz. The other growled.

"Then you are one without wit. I have said I desire the pistols. Is my will a light thing to be put aside?"

"And I have said I will keep them."

Dokadur Khan puffed at his pipe sulkily. Khlit regarded him calmly.

"So long as you are within the *yurt*," muttered the other, "I can not lay hand on you. It is written. But, when you leave the *yurt*, my men will follow and slay you for the weapons. If you give them now, you will not die, but there will be no payment."

Khlit's teeth gleamed under his mustache.

"A jackal snarls when it may not bite. But who fears a jackal, Dokadur Khan?"

The other's hand went to his sword, and his lip lifted in a snarl. But Khlit did not look at him.

"Nameless one of unmentionable fathers!" the Khirghiz swore. "It is well you are in the Togra. You can not leave unseen, and my men will take the weapons from your carcass before you are a mile into the defiles."

Khlit knew that Dokadur Khan would do his best to keep his promise. But he knew he was safe as long as he remained in the *yurt*. He leaned closer to the other.

"Harken, Khan," he said slowly, "we be two men with wise heads, you and I. Women quarrel over trinkets. I have heard that Dokadur Khan is skilled above other men in taking horses and in plundering where the danger and the spoil is the greatest. I have seen that this is true. Hey, you are a falcon that takes only the swiftest fox or the strongest antelope."

Mingled feelings showed in the Khirghiz' flat face. Pleasure combatted suspicion. His guest was one who cared nought for his feelings, yet who implied that they had common interests. A man of pride and, perhaps, one with a message.

"The falcon that flies highest," he responded surlily, "can best see the game afoot. Here in the Togra we hear of events in the steppe and over the frontier."

"Then you have heard when the Dragon Emperor comes to Liao to hunt."

"Within a week or less."

"With many followers?"

Dokadur Khan threw back his head with a roaring laugh.

"Nay, you must be from a distance, if you know not that Wan Li hunts with an army. Aye, an army of thousands; blue and yellow banners of spearmen, armor-arrayed beaters by the hundred; the nobility of Liao province. His pagoda is moved upon the backs of fifty oxen——"

"Rare plunder for a shrewd man."

The khan stared, his grievance forgotten.

"Wan Li's court! Nay—" he shook his head helplessly—"the Forbidden City itself is not safer than the imperial riches. A hundred beaters die in the time between sunrise and dark, for his sport. Have the *rakchas* sent madness upon your head?"

Khlit shook his head, and the Khirghiz saw that there was no folly in the keen, deep-set eyes under the tufted gray brows.

"Nay, Dokadur Khan, I would not steal, even from Wan Li. But spoil! There is the reward of the brave fighter. Is the Son of Heaven too high for the glance of a khan such as yourself? Nay, I have seen the citadel of an empire taken by men who had no other virtue than that they rode three hundred miles in three days."

The light of memory in his eyes, the Cossack told the plainsmen what he had seen—a part of it—in his journey from Russia, through Persia to Mongolia. As they listened, the men drew nearer the fire eagerly. Here was a tale fit for true men!

"Truly," protested the khan at the finish, "I fear not the men of the Dragon Emperor—even though the guards of the Golden Tomb be near at hand in the Liao Hills. But I have not two thousand men. It can not be!"

"Can a hooded falcon strike? Nay; only one that soars."

"But how?"

Khlit pointed across the fire to the west.

"A fool tells what he is about to do. From where I have come, are men who have no fear of the Dragon army. This much will I say. Be watchful during the hunt. For the end of the hunt will be the Seventh Moon, which is favorable to foes of the Dragon."

There was no mistaking Dokadur Khan's growing interest. Khlit's recital, capped by his vague promise, had fired his *tarasun*-heated brain.

"By keeping your men ready with arms at hand and your eyes keen. Is the Dragon the only one to hunt?"

Dokadur Khan pondered this with an air of wisdom. There was respect in the glance he cast at Khlit, also burning curiosity. He was aware that his followers were stirred by the words of their guest, and he did not wish to appear ignorant of what was afoot on the steppe.

When the talk ended, Khlit had gained two points. He had aroused the interest of the brigands and possibly gained himself allies, of a sort, if he should need them in the Togra. And he had taken the khan's mind from his pistols.

Of this last Khlit could not be sure. Morning might bring thought of his promise to take the weapons, to Dokadur Khan. Men of that type were fickle. It might be well not to put him to the test. His respect for Khlit had mounted; still. . . .

Khlit settled the matter himself by stealing from the tent long before dawn when the encampment was wrapped in sleep. He attracted no attention. Yet, when he walked to where his horse was picketed, he heard a step beside him and turned, hand on sword.

"Lord," a small, high voice came out of the darkness, "I had thought that the honorable one might leave before it was light. I read wisdom in his look, and those who are wise do not trust to Dokadur Khan. So I waited without the tent."

Khlit peered at the shadow beside him and made out the figure of the boy to whom he had thrown the meat. He laughed softly.

"Eh, little warrior," he chuckled, "you will be a leader of men some day, and perhaps a horse-thief."

"If the honorable one says that," cried the urchin proudly, "it will come true. I listened under the tent-wall, and surely the honorable one has the wisdom of the earth at his will. It was such a tale as I have never heard."

The boy kept close to the Cossack's side as the latter saddled his horse and mounted.

"Now," he whispered importantly, "I will show the khan a way to leave the Togra before the riders of Dokadur can reach him."

Khlit leaned down.

"Have you a horse, O one who will be great?"

"Nay," the lad muttered; "they say I am too young——"

"Come, then," chuckled Khlit.

He swung the child up to his saddle-peak. The lad gasped, half in fright, half in pleasure.

"Show me now this way from these cursed ravines."

By dawn they were many miles from the encampment. Khlit had little fear that his trail could be followed. Still he did not rein in his horse until they reached at midday the last of the ridges and came out on the level plain. Then, to the boy's sorrow, he set his comrade down.

"Harken, little khan," he growled. "Before many hours the men of Dokadur will come out near here. If not, go to one of the sentinels. Bear this as a free gift from me to Dokadur. Bid him not forget the seventh moon."

He put one of his pistols into the hand of the delighted lad and added some beef as an after-thought.

"It will earn you a better share of mutton," he laughed. "Say to the khan that I forced you to come with me. And remember the seventh moon."

"He shall hear," swore the child, "on my life!"

"I doubt it not. Health and honor to you!"

With that Khlit spurred off eastward across the plain in high good-humor. As long as he was in view, the boy stood in the defile holding the weapon clasped tight. Not until Khlit had vanished did he remember he was hungry and eat the dried meat. It was well, he thought triumphantly, that the old khan had not offered him reward. For true men do not reward one another, more than the trust between them, for a service asked and given.

II

A water-clock tells the passing of time: if the owner of the clock dies, it will not stop. Only when there is no more water will it stop.

Chinese proverb.

At one of the locks on the upper Liao stood the fish-house of Lun Chang, of lowly ancestors. When the crews of the outward-bound junks rested from their labors, they entered the fish-house of Chang to throw dice and to barter for dried fruit and salt fish. Thus it was that Chang prospered and heard much of what came to pass in Liao province. And, as with men of higher caste, his good fortune was his undoing.

It was late one afternoon of the sixth moon that Chang, his skinny hands folded in his sleeves and his straw-shod feet crossed under him, saw a small river-junk draw in to the bank and a tall plains-man with some difficulty land himself and his horse.

The stranger mounted at once, not clumsily, but with a leap that brought a glint to Chang's lined eyes. A horseman, thought the fish-dealer, and one from the plains. Undoubtedly possessed of a full purse of *taels*. Wherefore his kowtow was respectful.

"Health and an honorable life, uncle," he chattered; "is it your will to grace my insignificant shop with your presence? Food of the finest——"

Khlit scowled. He knew but a few words of Chinese, and the patois of Chang missed its mark. But the nature of the house was self-evident. He pointed to an armful of cherry branches not yet stripped of their fruit or leaves.

"Bring me these, Swine Face," he growled in the Tatar tongue.

Chang, however, knew the dialects of the frontier.

"It shall be as the lofty one desires," he said, picking up the branches. "Lo, here is luxuriant fruit, grown in the gardens of Wei Chung-hsien himself. Nay, will the honorable one——"

Khlit had caught the burden from him and placed it before his horse. Not until he saw that the animal was feeding well did the Cossack seat himself on a bench without the shop, calling for dried fish. When Chang had satisfied his wants, the shopkeeper lingered near, curious as to the man who fed his horse better than himself.

"You are from the plains, uncle. You come in good time, for the Son of Heaven himself, with many of his court, comes in the Dragon Chariot to Liao province to the hunting pavilion of Wei Chung-hsien."

Khlit tossed the man a coin and kept on eating. Chang stared curiously at his tanned face and gray mustache. His visitor, he was sure, was no Tatar; nor was he a Manchu. Then, what?

"You have come to take part in the hunt, uncle? Perhaps you are one of the plainsmen sent for by his Excellency, Wei Chung him-self, to tell of the whereabouts of game."

Khlit knew that it would be well to adopt some story as to his coming. The suggestion of Chang, he reflected, would serve very well. He had little fear of recognition by the Chinese, in his new attire. Few of the latter had seen him, and they were either dead or scattered with the armies of the empire. Still, his face and tongue would excite inquiry from the spies of the emperor. The fish merchant, doubtless, would repeat what he knew. And recognition would mean death to Khlit, who had fought against the Chinese more than once.

"Aye," he responded indifferently, "a plainsman."

"Then you will have honor at the hunting pavilion, good sir," gossiped Chang, "for the hunt must not fail of success, especially as it comes in the seventh moon, which some astrologers say is unpropitious for the emperor. It took all the arts of the beautiful Lady Li, the favorite, to bring him to Liao, it is said."

"Is the master of an empire obedient to the whim of a woman?"

Chang looked around him cautiously and lowered his voice.

"I have heard many rumors, honorable hunter. A junkman from the Forbidden City swore, when he had several beakers of wine, that the Lady Li, of the tiny feet, holds the heart-strings of Wan Li. In all but name she is empress. She is as fair as a pink sunrise—although that is a topic not for my profane tongue—even if she was once a harlot."

Khlit grunted with distaste of the man's whispering. Yet here was tidings Khlit needed. He tossed another coin to Chang. This time it was gold. The fish-dealer thrust it eagerly into his belt with a quick glance at his visitor.

"It is music in my ears," observed Khlit, "to hear such news of the Dragon court. There is little heard of such things on the steppe. Say on."

Momentary suspicion gleamed in Chang's faded eyes. It was dangerous to talk of those in power in Liao. But he loved gossip. And the stranger undoubtedly was a man from the steppe, and not a spy.

"Harken, uncle. Beyond the hunting pavilion of Liao is the Fourteenth Tomb of the Ming dynasty, called the Golden Tomb because of the treasures buried with the forefather of Wan Li. The Son of Heaven, in his august pleasure, is a lover of the chase. He was displeased when the astrologers declared that the seventh moon was one of bad omen. The emperor plans, it is rumored, to visit the pavilion in order to burn incense before the grave of his great ancestor, as is the custom. Then at the same time he will hunt. Thus, by his mission of prayer, the ill luck will be averted, and he may still enjoy a hunt."

Khlit did not smile at the manner in which the Dragon Emperor had saved his face. The ways of the Chinese were new to him, and he pondered.

"And Wei Chung—whatever the devil calls himself?" he asked. "Truly, you know many things, Chang."

The dirty fish-dealer was plainly flattered.

"Wei Chung-hsien," he explained, "is an honored eunuch and advisor of the munificent Wan Li. All unworthy, I speak the names of such great men. The home of Wei Chung-hsien is in the province here, and it is said he is head of the spies of the Dragon throne, besides being one of the clouds of Heaven. He has the trust of Wan Li—a mighty eunuch."

Khlit's probing brain pieced together the fragments of the fish-dealer's gossip—with a grim curiosity as to the land where such as Chang bandied rumors about the court.

The Lady Li, it appeared, owed much of her influence over Wan Li to the fact that she was the mother of a child—who was not the heir to the throne. Thus, without the title of empress, she was still the favored woman of the court—a court unequaled in the Ming dynasty for magnificence. Rumor stated that she was as ambitious as she was beautiful.

Wei Chung-hsien had been the emperor's friend from birth—a confidential advisor and intimate of the astrologers. His position as master of the spies naturally gave him access to all information that came to the court, wherefore he was much sought after by nobles who wished to better their fortunes.

"What kind of a man," broke in Khlit impatiently, "is this emperor who has women and near women for councilors?"

Horror showed in Chang's face at this remark. The fish-dealer might gossip concerning the Lady Li, but the person of the Son of Heaven was of celestial purity. A generous monarch, he cried, dutiful to the spirits of his ancestors and peace-loving, leaving the management of his armies in the hands of Wei Chung-hsien. Khlit tugged at his mustache moodily. The picture was not to his liking.

A sudden silence on the part of Chang caused him to look up. Along the bank of the river a small cavalcade was coming toward the inn. Several horsemen preceded a black sedan with yellow trimmings. Beside it walked two stout mandarins in gorgeous dress.

"A sedan of the court," whispered the fish-dealer hurriedly. "Bow!"

Khlit remained seated as he was, but the other advanced a pace and bent his head nearly to his knees. Not content with this, Chang kneeled in the dirt and pressed his head to the ground. Abreast of the shop the sedan halted, and one of the silk-robed personages approached them.

Khlit had not seen such an individual before. The man's sleeves hung below his knees; the blue-green of his robe was faced with yellow, and a tiny dragon was embroidered near the throat. A stout man, with smooth flesh hiding his eyes.

The newcomer halted and surveyed the prostrate fish-dealer, who bobbed his head without looking up. Then he said something Khlit did not understand. Chang rose on his haunches with a muttered reply. Khlit saw the figure of the fish-merchant stiffen.

Without further speech Chang got up and went into the house. He came out with a wooden spade. The man of the dragon robe pointed to the earth near the building, and Chang set to work to dig. Khlit saw that several sailors, who were looking on, had fallen to their knees. The face of Chang was dripping sweat, and in it Khlit read something akin to deadly fear. At times the dragon-robed individual kicked him.

Something was in the air. Khlit noted that the horsemen had come closer and were watching idly. From the latticed window of the sedan-chair he thought he saw a face peering, a small face, half-veiled by a fan held before it. A pair of dark eyes were visible over the fan. They belonged, thought Khlit, to a woman. He was not sure.

By now Chang had dug some two feet below the surface, for the ground was soft—a hole some six feet by two. He worked feverishly, aided by the kicks of the other. His legs were trembling. Then Khlit saw the dragon robe turn toward the sedan. Apparently some message passed between the occupant of the chair and the other, for the man stepped to Chang's side. The fish-dealer dropped his spade with a hoarse cry.

Quickly and without waste of effort the man of the dragon robe placed one hand over Chang's forehead, catching two fingers in the nostrils. A knife flashed in the other hand. The man then drew the knife deftly across the throat of the fish-dealer.

Khlit saw the legs of Chang crumple under him, and Chang himself fall into the newly-dug hole. The man in the dragon robe motioned to the onlookers, who took up the spade and began throwing the dirt back on the body. The slayer of the fish-dealer tossed the bloody knife down and turned to Khlit.

The Cossack, surprised at what had happened, understood that the other was asking his name. He thought quickly.

"I am a huntsman," he said in the dialect of the plainsmen of Dokadur Khan, "come to the pavilion."

The Chinaman's brow cleared.

"You are one of those—summoned?" he asked in the same dialect.

"To the hunt."

"By order of——"

"Wei Chung, of Liao," hazarded Khlit shrewdly.

The gossip of the slain Chang had served him well.

"Where do you come from?"

"The border. Is it not well? I have been told——"

The man held up his hand for silence.

"It is well, hunter. I am Ch'en Ti-jun, a eunuch of Wei Chung's. You can speak freely to me. What is your name and caste?"

Khlit glanced around at the watching sailors.

"That is for the ears of him who sent for me," he said slowly; "not for others."

The eunuch nodded approvingly.

"A fool is light of tongue," he commented. "Yonder carrion that was Chang, the fish-dealer, gossiped concerning the name of a woman high in favor in the eyes of the Son of Heaven. Now he is sped to his ancestors unhonored."

Khlit remembered the face he had seen behind the lattice of the sedan and guessed that the dark eyes might belong to the Lady Li. He said nothing, however, mounting his horse and joining the cavalcade which resumed its course away from the river. This he did at the bidding of Ch'en Ti-jun.

As he rode, he summed up what he had learned. Clearly, Wei Chung-hsien had sent for certain men from the border. Khlit had told the eunuch that he was one of this number. Ch'en Ti-jun would doubtless report as much to his master. Meanwhile, Khlit's position at the hunting pavilion would be safe.

What did Wei Chung desire of him? How would he explain his coming to the latter? Time would take care of that, thought Khlit, who was accustomed to rely on his wit. In this manner did Khlit come to match his skill against the men of the Dragon in the contest which only ended at the second gate of the Golden Tomb.

He found the pavilion of Wei Chung to be a *yâmen* of considerable size, an array of ornate buildings enclosed by a wall, the pavilion itself being a palace surrounded by gardens in the center of the enclosure. He was led by one of the horsemen to a low building beside the stables where the hunters were quartered. Entering, after caring for his horse, he found a motley assembly dicing and drinking.

Khlit selected a wooden couch in one corner of the hall where he could see what went on in the building, placing his saddle-bags and coat upon it. Among his companions he identified long-haired Manchus of the North, a few swarthy, fur-clad Tungusi hunters and the remainder squat Solangs of the border provinces. Hillmen and plainsmen, he thought, with few Chinese. Drunk, for the most part, and quarrelsome. He was content, however, to be here and not in the edifices of the Chinese, where spies were to be found.

His entrance had not passed unnoticed. A six-foot Manchu swordsman swaggered over to his couch and surveyed him, arms akimbo.

"Ho, good sirs," bellowed the giant, "a graybeard has fallen into our nest! Nay, look, he wears a full head of hair, unshaven on the forehead. By the sacred magpie, he is a cur among proper men. He will give us good sport! Shall we pluck out his hair or singe his beard?"

Several of the hunters strolled over at this, and gibes flew fast at the unconcerned Cossack. Among men such as these a graybeard was a rare sight, and Khlit belonged to none of the factions present. The drunken idlers welcomed the prospect of entertaining torment at the hand of the Manchu, who, by his size and manner, seemed to be a leader of his faction.

Khlit understood the speech of his persecutor, as the Manchu tongue was similar to the Tatar, but he made no response except to look up. To the Manchu this was a sign of weakness.

"Come, lads," he roared, "we'll singe the hair of his face and head. Ho, then he will be like a raven plucked of its feathers."

"An owl!" put in another gleefully.

"Here is fire!" added a third, handing to the Manchu a smoldering stick pulled from a brazier.

Khlit looked from one to the other. Loud-mouthed scoundrels, he thought, and therefore less dangerous. The Manchu thrust back the sleeves of his embroidered tunic with elaborate pretense and flourished the brand. The onlookers roared with glee at this by-play.

"I have no quarrel with you," growled Khlit, who had grown to dislike combat except where it served his own ends.

"Then I will pick one with you, grandfather of the owls."

Laughter greeted this sally. Attracted by the noise, a short figure in armor-stained undercoat of leather thrust through the group, a Manchu with a quiver slung over his shoulder and a guitar, at which he was plucking, under one arm. The newcomer stared at Khlit with a frown, and the Cossack returned his gaze curiously.

"Poor sport for you here, Kurluk," quoth the archer to the tall Manchu. He peered closer at Khlit. "May the devil mate with me! Nay, may I be born again as a woman, and queen of a pest-house, but here is an old friend!"

The man's voice stirred Khlit's memory. The short, tight-muscled form of the archer also was familiar. The latter, seeing his hesitation, plied the strings of the guitar.

> "When sober I feel,
> You are both my good friends.
> When drunken I reel,
> Our good fellowship ends!"

He sang, and recognition flashed into Khlit's eyes. He remembered a certain tower he had once held by good use of his curved saber, assisted by the shafts of the squat archer.

"Arslan!" he responded. "What do you here, minstrel?"

The singer kowtowed solemnly.

"Lord," he laughed, "I follow upon the scent of golden *taels*. Or silver, for that matter. Whoever pays, I am his servant; if he pays well, I am his slave. Here be women of the court in yonder palace who throw a worthy minstrel coins for a melodious song; likewise certain clouds of heaven who are pregnant with gold. As for Wei Chung, being neither man nor woman but a eunuch with a fat purse, I plant my shafts in the gizzards of his enemies."

"When last we met, Arslan," observed Khlit, recalling that the archer had been employing his arrows against the Chinese, "it was otherwise——"

"The dice of fate, lord," broke in Arslan hastily, "fall not always in the same manner. Like a horned ram, a poor mercenary does well not to look behind him——"

"Or to name those whom he met before, Arslan," growled Khlit meaningly, for fear the archer should reveal his identity. Arslan, however, he knew to be a man of wit and counsel, indebted to him for his life. "I, also, am a mercenary without title or honor other than my sword brings. Hey, that is a true word."

"You know this graybeard, Arslan?" put in Kurluk impatiently. "Nay, I shall make him croak like a sick raven. What name bears he?"

The slant eyes of the short archer narrowed shrewdly. Khlit's words had not been wasted.

"He has the surname of the Curved Saber, O light of skull," he laughed. "From that long weapon at his thigh."

"You called him 'lord,'" persisted the other suspiciously.

"Because he is a better fellow than you, Kurluk. Before this life you were an ape. You will be born again as a parrot, undoubtedly. But this old warrior has wisdom under his gray thatch."

Kurluk scowled, resenting Arslan's nimble tongue. The latter, however, he did not choose to antagonize.

"We will burn his roof for him," he muttered, flourishing the brand.

The onlookers guffawed.

Arslan's yellow teeth gleamed.

"Take care you scorch not your own thick fingers, Kurluk of the addle-pate," he retorted.

He had seen Khlit use his curved sword.

> "When a heaven-born fool
> Uses fire, in his folly,
> He will find it a tool
> Of dire melancholy."

He chanted, grinning. Kurluk scowled the more and advanced upon Khlit. The Cossack by a quick thrust of his scabbard knocked the burning stick to the floor. Kurluk swore and clapped hand to sword. The watchers drew back, sensing a quarrel. The noisy hunters fell silent, watching the two.

"I have done you no harm, Kurluk," said Khlit mildly, for in his present situation he disliked to attract attention to himself. "Leave the brand in the fire, and we will drink good wine together, you and I."

But the Manchu was not minded to forfeit his sport. His prestige was at stake, and Arslan's taunts had got under his thick skin. He jerked out his short sword savagely.

"Come, dog of the devil," he growled, "I am weary of hearing you bark. Let me see your teeth, if old age has left you any."

With that he spat in the direction of the Cossack, who rose from the couch at once, drawing his weapon. Arslan plucked rapidly at his guitar in high good humor.

As a rule, a Manchu was well-versed in use of the heavy, hatchet-shaped sword. There were no sturdier fighters among the men of the Dragon banners. But a Cossack is trained from infancy in handling his weapons and is a match for the skilled Osmanli and the best of the dangerous Tatars. His skill is that of one bred to no other purpose.

Khlit's shoulder and arm muscles were lean. He knew that his strength would last only a brief interval against the powerful swordplay of Kurluk. Wherefore he met the rush of his adversary in a manner that brought startled exclamations to the lips of the onlookers and a grin from Arslan.

Kurluk swung his weapon to beat down Khlit's guard. He found that the other's curved sword pressed against his own before his stroke gathered force. Lash and thrust as he would, the lighter sword formed a glittering guard before his face. When his strokes pierced the guard, the Cossack leaped to one side.

Not only that. Deftly Khlit was thrusting at Kurluk's head. His swift, short strokes cut the skin of the other's shaven head, drawing from one side to the other as a man uses a whetstone against a knife. Blood streamed from the Manchu's skull. Striving desperately to free his sword from the pressure of the other's blade, Kurluk was helpless to stop the deliberate slicing of his forehead.

A moment after the bout had begun, it ended. Kurluk stood cursing, his eyes and ears filled with blood that spattered from his face to the floor. Blinded by it, he was helpless.

"Come, Kurluk," cried Khlit, lowering his sword, "a skilled warrior like you should use his weapon against his enemies. 'Tis a waste of good blood between friends. Let Arslan pour water over your sore head, and we will drink a cup of wine. Truly, it was not by might but by a trick of the sword that I blinded you. So I would have you for a friend."

Kurluk growled irresolutely, rubbing at his smarting eyes.

"Nay, brain of an ox," mocked Arslan, "here is a true man. Sheathe your sword."

The Manchu did so. Thus it was that the Cossack found a friend in a land where he had few friends and many foes. But uppermost in his mind was the regret that the sword-bout had drawn widespread attention to him. He could no longer hope to remain unnoticed among the hunters.

III

On the first day of the seventh moon the beast *chilin* was sighted near the hunting pavilion of the Son of Heaven. Once before had the beast *chilin* been seen, and the omen was auspicious for the hunt. Yet at the same time a dark star was ascendent in the sky at night. How was it to be known which was the true omen, the good or the bad?
Annals of the reign of Wan Li.

In his silk-hung apartment Wan Li moved restlessly, glancing at the water-clock which showed it to be an early hour in the evening. A tall man in middle age with the full girth and broad, placid face of his race. He had discarded his robes of ceremony for a short dragon tunic.

Wan Li was impatient. For a week he had waited at the hunting *yâmen* of Wei Chung-hsien, and as yet there had been no decision from the court of astrologers regarding the omens of the coming hunt. And it was already the seventh moon. A verdict had been promised for that night, and it was already late. He halted impatiently by the two attendants at the door.

"Has Li Yuan F'o asked for admittance yet?" he asked.

One of the men kowtowed.

"May your Majesty live forever! Your servants have not seen the honorable astrologer——"

"Then go," commanded Wan Li, "and say it is my will that he come!"

He seated himself irritably on an ebony bench but looked up eagerly at the appearance of the astrologer. Li Yuan F'o, a venerable savant in ceremonial attire, made the nine obeisances and kneeled. His lined face was troubled.

"Your decision—the omens?" inquired Wan Li quickly.

"Lord of Ten Thousand Years!" began the man. "Your court of astrology has considered the omens with the greatest care, and our divination has been made. As the Son of Heaven in his wisdom knows, the augury of the stars is infallible. The lives of your ancestors of illustrious name have been safeguarded by the celestial omens."

"No one knows better than I, Li Yuan," assented Wan Li respectfully.

"We have used the utmost of our knowledge. The World Honored One must not undertake the hunt. The dark star of evil omens is in the ascendency during this moon. It is written that your Majesty must start upon no venture while this star is high in the heavens. That is the verdict of the court of astrology."

Wan Li frowned. Plainly he was not pleased.

"Yet I come here upon a sacred mission. To enter the tomb of my ancestor and burn incense before his coffin. Such an act is sufficient to abolish the evil influence of the star. Have you considered that, Li Yuan?"

The man kowtowed.

"We have considered, Lord of Ten Thousand Years. To open the grave door of the Golden Tomb, wherein no one but the Son of Heaven may come, is a holy act, but the omens are dark. Heed well the words of your faithful servants and close your ears to all others. There are some near you who think first of themselves, then of the Presence——"

Wan Li moved his head impatiently.

"I heed your words of wisdom as an astrologer, Li Yuan. But other advice I judge as I please. You are hostile to Wei Chung-hsien, who has my heart and ear. Is the decision of the astrologers final?"

Li Yuan's stately head bowed.

"It is final, except for divine intervention—such as the appearance of the celestial beast *chilin*, which is always auspicious to your dynasty. Your Majesty must not hunt. The Golden Tomb awaits you."

Both the astrologer and the emperor started at this unfortunate reference to the tomb of the Ming dynasty. Wan Li was impressed as well as disgruntled. He shook his sleeve, dismissing the savant.

"Very well," he muttered. "I had it in my heart to hunt, but, if the omens——"

Li Yuan departed hastily, a triumphant light in his faded eyes. In the outer hall he did not see the eunuch Ch'en Ti-jun step from a hidden door and follow him. Still less did the astrologer guess that this door gave access to a compartment directly behind the silk hangings of Wan Li's chamber. The eunuch laid his hand roughly on the savant's shoulder.

"Treacherous imbecile!" hissed the eunuch. "Is that the way you obey the command of Wei Chung-hsien? After a week's humbug!"

Li Yuan freed himself with dignity.

"The message of the stars," he said gravely, "is not subject to the will of men. I have told his Majesty the truth. Let him be warned by it. I care not for Wei Chung."

"You will think otherwise," assured Ch'en Ti-jun savagely, "if your old fingers are crushed slowly and your brains squeezed until they run through your nose. Go back and tell Wan Li you have reconsidered, or Wei Chung shall deal with you."

"Am I the servant of Wei Chung?" Defiance flashed in the eyes of the astrologer. "Is the Lord of Ten Thousand Years a slave to his own minion? Even if the court has become a hotbed of spies and false tales, forbidden to men of honor? Nay; I serve Wan Li and the stars."

The eunuch smiled.

"Even the decision of the stars, Li Yuan, can be bought by gold. You were witless to refuse Wei Chung's generous offer of rank and gold ingots. Truly, the matter is not important. What harm can come to Wan Li if he hunts?"

"I know not," the astrologer's voice trembled, and his glance fell. "But the stars do not lie. If the matter is so slight, why do you offer me so much to lie?"

Ch'en Ti-jun gnawed his lip; then he passed his long fingernails softly across the astrologer's thin throat.

"You know what happens to those who disobey Wei Chung? And how useless it is to oppose him? Are you entirely mad?"

Li Yuan's figure, which had fallen to trembling, stiffened.

"I shall be before long," he muttered angrily, "if these rats and foxes who are eunuchs of the court seize what power is left to the emperor. Already they have the command of his armies and the decision as to who shall be admitted to the Presence. They build triumphal arches for themselves, while the Son of Heaven, blind to their sins, goes unhonored. They wear the imperial yellow and forge orders in his name. Now they would control the immutable verdict of the stars——"

Still muttering, the old man moved away from Ch'en Ti-jun, down the passage. The eunuch looked after him, scowling. Then he turned swiftly and halted by the door from which he had come. He paused as if listening, nodding once or twice, as at a command from behind the hangings.

"But if they deny it?" he whispered.

Apparently the reply satisfied him, for he went to the attendants of the emperor's chamber. Wan Li acknowledged his subservient greeting with a gleam of anticipation. Experience had taught him that the eunuchs were quick to guess his pleasure and minister to it when he was displeased—more so than the hereditary members of his court, who persisted in troubling him with protests and state affairs.

"Lord of Ten Thousand Years," began Ch'en Ti-jun respectfully, "it is the honor of your slave to be the bearer of good tidings. Some members of the court of astrology have disagreed with the ancient Li Yuan. They say he has not interpreted the stars correctly. Your slave brings you their word."

"Is it favorable?"

"World Honored One, it is so. And this is the manner of it. While a certain star of ill omen is in the sky during the seventh moon, there is another star above it."

Wan Li nodded eagerly. The eunuch glanced involuntarily toward one of the silk hangings which swayed as if with a breath of air, although the chamber was closed on all sides.

"It is due to the zealous Wei Chung, whose happiness it is to serve the Son of Heaven, that the good tidings were learned," he continued smoothly. "He has questioned some of the astrologers and discovered this all-important fact. No less a star than that of good omen, your Majesty's birth-star, is now taking the ascendency over the dark orb of ill omen. He does not believe that the venerable Li Yuan knew of this."

"Li Yuan is old," agreed Wan Li eagerly; "he may have made a mistake."

"Doubtless unwittingly. But during the seventh moon, when the birth-star of the Son of Heaven is high, he may undertake a hunt in safety. His happiness is precious to those near the Presence. Excellent game has been sighted in the country between here and the Togra. Everything is prepared. Will your Majesty name the happy day of the opening of the hunt?"

Mingled feelings were reflected in the good-natured face of Wan Li.

"Is it not true," he questioned, "that a birth-star and the one of evil omen together in the sky may mean death?"

Ch'en Ti-jun shook his head with a smile.

"In the case of lesser men, perhaps—and then not always. But there is no power like that of the Dragon planet. Has not the star of your dynasty brought prosperity and long years to you? O Lord of Ten Thousand Years, has the word of the ancient Li Yuan more force than the good omen of your dynasty? Wei Chung-hsien would be grieved if he heard that the Son of Heaven had such a thought."

Wan Li shook his head dubiously. His better judgment told him that in matters of celestial omens the old astrologer would not deceive him. But he had the superstition of his time, and the prospect of the anticipated hunt was alluring. He dismissed Ch'en Ti-jun, unable to make up his mind.

Not more than five minutes after the hangings had fallen behind the eunuch, they parted again and revealed the smiling form of Wei Chung-hsien, clad in resplendent silks, embroidered as was the emperor's tunic with a yellow dragon. The large eyes of the chief eunuch were soft with pleasure as his massive figure made a slight obeisance.

"Glorious tidings for the ear of the Son of Heaven. All breathless, I hasten to bring them, to be the first to whisper the auspicious news. Your divine reign has been blessed by a true sign from heaven. A Manchu huntsman of my employ has sighted a *chilin* near the *yâmen*. The god-like beast that is an omen of celestial good-will."

Wan Li started and flushed.

"A Manchu huntsman! His name? Bring him to me that I may hear the story from his own lips."

Wei Chung shook his head regretfully.

"The fortunate man," he responded, "is drunk, overcome by his find, and can not come to the Presence."

A last doubt clouded the smooth brow of the emperor.

"How could a Manchu recognize the sacred beast?"

Wei Chung bowed with folded arms.

"O Lord of Ten Thousand Years, do you not see that the wonder is twofold thereby? For he, being of low birth, did not know what he had seen. Only when he described the strange beast to me, did I know of the good fortune of your Majesty. It is proof the man did not lie. As for the hunt——"

"The day after tomorrow," cried Wan Li joyfully, "I appoint as the beginning of the hunt. See that all is ready."

For a week the huntsmen had been idling in their quarters, and joyfully they received the tidings that night. The hunt was to begin at dawn on the second day. A eunuch of the court brought them the news, and they straightway fell to cleaning weapons and discussing the location of game on the plains beyond the Liao River.

To Khlit and Arslan the announcement brought relief. They had been chafing at the inactivity. Khlit especially found it irksome. He had tried to enter the imperial *yâmen* to satisfy his curiosity concerning the Dragon court. But every gate was guarded by the followers of Wei Chung. Nobles came and went in curtained sedans, surrounded by horsemen.

The atmosphere of the encampment beside the *yâmen*, where the soldiers of the emperor were quartered, was also strange to Khlit. The officers treated him with a contempt which he bore with grim patience. The Chinese men-at-arms were suspicious of his unusual face and figure and avoided him. Their weapons excited his amusement—armored head-pieces and vambraces guarding the arteries, huge quilted coats and two-handed swords, silken garments and black satin boots. The air of secrecy and distrust that pervaded the place was disagreeable to the open-handed Cossack.

Thus he was surprised when a messenger came from the *yâmen* summoning him to the hunting pavilion with Arslan. The archer touched him on the shoulder warningly as they followed their guide into the darkness.

"Silence is best, lord," he whispered. "Where we are going, the curtains have ears. If any ask, remember that you are one of the stout fellows sent for by Wei Chung from the plains. Kurluk and I are among them. None will know that you were not summoned with the rest."

Khlit grunted understanding. They were admitted by the sentinels at the gate and turned into a narrow passage that brought them to some stairs leading to the floor above. Here the floors were carpeted with costly Persian rugs, and the walls shone with lacquer and enamel. The scent of dried flowers was in the air.

A slender girl peered out at them from a curtain, which was drawn aside, and they stood in a dimly-lit chamber where the walls were veiled in shadows cast by a red-paper lantern overhead. Their guide had disappeared, but a squat eunuch took his place. Khlit felt that they were being carefully inspected by unseen eyes.

Presently he saw the eunuch kowtow and Arslan follow suit. Then he was aware that a woman had entered the room and was seated on a couch in front of them. In spite of the warning hiss of the eunuch, the Cossack scanned the shadowy figure.

He saw a slender form, erect, in a black silk dress, gold embroidered, with a yellow crêpe veil framing a delicate face. The tiny red lips were brilliant with paint; the dark eyes inscrutable. She was speaking in a low voice. Later Arslan interpreted what she had said.

They had been granted an audience by the Lady Li, favorite of the emperor.

She had heard, she said, that they were the leaders of the huntsmen who were to find game for the Son of Heaven. During the chase they would keep near the imperial sedan, pointing out the places where the finest animals were to be found. Such was the custom.

Before the chase began, said the Lady Li, the Son of Heaven would go to the tomb of his ancestor, a few hours' ride into the plain from the *yâmen*. There he would enter the grave chamber to burn incense and offer prayer, as was permitted once in ten years to the Ming monarchs. This duty performed, Wan Li would go to his sedan. Then the signal would be given for the beaters to begin their casts into the plains, and the hunt would go forward.

The departure from the *yâmen* would be after midnight so that the emperor would leave the Golden Tomb at dawn—such was his impatience to begin the excursion into the plains.

From the moment they left the *yâmen,* said the Lady Li, it was her wish that the worthy huntsmen, comrades of Khlit and Arslan, should ride close to the imperial chair. Darkness, she hinted, was a screen for the working of evil by traitors, of whom there were many in the court. The huntsmen could be relied on to be faithful to their salt. They must see to it that the emperor was not molested during the confusion of the hunt. Especially when the chase pushed into the rocky regions in the distant plains where ambuscades were possible.

The huntsmen must never leave the chair of the emperor.

This was the word of the Lady Li of the shell-tinted face and the dark eyes. At a signal from the eunuch Arslan and Khlit took their departure, walking backward. A light rain was falling without, and the archer drew the Cossack into a group of cherry-trees beside the pavilion gate while he told him the woman's message.

"Hey, old warrior," he chuckled, "you and I have been blessed with a rare sight, the face of the beautiful courtesan whose dainty hand upraised could slit the gullets of a thousand men if it pleased her. We shall have a fat purse of *taels* for this night's work. Nay, I marvel that she trusts us."

Khlit shook his head moodily.

"Think you so, Arslan? Why should she put faith in us? Are the words of such a woman to be believed?"

"She spoke us fairly. We are to watch over the emperor's person. Doubtless she has heard the tale of your sword-play with Kurluk. It may be she suspects evil of the fat Wei Chung."

"In whose pay you are."

"True. But the more masters, the more gold. The Lady Li has promised us costly emeralds and sapphires for doing her bidding. Wei Chung has not ordered otherwise."

Khlit stared at the lantern over the postern thoughtfully.

"It is said the Lady Li has a son. Is it true?"

"So the tale runs. A year ago the Lady Li announced that a son had been born, and the emperor burned incense before her tablet out of pure joy. Some said an infant had been smuggled into the woman's palace that night, but doubtless they were sliced in quarters for that calumny. Wan Li favors the child above his lawful heir, who has the support of the older nobles. There be rumors that Wan Li has signed a decree naming the son of Lady Li as his successor. I know not. In the Dragon court a decree is often a forgery at the hands of these foxes of eunuchs."

"Evil follows the destiny of a ruler who gives power to servants."

Arslan stared at his companion curiously. Khlit's keen insight into what went on about him was something of a mystery to the light-minded archer.

"You speak as one who knows the celestial omens, lord," he muttered.

The Cossack did not smile.

"Have you forgotten, Arslan," he responded, "that I have been, for a time, a leader of men?"

"Nay, I have not forgotten, Khlit. Nor that you once saved my life. Wherefore, I am your man, and your will is mine. Your peril is my peril. But why have you come to this nest of evil?"

This question had often troubled Arslan. Khlit did not reply at once.

"It is in my blood to wander, Arslan," he growled. "Why does a goshawk fly up into the sun? I have come to see the face of the Dragon Emperor, Lord of a Hundred Million Souls. When I have done so, I will be content."

Arslan shook his dark head dubiously. Why should a man risk his skin in such a profitless venture?

"I have a thought," mused Khlit, "that, if Wan Li died and the decree of which you speak could be produced, the Lady Li might claim the throne for her child. As the boy is an infant, she would then be empress-dowager, in possession of the Dragon throne."

The archer caught his arm hastily.

"Those words would earn us molten silver down our gullets, Khlit," he warned, anxiously. "Nay, you know not the power of the older nobles. If the Lady Li should be guilty of such a crime, all her influence at court would not save her life."

"Not if she were allied to Wei Chung?"

"The chief eunuch is his own master, Khlit. Nay, the slayer of Wan Li would be snuffed out like a candle in the wind, if he were the all-powerful eunuch himself."

"Wan Li might die by accident."

"Does the sun become dark by chance? To think that is madness."

The archer broke off, pointing to the postern. A sedan-chair had drawn up at the gate. The two watchers saw a robed figure descend from it hastily.

"That is the astrologer, Li Yuan," whispered Arslan, peering out between the tree trunks.

Khlit saw the face of the old man in the lantern light as he spoke to the guards. Li Yuan F'o seemed strongly agitated as he begged admittance. The attendants barred his passage.

"The old star-gazer is wroth," interpreted Arslan, who had caught the raised voices of the trio. "He asks why a noble of the court is barred from the presence of the emperor."

"What say the guards?"

"The Son of Heaven is asleep and must not be disturbed."

Li Yuan seemed to be protesting violently. He tried to push between the guards and was thrust back by their spears. Beating his forehead with clenched fists, he returned to his chair, which was borne off in the darkness by the bearers.

No sooner had he disappeared than the bulky figure of Wei Chung came to the doorway from within. The chief eunuch muttered something to the two guards, who seized their spears and ran after the sedan. Then Wei Chung retreated into the building.

To Arslan's horror Khlit emerged from the trees and sought the door, now empty of attendants. The archer followed unwillingly in time to see the tall Cossack peer up the stairs after the figure of the chief eunuch.

Not content with this, Khlit, motioning the archer to silence, slipped up the stairway. Looking into the silken hall, he saw Wei Chung vanish into the chamber where they had left the Lady Li. Arslan heard a moment later the shrill laugh of a woman.

"If we are found here," he whispered fearfully, "we shall be meat for the hunting-dogs on the morrow——"

This time Khlit accompanied Arslan to the door and out into the rain. His face was moody, and he did not speak until they regained the hunters' quarters.

"A woman and a eunuch," he said, "and well pleased."

The next day Arslan reported that an imperial decree had ordered

Li Yuan and the other astrologers from the grounds of the hunting pavilion. The name signed to the decree was that of Wei Chung.

It is written in the annals of Wan Li, of the Ming dynasty, that on the day before the hunt of the seventh moon, his Majesty out of generous good-will toward his subjects ordained that a puppet-show be given in the courtyard of the pavilion for the hunters. In the halls by the stables Arslan greeted the announcement of the servant with a loud shout of approval, while his black eyes snapped with excitement.

"Ho, brothers," he cried, "here will be merry music of fiddles and rare wine for the men of the chase. Let us go at once and seize the benches before the puppet-cage!"

His words were greeted by an answering shout from the idlers, whose interest was lightly stirred. The Manchus and plainsmen, Khlit among them, were early on the scene. They found the fruit-garden of the pavilion surrounded by eunuchs with drawn swords and the gates of the building itself heavily guarded by armed soldiery. But their anticipation was aroused by sight of a painted wooden structure among the trees in the courtyard.

The puppet-stage was curtained on three sides, the fourth presenting a miniature stage to the audience. Swaying of the draperies suggested to the eager audience of soldiers, huntsmen, and servants that the puppets were already in preparation for the show. Musicians tuned up squeaky fiddles at one side of the edifice. An imposingly garbed mandarin stood before the stage, ready to interpret the actions of the play. Wine was not lacking.

Wan Li had given especial orders that his huntsmen were to be well entertained. He himself deigned to appear behind the lattice screens of the pavilion balcony overlooking the court. Wei Chung and the Lady Li with her attendants were the only ones with him, for, since his decision to hold the hunt, the emperor had dismissed the nobles, who plagued him with matters of state, back to Peking. He sat expectantly on a couch, as eager as his servants for the play to begin.

At a signal from the mandarin by the stage the huntsmen arose and kowtowed respectfully in the direction of the concealed monarch.

"These worthies of the chase, sire," bowed Wei Chung, "express their hopes for a great kill of antelope, deer, tigers and the splendid wild camels for the morrow. They rejoice with the Presence in the good omen of the *chilin*."

Wan Li was still disappointed that he could not speak with the man who had sighted the legendary beast called the *chilin*—that left no footprint and conversed with human beings in their own tongue. He half hoped, however, aided by the flatteries of the eunuchs, that the *chilin* of good omen would be found in the hunt.

In the courtyard below the hunters were astir, for the mandarin had begun his chanting recital of the play, and the fiddles were sounding. Arslan listened with a critical ear and nudged Khlit.

"Harken, old warrior," he whispered, "the play will be about the coming visit of Wan Li to the grave of his ancestor."

Khlit looked up indifferently.

"Nay, we are like penned beasts, Arslan, guarded by drawn weapons. Since when have men been herded as animals?"

The archer motioned him impatiently to silence.

"Yon minstrel of the long robe chants," he explained, "how the tomb is watched night and day by chosen warriors of the Son of Heaven, for within it by the body of the illustrious dead man is a treasure beyond price. Harken—gold inlaid in enamel jars, and eternal candles that burn for ten years on pedestals of jade, also pearls and rubies of the rarest, and golden vessels. Small wonder it is called the Golden Tomb."

A puppet garbed in the imperial yellow appeared on the stage, manipulated by the hands of the men behind the edifice. It bowed before a candle and a black box, purporting to be the tomb, while the voice of the mandarin chanted on and the fiddles struck up a rude tune. Then a form with a gray beard descended from the ceiling of the stage and bent over the kneeling monarch.

"See," commented Arslan, "it is the dead emperor's spirit come from the ten courts of purgatory. No one but a Son of Heaven can set foot in the tomb. Even he does not approach the coffin but stands in the grave chamber. A pity such glorious riches should be buried. Only once in ten years are they seen. Ho, I see singing girls coming from the pavilion entrance!"

Khlit took no heed of what was happening. His thoughts were occupied by the request of the Lady Li that they guard the emperor during the hunt. Why had the favorite of Wan Li chosen them for this important post? Because she distrusted the usual guards? But these were the men of Wei Chung. And the Lady Li appeared on the best of terms with the chief eunuch.

Why had the old astrologer, Li Yuan, been kept from the emperor the previous night? Because the guards of Wei Chung were unwilling for him to deliver his message. What did the eunuch hope to gain from the hunt? Khlit did not know.

Memories of various things he had seen during his stay at the *yâmen* flocked upon him. Why had the veteran Ming generals of the Chinese army who had come with Wan Li been sent back to Peking on one pretext or another?

And why had Wei Chung sent out to the plains and the Northern provinces for Arslan and Kurluk and their comrades? The Lady Li had spoken truly when she said that the huntsmen, who had no interest other than their own skins, would be trustworthy guards of the imperial sedan. And, undoubtedly, they knew the whereabouts of game and could show Wan Li the best sport. Perhaps, after all, Wei Chung only hoped to make the chase a success.

Still Khlit was not altogether satisfied. His keen eyes had searched the faces of those in the *yâmen*, and he had been powerless to read the thoughts behind the inscrutable, slant eyes, but he had read deceit and consummate cunning of a kind strange to him.

He looked up as the puppets disappeared and a murmur from the huntsmen greeted the coming of the singing girls—delicate and fancifully-garbed damsels, who postured gracefully, swaying their supple bodies and chanting a shrill, melodious tune echoed by the fiddles. Arslan grinned with delight. Then, when the festival was almost at an end, one of the girls ran from the group and flung herself on her knees before the gallery where the emperor sat.

She stretched her slim arms upward imploringly, and Khlit, who was near, saw that her cheeks were blanched under their coating of red.

"Harken, Lord of Ten Thousand Years," she screamed shrilly, "to a low servant of your beneficence! Heed my message. Because it is a word from the dead for the ear of the Son of Heaven."

Sheer surprize silenced those around her. The singing ceased, and the fiddles broke off their tune. A movement behind the lattice showed that she was observed.

"Harken to a message from the unlawfully slain! Go not on the hunt at midnight. Your Majesty has been tricked with lies. The men of wisdom, who would have advised the Dragon faithfully, were sent away by forged decrees. Where are the generals of your army? They are dismissed. Only eunuchs and their followers remain. The story of the auspicious beast *chilin* was false, to delude the Son of Heaven. My father, the lowly Chang, was slain at his door because he voiced his suspicions——"

A heavy hand caught the daring girl by the hair and flung her to the earth. The high voice of Wei Chung rang out from behind the lattice.

"A knife for the mad wench! Her wails disturb the Son of Heaven."

The tall form of Ch'en Ti-jun strode to the side of the prostrate girl. Khlit saw him seize a sword and slash the unfortunate woman savagely. When the sword was running red, the eunuch tossed it aside and kicked the quivering form. The assembled hunters were hustled from the enclosure by the eunuchs.

In the balcony Wan Li had risen with a frown.

"Are you the emperor, Wei Chung?" he demanded, "to have power of life and death?"

The chief eunuch bowed his head abjectly, with a scornful look Wan Li did not see.

"If your servant has offended, may his head fall from his shoulders. I did but speak hastily, fearing lest your Majesty's peace be irked by the prating girl. For what is the like of such to the enjoyment of the kingly hunt that begins tonight?"

Wan Li surveyed him, hesitation mirrored in his good-natured face. The beautiful favorite stepped to his side.

"Lord of my life," she whispered, "I also have offended. It was I who slew the scurrilous Chang because he dared to breathe tales against my name. His madness has affected his child——"

"I forgive you," said Wan Li.

The courtyard was nearly deserted when Khlit and Arslan turned to go. To the archer's dismay Khlit picked up the body of the girl and stroke off with it to the gate.

"Have you love of the bow-string necklace?" whispered Arslan hurriedly. "Nay, the child is accursed now. Even while Ch'en Ti-jun was striking her, she cried that there was a conspiracy against Wan

Li and that those who honored him should not leave his side in the hunt——"

But Khlit shook his head.

"Dog!" he growled. "This is the body of a young girl. Would you leave it to be defiled? Nay; we will give it to a priest."

For all his protest the archer did not leave Khlit until the Cossack had seen to the burial of the slain girl at one of the temples. Then he followed as Khlit strode back to their quarters with moody brow.

"Truly, this is not such a great matter—a singing girl slain," quoth Arslan.

"It is devil's work."

Khlit swung around and grasped his companion's arm. Drawing the Turkish pistol at his belt, he thrust it into his hand.

"Will you serve me, Arslan?"

"My will is your will. Aye, that I shall do."

"Then seek out your horse. Say that you go on business of the hunt. Bear this weapon as a token from me to the Togra. You know Dokadur Khan?"

"The Khirghiz bandit? Aye."

"Bid him, if he values his life, assemble his men. Say to him that I, Khlit of the Curved Saber, sent you. Say that there may be rich spoil for the taking. But he must be watchful. Post sentries at the entrances of the Togra ravines. I will join you there tomorrow."

Arslan's eyes widened in surprize.

"But the hunt—who will guide the emperor?"

"I will—with Kurluk and some of the Manchus." Khlit's gray mustache twitched in a smile. "The hunt? Nay; it has begun. But other game is sought than antelope or tiger."

IV

The spirits of the everlasting dead have ascended on the Dragon. But in the tombs, hallowed by a thousand years, they are to be found. Humbly must the visitor come to the tombs.

For the mightiest emperor is a child before the faces of the invisible dead.

Li Yuan F'o, astrologer of the court.

In the plains beyond the Liao River the Golden Tomb had been built by one of the early Ming emperors. To guard against discovery, a half dozen tomb mounds were constructed of which only one was used. There was no visible monument, except the high mound of earth rising among some low, pine-clad hills.

In accordance with immemorial custom, an armed guard was stationed in the hills, a guard called the *kang leen* or watchmen at night. The captain of these picked soldiers himself did not know the location of the true grave—a precaution made necessary by the treasures housed within. But on the night of the seventh moon, when the hunt of Wan Li began, a confidential messenger came to the guard from the court bearing an order sealed by the ring at the emperor's girdle, commanding the captain to unearth the doorway of a certain tomb, buried underground.

So it was that, when the midnight gongs resounded in the *yâmen* of Wan Li, fifteen miles away in the plains, Chinese soldiers were working by moon and torchlight to uncover the stone door of the Golden Tomb. Under the pines they worked hastily, for the emperor was coming, and being alone in the hills they were gripped by fear of the dead man beneath the earth.

Wan Li entered his waiting sedan-chair with a light heart as the drums and gongs struck midnight. From the latticed gallery the Lady Li with her women watched his stately figure escorted through the courtyard, illumined by a hundred torches in the hands of mounted attendants.

A roll of drums announced to the waiting soldiery that the chair of the emperor was in motion. In front of it went a troop of armor-clad horsemen, under command of Ch'en Ti-jun. The sedan-chair of Wei Chung followed that of Wan Li. The quick glance of the Lady Li noted that the eunuch's chair was blazoned with the imperial dragon and possessed the same number of bearers as that of Wan Li. To all intents the two were alike, such was the presumption of the chief eunuch who had drawn to himself nearly all of the imperial power.

The lips of the dark-eyed favorite curled scornfully as she noted this proof of Wei Chung's arrogance, passed over by Wan Li. Truly, Wan Li was blind, she thought. A man enslaved by pleasures, bound by his own weak will. Her glance fell upon the group of fur-coated huntsmen riding on either side of the imperial chair, led by the tall rider whom she had heard called the Curved Saber.

Behind the emperor's cortège came an array of courtiers, robed for the chase, and such of the lesser nobles as Wei Chung had allowed to remain at the pavilion. Without the courtyard were waiting the ranks of soldiers and beaters who were to make a wide cast through the plains, hemming in the game to be killed in the presence of the emperor.

When the last torches of the cavalcade had vanished toward the plains, the Lady Li went to the chamber where she was accustomed to burn incense before the tablet of Wan Li. Instead of doing so, however, she locked the door and sank upon a couch, pressing her dainty hands against her temples, staring at a long candle, marked off at regular intervals to tell the passing of the hours.

Once clear of the pavilion, the imperial cortège fell into a swift trot, the sedan-bearers keeping up easily with the horsemen. On either flank the troops of soldiery spread out, their torches marking a line several miles from end to end. The huntsmen accompanying Wan Li kept their place in the procession silently. Their task would not begin until the ceremony at the Golden Tomb was completed.

Khlit rode at their head within a few yards of Wan Li's sedan. The emperor, he noted, kept himself hidden in the screened depths of the chair. Beside him rode the swaggering Kurluk, who had taken Arslan's place.

Khlit's thoughts were busy as he rode. Chiefly he wondered concerning the singing girl who had sacrificed her life to warn Wan Li against venturing on the chase. She must have known the danger she courted by her rash speech. Arslan had heard her speak of a conspiracy, even under the mortal blows of Ch'en Ti-jun. But he could see no evidence of a plot against Wan Li.

True, the emperor's immediate followers were all eunuchs, or nobles under the influence of Wei Chung. Yet he knew the main body of the soldiery would not countenance any violence to the person of Wan Li, sacred by the traditions of fifty generations. A weapon lifted against Wan Li would mean the death of the offender.

He believed that the Lady Li and the chief eunuch had joined forces. Both were interested in breaking the power of the emperor in order to install the favorite's child on the Dragon throne. With

Wan Li out of the way, this might be done. But how was the way to be cleared?

Khlit did not know. Were all his suspicions groundless? It seemed so. But the old Cossack was wise in the ways of evil, and he smelled treachery as keenly as he scented the damp night air.

Another thing that gave him food for thought was the treatment he and the Manchu mercenaries had received. Wan Li had given orders that the huntsmen should be honored. But was this the only reason that he and Arslan had been unmolested, although both must have earned the enmity of the all-powerful eunuchs?

They had been given a position of trust. And it was because Khlit's shrewd mind had guessed at the reason that he sent Arslan to Doka-dur Khan. If what he suspected came to pass, he and his friends would have need of aid, even from the bandits of the Togra.

Truly, thought Khlit, this would be a strange hunt. One where the hunters were silken-robed and inscrutable of eye, and where the lives of men counted as less than those of the beasts they sought.

He kept a keen lookout during the ride, but nothing occurred until they came to the pine hills that sheltered the tombs.

Here the soldiery on the flanks came to a halt, and the emperor's cavalcade went forward alone under the pines. A few minutes' trot, and they met the sentinels of the *kang leen* who accompanied them to the unearthed entrance to the tomb. The sedan-chairs of Wan Li and Wei Chung were deposited near the excavation. Khlit and the huntsmen dismounted and pressed forward curiously.

The torches of the *kang leen* lighted the place fitfully. Khlit saw that the courtiers and nobles remained at a distance in a semi-circle about the entrance. A flight of stone steps led down to what appeared to be a stone slab in the form of a door.

Wan Li had emerged from his chair, when he was approached by Wei Chung who escorted him to the tomb. Khlit was anxious to gain a better view of the Lord of Ten Thousand Years and made his way close to the entrance, in time to see his face clearly as he descended the steps and vanished in the shadows of the tomb.

Wei Chung was busied in arranging guards between the sedans and the gate. In doing so, the eunuch failed to notice Khlit, half-hidden in the shadows by the piles of freshly-dug earth. The other huntsmen had returned to their horses. Khlit was about to do like-wise, when he hesitated.

A sudden thought struck the Cossack. He was but a step from the sunken gate, and unobserved. It might be possible for him to slip into the tomb after the emperor. The risk would be great. But the Golden Tomb was a prize worth seeing.

Khlit did not waste a second thought on his venture. Bending low, he scrambled down the freshly-dug earth to the foot of the stairs. The huge stone gate was ajar, sixty feet below the earth's surface. It led into a passage built up with teakwood pillars, the ceiling supported by beams of the same wood, fifty feet above the Cossack's head. Some distance ahead of him light came through a door similar to the one he had entered. A glance showed Khlit the grave tunnel was empty as far as the further portal, and he walked forward quietly.

Midway he hesitated. He had heard a step on the stair behind him.

The sound caused the blood to quicken in Khlit's veins. The light ahead of him was faint, and, looking over his shoulder, he could see nothing in the shadows of the stairway. A moment he waited, then turned, reassured. No one had appeared in the grave tunnel. He remembered that the place was forbidden to all the Chinese except those of imperial blood.

He had little fear of being followed. And to the best of his knowledge no one had seen him enter the mausoleum. Ahead of him, Wan Li would be engaged in his devotions. Khlit made his way to the second door and looked within.

Unlike the first stone gate, the second portal swung on cleverly contrived hinges, making it possible for one man to open it. The hall that Khlit now saw was the grave antechamber, built of jade slabs and empty of ornament. In the center knelt the emperor.

Wan Li's back was toward the Cossack. He held a bronze bowl in which incense smoldered, sending thin spirals of smoke toward the ceiling. His face was toward the third chamber, which was the tomb, visible through half-drawn curtains of yellow silk, gold embroidered.

In a low undertone Wan Li was repeating a prayer, bending his massive back over the bowl. The glow from the grave illumined the dragon emblazoned on his robe. Beyond him Khlit saw the stone slab bearing the coffin of the Ming emperor. On either side of the slab were ranged sacrificial vessels of gold, emblems and ornaments of gold, studded with jewels.

The jewels reflected, with a hundred brilliant eyes, the light from the everlasting candles. These were huge masses of walrus fat, ascending in a pyramid, half-way to the ceiling. Khlit understood now why they were said to burn for ten years at a time beside the coffin.

Wan Li laid the bowl on the floor and touched his forehead to the stone. Silence reigned in the tomb. Khlit's gaze was fixed unblinkingly on the treasure of the grave chamber. The panoply of death meant nothing to him. The thought came to him that all this gold beside the dry bones of a dead man was like the dragon robe of the living Wan Li—the trappings of immortality decked about a human frame.

Khlit looked at Wan Li and smiled. A weak creature wielding the power of other men's making—a man ruled by women and courtiers, obedient to the words of astrologers. Was this the ruler of a hundred million?

Wan Li was praying again. Echoes in the rear chambers caught the murmur of his voice and whispered it back to Khlit. In spite of his scorn, the Cossack comprehended something of the spirit which had brought Wan Li to the tomb, the faithfulness to the memory of those who had worn the dragon robe before him. The link which bound Wan Li to the dead.

The emperor rose to his feet, and Khlit stepped back from the stone gate. He walked swiftly to the outer door and slipped through it as a sound behind him told him that Wan Li had closed the portal of the grave chamber.

The outer tunnel was now in darkness, and Khlit was forced to feel his way forward by the teakwood pillars. He went swiftly, not wishing to be observed by the man behind him. From the massive entrance gate he passed to the stairs, halting in the shadows at one side of the excavation.

It would be dangerous for him to walk out into the torchlight before the emperor came out. He reasoned swiftly that Wan Li would summon his men to help close the stone door. Then Khlit might make his appearance without exciting curiosity.

As he had thought, it happened. A resounding blow on the door by the man behind him brought Wei Chung with a dozen of the *kang leen* running to the stairs. As the dragon-robed figure passed up the steps within arm's reach of the Cossack, Wei Chung and his followers swung-to the door.

The gate thudded into place, and the fastenings were secured. Khlit joined the men, who retraced their steps as the task was performed. He was in time to gain his horse, held by Kurluk, and trot to where his men were waiting before the imperial cortège was in motion.

Surely, thought Khlit, Wan Li's mind had been fixed too long upon the dead, for his face was stony and drawn as that of a man who has seen his own grave.

He saw Wei Chung assist the imperial passenger into the sedan and lean within, as if to adjust the cushions, before he closed the door. Then the chief eunuch motioned to the courtiers; the drums sounded, and the chair-bearers broke into a trot. Khlit brought his men to their previous position, abreast the imperial sedan. They passed swiftly through the pines and out to the plains. The *kang leen* remained behind to guard the tomb.

It was near the hour of dawn. A fresh wind had sprung up in their faces, causing the torches of the cavalcade to flicker and the silk trappings of the sedan to rustle. The stars were dimmer overhead, and the spears of the horsemen who rode in the rear were outlined against the scarlet glow of sunrise in the east.

The huntsmen about Khlit were crying to each other, cheerful with the prospect of the coming hunt. Ch'en Ti-jun reined back his horse until he was within ear-shot of Khlit.

"Ride closer to the emperor's chair," he cried softly. "Remember the warning of the Lady Li."

Khlit made no response. The attending eunuchs and courtiers were a bow-shot length away; the soldiery even further. Only the hard-worked bearers and a half-dozen linkmen were between the huntsmen and the chair. There was no sign of any danger. Nevertheless, Khlit did as he was instructed.

The closer formation moved the Cossack slightly ahead of Wan Li's chair. His men formed a ring about it. He heard a sudden exclamation from one of the riders and turned.

A glance showed him what had happened. One of the torch-bearers, pressed closer to the sedan by the huntsmen, had allowed his brand to touch the side of the chair. Instantly the dry sandalwood lattice-work and the silk trappings caught. A cry of horror broke from the bearers.

The flame crackled in the high wind. It licked up the side to the roof of the chair. The shout of the bearers was echoed by the nobles who had sighted the fire.

"Treachery!" screamed Wei Chung, leaping from his sedan. "The dogs have attacked the emperor!"

"Slay them," shrilled Ch'en Ti-jun, striking at the nearest of the huntsmen. "Save Wan Li."

The man within the chair could not have seen the flames. The bearers, plainly paralyzed by fear, had let their burden fall to earth. One of the Manchu riders, endeavoring to wrap his cloak about the flaming wood, was struck in the face by an arrow launched toward the group. Kurluk beat at the mounting fire with his heavy hat, only to be almost unhorsed by the rush of Ch'en Ti-jun.

Khlit had wheeled his mount into the group. But by now the fire had caught about the door and roof of the sedan. The wind quickened its progress.

"To the emperor!" Wei Chung was shouting. "Treachery!"

"Aid for Wan Li!" screamed the nobles, charging into the dancing horses of the hunters.

Swords gleamed in the glow from the flames. Khlit saw that the huntsmen, surprized and surrounded, were being cut down. The Chinese appeared blinded by their excitement. Yet the Cossack noticed that their efforts were devoted as much to killing the riders as to quenching the fire that was consuming the remnants of Wan Li's chair.

By now it was impossible that the man within the imperial chair could be saved.

The lattice door had swung inward, its fastenings loosened by the flames. Khlit had a fleeting glimpse of a ghastly, round face and wide, staring eyes. Already the face was blackened by heat, and the dragon robe was shriveling.

What he saw made Khlit rein in his horse and wheel away from the chair.

"This way!" he cried above the tumult. "Kurluk, men of the hunt!"

Several of the riders heard him and spurred toward him. The giant Kurluk, however, was hemmed in by the Chinese, using his sword valiantly. Some nobles were beating at the flaming chair with their cloaks, but the eunuchs seemed intent on cutting down the riders who had been escorting the sedan.

Khlit rose in his stirrups after the fashion of the Cossacks and led his few followers into the group around Kurluk. The giant Manchu saw them coming and beat himself free from his antagonists, who quailed from his heavy sword.

Another moment and he had gained Khlit's side, cursing, his face streaked with blood.

"The devil himself set fire to Wan Li," he panted. "By my father's grave, it was no work of ours——"

Ch'en Ti-jun rode up to the Manchu, his seamed countenance alight with evil triumph. The eunuch pointed a pistol at Kurluk's shaggy head and fired. Khlit saw his friend sway in the saddle, eyes closed and chin on breast. Then he slid to the ground.

"Ride," shouted the Cossack to his remaining men, "or you are dead men!"

From three quarters the Chinese were closing in on them. But ahead of them a way was clear to the plains. Through the opening Khlit and his handful of hunters spurred, cutting down the few who tried to head them off. Cries and shots pursued them.

They were now free of the Chinese and settled down into a fast gallop, hugging their saddles to avoid the pistol-shots. A motley troop of soldiery galloped after them. But the huntsmen were well-mounted. Led by Khlit, they slowly widened the gap between them and their pursuers.

"Ho, comrade," snarled a bearded fellow close to the Cossack, "the accident to Wan Li will cost us dear. The Son of Heaven is burned to a crisp."

Khlit eased himself in his saddle, with a hard laugh.

"Have you lost your wits?" he demanded. "That was no accident."

"Be that as it may," growled the other, "we are dead men. Aye, dead by the rarest tortures known to those devils behind us. They will hunt us down like cornered antelope."

"Aye," muttered another, "there is no hope for us."

Khlit was silent, thinking grimly of the false words of the Lady Li. Truly, they had been trapped. The Chinese courtiers and soldiers, as well as the eunuchs, had seen the flames break out on Wan Li's chair in the midst of the hunters. The torch-bearer who had been responsible for the mishap was undoubtedly slain. Those of the sedan-bearers who lived would testify against the hunters to save their own skins.

He had suspected that they would be used in some such manner by the scheming eunuchs. But the swiftness of the catastrophe had surprized him. Wei Chung had planned well. There was no proof that the affair had not been an accident.

"Silence your loose tongues," he growled over his shoulder, "and you will yet save your skins."

In the plains ahead of him the dawn showed the rocky ridges of the Togra, still veiled in the distance by morning mists.

Arslan had ridden very rapidly to the Togra, for Khlit's words had been urgent. When he came to the first of the rocky defiles, the Manchu drew rein and halted his beast with a calculating glance of his black eyes over the heights in front of him. The midafternoon sun shone full in his tanned face. There was no sign of watchers in the defiles, but Arslan knew that the men of Dokadur Khan could not be far off. It was the season of the hunt, and at such times the riders of the Togra were accustomed to come forth from their haunts.

The experienced archer had no wish to be taken for a scout of the imperial forces, as might readily happen. So he slung his bow over his back, adjusted the quiver carelessly at his left hip and displayed his guitar ostentatiously. By these signs he hoped to make plain that his mission was one of peace. To leave no doubt in the mind of those watching him from the heights, he rode forward slowly, to all intents heedless of where he went.

His strategy had its reward, for, instead of a match-lock ball or an arrow in his back, he was accosted by a dark-faced Khirghiz, exceedingly well-mounted. In response to the other's questions, Arslan stated that his mission was to see Dokadur Khan; that it was imperative; that he was alone and without intention of spying on the men of the Togra. Only half satisfied, the Khirghiz bade him accompany him, and they presently came out into a large gorge in which some hundred men were dismounted about fires.

Here his guide left him, and it was only after a long delay that the man returned, accompanied by the broad figure of Dokadur Khan, whom Arslan easily recognized by the missing ear. The Togra chieftain inspected his visitor narrowly.

"What is your message, Manchu?" he growled.

Arslan, who had dismounted, returned the other's somber stare thoughtfully, his small head cocked to one side.

"In the last moon, Dokadur Khan," he began—Khlit had told him as much—"you had a guest at your *yurt* in the Togra, a gray-haired rider who was not Tatar nor Manchu."

"I remember. What of him?"

"He sends a message by me. Also a token. Do you recognize this, also?"

Arslan drew the chased Turkish pistol from his belt, being careful to handle it inoffensively, for the men of the Togra being outcasts were quick to suspect evil. Dokadur Khan's eyes lighted as they fell upon the weapon, perceiving that it was one he had coveted. He was now the owner of the brace, for the other reposed in his own belt. He accepted it without acknowledgment.

"And the message?" he asked again.

"Was one of pressing importance. The hunt of Wan Li has begun. The man who sent me bids you sharpen your eyes and ears and watch well from the Togra, or the Chinese swords will slit your jaws from your gullets."

"Does a goshawk need warning to watch its quarry?" snarled the chieftain. "You ride hard to say very little."

Arslan held up his hand as a sign he had further tidings. Khlit had had time to tell him few things that were in the Cossack's mind. But Arslan knew that Khlit would not send him on a venture that was not necessary, supremely so. There was no telling if Dokadur Khan was professedly loyal or not to the Chinese, for the moment.

"Heed this well, Dokadur Khan," he said impressively. "There will be taking of spoil before many suns. He who sent me, knowing this and trusting in the skill of the men of the Togra, will offer you a share in what is to happen."

The Khirghiz threw back his broad head with a growling laugh.

"Nay, small of wit! Does a man offer share in the spoil he has taken, if not from weakness. Has this old man of yours a tribe of horsemen? Nay, he is alone. How then can he take spoil? And where is it to be found?"

Arslan considered. Khlit had told him that they would have need of refuge in the Togra. And to bid Dokadur Khan be prepared with his men when he came to meet them. More than this he did not say. Arslan himself was curious as to why Khlit would come to the Togra; also, what he had meant by speaking of the hunt that had already begun. It would not do to promise anything, or the Khirghiz would suspect.

"There be matters, Dokadur Khan," he suggested, "that are best managed by one man alone. Where the stake is highest, a few players gain the best reward. Such a matter is this. The man who sent me has eaten at your fireside, and he has judged that you are one who may serve him. The honor is high."

"Nay, am I a jackal to feed from other's offal? In the Togra I am master."

"Be it so. You are a free man. You need not come to meet the one who sent me, if it pleases you not. Yet Khlit said you would be of service."

Arslan turned toward his horse indifferently. The Khirghiz halted him with an exclamation.

"Is this man Khlit of the Curved Saber? He who was master of the Jun-gar?"

"And of many others. Yet you need not join with him in this matter. The Khan Khlit deals with higher stakes than horseflesh or the plucking of a scurvy caravan. I will tell him that you will not see him."

Arslan made as if to mount. In his interest at the news he had just learned, Dokadur Khan went so far as to lay hand on his shoulder. The archer swung around with a scowl, hand at sword.

"Stay!" muttered the chieftain quickly. "I will not harm you, Manchu. So, I remember now the old warrior's face. It was like that of Khlit as it has been described to me. Dog of the devil! That is strange. What does the Curved Saber in the land of Wan Li?"

"That is for his telling," responded the Manchu curtly, not failing to note the other's quickened interest. His own indifference appeared the greater. Khlit had chosen his messenger well. "He comes to the Togra early tomorrow. I will meet him and say that you will not hear his tidings."

Dokadur Khan meditated, his thoughts mirrored in his swarthy, pock-marked countenance. Khlit he knew to be a warrior of note, one who had more than once caused grief to the men of the hat and girdle. What was he doing alone on the plains? Surely, it must be an important mission. He recalled that Khlit had hinted at a certain event that was to come to pass. What was this?

"He comes alone to the Togra?"

"What friends has he in the camp of Wan Li?" countered Arslan. "Nay, there will be few with him."

"He is the foe of Wan Li, without doubt."

"He has many enemies."

"And he schemes to take plunder from the Chinese courtiers during the hunt?"

Arslan laughed. Khlit had not told him what was in his mind, but the archer knew it was not that. He judged that the Cossack had come to Wei Chung's *yâmen* to gain sight of the Chinese court and that yesterday he had made up his mind on a course of action. What this might be, he did not know.

"Does a great khan seek for such plunder? In your village you know not the ways of the white-boned."

The Tatar tradition of believing nobles to possess white bones and their inferiors black was known to Dokadur Khan, who stared ominously at the archer, angered, yet curious and anxious to learn what was in his visitor's mind.

If Arslan had delivered his message outright, claiming refuge and aid for himself and Khlit against the men of Wan Li, Dokadur Khan would have given him a contemptuous refusal. This in spite of the magic of Khlit's name. For the slow-witted khan could have nothing but indifference for men who sought help from him. But an enterprise against Wan Li was another matter and familiar ground to him.

"I also am a khan not lightly named by men," he boasted, and Arslan smiled at the vanity of the man. "I have two thousand horsemen in the Togra, who are proved fighters, the chosen warriors of a dozen tribes."

Arslan looked fleetingly at the motley array of riders, lying about the fires, occupied with bowl and dice. Mongrels, he thought, but hardy.

"Hey," he growled as if disappointed, "no more? Khlit of the

Curved Saber has led fifty times as many. Nay, I was at his side in the pillaging of Shan-kiang. Still, he has said that the fewer men the larger portions of spoil."

Dokadur Khan scowled.

"What is his plan?"

"He will say. How should I know? Am I one of the white-boned? But this I will tell you. In the Ming court the leaders are no more of one mind. Wan Li is fast losing his grip on the Dragon throne. Others have their hands on it already. The factions may divide during the hunt. And while they fight among themselves— Nay, you are said to be quick of wit."

"Aye, that I am. If the Chinese quarrel, we may profitably join with one party, now that they are on the plains, far from their main armies."

Arslan laughed long.

"Have you forgotten the wisdom of Khlit? Would he waste thought on such a plan? Not so. I tell you he is foe to the end with the Dragon court. Can you not see what he means to do?"

The shrewd archer knew that others were within hearing and that Dokadur Khan would be loath to admit his stupidity. As he had fancied, it came to pass.

"Aye, Manchu. But I will speak only with Khlit. He and I are one kind."

"See that your men are ready when he comes. He will act quickly, or I know him not."

Hence it was that the band of Dokadur Khan watched expectantly from the defiles of the Togra the coming of Khlit. But at this time, although Arslan did not know it, the old Cossack was riding to them, hard-pressed and harassed, a man marked for death by a half million swords, and the outlawed foe of the Ming nobility, as well as the party of Wei Chung and the Lady Li.

V

Two men may have equal cunning, but he who can best look into the mind of the other shall be leader. Not otherwise.

The sun was near the point of midday the morning after Arslan's arrival at the camp of Dokadur Khan when Khlit and six followers spurred their wearied horses into a gallop within the shadows of the Togra ravines.

More men had been with the Cossack at dawn. Some had fallen by lucky pistol-shots of the pursuing Chinese—who were poor marksmen with this new weapon. More had dropped behind when their horses became exhausted. These, facing death with grim hardihood, knelt by their fallen beasts and shot what arrows remained to them into the ranks of their pursuers. Thus, each man lost in this manner had served to delay the Chinese as a straggling deer holds the wolf-pack for a moment until its flesh is torn from its bones.

Khlit had done his best for the men. Well-mounted himself, he stayed near the rear of his group of riders, encouraging them and directing their course. They knew as well as he that there was no hope of quarter at the hands of the Chinese soldiery. On the frontier of the Dragon empire war is carried out to its termination—the sword or bow-string for able-bodied men, the conqueror's *kang* for children and handsome women, and whatever spoil may be available taken to the last bit of bronze or of silk cloth.

The Cossack had taken responsibility for the betrayal of the huntsmen upon himself. He had suspected that they were to be tools in Wei Chung's intrigue. But how was he to foresee the manner of the eunuch's treachery?

The men were content to follow him. They knew the fate that lay upon them after the burning of Wan Li's chair. It mattered not if Wei Chung proclaimed it a plot on the part of the huntsmen or an accident. It meant death for them in the land of the Dragon. And Khlit had said they might yet be saved. By reason of his careful leadership during the pursuit, they had come to believe there might be truth in his words.

They rode into the nearest rock-bound defile with horses foam-flecked and dark with sweat. They splashed across a stream and wound into some scattered scrub larches. As they did so, one who had looked behind gave an exclamation.

Khlit glanced over his shoulder in time to see two of the pursuing Chinese drop from their saddles with the feathered ends of arrows sticking from their chests. The others drew rein. The arrows continued to fly from the larch clump with great accuracy, and presently the riders turned and galloped back the way they had come. They were lost to sight almost at once in a bend in the ravine.

The huntsmen walked their horses forward slowly. Out of the larches trotted Arslan, several of the bandits following.

"Ho, uncle and brothers," laughed the Manchu. "You bring a swarm of venomous insects into the Togra. Where are the others of our band?"

"Slain," said an evil-looking plainsman with an oath.

"Nay, devil take it—Kurluk?"

"Slain."

Briefly Khlit told Arslan what had happened at the beginning of the hunt and asked for Dokadur Khan. The sobered archer informed him that the master of the Togra with the bulk of his men was at the encampment, a short distance into the defiles. Also, that strong troops of Chinese had been sighted riding toward the Togra from the plain.

"It was an evil day we entered the service of the devil-begotten Wei Chung," he growled. "Kurluk and two-score brave fellows spitted like ripe fowls! Nay, that is an ill word. Bethink you, lord, our lives hang by a thin halter here. The Chinese will not lightly give up the pursuit. And Dokadur Khan has seen them and suspects that it is you they are after. He is like a weed moved in the wind, a friend to the strongest side. It may enter his fat head to give us up to the Dragon riders."

"I sent you with a message."

"It was faithfully delivered." Arslan recounted what had passed between him and the bandit chief. "Nay," he concluded, "where the saddle chafes is here. Dokadur Khan believes you have come to offer him a share in a rare *barranca*, with excellent spoil for the bait. Instead you come like a tired antelope, marked by the falcon——"

"You did well. What do the Chinese?"

"The yellow faces are spreading out to cover all approaches to the Togra on the east—whence you have come—so our lookouts report. Presently they will enter not one but several of the passes at once. They are many, with leaders."

"Then take me to Dokadur Khan."

Khlit was silent until they reached the encampment where the master of the Togra was seated on his horse, several hundred followers with him. He eyed Khlit blackly as the Cossack rode forward with his dust-coated men. He did not raise his hand in greeting, nor did he offer to speak. Arslan would have broken the silence but refrained at a quick glance from Khlit.

The huntsmen scanned the men of the Togra with the searching glances of those whose lives are at stake yet who hope little. It was clear that Dokadur Khan was not pleased at their coming.

"Have you no more men than these?" said Khlit suddenly. "I sent you a warning to be ready. These men are not enough."

Dokadur Khan grunted in sheer surprise. The Cossack had spoken like a leader who finds fault with a subordinate. Yet the Khirghiz saw that he had only seven riders with him and had come fleeing for his life.

"I have thrice this number," he assured Khlit; then he scowled, fearing to lose dignity before his men. "My sentries tell me you are followed by the Chinese. The Togra is no place for doomed men. Your archer lied to me. Why should I not give you to the Chinese —since he has lied?"

In spite of himself he had asked the question. Khlit had not the manner of a hunted man. And Dokadur Khan found it hard to forget the reputation of the Cossack leader.

"They will be here within the hour," he continued as Khlit was silent. "Already they form for attacking the defiles. We will bind you and give you to them, for thus we can save ourselves from attack and our villages from fire. I did not bid you come to the Togra with yonder hounds at your heels."

A murmur of assent from his men greeted these words. Arslan frowned. It was clear that the chieftain was excited, even frightened and thus dangerous. The huntsmen had dismounted and were watching Khlit.

The Cossack was still gazing at Dokadur Khan fixedly. Abruptly he laughed, and Arslan took a deep breath of surprise.

"We must make our peace with the Chinese," scowled Dokadur Khan. "We have no quarrel with them."

"In my first visit," said Khlit slowly, "I marked you as one light of wit, yet I did not think the leader of a thousand men was altogether a fool. I know not if that be true. Answer me a question, Dokadur Khan. Know you why the men of the Dragon seek our lives?"

"It matters not."

"Nay, it matters much. They believe, falsely, that we have slain Wan Li. But they believe."

In spite of himself the Khirghiz gaped.

"Wan Li—the Son of Heaven—slain?"

Khlit nodded grimly.

"Ask these men who came with me. The sedan-chair of the Lord of Ten Thousand Years was set fire to this dawn. There was a great killing of those around him at the time. By the speed of our horses we escaped."

The importance of the news was beginning to leak into the thick skull of the khan.

"And you rode here," he growled. "A dog without home or friends. Nay, you are accursed now. We must surely give you up."

"How?"

"Dog of the devil! I will see to it myself."

"And admit the Chinese to the Togra?" Khlit laughed again, and Arslan's black eyes gleamed, for he thought he saw light. "Nay, then you are altogether a fool, Dokadur Khan. Think you the men of the Dragon will stay their hand when they have slain us? Is the killing of an emperor so little a thing? Will they leave you and your villages unharmed? You know it is not so."

The khan glanced down the ravine blackly. He realized the truth of what Khlit said. The huntsmen of the Cossack were much like his own men in race and appearance. Moreover, his own reputation with the Chinese was hardly above suspicion. Once in the Togra, the Chinese would undoubtedly slay right and left until their bloodthirst was appeased.

"If we give you up and flee to the upper defiles of the Togra Nor, they will weary of the pursuit in time."

But in the eyes of Dokadur Khan and his men there was the glint of fear. They knew the numbers and strength of the men of Wan Li. In any case, their lot would be hard, and many would die.

Khlit leaned forward in his saddle and spoke quietly.

"Then you will lose the man who can aid you. I am that man. Fool! Do you think my coming of itself brought the men of Wei Chung hither? Nay, they would have come in any case, for the eunuch must have planned to slay hundreds of men on the frontier to bear out his scheme—to throw the blame for Wan Li's death on the bandits. I alone know something that will protect you and your men and their women. If you give me up, your hope of safety will be gone. For then I will not tell you what I know. Choose and choose quickly, for the Chinese are approaching the passes in force."

Dokadur Khan pretended to weigh the words of Khlit, while Arslan and the huntsmen watched without seeming to do so. In reality the mind of the Togra chief was tumultuous with uncertainty and fear. He had never been called upon to face the united strength of the Chinese forces. The fact that they were riding upon the defiles excited and flurried him. A bold enough man where a small *barranca* was concerned, the magnitude of the coming event confused him.

The calmness of Khlit further puzzled Dokadur Khan. How was it that the Cossack was untroubled, unless he knew of a secret reason by which he could win safety? It was true that the men of Wei Chung would lay waste the outlaw settlements of the Togra. And Dokadur Khan had no place to flee; no ally except Khlit.

"What is it that you know?" he demanded.

And Khlit knew that he had won his cause. But the way was not yet cleared.

"That which will save us—you and me and our men. What I know, no one else knows."

Dokadur Khan stirred impatiently.

"Already some Chinese have been slain in the Togra," added Khlit.

One of the Khirghiz riders who had been with Arslan spoke.

"It was the Manchu archer."

"Do the men of the Dragon know the difference?" asked Arslan logically, and by Khlit's silence he knew he had said the right thing.

The bandit khan scowled the more, and his followers swore. After this, they knew, there would be no escape from the Chinese.

"Nay, Khlit," he asked, "speak. What is your thought? There is no time to be lost."

The Cossack drew his whip slowly through his hand.

"We did not slay Wan Li, Dokadur Khan. The plot was the work of others. Of Wei Chung and his allies. They pursue us—and you. But other factions of the Dragon men do not yet know what is the truth of the event this morning. They would not slay us until they know what we know. From them we have not so much to fear. If

Wei Chung's guilt is proved, we are free men. I speak of the other Ming nobles and especially Li Yuan, the astrologer."

"Would you have us go to Li Yuan, the whole of us with women and children! Nay, how may that be? The men of Wei Chung are already on three sides of the Togra, and they number five times our strength. Li Yuan is at the Great Wall."

"By now, at the news of Wan Li's death, he will be riding toward the Liao *yâmen*."

"Even thus, how may we reach him?"

"In due time. That was not my plan."

The men of the Togra cursed uneasily. Each moment increased their fear, a fact which did not escape Khlit.

"Harken, Dokadur Khan," he continued. "My thought was that a picked few of us can win through the forces of Wei Chung tonight with darkness. The rest can hold the Togra. The ravines are well nigh impregnable if well held. Have you a place where the women and children can be concealed?"

"Aye, a rocky gorge near the lake. It is reached by a hidden tunnel."

"It is well." Khlit snapped his whip as if reaching a decision. "But this must be a fair bargain, Dokadur Khan. My men must have fresh horses and good ones. There must be no further talk of lies or treachery. We are of one race, we plainsmen, and the yellow faces are our enemies. If we hold together, we will win free. But you must do as I order."

The slant eyes of the khan narrowed as he considered this. Here was a request that endangered his own prestige. If Khlit took the reins of leadership and was successful, his men would hold him in contempt. The Cossack shrewdly guessed what was in his mind.

"We will do more than win free," he said. "We will gain spoil the equal of three years of your raids. I promised it, and it will come to pass. Thus your men will be rewarded."

"Where is this spoil?"

"The Golden Tomb. The gateway is unearthed."

To a man they stared at him, and Dokadur Khan gnawed his mustache. How might they go to the Golden Tomb when their own lives were in danger?

"The Togra is a natural fortress," explained Khlit, who was watching him. "None can defend it so well as you. Arrange the defense as best suits you. The Chinese attack upon us, under Wei Chung, will draw them all to the Togra. Wei Chung dares not turn back until we are slain, for we are witnesses against him when any can be found to hear us. In the excitement the Golden Tomb will be forgotten. It will be lightly guarded. With darkness I will take a hundred men, pass through the ranks of Wei Chung and ride to the tomb."

"I will go with you," meditated the khan.

"As pleases you. Tomorrow, when we have gained the ear of Li Yuan and the nobles, the attack on the Togra will be given up, for Wei Chung and Ch'en Ti-jun must hasten back to the Lady Li, their ally, if suspicion is aroused against them."

Dokadur Khan hesitated. If Khlit went with them, they need not suspect treachery from him, because he would be at their mercy. Yet the prospect of the ride across the frontier troubled him. For the third time Khlit guessed at his thought.

"In the Golden Tomb," he added, "is the wealth of an emperor, riches enough to load a dozen horses. We will take the extra horses with us. And at the Golden Tomb we may win safety from the wiles of Wei Chung."

"It will be dangerous," objected the Khirghiz, who nevertheless saw the eyes of his men glitter.

"Nay, Khan," growled Arslan suddenly, "if you follow not the plan of the Curved Saber, our heads shall decorate the saddles of Wei Chung's men in any case. Is there no danger in that? Are we sleek sheep to wait in a huddle for the happy dispatch of the butcher?"

A growl of agreement rose from the bandits. Dokadur Khan lifted his hand in decision.

"It shall be as you say, Khlit."

"Remember, Dokadur Khan," warned the Cossack, "there will be many slain. This is not a game of children. Ho, men of the Togra, have you good heart for kingly spoil and the clash of sharp swords? Will you put your strength against the evil brain of the eunuch?"

"Aye!" shouted those within hearing. "We be of good heart," added one. "We will follow the Curved Saber!" shouted another, the one who had been with Arslan.

"It is well," said Khlit, satisfied. "Now do you see to the defense of the ravines, Dokadur Khan. You have skill at that. I and those with me will sleep until the shadows are long in the afternoon, for we are weary. Then waken us, having picked a hundred good men."

And Arslan wondered to himself. He had seen a man worn and hunted, with only seven followers, win mastery over a thousand who wished him ill rather than good. And he had watched the plan of that man put into action over the objections of the khan of the Togra. Yet he had a doubt. Were they to face Li Yuan, loaded with the spoil of the Golden Tomb? If not, how were they to win back to safety with their burden? And what of the Lady Li, who was still at the *yâmen* with many followers?

The six who had ridden with Khlit to the Togra had not slept in thirty hours, and they quickly fell into a doze after retreating a short distance into the ravines to a cleared place which served as a meeting-spot for the tribesmen. The Cossack, however, did not join them until he had seen to the selection of eight fresh horses for himself and his followers and the preparation of a good meal against their waking. Arslan aided him in this, for the confusion in the place was great, owing to the preparations of Dokadur Khan.

Khlit did not rest until everything had been arranged to his satisfaction. This done, he seated himself on his saddle, back against a sheltering rock, and was asleep on the moment. Arslan noticed that a small urchin of the encampment stood beside Khlit, holding his horse, and refused to move. When he questioned the boy, the Khirghiz told him that he had once guided Khlit out of the Togra and was waiting in hopes of being taken on the expedition that night.

"Ho, small warrior," chuckled the archer, "we take no one who can not quaff a bucket of the Ming men's blood. But, if the jade Fortune blesses my bow, you shall have the skull of one Ch'en Ti-jun to play with ere nightfall."

With that he swaggered off to his horse, and sought the ranks of the tribesmen.

Dokadur Khan was a skilled leader at this form of warfare. Moreover, his men were fired by hatred of those who had invaded their fastness. It was too late to try to hold the entrances to the Togra, but within these Dokadur Khan had distributed his men in ambush at strategic points.

Arslan knew that the narrow, rocky gorges would afford little cover to the Chinese. Few trees grew in the place, and frequently the ravines contained streams up which Wei Chung's soldiers must force their way, coming as often as not to the blind barrier of a waterfall. The tribesmen knew the ground thoroughly and used their knowledge to good advantage.

Attracted by scattered shots, Arslan made his way to a height where a score of the Khirghiz held one of the main approaches of the Togra. Dismounting, the Manchu saw that the ranks of the mandarins' troops had been thinned by the arrows of those above and they were giving ground in confusion. Their few pistols and arquebuses, badly aimed, were not sufficient to annoy the concealed bowmen.

"This is but idle sport," laughed Arslan. "Come, we will make music for our friends below."

Unslinging the guitar from which he rarely parted, he struck the strings and sang, exposing himself recklessly.

> "In the land of the mighty bowmen
> The Ming men come,
> To find a doughty foeman
> In his Togra home."

Heedless of the pistol-balls which sped near him, he composed another verse.

> "The fox is in his burrow,
> O wise Wei Chung!
> Red wine will warm the furrow
> Of the Liao Tung."

He ceased his chant as the scattered soldiers in the ravine below gave back against the cliffs. The men beside him peered out from their concealment in time to see an array of armor-clad footmen advancing through the ranks of the routed horsemen. Over their vital parts they wore heavy-quilted pads. At their head went a banner of one of the armies of Wan Li.

"Oho," muttered Arslan, unslinging his bow, "here we have a goose that will require another kind of plucking. Fall to, good sirs, with your arrows and decorate yonder quilts for me."

The archers plied their shafts. A few of the foot-soldiers fell, struck in the face and throat, but the majority passed on, closing up their files. These were not the mounted rabble of the hunt, but paid soldiers of the emperor, intent, as they believed, on avenging his death.

"Drop your bows, good sirs," directed Arslan, noting the ill-success of the arrows, "and we will make cannon of ourselves and bump the helmets of the gentry beneath us."

The tribesmen caught his idea and fell to with a will, some of the older men and boys who had been hiding behind them dragging up the stones and the archers launching them over the cliff. Several rocks, bounding down the ravine, did good execution, but the trained soldiery parted their ranks to let them roll through and pressed forward, although more slowly.

Even Arslan's high good humor, bred by the prospect of battle, was beginning to fail when there was a shout from his companions. Down the ravine he saw a body of horsemen galloping, led by one of the lieutenants of Dokadur Khan. The mounted men struck the first ranks of the Chinese and crumpled them, pressing them back on those in the rear. Their armor was poor protection against the expert swords of the riders, and they gave ground.

It was not the custom of the tribesmen to continue such a hot hand-to-hand conflict, and they withdrew presently, leaving the Chinese badly cut up by their charge. The invaders halted where they were, waiting the coming of reinforcements before renewing their efforts. Seeing this, Arslan mounted and left the spot, seeking Ch'en Ti-jun.

Much the same kind of conflict was raging in the other ravines, the tribesmen inflicting heavy losses on the Chinese and withdrawing slowly when overmatched. The struggle was bitter, neither side asking quarter, but it was difficult for the Chinese to gain the heights as they were ignorant of the paths up the rocks. Whenever they attempted to climb the cliffs, old men and boys of the Togra greeted them with rocks and spear-points. By late afternoon the Chinese had won forward only a few miles at a heavy cost.

Arslan noted the success of his new companions with high glee. He was untiring in his efforts to locate Ch'en Ti-jun, and by diligent inquiries he was finally successful. The lieutenant of Wei Chung was directing one of the attacks against the heights from his sedan-chair, attended by a few followers. Arslan rode to the spot at once, and his slant eyes glittered evilly as he looked down from a nest of rocks upon the gilt chair of the eunuch.

The distance, however, was too great for an arrow. Arslan surveyed the scene before him carefully. The bulk of the Chinese soldiery were pressing forward with shouts and cries into one of the passes beside him, harassed as they went by the vindictive tribesmen. Other groups of the eunuch's horsemen were acting apparently as a reserve some distance in the rear. The sedan-chair rested in the center of a natural amphitheater, surrounded by rocky heights through which ran the pass the Chinese were assaulting.

The smile faded from the Manchu's dark face as he unslung his bow and saw to his saddle-girths. Gripping his steppe pony with his knees, he spurred forward quickly. The snorting horse slid and sprang downward among the rocks. Arslan kept his eyes fixed on the yellow sedan. So far he was unobserved.

"The philosophers have said," he muttered piously, "that with the slayer of his brother alive a man may not rest unavenged. May I prosper in my honorable purpose!"

He was now clear of the last of the rocks and spurred his mount forward. A shout told him that the men around Ch'en Ti-jun had seen him. As he rode, he fitted arrow to bowstring and bent low in the saddle. Other shafts flew around him. The servants seized spears and swords and ran toward him. But the experienced archer swerved his horse, to pass the sedan at a short distance from it.

Then he launched his shaft, reaching over his shoulder for another from the quiver. Swiftly he sent three other arrows crashing through the brittle lacquer-work of the sedan and grinned as he heard a shrill scream. His horse stumbled and fell, struck by a pistol-ball. The archer sprang clear nimbly and ran for the rocks on the further side of the clearing, waving his bow triumphantly. The servants pursued him.

From the sedan-chair the bearers saw dark drops falling to the earth. Ch'en Ti-jun no longer screamed.

Arslan had now gained the slope of the ravine, but a hue and cry was raised about him. He paused from time to time to discharge an arrow at his pursuers. The servants of the dead eunuch were soon distanced, but the Chinese men-at-arms nearby had observed him and were closing in.

The Manchu was forced to drop his bow and take to his sword. When a foeman appeared from behind the rocks, Arslan sprang at him with catlike agility, his small frame twisting and writhing.

From the first of these encounters he emerged successful. Men were now running toward him from all sides.

He stood in his tracks, swinging his short sword, his eyes red, agrin with the lust of slaying. Then he lifted his deep voice in song.

> "The tide of blood is flooding,
>   With the setting sun;
> When I see the ravens brooding
>   Over Ch'en Ti-jun."

He cut a menacing spear-point from its haft and slew the wielder. Then he hurled himself at the group of his enemies.

It was during the last of twilight that the Khirghiz lad, who had waited to see the departure of Khlit and his fellow horsemen, remembered the words of the Manchu archer. Arslan, the child reflected, had been missed when the picked horsemen under Khlit and Dokadur Khan rode off.

Searching among the slain where Arslan had last been seen the boy came upon the archer. The Manchu was half-sitting, half-lying against a stone, and at first the grin stamped on his dark face deceived the lad into thinking he was still alive. A second glance showed him the breastplate torn off and the body hacked from throat to belt.

The boy did not pause by his Manchu acquaintance. He was too busy despoiling the other slain of their weapons. But after a moment's consideration he left the body of Arslan unmolested. He remembered that he had heard that spirits of the unburied dead peopled the earth, and Arslan had been too hardy a warrior to risk enmity with his shade, fresh from the *rakchas* and the ten courts of purgatory.

Khlit had missed Arslan at the assembly and guessed that his comrade was slain when he did not appear. But the business of the hundred riders could not wait. When the men were equipped and ready, he followed Dokadur Khan out of the Togra at the head of the horsemen, noting that they took the hidden path through which the boy he had befriended had led him on his first visit to the place.

The men, numbering one hundred and seven, counting Khlit and his surviving huntsmen, were picked with care from the bands of the Togra and were well-mounted on fresh horses. Khlit had also seen that a score of led horses were brought. During the ride through the ravines, he let Dokadur Khan guide him, but once clear of the defiles he assumed the leadership himself. To this the Khirghiz made no objection. He had the good sense to see that the dice were now cast.

The safety of his own men, surrounded in the Togra, rested on the success of their expedition. The defenders of the wilderness could hold out for another day and night. After that they must have aid, or the forces of Wei Chung, embittered by their losses, must be withdrawn. His companions were satisfied that Khlit spoke the truth. The magic word, Golden Tomb, had been sufficient to still their doubts.

But, as Dokadur Khan rode after Khlit, who was leading them by landmarks and sight of the stars, through scattered bands of the Chinese, he bethought him. During the heat of the day's conflict the khan had had little time for consideration of Khlit's plan.

Now he reflected. It was true that Li Yuan and the older nobles would pay highly for proof of Wei Chung's guilt. It might be true, furthermore, that they were at the *yâmen* at Liao. And that Khlit might reach them there, since Wei Chung's party were at the outskirts of the Togra.

But would Li Yuan believe what they said? It would appear to the Ming nobles that the plainsmen were trying to throw guilt on the eunuch to save themselves. Lady Li was with the Ming party. Dokadur Khan had heard that the favorite had a guileful tongue. Who were they to confute her words? He knew that Wei Chung and the Lady Li were the ruling party at the court.

"I have considered all this," Khlit answered briefly when Dokadur Khan drew up beside him and voiced his doubts. "In the Golden Tomb is that which will save us."

Dokadur Khan weighed this laboriously in his mind and was not satisfied. Were they to plunder the tomb? That was well enough in its way. There would be much gold. But, once possessed of the treasure, after driving off or slaying the *kang leen*, they would be between the forces of Li Yuan and the eunuch.

How could they go to the Ming nobles with the wealth of the

Golden Tomb in their hands and say that they came as friends? This was a heavy doubt, and to the slow mind of Dokadur Khan it appeared insuperable. Apparently they were to go first to the grave and then to the *yâmen*. How would they guard the treasure when approaching the Ming party? In time it would be seen, and the truth would be known. Moreover, it would provide rare reasons for the nimble tongue of the Lady Li to pour into the ears of the nobles.

"Silence is best, Dokadur Khan," snarled Khlit when he explained what was in his mind. "Does the condemned criminal debate with himself whether the noose that will hang him shall be silk or horse-hair? Our plight, thanks to the evil Wei Chung, is no better than that. If we succeed, we shall save our skins and the lives of your folk in the Togra. If we fail, our fate will be no worse than in the Togra."

"Nay," growled the chieftain, "you have not heard of the torture of the red-hot nails driven slowly into the ears or that of the wooden donkey."

"Aye, I have heard. But, if we win what we seek, the ears may happily be those of Wei Chung."

"There may be truth in that. But harken, Khlit, you do not seek to hold the treasure of the Golden Tomb as ransom for our lives?"

"The treasure is vast. But thrice its worth would not serve to turn aside the vengeance of the Mings against those who have slain him they call the Son of Heaven."

Dokadur Khan considered this in silence.

"Then you have proof that will convict Wei Chung?" he asked.

To his surprize Khlit laughed.

"I have no proof."

"If that be so, you can not prove to Li Yuan that Wei Chung slew the emperor."

"Nay, I can not do so."

"Nor that the Lady Li is guilty?"

"How should I have such proof?"

"You swore——"

"That at the Golden Tomb we may yet save our lives. Harken, Dokadur Khan, if you must think, consider this. In this land it is said that the spirit of the unburied will be met with by those who are blood-guilty. Wei Chung and the Lady Li are guilty, and Li Yuan is a man of wisdom who knows the high arts of divination and magic."

Whereupon Dokadur Khan, who understood not what Khlit had said, was silent. Which was what Khlit desired, for their task in reaching the Golden Tomb was difficult.

They rode fast, avoiding the caravan tracks and keeping to the plains. Fortunately the countryside was aroused by the news of Wan Li's death, and such bands of soldiers as were in the vicinity of the *yâmen* were debating whether to take sides with the Ming nobles or Wei Chung. It was rumored that already the Lady Li had claimed the Dragon throne for her infant son and was gathering troops to support her cause.

On the other hand the Ming party, consisting of those sent from Wan Li by Wei Chung before the hunt, was already nearing the *yâmen*. This served to throw the province of Liao into confusion in which it was possible for the small band of tribesmen to make their daring ride unmolested and almost unnoticed.

Only once more did Dokadur Khan speak when Khlit had halted to inquire the way of a peasant.

"If there is no proof and the gold treasure will avail us naught," he said slowly, "what is it in the Golden Tomb that will save our lives?"

Khlit was silent for a moment.

"I followed Wan Li into the tomb entrance," he responded. "And, while the emperor was kneeling before the shrine of his ancestor, I saw what gives me hope now and what brings us here."

Dokadur Khan breathed quickly.

"Did you see Wan Li write something down and leave it in the tomb? He may have suspected Wei Chung."

"He wrote nothing. I have said he prayed."

"Then did Wei Chung leave proof of his guilt?"

"He has left no proof."

"What, then?"

Khlit turned irritably in his saddle.

"This. See you that star ahead of us?"

"Aye, Khlit."

"And its reflection in yonder pool of water?"

"Aye."

"It is the star called by the wise Li Yuan the star of evil omen. He spoke truly. What I saw in the tomb was not the star. But it was like to it. Ho, Dokadur Khan," laughed Khlit with sudden merriment, "I was looking at two emperors, one living and one dead. Yet before my eyes formed the image of death. When I tell what I know to Li Yuan he will understand. For he is a man of wisdom, while you are one without sense."

Surely, thought Dokadur Khan, Khlit was mad. For how could he have seen the likeness of death with his eyes? And how could a dead man come to life to save their lives? Nay, they were doomed to the fate of the red-hot nails. For the peasant had said that the Chinese army and many of those at court were joining the ranks of Wei Chung and the Lady Li, and the cause of the Ming nobles appeared lost.

VI

The wisdom of a shrewd man is like finely tempered steel. It is like to a sword of rare workmanship.

For it may slay its owner in the same manner as the enemies of its possessor. But it does not blunder amiss.

The excitement that held the Liao province in its grip had reached the *kang leen,* during that night in the seventh moon. The captain and soldiers who guarded the tombs in the pine hills were debating among themselves which party to join. In their quarreling they neglected to fill in the entrance to the Golden Tomb. It is not impossible that they considered, if civil war broke out in the Dragon empire, they might despoil the mausoleum for themselves.

It is related in the chronicles of Wan Li that because of this confusion the *kang leen* neglected to post the usual sentries. Even as late as the third hour of that night they were gathered in groups about the fires in front of their pavilion. Thus it was that they failed to see the troop of horsemen which approached swiftly from the plain, dividing at the first of the pine hills, to ride to either side.

Doubtless the neglect of the captain would have been punished by torture at the hands of his superiors if he had survived. It is written that the blight of an evil conscience falls upon a man without warning. In this case he had argued to his men that, by going over to the rising power of Wei Chung, whom he knew to be already hastening back to the *yâmen* and to Peking, they would be on the stronger side. And might also despoil the tomb without reproach, since they were no longer of the Ming party.

To this some objected that the spirits of the mighty dead might trouble them. But the treasure of the tomb, although they had not seen it, they knew to be of great value. Hence the majority sided with the captain. But, before they could act, the retribution for their evil intentions, as written in the annals of that year, was upon them.

From the pine clumps on either side of the fires came the hurried beat of horses' hoofs, followed by cries of the soldiers by the outer fires. The *kang leen* ran for their arms which were scattered around the camp, as they had become careless in their talk. They saw the flash of swords in the firelight, and two groups of horsemen rode among the fires, one from the north, one from the south.

The captain of the *kang leen* was among the first slain. His men, surprized and ignorant of their foes, made a poor defense for picked troops of the Liao province. Some formed in groups with their spears; others fled into the darkness, but the greater part submitted to slaughter with the fatality of their race. The invading horsemen made no prisoners. To the fleeing *kang leen* it seemed that the evil they had summoned upon their heads had been swift in coming.

Khlit saw to it that no fugitives were left, concealed in the pine clumps. He had lost few men in the attack. He sent some of his horsemen to harry the scattered guardians of the tomb and others to set fire to the pavilion so that they should have an abundance of light to work by. When he was satisfied that the place held no more of his enemies, he summoned Dokadur Khan with a few men and approached the entrance to the tomb.

The flames that rose from the pavilion that had sheltered the *kang leen* showed him that little earth had been restored to the excavation. Some had fallen in from the sides; that was all. Doubtless the news of Wan Li's death had interrupted the work of filling in the earth over the stairs.

With the tools that lay at hand he had his men clear the steps. By this time all the plainsmen had returned from their tasks and were clustered about the excavation, staring. Only Dokadur Khan and a few others went with him down the steps. They had heard what he had said about the spirits of the dead.

These few carried torches. By their light Khlit set about opening the massive stone gate. The fastenings were of heavy iron, and the gate itself was a foot or more in thickness. It was some time before the way was clear for it to swing back.

Then it took a dozen stout fellows to move it on its stone hinges. It creaked slowly open, and the tribesmen hung back. It was a place of the dead, and none of them cared to enter except Khlit, who lacked superstition. Nevertheless the Cossack's eyes shone strangely under their shaggy brows as he led Dokadur Khan and the torch-bearers forward into the grave tunnel.

The stale odor of cold and confined air struck their nostrils, and their boots echoed on the stone. The tribesmen glanced curiously at the lofty pillars of teakwood and at the further door.

Khlit walked the length of the grave tunnel in silence and pushed open the inner door, which was lighter, being designed to be swung back by one man. Standing within the threshold of the inner door, they now saw the cavernous grave chamber, lighted by the everlasting candles of the tomb. And the plainsmen halted in their tracks with muttered oaths. Before them glittered the wealth of the Golden Tomb.

And in the tomb stood Wan Li.

The Lord of Ten Thousand Years faced them impassively, his wide-sleeved arms folded across his deep chest, the candle-light caressing the sheen of his silk robe. Only his eyes moved, eyes under which were dark circles, searching from face to face.

Dokadur Khan recognized him and drew a deep breath of amazement. Here was the man the empire mourned as dead. Or was it really a living man? He swore softly but, looking long, was reassured. It was Wan Li, undoubtedly alive. His followers were uncertain, gaping and moving uneasily while they looked from Khlit to Dokadur Khan and from them to Wan Li. They had forgotten the wealth that they had first seen in their bewilderment. Only Khlit was tranquil.

"As I promised, Dokadur Khan," he said grimly, "here is what will save our lives. The Son of Heaven was left by Wei Chung in the tomb of his ancestor."

The emperor spoke sharply, but none among the plainsmen understood his words, which were in the dialect of Peking, the court speech. Dokadur Khan swore again; then he laughed gruffly. Then he stared at Khlit.

"How has this come to pass?" he asked, and the men hung upon Khlit's response, pressing forward.

"Stand back," commanded the Cossack sharply. "Wan Li is no foe of ours. Moreover, his safety means our lives. Nay, the matter is simple. I have said I came to the tomb, watching Wan Li from the shadows. As I said, I saw the dead emperor in his coffin and the living monarch, Wan Li. And also the image. For, as I watched, I saw another enter the tomb after me, unseen by Wan Li. It was a eunuch, much like the emperor in face, and dressed in similar robes. He it was who walked from the tomb, while Wan Li was shut within by his enemies. I saw it from the shadows of the stairs."

Dokadur Khan's mind moved slowly, and here was a weighty matter. He stared at the tall figure before him, wetting his bearded lips.

"And the other," he asked, "the false Wan Li——"

"Was a servant of Wei Chung's. He was not suspected by the soldiery without the tomb when he walked to the sedan-chair, for what reason had they to doubt he was Wan Li? The mind of Wei Chung is dark and evil as that of a serpent."

"Then he planned to have Wan Li die in the tomb?"

"Without doubt. Of starvation and thirst. Harken, O slow of wit. See you not he plotted the death of the emperor. But it was needful to do it without casting suspicion on himself. He could not slay the Son of Heaven. So he slew the servant, being treacherous even to his own men and heedless of the life of one who served him. It was when he helped the false Wan Li into the sedan that he slew him with a knife. I saw the wound by the light of the fire that consumed the sedan."

The emperor stared at Khlit, striving to fathom what he said. In spite of his plight, he did not lose his habitual dignity.

"In this way," concluded Khlit, "Wei Chung silenced the mouth of the servant that might have betrayed him—for the race is one without honor—and, if he should have been discovered in that act, he could have said he did it to punish one who had assumed the person of the emperor. But he was not seen, and the chair with its body was burned as he plotted——"

"To hide the body that might have bared the trick," swore Dokadur Khan.

"And to cast the guilt upon us to conceal what he had done. That was why he wished to slay all who were present."

"Aye," assented the khan, who saw light at last and could understand this. "Death silences tale-bearers."

In the annals of Wan Li it is written that during the hunt of the seventh moon, when the star of evil omen was ascendent, Wan Li was missed for a day and night, being thought slain, until he was restored to Li Yuan and other nobles by a band of huntsmen who had found him.

That is all that is written, because much was left out owing to the evil influence of the eunuchs about the emperor. Still, the chronicles state that an open rebellion by the forces of the Lady Li was only averted by the fortunate appearance of the Son of Heaven at the *yâmen*. Owing to this the silken cord of happy dispatch was sent to the Lady Li, for her slim throat, by order of Wan Li himself.

Khlit had kept his imperial prisoner by his side and, escorted by Dokadur Khan and the remaining huntsmen, sought for and found the party of Li Yuan and the Ming nobles who were encamped near the *yâmen*, a few hours' ride from the tomb. In the ranks of the Togra men a man was found who could converse with the emperor, and through him it was explained that his huntsmen had seen him imprisoned in the tomb and had rescued him. Whereupon they gave the Son of Heaven food and wine.

This done, Wan Li promised them that their lives should be safeguarded and they should receive a fitting reward. All this does not appear in the annals of his reign, owing to the power of Wei Chung, who censored all that was written.

Khlit and Dokadur Khan saw that Wan Li was delivered to Li Yuan, who greeted him on bent knees, accompanied by the other nobles of his party.

"It is a night of true beneficence," murmured the delighted astrologer. "Because the influence of the star of evil omen has been overcome by the rising birth-star of the Son of Heaven and the Lord of Ten Thousand Years."

Khlit did not understand this. He waited impatiently on his horse while the court kowtowed. He saw the silken cord of suicide sent to the beautiful favorite, without understanding what it meant.

But Wei Chung, who had arrived at the *yâmen*, heard, and sent a messenger to Wan Li bearing congratulations on his return and saying that his faithful servant, Wei Chung-hsien, had been striving to punish those who had conspired against the throne, the evil servants of the doomed Lady Li—so said the messenger—and who had nearly caused the Son of Heaven to lose his life while in the care of Wei Chung, who was innocent—thus ran the message—of all blame, because he had not been aware of the conspiracy of the Lady Li nor of the eunuch who had impersonated Wan Li.

"It is a lie!" Li Yuan had cried, lifting his clenched fists.

But Wan Li had hesitated. Nor would he give the word to slay the eunuch.

Hearing of what had passed from the plainsmen who understood the talk, Khlit did not at first believe that Wei Chung was actually to be spared. But his own eyes told him that Wan Li hesitated, unwilling to believe evil of the chief eunuch. Whereupon Khlit swore and whispered to Dokadur Khan to assemble his men. Unnoticed in the confusion, they left the *yâmen*. Riding swiftly, they gained the plain.

There they met the rest of their men with loaded pack-horses. Under cover of darkness they made their way out to the Togra. Dokadur Khan swaggered jubilantly in his saddle.

"Hey, old warrior," he cried familiarly to Khlit, "it is a good night's work. The spoil of the Golden Tomb, taken after we left with Wan Li, will well repay my men. Half of the treasure, as you have asked, will be sent to the Tatars, your old friends. You have served well me and mine, and I will see that the division is even, to the weight of a hair. The Tatars shall have a royal gift from you."

Khlit did not reply at once.

"I have seen the master of a million men," he said at length, "and he is a weaker man than you or Arslan or I. For he can not safeguard the lives of those who are his friends. Nor can he save his own. He will yet die by the hand of Wei Chung."

The tribesmen listened, for these were the words of one who had done them a great service. But they understood them not. At Khiit's next speech, however, they laughed with him.

"Hey, good sirs," he cried, leaning forward and patting the neck of his horse, "we have our lives and our good horses, and the free steppe is before us. It is well."

ADVENTURE SIX

THE RIDER OF THE GRAY HORSE

In the temples are the many-handed gods. High is the wisdom of the gods.

Is the wisdom of the gods one with Fate? Nay, how can it be known?

And in the palace is the face of a woman. There is perfume in her heavy hair, and the eyes of the maiden are dark, as with sleep. Her hand is small as a lotus blossom.

Yet in her petal-hand is the destiny of a man, of many men. The gods have ordained it, and it is true.

KHLIT, CALLED BY HIS ENEMIES THE COSSACK OF THE CURVED SABER, was followed.

He was aware of this. It caused him no uneasiness. For, he thought, if a rider carries nothing of value, should he fear thieves? He was not less watchful, however, on that account. It was the Year of the Rat, reckoned by the Chinese calendar—in the first decade of the seventeenth century of the Christian era—and the border of the desert of Gobi was a refuge of the lawless.

From time to time the Cossack reined in his horse and glanced backward over the wind ridges which formed an ocean of sand on three sides of the rider. On the fourth was the river Tarim. This Khlit was following, having heard that it would take him from the desert to the southern mountains. Beyond these mountains, he had been told by wandering priests, was the fair land of Ladak and Ind.

Wise in the ways of warfare and plunder, the old Cossack knew that only one rider followed him. Save for this half-perceived shadow that clung to his path, Khlit was alone. Such was his custom. Years since he had ridden from the war camp of the Cossacks—an outcast.

Now, disgusted with the silken treachery of the men of China, whither he had come from Tatary, the warrior had taken up his journey in a new direction, south. A veteran of many battles, impatient of authority, his shrewdness, enforced by very expert sword-play, had safeguarded him in a time when men's lives hung by slender threads. And had earned him enemies in plenty.

As he guided his mount beside the riverbank Khlit meditated. Why should one rider follow him? It was clearly to be seen that he carried no goods worthy of plunder. Merely some handfuls of dried meat and milk curds in his saddle-bags. Even his horse was not one to be coveted by a desert-man, being a shaggy steppe pony.

Perhaps the rider in his rear planned to wait until he dismounted at nightfall, slay him and take the horse. Yet it was not the custom of the Gobi bandits to hunt their prey alone.

Down a steep clay bank his pony slid, pursuing the half visible caravan track marked by dried bones and camel droppings. At the bottom of the slope, beside a stunted tamarisk, Khlit halted and faced about, drawing a pistol and adjusting the priming. He would see, he decided, what manner of man followed him.

Quietly the Cossack waited, his tall form upright in the saddle, sheepskin *svitza* thrown back to allow free arm play. His keen eyes peered under tufted brows at the summit of the mound down which he had come, searching the sky-line.

The stillness of the place was unbroken. The sluggish river moving through the waste was lifeless. There were no birds or game in the region. Even the warmth of a Summer sun was seasoned by the high altitude of the southern Gobi.

The horse pricked up his ears. Khlit lifted his weapon and scowled. By now the other rider must be near. His sharp ears had caught the impact of a stone dislodged from a near-by ridge.

Back and forth along the ridge summit his glance flickered. There was no sign of movement. A second sound arrested his attention. It was faint, coming from no definite direction. It was a low, whispering laugh.

The sound came from the stillness around him, softly mocking, almost caressing. It was a tiny sound, akin to the drip of sand. It might have issued from the ground under his feet. Then he heard a brief, dull mutter, as of a sword drawn from a rusted scabbard.

Still Khlit waited, impassive. His horse seemed to have lost interest in what was passing near at hand. In fact, Khlit himself was not oversure the sounds had not been a trick of the imagination.

With a stifled oath he swerved his mount and spurred up the ridge, his weapon ready in his free hand. His pursuer, apparently, had sighted him and turned back. The pony dug his leather-shod hoofs valiantly into the sand, which afforded evil footing, and gained the summit panting.

Khlit cast a quick glance over the plain. Nothing was to be seen of the other rider. True, the depressions between the ridges might shelter the other. But the scattered tamarisks and forlorn bushes by the river offered no concealment. Khlit was standing on the edge of the bank some hundred feet above the water, and the thickets in the region whence he had come were clear to view.

He looked down thoughtfully at his horse's tracks, outlined along the caravan trail. Then he swore aloud.

"Dog of the devil!" he grunted.

Beside his own tracks were those of another horse. They came within a yard of where he was, then ceased.

Khlit searched the summit of the ridge carefully. There was no mistaking the message in the sand. A second horse, making small, clearly indented tracks, had walked nearly to the crest of the sand. It had not returned, for there were no traces leading rearward. Nor had it passed him—his own eyes had been witness to that.

The Cossack replaced the pistol in his belt and tugged at his heavy mustache. The sounds might have been his imagining. Certainly the soft laugh had startled him. But the hoof-prints were not fancy.

Khlit thought briefly of the tales he had heard from the *gylongs* —wandering beggar priests of Buddha—concerning the *ghils* of the desert. These were spirits which followed the course of travelers, appearing beside them in the shape of men and luring them to destruction.

Woman's tales, he reflected, and not to be believed. The priests had warned him against the shrill cries of the *ghils* heard at night. But he was familiar with the strange noises the sands make at times, similar to the sound of drums or horse's hoofs.

The priests, he reasoned, would no doubt say that he had been followed by one of the spirits of the desert, which took flight into the air when he observed it. Khlit scowled at the tracks in the sand.

Undoubtedly another horse had come to the sand ridge. Since it was not to be seen, it had left. But where, and how?

Khlit laughed, a gruff hearty laugh, and slapped his thigh. Then he dug spurs into the pony's sides and as the animal sprang forward jerked the beast's head to one side. Down the embankment of sand into the river went pony and rider.

II

"Ho, one-without-sense!" growled Khlit as the pony struggled in the current of the Tarim. "Do you fear to do what another has done? Nay, we go not back here."

The thought had come to Khlit, standing on the ridge, of how the other rider had vanished. Only one way was possible—into the river. And a slope of loose sand, as the Cossack knew, left no tracks.

He guided his pony down the current in the direction he had been going. This way the other must have gone. Or Khlit would have seen the rider as he searched the riverbank to the rear. Clearly his companion of the desert path was anxious to pass him by rather than meet him. This stirred Khlit's curiosity the more.

As he crouched in the saddle, Cossack fashion, he scanned the shore keenly. His pursuer, he thought, must have been anxious to press ahead. And to escape observation. Otherwise the rider would have passed him by along the sand ridges instead of choosing the river. Of course, to do so would render the other visible to Khlit. Hence the leap into the Tarim.

Who, wondered Khlit, rode the caravan track alone and in haste, yet in fear of observation?

With difficulty Khlit kept the pony's head away from the bank. The water, in spite of the hot rays of the sun, was cold and torpid, winding between its banks with the silence of a huge reptile passing over the barren waste of the desert. A cold wind stirred the sand on the ridges and fanned Khlit's beard.

The Cossack presently gave an exclamation of satisfaction and headed for the bank. He had seen the tracks of a horse leading up the slope. Dark water stains showed that the horse and rider he was following had but recently passed that way. He had guessed correctly the maneuver of his erstwhile pursuer.

He urged his pony into a quick trot, following the traces in the sand. Before long he was convinced that the other's mount was fleet of foot, for he gained no sight of rider or beast, urge his horse as he would.

He saw only that the rider had returned to the caravan track. The sun, which had been low on the plain to the west, disappeared suddenly. The sky overhead changed from a clear blue to a dull purple. Khlit reined in his pony and dismounted.

Warmth, gathered during the day, was still exuding from the sand, but the Cossack knew that the night would be chill. He picketed his beast in the depression between two sand mounds, collected a bundle of tamarisk roots and kindled a small fire.

He placed his leather saddle-cloth between the sand slope and the fire and seated himself thereon with his saddle-bags, preparatory to making a meal of dried meat. The other rider, he thought, would not molest him, judging by what had happened at the river.

Khlit lay back on his heavy coat, gazing up into the purple infinity overhead. One by one the stars were glittering into being. Khlit knew them all. He had followed their guidance over the roof of the world into strange countries. Unlike most men, he was best contented when alone. His few companions in arms had been slain, and as for women, the Cossack regarded them as rather more troublesome than magpies or the inquisitive and predatory steppe fox.

The next instant he was on his feet, sword drawn, limbs taut and head sunk forward between his shoulders. A horse and rider had moved into the circle of firelight.

Khlit's first glance made sure that the intruder held no pistol. His second, that no weapons at all were visible. Nevertheless, he did not lower his sword. He had seen death reward imprudence too often.

And then he heard the echo of the soft laugh that had startled him by the river bank. Peering at the newcomer, he grunted. It was a woman, clad in a fur-tipped *khalat*, under which a silk shawl was wrapped over head and breast. Over a veil which shielded the lower half of her face two dark eyes scanned him calmly. Black hair of shimmering texture, evenly divided, crowned a high, fair forehead.

So much Khlit observed in surprise. He noted that the horse was a mettled gray stallion and the saddle trappings costly.

The rider of the horse spoke, in a limpid tongue unknown to Khlit. Then Khlit sheathed his sword.

"Nay, I know not your song, little night-bird," he said in Uigur, the semi-Turkish dialect of Central Asia. "Devil take me—I knew not the great desert breeds such as you."

The dark eyes snapped angrily.

"What matters your knowledge, O small-of-wit?" the rider lisped in the same tongue. "Among my people a gray horse is a sigil of wisdom. Here I find it on the mouth of a fool."

Khlit considered the woman in surprise. By the shifting firelight she appeared beautiful of face. Certainly her figure, under the *khalat* was rounded and slim. What was such a maiden doing alone on the desert? True, they were not two days' ride from the city of Khoten; but the caravan tracks were peopled with scoundrels, and Khoten itself was a rendezvous for the lawless of all nations.

Moreover, the woman puzzled him. She was not Chinese; her beauty was too great for a Khirghiz or flat faced Usbek. Her dress and imperious manner were not those of a Turk.

She leaned forward in the saddle, eyes bent intently on him. Her attitude suggested that she was ready to wheel and flee on the instant.

"Hey, you have truly the tongue of a magpie!" grumbled Khlit. "Were you the rider that braved the waters of the Tarim to pass me by along the caravan trail?"

"Aye, dullard. While you were swearing like a *caphar* and reading lies in the tracks in the sand. Now it is my whim to seek you. A fool, and an old fool, is harmless."

So saying she urged her horse nearer to the fire by a slight pressure of the knees—for she rode astride, as a man.

"Whence come you? Whither go you, in the great desert, O prattle-tongue?" asked Khlit.

The bright eyes over the veil were fixed on the fire, yet Khlit was aware that they kept him well in view.

"Nay, gray-beard, am I other than a *ghil* of the waste? Have you seen me come to your fire? I am here at the word of one who was master of the earth. Now he is dead, yet his word keeps me here."

"Ha! The fat Son of Heaven who is master of China?"

"Nay—" the black eyes half closed in a tantalizing smile—"a greater than Wan Li. Because of his death there is no bed where I am safe, nor any palace gate where I may enter. From beyond the grave his hand reaches out to me."

"Child's riddles," grumbled Khlit, striding to the fire.

He cared little that a woman of rank, and unescorted, should be in Gobi. One thing he had guessed. The soft, quick speech of the woman stirred his memory. He recalled another who had spoken similarly. His visitor was a Persian by birth.

She placed a jeweled hand lightly on his shoulder.

"I am hungry," she said plaintively. "And those who were to meet me here by the Tarim, two days' journey from Khoten, have not come. I have no food—and it grows cold."

"Dismount, then, and eat."

Long and earnestly the dark eyes scanned the tall Cossack. As if reassured, the girl slipped from saddle of the gray steed to ground, uttering an exclamation of pain as the circulation started in numbed feet. Khlit silently arranged a seat for her on his saddle-cloth and set about preparing a meal with the small means at his disposal.

III

"While I sleep, gray-beard, you may mount your horse and watch, lest others approach too near. With the dawn you should see two riders coming from the south in haste, for they are belated—a sin worthy of death by bastinado to those not of such high caste as these two."

Khlit eyed his companion grimly. Was he one to be ordered about by a woman? Even such as this one? For she had put down her veil on eating, explaining that, as he was a *caphar*—a Christian—there was no sin in his seeing the countenance of a woman who was a true believer. When Khlit asked how she knew he was a Christian she touched the miniature gold cross he wore at his neck with a ringed forefinger. Khlit saw that the ring bore an emerald of great size.

"There were some of your faith at the court of the great king," she remarked idly.

"What name bears this khan?"

She glanced at him and smiled fleetingly. Resting her rounded chin on her hand, she gazed at the fire. Khlit saw that her beauty was as fine as the texture of a peacock's plumage, as delicate as the tinted heart of a rare shell. Her eyes were not aslant, but level as his own.

The molding of the luminous brow and the tiny mouth bespoke pride and intelligence. The dark hair peering from under the hood of the *khalat* was abundant and silk-like.

The shawl about her slender shoulders was open at the throat, revealing a splendid throat ringed in pearl necklaces. Here was a woman who had undoubtedly been mistress of many slaves, who was a Mohammedan, with jewels to the value of many horses—even a principality.

"Akbar, of Ind," she said.

Khlit had heard of Ind as a land of many peoples and great treasure, whence caravans came to China. As far as he had a purpose in his wandering, he was bound there.

"Are there many *yurts* and tents in Akbar's camp?" he inquired.

The girl stared at him frankly and threw back her head with a musical laugh.

"O steppe boor! O one-of-small-wisdom! There be palaces in the empire of Akbar the Mogul as many as the tents of one of your dirty Tatar camps." The laugh ended abruptly. "Nay, he has a following of millions of many faiths, who obey his word from Samarkand to the Ganges' mouth. And his word has laid the seal of death on Nur-jahan——"

She broke off, biting her lip swiftly with a vexed frown.

"Hey—is that the name they have given you, little night-bird?" Khlit yawned indifferently. "It has a strange sound."

"It is mine at the bidding of a prince, dolt!" she cried. "And you have heard it. That is an evil thing, for I wish it not to be known."

"It matters not," growled the Cossack, lighting his long stemmed black pipe while the woman regarded him with vexed intentness. "I shall not speak it—nay, I care little for the secrets of a palace courtesan."

Nur-jahan leaned swiftly toward him. Khlit caught the glitter of metal in the firelight and threw up his hand in time to seize the slender hand that held a dagger a few inches from his chest. He turned the girl's wrist curiously to the light, inspecting the tiny weapon, scarce larger than the jade pendants that twinkled at her ears.

"Are these the weapons of Ind?" he asked mildly, a glimmer in his deep-set eyes. "And have you forgotten, Nur-jahan, the faith of a follower of Mahomet, who may not slay one with whom he has shared bread and salt?"

With that he released the Persian's wrist. The girl's cheeks were crimson and her eyes brilliant with anger. But the dagger fell to her lap.

Truly, thought Khlit, she was one of rank, for an ordinary concubine would not be so quick to resent a slight. The favorite of a prince, perhaps.

"Harken, little spitfire. Why did you leave the land of Ind for the foul Gobi desert—alone?"

"Nay, not alone. There was one with me who is worth ten other warriors. In the morning he will come, by the caravan track. Let him find you gone, *caphar*, or your life will cease as the flame of a candle in the wind, and the ravens will eat of your head!"

"He must be a brave khan, then. But he left you, Nur-jahan, alone in the lap of Gobi. How may that be?"

"He went to Khoten for news—of Ind. For tidings, and another who came over the mountains to join us. Also, to get food, which we lacked. As I said, Chauna Singh is belated and I shall scold him well. Nay, *caphar*, I could not go to Khoten lest I be seen; and Breath of the Wind—" she pointed to the gray horse—"is a stallion of Kabul, fleeter than the beasts of this country. He would keep me safe."

"A good horse, little night-bird. But fear you not I will slay you for those jewels—" Khlit nodded at her throat—"take the stallion and leave your fair body for the eyes of this Chauna Singh?"

Nur-jahan shook her dark head with a smile.

"What will be, will be. And it is not written that my grave lies in the desert. Besides, I read honesty in your dull eyes—honesty and stupidity. Strong men are my slaves. Speak, *caphar!*" She shifted on the robe until her head was near his shoulder. "Without doubt you are old in the ways of loves and have had many women to your will. Have you seen one so fair as I? Speak—is it not so? A prince, ruler of ten thousand swords, swore I was more lovely than the gardens of Kashmir in Spring. Aye, than the lotus and tulips of the divine wife of Prithvi-Raj. What say you, old warrior?"

There was assurance in the poise of the splendid head near Khlit, and a soft undertone to the musical voice. Nur-jahan spoke artlessly, yet with the pride of one whose beauty had brought to her—power. And great power.

Khlit was conscious of a perfume that came from the silken garments under the heavy *khalat*—a mingling of faint musk and dried rose-leaves. He looked steadily into the dark eyes, eyes that were veiled shadows changing to luminous pools, deep and full as the waters of quiet lakes.

"You are a child, Nur-jahan," he said gruffly, "and there is evil in you as well as beauty."

Nur-jahan considered him gravely, drawing the *khalat* closer about her, for it grew cold.

"What is evil, old warrior?" she mused. "The word of Allah the wise tells us that we know not what is before us or behind. We are wind-swept leaves on the roadway of fate. Our lives are written before we come to the world. Why do you call me evil? Nay, I will show you that it is not so."

She paused, making designs in the sand with the dagger point. Khlit threw some more wood on the fire.

"You know my name," she continued. "And that must not be. I am hiding, to save myself from the decree of Akbar, who, when he felt the angel of death standing near, ordered my execution. There was no place in Ind where I would be safe—nor in Tibet or Ladak. So I came with one other over the mountains into the desert. You go to Khoten, doubtless, and my enemies are there. So you may not live to say that you have seen me."

Khlit made no response. His indifference vexed the girl.

"By the face of the Prophet, you are witless!" she stormed. "Nay, since you have shared bread with me, I will offer you a chance of life before Chauna Singh comes. Or he will assuredly slay you. For the life of one such as you—and a *caphar*—is of trifling importance beside my secret. In spite of your sharing food with me he will slay you very quickly. He is a swordsman among a thousand."

"Then I shall wait until I see him, prattle-tongue. I have not seen a true swordsman since a certain Tatar khan died at my side."

"Fool! If you stay, your grave is dug here. Get you to horse. It will be several hours before Chauna Singh will sight our fire. If you ride north at once, he may not follow far, for he will not leave me again for long. So you may save your skin."

Khlit stretched his gaunt arms, for he was sleepy and the woman's talk disturbed him.

"I go south to Khoten—not north," he responded curtly. "As for

Chauna Singh, let him look to his own skin, if he stands in my way."

Nur-jahan stared at the Cossack as if she had not heard aright. She noted the deep-set eyes under gray brows, still alert in spite of their wrinkles, and the lean, hard cheeks, stretched firmly over the bones. A man not unlike her own people, she thought, yet one of rude dress and coarse bearing.

"Chauna Singh," she protested, "is a man in the prime of life, O one-without-wisdom, and you——"

"Truly, I am wearied of talk."

With this Khlit betook himself to the other side of the fire, where he rolled himself in his long coat and was asleep almost on the instant.

Thus it was that Khlit shared food and fire with the woman who came to him in the desert, whose name was strange to him. And Nur-jahan, watching sleepily by the tamarisk flames, thought that here was a man of a kind she had not met with, who cared not for her beauty and less for the threat of death, yet who gave up his shelter and the half of his food to her.

IV

It is written in the annals of the Raj that Pertap, the hero, gave his horse to a generous foe, thus risking death.

Wherefore do the men of the Raj cry: "Ho! Níla ghora ki aswár," when they ride into battle. For the memory of a Rájput is long.

The sound of voices wakened Khlit from a deep sleep. A glance told him that two riders had come up and were halted beside the woman, who was on her feet, talking to them.

Khlit rose leisurely and stirred up the remnants of the fire. This done, he scanned the newcomers. Both were well clad and mounted. One, a lean man of great height, bore a scar the length of his dark cheek. The Cossack noted that he sat his horse with ease, that the beast was of goodly breed, that the peaked saddle was jewel mounted and that gold inlaid mail showed under the white satin vestment over the rider's square shoulders. His turban was small and knotted over one ear, the end hanging over the right shoulder.

He was heavily bearded and harsh of face, thanks in part to the scar which ran from chin to brow, blighting one eye, which was half closed. The other man Khlit passed over for the time. He was bent, with the fragile frame of a child and a mild, wrinkled face.

Nur-jahan was speaking urgently to the man with the scar, who frowned, shaking his turbaned head. His glance searched Khlit scornfully. Apparently he was refusing some request of the girl's. Without taking his eyes from the Cossack, he dismounted and strode toward the fire.

"Ho! Rider of the mangy pony!" he cried, in broken Uigur. "One without manners, of a race without honor. I have heard the tale of Nur-jahan and your death is at hand."

Khlit lifted his arm, showing his empty hand.

"I seek no quarrel, Chauna Singh," he said slowly. "I am no old woman, to gossip concerning the affairs of others. Peace! Go your way, and I go mine."

"To Khoten?" The bearded lip of Chauna Singh lifted in a snarl. "It may not be. Nay, I do not desire your death; but the life of Nur-jahan is my charge, and the sword is the only pledge that seals the lips of a man. Come, take your weapon!"

Khlit stared at the other grimly. He had no wish to quarrel. And Chauna Singh was an individual of formidable bearing. There was no help for it.

"Be it so," he said briefly.

On the instant the two curved blades were flashing together, the two warriors soft-stepping in the sand. The weapons, like the men, were of equal size. Chauna Singh, however, wore a vest of fine mail, while Khlit was protected only by his heavy coat.

The warrior attacked at once, his scimitar making play over Khlit's sheepskin cap. A tall man, the champion of Nur-jahan was accustomed to beat down the guard of an adversary. Khlit's blade was ever touching the scimitar, fending it skillfully before a stroke had gained headway.

Chauna Singh's one eye glittered and his mustache bristled in a snarl. Here was not the easy game he had anticipated. Nor was the Cossack to be tricked into a false stroke by a pretended lapse on his part—as the other speedily learned.

The girl and the other rider watched in intent silence. Khlit had sufficient faith in the honor of his foes not to fear a knife in his back at the hand of Chauna Singh's comrade. He had eyes for nothing but the dazzling play of the other's weapon, which ceaselessly sought head, throat and side.

While Khlit's sword made play his brain was not idle. He saw that Chauna Singh appeared tireless, while his own arm lacked the power of youth. Soon he would be at a disadvantage. He must put the fight to an issue at once.

And so Khlit lunged at Chauna Singh—lunged and sank on one knee as if from the impetus of his thrust. His blade, for a second, was lowered.

Had Chauna Singh not held his adversary in mild contempt he would have known that a swordsman of Khlit's skill would not have made such a blunder. But the Rájput, heated by the conflict, uttered a cry of triumph and swung aloft his scimitar.

"Ho! Níla ghora ki aswár!" he shouted—the war-cry of his race.

Ere the blow he planned had been launched, Chauna Singh jerked himself backward. Khlit's weapon had flashed up under his guard, and the wind of it fanned his beard. Had the Rájput been a whit less active on his feet his chin would have been severed from his neck. As it was, the outer fold of his turban fell to his shoulders in halves.

A blow upward from the knee—a difficult feat—was an old trick of the Cossack.

Momentarily the two adversaries were apart, eying each other savagely. The voice of Nur-jahan rang out.

"Stay, Chauna Singh! Peace! Hold your clumsy hand and let me speak!"

Khlit saw the girl step between them. At her whispered urging Chauna Singh sheathed his weapon with a scowl.

"Harken, gray-beard, you be a pretty hand at sword-play. Almost you had dyed red the beard of stupid Chauna Singh. I have need of such men as you, and, verily, I can ill spare the big Rájput. You know my secret, and Chauna Singh, who has room for only one thought in his thick skull, will not consent to letting you go free. But come with us. Thus we can keep watch over your tongue."

The Cossack considered this, leaning on his sword.

"I go to Khoten, Nur-jahan," he made answer gruffly.

"And we likewise. These men have brought me news which takes us to the city. Come! In Khoten a lone man fares ill, for the place is a scum of thieves and slitthroats."

Khlit had no especial liking for company. On the other hand, Chauna Singh's sword-play had won his hearty respect. The Persian's words had not the ring of treachery. And her champion, although quick to draw blade, was not one to slay without warning.

"Whither go you from Khoten?" he asked.

Nur-jahan hesitated. But the man on the horse spoke, in a voice strangely musical.

"We go into the heart of peril, warrior—by a path beset with enemies. If you live, you will reach the hills of Kashmir and Ind and find honor at a Mogul's court. Have you heart for such a venture?"

Khlit glanced at the speaker curiously. The other could not have chosen words more to his liking. He saw a thin, dark face bent between slender shoulders, a sensitive mouth and shrewd, kindly eyes.

"Aye, khan," said Chauna Singh bluntly, "if you want good blows, given and taken, come with us—and gain a treasure of rare horses and jewels. But, give heed, your life will not be safe—for we face a thousand foes, we three, and a thousand that we see not or know not, until they strike."

"Be you men of the Mogul?"

Khlit saw the three exchange a curious glance. Nur-jahan's eyes lighted mockingly.

"If we live, khan—aye. But if we die we be foes of the mighty Mogul Akbar of Ind. Will you come, being our comrade-in-arms and the keeper of my secret?"

The Cossack sheathed his sword.

"Aye—be it so. Many enemies give honor to a man."

The Rájput strode forward, placing hand on lips and chest.

"By the white horse of Prithvi-Raj, I like it well! I have not met such a swordsman in a feast of moons. Ho! If we live, you will drink good wine of Shiraz and I will watch. If we die, we will spread a carpet of dead about us such as will delight the gods."

Nur-jahan's piquant face was smiling slightly, but the shrewd eyes of the man on the horse were inscrutable.

V

"And it was as the *mir* said. The word of a dead man has doomed her. Because of her beauty is she doomed. It is written that a fair maiden is like to a ruby-cup of wine that heats the brain of men while it stirs their senses."

Hamar, the companion of Chauna Singh, smiled meditatively at Khlit, stroking his mustache with a thin hand. The man, Khlit had discovered, was a musician of Hind, a wandering philosopher of Nur-jahan's country. He it was who had come from Kashmir to Khoten with word from the Mogul court that they were to hasten back.

The four were trotting along the caravan track, a day's ride nearer the city. Nur-jahan on her gray horse, was leading, with Chauna Singh at her side. Khlit and the minstrel followed at some distance, keeping a wary eye on the rear, for they had passed one or two cortèges of merchants, journeying from Aksu to Khoten.

"How may that be?" grunted Khlit, who had no liking for riddles and twisted words. "When a man is dead he can not work harm."

"Nay, but this is Akbar, lord of Delhi, ruler of the Raj, conqueror of Kashmir and Sind—monarch of five times a hundred thousand blades. His whispered word was law from Turkestan to the Dekkan. A mighty man, follower of Mahomet, achieving by his lone strength the mastery of the Mogul empire. He is dead, but his word lives."

"And that word——"

"To slay Nur-jahan." The faded eyes of the minstrel had gleamed at mention of the glories of Akbar; now they were somber. A man of wisdom, thought Khlit, considering his companion, and a dreamer.

"Harken, khan." Hamar roused himself. "This is the story. Akbar carved for himself the empire of the Moguls, following in the footsteps of his illustrious grandsire, Baber. Yet is the empire formed of races of many faiths—Moslems from Turkestan, Hindus of Ind, Jains and Buddhists of Ladak and priests of another temple who are masters in the hills. To hold together such an empire, the ruler must be one with his subjects—and Akbar, of blessed wisdom, was a patron of many faiths. Men say that he died calling upon the gods of Brahma, although a Moslem. I have seen him bow the head in many temples. So he held the jealous races of the empire together. And so must his successor, Jahangir, do."

Hamar paused, glancing over the waste ahead of them, where the barren trunks of dead trees reared themselves above the whitened bones of camels.

"When Jahangir was a youth of fifteen," he resumed, "he met the maiden Mir-un-nissa, now called Nur-jahan, in a palace festival. He gave the Persian girl two doves to hold for him. One escaped her grasp. Jahangir, angered, demanded how. Verily, then the proud temper of the maiden showed. 'Thus!' she cried and freed the other bird. From that moment the prince loved her—aye, stedfastly."

"The tale wearies me," growled Khlit. "Bah—doves and a maiden —what have they to do with an empire?"

"Much," smiled the minstrel patiently. "In our land men love passionately and long. Jahangir still desires Nur-jahan—and he is now Mogul. Akbar, foreseeing this in his wisdom, married the maiden to one Sher Afghan, a notable warrior and a proud man. Yet Nur-jahan fled from Sher Afghan when Akbar sickened."

"Wherefore?"

"Nay, you know not our people, khan. Jahangir, being ruler, will doubtless slay Sher Afghan, for the new Mogul's love for the maiden is great and they betrothed themselves, one to the other, when they were young. Again, Akbar thought of this and pledged the friends of his deathbed to slay the girl before she became the queen of Jahangir."

Khlit thought that Nur-jahan might well prove a disturbing influence over a young ruler. Yet surely there must be a further reason for Akbar's command of death. Hamar, as if reading his thoughts, pointed to the slim figure of the girl.

"Shall a serpent come into a nest of eggs? So reasoned Akbar. The maiden Nur-jahan is devoted to Islam and the rule of the Moslem. She is strong of will, and she would win Jahangir to her views. Then the Mogul would join himself to the Mohammedans and the empire of Baber and Akbar would vanish, thus!"

Hamar plucked a dried rose from a wallet at his girdle and tossed it into the air. The delicate petals fell apart and dropped into the sand. Hamar watched them moodily. His voice had been vibrant with feeling.

"Nur-jahan escaped death?" Khlit demanded, for the other's story had begun to interest him.

"Once, by aid of Chauna Singh, a follower of Sher Afghan. And fled over the mountains. Now Jahangir has sent me from the Agra court with word for her to return. Once in his palace, he will safeguard her."

"What of the knight, Sher Afghan?"

Hamar lifted his eyebrows slightly and waved a thin hand.

"A broken twig swept away by the current of a strong river—have you seen it, khan? Not otherwise is Sher Afghan. He is a proud man, who will not give up his wife—even if she be so only in name. His days are numbered."

Khlit nodded. He had seen a citadel stormed because of the beauty of an insulted woman and the emperor of Han pardon treachery because of the smile of a favorite. The witchery of such women, he reflected, was an evil thing.

"Hey," he laughed. "Then the matter is simple. We have but to take the maiden to Agra, to the embraces of her lover, the Mogul."

The minstrel smiled inscrutably.

"Think you so? You forget the word of Akbar. Among his followers are the priests of Kali, the four-armed, and—from the mountains—disciples of Bon, the Destroyer. They have sworn an oath to him that the girl shall not live. Their shrines are found from Khoten to Delhi and in the hills. Their servants are numbered as the sands of the great desert. Likewise they are priests of the gods, and the death of the Persian Moslem will safeguard their faith in Ind. Why did not Jahangir send an army to bring her to him? Nay, in the ranks would be assassins of Kali. The elephant drivers would see that she fell from the howdah."

Khlit grunted scornfully. Hamar's eyes flashed as he pointed ahead of them, where the dust of a caravan rose.

"If we drink from a cup, we must look for poison. If we sleep in a caravanserai, the camel men will come to us like evil *lings* with drawn knives. We be but four against a thousand. Aye, from his tomb, the hand of Akbar has set the seal of sacrifice on Nurjahan's forehead."

VI

In every Temple they seek Thee; in every language they praise Thee. Each faith says it holds Thee.

Thee I seek from Temple to Temple.

But only the dust of the Rose Petal remains to the seller of perfume.

Akbar, the Mogul.

The caravanserai was a low stone wall built around a well by the desert route. It was littered with dung and the leavings of former visitors. In the twilight it loomed desolate and vacant.

Chauna Singh had been unwilling to rest there the night, but Hamar pointed out that the sun was down, the air chill, and they had need of water. True, the caravan they had passed a short way back was hard on their heels; but they had been seen as they rode by it, and if danger was to be expected from the merchants and their followers it was better to face it in the lighted enclosure of the cara- vanserai than to journey further into the desert—where they could easily be traced.

Nur-jahan added her voice to Hamar's, and the Rájput, grumbling, bestirred himself to build a fire for the woman on the blackened débris of the hearth. Khlit tended the horses—a task readily yielded to him by Chauna Singh, who was not overfond of manual labor, except on the behalf of his mistress.

Khlit saw that the enclosure was similar to a Khirghiz *aul*—suffi- ciently large to accommodate them and the cortège which presently entered. Chauna Singh had shrewdly chosen a corner of the place farthest from the gate, where they could face the new arrivals. He aided the Cossack in preparing some rice over the fire, both appar- ently giving no heed to the other caravan but keeping a keen lookout.

"They be low-caste traders from the Han country," muttered the Rájput beneath his breath. "Men without honor, poor fighters; still —with ruffianly following."

"Hillmen—Khirghiz, a few," assented Khlit, who knew the folk of the uplands. "Hook-nosed Usbeks, a fat mandarin or two, some beg- garly Dungans—and a swine-faced Turkoman."

"Aye, the Turkoman may bear watching. He has a score of rascals."

Chauna Singh glanced at Khlit in some surprize at the Cossack's knowledge. The look was scornful, half askance, the look of a man who traced his ancestors to the gods and held honor dearer than life.

"Whence come you, khan, that you know the people of the hills? What is your caste?"

"For the present, Chauna Singh," said Khlit, "I come from Ta- tary. There I was but one among a hundred khans. They called me Khlit, of the Curved Saber."

"That is a strange name," meditated the Rájput. "Nay, by Shiva, you must be more than a small khan—a leader of a hundred! Surely, you had rank?"

Khlit stirred the fire calmly. He traced his ancestors to Ghenghis Khan, and the curved sword was that of Kaidu, overlord and hero of Tatary. Yet the Rájput's insolence irked him. Chauna Singh did not know that Khlit had been Kha Khan of the remaining tribes of Tatary.

"A leader of a hundred?" he growled. "Not so. I am lord of nothing save yonder pony. As for rank, I once spoke to the great emperor of Han—and he gave me some gold."

The Cossack's whiskers twitched in a smile, for he had saved the emperor Wan Li from burial alive in the tomb of his ancestors and had appropriated the treasure of the tomb as payment. But this he neglected to confide to Chauna Singh.

"Ho—gold!" The Rájput muttered, giving up his questioning as fruitless. "You will have rubies and sapphires if you live to reach Jahangir."

"You are a follower of Jahangir?" asked Khlit, eyeing the lean face framed in the firelight.

Chauna Singh's head snapped up.

"Since the breath of life was in Ind, a Rájput has been faithful to his lord."

Nur-jahan kept in the background as they ate. She had performed her after-sunset prayer as quietly as might be, keeping her veil drawn close. Hamar had impressed upon her the need of caution.

Even Khlit felt something of the alertness that possessed the two followers of the girl. Truly, they must fear the danger they stood from the priests of Akbar, the followers of Kali and Bon. When the Turkoman strolled over from the other fires with several men and stared at them, the Cossack saw Chauna Singh rise indolently, stretch and take up a position between Nur-jahan and the newcomers.

Hamar had drawn forth his *vina*—a guitar-like instrument—at which he was plucking softly. The Turkoman's slant eyes took in the scene and he swaggered forward.

Khlit did not hear what the caravan man said to Hamar, but Chauna Singh said in a whisper that he was asking if Nur-jahan were a slave.

The minstrel responded idly, without raising his eyes from the guitar. As he did so Khlit saw the ragged followers of their visitor edge to either side of the fire, as if to watch the musician.

Intently as he watched, he could not tell if the movement was preconceived or chance. The Turkoman spat into the fire, squatting opposite Hamar.

"He asked," whispered the Rájput to Khlit, "for a song. He has the face of a dolt, but—take care lest the followers get behind you. They have knives in their girdles."

The Turkoman, who announced that his name was Bator Khan, demanded in a loud voice that Hamar make them a tune and the slave girl dance. It was a breach of politeness that Chauna Singh and the minstrel passed over in silence. The attendants had ceased moving forward and were staring at them, chattering together, clearly waiting for a word from Bator Khan.

The conduct of the group did not impress Khlit favorably. They were too curious, too serious in what they did. Suppose that the evil-faced Turkoman should prove to be an enemy of Nur-jahan? They were four against a dozen.

The Cossack was too wise in the ways of violence to show his foreboding. He waited quietly, his hands near his sword hilt, for what was to come. Perhaps Bator Khan was merely a merchant who saw an opportunity to seize a slave girl. If so, he would not be likely to try force unless he thought he could take the three men unaware.

A silence fell as Hamar leaned forward to the fire. Khlit saw him lay a white silk scarf on the ground before him. Reaching behind him, the minstrel placed a crystal goblet on the cloth.

"Bring water," he said softly to one of the followers of Bator Khan. "And fill the goblet to the edge—no more. The water must be clean."

The man did as he was bid, with a glance at the Turkoman. All eyes were on the minstrel as he took up his guitar. His delicate hands passed lightly over the strings, which vibrated very faintly.

"You have asked for a song, Bator Khan," he said mildly. "So be it. I will play the *bhairov*, which is the song of water. Nay, you know not the high art of music—the training which enables one versed in the mysteries of tones to influence the elements—fire, air and water— which correspond to the tones. But watch, and you will see."

With a swift motion he tossed something from his hand into the flames. The smoke grew denser. A strong, pungent odor struck Khlit's nostrils. Some of the men of Bator Khan started back fearfully. Those who held their ground stared wide-eyed. Khlit knew the superstition of their breed.

Hamar closed his eyes. Sounds, faint and poignant, came from the strings under his fingers. Khlit had seen him exchange no word with Chauna Singh or Nur-jahan. Reflecting on this later, he reasoned that the other two must have known what the minstrel was about.

Bator Khan stared mockingly at the musician. Gradually, however, as the note of the guitar grew louder, the mockery faded and the Turkoman watched open-mouthed.

Hamar was repeating the same chords—varying them fancifully. The melody was like the tinkling of chimes with an undertone as of heavy temple gongs. It vibrated, caressing the same note, until it seemed to Khlit that the note hung in the air.

He had never heard the mystical Hindu music and he liked it little. Yet the impression of chimes persisted. Almost he could have sworn that bronze bells were echoing in the air overhead. And still Hamar harped on the vibrant note.

The ring of men was silent. Khlit saw that they were all staring at the goblet, save Chauna Singh and Nur-jahan who were in shadow. And he saw that the water in the glass was stirring, moving up and down.

The melody grew louder. Khlit swore under his breath. For the water was splashing about—although the goblet was steady and the cloth a good yard from Hamar. And then the water began to run down the sides of the vessel, staining the cloth.

It trickled down slowly, while the Turkoman's men drew back. One or two started away from the fire, staring at the cloth in fear. Even Bator Khan got to his feet and stepped back a pace.

The tune of Hamar ceased. And the water in the goblet was still. "Hide the devil!" swore the Turkoman. "It was a trick."

Hamar opened his eyes and smiled. Khlit saw him cast a half-glance behind him.

"Lift the cloth, then, O one-of-small-faith," said the minstrel. "How could it be a trick?"

Bator Khan did so, hesitantly. The whole of the scarf was wet through. But the goblet was still full to the brim. Hamar regarded him smilingly.

Khlit rose, intending to speak to Chauna Singh. He grunted in surprize. The Rájput and the girl were gone.

VII

They did not return to the caravanserai. Bator Khan, apparently in an ill humor, left the Cossack and Hamar to themselves. They spent the night in the enclosure. The dawn was yet cold in the sky the next day when Hamar roused Khlit and the two saddled their horses and rode from the place.

"It was agreed," explained the minstrel, "that if we separated I was to meet the Rájput and Nur-jahan at a certain tavern in Khoten. They must have ridden during the night and will be there ahead of us."

Khlit spurred his horse.

"Hey, minstrel!" he cried. "That was a rare trick you played the Turkoman."

Hamar's brow darkened.

"Call you that a trick? Dullard of the steppe! One without wisdom! Is my art like to a conjurer's mummery? I will teach you otherwise." His frown lightened, "Nay, Khlit, you know not our art. 'Tis true I played but to draw the attention of yonder fools while Nur-jahan slipped away. But as for the music——"

He smiled again, the sad, almost bitter smile that was the habit of the man. For the rest of the day they rode in silence. Khlit's thoughts turned on the man beside him.

Hamar perplexed him. Apparently a Hindu, the minstrel was familiar with the Moslem faith, a deep thinker, an ascetic. Khlit seldom saw him eat, and then only sparingly. His faded eyes, blank almost as those of a blind man, were masks for his thoughts. Khlit had not seen his like before.

At Khoten—a nest of hovels where four caravan routes met and crossed, yet some palaces and temples and a teeming population of every race—Hamar avoided the central squares and led Khlit down a bystreet to a low structure of sun-dried clay.

It was already evening, and they found the tavern half-filled with dirty camel drivers and some ill-favored merchants. Slaves were quartered in the courtyard with the horses.

Hamar left Khlit seated over a beaker of rank wine and a joint of meat, to seek out Chauna Singh and his charge. The Cossack beckoned the tavern-keeper—a silk-clad Chinaman.

"Hey, moon-face," he growled, "who is the master of this town?"

"May it please the illustrious khan," bowed the man, speaking in the Tatar tongue, as Khlit had done, "who has sullied his boots by entering my insignificant house—the city of Khoten is free of august authority, save for the Heaven-appointed folk of the temples."

"And what manner of scum are they?"

"Doubtless the illustrious khan has heard of the never-to-be-profaned Buddha and the many sects of the mountains, who are called the priests of the black hats. He may see for himself, for within two days there is the festival of Bon."

"A festival? Then there will be feasting in the streets of Khoten?"

The innkeeper, arms crossed in his wide sleeves, became silent. The Cossack, with a swift glance, threw a piece of gold on the board from his wallet. His host caught it up, thrusting it into a sleeve. The slant eyes scanned the room cautiously and he leaned nearer.

"May the liberal khan be blessed with many children and great honor. Lo Ch'un has kept his dirty house in Khoten for twice ten years, but he has not seen the rites of the august black hats—the *bonpas*. They are divine secrets. Yet it has been whispered by those loose of tongue that the masked slaves of Buddha sacrifice to their altars on the Year of the Rat."

Khlit nodded impatiently. He, also, had heard tales of the Khoten temples and those of the mountains but had set them down as idly spoken. Nevertheless, he had had reason to know the power of the Buddhist sects in Central Asia—different from the mild religion of the Chinese, and little better than demon worship.

Lo Ch'un continued with the same caution:

"It is not well to speak of such things, illustrious warrior, and my fear is greater than my yearning to be of service. But—" a crafty smile distorted his features—"I know what may be of value to you——"

Khlit laid another gold-piece on the table, and Lo Ch'un appropriated it with a claw-like hand, his bleared eyes gleaming covetously.

"Servants of Bon, the Destroyer, have arrived from Ladak and Ind and entered the Khoten temples. Men say they have censored the priests here for indolence in serving the faith. There are many black hats in the town and they have insolently—nay, augustly—made search of the caravans and taverns. They bear scowling brows. Harken, noble khan, to a word of wisdom from the lowly Lo Ch'un."

The tavern-keeper bent his evil smelling mouth close to the Cossack.

"The Khirghis and Usbek merchants and tribesmen are leaving Khoten before the festival of Bon. It would be well to go hence— say not that I have spoken thus!"

Khlit nodded indifferently. He had neither fear nor respect for the mummery of the priesthoods that influenced the borderland of China. Interpreting what Lo Ch'un had said in the light of Hamar's story, he guessed that the *bonpas* from over the mountains had been messengers of the sect bearing news of Nur-jahan. It was possible. And possible, also, that the Turkoman Bator Khan had been one of the slaves of the black hats.

Frequently, he knew, the priesthood controlled tribesmen through the bondage of fear.

A woman peered between the curtains of the further side of the room, her sallow cheeks crimson with paint, and faded flowers in her hair. She beckoned silently to Lo Ch'un, who pad-padded to her side. For a moment the two talked. Khlit drew out his pipe and scanty stock of tobacco. He began to wonder where Hamar had disappeared to.

When Lo Ch'un came to remove the joint of meat, Khlit stayed him.

"A word, moon-face," he growled. "Know you aught of the Turkoman merchant Bator Khan? Does he come often to Khoten?"

"I know not, honorable khan."

"Well, devil take you—do the caravan merchants stop here?"

"If it is their noble will."

"How dress these precious masked servants of Bon?"

"How should I know, honorable warrior?"

Khlit stared at Lo Ch'un, scowling. A change had come over the wrinkled face of the Chinaman. All expression had faded from his half-shut eyes. His voice was smooth as before, but less assured.

It was clear to the Cossack that his host regretted his speech of a moment ago. Wherefore? Perhaps the woman at the curtain had warned Lo Ch'un. Perhaps it was the mention of Bator Khan.

Khlit rose and grasped the shoulder of Lo Ch'un.

"Harken, keeper of a dirty house," he whispered. "I shall stay in Khoten. If I meet with ill treatment from those you call the black hats, I shall have a tale to tell them of a loose tongued Lo Ch'un.

Meditate upon that. The priests like not to have their secrets talked of."

The dim eyes of the tavern-keeper widened slightly and he licked his lips. With a sudden motion he shook himself from the Cossack and vanished behind the curtain.

VIII

Khlit smiled to himself, well pleased. If Lo Ch'un was actually under the *kang* of the priests, the man might tell them that Khlit purposed to remain in Khoten. Which would be well, considering that the Cossack doubted not Hamar planned to be on his way shortly.

Doubtless the three fugitives had stopped at Khoten but for provisions. Khlit turned this over in his mind. If he had been in Chauna Singh's place he would have sent one man in for the food and remained without the town. Surely it was dangerous for Nur-jahan here.

But then, he reasoned, Chauna Singh—shrewd in fighting—was a blunt man, of few brains. On the other hand, Hamar should have known better than to come to Khoten. Well, after all, the crafty minstrel had been obliged to follow the other two. He had had no chance, owing to the intrusion of Bator Khan, to confer with them before they left the caravanserai.

Where was Hamar? Had he found the other two? What was keeping him?

Khlit yawned, for he was sleepy. It would not do for him to fall asleep here in the house of Lo Ch'un. He determined to go forth and seek the minstrel.

As the Cossack pushed through the door, he saw, from the corner of his eye, a man rise from a table and follow. Khlit continued on his way, but once in the shadows beside the door frame—darkness had fallen on the town—he drew back against the wall. Experience had taught him it was not well to let another come after him from a place where were many enemies.

No sooner had he done so than another appeared in the doorway, peering into the dark street. Light shone on him from within and his features struck Khlit as familiar. It was a surly rascal in tattered garments—one of the men of Bator Khan.

The fellow looked up and down the street, muttering to himself.

He did not see the Cossack in the deep shadows beside him. Then he stepped forward into the gloom at a quick pace. It was clear to Khlit that the man was seeking to follow him and angered at having missed him.

Khlit wasted no time in slipping after the camel-driver. Two could play at that simple game, and if the other was interested in him he might do well to observe whither the man went.

The Cossack's keen brain was active as he pressed after the hurrying servant, keeping in the deep shadows of the low buildings. There was no moon, but occasional gleams from doorways served to reveal his guide.

Bator Khan must have arrived in Khoten. Moreover Khlit and Hamar had been traced to the tavern. How? Well, it mattered not. But Bator Khan alone could not have located them so speedily. Others must have given him information.

Here were tidings for Hamar and Chauna Singh when he met them. Khlit grinned to himself. The Rájput and the minstrel had shown little liking for his advice. Let them lie in the bed they had made for themselves! But there was the girl, Nur-jahan—aye, Nur-jahan.

Khlit paused. From a lighted door had come a fellow who spoke to the camel-driver. The two whispered together. At once the man he was following turned aside down an alley.

The Cossack did not hesitate. Freeing a pistol in his belt, he made after the man. Boldness was Khlit's policy in any hazard. He had learned that it paid best to be on the move when there was danger afoot and leave indecision to his enemies.

Gloom was thick in the alley, and thick also the stench of decayed meat, fish oil, and dirt that filled it. The man ahead was running now, which was fortunate, for Khlit traced him by ear, trotting as lightly as his heavy boots permitted.

Down the alley into another the two passed; from thence to a wide square—evidently a bazaar—where crowds loitered. The light was better here and the Cossack kept his man in sight until both halted before the shadowy pile of a massive building.

Khlit scanned the bulk of the place in the gloom. He made out a stone structure, windows unlit, a dim lantern over the postern door where his companion knocked.

A small panel opened in the upper half of the door and the camel-driver was subjected to a long inspection. Whispered words passed between him and the person within. Whereupon the door swung open, the servant passed inside and a tall form in mail and a black cloak appeared.

It was a spearman, helmeted and grim of visage. He yawned sleepily, leaning on the haft of his weapon.

So, Khlit thought, the place—whatever it might be—was guarded. A building of that size could only be a temple or palace. And it had not the look of the latter. Khlit yearned to see what was within. The spearman did not look overshrewd.

The Cossack had learned that it was easier to get out of a building than to get in—easier sometimes than to find a place of safety elsewhere among many enemies. Still, it would hardly do to use violence on the spearman. He might have comrades within.

Khlit swaggered up to the man.

"Bator Khan sends me," he said briefly in Uigur. "A message for those within."

He was watching the fellow's face keenly. At a sign of suspicion the Cossack would have turned back. But the bearded countenance was sleepily indifferent.

"It is well," the other growled. "If you see one of the black hats about, bid him send me a relief. The men within must have weighty business on hand, for they hum through the corridors like a swarm of insects. But I must eat and sleep."

Khlit passed him by without reply. He found himself in a low, long hall. At one side was a bare chamber, evidently a guard room, and empty. The Cossack paced the length of the corridor warily. At the end a flight of stone steps led upward.

These he ascended to an ill-lighted hall where two men—Chinamen—sat on benches that ran around the wall. They were dressed as servants, and unarmed. Khlit spoke to them gruffly.

"The man at the gate bids the black hats send him a relief."

One arose at this and Khlit motioned impatiently at the other. Both left the chamber with the submissiveness of the underlings of their race. Khlit judged them little better than slaves.

He was about to go forward, when he paused in his tracks. A strong, clear voice had spoken. Yet Khlit saw that there was no one in the room with him. The voice had seemed but a few paces distant.

Again it came, loud but muffled. Whispers repeated the words from the corners of the chamber, and fainter whispers down the stairs.

A cold tremor touched Khlit's back and he swore under his breath. Was the room filled with men he could not see? What manner of place was this?

Then he realized the cause of the mystery. The room was lofty, of bare stone. The voice came from an adjoining corridor and the echoes of the empty halls carried the sound to where he stood.

IX

Grim and desolate was the abode of Bon, the Destroyer, in the city of Khoten. Narrow embrasures formed the windows. In the great hall of the temple proper were ranged the fetishes—minatures of the monstrous idols in the main temple of Bon in the mountains.

In the annals of the ancient city of Khoten it is written that the secrets of Bon were safeguarded jealously. Access to the temple was difficult. Those who came to speak to the *bonpas*—priests—were not allowed to see the face of the man they conversed with. Especially was this true when one of the higher order of the mountain temple visited the Khoten sanctuary.

So a reception room was contrived, artfully designed so that the priest standing behind a curtain in the room would have his words carried to the ears of his visitor by echoes. The visitors stood sometimes in the chamber itself, on the outer side of the curtain, sometimes in the hall at the head of the entrance stairs—according to their degree of intimacy with the *bonpas*.

For the rest, the sanctuary was a place of silence, ill-omened. For the *bonpas* were worshipers not of Buddha or Brahma, but of Bon, the incarnate spirit of power, drawing strength through destruction and death. Thus they were allied to the *tantrik* sect of Kali, the four-armed.

In their halls few men showed their faces. By night men and women were brought into the halls, who left them cringing or laughing aloud, vacantly as those whose minds are disordered.

Bator Khan and his servant being followers of the *bonpas* were admitted to the reception chamber on the night that the Turkoman's caravan came to Khoten.

They stood uneasily before a heavy black curtain which stretched the length of the room. At one end of this curtain was placed a priest of Bon, masked—as was their habit during a ceremonial or a visit from their superiors of the mountain temple. This mask was merely a bag-like length of cloth, dropping over the face from the black hat and painted gruesomely to awe those who visited the sanctuary.

The black hat itself consisted of a helmet-like cap of felt—to distinguish the followers of Bon from the yellow hats, who were servants of the Dalai Lama of Lhassa. In addition, the *bonpa* by the curtain held—as sigil of his office—a trumpet of human bone.

"Your message!" he whispered to the two. "He who waits behind the curtain is impatient of delay."

Bator Khan's pig-like face was moist from perspiration.

"I was sent, O favored of Bon," he repeated huskily, "into the desert to seek the woman Nur-jahan. Behold, I was aided by the god, for I came upon them in a caravanserai. They be four—three men, two warriors and the third a wandering musician—and a woman. Surely this is Nur-jahan. I followed the four into Khoten, where I dispatched my men to find their abiding place."

He paused, licking his thick lips. The attendant by the curtain regarded him impassively from the mask.

"This man—" he pointed to the camel-driver—"found Hamar, the minstrel, and the old warrior at the noisome house of Lo Ch'un. Hamar went forth into the streets and we saw him not, owing to some black sorcery of which the man is master."

There was no response from the voice behind the curtain—naught save the echoes of the Turkoman's hurried words.

"As to Chauna Singh and the woman," continued Bator Khan, "they hide in the slave market. Truly, I do not think that Hamar has seen them yet. This man of mine has kept watch on the one at Lo Ch'un's. That is all, may it please the Presence."

Still there was no response. The camel-driver paled visibly and stared at the curtain. Bator Khan breathed heavily. The grim mask of the attendant leered at them sardonically.

"I found the woman Nur-jahan," protested Bator Khan defensively.

There was the sound of a laugh from the curtain, a sound taken up and passed down the corridor fitfully. The Turkoman shivered slightly.

"Dog of a dog's begetting," he heard, "think you to trick those who serve the gods—with lies? You were sent to find and slay the woman Nur-jahan. Have you done so? Blunderer—braggart—heart-of-a-jackal —vermin-of-a-dunghill! The enemies of Bon have clouded your wits. We have heard what passed at the caravanserai."

Bator Khan would have spoken, but the voice went on swiftly.

"In the desert you had the four at your mercy. By a device of the minstrel, Hamar, the woman escaped. You have not seen her since. Speak, is not this the truth?"

The Turkoman gulped and muttered—

"Aye."

"What has the camel-driver to say?"

The man started and glanced furtively to the door through which he had come. But a motion of the masked priest brought his gaze to the curtain.

"O exalted-of-the-gods, source-of-divine-wisdom," he chattered, "hear the follower who is less than the dirt beneath the hoofs of your horse. I watched the man Khlit at the tavern. He talked long with Lo Ch'un in a tongue I knew not. So I dispatched word to him by one of the harlots of the place to guard well his tongue. Then, when the tall plainsman left, I followed, and I—I——"

His eyes widened and he lifted hand to mouth as he sought for words.

"And he escaped your sight?"

"Aye—it was dark—a comrade of Bon sent me hither—I did my best!"

The man fell on his knees, raising arms over head.

"Fate has written a seal on your forehead, driver of camels," observed the priest behind the curtain.

"It was dark!" cried the ruffian.

"Is Bon to be served by such as you?" the voice rang out mockingly. "Nay, the god has better servants. Harken, Bator Khan. The day after the morrow is the feast-day of Bon, the Destroyer. You know the rites of the feast-day. The hand of Bon will be stretched over the city, and the god will rise in his strength. He must be worshiped. There will be a sacrifice."

Bator Khan lifted a hand to wipe the moisture from his brow.

"Votaries of the god," cried the voice, "will offer their lives. Lo, the home of the god is in the sacred mountains of Himachal, to the south. There is his sanctuary. The votaries will walk, unarmed and afoot, into the mountains, up, over the snow-line. No man—not even a priest of the temple may molest them. They will die in the summits of Himachal. Will you and the carrion that is your man offer yourselves as votaries?"

The echoes growled the words, drawn out into a long sound that was almost a shriek.

"Sacred Himachal is the abode of Mansarowar, the beast Mansarowar. Lo, the mountain abode is the fulfilment of human desires, Bator Khan—and human death. Those who journey up bearing the mark of Bon will not return. Should they come back—if they survived the cold of the summits—to Khoten, the hand of the *bonpas* would slay them, slowly as if they were smitten with leprosy."

The wretched men stared blindly at the black curtain. But when Bator Khan had made as if to speak, the voice went on.

"But you are too miserable an offering for Bon. Live then, for a time—it will not be long. Fate has set its mark on you. Meanwhile, the priest will see that Nur-jahan and her men do not leave the city. When the feast comes, they will be sought out and brought into the crowd of worshipers. There a cry will be raised against them, and they will have heart and bowels torn out by the followers of the god. It will be a pleasing sight. Now, away from here and live—if you can escape the writing of fate."

Whereupon the two turned and ran from the chamber. The masked priest watched them pass into the corridor. Then he moved his head alertly. From the outer hall, below the steps came the clash of weapons and a cry.

The priest hesitated, glancing at the motionless curtain. The ways of the man behind the curtain were sometimes secret and past knowing. Yet he had not known that the two were to be slain as they left. A second clamor, ended by a heavy fall, aroused his suspicions and he ran out into the hall above the stairs. Two frightened servants joined him.

The three descended the stairs and passed into the entrance corridor. There they halted. The bodies of Bator Khan and the cameldriver were prone on the stone floor. The mail-clad form of the spearman who had been sentry at the gate sprawled over them on hands and knees. His weapon lay beside him, the point severed from the haft.

The masked priest bent over him as the man sank to the floor,
groaning weakly. A thin stream of blood trinkled from his neck.

"Fool!" cried the priest. "Have you slain the Turkoman?"

The other coughed bestially, shaking his head. He was near death.
"Another—a curved sword."

He pointed to the door which was open.

The priest and the servants ran out. In the shadows of the street
a tall figure showed for an instant, then vanished.

The masked priest made as if to follow, then hesitated. Three
armed men had been struck down in the space of a minute—and
he did not follow.

X

Khlit and Hamar had waited in the ebony and lacquered room over
the tavern of Lo Ch'un for the space of a day. The Cossack liked
the room little. Tarnished silk covered the walls, and the varied odors
of the alley outside, issuing through a circular window, did not re-
lieve the smell of musk which pervaded the place.

Now and then the women of the place—girls of China, Samarkand,
with one or two Georgians—peered in through the hangings of the
single door but did not linger, seeing who was within. Khlit sat on
a bench against the further wall wiping his sword with a fragment
of silk and watching the door, while Hamar squatted beside him,
tuning his guitar softly.

They had seen nothing of Nur-jahan or Chauna Singh since
their arrival in Khoten. Hamar reported that the two must be among
the caravans of the slave market.

Evidently, thought Khlit, the girl and the Rájput had been kept
from coming to the tavern. That they had not fallen into the hands
of the bonpas he knew from the talk he had overheard in the temple
of Bon. Nur-jahan, he reasoned, had guessed at the peril she faced
in the streets of Khoten and had remained in hiding.

The death of the three in the hall of the temple caused him no
second thought. Not otherwise could he have escaped from the place,
and they had had time to draw their weapons.

He had told the minstrel of what passed the night before.

"It is fate." Hamar waved a lean hand, sniffing at a perfume he
carried in a flask about his throat. "Higher than the scheming of the

servants of the gods, khan, is the unalterable will which brings death to all things. What is to be, will be. What are the gods? Men worship them because they fear them. A dozen priesthoods wax fat on fear. They say there are good deities. How can it be so?"

Khlit fingered the gold cross at his neck.

"This is an evil place, Hamar," he observed. "A city in the waste of a desert—caravans that hold revelry herein—black priests that hold the city in their power. Hey! I have not seen the cross of a church for many Winters."

Hamar glanced at him curiously.

"A church. Nay, are there not temples enough for your liking about here?"

"Does a horse like the meat of a tiger?"

The minstrel fingered his guitar with a sigh. Suddenly Khlit found the man's faded, green eyes peering into his own.

"Yet you like danger, Khlit, khan, and the thrill of clashing swords. Tell me, why did you not heed the warning of Lo Ch'un and leave this place before the feast of tomorrow? What matters Nur-jahan to you? Our lives will be worth little more than the sand of the alley by another sun."

"Bah, minstrel," grunted the Cossack, "shall I ride hence while the woman—mischief-maker though she be—stays? Truly, it will not be easy to escape with whole skins on the morrow. Think you Nur-jahan is still in Khoten?"

Hamar nodded.

"Aye, the Persian is shrewd. Doubtless she has learned of the watch the *bonpas* keep on the place. If there be a way hence, she will find it."

He glanced again at Khlit thoughtfully.

"It is written that a diamond shines from a heap of dirt. Nay, khan, the woman reaches out to the rule of an empire with her small hand. She will have great honor—or death. And the issue lies on the dice of fate. Harken, khan. Sher Afghan, the husband of Nur-jahan, still lives. Chauna Singh is faithful to him. What if Sher Afghan is slain by Jahangir, the Mogul?"

"Then Nur-jahan will be free."

"But Chauna Singh? Since the name of Ind has been, a Rájput is faithful to his lord."

Khlit made no response. But he did not forget the words of Hamar.

The circle of the window darkened. Twilight was casting its veil over the city. From somewhere came the sunset cries of a *mullah*. Hamar rose and, striking flint on stone, lit a candle. In an adjoining room Khlit heard the wailing of a woman in grief. The sound had persisted for some time.

Hamar had paid no attention to it. Men were thronging into the place from the street, and the room below was a tumult of a score of tongues. Still the wail went on, shrill and dismal.

With an oath the Cossack sprang up and pushed through the curtains. Following the sound of the crying woman, he came to another chamber like the one he had left. Within he saw a carpet spread, and on the carpet a man.

Beside him knelt the woman who had beckoned Lo Ch'un from the tavern the night before. Her hair was disordered in grief and the stain on her cheeks showed vivid against a pallid skin. She raised inflamed eyes to the Cossack.

What drew Khlit's gaze and brought a second oath to his lips was the sight of a *bonpa* mask placed over the face of the man on the rug. It was the first that Khlit had seen, but he did not mistake it.

"Hide of the devil!" he muttered, for the painted fabric leered at him grotesquely.

Something in the loose position of the man's limbs and his dirty silk tunic aroused his suspicions.

Stepping over the prostrate form, Khlit lifted the black mask. The distorted face of Lo Ch'un stared up at him, eyes distended and flesh purple. It needed no examination to show that Lo Ch'un had been dead for some time—and Khlit remembered the long wailing of the woman.

"How was this done?" he asked the woman.

She shook her head mutely, not understanding what he said. Khlit perceived the end of a silken cord hanging from Lo Ch'un's mouth. The cord, he saw, was attached to a gag which had been forced far down the tavern keeper's throat.

Khlit flung the mask into a corner and turned from the room. Hamar looked up questioningly as he entered.

"Hey, minstrel," grinned Khlit, "there is a notable physician in the temple of the *bonpas* who has devised a cure for tongue-wagging. Doubtless—after the tidings brought to the temple by the man of

Bator Khan—the priests thought he was too free with their secrets."

"A fool has paid for his folly."

Khlit reflected moodily that Lo Ch'un had been slain in a room adjoining theirs without the sound of a struggle. They must have been within a score of feet when it was done. Yet they had not been molested. He scowled as he thought how the hand of the priests was everywhere in Khoten. Doubtless the men in the temple knew where they—Hamar and Khlit were—and, knowing, waited. For what? For the feast of the morrow, when the death of Nur-jahan was planned?

The words of Hamar returned to his memory. They were four against many, and their foes were not to be seen.

"Devil take it all!" he grumbled, for the thing was preying on his nerves somewhat. "Let us go below and eat, minstrel. Thus we will have a full meal under our belts. And it will be better so."

"I will not eat," said Hamar, "but I will go with you. If the *bonpas* have marked Nur-jahan's death for the morrow we have little to fear tonight."

With that the two descended to the tavern.

Unwatched by Lo Ch'un, a motley crowd was drinking and gorging at will. The women of the house were scattered among the benches, aiding the merriment with shrill laughter. Some looked up drunkenly at his entrance.

"Fill yourselves, dogs," muttered Khlit, "there will be none to tally the drinks——"

He broke off abruptly and clutched Hamar's arm. Among a crowd of men across the men he caught the veiled figure of Nur-jahan, with bearded Chauna Singh towering at her side.

"Here be our comrades, minstrel," he whispered. Hamar thrust his way through the crowd.

Then, as they approached the girl, she dropped her veil and smiled at them. Khlit heard Hamar draw in his breath in sharp surprize. Truly, it was a strange thing, for Nur-jahan was a Mohammedan and it was forbidden to such to show their faces before the eyes of strange men.

Chauna Singh flushed angrily, for Nur-jahan was wife to his lord, Sher Afghan, and it was not fitting that she should be seen by the drunken men of the brothel. He made as if to clutch her veil, but she stayed him with a whisper, speaking softly to Hamar also.

"Is the girl mad?" growled Khlit to the minstrel. "She hides herself for a day and two nights. Then, lo, she shows herself to these cattle. Look yonder!"

Hamar looked and saw the eyes of the men in the room turn to Nur-jahan and stare hotly. The girl's beauty stood out among the miserable women of the place in sharp contrast. A silence fell on the tavern.

Men pushed wine cups away from lips and gazed at Nur-jahan narrow-eyed. Bearded hillmen muttered to themselves. A sheepskin clad giant rose unsteadily, his pock-marked face flushed with drink, and lurched forward, grinning.

The fitful light of the place—from candle and hearth—gave the dark countenance of the girl a witchery that stirred the pulses of those who watched.

"She says," the minstrel whispered to Khlit, "that she wishes these dogs to see her beauty, that they may know her tomorrow."

"They seem little disposed to wait until the morrow, Hamar," said Khlit grimly.

He sensed trouble in the air, for the men were pressing closer. The Khirghiz giant planted himself in front of Nur-jahan, his small eyes a-light.

"Ho, comrades!" he bellowed. "A dainty morsel is here. By the bones of Satan, this is a face to delight the gods!"

Khlit moved closer to Chauna Singh. He was angry at Nur-jahan's prank. Not content with the enmity of the priests, the girl had dared the lawless crew of the tavern. She smiled at them coldly. And some who stared at her moved uneasily under her glance. Here, they thought, was no common courtesan. What manner of woman was she?

Thus it happened that while some pushed forward with silent intentness, others hung back, measuring the stature of Chauna Singh and Khlit and the bearing of the girl.

"Drink, men of the caravan trails!" cried the girl in her clear, commanding voice. "It is written that wine is the sweeper-away-of-care! Give them wine," she ordered the slaves. "Tomorrow they will see that which they will tell their children, and it will be a tale of many moons. Ha! Life is sweet when such deeds are in the air."

Her cry pleased many of the watchers and they roared approval.

"Lo Ch'un is dead—there be none to guard the wine!" cried one.

Over their heads Khlit could hear the faint wailing of the woman by the body. He glanced at Nur-jahan curiously. Mad the girl might be, but she was fearless.

Then silence fell again as the Khirghiz drunkard stretched out a heavy hand toward Nur-jahan. She drew back swiftly and touched Chauna Singh on the arm.

"Strike this dog," she cried softly, "but do not slay him."

At the words the scimitar of the Rájput flashed in front of her. No time had the Khirghiz to draw weapon. Khlit saw the scimitar turn deftly and smite the forehead of the man with the flat of the blade.

The knees of the Khirghiz bent under him and his bulk dropped heavily to the floor.

"He was a fool!" cried Nur-jahan aloud. "Harken, men of the desert, I am she who is called Nur-jahan, Light of the Palace. Look well, for you may not see my face again. I go from Khoten tomorrow, at the feast of Bon. Come to the feast, for there will be a sight worth seeing."

With that she turned swiftly and disappeared up the stairs. Chauna Singh followed with a black glance at the gaping crowd. Khlit watched until he was sure none of the caravan men would molest them further. Gradually they returned to their cups and their talk.

Khlit sought and found the joint of meat he had come for. Hamar had gone, and he ate alone, being hungry. His thoughts turned on the whim of Nur-jahan. She had shown her face to these men wilfully. They were, without doubt, devotees of Bon. Surely Nur-jahan had a reason for what she did.

What was it? At that time Khlit did not know.

XI

The midday sun was hot over Khoten's hovels and temples on the noon appointed as the feast of Bon. From the taverns and caravanserais issued a motley crowd—thin-boned Arabs, squat Khirghiz hillmen, hawk-faced Usbeks—a smattering of Hindus, cleanly robed.

And as they pressed into the streets leading to the temple of Bon, there came the low thrumming of stone drums beaten within the building.

The sound of the drums passed through the sand-swept alleys, out beyond the groves of wild poplars, leaves a-droop from lack of wind —out to the shimmering waste of the desert of Gobi to the north and the level plain that led to the mountains of the south.

Dimly in the heat haze these mountains were to be seen—gleaming snow summits flashing into the blue of the sky. The narrow embrasures of the temple looked out upon the hills. Men whispered to each other that the fetishes of the sanctuary faced toward the mountains, where was the home of the god Bon.

About the temple courtyard a throng was gathered, pushing and elbowing for a sight of the cleared space before the gate of the structure. A group of bearers set down the palanquin of a Chinese mandarin and escorted the stout silk-clad and crimson tulip-embroidered person of their master through the onlookers, striking aside those who stood in their way with their wands.

A continuous hubbub swelled over the monotone of the drums. By now half the men and women of the city were in the square before the temple—sleepy-eyed and quarrelsome from the revelry of the night before.

Bands of the black hats were passing through the streets. They were pale men, evil-eyed and complacent. Merchants who like them still journeyed to the square, for it paid to be friendly with the folk of the black hat on the feast-day of Bon. Votaries of the god went eagerly, driven by the blood-lust which yearned to see certain of their fellows marked for death.

In the throng were those who had come to Khoten with Nur-jahan —Chauna Singh, watchful and silent, disdainful of the multitude of low-caste—Hamar walking as if in a trance—Khlit, apparently oblivious of what passed, but inwardly observant.

The Cossack was ill-pleased with their position. He had seen enough of the handiwork of the *bonpas* to know that their lives were put to the hazard. Bator Khan was dead; but other servants of the priests, he knew, were not lacking. Any Arab or Khirghiz in the throng might be the bearer of a knife destined for them.

A crowd always disturbed the Cossack of the Curved Saber. Here there was no room for sword-play—no chance to set a horse to gallop and meet an enemy as he liked to do. He put little faith in his pistols.

Left to himself, Khlit would have ventured on a dash from the city, mounted on his pony. But the party of Nur-jahan was certainly shadowed by the priests—after the scenes in the tavern the night before there would be small difficulty in that.

So long, however, as Chauna Singh and Hamar remained with the girl, he was grimly resolved to see the matter through. He would not let the Rájput say that he had drawn back from danger.

"Give way, O born-of-a-dog and soul-of-swine!" snarled the Rájput at those in front as he drew Nur-jahan forward.

Hamar and Khlit pressed after them.

Oaths and threats greeted their progress. But here and there were men who had been in the tavern the evening before and these whispered to their neighbors, so that many turned to look after the girl. In this way they pushed to the first rank of watchers in the temple courtyard.

The crowd was already stirred by the ceremony of the priests. Khlit saw men staring, rigid-eyed, and others muttering fragments of prayers. The throb of the drums beat into his ears.

"It grows time for the servants of Bon to speak to us," he heard a Dungan say. "The dance is near its ending."

For the first time he had sight of what was going on in front of the temple.

An array of the black hats was sounding long trumpets, echoing the note of the drums—an insistent clamor that harped upon one note insidiously. Before them whirled and tossed a throng of the masked priests. In the center of the dances was the form of a woman, bare of clothing to the waist and streaked with blood.

Khlit watched the scene indifferently. It was evil mummery, this prostrating before a hidden god. Almost he laughed at panting priests in their painted masks. But, hearing the beat of the drums, he kept silence.

And, as at a signal from within the temple, the dancers ceased, flinging themselves on the ground.

A voice issued from the dark gateway of the temple, a voice measured and calm.

"On the summits of Himachal," it said, "is the abode of Bon, the Destroyer. There is the seat of happiness, the shrine of the ages. In the silence of the mountains the avalanches reveal the anger and power of the gods."

"Himachal!" the shout was taken up by the crowd. "In Himachal is life and the blessed death!"

Khlit caught Chauna Singh's eye and smiled without merriment.

"Has Nur-jahan come hither to be slain easily, as a white dove is caught by a falcon?" he growled.

Chauna Singh shook his head moodily.

"Nay, khan, I know not. It was her will to come. The city is guarded and we may not escape. But here is an evil place. Yet would she come, saying that we might yet live. Could I do otherwise? I am her man."

"Does she hope to awe these carrion with the name of Jahangir?"

"Nay," the Rájput grunted distastefully. "The Mogul is a stripling —and his power is distant."

"Then, what will we do?"

"Watch!"

"Aye—but not for long." Khlit motioned over his shoulder. Men of the black hats were edging through the crowd. "Look yonder."

"I see." Chauna Singh turned his back deliberately. "Nur-jahan has ordered that where she goes we must follow. Mark that, khan."

The voice within the temple rose to a hoarse cry. Khlit understood little of what it said, but the crowd surged excitedly.

"And the way to the hills is open," he heard. "Whoever offers his life to Bon—be he slave or khan—he will be put upon the path that leads past the shrine of Kedernath, by the lake of Lamdok Tso, to the home of the gods——"

A man sprang forward from the throng and cast himself in the sand before the woman.

"A sacrifice!" the gathering roared. "A life given to Bon."

Khlit saw the priests go to the man and take his weapons from his belt. Then he was led within the temple.

The Cossack snarled at the sight. Devilwork, he thought. The impulse to cast away life in religious frenzy was bred in the blood of the men around him.

Nur-jahan's hand clutched him swiftly.

"Come," he heard her whisper. "In this way we may win free!"

He caught at his sword-hilt, for the black hats about him had pressed closer. Nur-jahan's words had set him to thinking swiftly. He saw the girl, followed by her companions, step from the crowd.

Khlit stooped in the throng for a moment. Then he sprang erect and leaped after the others.

Nur-jahan's silvery voice came to his ears. The girl was standing among the priests before the gate of the temple.

"A sacrifice to Bon," she called clearly. "I, Nur-jahan the fair, offer myself to go into the mountains."

He saw Hamar's sensitive face pale and Chauna Singh scowl, as he joined them. The priests stared at them from their masks. A roar broke from the crowd.

"It is Nur-jahan!" he heard. "She of the tavern! Here is a fitting one to wander into the snows!"

The cries were taken up by others, stirred by zeal. Khlit wondered if it was for this that the girl had shown herself in the tavern. As he wondered, he was caught by the priests.

"To Himachal!" the crowd roared, as the black hats hesitated, glancing at the gate. "We will see them put afoot and weaponless at the foot of the holy hills. Let the men accompany her. Ho—she will be well attended in death!"

The eyes of the crowd were fixed in the black gate of the temple where was the hidden priest of Bon. A brief silence. Then:

"Let Nur-jahan be the sacrifice! Let the gods have the flower of the Mogul! We will see her put afoot in the hills, in the snows! None may molest her—she belongs to the gods!"

It was the cry of the camel-men who had seen the beauty of the girl the night before.

The shout was taken up by the multitude. The priests stepped forward and seized the four. At this there was a roar of approval.

"Bon has taken the woman!" shrieked a man. "Her limbs will wither in the snows!"

Khlit saw the girl poised proudly among the black priests, veiled head high. He saw Chauna Singh's scimitar snatched from him and felt his own pistols jerked from his belt. His scabbard hung empty at his side.

"To the camels!" cried the crowd.

They were led by the *bonpas* to the waiting beasts. They were not molested, for it was the law of the priesthood that the sacrifices were inviolate from harm by human hands.

Nur-jahan was cast upon the back of a kneeling camel. Khlit and the others followed her. At the eager urging of the throng, the beasts,

surrounded by mounted priests and their followers, were put into
motion away from the temple, to the south.

A black cloth was cast over Khlit's head and made fast.

For the rest of that day and the night the camels did not slacken
their pace. The next day many hands drew Khlit from the beast
and mounted him upon a horse.

They rode forward again—and upward. Still upward. The warmth
of the foot-hills gave place to the chill of the mountain slope.

XII

All things that die on Himachal, and dying think of his snows, are
blessed.

In a hundred ages of the gods the glories of Himachal could not be
told. Of Himachal, where Shiva lived and the Ganges falls from the foot
of Vishnu like the slender thread of a lotus flower.

Paradise is to be found on Himachal—even by the beast that bears the
name of Mansarowar.

Hymn to Himachal.

The shadows of the mountain slope were deepening, and the wind
that whispered down the pass was cold. Gaunt pine trees reared
overhead. Miles below, the level glow of the setting sun was still
on the plain.

Silence reigned in the forest—a silence broken only by the fitful
brush of pine branches, one against the other. The snow that had
glittered up the pass was a dull gray. In the distance, to right and
left, massive peaks reared their heads, and their snow crests caught
the last glimmer of the sun.

Standing in the ravine, Nur-jahan and her companions watched
a cavalcade move out on the plain. The tiny figures progressed slowly
across the brown expanse, horse and camel barely to be distinguished
at that distance. Light glinted from the pin-point of a spear or sword.

Then, as if by magic, the sun passed from the plain. The cavalcade
vanished in the shadows.

Nur-jahan turned to the men.

"With Allah are the keys of the unseen," she said softly. "Yonder
go the priests of Bon. Here we be, cast upon the mountain. What
say you?"

Chauna Singh brushed his hand across his eyes. Long muffled in a cloth, the watching had strained his good eye.

"Nay, *mir,*" he said slowly. "In my mind there is a thought. It is that the evil dogs have left some of their breed to spy upon us here."

Hamar roused himself from his reverie.

"The Rájput speaks truth, Nur-jahan," he assented meditatively. "The servants of Bon are accustomed to keep watch upon the men they cast out to die. If we turn back, our heads will be cut from our shoulders and sent to the Khoten temple. We have offered ourselves as sacrifices. We must go forward."

"To what?" snarled Chauna Singh. "Over our heads is the snow. It would be the work of four days to pass the peaks, by way of the lake of Lamdok Tso, to the further side—four days for strong men, with food and weapons. Nur-jahan is a woman—and we have not eaten since sunrise."

"Nay, more, Chauna Singh," laughed the girl. "Your weapons are in the hands of the *bonpas,* who have taken our horses. Recall the word of the priest who said our way lies onward, or death awaits us."

"It was your will, Nur-jahan," observed Hamar, "that we should do this. Wherefore?"

"Blind!" mocked the girl. "Allah has given you the gift of song, yet you are but a dreamer. Nay, we could not stand in Khoten. The knives of the black priests were already drawn for our slaying when I came forward from the crowd."

"A swift death is better than to be food for rooks," muttered Chauna Singh.

"Yet Sher Afghan gave you charge over me—to safeguard my life."

"Aye, Nur-jahan—it is so." Chauna Singh bent his head calmly. "And as I have promised, I will do."

"It is written," sighed the minstrel, "that death among friends is like to a feast."

"And it is also written," said the girl, "that Allah knows what is before us. Allah weakens the stratagems of misbelievers—and beyond the summits lies Kashmir."

She turned swiftly on Khlit, who had been moodily silent.

"What say you, old warrior?"

The Cossack stretched his big frame.

"I?" He laughed low. "I thirst to have yonder carrion priests at my sword's end."

"Ho, old khan, you are not faint of heart." She skipped from his side up the pass a pace. "Come, Hamar, Chauna Singh. Time passes and we must press on. We will see the heights where the god Bon dwells. Come, are you beasts of burden, to be whipped? Lead, Chauna Singh. I will follow with the khan."

The Rájput strode into the twilight without further word. Hamar accompanied him as best he could. The girl drew her *khalat* about her and followed, motioning Khlit to her side.

The sides of the gorge frowned down on them. There was no trail, the pass being rocky. The Cossack wondered if men hidden in the pines were watching them. The girl touched his arm.

"Harken, khan," she whispered. "Know you where we are?"

Khlit shook his head. The mountains were strange to him.

"We be below the Lake of Lamdok Tso, the blue lake. Here is where the votaries are led from Khoten in the evil ceremonies of the black priests. By the Lake of Lamdok Tso runs the pass of Kandrum, which leads from Kashmir. Hither we came to Khoten. There is no refuge for us in the pass—but at Lamdok Tso a man awaits us."

As Khlit was silent, she continued.

"Hamar came from Agra with the message from Jahangir, the Mogul—" she lingered on the name softly—"to hasten back to him. Chosen warriors of his are posted near to Leh to meet us. But Hamar fell in with a man of Sher Afghan in the outskirts of the town of Leh. The fellow said that Sher Afghan, the Lion-Slayer, would send a message to Chauna Singh—and to me."

"Where is this Lion-Slayer of yours?" grunted Khlit. "Will he not aid you against the devil priests?"

"Nay, you know not our people, khan." In the gloom he saw her smile. "My lord is proud—and I have fled from his side. I love him not—how may it be, when I was betrothed to Jahangir? After my flight with Chauna Singh, Sher Afghan would not lift a hand to aid me."

"Yet he sent the Rájput."

"Aye." The dark head tossed proudly. "I am honored of many men. Chauna Singh lives but to serve me—and Sher Afghan. He rode after me from the camp of my lord, saying that Sher Afghan had said that I should not go unattended. It is well."

Khlit was silent, turning the matter over in his mind. Verily, these were strange folk, proud and swift to act. Their love was as quick as their hatred.

"Hamar said to the man of Sher Afghan," continued the girl, "that if his lord would send a message, it might be dispatched to the Lake of Lamdok Tso, in the Kandrum Pass—for we must return by the pass to Kashmir. Now, when Hamar, riding but slowly, for he has a weak body, passed the trail by the border of the lake, he found the messenger already there. Sher Afghan had sent word swiftly."

"That was the time of one moon agone," observed Khlit.

"If it were a hundred days the man would still be there. And if we can gain the Kandrum trail, by the lake, we will find him—with food and a horse."

"Aye, food," growled the Cossack, who had already tightened his belt.

"Does Chauna Singh know this?" he asked after a while.

"Nay, why not?" said the girl lightly. Khlit glanced at her but could not see her face in the dim light. "Say not I have told you, khan," she added.

"In the mountains such as these," he meditated, "a man must carry food with him, for there is little game to be had. Either food—or a bringer of meat."

He halted, despite the girl's impatient exclamation.

"Go you with Chauna Singh," he continued. "I will follow—presently."

"May Allah the merciful forgive me!" cried Nur-jahan. "It is the hour of sunset prayer."

With a deft movement she undid the white veil from her head and spread it on the earth at her feet. Khlit fumbled under his heavy sheepskin coat. Nur-jahan saw that he drew forth something that gleamed whitely in the twilight. Seeing it, she caught her breath.

"How came that here, khan?"

"Hey, little song-bird," the Cossack laughed, "where else than beneath the tail of my coat? Think you the men of Bon could rid me of this?"

He swung his curved sword viciously about his head.

"It is good to feel it thus. Nay, I slipped it from scabbard in the throng in front of the temple and none saw it done."

"Whither go you?" whispered Nur-jahan, for Khlit had turned away.

"To see if the servants of the black priests follow us," he growled. "If it is so, then we may have food. If I come not back within an hour, go you ahead with the two."

Nur-jahan watched his tall figure fade into the gloom down the ravine. She called softly to Chauna Singh to linger and sank to her knees on the white veil, facing, as was the law, toward Mecca.

There was no cry of the muezzin to accompany her prayer. Nothing except the rising drone of wind in the tree-tops overhead, where the crests of the pines swayed and lifted.

When she completed her prayer she arose and joined her waiting companions, drawing the *khalat* close about her slender form, for the night wind was cold. Briefly she told the Rájput whither Khlit had gone. They watched the ravine to the rear, while darkness merged the outlines of tree and boulder. Stars twinkled out over their heads.

Chauna Singh was stirring impatiently when a form appeared beside them and they heard the Cossack's boots grating in the stones.

When he came nearer they made out that he held something in his hand, something bulky, that moved of its own accord. Chauna Singh bent closer. Then he stretched out his arm and touched what was on Khlit's arm.

"A bird!" whispered the minstrel.

"Nay," corrected the Rájput. "A falcon—a goshawk, unless I mistake its head. Whence came this, khan?"

"A rider of the black priests held it on his wrist, Chauna Singh. Lo, here is a getter of meat—if there be game hereabouts." He stroked the hooded and shackled bird, which clung to the gauntlet. "The men of Bon follow us—but they know not one of their number is missing. The horse escaped me. The man lies back among the rocks."

XIII

Dawn flooded into the gorge as the sun gleamed on the snow peaks overhead.

There was no mist as in the valleys of the foot-hills, yet the sun was long in dispelling the chill that clung to the rocks. The faces of the four were dark with chilled blood. Nevertheless, the light brought a certain amount of cheer.

They felt the brief exhilaration of those who have watched

through the night and feel the first warmth of the day in their veins. They had been stumbling ahead for the last few hours, making little progress, but Chauna Singh and Khlit had forbidden a halt. Sleep came with rest, and the two warriors knew that sleep, on stomachs long empty, lowered the vitality.

There were circles under Nur-jahan's fine eyes and her little feet limped in their leather slippers. Hamar's wrinkled face was a shade thinner. Of the four, he missed the absence of food the least, owing to his ascetic habits.

Khlit and Chauna Singh showed no trace of hardship so far. The night's march meant little to them and they were saving their strength with the experience of men accustomed to the hazards of forced journeys.

"We have not gone far, khan," muttered the Rájput.

Khlit cast a keen glance above and below. They were still in the forest belt, with the snow-line a bit nearer. He understood now why they had been placed in the ravine by the priests of Bon. The rock sides of the gorge were sheer. And impassable. They must go forward, or back.

And the men below would see that they did not go back.

"Hamar says," went on Chauna Singh, "that the pass leads up over the snow-line to the valley of the blue lake—Lamdok Tso. It is pleasing to Bon, the Destroyer, that his victims perish near the blue lake."

"One has perished already," laughed Khlit grimly.

"May he be born for a thousand years in the bodies of foul toads!" amended the Rájput. "Harken, khan. Let us loose the falcon. Soon we shall be above the place where game is to be found."

"Presently. Nur-jahan must press ahead now. When she tires we will unhood the goshawk." Khlit tightened the shackles of the sulking bird. "We have a greater enemy than hunger."

"Cold," assented Chauna Singh. His glance lingered on the form of the woman ahead of them. "So be it, khan."

They advanced up the defile steadily. Khlit, although he watched closely, saw no sign of those who were following. They had fallen back, he reasoned, trusting to the gorge to keep the four pent in.

So far they had advanced for a night and the part of a day. Nur-jahan had told him that the Lake of Lamdok Tso lay a journey of two nights, two days and part of a third night from their starting-point. And they still had the snow to face.

Khlit thought grimly that if the goshawk failed them it would go ill with the four. Yet he saw no chance of turning back. News of their venture would have spread through the foot-hills, and even if they succeeded in avoiding the guardians of the pass to their rear they would have no place of refuge to seek.

His talk with Chauna Singh convinced him that the Rájput did not know of the man awaiting them at the lake, in the Kandrum pass. Nur-jahan, then, had not told her follower what she had whispered to Khlit. Hamar knew.

The minstrel, his *vina* slung across his shoulders, kept pace with them silently. Like most men of small frame, once the first weariness had passed off, his limbs carried him forward lightly—as easily as the two stronger, who had more weight to carry.

Nur-jahan's strength surprised Khlit, who knew not that the Persian had been a wanderer in many lands before she met Jahangir. When the sun was high overhead that day and the woman's steps began to falter, he unhooded the goshawk, slipping the leash from the bird's claws.

Here was no opportunity to ply the art of falconry. They had sighted no quarry on the mountain slopes to fly the goshawk at. Khlit could only free the bird and pray that it would sight game for itself.

The four halted, watching the falcon ascend in wide circles. It rose until it had become a dark speck against the blue of the sky. Still it circled.

"Allah be merciful! Grant that it find prey," uttered Nur-jahan, eyes bent aloft.

"And near at hand," added Chauna Singh, pointing to the rock walls that shut them in on both sides. Hamar said nothing, watching the bird with the calm of the fatalist.

"It must be well hungered," observed the Rájput, who understood the pastime of falconry, "and it will not return until it has sighted quarry. Ho—look yonder!"

The goshawk had darted downward, wings folded. When it was once more well within sight it fluttered and circled, quartering across its previous course.

"It has sighted quarry!" cried Chauna Singh, moved out of his habitual quiet. "Now, it seeks it out—nay, it points to the thicket ahead of us. Ho—it strikes!"

The bird had disappeared among a clump of trees at one side of the ravine, some distance ahead. Chauna Singh and Khlit ran forward, scrambling over rocks and plunging across a freshet to the trees.

"Shiva send it be a mountain sheep. The bird was hungry!"

Pushing into the bushes, the two cast about for the falcon.

Presently the rustling of leaves attracted their attention and Chauna Singh pointed to where the bird was tearing at the body of a hare, shredding the flesh with its beak, fierce eyes gleaming redly at them.

"A hare!" growled the Rájput, angrily. "A hare among four!"

Nevertheless, he tore the bird from its hold on the warm quarry, hooded and shackled it. When Nur-jahan and Hamar came up, Khlit had prepared the flesh of the animal, roughly, for eating. The girl shivered at sight of the blood.

"Eat," said Chauna Singh, almost roughly. "It is not only food—but warmth."

Obediently, she swallowed some mouthfuls of the meat, until sudden sickness stayed her. Hamar refused his portion.

"What need have I of such?" he said tranquilly. "My strength lies not in meat."

Whereupon Chauna Singh, staring, put aside the minstrel's share for Nur-jahan. What remained he placed in a fold of his tunic. He and Khlit ate sparingly and urged the others ahead.

The ravine they had been following through many valleys gave way to the broad shoulder of the mountain. The last trees disappeared. The wind that pressed steadily in their faces grew colder. Standing in the open, they saw a score of mighty peaks stretching away on their left hand.

On their right Khlit saw a small pile of stone, topped by a flat slab, on which were graven some signs unknown to him.

"A shrine of the god Bon," whispered Nur-jahan, breathing heavily because of the thin air into which they had come.

"Here be none but the god!" cried Hamar aloud. He pointed down the gorge behind him. "There our guards wait. Ahead is the heart of Himachal, home of the many-faced gods!"

Khlit glanced at him sharply. The man's eyes were glowing somberly and his voice was shrill. The Cossack wondered if the lack of food had not done him harm.

Nevertheless, it was Hamar who took the lead, guiding them upward among the ridges.

At sunset Nur-jahan's knees gave way and she sank to the ground, uttering no cry. When Khlit and Chauna Singh touched her they saw that she was shivering.

The two glanced at each other significantly. Khlit took off his sheepskin *svitza* and cast it over the girl. Seeking a sheltered spot among the rocks, they rested, placing the girl between the three men.

Khlit fell asleep at once, to be roused shortly by Hamar. Chauna Singh had also slept. The Rájput gathered the passive woman in his arms and strode forward, Hamar leading.

In this fashion, relieved at times by Khlit, the man carried Nur-jahan through the night. He spoke no word, nor did he offer to rest. Only his heavy breathing testified to the effort Chauna Singh was making.

The silence of the higher spaces closed around the four. Khlit, plodding after the Rájput, throught of the sacrifice Nur-jahan had offered at Khoten to the gods of Himachal. Were there gods on Himachal? The icy fingers of cold plucked at his veins—the girl had his coat—and he shook his head savagely.

They had ventured into forbidden places, he thought. Here they were cast upon the roof of the world. Their lives had passed out of their keeping.

From the darkness ahead came the sound of a soft melody. The wind carried it clearly to Khlit. It was Hamar, striking upon his *vina*.

XIV

There are three things that change not—the will of the gods, the mountains of Himachal and the word of a Rájput.

Bengal proverb.

The Lake of Lamdok Tso lies in the heart of the Himalayas, below the line of perpetual snow, and it is said by some that the sacred Indus, called by the disciples of Bon the Sing Chin Kamba—Lion's Mouth—rises therein.

It is written that the Indus, blessing the happy land of Kashmir and moistening the purple iris fields from the Dhal Lake to the Grove of Sweet Breezes, falls from the skies through the waters of Lamdok Tso.

In the time of the Mogul Jahangir, the Kandrum Pass, leading from Leh to Khoten, ran by the left bank of the lake. Midway along the shore the trail crossed a promontory of rocks. This height could be seen from both ends of Lamdok Tso.

And so it happened that when Nur-jahan and her companions wandered down from the snow-line on aching feet bound by strips of Chauna Singh's turban, into the Kandrum gorge, they saw ahead of them the pin-point of a fire, as if hung above the shore of the lake.

Nur-jahan sighted it first, with a low cry.

"Look yonder!" she whispered, for her lips were stiff with cold. "A fire—and aid. It is not far."

Hamar halted at her cry, peering ahead through the darkness. Khlit swore joyfully, although weakly, for since the slaying of the hare they had walked steadily for a day and a half. Chauna Singh had not spoken since the dawn of the last day. He had carried Nur-jahan when she could not walk and aided her when she ventured afoot, her slippers bound by the cloth from his turban.

In this fashion they had crossed the snow field, eating the last of the meat as they went and satisfying their thirst with snow. Hamar had not eaten. How the minstrel retained his strength Khlit did not know—not understanding the control over their bodies possessed by the ascetics of India.

As they pressed forward toward the fire he pondered. Nur-jahan had spoken the truth when she said that the messenger from Sher Afghan would wait. If he were another such as Chauna Singh he would remain in the pass until he had lost hope of meeting those to whom he was sent.

Yet what was the message he bore? Hamar had seen him, spoken to him, but had said naught to Nur-jahan of the message. It was possible the other had wished to deliver it to no one but the woman.

Another thing. Here was a fire—some food—and a horse. But there also was the man who possessed them. How were five to live through the journey down the mountains to Kashmir? No other dwellers were in the heights. The chances of meeting with other travelers was slight. And four of the five were already greatly weakened.

Even the falcon was gone. When the meat gave out they had unhooded it again, but the bird had flown far from where they were.

Up the rising ground to the promontory they went, as quickly as might be. On their left hand the cold surface of the lake dropped further beneath them. On the right a precipice rose sheer. As they advanced the fire loomed larger—grew into a nest of flames, by which slept a man wrapped in a heavy cloak.

A rock, dislodged by Khlit's boots, fell into the lake and the man awoke. He sprang to his feet, staring into the darkness—a short, bearded warrior, clad in fine mail, who fingered the hilt of a jeweled sword.

Chauna Singh and Nur-jahan stumbled into the light and the man by the fire gave a cry of recognition. As Khlit stepped forward to warm himself at the flames Hamar joined him. Chauna Singh and the girl had paused by the stranger. They spoke together in a tongue Khlit did not understand.

He saw that Hamar watched out of narrow eyes, swaying the while with the movement of one who has been in motion for so long that his limbs are not readily brought to rest. The minstrel's eyes were sunk in his head, but they were quick and alert.

Nur-jahan had caught the arm of the messenger and was peering into his face intently. She had cast away her veil and the dark hair flooded about her pale cheeks.

Khlit saw the man glance from her to Chauna Singh. Then silence fell upon the group.

"Now we will hear the message," whispered Hamar. "He would not tell me."

Khlit had turned to the fire, when he heard a cry from Nur-jahan. In it dismay and joy were strangely mingled. He saw the girl draw back as if she did not wish the others to behold her face. Chauna Singh thrust his scarred face close to the man by the fire, questioning him fiercely. Hamar laughed softly.

"The Lion-Slayer is dead, khan," he whispered. "Sher Afghan has felt the hand of the Mogul—he who stood in the way of the love of the Mogul—he was sent for, resisted, and the men of Jahangir slew him in the fight that followed. That is the message. But give heed. There is a debt yet to be paid. The threads of fate must be knitted together."

"What mean you, minstrel?" growled the Cossack.

"This!" Hamar laughed again. "I have known Sher Afghan. And Chauna Singh is his man, pledged to serve him to the death. When Nur-jahan fled from the lord, he hated her—for his pride was stricken. And so he sent Chauna Singh. That much I know. Wherefore was the Rájput sent? Sher Afghan knew the love bond between the woman and Jahangir. He is not the man to see Nur-jahan belong to another after his death."

Khlit scanned the group by the fire, frowning. Chauna Singh and his comrade had ceased talking. The Rájput passed his hand across his eyes—once—and fumbled at his girdle. It was the gesture of a man feeling for a sword.

"See you that, khan?" muttered the minstrel. "Sher Afghan is dead. Chauna Singh has sworn an oath to his lord. Nay, I can guess what it was! Sher Afghan, as well as Jahangir, loved Nur-jahan—and love knows no pity——"

Khlit had left his side. The Cossack strode to the girl, who had drawn nearer the precipice, looking out over the lake. But Chauna Singh was as quick as he.

The Rájput had placed his hand on the girl's shoulder, not roughly, but gently. Khlit caught his wrist and held it firmly. The eyes of Chauna Singh burned into his own, the blind eye dull and lifeless. Nur-jahan turned and seeing the two men, was silent.

"Nay, Chauna Singh," growled the Cossack. "Are you a man to do a thing such as this?"

The lips of the Rájput curled angrily.

"Back, khan," he snarled. "Fool of the steppe! This is a matter which concerns you not."

Nur-jahan drew a quick breath. Hamar and the other stared, surprized into silence. Khlit's gaze did not flinch.

"The woman came to me in the desert," he said calmly. "We have shared bread and salt. You and I, Chauna Singh, have fought the same foes. We be true men—you and I. You will not harm the woman."

The Rájput wrenched himself free.

"I have sworn an oath, O one-without-understanding!" he hissed. "Is the word of a Rájput to his lord to be broken? Nay, since my birth it has not been so. When Sher Afghan's death should be known to me, I swore that Nur-jahan should die. Thus does widow of the

Ráj join her lord. The lake will give her a grave. Back! I have sworn. Ho—" Khlit had drawn his sword—"Ramdoor Singh!"

Fiercely the Rájput cast himself empty-handed upon Khlit. As swiftly the Cossack struck. Chauna Singh's turban had been used to cover the feet of his mistress and his head was bare. The curved blade fell upon his temple, sending him reeling to the earth.

As he struck, Khlit had deftly turned his weapon, so the flat of the blade had met the other's brow.

The next instant, at a warning cry from Nur-jahan, he had turned in time to ward a powerful sweep of Ramdoor Singh's weapon. The stocky warrior leaped back from Khlit's counter-thrust and the two circled warily, striving to get the light of the fire in the other's eyes.

Again the weapons clashed. Weariness smote through Khlit's lean frame. He saw the dark face of the other framed against the black expanse of darkness over the lake.

Then Ramdoor Singh cast up his arms. His sword flew from his grasp. His body sank backward and away—and Khlit was gazing into the dark where his foe had been.

A second passed—and he heard a splash over the precipice, far beneath. Hamar came to his side and peered over the edge of the cliff.

"Ramdoor Singh wore mail," the minstrel said slowly. "His death will be swift. I saw him slip on a little stone at the edge. Truly, the ways of fate are past knowing."

XV

Khlit had seated himself on a stone, for he was weary, nursing his sword. And as he did so he watched Nur-jahan. The woman had Chauna Singh's bleeding head on her knee. With strips torn from her undergarments and moistened in melted snow she bathed the dark bruise where Khlit's blade had crushed the skin.

From the other side of the fire Hamar watched, his thin frame sunken together with fatigue, his eyes bright as with fever. Chauna Singh stirred, moaned, and lifted a hand that trembled to his head.

"Ramdoor Singh!" he muttered. "Ramdoor Singh—to me! Ha—am I blind?"

"Nay, Chauna Singh," said the girl softly, "you are hurt."

The lips of the Rájput moved and his good eye opened, only to close at once. With returning consciousness the warrior stifled his groans. But the Cossack saw that he was in pain.

"Ramdoor Singh is dead—in the waters of Lamdok Tso," went on Nur-jahan, "and you would be likewise but for the mercy of the khan. He stayed his hand when he might have slain. That is well, for I would speak with you, Chauna Singh. Look at me!"

The man opened his eye and peered about him dully. A wrinkle of pain crossed his swollen forehead.

"I can not see—yet," he said calmly.

Nur-jahan searched his bearded face intently, as if striving to read therein what she wanted to know.

"Tell me, Chauna Singh, warrior of Jhelam, man of Sher Afghan, who is dead—is it your will still to slay me? When have I done you ill? Nay, I thought that you had love for Nur-jahan, the betrothed of Jahangir the Mogul."

"By the sack of Chitore, I swore it—that I would safeguard you for him that was Sher Afghan, protect you and keep your honor with my life—until the death of my lord. I made him this oath when he set me after you, knowing that his life was no longer safe. Then, when I had news of his death, I was to slay you. By the sin of the sack of Chitore, on the word of a Rájput, it was sworn."

Silence followed upon this. Khlit, meditating, recalled the speech of Chauna Singh—*since life was in Ind, a Rájput has kept faith.*

And Nur-jahan had suspected something of this, for she had not told Chauna Singh that a man of Sher Afghan awaited them. Chauna Singh had done his best to keep his oath. Nay—knowing the man, Khlit felt this to be true—he would still strive to carry out his word.

"What care I for Jahangir," the Rájput muttered fiercely, "the Mogul—a Moslem without doubt—a stripling? Nay, Sher Afghan is dead."

Nur-jahan stroked his forehead idly with the cloth. Fatigue had drawn the flesh of her round face close upon the bones—yet had increased the beauty of the lovely mouth and dark eyes.

"The time came," spoke Nur-jahan softly, "and you attacked me, Chauna Singh. If I live, I shall be mistress of many thousand swords. Will you not forget and have the honor that I can give you?"

"I will not forget."

"You can not carry out your promise to—to Sher Afghan. Unwillingly I was forced to cross the threshold of the Lion-Slayer's home. Chauna Singh, my heart has been in the keeping of Jahangir —although I have seen him not for years. We were betrothed. Allah's mercy may bring me safe to the court of the Mogul. Think upon that, Chauna Singh—and say if you will not forget. You have not known the bond of love?"

"Aye, for my lord. He was a true man."

"And you can be to me what you were to him."

A mute shake of the head was her answer.

"We have shared peril together, Chauna Singh."

The Rájput was silent, his dark face impassive.

"Harken, Chauna Singh—" the beautiful head lifted proudly—"it is Mir-un-nissa who asks, Nur-jahan, Light of the Palace and Flower of the World. I ask it of you. Forget the oath."

"It may not be."

Across the fire Khlit saw Hamar watching keenly what passed. The face of the minstrel was inscrutable. A thought came to Khlit. Chauna Singh would be faithful to his word. And this must cost him his life.

Nur-jahan could not carry the wounded man down the mountain slopes to safety. Chauna Singh was strong, and the wound was not severe. The girl's life would not be safe in his company.

Khlit had discovered Ramdoor Singh's horse picketed in a clump of willows not far from the fire—and some dried dates and rice in the saddle-bags. Enough to get them alive into Kashmir. But they could not take Chauna Singh.

What then? Leave him by Lamdok Tso? That meant death, for the warrior was half starved, and hurt, and travelers in the Kandrum pass were few.

It was for Nur-jahan to decide, thought Khlit. And he watched the girl. She shook back the dark hair from her eyes and stretched out her small hand.

"Give me the curved sword, khan."

Khlit handed her the blade without a word. The girl fingered it quietly. Then laid it against the side of Chauna Singh's throat. The Rájput gave no sign he had heard, or felt.

"Look at me, Chauna Singh," she said.

The man shook his head slightly.

"I can not see. The hurt is above my eye."

"You can feel. I hold the curved sword of the khan, Khlit. Speak, Chauna Singh! Since you will not forget the oath, you must choose. Shall it be death here, at my hand—or to be left when we go down the pass at dawn? As you choose, it shall be."

Chauna Singh raised himself unsteadily on one arm.

"I do not offer you life, Chauna Singh—for I know that you may not be bought. Choose!"

The Rájput laughed and lay back on the earth wearily.

"Shall I be food for the ravens, Nur-jahan? Nay, let it be death by the sword. It is well. And then the waters of the lake."

The girl brushed the sword against his throat. And Khlit saw her smile.

"Give heed," she said softly. "Your life is mine. You have said it. And—I spare it. I have taken from Sher Afghan the life of his follower that was his. And I have given you fresh life. Remember—for it is a debt—and you are a man of the Ráj."

No muscle moved in the warrior's face. In the silence Khlit heard the murmur of water against the lake shore beneath them.

"It is a debt, Chauna Singh. Your life is mine, and I am safe henceforth from harm at your hand. Some day you will pay back the debt. That is the way of the Ráj." She turned to Khlit wearily. "You have found food, khan. We must eat and sleep. For we must be on our way at dawn."

Khlit wondered but said nothing as he took back his sword. For the first time in many days he saw Hamar eat—but sparingly.

So it happened that when the pale dawn touched the peaks above them and the faint reflections took shape in the dark pool of Lamdok Tso, Nur-jahan had Chauna Singh placed upon the horse and they set their faces toward Kashmir. Now Chauna Singh's scarred face was somber, for he saw nothing of the dawn. And Hamar, walking before them, did not make music upon his *vina.*

"Here is talk of a debt," Khlit heard the minstrel mutter, "but who shall give the gods what is owing to them?"

XVI

It had rained for a day and a night and part of the next day. Hamar, who led the four, shivered beneath his thin garment. The horse under Nur-jahan and Chauna Singh slipped and floundered down the mud of the trail.

Khlit, walking beside the minstrel, moved ahead mechanically, as he had done for many days. He could see little of their surroundings, for a wall of rain closed them in. He noticed that the crags and ravines of the mountains had given way to dark-green woods, traversed by foaming freshets. The air was warmer. This was well, he thought, for Nur-jahan could not have lived through the rain, had the cold of the mountain peaks been upon them.

He guessed—since the minstrel was silent and Nur-jahan in the stupor of weariness—that they were among foot-hills. But as yet there was no sign of dwelling or human being.

Chauna Singh had not spoken since the night of Ramdoor Singh's death. But Khlit fancied that the Rájput's sight had healed in his good eye. Nur-jahan seemed to have no fear of Chauna Singh since she had spared the warrior's life. She had laid a debt upon the man.

They were content to follow Hamar, who had said that there was a building near at hand.

Khlit was weary, and he knew that Nur-jahan's slender strength was only upheld by the thought of her nearness to Jahangir and the Mogul court. Hamar's endurance amazed him—when he roused himself to think collectively. The man pressed ahead as if driven by a will more than human—stumbling and shivering as he went, but with eyes fastened on the rain mist in front of them.

In this manner out of the breast of Himachal came the four—to where a wall loomed out of the mist. A wall of stone, carved with characters unknown to Khlit.

Hamar greeted the stone inscription with a glad cry and hastened his steps, turning off to one side of the way, to follow the wall which stretched before them, endlessly graven with the carven letters.

Chauna Singh had not looked up.

"Here is the place we seek!" croaked the minstrel. "Lo, the prayers to a great god are upon the stone. Come, we must hasten! We have been long."

And he shivered again, raising trembling hands to his head. The man's eyes were alight as if from fever. Khlit thought that it was a strange fever—not knowing the manner of strength which had sustained the fragile man for so long.

Above their heads the dark pile of a building took shape amid the rain. It was lofty, rising from a walled courtyard. A tower surmounted the gateway.

For an instant the rain dwindled, and, a fresh wind springing up, Khlit saw that the wall they had been following shielded a cliff. The mass of the building they had come to lay against the edge of the cliff.

Out and below them he glimpsed a level plain cut by a winding river.

"The valley of the Indus!" cried Nur-jahan, stirring in the Rájput's hold. "We must be near to Leh!"

Hamar laughed and stretched his thin arms overhead.

"Aye—near!" he muttered. "A slave upon a buffalo might ride to Leh within two days—but we are not at Leh. Ho, between us and there be the men of Jahangir. But we be here. Come, we are late!"

With that he hurried under the gate into the courtyard, pulling at the bridle of the horse. As he did so the rain closed in again, shutting off the sight of the valley. Khlit stumbled after the horse. But within the court he hesitated.

No men were to be seen. No windows showed in the stone walls which disappeared into the mist overhead. Shadows wreathed the corners. Before them was an iron-studded door. Complete silence reigned in the place.

For a moment the mind of the Cossack was prey to illusion. He had a fancy that their week's journey had taken them nowhere—that they were still at Khoten. A chord of memory had been touched and wrought the illusion. Then again, in the shadows of the court he fancied shapes appeared and moved.

Against the wall was a shadowy form, monstrous and cold. It was an animal of gigantic form—or was it an animal? He had heard priests tell of Ganesh, the elephant-headed god, and Hanuman, the monkey-god.

Then Khlit shook his head savagely and saw that what he beheld was a stone image at one side of the door—an elephant of red sandstone with a figure mounted astride its neck.

Other shadows issued from the door—a light gleamed within. The people of the place had sighted them and were coming out. Khlit saw Nur-jahan slip from the horse. It was well, he thought, for the woman must be faint. And he swore gruffly, because he had shivered again.

Then a gray shadow wheeled and brushed past him. Khlit drew back, staring. Surely this was Chauna Singh bent over the neck of the horse, riding from the place!

He drew his hand across his brow, cursing. The form was gone. But hoofs echoed on the road behind him, fading into the distance.

Why had Chauna Singh done this? Khlit knew not. He felt hands touch him and stumbled forward again.

These were shadows, he told himself. Yet without doubt they were men, for they touched him. Why could he not see their faces? Again came the illusive memory—this was Khoten, not Kashmir.

How could that be? Khlit summoned his strength and tried to see what was around him. He wished to see the men, not shadows. Yet they were not all men—some were women. Torchlight was in his eyes now, blinding him, for he had been in semidarkness for many hours.

The hands that were guiding him pushed him forward. A door closed behind him. The torches went before him down a hall—up some steps—into another hall. He heard voices which he did not understand.

His knee touched a bench and he sat upon it, for he was very weary. So much so that he had no desire for food. He craved rest and sleep. Here was warmth and shelter from the rain that had beat upon him for two days and a night. Rest—and sleep.

The torches went away. Khlit's head dropped on his shoulder—and he slept.

Only fitfully. For he woke from time to time, hearing a noise which disturbed him. It was a deep, echoing sound, like the beat of temple drums. After a long while Khlit lifted his head. Men were standing near him and the torches had come again.

Then Khlit knew what his memory had been trying to tell him. The place they had come to in the mist was like to the temple of Khoten—the sound of the drums was the same. The courtyard had been the same.

He looked full into the face of Hamar.

"Tell me, minstrel," he muttered, "be we in Kashmir or back in the devil temple of Khoten?"

Hamar smiled, and the fever was still in his eyes.

"We were long in coming, khan. But I guided you truly. You and Nur-jahan are in a temple—aye, but not that of Khoten. 'Tis the home of the god Bon, the shrine of the master of Himachal in Kashmir—and I have brought you here."

XVII

Then Khlit looked about him. Several men in dark robes stood near, bearing torches. By their light he saw Nur-jahan beside him, erect and silent, his sheepskin coat thrown from her shoulders, her garments shrunk to her slender body by the wet.

Others sat on benches in the shadows by the walls. They were white of face and wore the dress of the black priests. A long chamber stretched before him, lighted after a fashion by candles. At the end of the chamber was a dais of stone.

On this pedestal Khlit could see twin shapes that resembled feet, of monstrous size. The rest of the form was hidden by a curtain which hung from the ceiling.

Again the sound of the gongs came to him, and Nur-jahan spoke.

"You have brought us—here—Hamar? You who were my friend?"

"Aye," said the minstrel slowly. "But what is friendship? Two leaves drifting together down the highway at the wind's touch. Lo, I am a servant of Bon. The other gods are small beside Bon. For greater than the many-faced gods is fate. And death is one with fate. Death is the power that holds us in its grasp—and I am a servant of death."

He paused, to glance fleetingly at the curtain in the shadows. When he spoke again his voice was gentle.

"There lived one man, Nur-jahan, who was strong enough to wrestle with fate. That was Akbar, the Mogul. Out of the threads of life his hands wove the fabric of an empire. He saw beyond the many shrines of the gods—Moslem or Brahman. He sought a greater wisdom than theirs. Even to the temple of Bon he came and bent his head."

A murmur of assent issued from the lips of the men who sat by the wall. Nur-jahan stared at them proudly.

"The word of Akbar was law among us, Nur-jahan," went on the minstrel. "His last thought was for his empire. A mighty man and strong, he. But he yielded to the call of death. And he ordered your death, for he foresaw trouble if you were joined to Jahangir."

Khlit rose to his feet, the stupor of sleep clearing from his brain.

No one heeded him. The passive silence of the watchers irked him. Here was an evil place.

"The servants of Bon," cried a voice from the gloom, "are enemies of the Moslems. The death of Nur-jahan will be pleasing to the god."

"Aye," assented Hamar softly, "it is so. You have sharp eyes and wit, Nur-jahan, beloved of the Mogul. But you were blind—you and the two fools who served you. I was the messenger of Bon, sent to Khoten to bring you hither. It was I who kept Bator Khan from striving to take your life in the desert of Gobi. For your two fools are strong of limb and they were watching the dog of a Turkoman. So I waited."

"False to your salt!" mocked the girl.

"Nay, what is faith among men but an idle word? At Khoten I sought for you long, but Chauna Singh had hidden you well, and so I and those who served me might not harm you—then. Before the temple of Bon in the city your death was decreed. Yet, for once, your wit saved you—when you offered yourself a sacrifice."

"Was I one to be a victim to the mummery of the black priests?"

"Nay, Nur-jahan, it is better so. You have given yourself to Bon, and the god will have your sacrifice. In the mountains I feared lest my feeble strength fail, and I should not guide you here. So I played the mystical music of Bon and was heartened."

Khlit held himself erect by an effort of will. His endurance had been sapped by the last three days, and he knew that he had not the strength to lift a weapon. Age had taken from him the vigor that was Chauna Singh's. Indeed, the priests had not troubled to take his sword. In the brief silence came the ceaseless beat of the temple gongs.

"By the Lake of Lamdok Tso," smiled Hamar, "I thought that the will of the Rájput would rob me of your death. But fate had willed that it was not to be by his hand."

"Aye," said a voice, "they bound themselves over to the god, and thus it shall be."

"Well I knew the way to this temple, Nur-jahan. I prayed for strength to finish my task—and it was given me."

XVIII

Khlit glanced around from face to face. He saw the same thing mirrored in all—the blood lust that had stirred the crowd in Khoten.

The beauty of Nur-jahan only excited them further. The girl was pale, her thin cheeks ringed by dark, wet hair. But her eyes were proud.

Here was a true daughter of kings, thought the Cossack. Worn by the hardships they had been through, she still had spirit to confront those who hungered for her death.

"Better the swift hand of the Rájput!" she cried. "Than this thing of evil!"

"Nay, Nur-jahan, queen among women," smiled the minstrel-priest. "Chauna Singh is but a man. When he lifted his eyes in the courtyard and saw whither he had been brought, he fled. Here your blood will be laid before a god. You have sought to grasp the scepter of an empire in your lotus-hand, Nur-jahan, but no one can wrest life from death. That which causes life causes also death."

Khlit missed the sound that had been echoing through the hall. The temple gongs were silent.

"We shall not delay further, Nur-jahan," said a hard voice.

Khlit swayed and cursed his weakness. If he had been able to lift sword he would have flung himself upon the man who had betrayed them. But such was his weakness that he could not speak. Not so Nur-jahan. The girl's dark eyes flashed.

"Ho, priest!" she cried. "Your folly has made you mad. Think you, when Jahangir hears of this, he will leave one stone upon another, of this temple? Will one of you—" she swept an arm at the watchers —"save his life, if you slay me? The arm of the Mogul is long, and his love is everlasting as the hills."

"How shall he know?" Hamar smiled. "The khan who came with you will die at the same time. And Chauna Singh, remembering what he himself had planned to do, will not dare speak. Jahangir will not know. No tales pass beyond the walls of this temple."

Khlit shook his head, for he thought that the illusions of a few hours ago were returning. Voices came to his keen ears from without, and the halls of the temple echoed strangely. Nur-jahan's cheeks, instead of being pale, had flushed, suddenly.

"Will you slay a woman, Hamar," she cried loudly, "in this place of evil—and a woman who is loved of the Mogul?"

"Aye!" cried the voices around the wall, "for she has given herself!"

The sounds without grew in volume, swelling over the cries of the priests. Khlit wondered if many were coming to the hall. He knew not the customs of these temples. And still the clamor grew. Men rose along the wall and slipped from the door. Others glanced about uneasily.

Nur-jahan had not ceased speaking. But Khlit paid no further heed to her. He had heard a sound which stirred his blood. Was it more of the mummery of the black priests? He knew not.

And then the girl fell silent. And silence held the room, with those who remained within it.

Hamar's eyes turned from them to the door. And Khlit saw that he was troubled. The gaze of the others followed that of the minstrel.

A crashing blow sounded somewhere below them. At once the muffled sounds swelled clearer, as if a gateway had been opened. And Khlit laughed. He had heard what he knew well—the echo of horses' hoofs—many of them—upon stone.

The priests rose and hurried to the door. Hamar stared blankly. Came a pistol shot, followed by the ring of weapons. Nur-jahan caught Khlit's arm.

"Back!" she whispered. "Into the shadows."

And then Khlit was standing, sword in hand, in the gloom by the foot of the god Bon. The tumult increased to a roar—a shout from many throats.

"Ho! Níla-ghora ki aswár!"

"The battle-cry of the Rájputs, khan," whispered the girl, her eyes proud. "Said I not Jahangir was lord of swift swords? Harken—they are riding their horses into the temple. They have come to meet me —Jahangir has sent his men to meet me!"

Khlit saw the bent form of Hamar scramble to the door, then pause, looking around wildly. A pistol cracked without the door and the man clutched the air, screaming. A wind swept into the place, blotting out many of the candles. On the stone floor the scattered torches were smouldering into embers.

Khlit roused himself to understanding of what had happened.

"Nay," he laughed, "Chauna Singh has paid his debt. The Rájput has brought hither the men from Leh. It is well."

Whereupon, being weary, he sat down on the dais. And was asleep on the instant, his head pillowed on the foot of the god Bon.

ADVENTURE SEVEN

THE LION CUB

Who can lift the veil of the unseen? And who can read the hand-writing of Fate?

Jhilam the Mighty, the stronghold of the hills, had been fief of the sires of Sattar Singh since the time of Ram. Now Sattar Singh, Lord of Jhilam, was dead.

And Rani Begum, wearing the white robe of widowhood for Sattar Singh, brought the keys of Jhilam castle and laid them before Jahangir, the Mogul, as was the law. But her heart was heavy.

"Lord of the World," cried Rani Begum—and her fear was a great fear at sight of the mask of anger that overspread the face of the Mogul—"my Lord Sattar Singh swore that the keys of Jhilam of the Hills should be held by none but our son Rao Singh. Such is our right."

"Is the oath of a hill chief greater than the word of the Mogul?" said Jahangir.

So it came to pass that Jahangir the Mogul, Lord of the Punjab, of the Dekkan, of Sind and all Hindustan, gave the fief of Jhilam to one Shaista Mirza, a Persian. But the allegiance of the men of Jhilam he could not give.

Allah in his mercy laid the hand of death upon Rani Begum. It was written that this should be.

Who can look beyond the veil of the future? Yet the thought came to me in a vision that the treasure of Jhilam should be found. And in the vision was the dark form of the Angel of Death.

From the tale of Ahmad Rumi.

THE HOUR OF SUNSET PRAYER WAS PAST. AHMAD RUMI, TELLER OF legends, folded his prayer-carpet neatly and placed it within his bundle and seated himself at the side of the caravan-track. This was the trail from the Wular lake to the southern border of Kashmir. And it was the year 1609 of the Christian era.

Carefully the legend-teller adjusted the folds of his white turban and ate sparingly of dates which he took from his girdle, leaning on his staff the while. The sun had gone down behind the willows at his back; the shadows lengthened, dwindled and formed again under the pale light of a new moon.

Except for the loom of the turban against the underbrush, touched by the faint fingers of moonlight, the form of Ahmad Rumi was invisible. He sat very quiet, sensing the change of hour by the night chill. For Ahmad Rumi was blind.

He lifted his head at a sound from above him on the caravan-track. Other sounds reached him, blended and confused, but clear to the blind man. Three horses were approaching.

Three Arabian horses, bearing heavy men perhaps in armor. So reasoned Ahmad Rumi and drew farther back into the willows. Years had taught him the different tread of a Turkoman's pony, a Kirghiz' quick-moving horse and the stolid gait of a Kabul stallion. He could distinguish between the bell-bearing mules of a Bokharan caravan and the laden beasts of Chinese merchants.

Slowly the three Arabs passed. They minced along after the manner of their kind, and their riders spoke Persian. The horsemen did not perceive Ahmad Rumi.

"Fresh horses, held in check," muttered the legend-teller to himself, "and going warily. Aye, verily, the tale of the Wular peasants was true. *Insh'allah!*"

He leaned slightly forward, facing up the trail expectantly and stroking the gray beard that fell to his girdle. His wide, brown eyes were closed, and the moonlight outlined shadows under his high cheekbones. Then he lifted his head again eagerly.

This time he scrambled to his feet, aided by his staff, and stepped into the highroad to confront the rider who trotted swiftly under the willows.

"Back, beggar," cried a high voice, not unkind nor harsh. "I have no silver——"

"I am blind," responded the teller of legends quickly.

He felt for the bridle of the horse that had been reined in sharply.

His lean hand touched the bridle and the silk shoulder-straps, halting at the wrought silver ornaments.

"The Wular stallion," he muttered. "Allah is merciful."

A quick indrawing of breath escaped the rider.

"Back, Moslem. I must pass."

"Nay, Rao Singh. Not until you and I have spoken together."

For a space the rider was silent, peering at the fragile form in his path. He sat his mount easily, a slender figure nervously erect, in a plain white tunic with silk girdle bearing a light sword and a small, peaked turban.

"What seek you? How knew you my name?" he demanded suspiciously.

Ahmad Rumi felt for the hand of Rao Singh and pressed it to his forehead.

"Thrice blessed is this hour!" he exclaimed joyfully. "*Aie*—should I not know the name of the son of my lord? It is sweeter than the wind in the pine-tops in the hills and more fragrant than the scent of the lotus by the lake.

"Dismount, Rao Singh; dismount! At a distance of a bowshot wait those who would slay you and scatter your ashes on the wind of death. By the ford they watch—three, with arms and perhaps coats of mail."

Rao Singh lifted his dark head and glanced warily about into the thickets. In that age it was well to keep to horse on the caravan-routes, even within sight of the camp of the Mogul, as he then was.

But Ahmad Rumi was alone. Youth and aged man seated themselves on the bank by the willows.

"How know you this thing?"

Rao Singh spoke with the directness of a boy—which he was, barely attained to man's figure.

"You could not see them?"

Suspicion was in the last words and Ahmad Rumi smiled gently.

"They spoke Persian, which I know. They will wait at the ford for the one they seek. I heard the rattle of their weapons. Death is in the air tonight—for Rao Singh."

"Whence came the three?"

"From the Jhilam path."

"How knew you I should come?"

The teller of legends sighed, stroking his beard.

"Many are the mouths that will utter evil. The master of horse of the Lord of Jhilam spake to the slaves, the stable slaves, and they whispered to the cutters of wood, who bore the news to the forest men. Hence I, who wait at the Wular gate, heard that this night Rao Singh was to be slain at the ford near the outpost of Mogul camp.

"So I came hither with a caravan from Khoten, bound for the camp. Even as I heard the thing has come to pass."

"Three common retainers from Jhilam," meditated Rao Singh.

"Nay; one was noble, for I caught the scent of musk as they passed."

"Nevertheless I must ride on."

The boy glanced up anxiously at the moon. "May the gods reward you for your tidings——"

"*Aie,* say not thus, my lord! For the space of four Winters since the death of Sattar Singh, who was master of Jhilam, I have lived but for one thing—to embrace the hand of the son of Sattar Singh, telling him the while that there are those at Jhilam who have not forgotten. It was our fate to suffer, and we have endured much, but we have not forgotten——"

"Peace!" whispered the boy.

Ahmad Rumi's keen ears had caught the sound—the swift clatter of horse's hoofs down the trail. But this time his memory was at fault. The gait was not that of Arab or Persian beast, nor yet that of a steppe pony.

Rao Singh had sprung to his feet, hand on sword. He saw a black horse sweep by bearing a tall form in sheepskin *khalat* and black hat. The rider glanced at him but did not pause.

"A hillman," he whispered to Ahmad Rumi, "perhaps a Kirghiz, yet I think not. Presently he will be at the ford."

"The trees are thick there, I have heard. It may be written that this one should be attacked and perish in your place——"

"Then must I mount and warn," cried the boy.

"You are too late, my lord."

The teller of legends raised his hand. From below came the sound of horses plunging in shallow water, a cry and the sharp clash of weapons.

"Siva! It is one against three."

Shaking off the protesting beggar, Rao Singh leaped to saddle and spurred down the track, drawing his sword as he went. Again the noise of steel striking steel, again a cry of pain, followed this time by the sound of a heavy body breaking through brush.

In the edge of the stream Rao Singh reined his mount and stared about him. A riderless horse, trembling with excitement, stood near by, its reins tangled in a human body stretched on the grass.

Under the surface of the shallow water where a moonbeam pierced the curtain of trees he saw a second form that seemed to move as he watched. Then it was still. Silence held the ford, and he wondered at the swift change from tumult to quiet.

Not more than two minutes had passed since the first shout, and two men were dead and two had fled beyond sight and hearing. Into the silence, however, crept a *tap-tap*. It came nearer and Rao Singh's eyes widened as he gripped his weapon.

The *tap-tap* changed to a rustle, and as Rao Singh was about to voice a prayer to ward off the evil influence of a *rakzhas*—a malignant demon—he saw Ahmad Rumi's lean figure approach along the way he had come.

Reassured, the boy dismounted and guided the Moslem to the edge of the stream.

"Heard you the sword-blows, Ahmad Rumi?" he questioned uneasily. "All was over ere I reached the ford. 'Tis like to demonwork, for here be two slain as by magic. By Kali and Durga, protectress of the two worlds, 'twas magic!"

"Nay," returned the beggar calmly, "there is no enchantment save the will of Allah and the handwriting of fate, lord. I heard steel strike upon steel. Is the rider who passed us by slain?"

Rao leaned over the body by the horse. It was that of a commoner —a harsh face stared up at him above a blood-stained quilted tunic. Satisfied as to this, the boy inspected the form in the water. Caste prevented him from touching the dead. A strong smell of musk assailed him.

"The noble who rode with the three," Ahmad Rumi informed him promptly.

"Aye, he wears a gold chain, and the moonlight shows mother-of-pearl inlaid upon the scabbard at his girdle."

The blind man had run his delicate hand over the features of the bearded soldier. He drew in his breath sharply.

"Bairam, master of horse of Shaista Mirza, will breed no more foals," he muttered. "Just so was his beard ever trimmed and this is his Damascus steel cap. Little it availed him."

The two were silent a space, pondering what had passed at the ford. Plainly the rider of the black horse had been set upon by the three Persians ambushed at this spot. In all probability he had been mistaken in the deep shadows under the trees for Rao Singh. Yet he had fought off the three sharply, killing two, and had passed on his way.

"Truly a swordsman, he," sighed the boy. "Would I had seen him more closely and that he had joined his blade to mine, for I have need of such a one."

"You have many foes, lord," mused Ahmad Rumi, seating himself, for his aged limbs were not strong. "There be jackals aplenty who would pull down the lion cub of Jhilam. Aye, in the Mogul camp. After what has passed, is it safe to draw your reins thither?"

Rao Singh smiled, his white teeth flashing gaily from his dark face. His countenance was immature; the chin weak, the mouth delicate, the eyes somber. Like his slender figure, it bespoke nervous energy and wilfulness rather than strength. There was pride in the lines of the thin nostrils, and the imprint of sorrow in the creased brow.

Rao Singh was eighteen years of age, yet he bore the cares of a man of thirty—not an uncommon thing in the Mogul era when fortune or exile hung upon the fancy of an emperor and death was the reward of a slight offense.

"Nay," he laughed, "have not the gods favored me, Ahmad Rumi, this night? It is well, for I must accomplish a great thing before dawn—" He broke off to stare at the placid beggar suspiciously.

"Ho, Ahmad Rumi, how shall I trust you? You have come upon my path like a spy. You—a follower of the Prophet—claim allegiance to my father, who holds sacred the books of the Veda and the many-armed gods. That is not wonted."

The legend-teller leaned on his staff, his blind eyes seeking the boy with uncanny exactitude. Rao Singh fingered his sword nervously.

"Siva!" he muttered. "You have not the look of one who is blind." Ahmad Rumi smiled patiently.

"Your temper, lord," he said slowly, "is like to that of noble Sattar Singh. He was ever swift to draw weapon, and heedless of danger.

Wherefore his followers loved him and his name is still whispered among the forest men of Jhilam, who are of his faith."

He nodded slowly, pondering as the aged will on events that were past.

"I am not one of them, Rao Singh. That is true. But there was a day when I journeyed barefoot to Mecca, to the holiest of the holy. It was the sacred month of Ramazan.

"There came a Mogul noble with his followers—one who was hunting with falcons and had had poor sport. He mocked me and set his dogs upon me, who was in rags. With my staff I slew one of the dogs, wherefore the noble grew great in anger, and his servants pierced my eyes with the fire pencil."

Rao Singh leaned uneasily against his horse, glancing from the lean face of the beggar to the dead body in the shallow water, and up to where the round sphere of the moon showed through the trees.

"Came one who rode hastily and cried out in hot accusation against the noble," continued the teller of legends. "He cried that I had been wronged, and weapons clashed. I heard little, for the pain was great.

"Then the rider spake to me gently and had a skilled *hakim* make me a healing bandage. Eh—for that I blessed him and asked that I might be the servant at his doorpost."

There was a silence while Ahmad Rumi paused as if listening—a silence broken by the whimper of the stream and the rustle of the bushes in the night wind.

"I thought footsteps sounded," he observed. "Nay, what is written is written. It was written that I should be blind.

"Since that day I learned that the noble who hunted was Shaista Mirza of Rudbar, and the one who took up my quarrel was Sattar Singh; and men said that both had long been enemies at the court of Akbar, on whom be peace."

"Did you ask punishment for the wrong done?"

"Am I a paladin of Mogulistan or Hindustan to accuse those of high blood? Nay; Shaista Mirza is a Persian and the Mogul favors his race for their learning and their political power.

"But since then I have had a hut where the Jhilam road joins the Wular lake, and the fishers of the Wular have brought me food—until the evil day when Shaista Mirza became master of Jhilam. Since then there has been little food and my hunger has been great."

He stretched a trembling hand toward the boy.

"Come to the Wular lake, Rao Singh. I have heard evil spoken of you at Jhilam. Those who hold the fortress are powerful. The sword-arm of Shaista Mirza is long—enough to reach to the court of the Mogul. He and his astrologer Nureddin are very shrewd.

"In the Wular forest you will be safe, for there are those who will guard the path to your hut and watch while you sleep. The forest men and the fishers—who are Kashmiris—remember Sattar Singh. And they ask for Rao Singh, his son."

He salaamed before the youth.

"To those who asked I said that Rao Singh would come. The lion cub of Jhilam would come, and with their own eyes they would see he was like to his father. This thing I have sworn upon the *kaaba* and the holy names of Omar and Welid.

"I have told them the legends of Jhilam. Yet they have doubted. They have not seen the face of Rao Singh. Shaista Mirza they see and know his power. *Aie,* too well!"

"Has the Persian put hardships on the bent neck of the Jhilam people?"

"Aye, it was our fate that he should do so. The slaves he brought with him have been made overseers with whips in their hands. The eunuchs who guard his women have the power of life and death."

Words tumbled eagerly from the beggar's beard.

"The tithes of rice are doubled; men no longer work the soil, for the tithes are ruinous; instead they have turned wolflike into rob-bers and as such are slain daily by the retainers of the Persian. The village oxen are taken without pay——"

"How could I alter this, Ahmad Rumi?" cried the boy. "Am I one to share the lot of peasants?"

"They ask but to see you. They would look upon the face of the son of Sattar Singh who was their lord."

And the boy laughed with bitterness.

"Truly a poor sight that, Ahmad Rumi—to see the blank eyes and woful mouth of him who is poverty-ridden hostage to Jahangir the Mogul."

The beggar touched the other's foot hopefully.

"Nay, lord. Is it not written that an omen may bring good? It would be an omen—for the forest men and the outcasts of Jhilam.

They would know that you live, and their hearts would be lifted up as flowers at sight of the sun.

"This was the message I was to bring. And—our need is great."

He waited patiently while Rao bent his head in thought. Once he looked up hastily at the moon as if to mark the passage of time.

"Men starve in the forests of Jhilam, and the hills that are sacred to you and yours, Rao Singh, see nightly hunting of men like beasts along the lake. A pavilion of pleasure has been built by Shaista Mirza on the floating garden of the Wular and there Kashmiri women die slowly so their agony shall be longer and the pleasure of their lord the greater——"

In his earnestness Ahmad Rumi did not hear the slight crackle of brush that drew nearer the two.

"Verily, Rao Singh—" he rose to his full height and extended an imploring hand—"Jhilam cries for the son of Sattar Singh!"

The boy did not move, nor did his expression change. Meditating as he was, he did not hear the sounds in the thicket.

Rao Singh had the faults and the splendid virtues of his race. Proud, intolerant of personal wrong and brave in battle to the point of folly, he was passionate, short-tempered and as yet indifferent to the misfortunes of those of baser birth.

His years of semi-captivity at the Mogul court had not made him a satellite of the throne, bred to flattery and intrigue; but they had branded suspicion into him, and boyish selfishness. And one other thing.

He was unwilling to take up the cause of his hereditary vassals as Ahmad Rumi had hoped; yet he saw in the suggestion of the blind man a possibility of obtaining new followers. The inbred restriction of caste kept him from association with outlaws and the poorer orders; yet his hopes were stirred of taking up arms against Shaista Mirza.

"Whither lies the place I should come—to the Wular?" he asked.

"At the end farthest from the palace and the pleasure island, lord," chanted Ahmad Rumi. "Up the course of a stream, an hour's fast ride, to where the pines give way to a cleared place. There is a place of many rocks called the Wular *davan*—where I have my hut."

Again the boy laughed softly.

"I have prayed to the many-armed gods, Ahmad Rumi. The time

has come when I am no longer child but man. Tonight I ride to
claim what is mine——"

"Allah is merciful——"

"Nay, it is a woman. There is one in the Mogul camp who has
looked at me, and in her eyes burned the fire of love. I also feel love,
and it is strange. I will take her from her guards, and I shall turn
my horse from the court. If Jahangir's men would seek me they must
come into the hills."

The teller of legends plucked at his beard, considering this. He shook
his head doubtfully. Rao Singh had no friends in the court—such
was the weight of Jahangir's displeasure—and women were ever the
harbingers of strife.

Moreover the boy had not said that the woman was to be given
him; he had declared that he would take her in spite of guards.
Whoever stole the woman of another ran a great risk, for the Mo-
gulis were even more jealous of their womenkind than the Hindus.

"A slave, lord?" he questioned.

"Nay."

Rao Singh threw back his head proudly.

"A free-born maiden, fairer than the lotus."

"A concubine?" persisted the blind man.

"Not so. Kera of Kargan is hostage for her tribe. Her lot is like to
mine."

"Aie!"

Ahmad Rumi wrung his hands against his lean chest.

"The maiden of Kargan Khan, hill chief of the Kirghiz, master of
a thousand riders and lord of the northern hills beyond Jhilam. Aie!
Verily Allah has thrown the dust of madness into the pool of your
wisdom."

Rao Singh paid little attention. The rustle in the thicket had
ceased save for a dull impact that might have been the stamp of a
horse's foot.

"Kera of Kargan," he murmured. "Beautiful as the solitary moon
at midnight. Fragrant as the jasmine—her lips like coral, teeth white
as water-lilies.

"Her figure is slender as the young pine. And her eyes—dark as
shadows in a forest pool at night."

"Hostage for the allegiance of Kargan Khan, who is ruthless as the storm-wind——"

"A pearl set in base silver. And Cheker Ghar, her buffoon, brought me word that she would mount my horse and go where I willed."

"Kargan Khan esteems the maiden as the jewel in the hilt of his sword. Only when Jahangir pledged her safety did he render her to the Mogul."

"Tonight I will seek her among the tents, and she will come."

Ahmad Rumi tore at his beard as he grasped the meaning of this.

"Eh—then she must be in the imperial seraglio. She is among those in the red imperial tents. Rao Singh, snatch from the jaws of a lion the calf which it is devouring, touch the fang of an angered cobra, but do not raise your eyes to a woman of the Mogul's tents!"

"Nay, she put on her ornaments that she should be fair in my eyes. Twice I saw her face, for she is not like the veiled mistresses of the Moslems."

"Kargan Khan will hunt you, and when he has found you cut you in many pieces which he will throw to the fish of a mountain lake."

"I have sworn to the conjurer that I would come this night to the imperial tents."

Ahmad Rumi sighed, hearing the wilful pride that rang in the youth's words.

"It was the way of Sattar Singh to be rash," he mused, "yet this is madness—and death for the sake of a woman. Surely there be slave girls that can be bought——"

"I have spoken," said Rao Singh shortly. "It is late——"

He had turned to his horse when his figure tensed and his hand flew to his sword.

"Siva!" he cried softly.

Not ten paces away a man stood in the shadows, afoot, one hand holding the bridle of a horse, the other closed over the beast's muzzle. He was a tall man with high shoulders, wearing a long-sleeved sheepskin *khalat,* heavy horsehide boots and a black sheepskin hat.

"It is he of the black horse," the boy whispered to Ahmad Rumi, who had turned his head inquiringly.

The stranger had made no move. He stood with powerful legs wide apart, the set of the shoulders suggesting strength, although his figure was spare. The hat was perched on one side of his head. Rao Singh could make out that the stranger had long, gray mustaches, and a beard.

Both men measured glances in silence. The boy was the first to speak.

"Whence came you?" he cried shrilly. "What seek you here?"

He had whipped out his sword and poised watchfully, one foot in stirrup.

"A jackal comes in silence," he repeated angrily, for he was startled.

"And jackals lie in wait," responded the other.

He spoke slowly in the deep voice of one well on in years, yet almost indifferently. He seemed careless of the threatening attitude of Rao Singh.

"What mean you? I wait for no one."

"This."

The man by the black horse spoke Moguli somewhat brokenly. He moved forward and touched the dead Bairam with his foot.

Out in the moonlight his true height was revealed. He towered over the boy and the legend-teller. He glanced at the Hindu's mount appraisingly.

"A good horse, that," he grunted. "Yet the other three were ill mounted and worse swordsmen."

Rao Singh hesitated. The swaggering, powerful figure was that of a warrior conscious of his power—resembling somewhat a Turkoman or Kirghiz. But the man's eyes did not slant, nor had he the furtive manner of a hill bandit.

His dress was rough, yet the curved sword in his leather girdle was richly chased and he had besides two costly Turkish pistols. His skin was lighter than that of an Afghan. Moreover his speech was strange.

"Dog of the devil," he observed meditatively, "this is a cursed spot. Here the three set upon me in the stream. When two were slain the third fled and won free in the thickets. I saw you and yonder beggar standing at the ford and returned to see whether you were kin to the three——"

"Nay, they waited here to set upon me."

The stranger looked at the boy keenly, but held his peace. Rao Singh wondered how much of their talk he had heard. The man had come from the brush with uncanny quietness, after the manner of one who was at home in such paths.

"Warrior," spoke Ahmad Rumi, "this youth mounted and rode to aid you when you were attacked."

"He came not overswiftly."

Rao Singh bit his lip.

"No fault of mine—you rode with speed."

He frowned.

"Are you a Moslem?"

"Nay."

The stranger spat into the stream indifferently.

"Perchance a man of the Mogul."

"Nay."

Rao Singh sheathed his sword with sudden decision.

"Verily you are blunt of speech. Yet you did me a service. And—" condescendingly—"'tis plain you are not an ill swordsman. Will you enter my service? I have need of a keen sword this night."

At this the owner of the black horse tugged at his mustache thoughtfully. From far below the three came the shrill cry of the Mogul's sentries. The wind bore a faint echo of the imperial kettle-drums and brass cymbals playing a festive measure.

"Harken, stripling," growled the stranger abruptly, "I like not many words. I eat the bread of Jahangir——"

Rao Singh stepped back instinctively, but the other waved a gnarled hand impatiently.

"I am no follower of the Mogul. In the Summer I came to his court from—another court. Because of a service Jahangir, who is lord of these lands, gave some horses and gold. Despite that his minions came near to slaying me."

He pointed down to the south, where lay the border of Kashmir.

"I saw some elephants bearing gilt castles, surrounded by fat horsemen, and watched, for I had not seen the elephants before. Then the horsemen and slaves with staffs began to strike me, crying that the Mogul's women rode upon the elephants.

"Blood of Satan! I cared not to see the women. The Mogul is tenderer of his women than a bear of a bruised paw. Bethink you and molest them not."

"Then you heard?"

Rao Singh gnawed his lip and sprang suddenly to saddle.

"Ho—wait here and you will see Kera of Kargan. Eunuchs are fat; they will make good slicing with a sharp sword!"

The stranger grunted, either in agreement or dislike.

"Wait here, Ahmad Rumi," cried the boy, fired with his purpose. "And at dawn you shall hear the music of the voice of the Flower of Kashmir. Aye, then we shall ride to the hills."

He spurred forward with a wave of the hand and vanished down the caravan path.

"Allah be kind to the youth!" cried the blind man.

"A pity," mused the stranger, "to hazard such a horse for a woman."

The stranger stared after Rao Singh, then glanced at the legend-teller's blind countenance. He tethered his horse carefully, then led Ahmad Rumi to a seat against a rock by the brook bed. He sat near by, leaning upon the trunk of a fallen willow, his long, booted legs stretched idly before him. Here he could see both up and down the trail. Although his posture indicated idleness, even physical laziness, his eyes under tufted brows were keenly watchful.

Ahmad Rumi squatted passively on his heels, his gentle face turned upward as was his wont to the stars he could not see, and waited what was to come with the calm of a fatalist. He made a strange contrast to the scarred, moody face of the warrior.

"Ho, Ahmad Rumi," said the stranger at length, "you spoke of Jhilam and its lord. Something I have heard of it in the prattle of yonder courtiers. What is the true tale?"

Thus did Khlit, the wanderer and the seeker after battles, hear the story of Jhilam. While the two waited the return of Rao Singh they talked, and Khlit learned much of what went on in the hills by the Wular lake and how Shaista Mirza scourged the villages of Jhilam with the whip of fear.

II

It was the beginning of the third watch of the night and the revelers had retired from the imperial *kanates* when Cheker Ghar poked his head from his ragged shelter.

He scrambled nimbly to his feet, then drew a heavy pack wrapped in leopard-skin tenderly from the tent. Cheker Ghar was a wiry, bare-legged man of uncertain age with a crafty, fox face whitened with powder as a mark of his profession—conjuring.

With a sigh he shouldered his pack and began to trot through the tents, keeping well in the shadows and avoiding the slaves who guarded the barriers of each noble's camping-site.

The dense smoke rising from fires of dried dung and green wood had cleared away with the advent of early morning but a faint mist hung about the tents. Cheker Ghar sniffed the air as a dog does.

He marked the position of the Light of Heaven—the lantern on the lofty pole erected beside the imperial yak-tail standard at the gate of the Mogul's pavilions. Toward this he made his way, skipping over tent-ropes and avoiding snarling dogs with the skill of one familiar with encampments.

He avoided the avenue of torches by the imperial gate, and the tent of the ameer who was on guard that night. His way led to the *kanate*—the barrier of cotton cloth printed with flowers and supported by gilded poles—which surrounded the Mogul's enclosure. And to that portion of the cotton wall which veiled the tents of the seraglio.

Outside the *kanate* were no sentries, for the ameer on guard was supposed to make the rounds with a troop of horsemen from time to time. Within however were stationed wakeful eunuchs, armed. Cheker Ghar shivered. He knew the cruelty of the eunuchs.

But a stronger impulse than his own will drew him to the barrier. Here he listened attentively. Occasional voices reached him, showing that the guardians of the women were awake. Cheker Ghar glanced swiftly behind him to reassure himself as to his position.

About the *kanate* was a cleared space, on the farther side of this the horse artillery that always accompanied the Mogul was parked. Through the mist reared the summits of the tents of the ameers and *mansabdars,* illumined by the pallid moonlight. For several miles the camp extended, to the hills.

The only sounds were the measured cries of the outer sentries, the howl of a dog, the mutter of the hunting-beasts prisoned in the Mogul's menagerie, or the snort of a horse. The air was chill with a hint of coming dawn.

There was no time to be lost. Satisfied as to his position, Cheker

Ghar bared his teeth and, taking his pack in his arms, slipped under the *kanate*.

He crept slowly into the moonlight on the farther side. A stout eunuch poised not twenty feet away saw him and squealed shrilly—then his warning cry changed to a laugh.

"El Ghias," the guard called softly to his companions. "The buffoon."

"Aye, gracious masters," bowed the conjurer; "aye, here is poor El Ghias. Eh—I starve for food. There is scanty picking among the dogs this night, and my belly yearns. I remember the gracious masters who gave me silver——"

"Begone," warned the eunuch carelessly. "Misgotten cur—mongrel of a jackal's begetting! We have no silver for you. Entrance here is forbidden——"

"O unutterable vileness, bred of dishonorable fathers and unknown mothers," said Cheker Ghar to himself. Aloud:

"By the gods, 'tis a dreary night, masters. See, I would beguile the hour with a clever trick. A rare sight, noble swordbearers of Jahangir!"

He shifted his pack from his shoulders to the ground, prostrating himself before the guardians. It was not the first time he had come, for he had prepared craftily for this night. The eunuchs had been amused at his arts.

"O thrice-defiled maggot of a dung-hill," he whispered under his breath, adding:

"Bara, grant me but a moment. I have an artful trick, taught me by my father's wisdom. The hour is fitting for such a feat. Watch in silence——"

He swiftly unstripped his pack, disclosing a pot of earth and a white silk cloth. Bara and the others drew near, fired with curiosity. They ran great risk in allowing the conjurer to stay, but his cleverness had whiled away weary hours before this, and now he promised a rare trick.

"In this pot," said Cheker Ghar solemnly, "aided by Hanuman, the monkey-face, and Ganesh, the elephant-head, I can make to grow—a tree. Name what tree you will, noble masters, and it will grow and bear fruit."

He squatted behind the pot, glancing up at them. From the corner of his eye he saw a shadow appear under the awning of the tent

nearest on the right—the one that sheltered the women in attendance on the seraglio. Four eunuchs now stood about him, leaving a
bare space of some two hundred yards along the tent-line.

"A lie," chattered Bara. "A tree! Nay, it can not be, base-born."

"Even as I say," nodded Cheker Ghar, "it will appear. Name but
the tree."

Incredulity, curiosity and uneasiness were in the black faces that
bent over the conjurer.

"A plane-tree," hazarded one.

"Nay, a mulberry," broke in Bara, grinning. "Wretched one,
sweeping of the offal-heap, noisome breeder of evil smells, grow me a
mulberry-tree with fruit! Six silver dinars if I taste of the fruit. The
bastinado if you fail."

The others laughed and pressed closer.

Cheker Ghar did not laugh. Nor did he look up at Bara. Perhaps
—for the conjurer had a way of hearing all the news of the imperial
bazaars—Cheker Ghar had known Bara was fond of mulberries.

"Take heed, exalted ones," he muttered, "and speak not."

Whereupon he cast the white cloth over the pot. The trick was a
favorite with Hindu conjurers but so difficult that it was not performed on ordinary occasions. The eunuchs had never witnessed it
although they had heard of it.

Cheker Ghar raised his bare, brown arms and lifted the cloth. A
tiny green shoot was disclosed.

"Nay," shrilled Bara, "that is no tree but a weed——"

"It is the seed-shoot of the mulberry," reproved the conjurer
sternly.

Again he replaced the cloth with tense face. His half-closed eyes
shot to the tent on the right. The slender shadow was still there.
Without the enclosure sounded the trot of horses.

"The horsemen make their rounds," observed Bara.

He was unconcerned, for none of the outer guard would have
dared look within the *kanate*.

"Behold!"

Cheker Ghar's bare arms writhed above his head and the cloth
seemed to rise of itself into his hand. A young tree perhaps three
feet in height stood in the pot.

"*Karamet, karamet!*" cried the onlookers. "A miracle!"

The conjurer's keen ears had noted that one horse lagged behind the others. A gleam of moonlight appeared against the *kanate* as if a weapon wielded from without had slit the cotton fabric. The eunuchs, absorbed in the tree, had sensed nothing untoward.

"Pluck the fruit, noble Bara," he wheedled. "See, within the leaves. The six dinars are mine."

Incredulously the chief eunuch, who bore the honorary title of Purified One of Paradise, felt among the branches of the tree. He plucked craftily at the stem, but it did not yield. The tree was in fact a mulberry.

He stared angrily at the ripe fruit he had found and fumbled in his girdle for coins which he flung down with an oath. Cheker Ghar clutched them eagerly.

Then the shadow flitted from the canopy toward the barrier. In the moonlight it was revealed as a veiled woman.

A eunuch saw her and cried out. At once with incredible swiftness Cheker Ghar clutched his pot, thrust it into the pack and gained his feet, holding the leopard-skin.

"Fools!" he chattered. "Offspring of swine!"

Bara's sword whirled at him but the conjurer leaped back still reviling his enemies and scurried under the barrier with crab-like agility.

The woman who had fled from the tent had passed through the opening in the cotton wall. Bara sprang after her, storming curses. As he plunged into the slit cloth a hand appeared in the aperture—a hand that grasped a dagger.

Bara staggered back with the haft of the dagger sticking from his broad girdle. He gripped the haft moaning and sank to his knees. His companions hesitated, making the night shrill with their screams. Others ran up.

On the outer side of the *kanate* the girl had been caught up in strong young arms.

"Kera! Flower of my heart!"

She lay trembling in Rao Singh's grasp as the boy ran to his horse and swung into the saddle. He set spurs to his horse and wheeled away from the imperial enclosure as the beat of approaching hoofs neared them—but not before a diminutive figure had secured a firm hold on his stirrup and raced beside him, barelegged, a leopard-skin on its shoulders.

"Into the cannon, noble lord," warned Cheker Ghar. "The ameer's guard is close behind."

Rao Singh swerved and traced his way among the picketed horses. Slaves started up to gaze, but hung back perceiving a nobleman with a woman on his saddle peak.

Behind them echoed the shouts of pursuers. Eunuchs and soldiers swept through the parked cannon, questing for the horseman they had glimpsed for a moment.

Out of the red imperial tents came women slaves who gathered together and stared at a fat figure prone on the earth, hands clasped about a dagger-hilt and wide eyes staring up into the moon with a kind of helpless surprise.

III

Khlit was making his morning meal at the ford in the Jhilam caravan-trail. The sky overhead had changed from gray to blue and the stars had paled before a rush of crimson into the eastern sky.

The wanderer had drawn rice-cakes and portions of dried mutton from his saddlebags and was eating hungrily, cutting the food with his dagger. He was alone at the ford. Fresh hoof-prints showed on the farther bank. But here two trails crossed and the marks could not be traced beyond the stream edge.

Khlit eyed the stream meditatively. Often he frowned. He had much to think about.

From the Cossack steppe he had journeyed to the Tatar plains, where he had found men to his liking—indeed of his own blood. He had liked the life on the open steppe where men lived on horseback and there were no cities.

Here matters were different. Wherever Jahangir the Mogul went, there was a city of tents. And a myriad courtiers, ambassadors from outlying tribes, trade cities and kingdoms.

Khlit had been interested at first in the splendor of the palaces and the temples of the Land of the Five Rivers (The Punjab). He had never seen such an array of soldiery assembled in one place. The very numbers oppressed him. Here was luxury, food in plenty. Here beat the pulse of the southern Asiatic world.

He had been favored with gifts at first—slaves, which he gambled away, and horses, which he liked and kept. But since the affray

with the guards of the seraglio had been ignored although he might
still claim the favor of Jahangir in memory of the deed that had
brought the wanderer to Hindustan.

The heat of the plain had annoyed him and he was glad when
the Mogul's court moved to the cool hills of Kashmir. And Khlit had
been thinking. He saw unending caravans bear wealth to the Mogul;
but he had noticed that Jahangir drained the nobles of their wealth
to pay his enormous army.

He had seen a fortunate Rájput chief raised at a word to the rank
of two thousand horse; yet another of the same clan had been
beheaded as promptly for a whispered word against the Mohammedans. He had listened while emissaries from Khorassan called Jahangir monarch of the world to his face and debated among themselves
whether they should shake off the Mogul's yoke and throw their
fortunes with the Persians.

Curiously he had noted that Jahangir and his followers uttered
their prayers even while drunk, yet massacred the garrison of a hill
town with bland treachery when inviolability had been promised.

Khlit perceived the greatness of the empire of Hindustan, and
marveled. Yet these hive-like human beings were not of his race. And
he was weary of the silken luxury which enwrapped the camp.

The high civilization of the court held no interest for him. Khlit
had seen too much of the evil ambition of the priests—for the most
part—the astrologers and the physicians. With very few exceptions
each man had his price.

These matters and others Khlit considered while the light grew
in the east and he listened to the approach of a large body of horsemen. They came swiftly, but Khlit was not disturbed. He was not
accustomed to yielding his place at the approach of strangers. Furthermore he had a purpose in staying where he was.

The leaders of the cavalcade swept up to the ford and reined in
with a shout.

"Ho, graybeard!" one cried. "Saw you a horseman with a woman
in his arms pass this way?"

Others appeared—cavalry of the imperial guard, eunuchs, archers
and one or two ameers of rank gorgeously clad and profane in their
anger and haste.

"Speak, dullard!" exclaimed another. "A woman has been stolen from the exalted seraglio. Men will die for this. Saw you the traitorous rider?"

Khlit surveyed them in silence. He had watched while Rao Singh with Kera and Ahmad Rumi, mounted behind Cheker Ghar, had taken the upper turn to the hills. Both horses—they had availed themselves of the animal belonging to the slain Persian master of horse—had been carrying double and they had but a brief start.

If the pursuers were set on their tracks at once they must be overhauled. But Khlit was not minded that this should happen. His talk with Ahmad Rumi had not been in vain. Moreover, he had been pleased with the youthful Rao Singh.

"How should I know?" he growled. "I am no stealer of women."

The ranking ameer glanced anxiously at the divided trails and gnawed his lip. He had been commander of the guard when Kera escaped.

"Perchance this will quicken your memory, warrior," he cried, fingering a gold mohar.

Khlit's eyes gleamed shrewdly under their shaggy brows.

"Aye, that is well spoken," he responded. "A rider with a woman across his knees passed this way and took the lower turn."

He pointed to where the cross-trail led into the thickets, away from the path to the hills where Rao Singh had gone.

The ameer who was leader of the party was about to sign for an advance after tossing Khlit the coin when a small, dun Arab pushed in front of him and a high voice not unlike a woman's addressed him.

"Lord, I, all unworthy, have a word for your ear."

Khlit looked up swiftly, sensing a new development. He saw a withered, bent frame of a man with a singularly light complexion and sharp eyes. He wore a skull-cap, and his frail figure was enveloped in a white cloak, a garment of rich texture, with bracelets of pearls at the wrists.

"Speak, Bember Hakim—waste no words."

The ameer glanced at the newcomer half-scornfully.

"Lord, I spake with one who was sentry at the foot of this path. He said that when the moon was very bright there came two who stood on the hill above him and looked toward the camp. One wore the turban of an Afghan, the other was yonder graybeard.

"They watched, lord. For what? Perchance for the coming of one in haste from the camp."

The ameer glanced at Khlit, fingering his sword. The wanderer met his gaze squarely.

"This one remained at the ford," continued Bember Hakim shrewdly. "Wherefore if not to turn us aside from the fleeing rider? It is written that the evil-doers shall trip in their own snare. Why should the man we seek take the lower turn, which leads but to villages? Nay, we shall find him riding into the hills——"

"By the beard of the Prophet!"

The ameer's dark face twisted in a snarl. He signed to his men.

"Seize me this traitor and squeeze his gullet until blood or the truth come from his lips."

Khlit saw that others rode past him to the farther side of the ford to hem him in. His horse stood behind him, but he was surrounded save for the stream.

He did not move as two warriors approached; looking up instead at Bember Hakim.

"You be men of the Mogul's," he said slowly. "Know you Jahangir has promised me safeguard? Aye, his safeguard to Khlit. I have his oath."

The soldiers hesitated, but the ameer scanned Khlit sharply and bared his teeth in a grim smile.

"A favorite of Jahangir? In common garments? Nay, you be no Moslem."

"Nevertheless it is the truth. I give you warning."

"A woman has been taken from the imperial seraglio," broke in the Arab. "This man is a *caphar,* an unbeliever, by dress and speech. What matters a safeguard if he be a traitor?"

Khlit rose and faced the two.

"Take me then to Jahangir," he ventured. "He will remember the one who befriended Nur-jahan."

"Spawn of an unbeliever!"

The ameer gripped his sword.

"Nay, I waste not words with such. Speak us the truth and you may save your life. Jahangir's memory is short."

"I have spoken."

Khlit noted that the ring of men pressed closer, and he saw a smile creep upon the thin face of the *hakim.* In a calmer mood perhaps the horsemen would not have dealt so harshly with him; yet it was a vital matter—since favor at court rested with the outcome—that they should find Kera and Rao Singh. Moreover the nobles of Jahangir were scarcely tolerant.

"We waste time!"

The ameer reined his horse forward.

"Bind me this wretch——"

"And the word of Jahangir?"

"Is a thing that is past. If you have aided the misdeed this night you will be given to the elephants to trample——"

Khlit had been thinking while he talked. In fact he had played with words while he considered the situation. To his ability to weigh chances and to act swiftly in the face of danger he owed his long life.

If the ameer's men had realized the character of the wanderer they would not have given him the chance to mount his horse. Khlit's enemies frequently underestimated his strength, and still more frequently his intelligence.

"Stay!"

Khlit grasped the reins of the leader's horse, forcing the beast back on its haunches.

"Behold what lies underfoot!"

Before this the newcomers had not observed the body in the deep pool where the current had washed it. The body of the Persian. They were startled, and their eyes were drawn to it for a brief second.

Time enough for Khlit to spring bodily into the saddle of his horse and plunge spurs into flank. Perfect rider as he was, trained in the Cossack school, it was no difficult feat to avoid the other horses and gallop up the bed of the stream.

A pistol echoed behind him. He bent low, avoiding the sweep of the branches overhead. The others were after him at once. But his course had surprized them, and the footing was of the poorest.

Khlit had chosen his present horse with care, and by keeping well in to the bank he drew ahead of his pursuers, who were on spent beasts. Their pistol-shots went wide.

Only one kept close to him. After an interval Khlit looked behind.

He saw the little Arab galloping through the brush by the stream, and he put spurs again to the black horse.

The stream turned into an open glade. Once this was passed, and the thicket on the farther side, Khlit reined in sharply. He drew a pistol from his belt and awaited the approach of the *hakim,* satisfied that the others had been left in the rear.

The Arab came into view and the rider slowed to a walk as he neared the Cossack. He seemed to be unarmed, wherefore Khlit did not fire his weapon but waited alertly.

The little man in the cloak surveyed him shrewdly and held up an open hand.

"Peace!" he cried.

He sighed, glancing back the way he had come.

"*Aie*—you can slay me if you will. By the holy names of Allah, I am a doomed man."

He faced Khlit with the calm of a fatalist and smiled. The Cossack lowered his weapon, frowning.

"By the delay," explained Bember Hakim, "the rider and the maiden will win free, and you also are safe—although you had best ride farther. But I am doomed."

"Wherefore?"

"Eh—you know not the Mogul. The girl is lost. And I was the physician, chosen last night to minister to the ills of the women. By the will of Allah I spoke blindfolded with Kera of Kargan. This will come to the ears of Jahangir, and I——"

He drew a lean finger across his throat and sighed.

"*Caphar,*" he added reflectively, "I would have accomplished your death. That is a thing like to writing on the sand when the wind has passed. Will you grant me the hand of friendship? We be both branded men."

Khlit surveyed him with some surprise. Verily Bember Hakim was a strange philosopher. Then he laughed. The offer appealed to his fancy.

"Come then, if you will," he said gruffly and wheeled his horse into the brush.

The physician trotted after moodily on his small horse.

Thus did Khlit leave the camp of the Mogul and lose the favor of Jahangir. But as he put the miles between himself and the imperial pavilions his contentment grew, so that he laughed. Whereupon Bember Hakim looked at him curiously, not knowing Khlit was glad to be his own master again with a horse between his knees and open spaces ahead.

IV

In the lake waters glimmer the snow-crests of the mountain peaks. In a mirror a woman looks upon her beauty and smiles.

Within a mirage over the desert are caravans that leave no trace, and wells that are barren of water.

But how shall we see the faces of the gods?

Hindu saying.

The Wular lake was very old, older than the floating island and older than the pillared halls of Jhilam. Older than the first myths of the Hindus—than the ancient story of the *Ramayana*.

It was high in the mountains north of the pasture-land of Kashmir. Yet it was below the Summer snow-line—low enough in altitude to escape freezing in Winter. It was a sheet of turquoise-blue water fed by cascades descending from the snow-line.

The southern end of the lake was occupied by the castle of Jhilam with its gardens and the native village. At this point of the lake was the floating island on which Shaista Mirza had built his pleasure pavilion. Around Jhilam were the rice-fields, the beehives—famous in Kashmir—and the fruit-groves that had once belonged to the natives and now were the property of the Persian lord.

At the northern tip of the Wular rose the mountains which formed the foot-hills of the Himalayas—pine-clad and rocky, yet richly verdant. Of late years many of the Hindus of the Jhilam village, as told by Ahmad Rumi, had forsaken their huts to flee from the ruinous taxes of their overlord and to take refuge in the pine forest where game was moderately plentiful.

So it happened that the village of Jhilam came to be overrun by slaves of the Persian and in the castle proper were only adherents of Shaista Mirza—soldiers, Khorassanis, a few Pathans, Hazaras and the Persians. And as Jhilam was the fortress of northern Kashmir all the province from the lowlands to the boundary of Kargan Khan's territory had come under the Persian's sway.

It was a clear morning in early Winter with a hint of snow in the air when a man in armor on an exhausted horse rode up the avenue of aspens through the gardens and dismounted hastily at the castle gate.

He was recognized by the guards and passed into the main hall by a gigantic Turk, Jaffar, sword-bearer of Shaista Mirza.

"The master!" cried the rider. "The master! I bear ill news."

Jaffar grunted as he parted the satin hangings over the portal of Shaista Mirza. The soldier, dust-stained and streaked with sweat, prostrated himself.

"Lord," he cried, "may your shadow ever be over us. Lord, I bring word from the Jhilam road."

Jaffar eyed him eagerly, but Shaista Mirza did not look up from his study of the chess-board. He sat on his heels on the tiled floor by the ivory chessmen—a lean man, wasted by illness, pock-marked and pallid with the expressionless gaze that is sometimes seen in animals.

Shaista Mirza was neither Moslem nor sun-worshiper. Some said that he was a survivor of the *Refik*, a follower of the Assassins, the secret order that had held power in northern Persia during the twelfth century. Shaista Mirza never admitted this, and those who knew him best—among them the astrologer Nureddin—said that the Mirza liked the title of Assassin yet did not belong to the order.

He was a man who chose to inspire fear among his followers and his enemies. He did this in a number of ways—availing himself sometimes of the arts of Nureddin, who was skilled in the magic of the time, and maintaining a network of spies among the Kashmir hills as well as in the Mogul court. He had chosen Jaffar with this end in view, and Jaffar's congenital cruelty fitted well with the needs of his master.

Such was Shaista Mirza's shrewdness that Jahangir saw fit to conciliate the Persian, fearing him more than a little and allowing him to accomplish his own ends in Kashmir. This was what the Mirza sought, and he sent the Mogul a small yearly tribute from the rich fief of Jhilam.

Beside the chess-board burned a brazier, tended by Nureddin, giving out the scent of sandal-paste and aloes. The Persian's gaze shifted from the mimic warriors of the board to the smoke of the brazier—a fixed, cold stare that resembled the unblinking scrutiny of a snake.

Beyond the brazier stood a small mirror, and in this mirror Shaista Mirza could watch the prostrate soldier.

"You have no weapon," he said slowly, and the man squirmed, for the Mirza—so he thought—had not glanced at him.

How then was he to know that of which he spoke?

"*Akh!*" he cried. "Lord of Exalted Mercy and River of Forgiveness, my sword was taken from me by a demon on a black horse. Verily it was a demon, for it slew Bairam with one stroke and my comrade with another. In the time it takes to draw breath it slew the twain. Verily it was a demon."

Jaffar grunted at this, and Nureddin glanced up fleetingly. The astrologer was a handsome man, ruddy of cheeks, with black beard curled and scented—a man of manifest vitality. Some who stood in awe of Shaista Mirza whispered that the wasted master of Jhilam sucked blood and strength from the strong body of Nureddin.

Shaista Mirza did not look up, but toyed with the links of a gold chain about his lean throat.

"*Akh,*" protested the soldier volubly, "the demon warrior flung a black cloak of darkness about him—and how was I to see where to strike? By the ashes of death, I struck, and fire darted from the nostrils of the black horse and turned the blade, which fell into the stream."

Jaffar scowled, but the expression of the pale Persian did not change.

"Verily—" the soldier plucked courage from the silence—"a troop of accursed spirits were abroad in the night. At one stroke was Bairam slain—his head hanging to his shoulder by the windpipe. I rode without stopping for drink or meat until I should bear the news to my lord."

Shaista Mirza signed to the Turk.

"This man thirsts," he whispered. "See that he has drink. Wine he may not drink because of his faith, but water; ah, water, Jaffar. Bind a rope about his ankles and tie the rope to a branch of a tree overhanging the lake in the pear-garden. Thus may his head hang in the water, and he will drink—much."

A wail from the suppliant was interrupted by the sword-bearer, who jerked the soldier to his haunches. Jaffar had learned to obey Shaista Mirza swiftly—hence he was alive and in favor.

Fear lent the soldier brief courage.

"Lord," he cried, "Lord of Rudbar—I have further news. Grant me release from this punishment and you shall hear it."

Shaista Mirza lifted an ivory castle delicately from the board and set it down on another square.

"Wretched one," he said softly, "you and the twain were sent to slay me and the stripling Rao Singh. Yet did you attack another man. The twain have atoned for their mistake. Shall you fare better?"

"Lord, I have rare news."

The Persian glanced at him fleetingly and the man shivered.

"Speak!"

"Lord, will your exalted mercy pledge me life——"

"Speak!"

"Give tongue, dog."

Jaffar struck his prisoner with a heavy fist.

"My lord of Jhilam loves not to wait."

"This is the word, master," the man exclaimed, his eyes rolling from one to another of the group in feverish supplication. "In the third watch of last night Rao Singh did seize the woman Kera of Kargan from the imperial tents and bear her away."

Nureddin sucked in his breath with sudden interest and was silent, watching his master.

"He escaped?" demanded Shaista Mirza.

"Aye, lord."

"How heard you this?"

"From certain eunuchs who rode in pursuit."

"Whither went Rao Singh?"

"North into the hills, they knew not where."

"How large a following?"

"Lord, they knew not. A wild figure clung to his stirrup. Perhaps others went also. Allah alone knows the truth."

"Darkness doubles numbers—if they be enemies," smiled Nureddin, speaking his limpid mother-tongue. "Also—creates demons, my lord."

Shaista Mirza turned to Jaffar.

"Strip this scion of purgatory and bind him upon an ass with his face to the tail. Then summon the archers to feather him thick as a falcon is feathered with their shafts. Let the body be led through the village as a warning."

"*Akh!* My life was pledged——"

"Fool and nameless one," pointed out Nureddin coolly, "Shaista Mirza did but grant your prayer that the punishment be altered."

When Jaffar and his prisoner had gone—the man silent with the hopelessness of the fatalist—Nureddin lowered his voice.

"'Tis well, my lord. Wisdom teaches that a broken arrow should not be kept in the quiver. Rao Singh has scant friends, yet it were not well to have knowledge of your attempt on his life get abroad."

Shaista Mirza made no reply, whereupon Nureddin glanced at him appraisingly and bent over the chess-board.

Not until the last move had been made and the Mirza's king had been mated beyond all doubt—it was significant of the relations between the two men that the Persian would have flown into a rage had Nureddin not played his utmost, oblivious of the result—that Shaista Mirza leaned back on his cushions and allowed his mind to wander from the game.

"Aye," he mused, "the stripling lacks favor at Jahangir's court. Eh, at one stroke he has flown from his gilded cage and taken a mate. What think you of that?"

Nureddin smiled, stroking his beard.

"Never, my lord," he responded slowly, "will you occupy Jhilam in peace until the last of the brood of Sattar Singh has been laid in death. And now Kera of Kargan is one of the brood.

"The blood of youth is traitor to its own cause, lord. Rao Singh has stepped to the brink of a deadly cliff, whence by good fortune and some small arts of ours he shall doubtless tumble to his death."

Shaista Mirza was silent for a space. Then:

"Jahangir will give much for his punishment. Yet the Mogul departs with his following for the plains of Hindustan. It is my thought that Rao Singh will escape capture—by the Mogul's men."

Nureddin bowed assent, thrusting his hands—now that the game was ended—in his wide sleeves, as etiquette prescribed.

"The essence of truth, my lord. Yet perchance he will not escape —us."

Shaista Mirza tapped his chain meditatively.

"Nor will Kera of Kargan. Verily the fool has dug a pit in which he shall be caught. Know you Kargan Khan?"

"Aye, being sharer of the wisdom of the Lord of Rudbar. A brainless hill chief blind in one eye because of a spear-thrust and likewise blind in his brain. Kin to his own clumsy yaks, my lord, he has room but for one thought at a time."

"And that thought?"

"To rend the man who has carried off his child. Kargan has love for his daughter."

Shaista Mirza made no response. Love was a feeling he had never possessed. Wasting sickness had stripped him of vitality, leaving a burning sense of injury—a craving to overmaster the happiness and the lives of others. Ambition and cruelty were the twin forces that gripped the Persian's keen brain.

Yet he was shrewd enough to make allowance for such feelings—in others. He had studied the human emotions, aided by Nureddin's knowledge of the sciences, of Avicenna's Law, and Galen's, and even Aristotle.

"Nureddin, you boast the foreknowledge of the stars. Can you answer me this: Where will a fox flee when pursued?"

"Nay," smiled the astrologer, "no divination is needed to speak you that. To his burrow."

"And when the goshawk mates, where will you find the female bird?"

"In the eyrie of her mate."

"Aye, Nureddin. Now while the heat of love, rising from the center of life in the human body, which is the stomach——"

"Nay; the kidneys." This was a debated point between the two.

"Nay; the Frankish philosophers claim the heart, yet the wisdom of Arabia, allied to the lore of Avicenna, proclaims it the stomach. The heat of love dulls the keenness of the brain. Yet Aristotle, who is the master of learning, proves by experiment that when animals mate the male is rendered doubly alert and jealous of danger. So with human beings, Nureddin—for we are naught but higher beasts——"

"The Buddhist priests claim we are animals reincarnate——"

"Then Kargan is a buffalo reborn. Yet what I would say is this: Rao Singh will be thrice as wary now as heretofore, on behalf of Kera, whom he has taken to himself. Therefore he will be crafty in selecting a retreat. Yet his instincts will lead him to flee near his homeland."

Nureddin raised his brows.

"Jhilam?"

"Not near the castle. That were madness. Or supreme cleverness, such as——"

"Only Shaista Mirza possesses."

"Nay, but near to Jhilam are barren hills."

"Aye, lord; north of the lake."

"Yet he will not ride to the country of Kargan Khan. So perchance Rao Singh may be found north of the lake. Send riders out to overcast the countryside."

Shaista Mirza stretched back on his cushions, his eyes closed. Frequently he was in bodily pain bred of his disease.

"Send a messenger to the Mogul saying that by his favor I, Shaista Mirza, will hunt down the lawless defiler of the seraglio."

"And Kargan Khan?"

The Persian opened his eyes, and their stare was baneful.

"Nureddin, I have a thought that mighty omens are foreboding events in my favor. I asked for your wisdom, gleaned from the stars. Are the coming days favorable to me? Is my star ascendant?"

There was genuine anxiety in his voice. Like many men of genius Shaista Mirza trusted much in the potent element of destiny. Nureddin considered.

"The season of Taurus is past, lord," he responded. "Yet the days of Capricorn, of the Goat, are auspicious. Aye, your birth-star is high. Great events may be forthcoming."

"Then," cried Shaista Mirza, "we will deal with Kargan Khan—not now but later. First we will find Rao Singh."

V

It was cold among the deodars midway up the long slope that led to the Himalaya peaks. Animals here bore a thicker coat than those south of the Wular lake.

Yet in the Wular *davan*—valley—towered precipices, and in the base of these were caves. It was at the upper end of the *davan* where the gorge terminated in a rock-tangle that Ahmad Rumi had his hut, and the hut was but cedar slabs placed across the entrance of a cavern with skins of mountain sheep within to lie upon, and a cleft in the rock overhead to carry off the smoke from the fire.

Not that Ahmad Rumi could cut himself firewood. The Kashmiris of the forest saw to that—and likewise brought fish at intervals. But now in the first moon of the early Winter of the year 1609 they brought also smoke-cured mutton and goat's milk.

For instead of one there were now four in the Wular *davan*. And the Kashmiris ran from a great distance a few at a time to look upon the face of the son of Sattar Singh and his bride.

They were small squat men in ragged gray woolen tunics and round hats, and their women in shawls. They came a few at a time in spite of the cold. They came from their mountain nests, from the caverns by the lake and from the valleys as far distant as the border of Baramula, which was the land of Kargan Khan and his Kirghiz.

In fact many of them were Kirghiz—those that boasted ponies and felt *yurts*, and were of the breed of the northern steppe. And so it happened that Kera of Kargan, who was the mate of Rao Singh, felt no terror at sight of the ragged groups, for they were like to her own people the Kirghiz, whom she remembered from her child-days.

They asked no gifts from Rao Singh, knowing the tale of his misfortune—how he had been kept as a prisoner at the Mogul's camp. In that Winter the verdant land of Jhilam was rife with poverty, arisen from the tithes of Shaista Mirza, and few but the *aksakals* of the Kirghiz *yurts* possessed two horses.

It was a strange court that Rao Singh held. His bride, daughter of a Kha Khan and a beauty among the women of the Mogul, had no better quarters than the hut of Ahmad Rumi, which had been given up to her and her lord. She lacked the jewels and the perfumes bestowed upon their women by the southern ameers.

Her lord owned but two horses, and only one of these better than the average—and his sword. He had no wealth, for he had been shown no favors by Jahangir—consequently none by the nobles of the empire, to whom Jahangir's disfavor was a potent ban.

Yet Kera of Kargan did not complain. She was happy in Rao Singh. Kera was barely at the verge of womanhood—a shy, dark-faced girl with splendid black hair that matched her eyes and a free spirit bred of her early life on the steppe. She was round of arms, with strength in her youthful limbs. This was well, since a woman of the hotter climate, accustomed to the luxuries of Hindustan, could not have survived the days in the hills.

She sang to herself and bound her silver ornaments in her long hair by aid of the mirror of the spring near the cavern. This she did to make herself fair in the sight of Rao Singh, who was her lord.

"Eh, my lord," she had said, "may it not be that we can ride to the encampment of Kargan? It would be well that we should do this, for evil tales will be whispered to him and he will hear naught that is good of you if I am not the messenger. Yet great is his love for me, and he will take heed when I speak."

"Nay; you are mine, no longer Kargan's," Rao Singh had replied fiercely.

He did not add that patrols of horsemen had been seen near the lake, nor that the Kashmiris had reported search being made for the two. It would have been courting danger to venture from the valley. Here the forest men kept guard vigilantly, and they were reasonably safe. Moreover the chance of discovery was lessened if they stayed in one spot.

"Who shall safeguard you, Light of my World," whispered Rao Singh, his dark eyes aflame with the beauty of the girl, "but me?"

Kera sighed.

"We have many enemies, my lord. I have a woman's thought and wish that we could seek the Baramula and the might of Kargan. He has many horsemen—and his anger is quick. Who can pen the waters when the dam has burst? Let me speak with him and win his pride to our favor?"

"Nay," said Rao Singh again, "will the Khan of Baramula look with favor on one who is an outcast? The time will come—so says the wise Ahmad Rumi—when I shall ride to meet Kargan with horsemen at my back as one chief to another."

So it happened that the pride of the youth kept Kera from sending a messenger to the Kirghiz. In this he blundered perhaps. If Kera had had her way it might have altered the events that came to pass in Jhilam during the space of that moon.

Kera was content to obey her lover. Cheker Ghar, who liked the cold little, still bestirred himself to amuse her—saying naught of his disappointment at the poor fortunes of Rao Singh.

"Ho, Flower of the Hills," he would cry, "when had a woman such rare followers? Here is Ahmad Rumi, who is councilor of owl-like wisdom and can repeat his Moslem proverbs and legends with the

art of one who is schooled in chronicles and books. And I, my lady
—behold the chosen buffoon of the imperial bazaar!"

He waved his lean hand toward his precious leopard-skin and
salaamed.

"Aye, even unworthy I—unworthy in the fragrant splendor of your
beauty—yet a paladin among conjurers, buffoon and mimic without
a peer——"

Whereupon he gathered his cloak about his scant form and strode
about in the semblance of an ameer until Kera clapped her hands
in delight.

"Behold," he chattered, rejoiced to see her merriment, "a eunuch
of the royal seraglio."

He puffed out his dark cheeks and bound his voluminous turban
in the Turk fashion and clutched a stick, which he bore before him
like a scimitar, scaling his voice to the shrill pitch of one of those
unfortunate creatures. Rao Singh, even, smiled at his performance,
and Ahmad Rumi turned his sightless eyes toward the mimic in
gentle approval.

Secretly Cheker Ghar turned up his nose at association with the
blind Moslem; yet he spoke not of this dislike, nor of the many
things he did in defiance of the dictates of his caste for the sport of
Kera of Kargan.

"If," ventured Rao Singh, "that was the likeness of him you named
Bara you need not fear he will call you to account. I left my knife in
the chief eunuch's ribs."

"Ho, verily?"

Cheker Ghar smiled broadly.

"Then my heart is light, for the Purified One was such but in
name, and he was like to a thriced-defiled swine that has eaten of
filth."

The conjurer had an uncanny knack at mimicry. So great was his
skill that he frequently confounded Ahmad Rumi, who thought that
Rao Singh or another addressed him when Cheker Ghar spoke.

With others than the light-hearted Kera he took his profession
with grave seriousness. He was at such times not so much the buffoon as the Hindu master of magic. Only for her would he powder

his face white and make idle sport. Cheker Ghar loved her as a
dog loves its mistress, and this love was to bear fruit in due course.

Often he would sit squatted opposite the fire from the legend-
teller while Kera and Rao were together on the hillside and their
Kashmiri followers were on watch.

"Harken, Son of the Owl," Cheker Ghar whispered to the Moslem, "and tell me what is this you hear——"

A plaintive cry floated through the cavern, coming apparently
from the cleft overhead.

"It is *kulan,* the wild ass, calling."

The cry changed to a grunting, snapping torrent of sound, echoing
from a corner of the cave.

"The wild pig of the jungle!" muttered the blind man. *"Bismillah*
—does such an animal of filth approach?"

"Nay," said the mimic seriously; "have no fear; I will guard you
from defilement."

He bellowed suddenly, hoarsely.

"The mountain buffalo, the yak, calling to its mates, Cheker
Ghar."

A shrill, grunting moan issued from the Hindu in such a fashion
as to appear as from a distance. Ahmad Rumi lifted his white head.

"A camel complains under its load as the pack is bound on by
the camel man."

"Aye," assented Cheker Ghar, pleased. "Yet there is no yak, and
no camel in the valley. Is it not magic then?"

"There is no magic but the will of Allah."

And so the days passed under the cloud of danger with scant food
and comforts until Bember Hakim found his way to the hut; and
with him came Khlit.

The wanderer entered quietly into the life of the valley, asking
nothing from Rao Singh and providing his own meat, which he obtained in ways best known to himself.

He constructed a shelter of sheepskins not far from the cavern.
Khlit disliked to live under a roof, and so pitched his *yurt* in a pine
grove where his horse could be picketed.

Ahmad Rumi removed his prayer-carpet and skins to the *yurt,* where he fell to talking much with Khlit. The life suited the Cossack, and the *davan* provided good concealment from the riders who searched the hills.

The Kashmiris had reported that the Mogul cavalry were no longer questing for Rao Singh; but others kept up the pursuit. So well chosen was the hiding-place in the valley that it had not been noticed. The rock walls were sheer on one side, and on the other was dense forest. Nothing was to be seen from the lake side, and from the overhanging peaks the *davan* appeared nothing more than a break in the forest.

By now the searchers were striking farther afield to the north, and Rao Singh felt that they had escaped discovery. He himself began to make excursions to the haunts of the Kashmiris at the urging of Ahmad Rumi, who felt that the coming of Rao Singh would work a miracle of some kind and aid the suffering peasants of Jhilam.

"Verily," he assured Khlit, "is he not the son of Sattar Singh, who extended the hand of mercy to the wound of my suffering?"

"He is a man half-grown," grunted Khlit, "who loves a woman. What skill has he in warfare?"

"Eh, he may adorn the pearl of love with the diamond of mercy," said the legend-teller wistfully. "Allah grant I may see him Lord of Jhilam. I have prayed much, but the span of my life draws to an end."

He showed the Cossack a white garment wrapped beneath his clean tunic. It was a winding-sheet.

Except with Ahmad Rumi Khlit talked little. Rao Singh and Kera were wrapped up in each other, and Cheker Ghar in Kera. Khlit from long habit made no advances and kept to himself.

Rao Singh and his small colony entertained no distrust of the wanderer, for the reason that Khlit was an outcast such as they. They had heard from the Kashmiris that he was banned by the Mogul, and they knew that, having slain by chance two men of Shaista Mirza's, he could claim no alliance with the Persian.

As for Bember Hakim he occupied himself in collecting herbs, a task which took him away from the valley for long intervals, and otherwise accepted his hard lot with characteristic philosophy.

"Now, my lady," quoth Cheker Ghar, squatting at the feet of Kera, "we have a physician of the court. What lack we now?"

He rose and began to move around, limping after the manner of

Bember Hakim and uttering pseudo-learned remarks on the Arabic sciences until he saw her smile.

"Naught save the protection of Kargan Khan," she said, leaning her smooth chin on her arms. "Would I might send Khlit to him with word from me!"

"The rider of the black horse performs errands for no one, O Flower of the Hills. His look fills me with a fear. It is like a wolf, looking into the distance."

He shook his turbaned head moodily.

"A wolf—aye, for he is not one of us. And when did a wolf do a kindness to others?"

He sighed.

"As for Kargan Khan, methinks the Kirghiz would welcome you to his *yurt*, my lady, but we others would have our blood let from our veins by his sharp sword."

Now it happened that it was night when Cheker Ghar said this, and they were seated by the fire in the cavern, Rao Singh being absent on one of his rides.

The hour grew late, and Kera, wearied with the tricks of the conjurer and becoming anxious for her lover, left the fire and sought the sheep path by which Rao Singh would ride back to the *davan*.

She walked swiftly for the night was cold and she knew the way leading to a rock—a favorite resting-place of their guards—by the trail. But recently the Kashmiris had given over their vigil as the pursuing bands had not visited the vicinity.

Kera wrapped her sheepskin *khalat* about her slender shoulders and tripped along in her light leather boots. Unlike the women she had lived with in Hindustan, the solitudes of the forest held no fear for her. She passed between giant pine-trunks and slipped around trailing junipers. A scanty fall of snow had rendered it easy to follow the trail, outlining the bulk of tree and rock.

She seated herself on the stone she sought, drawing up her knees under her chin for warmth. Then she lifted her head alertly. She had heard a heavy tread along the sheep path. Her pulse quickened at the sound.

She had been moody that night, perhaps because of the absence of Rao Singh, perhaps because of the tales of Ahmad, who had been depressed in spirit. The legend-teller had said that he had a premonition of danger.

Kera stared at the dark form that paced toward her, coming from the valley. Opposite the rock it halted, and she heard Khlit's voice.

"Have you a fear, little girl?"

It was a deep voice without pretense of anything but gruffness. Kera sat up straight, her heart still beating swiftly.

"What seek you?"

Up to now she had felt more uncertainty than pleasure at Khlit's presence. The Cossack was not one to impress women favorably. Yet Kera was not afraid of him. She watched—seeing him dimly—while he scanned the trail, then leaned against the rock with folded arms, his head on a level with her own.

"I seek that which is a thorn in the side of Rao Singh," he said slowly.

Kera hissed angrily.

"I? A thorn? Dolt! One without understanding!"

She fumbled in her girdle for the dagger that she carried; but Khlit did not move, nor did he look at her. He was watching where the pine-branches took shape slowly against the sky and the gleam of the many stars paled as the moonlight flooded the vast spaces of the air from a hidden quarter somewhere behind the hills.

The snow-summits were turning from dull gray to silver, and the shadows deepened. Shafts of silver shot through the branches, forming a tracery in the snow, outlining the sticks and rocks that had been invisible before.

"A thorn, Kera of Kargan. You are a woman and you love. See you not that Rao Singh is brooding?"

The girl considered this silently, peering at Khlit as if she tried to read his meaning in his face. She no longer felt disturbed at his presence.

"Aye, Khlit, my heart has told me that. Yet it is for me that Rao Singh has a foreboding."

"Ahmad Rumi has talked much. He is full of words. He has told me you left a silk couch in a velvet tent to be by the side of Rao Singh. Yonder hut is a poor shelter for a woman—they are like to birds who seek a soft nest. Is it not so?"

The Kirghiz girl laughed softly.

"Who does not like the touch of silk? Yet with Rao Singh lies my path and my heart. My pride is his strength; he is a mighty lord."

"Without a follower save for yonder mummers. Kera, would you ride back to the tents of the Mogul? Then your body would again lie in ease."

Again Kera laughed, resting her face sidewise on her arms, which were clasped over her knees.

"Ho, the fool is a mighty fool," she whispered softly. "He is blinder than the poor Moslem. He has the wisdom of the dullard yak. Aye, though Ahmad Rumi said that he had once been Khan of the Horde. Nay, Ahmad Rumi lied, for you, Khlit, are the one that is—" again her laugh echoed softly—"blind. More blind than the teller of legends."

She glanced up the trail hopefully at the sound of a falling twig, and sighed.

"Aye, Ahmad Rumi is like to one that sits in the dark; still in his spirit there is a lamp by whose rays he sees an assemblage wherever he looks. So he said, and I wondered. Now I understand that he has within him a vision, while you——"

She broke off in contempt. Other women of her race perhaps would have cursed Khlit, being angry. Kera however was gentle.

"Where Rao Singh goes I guide my horse," she added as he did not speak. "His smile opens my heart like a flower. Why should it be otherwise?"

Khlit was satisfied. He had thought to test the girl's feeling for the Hindu. He had done so crudely. But it did not occur to him to explain this to her. He was indifferent to what she might think of him.

He returned to the thought that had impelled him to follow her along the sheep path.

"Kera, the thorn of unrest is in the side of the son of Sattar Singh. He has seen the evil that is wrought upon his people. And he is angry. He knows not the path he should follow."

The Cossack spoke gruffly.

"Likewise his thoughts are bound up in a woman."

The girl made no response, and Khlit went on.

"What has the stripling learned of war? He can think of naught but to find the path to your hut and to lie with your arms about him.

Yet it is time he should mount and take up his sword. There be those who will follow."

"Nay."

Timidity—the shrinking of a woman who loves—gave Kera speech.

"Here he is safe. If he rode far the men of Shaista Mirza would hear of it."

"The time must come, little sparrow," growled Khlit, "when your lord will try sword-strokes with this same Mirza. It would be well were he to strike first."

"It may not be, baba-ji. Aie, how should that come to pass? The Persian is friend to Jahangir."

"Not so. The master of Jhilam—whatever name he bear—will be well treated by Jahangir. For Jhilam is a key to the hills. It lies too far to the north for the Mogul to muster his banners to attack it. So 'tis said, but I have a thought the Mogul fears to leave the Delhi court, and those who would plot against him, so far in his rear. So he must conciliate him who is lord of the fortress."

Out of his wisdom, hard-won in dealing with merciless foes, Khlit spoke. Out of her love for Rao Singh—blind love—the girl responded.

"Does a hunting-dog walk into the den of a lion?"

"Aye, when death awaits him without."

"No danger lies about the davan. The riders have drawn their reins from these hills."

Khlit moved angrily.

"It is not I who am blind, Kera. Hide of Satan, see you not that Rao Singh must slay Shaista Mirza, or the Persian will sprinkle the cub's blood on the snow of his native hills?"

Kera drew back with a shiver.

"Aie—it is cold! Nay, baba-ji, it is said you are wise in battle. The gods may have so willed. Yet it is but the space of a short day I have Rao Singh at my side."

"The time for sword-strokes has not yet come—he lacks followers —perchance time will bring Kargan's riders to his aid—then—" proudly—"shall I gird the belt of war on the twain. Ahmad Rumi has said that this would come to pass."

Khlit would have turned away angrily, not knowing that the words of the woman were to come true. Yet in a manner such as he had not conceived. Ahmad Rumi possessed something of the gift of prescience which is found at times in men of frugal life and intensity of thought.

"Stay!"

The girl touched his shoulder.

"Shaista Mirza has five hundred horsemen under Jaffar his sword-bearer. I pray the gods that he will fall in the dust of defeat."

"I have heard it said that you are a father of battles. Will you ride with Rao Singh against Shaista Mirza when it is his fate that this should come to pass?"

The Cossack shook off the girl's hand impatiently.

"When Rao Singh is—a man," he growled.

"My lord will be a great *ghazi* conqueror," she cried proudly. "He is one among a thousand, and like to his father. So Ahmad Rumi swore."

Her mood changed swiftly and she looked up beyond the trees where the stupendous mountain peaks of the Himalayas were coming into view under the silver torch of the moon like sentinels taking their posts. A breath of the cold air from the heights above brushed her long hair across her face and she pushed it back, gazing up with eyes dark as fate.

"*Aie*—on the high places of the hills live the gods. Who knows what is in the heart of the gods? Who can pierce the cloud that covers the will of the many gods?"

"I have prayed that they will be kind to Rao Singh! I have bent my head on the footstools of the gods, but they will not answer—save to send the wind and the cold."

She stretched up her slim arms.

"Why will the gods not answer? They hide their faces. Once I thought that they were near. *Aie*—they are cold, and I have naught to offer them. There is no mountain sheep to be slain for their pleasure. If they had an offering then they would turn the sun of their kindness on Rao Singh——"

She broke off in a moan that changed to a cry of delight as a rider came trotting down the trail on a spent horse, passing swiftly under the changing shadows of the moon.

Long after Rao Singh and Kera had gone, Khlit leaned against the rock, pondering many things. And in his thought Kera and her plaint had no place.

Khlit was not content with their position in the valley. The next day he went on a tour of inspection down to the lake. As usual, he went alone. The ride warmed his blood, and he sought for a fishing settlement that Ahmad Rumi had mentioned.

He was unable to locate it and wasted several hours, so it was late in the afternoon when he returned, hungry, for he had not eaten that noon. He was in high spirits, being naturally suited by a cold climate, and he had formed a plan which he intended to confide in Rao Singh.

The sun had set and Khlit had put his horse to a swift trot when he halted abruptly at sight of a body in the path. It was a peasant, an arrow projecting from his side. The man had been dead some time.

Khlit passed him by silently after observing that the trail of several horsemen led from the body away in the direction of the lake.

He was now in the *davan*, and scented smoke from the fire in the hut. He pushed his horse forward, rounded the turn by the spring and then set spurs to flank.

Prone on his face in the snow lay Cheker Ghar, his small limbs twisted strangely. Beside the body of the conjurer were the tracks of many horses. Yet the valley was silent, strangely so. Khlit uttered a gruff exclamation. He was now before the cave entrance. Here the horse-tracks ran, and among them the imprint of booted men. These footsteps led to the cavern.

The snow was gray with early twilight and trampled in spots as if men had struggled. And here and there were dark blotches of blood.

Just outside the door lay Ahmad Rumi, his white beard ominously stained. His turban was askew over one ear and the front of his tunic was slashed in a dozen places. From the pallor of his thin face Khlit knew that he was dead.

And beside the legend-teller was the form of Kera.

Khlit dismounted and stepped to the girl's side. Her dark hair flooded over the snow. She lay on her back, one hand clenched on her breast. And Khlit saw that her dark eyes were half-closed, the small, red mouth half-shut as if in a deep breath.

A scimitar stroke had slashed the base of her throat, severing the jugular vein. Her *khalat* was thrown back, revealing the grim message of death embodied in her torn and pierced chest:

Shaista Mirza has found those whom he sought.

Bember Hakim hobbled from the near-by thicket fearfully and stared at the form of the girl and the blind man.

The story written in the snow was plain for Khlit to read. A group of horsemen had ridden swiftly up the valley, encountering Cheker Ghar on the way, and had surrounded the hut entrance. Some had dismounted and dragged Ahmad Rumi from the cavern.

Kera seemed to have attempted to flee but had been struck down beside the blind man. Her slender dagger lay near her clenched hand.

Then the riders had passed out by the way they came in, leaving the valley desolate with its dead. Of the Hindu youth there was no sign.

"Eh," cried the Arab, "I was at the cliff summit—Allah be praised—and I saw Jaffar and his men ride hither. It was an evil deed——"

"Rao Singh?" questioned Khlit sharply.

"He ran from the cavern at the cry of Cheker Ghar. Two horsemen rode him down and his weapon broke upon the sword-hilt of one. Then many seized him and he was bound. Allah the merciful laid the shadow of a swoon upon the youth—for he was struck heavily on the head with the flat of a blade—and he saw not the fate of Kera. Eh, it was a deed of shame——"

"They took Rao Singh?"

Bember Hakim's shrewd, dark eyes searched Khlit's face.

"Aye. Jaffar cried that Shaista Mirza would take pleasure in the sight of his foe."

Khlit said no more but walked heavily to the cavern, glancing within at the embers of the fire. Ahmad Rumi's prayer-carpet was in its place by the coals, and there also lay the sack of the conjurer. The Cossack stared at them meditatively. Then he flung up his head. From down the valley came a mournful cry, rising and falling. It was like the cry of a madman. As it neared him Khlit could distinguish words:

"Wretched one, child of a thieving slave! O faithless and thrice accursed! O traitor to thy bread and salt! O snake that crawled from defiled flesh!"

It was a voice shrill, incoherent with rage. It panted as it cursed. And Khlit, striding from the cavern, swore in surprize.

Cheker Ghar was running up to the cavern, his puny fists clenched overhead. In the failing light his features showed distorted with anger. He was looking not at Khlit but a form that climbed the opposite rock wall, where a cleft offered foothold.

Khlit peered doubtfully at the climber and recognized Bember Hakim, who passed from view behind boulders on the summit as he watched.

"O unutterable filth! O blood-guilty, and dog without a name!"

Cheker Ghar shook his fists at the spot where the fugitive had vanished.

Abruptly he fell silent and sank on his knees by the body of Kera. He raised a twisted face to Khlit.

"Thus does one without honor reward the hand of mercy. I have seen what I have seen. The Turk and his men were led to this spot by Bember Hakim, accursed by the gods. Aye, for when the slaying was done he crept like a lizard from behind the warriors and smiled."

The conjurer moaned, touching the garment of his mistress.

"Bember Hakim set his foot upon the breast of the slain Flower of the Hills. For that I will follow the pursuit of blood. Aye, if the gods are kind I will tear open his breast and let his life run forth like water. Traitor to his salt——"

"Stay!" broke in Khlit gruffly. "Hide of the devil, how comes it that you live? With my eyes I saw you dead."

"A simple feat, lord, for one of my profession. When I saw the riders sweep up the valley I cried out. They would have seized me in their hands, but I slipped away. When they bore off Rao Singh I ran after, keeping to the forest, until my strength was spent.

"When I came hither again to bury my mistress I heard hoofs and lay like one dead. I saw not it was you until you had passed——"

"Then Bember Hakim was a man of Shaista Mirza?"

"Aye, yet we knew it not."

Khlit thought of the meeting at the ford when Bember Hakim had ridden after him. Seldom had Khlit been tricked by the art of another. But the physician was crafty and quick of wit and had told his lies readily.

Bember Hakim had guessed that the Cossack knew the hiding-place of Rao Singh. And his pretended search after herbs had afforded the opportunity to communicate with his master. Khlit had wondered when the other spoke the name how Bember Hakim had known it was Jaffar who led the riders.

Mechanically he seated himself by the fire and added fuel to the embers while Cheker Ghar labored at digging a grave with a Kashmiri tool.

Khlit had not eaten but he felt no desire for food. As was his habit when thinking deeply he drew his curved sword and laid it across his knees, stroking it absently. He felt no immediate fear that Jaffar and his party would return, for they must take Rao Singh to Jhilam. It was useless to follow Bember Hakim, who had gained a good start among the rocks, where there was little snow to reveal his course.

Several things puzzled Khlit. Why had Bember Hakim remained in the valley? Perhaps the Arab sought to trap him—believing all the others dead.

If so, why? Shaista Mirza would not want a living witness to the deed in the valley—one like Khlit who might bear the news to others.

Still Khlit was not satisfied with this reasoning. And it was not likely that Bember Hakim had remained to guard the bodies from the beasts.

Why had the Arab told Khlit the truth—in part—of what had happened? It seemed illogically cruel moreover that Kera should have been slain as she was. Why had she not been kept as a hostage? Surely by all accounts Kargan Khan was not lightly to be made an enemy of.

Khlit perceived that the Persian was a crafty foe. And his servants were like to him. In reasoning thus the Cossack came near to the truth. But he did not yet understand the masterly mind of Shaista Mirza.

He rose presently and aided Cheker Ghar in his toil. They worked in silence by the glow from the cavern mouth. Snow began to fall lightly. There was no moon.

When they had buried the two they rolled rocks to the spot to protect it from the prying claws of jackals. This done, Khlit touched the shoulder of the conjurer, who squatted by the mound.

"We can not stay," he pointed out. "By dawn Bember Hakim will bring others with him to search us out."

Cheker Ghar prostrated himself in the snow and clasped the boot of the Cossack.

"Lord," he whispered, "I heard it said in the Mogul's camp that you were crafty as the steppe fox and wise in war. Aid me to bear tidings of this thing to Kargan Khan over the Baramula trail. He will mount for vengeance, for Kera was his child."

"Nay," said Khlit.

Then, seeing the despair in the conjurer's dark face, he added: "Kargan Khan will not believe our tale. Shaista Mirza will send emissaries to the Kirghiz tribe. They would say that we lied."

He withdrew his foot from the other's grasp.

"Come, Cheker Ghar. Gird on your pack."

"*Aie,* lord! Whither should I go, if not in the pursuit of blood? I have sworn an oath to the gods——"

"And I, too, swear an oath, Cheker Ghar, though to another God." Khlit's voice deepened with involuntary feeling.

"This thing I swear: I will not turn my horse's head from the Wular lake until Shaista Mirza be laid in death."

VI

In the end, a lion's cub becomes a lion, although brought up a slave.

Hindu proverb.

The floating island of the Wular lake had been built by human hands. The stalks of the rushes that lined its banks had been cut and fastened into bundles by withes. Rows of these bundles had been laid one upon the other, and over all earth. Under the reed bundles were the trunks of trees.

So it was that a grass carpet covered the floating island. And gardens bloomed with jasmine and wild rose in the Summer—gardens built upon the roofs of the arbors that surrounded the kiosk. This kiosk had been fashioned by artisans from Persia.

Slender pillars of marble—delicate, so that the foundation of the pleasure island should not be overbalanced—supported a cedar roof, the under side of which was enameled. Between the pillars were ranged gilded squares of wood upon which were blazoned certain words of the poets, and paintings from the Persian annals.

The porticos were hung with brocaded silk. In the center chamber were placed brass braziers and incense pots that filled the air with a hot scent. Also they served to lessen the chill of the kiosk, for snow lay without on the bare rose-bushes; and Shaista Mirza had chosen to visit the pleasure island alone with Nureddin.

"By slitting the tongue, O learned interpreter of the stars," he confided, "men may be made voiceless, and by piercing the inner ear, deaf. Yet it is well sometimes to go where there are none to hear or to speak."

Satisfied that the slaves had stocked the braziers well, Shaista Mirza lay back on his cushions, eying the vista of the lake through the open portal. The Persian was habitually watchful, for he did not fail to credit others with his own crafty nature. By virtue of this he was still alive.

Moreover he was well content this day. He scanned the kneeling astrologer through half-closed eyes, and Nureddin did not return his gaze. The astrologer had partaken of bhang to stimulate his brain.

Shaista Mirza however did not use opium, hashish or bhang. He was sparing of wine, for he would say that a man was witless to soften his brain with false pleasures.

"Verily, Nureddin," he mused, "my star is ascendant. Rao Singh lies in chains in the tower of Jhilam. Aye, the lion cub has dragged his limbs to the den of his sire. And his mate is where she will work us no harm."

"It was fated."

"Nay, I willed it. What is fate, Nureddin, but the whine of the low-born? When I placed my yoke on the neck of the Kashmiris, behold, they cried that it was fate. Believing this thing, they will not attempt to rise against me."

"Men do not rebel, my lord, without a leader. And you have the body of him they call master."

"A stripling, Nureddin; a broken pine that leans to the wind; aye, a weakling who found his happiness in the arms of a woman."

He stirred the coals of a brazier with his dagger and drew his cloak about his shoulders. He loved better the sun of Persia than the winds of Kashmir.

"Sattar Singh was a man, Nureddin," the high, soft voice went on, "a man of strength whose greatest foes were his own passions. Rao Singh is a child. I feared his mother more than the boy. So it happened that she partook of hashish from Rudbar in Persia——"

He broke off with a wave of the thin hand. The astrologer started. He had not thought until then that Shaista Mirza had conceived the death of the woman. He was not sure whether this was the case or not. The Persian, a master of intrigue, liked to be mentioned as the author of violence in which he had no hand, and likewise was silent about many deeds of which he was the author.

"Power, Nureddin, is built upon a multitude of swords. Sword-arms can be bought. Wealth we must have, and it comes from the labor of the low-born who are the peasants of Jhilam, and now——"

"The Kashmiris mutter and shirk, feeling the breath of the wind of rebellion, my lord."

"Aye, due to sight of Rao Singh, who is of the accursed brood of Sattar Singh. Verily they shall not see him long."

He leaned closer to the astrologer.

"The Mogul must have his tribute—silver coins, while gold mohars accumulate in the treasury of Jhilam."

He threw back his head with a silent laugh that changed to a grimace of hate.

"Nureddin, how shall we deal with the lion cub of Jhilam?"

The courtier meditated, seeking a clue in the face of his master.

"'Tis plain, my lord, the scoundrel came to Jhilam to stir the fires of strife. Is he not then a rebel against the Mogul? Should he not be impaled upon a spear and left to rot where the kites and the low-born may find him?"

Shaista Mirza smiled grimly.

"The stars have not taught you—policy, Nureddin. Nay, is it well to mention the Kashmiris to Jahangir? He is their overlord—though he keeps his army south of the hills."

"Harken—Rao Singh has outraged the seraglio of the Mogul. So shall we send a rider in haste with news of his capture and a prayer that Jahangir name the manner of his punishment. Thus will we have the sanction of the Mogul for our action. And the Kashmiris shall know this."

The astrologer bent his head and touched the floor with the tips of his fingers as a sign of mute admiration.

"O wise reader of men! 'Tis an excellent plan. But if the punishment be not—death?"

"A simple matter. The boy will sicken and—follow the shadow of his mother. He mourns for Kera—the wanton. So shall he welcome the false contentment of hashish."

"And Kera of Kargan?"

Nureddin looked up curiously. He had not understood why Shaista Mirza had ordered Jaffar to slay the girl brutally.

Moreover Nureddin was a trifle anxious concerning Kargan Khan. If the truth were known the Kirghiz could muster a force of warriors who were hardy men, bold riders and fearless.

"Jaffar mutilated the maiden as I bade him," responded the Persian softly. "Already I have decided to send a messenger to the Kirghiz tribe, relating how Kera was laid in the dust of death by—a certain one. Bember Hakim, our worthy physician, saw the deed."

The astrologer glanced admiringly at his lord. Truly Shaista Mirza was a master of human fate.

"Then will come Kargan Khan to Jhilam like the breath of the storm-wind to see vengeance done. And when he comes he will look upon the body of the slayer of Kera. Because of this he will yield me the hand of friendship which he has withheld until now——"

Sudden suspicion flared in the cold eyes of the Mirza and an oath trembled on his lips as he stared through the portal. A fisher-boat had drawn in to the landing-stage of the floating island.

Then he saw that the figure in the boat was Bember Hakim, escorted by the mighty Jaffar.

The physician performed the triple salaam as he came into the presence of his master. As a mark of favor Shaista Mirza bade him be seated on the carpet. Bember Hakim's white cloak with the pearls was stained with mud and his thin face was blue with cold.

"Wherefore are you late?" demanded Nureddin sharply.

"Lord, and Monarch of Exalted Mercy," said the physician to Shaista Mirza, "as you bade me, I awaited the gray rider of the steppe. The words that you were divinely pleased to utter I repeated to him."

"What thinks the unbeliever?"

"Lord, one escaped death—a wretched Cheker Ghar, the buffoon. He upbraided me with treachery, and barely I escaped with my life. Yet even in the cold—and the snow fell—I crept back to the cavern from the rocks above and heard the Cossack vow——"

He hesitated in fear of the man who watched him silently.

"What, fool?"

"He vowed, lord, to seek vengeance for Kera, and to—slay the master of Jhilam."

Nureddin laughed, but Shaista Mirza moved no muscle of his face.

"It is well, Bember Hakim," he said, and the Arab knew he was pleased.

After a moment's thought he continued.

"Thus we have two alive who are our foes. Of Khlit of the Curved Saber I have heard some talk. A wandering Christian who was once khan of a northern clan. He dares not ride to the Mogul with his news, for he is under the ban of outcast."

He played with the golden chain at his throat, frowning slightly.

"'Tis unlikely that this aged unbeliever will seek Kargan Khan, yet—shall we leave no hole through which the fox could creep. Mount, Bember Hakim, this day, and ride by the Baramula caravan-trail to the Kirghiz tribe.

"Seek Kargan and say to him that if he would look upon the murderer of his daughter to come to the Wular *davan* with speed. Your tongue is shrewd, Hakim—speak him well, but haste."

He sighed and fell to stirring the brazier.

"Nureddin, the dice fall as we wish—since we have doctored them. For who would play with life with unloaded dice? A fool! And who would invoke a god to aid him? A simpleton.

"Yet is this Khlit crafty after a fashion. Nureddin, talk with Rao Singh. The youth saw not the death of his wanton. Declare that Khlit sabered her. Thus will we plant a seed that may bear fruit."

"If he doubts, my lord——"

"Eh—remind him that Khlit owes his outlawry to Kera—" Bember Hakim had told his master all that had passed—"also that Khlit escaped hurt when Jaffar attacked Rao Singh."

"Yet the fight at the ford——"

"He saw it not."

Shaista Mirza turned to the waiting sword-bearer.

"Jaffar, choose a following—nay, t'were best to ride alone. Fear you the Curved Saber?"

The broad Turk bared his teeth and touched his scimitar significantly.

"Then seek the man about the northern end of the lake. Take with you some trinket from Rao Singh. Say that the youth sends a message to the ear of Khlit, having promised you the jewel as reward. If he is puzzled in spirit by this and relaxes his guard—slay him. Do not fail this time."

Now as the four were ascending the bare gardens of Jhilam over the terraces to the palace proper Jaffar espied in the distance on the crest of a hill something that might have been a rider on a dark horse.

Whereupon, after marking the position of the watcher at the forest edge, he mounted hastily without waiting to don his armor and spurred to the spot.

Here he found tracks in the snow made apparently by two animals. Doubtful now of what he had seen, he went forward into the pines, following the tracks leisurely. After a while they separated.

Jaffar turned his horse after one trail, taking the precaution of poising a primed pistol in his free hand. He was an experienced warrior, yet too vain of his strength, which was bred more of flesh than of spirit.

He hastened forward at a curious sound. It resembled the groan of a man. It proved to be but a mule.

A sick mule, wasted and trembling upon its legs. On its back was bound the blackened body of a man long, long dead, with arrows sticking from its chest. Jaffar's eyes widened and he cursed aloud until he remembered the soldier slain by order of Shaista Mirza a fortnight ago.

Then he thrust his pistol back into his girdle and had turned homeward something hastily, for the sight of his own handiwork was not pleasant, when he saw a strange form creeping from the thicket at his side.

It was a lean man in a green cloak, a knife between his teeth, which were set in a grin of hate. Seeing that he was observed, the man leaped forward, running with bent knees, silently intent.

Jaffar plucked the pistol from his belt and fired, only to see one corner of the cloak jerk. He had no time to draw a second weapon. A black horse burst from the farther side of the thicket, snorting under the spur.

The Turk whirled to meet the rider of the black horse. Another second and his own mount had been knocked from its feet by the impact of the other's horse and Jaffar with a shrill cry of terror fell headlong.

For an instant before the creeping man with the knife reached him Jaffar's eyes rolled in fear while he fumbled with his sword. Then Cheker Ghar with a low chuckle of joy sprang upon the powerful Turk, knife in hand.

That night Jaffar returned on his horse to his lord and to Jhilam. His horse wandered back to its stable by instinct. Yet slowly, for tied to the saddle-girth of Jaffar was the halter of the mule. Upon the back of the mule was the victim of Shaista Mirza.

And, as Nureddin observed sagely, the one was not more dead than the other.

Thus did Khlit throw down the gage of war to Shaista Mirza and did Cheker Ghar avenge her to whom he had given his allegiance and whom he still praised as the Flower of the Hills.

It was long before the conjurer was seen in the vicinity of the Wular.

VII

Jaffar's death did not disturb Shaista Mirza, after the first moment when the body of his sword-bearer was brought to him. His anger had blazed up at sight of the dead Turk and he spurned the body with a slippered foot.

"Fool," he whispered, "to be outwitted by a mummer and a graybeard. Waste not a dinar on burial, but cast this carrion into the lake."

Whereupon he fell silent and retired to his chamber, playing long games of chess with Nureddin while he awaited word from his messengers.

The first to arrive was the rider he had dispatched to the Mogul. Jahangir was rejoiced at the capture of Rao Singh. In the royal firman were many words of flattery and praise for Shaista Mirza.

Jahangir ordered that Rao Singh be confined in the prison cells of Jhilam. Death was the penalty for breaking into the imperial seraglio, but the cautious monarch suggested that the Kashmiris might resent the infliction of such a punishment on the son of Sattar Singh. Hence the decree of imprisonment.

Shaista Mirza spat upon the firman, then tossed it contemptuously to the astrologer.

"Behold the word of a monarch who is bound by the cords of his fear! Still it must suffice. When Bember Hakim returns bid him prepare the drug that eats into the brain and creates a fever in the limbs—a wasting sickness. Did not the *hakim* prepare this physic for Rani Begum?"

Nureddin bowed in understanding. So the Mirza had been the author of Rani Begum's death! After all, the astrologer reflected, it was wise, for so long as the brood of Sattar Singh lived the Persian's seat upon the throne of Jhilam was not secure.

But Bember Hakim was slow in making his appearance. Knowing the uncertainty of travel over the northern passes where only the horns of mountain sheep and stags marked the caravan-trails, Shaista Mirza was not disturbed. The man's patience where his schemes were involved was as great as his anger at the failure of a subordinate.

Yet he did not go again to the floating island, having in mind perhaps the death of Jaffar. He sat on the carpet of his sleeping chamber, hearing the reports of his vizier, the treasurer of the Jhilam fief, and playing at chess often—sometimes discussing with Nureddin the science of the stars.

Although a keen watch was kept around the outer gardens of Jhilam, Khlit was not to be seen.

Shaista Mirza had issued a firman declaring death the penalty for any Kashmiri to give food or shelter to the outcast, also promising a *mohar* of rupees to whoever would bring tidings of Khlit.

No one came to claim the gold, and it is certain that the Cossack was given fodder for his horse at the Wular villages. The Cossack kept to the forest, pitching his *yurt* where he could watch Jhilam without danger of discovery.

This course of action suited Khlit well. He was accustomed to playing a lone hand, and the numerous followers of the Persian gave him no cause for concern. He hunted occasionally when he needed meat, and slept little, sitting in the door of his *yurt*, his sword across his knees and the brace of pistols on a sheepskin at his side. And he groomed and fed his horse painstakingly.

"Hey, black imp of hell," he observed caressingly, "eat well—yet not too much; for the day will come when you must gallop with the dogs of Satan at heel. Hey, that will be a ride of rides."

So Khlit waited in his *yurt* overlooking the fortress, and Shaista Mirza sat in an inner room and meditated.

Then came Nureddin to his master, smiling, with news on his bearded lips.

"O Lord of Exalted Wisdom," he announced, "there came Bember Hakim alone and pale with the cold of the hill passes. Verily the thin blood has dried in his veins and the fingers of one hand are scourged with frost. Barely he could whisper his message——"

"What said he, parrot-tongue?"

"This, my lord. He gave me a signet from Kargan Khan—" Nureddin handed the Mirza a ring which his master scanned keenly and placed in his girdle, satisfied—"and reported that the wrath of the Kirghiz hill chief was like the blind rage of a wounded tiger——"

"Nay, a witless buffalo!"

"Aye, my lord. Kargan Khan musters his riders and girds on the sword of vengeance. In spite of the snow he will ride down the Baramula trail to the Wular *davan*, even as you advised."

The hard eyes of the Persian gleamed.

"Furthermore Kartan Khan would look upon the body of his child, so that the edge of his anger shall be sharp. Even now he tears his beard and cries upon his gods to speed the arrow-stitches of retribution."

Shaista Mirza stroked the wrinkled skin of his forehead reflectively.

"Why do men utter the name of a god when they feel pain? 'Tis like to the vain cry of a child new-born, Nureddin. Aye—not even the hand of a god may lift the shadow of destiny. Say on."

"On the fifth day will Kargan Khan be at the Wular *davan* by the grave of Kera. So said he at the border of his land. For three days Bember Hakim rode hither."

"Then," calculated the Mirza, "on the second day from now will we meet with Kargan Khan. It is well. You have talked with Rao Singh?"

"Aye. Yet not as if there was a purpose in my mind. I spoke as if by chance, saying that Khlit had slain the woman. At first he believed not."

Shaista Mirza frowned, but Nureddin raised his hand deprecatingly.

"Not in vain have I knelt at the feet of the master of wisdom of Rudbar, and disciple of the *Refik*. A thought came to me, and I had slaves fetch the body of Jaffar—before it was thrown to the Wular—as if by chance. And the slaves told the boy that Khlit had slain Jaffar. They told how the unbeliever was an outcast in the hills."

Shaista Mirza leaned forward expectantly.

"My lord," continued Nureddin smilingly, "the slaves were simple folk and Rao Singh saw that they lied not. Wherefore a doubt seized upon his spirit as the first sore of disease appears upon the body."

"And then——"

"I sought out Bember Hakim's accursed store of herbs and powders. I bade the warders give him opium, a little at a time. And Rao Singh began to brood. His doubt is heavy upon him. He remembers little of the fight in the valley, for his brain is dulled with the blow and with mourning for Kera of Kargan."

Nureddin stroked his beard tranquilly, aware that Shaista Mirza was pleased.

"One thing further shall I do before the day of—triumph. Bember Hakim now lies abed, gripped by the demons of sickness, for his body is frail and he has endured much.

"The malady has affected his tongue, but he is doctoring himself with rank-smelling herbs and by the second day he will recover. Then shall I send him to the chamber of Rao Singh, and his words will bear out my tale."

"Aye," assented Shaista Mirza; "Rao Singh knows that the Arab saw the affray in the Wular *davan*."

"The boy is feverish with his grief. Truly it is strange that he should grieve for one woman.

"Are there not round-faced maids of Persia to be bought as slaves? Or pale and handsome maidens from Georgia? And even the Kashmiris are not ill shaped, for I have seized certain——"

Shaista Mirza waved his hand impatiently and the astrologer was silent.

"Rao Singh is not like to Sattar Singh, Nureddin," he meditated. "He is empty of mind and foolish as a young stag—eh, thereby we shall profit. For by your arts Rao Singh will believe Khlit slew the woman."

He glanced up at the water-clock that marked the passage of the hours.

"Soon, Nureddin, we shall take Rao Singh to the Wular *davan*, and with him Bember Hakim. Then shall they bear witness that Khlit is the slayer of Kera. And Kargan Khan shall hear."

"Most wise lord!" mouthed the astrologer.

"Take care that the Hindu is plied well with opium. Thus by the arts of Bember Hakim he shall say what we will that he should. And Kargan Khan with his steppe wolves will scour Kashmir until he hunts down Khlit."

"Aye, lord, and with Rao Singh gone to the portals of death you will be purged of the brood of Sattar Singh."

"And sole master of Jhilam, in favor both with the Mogul and Kargan Khan."

He looked up where the sky showed through an embrasure in the wall. Suspense crept into his crafty face.

"The omens are good, Nureddin? My star will be ascendant in the constellation of the east?"

"Lord, the star of your birth will rise that night, foretelling a mighty event."

In a bed-chamber of the Jhilam palace a wizened man coughed and muttered on the cushions of the floor, wrapped in his cloak, while he prepared certain mixtures of powders which smoked in a brass pot over the flames.

He ordered his trembling slaves to fetch a young goat, living, and to let some of its blood run into a dish. Whereupon he consulted the book of the two hundred and sixty medicinal substances as written by the Arab scientists. He prepared a broth of the goat-blood and the contents of the vials at his girdle.

The slaves cringed and choked in the smoke from the foul mixture in the pot. Then he drank the broth and sighed, announcing that the elements of disease had been vitiated and that he would sleep until Shaista Mirza summoned him.

During that night and the next day fur-clad riders threaded through the lower passes of the Himalayas on ponies that stumbled ahead in blinding snow and a sharp wind that swept in their faces like a keen sword.

The riders bore spears at their shoulders, and under their furs wore shirts of Kallmark mail. They stopped only to make an offering of food before the shrine of the Altai-Nor god—a felt image fastened to a tree-trunk beneath a rough wooden roof—to insure their safe descent of the dangerous pass.

They dismounted only to run beside their horses and stir the heat of their bodies. They ate sparingly of dried horseflesh and frozen mare's milk.

Kargan Khan, who led the troop, had said that they would not rest until they reached the *davan* where his daughter was buried.

And during that interval Khlit sat by his horse in the snow-storm, having raised one side of the sheepskin shelter so that it partly covered the black stallion. His food was nearly exhausted but he did not venture abroad for more, having decided that the next day was the one in which he would seek out Shaista Mirza.

During the last week Khlit had formulated a plan. He had pondered it carefully and was content. It was a bold venture, depending for success upon the speed of his horse. Yet in his plan Khlit had been unaware of one thing—the consummate cleverness of the Persian, and the craft of his servants.

Khlit had faced many enemies and had lived while they had died by virtue of his shrewd brain. In Shaista Mirza however he had a foe who was no less shrewd, who planned as carefully and who was master of many swords.

Yet Khlit did not intend to trust to his sword. Rather he put his trust in his horse, and in a thing that Shaista Mirza would have scorned—the faith of another man.

VIII

When the dead are placed in the earth or upon the burial-fire, they are not. Then is the burial-place a place of shadows. The caravan will pass by and see not the shadows. The singer will strike upon the guitar, and heed them not. The women will bear jars to the near-by well and know them not.

Yet there is one who will heed the shadows. Aye, the slayer of the dead!

Kirghiz proverb.

The snow ceased not long after dawn, leaving its carpet over the breast of the Jhilam hills and its tracery upon the laden branches of the pines. With the clearing of the weather Shaista Mirza ordered the kettle-drums of the fortress to sound the muster of his forces.

The riders assembled in the snow-covered gardens—Persians in elaborate armor, Pathan mercenaries in cloak and hood, lean Hazaras in quilted corselets with quivers slung at the saddles.

The Mirza inspected his men with care to see that they were well armed and mounted. It was well, he thought, to make a good showing of force before Kargan Khan.

He was mounted on a beautiful Arab, his thin body wrapped in furs that covered all but his sharp face. Nureddin accompanied him, a handsome figure with jeweled saddle-peak and sword-belt.

Only a small force was left with the slaves in the fortress. Shaista Mirza completed his muster. He selected a group of heavily armed Persians—among them a few musket-men—as bodyguard for himself. Others he told off under Nureddin to escort Rao Singh and the master of physics, who was muffled in his soiled white cloak because of his recent malady.

The Pathan mercenaries Shaista Mirza placed in the vanguard, and he threw out two flanking parties of Hazara archers. In this manner they set out along the Jhilam road around the lake, leaving only slaves, servants and a few soldiers under a Persian captain to guard the castle. On that day the Mirza's riders numbered twenty-five score.

They rode through the village, flinging gibes at the few emaciated women who with children clinging to their shawls came to look impassively at the cavalcade. The men of the village were not to be seen.

Along the lake-shore the huts of the fishermen were empty, so the sharp-eyed vizier whose duty was to assess the taxes noted. Here the road wound into the pines.

The sun was high by now, giving out a cheering warmth. The riders, now that the early-morning chill had been shaken from their limbs, laughed and sang snatches of ballads, restraining their fresh horses with difficulty. Shaista Mirza smiled and plucked at his cheeks. He was treading the path of his destiny, and his plans were well laid.

Rao Singh, his arms bound behind him, rode with head downcast, saying nothing and only looking up at intervals to stare at the thickets that bordered the road. He paid no heed to the witticisms of Nureddin, who was in a high good humor.

Then Khlit rode into the path ahead of the vanguard.

A shout went up from the Hazaras, a shout which was repeated back until it reached Shaista Mirza.

"Let the archers pursue!" he cried shrilly. "Yet not more than a ten—all others keep to their files."

The black horse wheeled under spur as the nearest Hazaras urged their mounts forward. Khlit waved his arm as if making a sign to some one hidden from view. He bent low in the saddle, for the archers had sped a few haphazard shafts, and gave the black horse its head.

Rao Singh had raised his head dully at the shout, but seemed not to grasp its meaning.

"Eh, the wolf is seen by the pack, Bember Hakim," chuckled the astrologer. "The stars are kind to Shaista Mirza."

"Nay, 'tis a shrewd wolf," muttered the other, "and Jaffar sleeps with the fish for bedfellows."

Nureddin shrugged his plump shoulders, yawned and glanced appraisingly at Rao Singh.

"Gave you the youth opium?" he whispered.

"He is made ready for what is to come. See, where he reels in his saddle."

Khlit rode well ahead of the pursuers, keeping beyond bow-shot. His horse was fresh and had the legs of the others. Little by little he increased his lead, turning easily in the saddle to measure the distance.

He had lost sight of the main body of his enemies. He rose in his stirrups, plucking his curved sword from its scabbard and swinging it around his head, feeling the exhilaration of being again in the saddle and tasting the keen delight of peril.

Yet as he did so—obeying one of the instincts that were his heritage from his Cossack forebears—he sheathed his weapon and crouched forward watchfully. In the snow before him he had seen the tracks of many horses.

Into the broad trail left by these riders he urged his own mount, and a cry went back from the speeding archers to the men around Shaista Mirza.

"The outcast has turned into the Wular *davan*."

The Persian laughed, then scowled and snapped an order angrily. "Summon back the archers! Form in close files."

He was wary of riding haphazard into the valley where the men of Kargan Khan were waiting. And he knew that Khlit once in the *davan* was between his own men and the Kirghiz and could not escape without leaving his horse and climbing the slope—a course of action that would leave him afoot and consequently an easy prey.

Shaista Mirza was willing to believe that sheer good fortune had thrown the Cossack before his men. Yet his suspicions were sharp and he had heard how Khlit had once led two bands of soldiers into conflict with each other by just such a trick. He knew his own strength and the weapons he could employ to sway the mind of Kargan, and he could afford to be cautious.

"Perchance the outcast thought to bait a trap," he muttered to the leader of his musket-men. "If so he must be without hope, for he has ridden ahead of us into the *davan*."

It occurred to Shaista Mirza that Khlit might have hoped that Rao Singh could escape in the excitement that arose on his appearance. But the Hindu was in his place, leaning heavily on the peak of his saddle.

"If we find the Cossack in the *davan*," he called to Nureddin, "make no move to seize him until I command."

Whereupon he set his men in motion in orderly ranks, close knit now that they ascended the slope that led from the lakeshore to the *davan*.

Meanwhile Khlit had not slackened the pace of his horse. The way was familiar, and those who had gone before him had trampled the snow-crust into a compact footing.

He passed two sentinels—bearded men mounted on shaggy steppe ponies—without pause, only shouting the name of Kargan Khan. The two, seeing that he was alone, permitted him to ride on.

Now he saw slender blue spirals of smoke rising from the head of the valley and caught the stamp of horses' hoofs and the jangle of bits. Rounding the turn where he had once passed the form of Cheker Ghar, he came full upon the Kirghiz.

They filled the valley-head from cliff to cliff, squatting in circles around the fires, yet with their horses' bridles near at hand and their weapons across their knees—stalwart men roughly clad in furs and horsehide boots, their broad faces set with slant eyes that turned inquiringly upon Khlit.

The Kirghiz had come in peace to the Wular; still the tribesmen had no love for the mercenaries of Jhilam and they trusted no man's word—save only Kargan Khan's.

And Khlit reined in sharply, beholding one who sat upon a stone and watched him under shaggy brows. It was a man whose heavy head seemed sunk into massive shoulders; whose bent and mightily thewed frame was enclosed in a supple corselet of Turkish mail without the customary *khalat*.

A bronzed and hairy hand gripped each knee of the sitter, and Khlit saw that one eye was closed beneath a vivid scar that ran from chin to brow. By this Khlit knew that he faced Kargan, chief of the Baramula horde.

But already he had seen where the rocks over the grave had been rolled aside and the earth upturned. The *khalat* of the khan lay on the snow before him, and under the *khalat* the outline of a slender figure.

Thus did Khlit ride to meet Kargan Khan on the day that gave to the Wular valley the name of Kizil Yar, or Red Pass, in the tongue of the Kirghiz.

He lifted his right hand to show that he held no weapon and walked his horse forward slowly. The warriors on either side of the khan observed him intently but made no hostile move.

"Dismount!" cried one gruffly.

Khlit made no move to do so.

"Shall a kha khan dismount before a khan, even the chief of a horde?" he asked, speaking directly to Kargan. "I am Khlit, called by some the Curved Saber, and once the yak-tail standard of the Jungar horde followed me."

A murmur went through the assembled warriors at this. The southern Kirghiz had never seen Khlit, but his name was known by hearsay. Many tales concerning the Cossack had been repeated throughout the nomad tribes.

Kargan Khan's harsh face showed no indication of his thoughts. "What seek you, Khlit?"

"I ride to Kargan Khan with a message. Behind me, in the space milk takes to boil, will come the slayer of Kera."

The muscles under the jaw of the Kirghiz tightened and the skin of his face darkened.

"It is well," he rumbled, the words rolling from his thick chest—the only sign of his emotion. "For I have come in the pursuit of blood. I have looked upon the dead body of Kera."

Shaista Mirza took in the scene at the valley-head with a swift glance. He sought out Khlit, noting his position a few yards from and slightly back of Kargan Khan.

He saw that the Kirghiz had mounted but were not formed in any order. They sat silently on their wearied ponies, staring at the gaudily attired Persians. Shaista Mirza reflected smilingly that they resembled a pack of wolves.

Whether Khlit was Kargan's prisoner or not Shaista Mirza could not guess. He considered it a stroke of rare good fortune that Khlit should have walked into the trap. Perhaps, he reasoned swiftly, the Cossack planned to denounce him—Shaista Mirza.

For this Shaista Mirza was prepared. Hidden among his followers, he reflected, were Rao Singh and Bember Hakim, whose testimony united to his own would overbear anything the solitary outcast might say.

So Shaista Mirza smiled and bent his head slightly in greeting to the khan.

"Hail, Kargan Khan," he began smoothly, "master of the Baramula and lord of the Kara Kirghiz. Auspicious is the day we can meet in friendship. Favorable are the omens for this day, and fain would Jahangir himself have been present to greet the chieftain he holds in honor."

He paused for a response, but Kargan Khan spoke not. The single eye of the Kirghiz roved over the Persian ranks as if seeking that which he found not.

"Happy am I, Kargan Khan, to bid you and your followers welcome to Jhilam, and to the castle."

Shaista Mirza's courteous words thinly veiled the scorn in which he held the clumsy figure on the rock. His glance wandered to the *khalat* and the form beneath it, and wavered. Then he summoned a ready smile.

"Think not, Kargan Khan, because I sent a single man to your encampment that I am unmindful of the honor due the Lord of the Baramula. Nay, Bember Hakim is the trusted servant of the Mogul himself, and a worthy messenger."

The Kirghiz lifted his shaggy head impatiently.

"Aye," he responded, "the *hakim* swore that when I rode to this spot I would set hand on the slayer of my child. Name the man!"

The last words echoed forth as if torn from the muscles of the warrior's chest.

Shaista Mirza bent his head and glanced sidelong at Khlit. The Cossack sat his horse impassively, apparently indifferent to what was said. He also was scanning the Persian ranks.

In spite of himself the Mirza wondered at the outcast's calm. He reflected that Khlit must be in truth dull of wit and not as the tales had painted him. Once Kargan Khan heard Shaista Mirza speak the name of Khlit, the Cossack would die as swiftly and mercilessly as a cornered roe deer is torn by dogs.

Wherefore Shaista Mirza smiled—a smile that ended in a sneer. He liked well to play with a victim, to tie slowly the knot of death upon the condemned.

Truly, he would have preferred to see a woman die rather than the gray-haired warrior. He regretted that he had not seen Jaffar deal with Kera. It would have been a dainty sight.

"My heart is heavy with your sorrow, O khan," he lisped. "And I have come prepared to see vengeance done. Aye, to see the end of the pursuit of blood. Yet you are a chief and a judge.

"Behold then, I would have the matter clear and purged of the cloud of doubt, so that none may whisper Kargan Khan slew wrongly."

He turned in his saddle.

"Nureddin!"

The astrologer pushed forward.

"Fetch Rao Singh and Bember Hakim."

Softly he added—

"You have made certain the stripling is heavy with opium?"

"Aye, my lord. These past six hours has Bember Hakim been plying him with noxious physics and nostrums, so that he knows not his right hand from his left."

Satisfied, Shaista Mirza watched his two witnesses dismount and advance until they stood beside the *khalat*. Rao Singh, whose arms had been freed, stumbled, and was supported by the other. Khlit was watching not Rao Singh but the face of Kargan.

By now the sun was well down behind the mountain peaks and the shadows were gathering under the pines. Sometimes the shadows shifted as if wind had moved the pine-branches. But there was no wind.

From a cleft in the rock—the same as that by which Bember Hakim had made his escape—yellow rays of the sun shot across the ravine, falling athwart the figure of Rao Singh.

Kargan Khan had gripped his weapon spasmodically as the boy stood before him, wondering if the Hindu who had carried Kera from the seraglio was the one he sought.

Rao Singh looked up, and father and lover of Kera stared long into each other's eyes. Then the boy's drooping figure straightened and he flung back his head, crossing his arms on his chest.

Nureddin frowned, for he could see that a change had come over the face of Rao Singh. The lips had drawn firmly together. Suffering had wiped out the lines of youthful indolence. The eyes were level and purposeful.

Into the face of Rao Singh had come the stamp of grief and the strength that changes boy to man. Nureddin moved uneasily and would have spoken, but Rao Singh was before him.

"Kargan Khan," he said slowly, "the Flower of the Hills was my bride. Aye, she was the rose that made fragrant the garden of my heart. And she called me lord."

In the dark eyes of the Hindu shone a steadfast purpose. Kargan Khan stared at him with fierce intentness, his savage anger challenging the pride of the Hindu.

Shaista Mirza had not thought to find Rao Singh master of his senses and would have spoken, but the Kirghiz motioned him aside without taking his gaze from the Hindu.

"You feared to ride to me—Kargan—with Kera upon your saddle-peak."

"Nay," retorted the Hindu proudly; "that I could not do until Kera was mistress of Jhilam as was Rani Vegum, my mother."

Long and steadily the Kirghiz measured Rao Singh, and a new gleam crept into his single eye.

"By the gods—name me the slayer of my child!" he roared, whipping out his sword.

Shaista Mirza put out his hands, then licked his dry lips softly, studying his prisoner craftily—as a man who scans the dice he is about to cast.

Rao Singh wheeled and pointed.

"Shaista Mirza," he said.

A rising mutter of anger from the ranks of the Kirghiz—a quick flash of weapons—ponies capered under the spur—an exclamation from the Persians—and Kargan Khan sprang to his feet. Then Shaista Mirza lifted his hand. Except for a quick spasm his face showed nothing of the rage he felt.

"Stay," he cried harshly, his high voice rising over the tumult. "Would you listen to one who speaks in the stupor of opium? Rao Singh has partaken of the drug. He knows not what he is saying."

The Persian would have urged his horse upon Rao Singh, but the Hindu leaped back and the Kirghiz interposed his bulk between them. The sword that the chief held was a heavy blade, but it trembled with the force of his anger and the strength that held the anger in check.

Khlit had not moved. Nor did he seem surprized by the speech of the boy.

"Nay, Kargan Khan," pursued Shaista Mirza swiftly; "is not Rao Singh my foe? Did he not seize your child? His false lips frame lies."

He clutched the khan's massive shoulder and whispered:

"Yonder sits the scoundrel. Aye, Khlit—he of the Curved Saber— is the man you seek!"

The Kirghiz shook his head angrily like the buffalo that Shaista Mirza was fond of calling him.

"Death of the gods!" he cried. "Would the slayer of Kera ride alone into my array?"

Then for the first time Shaista Mirza felt the chill of doubt, and paled. His voice broke as he called for Bember Hakim.

"Aye," said Khlit.

This was the only time he spoke during the judgment in the Wular *davan*.

"Let us hear Bember Hakim."

"Bember Hakim is the man of the Mogul," shrilled Shaista Mirza.

"He is the faithful servant of Jahangir. His words are as the pearls of truth, for he saw the death in this valley——"

"He will say that Rao Singh is in a stupor," cried Nureddin.

"Let him speak!" growled the khan.

The wizened figure in the white cloak fell on its knees before the Kirghiz.

"Rao Singh spoke not the truth," he cried.

Shaista Mirza smiled while the witness crawled closer to the khan and embraced his boots.

"*Aie,*" chanted the figure at the feet of Kargan Khan, "I have seen what I have seen. I saw the fair head of the Flower of the Hills sink in death under the sword of the miserable Jaffar. I have heard Shaista Mirza boast that he ordered the death.

"*Aie!* My spirit is parched with the thirst of vengeance. Jaffar is slain. But Shaista Mirza lives——"

The pale face of Shaista Mirza flushed and his eyes widened.

"Traitor! False to your bread——"

Shaista Mirza struck at the prostrate form with his dagger, realizing that the man had betrayed him and understanding now why Rao Singh, who had been placed in his care, was free from opium. The Persian's dark brow was rife with hatred and fear as he thought how Bember Hakim must have fallen in with Khlit at the Baramula trail on his quest to Kargan Khan. Kargan Khan read this swiftly.

The next instant Shaista Mirza reined back sharply among his bodyguard, who had pressed forward. For Kargan Khan had bounded upon him and struck down a shield that was interposed. His second blow felled the holder of the shield to earth and he sprang after the Persian, slashing at the spears of the riders who sought to ward him off and bellowing his war-cry.

And after Kargan came Rao Singh, who had snatched up the weapon of the felled rider. And upon his heels came the mass of the Kirghiz, fearful for their chief.

In an instant the valley resounded with the clash of steel, the frenzied snorts of horses and the cry of the injured.

The Kirghiz had attacked with fury, led by Kargan, who had mounted. In the confined space was no room for maneuvering or for the use of arrows. The compact bands of horsemen made one struggling mass, where knee pressed knee and shield clashed against shield.

Khlit had set spurs to his horse and forced his way into the center of the ranks. He found Rao Singh and drew the Hindu away from the Persian files, protesting.

"Have you forgotten?" the Cossack cried sternly. "There are those who await your coming."

At that Rao Singh had turned and sped to the cleft in the slope where he disappeared behind the rocks.

One other man had parted from the battle. Nureddin after a glance around had wheeled his horse and slipped back through the array of the Persians. Once clear of the valley he set out swiftly down the Jhilam road.

Kargan Khan had flung himself into battle with the sole thought of finding and striking down the Mirza. His men had attacked readily, savagely, but without plan or formation.

The Persian's forces had given back at first; then closed in with the armored horsemen in front. Shaista Mirza, safe behind the cordon of his men, directed the fight craftily.

In the narrow quarters the Kirghiz could not employ their favorite tactics of enveloping their foe, and were forced to fight hand to hand. They had little armor, and their horses were wearied. The fury of their first onset waned, and they split up into knots of horsemen, wheeling and plunging at superior numbers.

All this Khlit noticed, and frowned.

Then that for which he watched came to pass. Down the cleft in the ravine, down the rock-slope, even down the cliff itself, swarmed dark figures chattering with eagerness and bearing knives, rusted spears, clubs or stones. And at their head was Rao Singh.

They raced behind the Hindu brandishing their makeshift weapons, and fell upon the flanks and rear of the Persians.

Thus did Rao Singh put himself at the head of the forest men of Jhilam even as his father Sattar Singh had done before him, though under different circumstances.

The Kashmiris were unskilled warriors but they had the agility of their kind, and their anger against the Persians was a great anger. With their coming the Kirghiz pressed in, raising their war-cry anew. Khlit could see the broad figure of Kargan Khan at their head, his weapon flashing.

"Hey," he meditated, "it is a good fight. Yet it is the fight of Rao Singh and Kargan Khan."

He fingered his sword, swearing anxiously. Never before had he been a spectator of a battle. Then he sheathed his sword and sighed.

The fight—the first phase of it—was over. The Persians, their ranks broken, were streaming back toward the valley-entrance. By their flanks, clutching and stabbing, went the Kashmiris, and in their rear the Kirghiz struck down the fleeing riders. Half of Shaista Mirza's men lay in the *davan*.

Khlit, galloping among the Kirghiz, caught up with Kargan Khan at the edge of the lake. Twilight had fallen, and the cries of the stricken mercenaries were growing fainter down the Jhilam road.

Kargan Khan with a band of his men had halted to stare at a red glow on the lake. In the dusk it flickered from the surface of the water.

" 'Tis witchcraft!" muttered Kargan Khan.

"Nay," laughed Khlit, " 'tis but the pleasure island of Shaista Mirza gone up in flames after the visit of the fisher-folk. The villagers have attacked the castle and overcome the scanty garrison."

"Praise be to the gods!"

Kargan Khan looked at Khlit curiously.

"Nay, did you plan this rising of the Kashmiris? It served us well."

"Rao Singh leads them," said Khlit, and was silent.

Then he laughed.

"Nureddin—I saw the rascal flee—will be well greeted at the castle. And those of Shaista Mirza who reach there will fare little better."

While he trotted beside the Kirghiz after the fugitives Kargan Khan looked at Khlit long, wondering how much Khlit had foreknown of what came to pass at the Kizil Yar.

There were few of the Persians who escaped from Jhilam that night, and Shaista Mirza was not among them. And that night Rao Singh took the chair of his father in the council-hall of Jhilam.

Concerning Bember Hakim there is a strange tale. A forest man of Jhilam tells the tale. It was the day after the battle, at dawn, and he saw Khlit and Bember Hakim go into the forest along the Baramula trail.

Being curious, the man followed. He saw the two come to a heap of stones that seemed to mark a grave. There, so says the Kashmiri, Bember Hakim threw off his cloak, tunic and sandals and washed some stains from his face with snow.

Then—such is the tale—Bember Hakim rewound his turban in a different fashion and took from the rocks a green cloak and other garments, which he put on, shouldering also a heavy leopard-skin pack.

Thus Bember Hakim the Arab physician became in the eyes of the Kashmiri Cheker Ghar, the conjurer and mimic—Cheker Ghar, who pressed Khlit's hand to his forehead and departed to the south, while Khlit rode alone to the north.

This tale of the Kashmiri was adjudged a lie by those who heard. For how could one man be like to two?

Doubtless, said those who heard, the Kashmiri had partaken of the good wine of Shiraz, for that night there had been great feasting in Jhiiam, and much rejoicing among the men of Jhilam.

THE BRIDE OF JAGANNATH

Down past the stone shrine of Kedarnath, down and over the tall grass of the Dehra-Dun, marched the host of the older gods. The Pandas marched with feet that touched not the tall grass. Past the *deva-prayag*—the meeting-place of the waters—came the older gods bearing weapons in their hands.

In the *deva-prayag* they washed themselves clean. The gods were very angry. The wind came and went at their bidding.

Thus they came. And the snow-summits of Himal, the grass of the valley, and the meeting-place of the waters—all were as one to the gods.

The Vedas.

THE HEAVY MORNING DEW LAY ON THE GRASS OF THE LAND OF THE Five Rivers, the Punjab. The hot, dry monsoon was blowing up from the southern plain and cooling itself among the foot-hills of the Siwalik in the year of our Lord 1609 when two riders turned their horses from a hill-path into the main highway of the district of Kukushetra.

It was a fair day, and the thicket through which the trail ran was alive with the flutter of pigeons and heavy with the scent of wild thyme and jasmine and the mild odor of the fern-trees. The sun beat on them warmly, for the Spring season was barely past and they were riding south in the eastern Punjab, by the edge of Rajasthan, toward the headwaters of the Ganges, in the empire of Jahangir, Ruler of the World and Mogul of India.

"A fair land," said one. "A land ripe with sun, with sweet fruits and much grain. Our horses will feed well. Here you may rest from your wounds——"

He pointed with a slender, muscular hand to where a gilt dome reared itself over the cypress-tops on a distant hill-summit.

"*Eh*, my Brother of Battles," he said, "yonder shines the dome of Kukushetra. Aye, the temple of Kukushetra wherein dwells an image of Jagannath——"

"*Jagannath!*"

It was a shrill cry that came from the roadside. A small figure leaped from the bushes at the word and seized the bridles of both horses. They reared back and he who had pointed to the temple muttered a round oath.

"Jagannath!" cried the newcomer solemnly.

He was a very slender man, half-naked, with a gray cloth twisted about his loins. The string hanging down his left chest indicated—as well as the caste-mark on his forehead—that he was a Brahman, of the lesser temple order.

"The holy name!" he chanted. "Lord of the World! Brother to Balabhadra and to Subhadra! Incarnation of the mighty Vishnu, and master of the Kali-*damana!* Even as ye have named Jagannath, so must ye come to the reception hall of the god——"

"What is this madness?" asked the elder of the two riders gruffly.

The Brahman glanced at him piercingly and resumed his arrogant harangue.

"The festival of Jagannath is near at hand, warrior," he warned. "This is the land of the mighty god. Come, then, to the temple and bring your gift to lay at the shrine of Jagannath of Kukushetra, which is only less holy than the shrine of Puri itself, at blessed Orissa. Come——"

"By Allah!" laughed the first rider. "By the ninety-nine holy names of God!"

He shook in his saddle with merriment. The Brahman dropped the reins as if they had been red hot and surveyed the two with angry disappointment.

"By the beard of the Prophet, and the ashes of my grandsire—this is a goodly jest," roared the tall warrior. "Behold, a pilgrim hunter come to solicit Abdul Dost and Khlit of the Curved Saber."

He spoke Mogholi, whereas the misguided Brahman had used his native Hindustani. Khlit understood Abdul Dost. Yet he did not laugh. He was looking curiously at the marked brow of the priest, which had darkened in anger at the gibe of the Moslem.

"*Eh*—this is verily a thing to warm the heart," went on Abdul Dost. "A Brahman, a follower of Jagannath, bids us twain come to the festival of his god. He knew not that I am a follower of the true Prophet, and you, Khlit, wear a Christian cross of gold under the shirt at your throat."

He turned to the unfortunate pilgrim hunter.

"Nay, speaker-of-the-loud-tongue, here is an ill quarter to cry your wares. Would the wooden face of armless Jagannath smile upon a Moslem and a Christian, think you?"

"Nay," quoth the priest scornfully, "not so much as upon a toad, or a pariah who is an eater of filth."

In his zeal, he had not taken careful note of the persons of the two travelers.

He scanned the warriors keenly, looking longest at Khlit. The elegantly dressed Afghan, with his jeweled scimitar and his silver-mounted harness and small, tufted turban, was a familiar figure.

But the gaunt form of the Cossack was strange to the Brahman. Khlit's bearded cheeks were haggard with hardship and illness in the mountains during the long Winter of Kashmir, and his wide, deep-set eyes were gray. His heavy sheepskin coat was thrown back, disclosing a sinewy throat and high, rugged shoulders.

In Khlit's scarred face was written the boldness of a fighting race, hardened, not softened by the wrinkles of age. It was an open face, lean and weather-stained. The deep eyes returned the stare of the priest with a steady, meditative scrutiny.

Abdul Dost was still smiling. His handsome countenance was that of a man in the prime of life, proud of his strength. He sat erect in a jeweled saddle, a born horseman and the finest swordsman of northern Hindustan. He rode a mettled Arab. Khlit's horse was a shaggy Kirghiz pony.

"It is time," broke in Khlit bluntly—he was a man of few words—"that we found food for ourselves and grain for our horses. Where lies this peasant we seek?"

Abdul Dost turned to the watching priest, glancing at the sun.

"Ho, hunter of pilgrims," he commanded, "since we are not birds for your snaring—and the enriching of your idol—tell us how many bow-shot distant is the hut of Bhimal, the catcher of birds. We have ridden since sunup, and our bellies yearn."

The Brahman folded his arms. He seemed inclined to return a sharp answer, then checked himself. His black eyes glinted shrewdly. He pointed down the dusty highway.

"If the blind lead the blind, both will fall into the well," he chanted. "Nay, would you behold the power of the name of Jagannath whom you foolishly deride? Then come with me to the abode of this same Bhimal. I will guide you, for I am bound thither myself on a quest from the temple."

"So be it," nodded Abdul Dost carelessly and urged his horse forward, offering the pilgrim hunter a stirrup which the Brahman indignantly refused.

Abdul Dost was not the man to repent his own words, spoken freely. But he understood better than Khlit the absolute power of the Hindu priests in the Land of the Five Rivers.

The fertile province of Kukushetra was a favorite resort for the Hindu pilgrims of the highlands. Here were the ruins of an ancient temple, near which the new-gilded edifice—a replica of that at Puri at the Ganges' mouth—had been built. Here also were gathered the priests from the hill monasteries, to tend the shrine of the Kukushetra Jagannath.

Religious faith had not made a breach between Khlit and Abdul Dost. The Cossack was accustomed to keep his thoughts to himself, and to the *mansabdar* friendship was a weightier matter than the question of faith. He had eaten bread and salt with Khlit.

He had nearly slain the Cossack in their first meeting, and this had made the two boon companions. Khlit had treated his wounds with gunpowder and earth mixed with spittle—until Abdul Dost substituted clean bandages and ointment.

The two ate of the same food and slept often under the same robe. They were both veteran fighters in an age when a man's life was safeguarded only by a good sword-arm. Abdul Dost was pleased to lead his comrade through the splendid hill country of northern India perhaps influenced—for he was a man of simple ideas—by the interest which the tall figure of Khlit always aroused among the natives.

Khlit was well content to have the companionship of a man who liked to wander and who had much to say of India and the wars of the Mogul. Khlit himself was a wanderer who followed the path of battles. From this he had earned the surname of the "Curved Saber."

It was the first time that Khlit had set foot in Hindustan, which was the heart of the Mogul empire.

The priest, who had maintained a sullen silence, halted at a wheat-field bordering the road. Here a bare-legged, turbaned man was laboring, cutting the wheat with a heavy sickle and singing as he worked.

The Brahman called, and the man straightened, casting an anxious eye at the three in the road. Khlit saw his eyes widen as he recognized the priest.

"Greeting, Kurral," spoke the man in the field; "may the blessing of divine Vishnu rest upon you."

"Come, Bhimal," commanded the Brahman sharply; "here be barbarian wayfarers who seek your hut. Lay aside your sickle. Your harvesting is done."

With a puzzled glance over his shoulders at the half-gathered grain Bhimal the *chiria mars*—Hindu of the bird-slaying caste—led the way to his cottage beside the field. It was a clay-walled hut with roof of thatched roots, under the pleasant shade of a huge banyan.

On either side the door within the shade grapevines were trained upon a lattice; in the rear an open shed housed two buffalo—the prized possession of Bhimal and his brother.

At the threshold, however, the slayer of birds hesitated strangely and faced his companions as if unwilling for them to enter. Khlit and Abdul Dost dismounted, well content with the spot, where they had heard a good breakfast for a man and beast might be had from the hospitable Bhimal. They had unsaddled and were about to request a jar of water from the cottage tank under the banyan when a word from Kurral arrested them.

"Stay," muttered the Brahman.

Turning to Bhimal, he smiled, while the simple face of the old peasant grew anxious.

"Is it not true, Bhimal, that this cottage belongs to you and your brother, who departed long ago on a pilgrimage to Puri?"

"It is true, Kurral," assented Bhimal.

"That you own two fields and a half of good wheat ready for the harvest? And two buffalo? This cottage?"

At each question the peasant nodded.

"And a few rare birds which you caught in snares?"

Kurral drew a folded parchment from the robe at his waist and consulted it. Then he tossed it to Bhimal.

"You can not read, O slayer of birds," he smiled. "But this is a bond signed by your brother. You can make out his scrawl, over the endorsement of the holy priest of Puri, the unworthy slave of Jagannath. The bond is for the cottage and all the goods, animals and tools of your brother and yourself. It was sent from the mighty temple of Puri to the lesser shrine at Kukushetra. And I am come to take payment."

Khlit, not understanding Hindustani, yet read sudden misery in the lined face of Bhimal.

"How fares my brother?" cried the peasant.

"He brought fitting gifts of fruit, grain and oatmeal to the shrine of Jagannath, Bhimal. His zeal was great. All the coins that he had, he gave. But mighty Jagannath was ill rewarded by your brother, for you come not with him on the pilgrimage."

"Nay, I am sorely lame."

Bhimal pointed sadly to a partially withered leg.

"No matter," declared Kurral sternly. "Is Jagannath a pariah, to be cheated of his due—by miserable slayers of carrion birds? Your brother wrote the bond for this cottage and the fields. He offered it to the priest and it was taken. Thus he gained the blessing of all-powerful Jagannath."

"Then—he is ill?"

"Nay, I heard that he died upon the return journey, in the heat. By his death he is blessed—as are all those who perish on behalf of the All-Destroyer, whether under the wheels of the sacred car or upon the path of pilgrimage."

Bhimal hung his head in resignation. Abdul Dost, with a shrug of his slender shoulders, was about to take the jar of water from the tank when Kurral wheeled on him vindictively.

"Stay, barbarian!" he warned. "This tank and the cottage and the food within is now the property of the temple of Kukushetra. No unclean hand may be laid upon it."

Abdul Dost stared at him grimly and glanced questioningly at Bhimal.

"It is true," admitted the peasant sadly. "A bond given to the god

by my brother is binding upon my unworthy self. Yet—" he faced
Kurral beseechingly—"the wheat and the rare birds are all that I
have to live through the season of rains.

"Suffer me to stay in the cottage and work on behalf of the god.
I shall render you a just tribute of all, keeping just enough for
my own life. I would strew the ashes of grief upon my head in soli-
tude——"

"Nay," retorted Kurral; "would you mourn a life that has passed
to the keeping of the gods? I have marked you as one of little faith.
So you may not tend this property. Another will see to it."

A rebellious flicker appeared in the dim eyes of the peasant.

"Has not Jagannath taken the things that are dearest to me, Kurral?" he cried shrilly. "My brother's life and these good buffaloes?
Nay, then let me keep but one thing!"

"What?" demanded the priest, still enjoying his triumph over the
two warriors.

"A peacock with a tail of many-colored beauty. I have tended it
as a gift to my lord, the Rawul Matap Rao, upon his marriage. I
have promised the gift."

Kurral considered.

"Not so," he decided. "For the Rawul—so it is said—has not bent
his head before the shrine of Kukushetra in many moons. It is rumored that he inclines to an unblessed sect, the worshipers of the sun-
image of Vishnu—the followers of the *gosain* Chaitanya. He is
unworthy the name of Hindu. Better the peacock should adorn the
temple garden than strut for the pleasure of the bride of Rawul
Matap Rao."

Then Khlit saw a strange form appear from within the entrance
of the hut. In the dim light under the great tree it appeared as a
glittering child with a plumed headdress. Kurral, too, saw it and
started.

"Who names the Rawul with false breath?" cried the figure in a
deep melodious voice. "Ho—it is Kurral, the pilgrim hunter. Me-
thought I knew his barbed tongue."

By now Khlit saw that the figure was that of a warrior, standing
scarce shoulder high to the Cossack and the tall Afghan. A slim,
erect body was brightly clad, the legs bound by snowy white

muslin, a shawl girdle of green silk falling over the loins, a shirt of finely wrought silvered mail covering the small body, the brown arms bare, a helmet of thin bronze on the dark head.

The man's face was that of a Hindu of the warrior caste, the eyes dark and large, the nostrils thin. A pair of huge black mustaches were twisted up either cheek. A quiver full of arrows hung at the waist-girdle.

In one hand the archer held a bow; under the other arm he clasped a beautiful peacock, whose tail had stirred Khlit's interest.

"Sawal Das!" muttered Kurral.

"Aye, Sawal Das," repeated the archer sharply, "servant and warrior of the excellent Rawul Matap Rao. I came to Bhimal's hut at sunup to claim the peacock, for my lord returns to his castle of Thaneswar tomorrow night. And now, O beguiler-of-men, have you wasted your breath; for I have already claimed the peacock on behalf of my lord."

"Too much of the evil juice of the grape has trickled down your gullet, Sawal Das," scowled the priest. "For that you came to the hut—under pretense of taking the bird. You are a dishonor to your caste——"

"Windbag! Framer of lies!"

The archer laughed.

"*Ohé*—are you one to question a warrior? When the very clients that come to your cell will not take food or water from the hand of a *Barna** Brahman. *Oho*—well you know that my master would hold himself contaminated were your shadow to fall across his feet."

He paused to stare at Khlit and Abdul Dost, whom he had not observed before.

"So you would steal from Jagannath!" fumed the priest.

"Nay."

The white teeth of the archer showed through his mustache.

"Am I one of the godless Kukushetra brethren who gorge themselves with the food that is offered to Jagannath? I plunder none save my lawful foes—behold this Turkish mail and helmet as witness!"

"Skulker!"

The hard face of the Brahman flushed darkly.

"Eavesdropper!"

---

* One of the lowest orders of the priesthood.

"At least," retorted the warrior, "I take not the roof from over the head of the man whose guest I am."

He turned to the mournful Bhimal.

"Come, comrade, will you let this evil lizard crawl into your hut? A good kick will send him flying."

"Nay—" the peasant shook his head—"it may not be. My brother gave a bond."

"But your brother is dead."

"He pledged his word. I would be dishonored were I not to fulfil it."

Sawal Das grimaced.

"By Siva!" he cried. "A shame to give good grain and cattle to these scavengers. Half the farms of the countryside they have taken to themselves. Even the might of my lord the Rawul can not safeguard the lands of his peasants. If this thing must be, then come to Thaneswar where you will be safe from the greed of such as Kurral."

"I thank you, Sawal Das."

Bhimal looked up gratefully.

"But I would be alone for a space to mourn my brother who is dead."

"So be it," rejoined the archer, "but forget not Thaneswar. Rawul Matap Rao has need of faithful house-servants."

"Aye," observed the priest; "the time will come when he who sits in Thaneswar will have need of—hirelings."

Khlit, indifferent to the discussion which he did not understand, had watered his horse and searched out a basket of fruit and cakes of jellied rice within the hut. Coming forth with his prize, he tossed a piece of silver money to Bhimal.

The peasant caught it and would have secreted it in his garments, but Kurral's sharp eye had seen the act.

"Take not the silver that is Jagannath's!"

He held out his hand.

"Or you will be accursed."

Reluctantly the peasant was about to yield the money to the priest when Sawal Das intervened.

"The bond said naught of money, Kurral," he pointed out. "Is your hunger for wealth like to a hyena's yearning for carrion? Is there no end of your greed? Touch not the dinar."

The priest turned upon the archer furiously.

"Take care!" he cried. "Kukushetra has had its fill of the idolatry of the Rawul and the insolence of his servants. Take care lest you lose your life by lifting hand against mighty Jagannath!"

"I fear not the god," smiled Sawal Das. "Lo, I will send him a gift, even Jagannath himself, by the low-born Kurral."

So swiftly that the watching Abdul Dost barely caught his movements, the archer dropped the peacock and plucked an arrow from its quiver. In one motion he strung the short bow and fitted arrow to string.

Kurral backed away, his eyes widening in sudden fear. Evidently he had reason to respect the archer. A tree-trunk arrested his progress abruptly.

Sawal Das seemed not to take aim, yet the arrow flew and the bowstring twanged. The shaft buried itself deep into the tree-trunk. And the sacred cord which hung to Kurral's left shoulder was parted in twain.

Kurral gazed blankly at the severed string and the arrow embedded not two inches from his ear. Then he turned and fled into the thicket, glancing over his shoulder as he went.

"A good shot, that, archer," laughed Abdul Dost.

"It was nought," grinned Sawal Das. "On a clear day I have severed the head from a carrion bird in full flight. Nay, a good shaft was wasted where it will do little good."

He strutted from the hut, gathering up the peacock.

"If you are strangers in Kukushetra," he advised, "you would do well to seek the door of my master, Rawul Matap Rao. He asks not what shrine you bow before, and he has ever an ear for a goodly song or tale, or—" Sawal Das noted the Afghan's lean figure appraisingly—"employment for a strong sword-arm. He is a just man, and within his gates you will be safe."

"So there is to be a marriage feast at Thaneswar?"

"Aye," nodded the archer, "and rare food and showers of silver for all who attend. This road leads to Thaneswar castle by the first turn up-hill. Watch well the path you take, for there are evil bandits—servants of the death-loving Kali—afoot in the deeper jungle."

With that he raised a hand in farewell and struck off into a path through the brush, singing to himself, leaving Bhimal sitting grief-stricken on the threshold of the hut and Khlit and Abdul Dost quietly breakfasting.

II

On that day the young chieftain of Thaneswar had broken the *torun* over the gate of Rinthambur.

The *torun* was a triangular emblem of wood hung over the portal of a woman who was to become a bride. Matap Rao, a clever horseman, rode under the stone arch, and while the women servants and the ladies of Rinthambur laughingly pelted him with flowers and plaited leaves he struck the *torun* with his lance until it fell to earth in fragments.

This done, as was customary, the mock defense of Rinthambur castle ceased; the fair garrison ended their pretty play and Rawul Matap Rao was welcomed by the men within the gate.

He was a man fit to be allied by blood even with the celebrated chiefs of the Rinthambur clan—a man barely beyond the limits of youth, who had many cares and who administered a wide province— Thaneswar—with the skill of an elder.

Perhaps the Rawul was not the fighting type beloved by the minstrels of the Rinthambur house. He was not prone to make wars upon his neighbors, choosing rather to study how the taxes of his peasants might be lightened and the heavy hand of the Kukushetra temple be kept from spoliation of the ignorant farmers.

The young Rawul, last of his line, was a breeder of fine horses, a student and a philosopher of high intelligence. He was the equal in birth to Retha of Rinthambur—the daughter of a warlike clan of the sun-born caste. She had smiled upon his wooing and the chieftains who were head of her house were not ill content to join the clans of Rinthambur and Thaneswar by blood.

War on behalf of the Mogul, and their own reckless extravagance with money and the blood of their followers, had weakened the clan. The remaining members had gathered at Rinthambur castle to pay fitting welcome to the Rawul.

"We yield to your care," they said, "her who is the gem in the diadem of Rajasthan—Retha of Rinthambur—who is called 'Lotus Face' in the Punjab. Guard her well. If need arise command our swords, for our clans are one."

So Matap Rao joined his hand to that of Retha, and the knot in their garments was tied in the hall of Rinthambur before the fire altar. Both Matap Rao and the Rinthambur chieftains were descendants of the fire family of the Hindus—devotees of the higher and milder form of Vishnu worship.

"Thaneswar," he said, "shall be another gate to Rinthambur and none shall be so welcome as the riders of Rinthambur."

But the chieftains after bidding adieu to him and his bride announced that they would remain and hold revelry in their own hall for two days, leaving the twain to seek Thaneswar, as was the custom.

Thus it happened that Matap Rao, flushed with exultation and deep in love, rode beside his bride to the boundary of Rinthambur, where the last of the bride's clan turned back. His followers, clad and mounted to the utmost finery of their resources, fell behind the two.

The way seemed long to Matap Rao, even though a full moon peered through the soft glimmer of twilight and the minstrel of Thaneswar—the aged *Vina*, Perwan Singh—chanted as he rode behind them, and the scent of jasmine hung about their path. In the Thaneswar jungle at the boundary of the two provinces a watch tower stood by the road, rearing its bulk against the moon.

Here were lights and soft draperies and a banquet of sugared fruits, sweetened rice, jellies, cakes and curries, prepared by the skilled hands of the women slaves who waited here to welcome their new mistress. And here the party dismounted, the armed followers occupying tents about the tower.

While they feasted and Matap Rao described the banquet that was awaiting them on the following night at Thaneswar hall, Perwan Singh sang to them and the hours passed lightly, until the moon became clouded over and a sudden wind swept through the forest.

A drenching downpour came upon the heels of the wind; the lights in the tower were extinguished, and Retha laid a slim hand fearfully upon the arm of her lord.

"It is an ill omen," she cried.

"Nay," he laughed, "no omen shall bring a cloud upon the heart of the queen of Thaneswar. Vishnu smiles upon us."

But Retha, although she laughed with her husband, was not altogether comforted. And, the next morning, when a band of horsemen and camels met them on the highway, she drew closer to Matap Rao.

A jangle of cymbals and kettle-drums proclaimed that this was the escort of a higher priest of Kukushetra. Numerous servants, gorgeously dressed, led a fine Kabul stallion forward to meet the Rawul, and its rider smiled upon him.

This was Nagir Jan, *gosain* of Kukushetra and abbot of the temple.

He was a man past middle life, his thin face bearing the imprint of a dominant will, the chin strongly marked, the eyes piercing. He bowed to Retha, whose face was half-veiled.

"A boon," he cried, "to the lowly servant of Jagannath. Let him see but once the famed beauty of the Flower of Rinthambur."

Matap Rao hesitated. He had had reason more than once to feel the power of the master of the temple. Nagir Jan was reputed to be high in the mysteries of the nation-wide worship of Jagannath.

Owing to the wealth of the priests of the god, and the authority centered in his temples, the followers of Jagannath were the only Hindus permitted by the Mogul to continue the worship of their divinity as they wished. The might of Jagannath was not lightly to be challenged.

But Nagir Jan was also a learned priest familiar with the Vedas and the secrets of the shrine of Puri itself. As such he could command the respect of Matap Rao, who was an ardent Vishnu worshiper. For Jagannath, by the doctrine of incarnation, embodied the worship of Vishnu.

"If Retha consents," he responded, "it is my wish."

The girl realized that the priest had come far to greet her. She desired to please the man who was more powerful than the Rawul in Thaneswar.

So she drew back the veil. But her delicate face wore no smile. The splendid, dark eyes looked once, steadily into the cold eyes of the priest.

"Truly," said Nagir Jan softly, "is she named the Lotus Face. The lord of Retha is favored of the gods."

While the twain rode past he continued to look after the girl. Glancing over his shoulder presently, the Rawul saw that Nagir Jan was still seated on his horse, looking at them. He put spurs to his horse, forcing a laugh.

But after the festival at Thaneswar Matap Rao would have given much, even half his lands, if he had not granted the wish of Nagir Jan.

The same thunder-storm that so disturbed the young bride of the Rawul caught Khlit and Abdul Dost on the open road.

The warriors had lingered long at the hospitable hut of Bhimal to escape the mid-day heat. So the sun was slanting over the wheat-fields when they trotted toward the castle of Thaneswar. It was twilight when they came upon the cross-roads described by the archer, Sawal Das.

Here was a grimy figure squatted upon a ragged carpet, the center of interest of a group of naked children who scampered into the bushes at sight of the riders.

The man was a half-caste Portuguese, hatless and bootless. On the carpet before him were a mariner's compass, much the worse for wear, and one or two tattered books, evidently—as Khlit surmised—European prayer-books. He glanced up covertly at the warriors.

"What manner of man is this?" wondered Abdul Dost aloud in Hindustani.

"An unworthy astrologer, so please you, great sirs," bowed the half-caste.

He closed both eyes and smiled.

"My mystic instrument of divination—" he pointed to the compass —"and my signs of the Zodiac."

He showed illuminated parchment pictures of the saints in the prayer-book.

"It is a goodly trade, and the witless ones of this country pay well. My name is Merghu. What can I do for the great sirs?"

"*Jaisa des waisahi bhes!*" (For such a country, such a masquerade) responded the Afghan contemptuously. "Will not the priest of Ku-kushetra beat your back with bamboos if they find you here at the cross-roads?"

Again the man's eyes closed slyly and his sullen face leered. He lifted a corner of his cloak, disclosing a huge, ulcerous sore.

"Nay, noble travelers. They may not touch what is unclean. Besides the festival of *Janam* approaches, and the priests are busied within the temple——"

"Enough!" growled the Afghan at a sign from Khlit, who had marked a cloud-bank creeping over the moon that was beginning to show between the tree-tops. "We are belated. We were told to take the upper hill trail to Thaneswar castle, but here be two trails. Which is the one we seek?"

"Yonder," muttered the astrologer, pointing. "The other leads to the temple."

Khlit and Abdul Dost spurred up the way he had indicated. Glancing back at the first turn in the trail, the Cossack noticed that the sham astrologer had vanished, with all his stock in trade.

But now wind whipped the tree-tops that met over the trail. Rain poured down in one of the heavy deluges that precede the wet season in this country.

Khlit rode unheeding, but Abdul Dost swore vehemently as his finery became soaked. He spurred his horse faster into the darkness without noticing where they went save that it was upward, trusting to the instinct of his mount to lead him safely.

So the two came at a round pace to a clearing in the trees. A high, blank wall emerged before them. This they circled until a gate opened and they trotted past a pool of water to a square structure with a high peaked roof whence came sounds of voices and the clang of cymbals.

"The wedding merriment has begun!" cried Abdul Dost.

He swung down from his horse and beat at a bronze door with fist and sword-hilt. Khlit, from the caution of habit, kept to his saddle. The door swung inward. A glare of light struck into their faces.

"Who comes to the hall of offerings of Jagannath?" cried a voice.

Khlit saw a group of Brahmans at the door. Behind them candles and torches lighted a large room filled with an assemblage of peasants and soldiers who were watching a dance through a wide doorway that seemed to lead into a building beyond.

In this farther space a cluster of young girls moved in time to the music of drums and cymbals, tossing their bare arms and whirling upon their toes so that thin draperies swirled about their half-nude forms.

Abdul Dost, who was a man of single thought, stared at the spectacle in astonishment, his garments dripping and rain beating upon his back.

"Who comes armed to the outer hall of the Lord of the World?" cried a young priest zealously. "Know ye not this is the time of the *Janam?*"

"I seek Thaneswar castle," explained the Afghan. "Is it not here? Nay, I am a traveler, not a slave of your god——"

"Begone then from here," commanded the young priest. "This is no place for those of—Thaneswar. Begone, one-without-breeding—low-born——"

"By Allah!" shouted Abdul Dost angrily. "Is this your courtesy to wayfarers in a storm!"

He swung back into his saddle, drawing his sword swiftly. Khlit, lest he should ride his horse into the throng, laid firm hand on the arm of the irate Moslem. They caught a passing glimpse of the dancing women staring at them, and the crowd. Then the door swung to in their faces with a clang.

"Low-born, they said in my teeth!" stormed the Afghan. "Base mouthers of indecency! Mockers of true men! Saw you the temple harlots offering their bodies to feast the eyes of the throng? Saw you the faithless priest offering food to the sculptured images of their armless gods——"

"Peace," whispered Khlit. "Here is an ill place for such words."

"Why laid you hand on my rein?" fumed Abdul Dost. "If you had fear in your heart for such as these—offscourings of thrice defiled dirt—why did you not flee? I would have barbered the head of yon shaven villain with my sword. *Eh*—I am not an old woman who shivers at hard words and sword-strokes——"

Khlit's grasp on his arm tightened.

"The rain is ceasing," growled the Cossack. "I can see the lights of Kukushetra village through the farther gate in the temple wall. Many men are afoot. Come. Thaneswar is a better place than this."

While the Cossack eyed the surroundings of the temple enclosure curiously Abdul Dost shrugged his shoulders.

"Age has sapped your courage, Khlit," muttered the *mansabdar*. "Verily, I heard tales of your daring from the Chinese merchants and the Tatars. Yet you draw back before the insult of a stripling priest."

Khlit wheeled his horse toward the gate jerking the bridle of the Afghan's mount.

"Aye, I am old," he said, half to himself. "And I have seen before this the loom of a man-trap. Come."

Sullenly the other trotted after him. Back on the trail the moon, breaking from the clouds by degrees, cast a network of shadows before them. The two rode in silence until Abdul Dost quickened his pace to take the lead.

"Perchance," he observed grimly, "that miscreant astrologer abides yet at the cross-roads. The flat of my sword laid to his belly will teach him not to guide better men than he astray."

Khlit lifted his head.

"Aye, the astrologer," he meditated aloud. "Surely he must have known the way to Thaneswar, as well as the temple path. It would be well, Abdul Dost, to watch better our path. Why did he speak us false? That is a horse will need grooming."

"Aye, with a sword."

The *mansabdar* rode heedlessly forward until they had gained the main road. Khlit, looking shrewdly on all sides, thought that he saw a figure move in the thicket at the side of the path. He checked his horse with a low warning to his companion.

But Abdul Dost, lusting for reprisal, slipped down from his saddle and advanced weapon in hand to the edge of the brush, peering into the shadows under the trees, which were so dense that the rain could barely have penetrated beneath their branches. Standing so, he was clearly outlined in the moonlight.

"Come forth, O skulker of the shadows!" he called. "Hither, false reader of the stars. I have a word for your ears— *Bismillah!*"

A dozen armed figures leaped from the bush in front of him. Something struck the mail on his chest with a ringing *clang,* and a spear dropped at his feet. Another whizzed past his head.

Abdul Dost gave back a pace, warding off the sword-blades that searched for his throat. Excellent swordsman that he was he was hard pressed by the number of his assailants. A sweeping blow of his scimitar half-severed the head of the nearest man, but another weapon bit into his leg over the knee, and his startled horse reared back, making him half-lose his balance.

At this point Khlit spurred his horse at the foes of Abdul Dost, riding down one and forcing the others back.

"Mount!" he cried over his shoulder to the Afghan.

Abdul Dost's high-strung Arab, however, had been grazed by a spear and was temporarily unmanageable. Khlit covered his companion, avoiding the blows of the attackers cleverly. They pressed their onset savagely.

Abdul Dost, cursing his injured leg, tossed aside the reins of his useless mount and stepped forward to Khlit's side, his sword poised.

Then, while the two faced the ten during one of those involuntary pauses that occur in hand-to-hand fights, a new element entered into the conflict at the cross-roads.

There was a sharp twang, a whistling hum in the air, and one of the assailants flung up his arms with a grunt. In the half-light Khlit saw that an arrow had transfixed the man's head, its feathered end sticking grotesquely from his cheek.

A second shaft and a third sped swiftly, each finding its mark on their foes. One man dropped silently to earth, clutching his chest; a second turned and spun dizzily backward into the bush.

One of the surviving few flung up his shield fearfully in time to have an arrow pierce it cleanly and plant itself in his shoulder.

There was something inexorable and deadly in the silent flight of arrows. Those who could stand, in the group of raiders, turned and leaped into the protecting shadows.

Khlit and Abdul Dost heard them running, breaking through the vines. They stared curiously at the five forms outstretched in the road. On the forehead of one who faced the moon, a shaft through his breast, they saw the white caste-mark of Jagannath.

Already the five had ceased moving.

"Come into the shadow, O heedless riders of the north," called a stalwart voice.

Khlit turned his horse, and was followed by Abdul Dost, who by this time had recovered his mount.

Under the trees on the farther side of the road they found Sawal Das, chuckling. The archer surveyed them, his small head on one side.

"Horses and sword-blades are an ill protection against the spears that fly in the dark," he remarked reprovingly.

"How came you here?" muttered Abdul Dost, who was in an ill humor, what with his hurt and the events of the night.

"Ohé—Oho!" Sawal Das laughed. "Am I not the right hand man of my lord, the Rawul? Does he not ride hither with his bride to-morrow? Thus, I watch the road.

"A short space ago when the rain ceased I heard an ill-omened group talking at the cross-roads. There was a half-caste *feringhi* who said that the two riders would return to seek the Thaneswar path——"

"The astrologer!" muttered Abdul Dost, binding his girdle over his thigh.

"Even so, my lord. Who is he but a spy of the temple? Ah, my bold swordsman, there be jewels in your turban and sword-hilt.

"Likewise—so Bhimal whispered—the low-born followers of the temple have orders to keep armed men from Thaneswar gate. I know not. But I waited with bow strung, believing that there would be sport——"

"Bravely and well have you aided us," said Khlit shortly in his broken Mogholi. "I saw others moving in the bush——"

"Perchance the evil-faced Kurral and his friends," assented Sawal Das, who understood.

"I will not forget," grunted the Cossack.

"Nay."

The archer took his rein in hand.

"This is no spot for our talk. I will lead you to Thaneswar, where you may sleep in peace."

He led them forward, humming softly to himself.

"Men of Jagannath have been slain," he murmured over his shoulder. "That will rouse the anger of the priests. Already the hot blood is in their foreheads at thought of the honor and wealth of my lord the Rawul. We will not speak of this, lest a cloud sully the bride-bringing of my lord.

"Verily," he said more softly, "did Perwan Singh, the chanter of epics, say that before long this place will be as it was in the days of the Pandas and the higher gods. Aye, Perwan Singh sang that blood would cover the mountains and bones will fill the valleys. Death will walk in the shadows of the men of Thaneswar."

Now, after they had gone, a form scurried from the thicket down the muddy highway, a heavy pack on its back. It paused not, nor looked behind. Merghu, the astrologer, was leaving Kukushetra.

III

There is One who knows the place of the birds who fly through the sky; who perceives what has been and what will be; who knows the track of the wind——

He is named by many names; yet he is but one.

Hymn to Vishnu.

Khlit was disappointed in the sight of Thaneswar castle. On the day following the affray of the cross-roads the Cossack was early afoot, and as the retainers were busied in preparing for the coming of their lord he was able to make the rounds of the place undisturbed save by a few curious glances.

The abode of Rawul Matap Rao was not a castle in the true sense of the word. In the midst of the wheat-fields of the province of Kukushetra a low wall of dried mud framed an enclosure of several buildings. The enclosure was beaten smooth by the feet of many animals, and against the wall were the stables, the elephant-stockade, the granaries and the quarters of the stable servants and the mahouts.

In the center of the site grew the garden of Thaneswar, a jumble of wild flowers, fern-trees and miniature deodars cleverly cultivated by gardeners whose hereditary task it was to tend the spot and keep clean the paths through the verdure, artfully designed to appear as if a hapazard growth of nature.

An open courtyard ornamented by a great pool of water shadowed by cypresses fronted the garden. At the rear of the courtyard, it was true, a solid granite building stood—the hall of the Rawul.

Pillars of the same stone, however, supported a thatched roof, under which ran layers of cane. Numerous openings in the granite wall provided sleeping-terraces.

The inner partitions were mainly latticework, and only one ceiling —that of the main hall—was of stronger material than the thatch. This was of cedar, inlaid with ivory and mosaic, and brightly painted.

To Khlit, accustomed to the rugged stone structures of Central Asia, the small palace was but a poor fortress. He had no eye for the throng of diligent servants who were spreading clean cotton cloths over the floor mattresses or placing flowers in the latticework.

"The temple of the hill-god, yonder," he muttered to Sawal Das, who had joined him, "was stronger."

The archer fingered his mustache.

"Aye," he admitted restlessly. "I would that the Rawul had kept the heavy taxes upon the peasants, so that the armed retainers of Thaneswar would be more numerous and better equipped. I have scarce twoscore able men under me. And my lord has not many more men-at-arms to attend him. He would give the very gold of his treasury to the peasants, if need be.

"When I say that we should have more swords—when yonder

eagle—" he pointed to the glittering dome of the temple—"cries out in greed—he laughs and swears that a word will rouse the peasantry and villagers of Kukushetra on our behalf. But I know not."

He shrugged his shoulders and dismissed his forebodings.

"Ah, well, warrior, who would dare to lift hand against Rawul Matap Rao, the last of the Thaneswar clan? Come, here is the choicest defender of Thaneswar, with his companions."

Sawal Das pointed to the stockade in one corner of the great enclosure. Here a half-dozen elephants were being groomed for the reception of the chieftain and his bride.

It was the first time that Khlit had seen the beasts near by and he strode over to gaze at them. Seeing his absorption in sight, the archer left to attend to his own affairs.

First the elephants were washed down well in a muddy pool outside the enclosure, reached by a wide gate through the wall. Then their heads, trunks and ears were painted a vivid orange, shaded off to green at the tips of the flapping ears and at the end of the trunk.

Then crimson silk cloths were hung over their barrels, and a triangular piece of green velvet was placed over their heads between the eyes. This done, silk cords with silver bells attached were thrown about their massive necks.

The largest of the huge animals, however, was attired in full war panoply. Bhimal, who had come with several of the household to gaze at the sight, touched Khlit's elbow.

"Behold Asil Rumi," he said in Mogholi.

Khlit and Abdul Dost had treated the lame peasant kindly—something rare in his experience—and he was grateful.

"The favorite elephant. He was a gift to the grandfather of the Rawul from a raja of Rinthambur. He has not his match for strength in this land. He is mightier than the storm-wind, which is the breath of the angry gods, for he can break down with his head a tree as big as my body."

The peasant sighed.

"Oftentimes, when the Rawul hunted tiger toward Rinthambur, Asil Rumi has trod down my wheat. But always the Rawul flung me silver to pay for the damage. A just man."

Khlit glanced at the old peasant.

"Have you left your farm?"

"Is it not Jagannath's? I would not dishonor the faith of my dead brother. See!" he cried.

Asil Rumi, with a thunderous internal rumbling, had planted his trunk against a post of the stockade a few yards from them. The elephant wore his battle armor—a bronze plate, heavily bossed, over his skull, stout leather sheets down either side, and twin sword-blades tied to his curving tusks.

Under the impact of the elephant's bulk the post creaked. Khlit saw it bend and heard it crack. The house servants ran back.

Asil Rumi leaned farther forward and the post—a good yard thick—gave as easily before him as an aspen. Then his mahout ran up. Khlit was surprized to hear the man talk to the beast urgently. The mahout held a silver prong, but this he did not use. Asil Rumi drew back.

At a second word from his master the elephant coiled his trunk about the post and straightened it. Then he stood tranquil, his huge ears shaking, muttering to himself.

"How is it," asked Khlit, "that a small man such as that can command a beast like Asil Rumi? The beast could slay him with a touch of the tusk."

"Aye," assented Bhimal gravely, "the father of this mahout was slain by Asil Rumi when he was angry. But today he only plays. So long as this man speaks to him Asil Rumi will obey because of his love for the man."

And Bhimal told how two generations ago the elephant had taken part in one of the battles of Rajasthan. The standard of the warlike Rinthambur clan had been placed on his back, and his mahout had led him well into the van of the Rajputs, ordering him to stand in a certain spot.

The battle had been closely fought about the beast, and the mahout slain. The elephant had been wounded in many places and the greater part of the Rinthambur Rajputs slain about him. Still Asil Rumi had remained standing where he was placed.

The Rajputs had won the battle, so Bhimal said. The soldiers had left the field during the pursuit, but Asil Rumi had stayed by the body of his mahout, refusing food or water for three days in his sorrow for the man who had been his master.

Then they had brought the boy who was the son of the mahout. Him the elephant had recognized and obeyed.

"Asil Rumi will go to meet the bride of Rinthambur," concluded Bhimal. "She will mount his howdah, with her lord. It will be a goodly sight."

Presently came Abdul Dost, resplendent in a fresh tunic and girdle, to announce that it was time they should groom their horses for the ride to meet the Rawul.

But Khlit remained in the elephant-stockade watching the beasts until the household cavalcade had actually mounted, when he left the animals that had so stirred his interest. He washed his face hastily in the garden pool, drew his belt tighter about his *khalat*, pulled at his mustache and was ready to ride with the others.

Bhimal excused himself to Sawul Das from accompanying the leaders of the peasants, saying that he was too lame to walk with the rest. Khlit, however, noticed that Bhimal kept pace with them as far as the cross-roads.

The bodies had been cleared away, and the feet of men and beasts had obscured the imprint of blood here. Bhimal lingered.

"So," said the Cossack grimly, "you go to Jagannath, not to your lord."

"Aye," said the peasant simply. "In the temple above is *he* who is greater than any lord. *He* is master of death and life. My brother died in his worship. Wherefore should I not go?"

Khlit lingered behind the other horsemen, scanning Bhimal curiously. As the elephants had been strange beasts to him, so Bhimal and his kind were a new race of men.

It was Khlit's habit to ponder what was new to him. In this he differed from Abdul Dost.

"Have many of the Thaneswar peasants gone to the temple festival?" he inquired, noticing that the foot retainers with the cavalcade were few.

"Aye."

"What is the festival?"

"It is the great festival of Jagannath. *Janam,* the holy priests call it. They say it is to honor the birth of the god. It has always been."

"Will the Rawul and his woman go?"

Khlit did not care to revisit the temple after the episode of the night before.

"Nay. The Rawul has no love for the priests of the temple. He has said—so it is whispered through the fields—that they are not the true worshipers of Vishnu."

Down the breeze came the sound of the temple drums and cymbals. Khlit thought grimly that he also had no love for the servants of Vishnu.

"What is this Jagannath?" he asked indifferently.

To Khlit the worship of an idol by dance or song was a manifestation of Satan. He was a Christian of simple faith.

His tone, however, aroused the patient Hindu.

"Jagannath!" he cried, and his faded eyes gleamed. "Jagannath is the god of the poor. All men stand equal before him. The raja draws his car beside the pariah. His festival lasts as many days as I have fingers, and every day there is food for his worshipers. It is the holy time when a bride is offered to Jagannath."

He pointed up to the temple.

"A woman is chosen, and she is blessed. She is called the bride of Jagannath. Food and flowers are given her. She rides in the front of the great car which we build with our hands when Jagannath himself comes from his temple and is borne in the car to the ruins of the holy edifice which was once the home of the older gods themselves.

"The woman—so Kurral said—abides one night in the shrine of the god. Then Jagannath reveals himself to her. He tells the omens for the coming year, whether the crops will be good, the rains heavy and the cows healthy. Then this is told to us. It is verily the word of the god.

"Ah!" He glanced around. "I am late."

He hobbled off up the path, leaning on his stick, and Khlit spurred after the others, dismissing from his mind for a time what he had heard about the festival of *Janam*.

He soon forgot Bhimal in the confusion attending the arrival of the Rawul, and the banquet that night.

There was good cheer in Thaneswar. The young Rawul with his bride and his companions feasted on the gallery overlooking the main hall. The soldiery and retainers shared the feast at the foot of the hall, or without on the garden terrace.

Khlit and Abdul Dost had discovered that wine was to be had by those who so desired, and seated themselves in a corner of the hall with a generous portion of the repast and silver cups of sherbet between them.

"*Eh*," cried the *mansabdar*, "these Hindus lack not a free hand. Did you mark how the Rawul scattered gold, silver and gems among the throng? The beauty of his bride has intoxicated him."

Khlit ate in silence. The music of Hindustan—a shrill clatter of instruments—held no charm for him. Abdul Dost, however, was accustomed to the melodies and nodded his head in time, his appreciation heightened by the wine.

"Last night," he said bluntly, "I spoke in haste, for I was angry. You are my brother in arms. By Allah, I would cut the cheek-bones from him who dared to say what I did."

He emptied his cup and cast a pleased glance over the merry crowd.

"It was a good word you spoke when Sawal Das led you to the horse of the Rawul and spoke your name to Matap Rao. *Eh*, Matap Rao asked whether you had a rank as a chieftain."

He smiled.

"You responded that a chieftain's rank is like to the number of men who will follow his standard in battle. That was well said.

"I have heard tales that you once were leader of as many thousands as Matap Rao numbers tens among his men. Is that the truth? It was in Tatary, in the Horde."

"That time is past," said Khlit.

"Aye. Perchance, though, such things may arise again. Sawal Das says that there may be fighting. Yet I scent it not. What think you?"

Abdul Dost glanced at Khlit searchingly. Much he had heard of the Cossack's craft in war.

Yet since their meeting Khlit had shown no desire to take up arms. Rather, he had seemed well content to be unmolested. This did not accord with the spirit of the fiery Afghan, to whom the rumor of battle was as the scent of life itself.

"I think," said Khlit, "that Matap Rao had done better to leave guards at the gate."

The Afghan shrugged his shoulders. Then lifted his head at the sound of a ringing voice. It was aged Perwan Singh, and his song was the song of Arjun that begins:

> As starlight in the Summer skies,
> So is the brightness of a woman's eyes—
> Unmatched is she!

Silence fell upon the hall and the outer corridors. All eyes were turned to the gallery where behind a curtain the young bride of Thaneswar sat beside the feast of Matap Rao and his companions, among them Perwan Singh.

> The sunbeam of the morning shows
> Within her path a withered lotus bud,
> A dying rose.
>
> Her footsteps wander in the sacred place
> Where stand her brethren, the ethereal race
> For ages dead!

A young noble of the household parted the curtain at the song's end. He was a slender man, dark-faced, twin strings of pearls wound in his turban and about his throat—Serwul Jain, of Thaneswar.

"Men of Thaneswar," he cried ringingly, "the Lotus Face is now our queen. Happy are we in the sight of the flower of Rinthambur. Look upon Retha, wife of your lord."

There was a murmur of delight as the woman stood beside him. She was of an even height with the boy, the olive face unveiled, the black eyes wide and tranquil, the dark hair empty of jewels except for pearls over the forehead. Her thin silk robe, bound about the waist and drawn up from feet to shoulder, showed the tight underbodice over her breast and the outline of the splendid form that had been termed the "tiger-waisted."

"Verily," said Abdul Dost, "she is fair."

But Khlit had fallen asleep during the song. The minstrelsy of Hindustan held no charms for him, and he had eaten well.

A stir in the hall, followed by a sudden silence, aroused the Cossack. He was wide awake on the instant, scenting something unwonted. Abdul Dost was on his feet, as indeed were all in the hall. Within the doorway stood a group of Brahmans, surrounded by representatives of the higher castes of Kukushetra.

The castle retainer stood at gaze, curious and expectant. Through the open gate a breath of air stirred the flames of the candles.

"What seek you?" asked Serwul Jain from the gallery.

"We have come from the temple of Kukushetra, from the holy shrine of the Lord of the World," responded the foremost priest. "Rawul Matap Rao we seek. We have a message for his ears."

By now the chieftain was beside Retha. The eyes of the throng went from him to the Brahman avidly. It was the first time the Brahmans had honored Thaneswar castle with their presence.

"I am here," said the Rawul briefly. "Speak."

The Brahman advanced a few paces, drawing his robe closer about him. The servants gave back respectfully.

"This, O Rawul," he began, "is the festival of *Janam*. Pilgrims have come from every corner of the Punjab; aye, from the Siwalik hills and the border of Rajasthan to the temple of Jagannath. Yet you remain behind your castle wall."

He spoke sharply, clearly. No anger was apparent in his voice, but a stern reproach. Behind him Khlit saw the gaunt figure of Kurral.

"The day of my wedding is just past," responded Matap Rao quietly, "and I abide here to hold the feast. My place is in my own hall, not at the temple."

"So be it," said the priest.

He flung his head back and his sonorous voice filled the chamber.

"I bear a message from the shrine. Though you have forgotten the reverence due to the Lord of the World, though you have said harsh words concerning his temple, though you have neglected the holy rites and slandered the divine mysteries—even though you have forsworn the worship of Jagannath—the Lord of the World forgives and honors you."

He paused as if to give his words weight with the attentive throng.

"For the space of years your path and that of the temple have divided. Aye, quarrels have been and blood shed. Last night five servants of the temple were slain on the highroad without your gate."

A surprized murmur greeted this. News of the fight had been kept secret by the priests until now, and Sawal Das had held his tongue.

"Yet Jagannath forgives. Matap Rao, your path will now lead to the temple. For tonight the bride of Jagannath is chosen. And the woman chosen is—as is the custom—fairest in the land of Kukushetra. Retha of Rinthambur."

Complete silence enveloped the crowd. Men gaped and started. Youthful Serwul Jain started and clutched at his sword. The lean hand of Perwan Singh arrested midway as he stroked his beard. The girl flashed a startled glance at her lord and drew the silk veil across her face.

A slow flush rose into the face of Matap Rao and departed, leaving him pale. He drew a deep breath and the muscles of his figure tightened until he was at his full height.

To be selected as the bride of the god on the *Janam* festival was held a high honor. It had been shared in the past by some of the most noted women of the land. The choice of the temple had never been denied.

But in the mild face of the Rawul was the shadow of fierce anger, swiftly mastered. He looked long into the eyes of the waiting priest while the crowd hung upon his word.

"Whose is the choice?" he asked slowly.

"Nagir Jan himself uttered the decree. The holy priest was inspired by the thought that Retha, wife of the Rawul, should hear the prophecy of the god for the coming year. Who but she should tell the omens to Kukushetra?"

Matap Rao lifted his hand.

"Then let Nagir Jan come to Thaneswar," he responded. "Let him voice his request himself. I will not listen to those of lower caste."

IV

Upon the departure of the priests the curtain across the gallery was drawn. A tumult arose in the hall. Many peasants departed. The serving women fled back to their quarters, and the house retainers lingered, watching the gallery.

Abdul Dost leaned back against the wall, smiling at Khlit.

"By the beard of my grandsire! If I had such a bride as Retha of Rinthambur I would yield her not to any muttering Hindu priest."

He explained briefly to Khlit what had passed. The Cossack shook his head moodily.

"There will be ill sleeping in Thaneswar this night, Abdul Dost," he said grimly. "The quarrel between priest and chieftain cuts deeper than you think."

"It is fate. The Rawul may not refuse the honor."

Khlit stroked his gray mustache, making no response. The prime of his life he had spent in waging war with the reckless ardor of the Cossack against the enemies of the Cross. The wrong done to Bhimal had not escaped his attention. Nor had the one glimpse of the Kuku-shetra temple been agreeable to his narrow but heartfelt idea of a place of worship.

"When all is said," meditated the Afghan, "this is no bread of our eating."

"Nay, Abdul Dost. Yet we have eaten the salt of Matap Rao."

"Verily, that is so," grunted the Afghan. "Well, we shall soon see what is written. What is written, is written. Not otherwise."

Khlit seated himself beside his comrade and waited. Soon came Sawal Das through an opening in the wall behind them. Seeing them, he halted, breathing hard, for he had been running.

"*Aie!*" he cried. "It was an ill thought that led Matap Rao to thin the ranks of his armed men. Nagir Jan has watched Thaneswar ripen like a citron in the sun. He has yearned after the wheat-fields and the tax paid by the peasants. Truly is he named the snake. See, how he strikes tonight.

"*Aie!* He is cunning. His power is like that of the furious *daevas*. His armor is hidden, yet he is more to be feared than if a thousand swords waved about him."

Abdul Dost laughed.

"If that is the way the horse runs, archer, you could serve your master well by planting a feathered shaft under the ear of the priest."

Sawal Das shook his head.

"Fool!" he cried. "The Rawul would lose caste and life itself were he to shed the blood of a higher priest of Jagannath. He would be left for the burial dogs to gnaw. The person of Nagir Jan and those with him is inviolate."

"Then must Matap Rao yield up his bride."

The archer's white teeth glinted under his mustache.

"Never will a Rawul of Thaneswar do that."

Both men were surprized at the anger of the slender archer. They knew little of the true meaning of the festival of Jagannath.

"Perchance he will flee, Sawal Das. Khlit and I will mount willingly to ride with him. Your shafts would keep pursuers at a distance."

"I have been the rounds of the castle enclosure," observed Sawal Das. "The watchers of the temple are posted at every gateway and even along the wall itself. Their spies are in the stables. Without the enclosure the peasants gather together. They have been told to arm."

"On behalf of their lord?"

"Vishnu alone knows their hearts."

Abdul Dost reached down and gripped the arm of Sawal Das.

"Ho, little archer," he growled, "if it comes to sword-strokes—we have eaten the salt of your master, and we are in your debt. We will stand at your side."

"I thank you."

The Hindu's eyes lighted. Then his face fell.

"But what avail sword-strokes against Jagannath? How can steel cut the tendrils of his temple that coil about Thaneswar? Nay; unless my lord can overmaster him with fair words it will go ill with us."

He shook both fists over his head in impotent wrath.

"May the curse of Siva and Vishnu fall upon the master of lies! He has waited until the people of the countryside are aflame with zeal. He has stayed his hand until the Lotus Face came to Thaneswar as bride. Did not he ask to look upon her when she rode hither? *Aie*, he is like a barbed shaft in our flesh."

Came Bhimal, limping, to their corner.

"Nagir Jan is at the gate, Sawal Das," he muttered. "And behind him are the peasantry, soldiers and scholars of Kukushetra, many of them armed, to receive Retha as the chosen bride."

The archer departed. Bhimal squatted beside them, silent, his head hanging on his chest. Abdul Dost glanced at Khlit.

"Your pony is in the stable," he whispered. "Perchance if you ride not forth now the going will be ill."

"And so is yours, Abdul Dost," grunted Khlit. "Why do you not mount him?"

The Afghan smiled and they both settled back to await what was to come.

Nagir Jan entered the hall alone. Matap Rao advanced a few paces to meet him. Neither made a salaam. Their eyes met and the priest spoke first, while those in the hall listened.

"I have come for the bride of the *Janam*. Even as you asked it, I have come. Tonight she must bathe and be cleansed of all impurity. The women of the wardrobe and the strewers of flowers will attend her, to prepare her to mount the sacred car on the morrow. Then will she sit beside the god himself. And on that night will she kneel before him in the chamber in the ruins and the god will speak to her and manifest himself in the holy mystery. Where is the woman Retha?"

Matap Rao smiled, although his face was tense and his fingers quivered.

"Will you take the veil from your face? Will you withdraw the cloak from your words, Nagir Jan?"

The cold eyes of the priest flickered. His strong face showed no sign of the anger he must have felt.

"Nagir Jan, I will speak the truth. Will you answer me so?"

"Say on," assented the Brahman.

The young lord of Thaneswar raised his voice until it reached the far corners of the hall.

"Why do you hold me in despite, Nagir Jan? You have said that I am without faith. Yet do I say that my faith is as great as yours. Speak!"

A murmur went through the watchers. The youths standing behind Matap Rao glanced at each other, surprized by the bold course the Rawul had taken.

"Does a servant of Jagannath speak lies?" Nagir Jan smiled. "Is the wisdom of the temple a house of straw, to break before the first wind? Nay."

He paused, meditating. He spoke clearly, forcibly in the manner of one who knew how to sway the hearts of his hearers.

"Is not Jagannath Lord of the World, Matap Rao? In him is mighty Vishnu thrice incarnate; in him are the virtues of Siva, protector of the soul; and the virtues of Balabhadra and Subhadra. Since the birth of Ram, Jagannath has been. The power of Kali, All-Destroyer, is the lightning in his hand. Is not this the truth?"

Nagir Jan bowed his head. Matap Rao made no sign.

"Surely you do not question the holiness of Jagannath, protector of the poor, guardian of the pilgrim and master of our souls?" continued the priest. "Nay, who am I but a lowly sweeper of the floor before the mighty god?"

He stretched out a thin hand.

"Jagannath casts upon you the light of his mercy, Rawul. He ordains that your faithlessness be forgiven. Thus does Jagannath weld in one the twin rulers of Kukushetra.

"If you seek forgiveness, Kukushetra will prosper and the hearts of its men be uplifted. To this end has Jagannath claimed the beauty of Retha. Your wife will be the bond that will bind your soul to its forgotten faith."

He smiled and lowered his hand. Dignified and calm, he seemed as he said, the friend of the Rawul.

"Is not this the truth, Matap Rao? Aye, it is so."

The priest ceased speaking and waited for the other to reply.

In his speech Nagir Jan had avoided the issue of Matap Rao's faith. He had spoken only of the claim of Jagannath. And a swift glance at his hearers showed him that his words had gone home. Many heads nodded approvingly.

The Rawul would not dare, so thought Nagir Jan, to attack the invisible might of Jagannath. By invoking the divinity of the god, Nagir Jan had made Matap Rao powerless to debate. And personal debate, he guessed, was the hope of Matap Rao.

Something of triumph crept into his cold face. Matap Rao was thoughtful, his eyes troubled. The chieftain was an ardent Hindu. How could he renounce his faith?

Abruptly his head lifted and he met the eyes of the priest.

"What you have said of Jagannath, incarnation of Vishnu, is verily the truth, Nagir Jan," responded the Rawul. "Yet it is not all the truth. You have not said that the *priests* of Jagannath are false. They are false servants of Vishnu. They are not true followers of the One who is master of the gods."

He spoke brokenly, as a man torn by mingled feeling.

"Aye. Wherefore do the priests of Kukushetra perform the rites in costly robes? Or anoint themselves with oil? With perfume, with camphor and sandal? Instead of the sacred Vedas, they chant the *prem sagar*—the ocean of love. The pictures and images of the temple are those of lust."

His voice was firmer now, with the ring of conviction.

"Aye, you are faithless servants. The rich garments that are offered by pilgrims to the gods, you drape once upon the sacred images. Then you wear them on your unclean bodies.

"What becomes of the stores of food yielded by peasants for the meals of Jagannath? Four times a day do you present food to the wooden face of the god; afterward you feast well upon it."

Nagir Jan showed no change of expression; but he drew back as if from contamination.

"You have forgotten the wise teachings of Chaitanya, who declared that a priest is like to a warrior," continued the Rawul. "The *gosain* preached that sanctity is gained by inward warfare, by self-denial and privation.

"You of Kukushetra follow the doctrine of Vallabha Swami. He it was who said that gratified desire uplifts the soul. And so do you live. What are the handmaidens of Jagannath but the prostitutes of the temple and its people?"

An uneasy stir among the listeners greeted this. Many heads were shaken.

"It is the truth I speak," cried the Rawul, turning to them. "Nagir Jan claims to be the friend of the poverty-afflicted. Is it so? He seeks devotees among the merchants and masters of wealth.

"He takes the fields of the peasants by forfeiture, contrary to law. He has taken much of my land. He seeks all of Thaneswar."

The young chieftain spread out his arms.

"My spirit has followed the way of Chaitanya. I believe that bloodshed is pollution. My household divinity is the image of the sun, which was the emblem of my oldest forebears, whose fields were made fertile by its light. Is it not truth that a man may uplift his spirit even to the footstool of the One among the gods by *bahkti*—faith?"

While the watchers gazed, some frowning, some admiring, Abdul Dost touched the arm of Khlit and nodded approvingly.

"An infidel," he whispered, "but—by the ninety-nine holy names— a man of faith."

Nagir Jan drew his robe closer about him, and spoke pityingly.

"Blind!" he accused. "Does not the god dwell in the temple?"

"Then," responded Matap Rao, "whose dwelling is the world?"

He pointed at the priest.

"What avails it to wash your mouth, to mutter prayers on the pilgrimage if there is no faith in your heart, Nagir Jan? For my faith, you seek to destroy me, to gain the lands of Thaneswar. And so, you have asked Retha as the bride of Jagannath."

The shaven head of the priest drew back with the swift motion of a snake about to strike. But Matap Rao spoke before him.

"Well you know, Nagir Jan, that I will not yield Retha. If it means my death, Retha will not go to the temple."

"Thus you defy the choice of Jagannath?"

"Aye," said Matap Rao, and his voice shook. "For I know what few know. Among the ruins will the bride of Jagannath remain tomorrow night—where you and those who believe with you have said the god will appear as a man and foretell the omens, in the mystery of *Janam*. But he who will come to the woman is no god but a man, chosen by lot among the priests—perhaps you, Nagir Jan."

His tense face flushed darkly. He lowered his voice, but in the silence it could be heard clearly.

"The rite of *Janam* will be performed. But a *man* violates the body of the bride. It is a priest. And he prophesies the omens. That is why, O Nagir Jan, I have called the priests false.

"Never will the Lotus Face become the bride of Jagannath," he added quietly.

"Impious! Idolator!"

The head of Nagir Jan shot forward with each word.

"It is a lie, spoken in madness. But the madness will not save you."

His eyes shone cruelly, and his teeth drew back from the lips.

"You have blasphemed Jagannath, O Rawul. You have denied to Jagannath his bride."

He turned swiftly.

"Thaneswar is accursed. Who among you will linger here? Who will come with me to serve Jagannath? The god will claim his bride. Woe to those who aid him not——"

He passed swiftly from the hall and a full half of the peasants as well as many of the house servants slipped after him. The soldiers around the Rawul stood where they were.

Rawul Matap Rao gazed after the fugitives with a wry smile. Old Perwan Singh laid down his *vina* and girded a sword-belt about his bony frame. Serwul Jain drew his scimitar and flung the scabbard away.

"The battle-storm is at the gate of Thaneswar," he cried in his high voice. "Ho—who will shed his blood for the Lotus Face? You have heard the words of your lord."

A hearty shout from the companion nobles answered him, echoed by a gruffer acclaim from the soldiery, led by Sawal Das. Matap Rao's eyes lighted but his smile was sad.

"Aye, blood will be shed," he murmured. "It is pollution—yet we who die will not bear the stain of the sin."

He laid an arm across the bent shoulder of the minstrel.

"Even thus you foretold, old singer of epics. Will you sing also of the fate of Thaneswar?"

Abdul Dost spoke quickly to Khlit of what had passed. His face was alight with the excitement of conflict. But the shaggy face of Khlit showed no answering gleam.

"There will be good sword-blows, O wayfarer," cried the Moslem. "Come, here is a goodly company. We will scatter the rout of temple-scum! *Eh!*—what say you?"

Khlit remained passive, wearing every indication of strong disgust.

"Why did not yonder stripling chieftain prepare the castle for siege?" he growled.

"Dog of the devil—he did naught but speak words."

He remained seated where he was while Abdul Dost ran to join the forces mustering under Serwul Jain at the castle gate. He shook his head moodily.

But as the Rawul, armed and clad in mail, passed by, Khlit reached up and plucked his sleeve.

"Where, O chieftain," he asked bluntly, "is Asil Rumi, defender of Thaneswar? He is yet armored—aye—the elephants are your true citadel——"

Not understanding Mogholi, and impatient of the strange warrior's delay, the Rawul shook him off and passed on. Khlit looked after him aggrievedly.

Then he shook his wide shoulders, yawned, girded his belt tighter and departed on a quest for food among the remnants of the banquet. It was Khlit's custom, whenever possible, to eat before embarking on any dangerous enterprise.

V

And they paused to harken to a voice which said, "Hasten."

It was the voice of the assembler of men, of him who spies out a road for many, who goes alone to the mighty waters. It was Yama, the Lord of Death, and he said:

"Hasten to thy home, and to thy fathers."

Nagir Jan was not seen again at Thaneswar that night. But his followers heard his tidings and a multitude gathered on the road.

Those who accompanied the Brahman from the hall could give

only an incoherent account of the words Matap Rao had spoken. The crowd, however, had been aroused by the priests in the temple.

It was enough for them that the Rawul had blasphemed against the name of Jagannath. They were stirred by religious zeal, at the festival of the god.

Moreover, as in all mobs, the lawless element coveted the chance to despoil the castle. Among the worshipers were many, well armed, who assembled merely for the prospect of plunder. They joined forces with the more numerous party.

The ranks of the pilgrims and worshipers who had been sent down from the temple by the Brahmans was swelled by an influx of villagers and peasants from the fields—ignorant men who followed blindly those of higher caste.

The higher priests absented themselves, but several of the lower orders such as Kurral directed the onset against the castle. Already the enclosure was surrounded. Torches blazed in the fields without the mud wall. The wall itself was easily surmounted at several points before the garrison could muster to defend it—even if they had been numerous enough to do so.

"Jagannath!" cried the pilgrims, running toward the central garden, barehanded and aflame with zeal, believing that they were about to avenge a mortal sin on the part of one who had scorned the gods.

"Jagannath!" echoed the vagrants and mercenary soldiers, fingering their weapons, eyes burning with the lust of spoil.

"The bride of Jagannath!" shouted the priests among the throng. "Harm her not, but slay all who defend her."

Torches flickered through the enclosure and in the garden. Frightened stable servants fled to the castle, or huddled among the beasts. The neighing of startled horses was drowned by the trumpeting of the elephants. A mahout who drew his weapon was cut down by the knives of the peasants.

But it was toward the palace that the assailants pressed through the pleasure garden; and the palace was ill designed for defense. Wide doorways and latticed arbors guided the mob to the entrances. The clash of steel sounded in the uproar, and the shrill scream of a wounded woman pierced it like a knife-blade.

The bright moon outlined the scene clearly.

Khlit, standing passive within the main hall, could command at once a balcony overlooking the gardens and the front gate. He saw several of the rushing mob fall as the archers in the house launched their shafts.

A powerful blacksmith, half-naked, appeared on the balcony, whither he had climbed, dagger between his teeth. A loyal peasant rushed at him with a sickle, and paused at arm's reach.

"Jagannath!" shouted the giant, stepping forward.

The coolie shrank back and tossed away his makeshift weapon, crying loudly for mercy. He stilled his cry at a melodious voice.

"Chaitanya! Child of the sun!"

It was old Perwan Singh, walking tranquilly along the tiles of the gallery in the full moonlight. The smith hesitated, then advanced to meet him, crouching. The minstrel struck down the dagger awkwardly with his sword. Meanwhile the recalcitrant peasant had crept behind him, and with a quick jerk wrested away the blade.

Perwan Singh lifted his arm, throwing back his head. He did not try to flee. The black giant surveyed him, teeth agrin, and, with a grunt, plunged his dagger into the old man's neck. Both he and the coolie grasped the minstrel's body before it could fall, stripping the rich gold bangles from arms and ankles of their victim and tearing the pearls from his turban-folds.

Before they could release the body an arrow whizzed through the air, followed swiftly by another. The giant coughed and flung up his arms, falling across the body of the coolie. The three forms lay on the tiles, their limbs moving weakly.

Sawal Das, fitting a fresh shaft to string, trotted by along the balcony, peering out into the garden.

The rush of the mob had by now resolved itself into a hand-to-hand struggle at every door to the castle. The blood-lust, once aroused, stilled all other feelings except that of fanatic zeal. Unarmed men grappled with each other, who had worked side by side in the fields the day before.

A woman slave caught up a javelin and thrust at the assailants, screaming the while. For the most part the house-servants had remained loyal to Matap Rao, whom they loved.

By now, however, all within the castle were struggling for their lives. A soldier slew the woman, first catching her ill-aimed weapon coolly on his shield. Khlit saw a second woman borne off by the peasants.

At the main gate the disciplined defenders under Matap Rao,

aided well by that excellent swordsman, Abdul Dost, had beaten off the onset. Serwul Jain and several of the younger nobles had been ordered to safeguard Retha.

They stood in the rear of the main hall, the girl tranquil and proud, her face unveiled, her eyes following Matap Rao in the throng. The Rawul, by birth of the Kayasth or student caste, proved himself a brave man although unskilled.

It was when the first assault had been beaten off and the defenders were gaining courage that the crackle of flames was heard.

Agents of the priesthood among the mob had devoted their attention to firing the thatch roof at the corners. Matap Rao sent bevies of house-servants up to the terraces on the roof, but the flames gained. A shout proclaimed the triumph of the mob.

"Jagannath!" they cried. "The god claims his bride."

"Lo," screamed a pilgrim, "the fire spirits aid us. The *daevas* aid us."

Panic, that nemesis of ill-disciplined groups, seized on many slaves and peasants who were in the castle.

"Thaneswar burns!" cried a woman, wringing her hands.

"The gods have doomed us!" muttered a stout coolie, fleeing down the hall.

Serwul Jain sprang aside to cut him down.

"Back, dogs!" shouted the boy. "Death is without."

"*Aie!* We will yield our bodies to Jagannath," was the cry that greeted him.

"Jagannath!"

Those outside caught up the cry.

"Yield to the god."

The backbone of the defense was broken. Slaves threw down their arms. A frightened tide surged back and forth between the rooms. A Brahman appeared in the hall and ran toward Retha silently. A noble at her side stepped between, taking the rush of the priest on his shield.

But the Brahman's fall only dispirited the slaves the more.

Khlit saw groups of half-naked coolies climbing into the windows—the wide windows that served to cool Thaneswar in the Summer heat. He walked down the hall, looking for Abdul Dost.

He saw the thinned body of soldiers at the gate struggle and part before the press of attackers. Then Bhimal, who had remained crouched beside him during the earlier fight, started up and ran, limping, at Serwul Jain.

"Jagannath!" cried the peasant hoarsely. "My brother's god."

He grappled with the noble from behind and flung him to the stone floor. Coolies darted upon the two and sank their knives into the youth. Bhimal stood erect, his eyes staring in frenzy.

"Jagannath conquers!" he shouted.

Khlit caught a glimpse of Matap Rao in a press of men. He turned in time to see Retha's guards hemmed in by a rush of the mob, their swords wrested from their hands.

Retha was seized by many hands before she could lift a scimitar that she had caught up against herself. Seeing this and the agony in the girl's face, Khlit hesitated.

But those who held the wife of the Rawul were too many for one man to encounter. He turned aside, down a passage that led toward the main gate.

He had seen Abdul Dost and Matap Rao fight loose from the men who caught at them.

Then for a long space smoke descended upon the chambers of Thaneswar from the smoldering thatch. The cries of the hurt and the wailing of the women were drowned in a prolonged shout of triumph.

The Rawul and Abdul Dost, who kept at his side, sought fruitlessly through the passages for Retha. Those who met them stepped aside at sight of their bloodied swords and stern faces. They followed the cries of a woman out upon the garden terrace, only to find that she was a slave in the hands of the coolies.

Matap Rao, white-faced, would have gone back into the house, but the Moslem held him by sheer strength.

"It avails not, my lord," he said gruffly. "Let us to horse and then we may do something."

The chieftain, dazed by his misfortune, followed the tall Afghan toward the stables, which so far had escaped the notice of the mob, bent on the richer plunder of the castle. Here they met Khlit walking composedly toward them, leading his own pony and the Arab of Abdul Dost, fully saddled.

"Tell the stripling," growled Khlit, "that his palace is lost. Retha

I saw in the hands of the priests. They will guard her from the mob. Come."

He led them in the direction of the elephant-stockade. He had noted that morning that a gate offered access to the elephants' pool. Avoiding one or two of the great beasts who were trampling about the place, leaderless and uneasy, he came upon a man who ran along the stockade bearing a torch.

It was Sawal Das, bow in hand. The archer halted at sight of his lord.

"I had a thought to seek for Asil Rumi," he cried. "But the largest of the elephants is gone with his mahout. *Aie*—heavy is my sorrow. My lord, my men are slain——"

"Come!" broke in Abdul Dost. "We can do naught in Thaneswar."

Even then, loath by hereditary custom to turn their backs on a foe, the chieftain and his archer would have lingered helplessly. But Abdul Dost took their arms and drew them forward.

"Would you add to the triumph of Nagir Jan?" he advised coolly. "There be none yonder but the dead and those who have gone over to the side of the infidel priests.

"This old warrior is in the right. He has seen many battles. We be four men, armed, with two horses. Better that than dead."

A shout from the garden announced that they had been seen. This decided the archer, who tossed his torch to the ground and ran outward through the stockade and the outer wall.

Avoiding their pursuers in the shadows, they passed by the pool into the wood beyond the fields. Here a freshly beaten path opened before them. Sawal Das trotted ahead until all sounds of pursuit had dwindled. Then they halted, eying each other in silence.

Matap Rao leaned against a horse, the sweat streaming from his face. His slender shoulders shook. Khlit glanced at him, then fell to studying the ground under their feet.

Sawal Das unstrung his bow and counted the arrows in his quiver.

"Enough," he remarked grimly, "to send as gifts into the gullets of the Snake and his Kurral. They will not live to see Retha placed upon the car of Jagannath. I swear it."

Abdul Dost grunted.

Matap Rao raised his head and they fell silent.

"In the fall of my house and the loss of my wife," he said bitterly, "lies my honor. Fool that I was to bring Retha to Thaneswar when Nagir Jan had set his toils about it. I can not face the men of Rinthambur."

"Rinthambur!" cried Abdul Dost. "Ho—that is a good word. The hard-fighting clan will aid us, nothing loath—aye, and swiftly. Look you, on these two horses we may ride there——"

"Peace!" said the Rawul calmly. "Think you, soldier, I would ride to Rinthambur when they still hold the wedding feast, and say that Retha has been taken from me?"

"What else?" demanded the blunt Afghan. "By Allah—would you see the Lotus Face fall to Jagannath? In a day and a night we may ride thither and back. With the good clan of Rinthambur at our heels. *Eh*—they wield the swords to teach these priests a lesson——"

"Nay, it would be too late."

"When does the procession of the god——"

"Just before sunset the car of Jagannath is dragged to the ruins."

"Then," proposed the archer, "if Vishnu favors us we may attack— we four—and slay many. Twilight will cover our movement near the ruins. Aye, perchance we can muster some following among the near-by peasants.

"Then will we provide bodies in very truth for the car of Jagannath to roll upon. From this hour am I no longer a follower of the All-Destroyer——"

Matap Rao smiled wanly.

"So have I not been for many years, Sawal Das. My faith is that of the Rinthambur clan, who are called children of the sun. I worship the One Highest. Yet what has it availed me?"

He turned as Khlit came up. The Cossack had lent an attentive ear to the speech of the archer. He had completed his study of the trail wherein they stood. He swaggered as he walked forward—a fresh alertness in his gaunt figure.

"It is time," he said, "that we took counsel together as wise men and as warriors. The time for folly is past."

Abdul Dost and Sawal Das, nothing loath, seated themselves on their cloaks upon the ground already damp with the night dew. Matap Rao remained as he was, leaning against the horse in full moonlight notwithstanding the chance of discovery by a stray pursuer.

The mesh of cypress and fern branches overhead cast mottled shadows on the group. The moon was well in the west and the moist air of early morning hours chilled the perspiration with which the four were soaked. They drew their garments about them and waited, feeling the physical quietude that comes upon the heels of forcible exertion.

Khlit, deep in the shadows, called to Sawal Das softly.

"What see you here in the trail?" he questioned. "This is not a path made by men, nor is it a buffalo-track leading to water."

The archer bent forward.

"True," he acknowledged. "It is the trail of elephants. One at least has passed."

He felt of the broad spoor.

"Siva—none but Asil Rumi, largest of the Thaneswar herd, could have left these marks. They are fresh."

"Asil Rumi," continued Khlit from the darkness. "It is as I thought. Tell me, would the oldest elephant have fled without his rider?"

"Nay. Asil Rumi is schooled in war. He is not to be frightened. Only will he flee where his mahout leads. Without the man Asil Rumi would have stayed."

"This mahout—is he true man or traitor?"

"True man to the Rawul. It is his charge to safeguard the elephant. He must seek to lead Asil Rumi into hiding in the jungle."

"A good omen."

Satisfaction for the first time was in the voice of the Cossack.

"Now may we plan. Abdul Dost, have you a thought as to how we may act?"

The Moslem meditated.

"We will abide with the Rawul. We have taken his quarrel upon us. He may have a thought to lead us into the temple this night, while the slaves of Jagannath sleep and the plundering engages the multitude——"

"Vain," broke in the archer. "The priests hold continued festival. The temple wall is too high to climb and the guards are alert. Retha will be kept within the sanctuary of the idols, under the gold dome where no man may come but a priest.

"The only door to the shrine is through the court of offerings, across the place of dancing, and through the audience hall——"

"Even so," approved Khlit. "Now is it the turn of Sawal Das. He has already spoken well."

"My thought is this," explained the archer. "There will be great shouting and confusion when the sacred car is led from the temple gate. A mixed throng will seek to draw the car by the ropes and to push at the many wheels.

"We may cover our armor with common robes and hide our weapons, disguising our faces. Men from the outlying districts will aid us, for they are least tainted by the poisonous breath of the Snake——"

"Not so," objected the Afghan, ill pleased at the archer's refusal of his own plan. "Time lacks for the gathering of an adequate force. Those who were most faithful to the Rawul have suffered their heads and hands cut off and other defects.

"Besides, the mastery of Thaneswar has passed to the Snake. When would peasants risk their lives in a desperate venture? *Eh*—when fate has decreed against them?"

"Justly spoken," said Khlit bluntly. "Sawal Das, you and the Rawul might perchance conceal your likeness, but the heavy bones of Abdul Dost and myself—they would reveal us in the throng. It may not be."

"What then?" questioned the archer fiercely. "Shall we watch like frightened women while this deed of shame is done?"

"Has the chieftain a plan?" asked Khlit.

Matap Rao lifted his head wearily.

"Am I a warrior?" he said calmly. "The Rinthambur warriors have a saying that a sword has no honor until drawn in battle for a just cause. This night has brought me dishonor. There is no path for me except a death at the hands of the priests——"

"Not so," said Khlit.

The others peered into the shadows, trying to see his face.

"You have all spoken," continued the Cossack. "I have a plan that may gain us Retha. Will you hear it?"

"Speak," said Abdul Dost curiously.

"The temple may not be entered. The multitude of worshipers is too great for the assault of few men. Then must the chieftain and Abdul Dost ride to Rinthambur as speedily as may be."

"And Retha?" questioned the Rawul.

"Sawal Das and I will fetch the woman from the priests and go to meet you, so that your swords may cover our flight."

Matap Rao laughed shortly. To him the rescue of Retha seemed a thing impossible.

"Is my honor so debased that I would leave my bride to the chance of rescue at other hands?"

Whereupon Abdul Dost rose and went to his side respectfully. He laid a muscular hand on the shoulder of the youth.

"My lord," he said slowly, "your misfortune has befallen because of the evil craft of men baser and shrewder than you. Allah—you are but a new-weaned boy in experience of combat. You are a reader of books.

"Yet this man called the Curved Saber is a planner of battles. He has had a rank higher than yours. He has led a hundred thousand swords. His hair is gray, and it was said to me not once but many times that he is very shrewd.

"It is no dishonor to follow his leadership. I have not yet seen him in battle, but I have heard what I have heard."

The Rawul was silent for a space. Then, "Speak," he said to Khlit.

While they listened Khlit told them what was in his mind, in few words. He liked not to talk of his purpose. He spoke to ease the trouble of the boy.

When he had done Sawal Das and Abdul Dost looked at each other.

"*Bismillah!*" cried the Afghan. "It is a bold plan. What! Think you I would ride to Rinthambur and leave you—Khlit—to act thus?"

"Aye," said the Cossack dryly. "There is room for two men in my venture; no more. Likewise two should ride to the rajas, for one man might fail or be slain——"

Matap Rao peered close into Khlit's bearded face.

"The greater danger lies here," he said. "You would take your life in your open hand. How can I ask this of you?"

Khlit grunted, for such words were ever to his distaste.

"I would strike a blow for Retha," he responded, but he was thinking of Nagir Jan.

His words stirred the injured pride of the Hindu.

"By the gods!" he cried. "Then shall I stay with you."

"Nay, my lord. Will the chieftains of Rinthambur raise their standard and mount their riders for war on the word of a stranger—a Moslem? So that they will believe, you must go," adding in his beard, "and be out of my way."

So it happened before moonset that Abdul Dost and the Rawul mounted and rode swiftly to the west through paths known to the chieftain.

At once Khlit and Sawal Das set forth upon the spoor of Asil Rumi, which led north toward the farm of Bhimal. Now as he went the little archer fell to humming under his breath. It was the first time he had sung in many hours.

VI

When the shadows lengthened in the courtyard of the temple of Kukushetra the next day a long cry went up from the multitude. From the door under the wheel and flag of Vishnu came a line of priests.

First came the strewers of flowers, shedding lotus-blossoms, jasmine and roses in the path that led to the car of Jagannath. The bevy of dancing women thronged after them, chattering excitedly. But their shrill voices were drowned in the steady, passionate roar that went up from the throng.

The temple prostitutes no longer drew the eyes of the pilgrims. Their task in arousing the desires of the men was done. Now it was the day of Jagannath, the festival of the *Janam*.

Bands of priests emerged from the gate, motioning back the people. A solid wall of human beings, straining for sight of the god, packed the temple enclosure and stretched without the gates. A deeply religious, almost frenzied mass, waiting for the great event of the year, which was the passage of the god to his country seat—as the older ruined temple was termed.

A louder acclaim greeted the appearance of the grotesque wooden form of the god, borne upon the shoulders of the Brahmans. The figure of Jagannath was followed by that of the small Balabhadra, brother to the god, and Subhadra, his sister.

Jagannath was carried to his car. This was a complicated wooden edifice, put together by reverent hands—a car some fifteen yards long and ten yards wide, and lofty. Sixteen broad wooden wheels, seven feet high, supported the mass. A series of platforms, occupied by the women of the temple, hung with garlands of flowers and with offerings to the god, led up to a wide seat wherein was placed Jagannath.

This done, those nearest the car laid hold of the wheels and the long ropes, ready to begin the famous journey. The smaller cars of Balabhadra and Subhadra received less attention and fewer adherents.

Was not Jagannath Lord of the World, chief among the gods, and divine bringer of prosperity during the coming year? So the Brahmans had preached, and the people believed. Had not their fathers believed before them?

The decorators of the idols had robed Jagannath in costly silk and fitted false arms to the wooden body so that it might be sightly in the eyes of the multitude.

The cries of the crowd grew louder and the ropes attached to the car tautened with a jerk. A flutter of excitement ran through the gathering. Had they not journeyed for many days to be with Jagannath on the *Janam*?

As always in a throng, the nearness of so many of their kind wrought upon them. Religious zeal was at a white heat. But the Brahmans raised their hands, cautioning the worshipers.

"The bride of Jagannath comes!" they cried.

"Way for the bride of the god!" echoed the pilgrims.

The door of the temple opened again and Retha appeared, attended by some of the women of the wardrobe. The girl's slim form had been elaborately robed. Her cheeks were painted, her long hair allowed to fall upon her shoulders and back.

A brief silence paid tribute to the beauty of the woman. She glanced once anxiously about the enclosure; then her eyes fell, nor did she look up when she was led to a seat beside and slightly below the image of the god.

Once she was seated the guardians who had watched her throughout the night stepped aside. In the center of the crowd of worshipers Retha was cut off from her kind, as securely the property of the god as if she still stood in the shrine. For no one among the throng but was a follower of Jagannath, in the zenith of religious excitement.

The priests formed a cordon about the car. Hundreds of hands caught up the ropes. A blare of trumpets from the musicians on the car, and it lurched forward, the great wheels creaking.

"Honor to Jagannath!" screamed the voice of Bhimal. "The god is among us. Let me touch the wheels!"

The machine was moving forward more steadily now, the wheels churning deep into the sand. The pullers sweated and groaned, tasting keen delight in the toil; the throng crushed closer. A woman cried out, and fainted.

But those near her did not give back. Instead they set their feet upon her body and pressed forward. Was it not true blessedness to die during the passage of Jagannath?

Contrary to many tales, they did not throw themselves under the wheels. Only one man did this, and he wracked with the pain of leprosy and sought a holy death, cleansed of his disease.

Perhaps in other days numbers had done this. But now many died in the throng, what with the heat and pressure and the strain of the excitement, which had continued now for several days.

Slowly the car moved from the temple enclosure, into the streets of the village, out upon the highway that led to its destination. The sun by now was descending to the horizon.

But the ardor of the pilgrims waxed higher as the god continued its steady progress. For the car to halt would be a bad omen. And the dancing women, stimulated by *bhang*, shouted and postured on the car, flinging their thin garments to those below and gesturing with nude bodies in a species of frenetic exaltation.

Those pushing the car from behind shouted in response. The eyes of Nagir Jan, walking among the pilgrims, gleamed. Kurral, crouched on the car, had ceased to watch the quiet form of Retha.

Rescue now, he thought, was impossible, as was any attempt on her part to escape. For the car was surrounded the space of a long bow-shot on every side.

The wind which had fluttered the garlands on the car died down as the shadows lengthened. The leaders of the crowd were already within sight of the shrine whither they were bound.

Retha sat as one lifeless. Torn from the side of her husband and carried from the hall of Thaneswar, she had been helpless in the hands of the priests. A proud woman, accustomed to the deference shown to the clan of Rinthambur, the misfortune had numbed her at first.

Well knowing what Matap Rao knew of the evil rites of Jagannath, to be exhibited to the crowd of worshipers caused her to flush under the paint which stained her cheeks.

She would have cast herself down from the car if she had not known that the Brahmans would have forced her again into the seat. To be handled by such a mob was too great a shame.

She had heard that Matap had escaped alive the night before. One thought kept up her courage. Not without an effort to save her would the Rawul allow her to reach the shrine where the rites of that night were to take place.

This she knew, and she hugged the slight comfort of that hope to her heart. Rawul Matap Rao would not abandon her. But, seeing the number of the throng, even this hope dwindled.

How could the chieftain reach her side? But he would ride into the throng, she felt, and an arrow from his bow would free her from shame.

At a sudden silence which fell upon the worshipers she lifted her head for the first time.

Coming from the shrine of the elder gods she saw a massive elephant, appareled for war, an armored plate on his chest, swordblades fastened to his tusks, his ears and trunk painted a bright orange and leather sheets strapped to his sides. And, seeing, she gave a low cry.

"Asil Rumi!"

The elephant was advancing more swiftly than it seemed at first, his great ears stretched out, his small eyes shifting. On his back was the battle howdah. Behind his head perched the mahout wearing a shirt of mail. In the howdah were two figures that stared upon the crowd.

Asil Rumi advanced, interested, even excited, by the throng of men. Schooled to warfare, he followed obediently the instructions of his native master, scenting something unwonted before him. Those nearest gave back hastily.

For a space the throng believed that the elephant was running amuck. Never before had man or beast interfered with the progress of the god. But as Asil Rumi veered onward and the leading pullers at the ropes were forced to scramble aside an angry murmur went up.

Then the voice of Kurral rang out.

"Infidels!" he cried. "Those upon the elephant are men of Matap Rao."

The murmur increased to a shout, in which the shrill cries of the women mingled.

"Blasphemers! Profaners of Jagannath! Slay them!"

Nagir Jan raised his arms in anger.

"Defend the god!" he shouted. "Turn the elephant aside."

Already some men had thrust at Asil Rumi with sticks and spears. The elephant rumbled deep within his bulk. His wrinkled head shook and tossed. His trunk lifted and his eyes became inflamed. He pushed on steadily.

A priest stepped into his path and slashed at his trunk with a dagger.

Asil Rumi switched his trunk aside, and smote the man with it. The priest fell back, his skull shattered. A soldier cast a javelin which clanged against the animal's breastplate.

Angered, the elephant rushed the man, caught him in his trunk and cast him underfoot. A huge foot descended on the soldier, and the man lay where he had fallen, a broken mass of bones from which oozed blood.

Now Asil Rumi trumpeted fiercely. He tasted battle and glanced around for a fresh foe.

The bulk of the towering car caught his eye. With a quick rush the elephant pressed between the ropes, moving swiftly for all his size and weight.

The clamor increased. Men dashed at the beast, seeking to penetrate his armor with their weapons; but more hung back. For from on the howdah a helmeted archer had begun to discharge arrows that smote down the leaders of the crowd. The mahout prodded Asil Rumi forward.

The elephant, nothing loath, placed his armored head full against the car. For a moment the pressure of the crowd behind the wooden edifice impelled it against the animal. Asil Rumi uttered a harsh, grating cry and bent his legs into the ground.

He leaned his weight against the car. The wooden wheels of

Jagannath creaked, then turned loosely in the sand. The car of the god had stopped. A shout of dismay went up.

Then the mahout tugged with his hook at the head of Asil Rumi. Obedient, even in his growing anger inflamed by minor wounds, the elephant placed one forefoot on the shelving front of the car. The rudely constructed wood gave way and the mass of the car sank with a jar upon the ground, broken loose from the support of the front wheels.

By now the mob was fully aroused. Arrows and javelins flew against the leather protection of the animal and his leather-like skin, wrinkled and aged to the hardness of rhinoceros hide.

A shaft struck the leg of the native mahout and a spear caught in his groin under the armor. He shivered, but retained his seat. Seeing this, Khlit clambered over the front of the howdah to the man's side.

"Make the elephant kneel!" he cried.

Asil Rumi knelt, and the fore part of the car splintered under the weight of two massive knees. It fell lower. Now Asil Rumi was passive for a brief moment, and Sawal Das redoubled his efforts, seeking to prevent the priests with knives from ham-stringing the beast.

"Come, Retha!" cried Khlit, kneeling and holding fast to the head-band beside the failing native.

The woman was now on a level with him. She understood not his words, but his meaning was plain. The shock to the car had dislodged many of the men upon it.

The temple women clutched at her, but she avoided them. She poised her slender body for the leap.

"Slay the woman!" cried Kurral, scrambling toward her.

A powerful Bhil perched beside the head of the elephant and slashed once with his scimitar. The blow half-severed the mahout's head from the body. Before he could strike again Khlit had knocked him backward.

Retha sprang forward, and the Cossack caught her with his free arm, drawing back as Kurral leaped, knife in hand. The priest missed the woman. The next instant his body slipped back, a feathered shaft from the bow of Sawal Das projecting from his chest.

"Ho—Kurral—your death is worthy of you," chanted the archer. "Gully jackal, scavenger dog——"

His voice trailed off in a gurgle. And Khlit and the girl were flung back against the howdah. Asil Rumi, maddened by his wounds and no longer hearing the voice of his master, started erect.

He tossed his great head, reddened with blood. His trumpeting changed to a hoarse scream. The knives of his assailants had hurt him sorely.

The sword-blades upon the tusks had been broken off against the car. The leather armor was cut and slashed. Spears, stuck in the flanks of the elephant, acted as irritants. His trunk—a most sensitive member—was injured, and his neck bleeding.

While Khlit and Retha clung beside the body of the mahout Asil Rumi shrilled his anger at the throng of his enemies. He broke crashing from the ruins of the car wherein lay the unattended figure of Jagannath, and plunged into the crowd. Weaving his head—its paint besmirched by blood—Asil Rumi raced forward.

He rushed onward until no more of his tormentors stood in his path. Then the elephant hesitated, and headed toward the trail up the hill which led down to his quarters at Thaneswar.

"Harken," said a weak voice from the howdah.

Khlit peered up and saw the archer's face strangely pale.

"Asil Rumi will run," said Sawal Das, "until he sees the body of the native fall. Hold the mahout firmly."

A few foot soldiers had run after the elephant in a half-hearted fashion. There were no horsemen in the crowd, and few cared to follow the track of the great beast afoot. Asil Rumi had struck terror into the worshipers.

His appearance and the devastation he had wrought had been that of no ordinary elephant. Among the Hindus lingered the memory of the elder gods of the ruins from which Asil Rumi had so abruptly emerged. And some among them reflected that Vishnu, highest of the gods, bore an elephant head.

So had the deaths inflicted by Asil Rumi stirred their fears.

The sun had set, and the crimson of the western sky was fading to purple. The calm of twilight hung upon the forest through which Asil Rumi paced, following the trail. A flutter of night birds arose at his presence, and a prowling leopard slunk away at the angry mutter of the elephant, knowing that Asil Rumi was enraged and that an angry elephant was monarch of whatsoever path he chose to follow.

Again came the voice of Sawal Das, weaker now.

"My heart is warm that the Lotus Face is saved for my lord," it said—neither Khlit nor the girl dared to look up from their precarious perch where the branches of overhanging cypresses swept.

"An arrow—" the voice failed—"tell the Rawul how Sawal Das fought—for my spirit goes after the mahout——"

A moment later a branch caught the howdah and swept it to earth. Retha and Khlit clung tighter to the head-straps, pressing their bodies against the broad back of Asil Rumi. Khlit did not release his grasp on the dead native.

The wind of their passage swept past their ears; the labored breath of the old elephant smote their nostrils pungently. Ferns scraped their shoulders. They did not look up.

It was dark by now, and still Asil paced onward.

Dawn was breaking and a warm wind had sprung up when Matap Rao and Abdul Dost with the leaders of the Rinthambur clan passed the boundary tower of Thaneswar. A half-thousand armed men followed them, but few were abreast of them, for they had ridden steadily throughout the night, not sparing their horses.

Dawn showed the anxious chieftain the unbroken stretch of the Thaneswar forest through which he had passed on his bridal journey. He did not look at those with him, but pressed onward.

So it happened that Rawul Matap Rao and two of the best mounted of the Rinthambur riders were alone when they emerged into a glade where a path from Thaneswar crossed the main trail. And here they reined in their spent horses with a shout.

In the path lay the body of a native. Over the dead man stood the giant elephant, caked with mud and dried blood, his small eyes closed and his warlike finery stained and torn. And beside the elephant stood Khlit and Retha.

What followed was swift in coming to pass. After a brief embrace the Rawul left his bride to be escorted back to Rinthambur by Khlit and Abdul Dost at the head of a detail of horsemen while he and the Rinthambur men wrested Thaneswar from the priests.

It was a different matter this, from the assault upon the palace by Nagir Jan, and the followers of the temple were forced to give way before the onset of trained warriors.

The religious fervor of the Kukushetra men had suffered by the misfortune that befel their god before the ruins, and the fighting was soon at an end.

But it was not until Matap Rao was again in Thaneswar with Retha that Khlit and Abdul Dost turned their horses' heads from the palace. Peace had fallen upon the province again, for Matap Rao had sent a message to the shrine of Puri, and the high priests of Vishnu, among whom the ambitions of Nagir Jan had found no favor, had judged that Nagir Jan had made wrong use of his power and sent another to be head of the Kukushetra temple.

"Aye, and men whispered that there was a tale that the mad beast of the ruins was the incarnate spirit of an older god," laughed Abdul Dost, who wore new finery of armor and rode a fine horse—the Rawul had been generous. "Such are the fears of fools and infidels."

Khlit, who rode his old pony, tugged his beard, his eyes grave.

"It was not the false gods," he said decidedly, "that saved Matap Rao his wife. It was verily a warrior—an old warrior. But how can the Rawul reward him."

Abdul Dost glanced at Khlit curiously.

"Nay," he smiled; "you are the one. You are a leader of men, even of the Rawul and his kind—as I said to them. Belittle not the gratitude of the chieftain. He would have kept you at his right hand, in honor. But you will not."

"Because I am not the one."

"Sawal Das?"

"Somewhat perhaps."

Khlit's voice roughened and his eyes became moody.

"Asil Rumi is the one. Truly never have I seen a fighter such as he. Yet Asil Rumi is old. Soon he will die. Where is his reward?"

Whereupon Khlit shook his broad shoulders, tightened his rein and broke into a gallop. Abdul Dost frowned, pondering. He shook his handsome head. Then his brow cleared and he spurred after his friend.

BOGATYR

When the trail is lost and the stars are hidden, the warrior looks in vain to his right hand and his left. When there is neither meat in the saddle bags, nor grain in the sack—let the horse show the way.

Tatar proverb.

AYUB, THE ZAPOROGHIAN COSSACK, WAS LOST. AS FAR AS HE COULD see in every direction the sea of grass stretched, rippling under the gusts of wind, brushing against his shoulders, although he was a big man and the stallion he bestrode a rangy Kabarda.

Behind him the sun was setting and the whole steppe was turning swiftly from green to purple. The wind had a cold bite to it, and Ayub, all the three hundred pounds of him, ached with hunger. In the chill air of evening an old wound twitched painfully. He wanted very much to build a fire and lie down under shelter for the night.

But how the — was a warrior, even a Zaporoghian—a free Cossack from the war encampment on the river Dnieper—to make a fire when there was not wood? And grass and tamarisk bushes would not make a shelter fit for a dog.

"*Tà nitchogo!*" he muttered to the silky ear that the black stallion turned back, "it doesn't matter."

He pulled the soiled sheepskin over his shoulders and crossed heavily thewed arms on a chest burned as dark as the *svitka* by the sun's rays. His nankeen trousers, a prized possession, fell in wide baggy folds to the tops of costly red morocco boots with high silver heels. Not in all the steppe that stretched from the Black Sea of the

Tatars to Moscow, the city of the Muscovite lords, was there another such pair of trousers. Ayub had found them on a dead Tcherkessian chief.

The black Kabarda he had taken in a raid on the horse herd of Ghirei Khan, the Nogai Tatar, and it was the pride of his heart. Although the horse had come a hundred leagues in four days, it was only sweating under the saddle; a wise and stout stallion of the breed known as wolf hunters. Ayub stood up in the stirrups and looked north and south in the last level gleam of the sunset. And he saw no trace of smoke from a hamlet in some distant gully, no glint of light from the horns of straggling cattle.

"—— take you, steppe!" he said, angrily. "You are fragrant and smooth as a Tcherkessian maiden, and I know none fairer. You are full of tricks. You beckon and smile like the maiden, then leave a warrior to sleep in a cold bed."

Laughing, he sank back in the saddle that creaked under his weight. Although there were gray hairs in the scalp-lock curled under his black *kalpak*, his Cossack hat with the red crown, Ayub never bothered his head about anything. It was easier not to think about things and to follow where others led. For this reason the Zaporoghian Cossacks who held the frontier of the steppe had never made him an *ataman*, though few warriors could stand up to Ayub with the sword, or ride more swiftly or drink more corn brandy.

Ayub had a way of trusting everything to luck, and so he got into more scrapes than a drunken bear. Somehow he had kept life in his body in an age when men rode with death at their shoulder on this steppe where the vultures circled over the scurrying quail and Cossack and Tatar alike left their white bones to be washed by the rain. But if he had been put in command of a regiment of warriors there would have been nothing left of the regiment.

In fact, he could not remember how he had left his comrades at the Zaporoghian Siech. He had been drunk when he saddled his horse, and he recalled vaguely a tavern a couple of days later where he had thrown coins to the musicians and had led out the prettiest girls to the cleared space between the tables. At his belt hung a heavy pouch of silver, and he did not know how it had come there.

Reaching over his shoulder he touched the cross on the hilt of his sword and reflected. A sunset like this, the Moslems said, was an omen—Allah had hung the banners of death in the sky. He had seen such sunsets before and always men had yielded up their breath before the night was done. Where was he to find shelter?

As nearly as Ayub could remember he had ridden east and a little north from the war camp. He was at the edge of the salt barrens where sage begins to appear. Ahead of him somewhere should be a small river, the Donetz. Beyond that should be the *auls* of the Nogai Tatars, though God alone knew just where those tent villages were, since they moved around like wolf packs. In fact Ayub suspected that he had come too far into Tatar country, and this put a new thought into his head.

Not far from the Donetz in this part of the steppe was an abandoned wooden castle, built in forgotten times by the hordes that had followed Tamerlane to the very gates of Moscow. The log castle would provide him with firewood and shelter, and as for the Tatars, they avoided it for superstitious reasons. But where was it?

"*Tchorttielya vosmi dvortzi!*" he grunted. "—— take you, castles! The stallion will find you before I will."

So he tossed the reins on the Kabarda's neck and settled back in the saddle.

The stallion was trotting along a lane in the grass with the purposeful gait of a horse that knows very well where it is going to be quartered that night. They were approaching a river because wild ducks rose with a discordant clamor from the reeds far ahead of them. By the time the last streak of orange had faded in the sky behind them, Ayub's keen eyes picked out the glimmer of fire on a knoll near the spot where the ducks had started up. Toward this speck of light the Kabarda headed with a rush, as if to say the day's ride was over.

But Ayub, who had no desire to stumble into a Tatar ambush, reined in the horse while he studied the light.

Many ruddy gleams pierced the darkness on the hillock, and a vague glow rose from the earth, as if the summit of the mound had been hollowed out and a fire kindled in its depths. A mutter of voices and a hammering of axes reached the Cossack.

The steppe around here should be deserted—he had not seen a living man for days.

"Can't be Tatars," he reflected. "They wouldn't make such a —— of a racket after dark. Can't be any honest folk out here either—"

With a prickling of the scalp, he remembered the evil omen of the blood-red sunset and wondered whether the knoll might not be in possession of hob-goblins and gnomes. Such mounds, common enough on the great steppe, were often burial places of the tribesmen. In other ages the conquering Mongols had interred their dead in mounds, with gold and silver plate and jeweled weapons, and had slain war horses to bear the dead company to the kingdom of Erlik below the earth. Ayub had seen hardy spirits, Muscovite merchants who came from the cities of the north, dig up such bones and buried riches. For his part he did not fear the live Tatars half as much as the dead.

He was on the point of turning back when he reflected that his horse showed no uneasiness. The stallion always shied when a vampire was about at night. Besides, ghosts did not chop wood to start fires going. Cautiously—for a man who did not know the meaning of caution otherwise—Ayub advanced until he made out a palisade on the hillock and the shapes of wooden towers.

The ruddy glow came from large fires within the wall and the light he had first seen from the openings that served for windows in the blockhouse. This was the abandoned stronghold of the Tatars for which he had been searching. Reassured, the Cossack went around to the gate and found a man on guard.

"Health to you, brother," said Ayub. "What company is this?"

Either the sentry did not understand or would not answer. He leaned on his spear, looking up at the Cossack sidewise, so that Ayub did not know if he were friendly or not. But inside the palisade were other men-at-arms and slaves sitting about the fires where quarters of sheep and joints of beef were roasting. Spears were stacked in the corners and rusted iron helmets lay beside some of the warriors. A line of carts, heavily loaded, stood by the stables. Some of the slaves wore wolfskins, but many were nearly naked. All of them stared at the horseman who had appeared in the gate—evidently they had never seen a Zaporoghian Cossack in his regalia before.

At the doorway of the main building, a rambling one-story log structure, Ayub dismounted and found that an officer had come out to look at him—a black-browed giant who carried a whip and a battle ax.

"What fellow are you?" demanded the stranger, scowling. "Where are you from?"

Light dawned on Ayub. By his accent the captain of the warriors was a Muscovite, a Moskya in Cossack speech. So this company was from the northern towns, a long journey. What was it doing in the steppe?

"Are you the master here?" retorted Ayub who did not relish the other's surly tone. "Hey, *Krivonos*—Crooked Nose?"

For a moment the two warriors exchanged glances without the slightest change of expression, the impatient Cossack repressing a broad grin and the stalwart Muscovite wrestling with his own thoughts.

"How could I be master?" he responded. "My lord the prince is within."

Ayub had seen Muscovite merchants before, but never one of the grandees, though he had heard of their growing power. Tempted by curiosity and the smell of roast meats and fragrant wine, he thrust Crooked Nose aside and stalked into the log fortress.

The roof had fallen in long since and trees were growing within the ruins, but the tall grass had been trampled down and the *débris* of rafters had been heaped on two great fires. Tables had been built out of the timber, and at these tables sat thirty or forty men, some wearing mail that had once been gilded, others in long tabards with painted collars, their armor thrown carelessly underfoot.

Their leader, a young man, sat at the head of the higher table where the firelight struck full on his red-gold hair that hung to his shoulders, and his face as colorless as wax. His head, jutting forward as if he could not manage to hold it erect, was turned toward the Cossack who, cap in hand bowed low, expecting an invitation to seat himself at one of the tables—perhaps to be offered a goblet of wine by the young lord. Such was the custom and the hospitality of the Zaporoghians, who would never suffer a stranger to go unfed at meal time.

Servitors in long blue coats ornamented with gilt braid, and wearing green slippers, glanced at him apathetically as they hurried about with flagons to fill the cups of the vassals.

A steward who wore a hat trimmed with sable and as high as a minaret—as Ayub thought admiringly—and who carried a staff came over to him and announced that His Illustriousness, the Prince

Vladimir was pleased to ask a question of the stranger, and Ayub bowed again, to his girdle, at the bench where the young lord was seated.

"You are wearing a sword, Cossack—such a sword!" observed Vladimir.

"Aye, noble sir," Ayub admitted, scenting a chance to tell one of his stories.

No other Cossack had a sword like this one, for he had taken it from a Walloon, and it was a two-handed affair, as heavy as a sheep and as long as a pike. Only a man of really great strength could make it whistle around his head, and Ayub wore it slung on his back.

"By your top-knot you are a Zaporoghian. I warrant you are one of the hero-warriors they call *bogatyr*."

"Nay, God knows, your highness, no such luck is mine. In our Siech only the wisest and most famous knights are given that title."

Ayub stared thoughtfully at the gold goblets on the white cloths, and the steaming platters. Before Vladimir a whole swan had been set, and two of the slaves were hard at work carving it. Many of the vassals had fallen asleep, overcome by the wine that stained their rich linen and damask. In one corner, where the prince's bed had been set up under a canopy, he saw several leather chests, and Ayub wondered what they contained. Either this was a wealthy lord, traveling in state or a notable brigand. Truly a notable robber because a dozen *boyars* sat at his table—nobles who did not wear the iron collar of slavery.

"They drink like lords," he thought, admiringly. "Only they don't talk or sing at all—just drop off."

Struck by a sudden impulse, he turned again to the young noble who was watching the carving of the swan.

"Your pardon, *kniaz grodny*," he muttered, "but this is an ill place to camp for long. The frontier posts are far off—far off. You'll have Tatars around like bees."

One or two of the soberest vassals looked up at him angrily, but Vladimir laughed.

"What a dolt you are, Cossack! There are no Tatars on this bank of the Dnieper."

Ayub fancied that he must be jesting, until he looked into the vacant gray eyes.

"Noble sir, may I roast in a brazen ox, but this is not the river

Dnieper. Nay, Father Dnieper lies a hundred leagues to the west. This is the Donetz, beyond the frontier."

One of the *boyars*, a gentleman in attendance on the prince, rose from his place and struck his fist on the table.

"How could this river be the Donetz?"

"Because it is, noble sir," responded Ayub bluntly. "God be my witness, I have slept in this *dvortza* many a time after shooting wild ducks in the reeds."

"You dolt!" The *boyar* ran his words together, being heavy in drink. "We can not be beyond the frontier, because His Illustriousness, the Prince led us himself, taking no other guide, from his estates near Moscow over the devil knows how much accursed barren plains to this place. Here is the Dnieper, our destination. No doubt other Christians will come to greet us before long."

Ayub shook his head.

"Not other Christians, noble sir, but heretic Muhammadans will greet you. You will hear their shout—*ghar—ghar—ghar!* Then they will take your horses and cut you up like hares; that is how they will greet you."

The stout *boyar* blinked his good-natured, watery eyes and thrust both hands into his beard, looking at his lord for support in the argument. Instead, Vladimir saw fit to ask a question.

"You speak of the Tatar hordes, Cossack. Why do you think they will raid this place?"

"Because it is the month for them to come. When the snow melts and the steppe dries out enough for horses, noble sir, the Tatar comes across the line for cattle and prisoners to sell as slaves. You see, after the winter they need beef and money. Later, when the harvests are being gotten in, we look for him again."

"*Gospody batyushka!*" said the young prince. "God save us! Would the Tatar hordes, think you, attack a hundred men in a walled place like this?"

"Well, not here perhaps."

The Cossack remembered that the tribesmen avoided the ruined castle.

"Why not here?" Vladimir pressed.

"Because this place—Sirog they call it—has some of their graves in it."

Vladimir waited until the cup-bearer behind him had filled his goblet with foaming spirits before he answered, the shadow of a smile in his gray eyes:

"This is the Dnieper right enough. They all look alike, the rivers in this wilderness. You've got them mixed, that's all. Ah, what a splendid horse!"

Hearing a scuffling behind him, Ayub glanced over his shoulder. The Kabarda stallion, hungry and restive, had come through the door to look for his master—to be unsaddled and have the bit taken out of his mouth. On the rare occasions when he slept within walls, Ayub permitted the horse to share his quarters, to make sure that the stallion was comfortable and safe from thieves.

Tossing his small, lean head and avoiding the servitors and the fires, the stallion came up to Ayub, snuffling the back of his neck.

"Go along, you devilkin!" grunted Ayub, vastly pleased, nevertheless. "A wolf hunter, this!"

The prince had not taken his eyes off the Kabarda, and now he spoke a word to the cup-bearer who offered Ayub the untasted goblet that had been on the table before Vladimir. Ayub stroked his mustache down, lifted the goblet in both hands and drank the health of the company, while the indolent glance of the prince dwelled on his long sword.

"Now go," said Vladimir, "look at the river again, and tell me if it is not the Dnieper."

After quaffing the heated spirits Ayub swaggered through the gate, accompanied by Crooked Nose. They went out of the palisade and the Cossack stared up at the towers, painted crimson by the glow of firelight. Then he studied the strip of gray that was the distant river.

"That is the Donetz," he observed decidedly. "What kind of a game is the young lord playing, eh, Crooked Nose?"

The man from the north seemed to be enveloped in impenetrable silence. Leaning on his battle ax, he loomed over the powerful frontiersman, his small eyes shifting from one thing to another.

"My name," he growled at length, "is not Crooked Nose. They call me Durak, the Idiot."

"They named you well," acknowledged Ayub, striding back to the fort. As he drew near the entrance he shouted suddenly:

"Look out for his heels—keep your hands off him, fools! Stand back!"

Some of the servitors who wore the iron collars about their necks had attempted to take the saddle off the stallion within the block-house. The horse was tossing his head and circling, and when his leather shod hoofs lashed out, a luckless slave was knocked prone, his ribs crushed.

"Out of the way!" Ayub repeated impatiently to the dozen men-at-arms who had taken position in front of the door. Instead of stepping aside, they unsheathed their swords and lifted their shields. Stopping in his tracks, Ayub grunted and shaded his eyes to look into their faces.

"You may not go back," Durak cautioned him. "The lord prince has taken a fancy to your nag. Half a verst away is a settlement of your fellow Cossacks. Go thither and give thanks to the Saints that your skin hasn't been slit."

It did not enter his head to take the Muscovite's advice. Quick-tempered as the Kabarda that had carried him over the steppe trails for half a dozen years, Ayub was gripped by hot anger that left him quivering and snorting. His horse could be taken from him in only one fashion.

Reaching back over his right shoulder with both hands, he gripped the hilt of the heavy sword and pulled it clear. With the blade swinging in front of him in glittering circles he stepped forward. Two shields splintered under the edge of the sword and the Musco-vites slipped apart, to run at him from the side.

But Ayub had been at hand blows too many times to be cut down in this fashion. Leaping to the right he knocked a man prone with the flat of the blade, and whistled shrilly.

The Kabarda answered the whistle instantly. Rearing and avoid-ing the hands that clutched at the rein, the horse galloped through the entrance, and no Muscovite had hardihood to stand in his way. With a final flourish of the long sword Ayub ran to the stallion, grip-ping the saddle horn with his left hand.

He crouched for the leap into the saddle, and something crashed down on his skull. Flames spread before his eyes, and he pitched forward. Nor did he feel the earth upon which he sprawled without consciousness. Durak had picked up a small log and had thrown it with all his strength at the Cossack.

II

Ayub was not long in coming to himself, because the blood on his neck had not dried yet. It was still dripping from his broken scalp, and he sat up, spitting it out savagely. His head hurt him and he swallowed a groan when he stood up, leaning on the sword that was still fast in one fist.

To take a man's horse—to set him afoot in that part of the steppe—was something beyond belief. To take a horse like the Kabarda stallion was a blacker crime, to Ayub's way of thinking, than to strip him naked. They had carried him a good way from the palisade. Possibly they had meant to toss him into the river but had found him too heavy to carry.

Better for them, perhaps, if they had. Because the Cossack had no intention of leaving Sirog until he had recovered his horse or settled the account.

He remembered that the man-at-arms, Durak, had said something about a camp near at hand, and he could see, in the half light of a quarter moon, a road leading from the blockhouse off into the tall grass. Sheathing his sword, he began to walk away, cursing the weight of the heavy blade, his silver heels that were made to grip the stirrup, not the earth, and all Muscovites of past and future generations.

In a little while he came to the lights of a village. A cluster of wattle and daub huts stood around a log *kortchma*, a tavern, and a half finished church. Farther off were sheep folds and cattle pens. It was plainly a frontier settlement, like a thousand others that had crawled out into the plain protected by Cossack outposts. But he did not understand what it was doing on the Donetz.

When he kicked open the tavern door a half dozen men stared at him apathetically. They had long, unkempt hair and hollow cheeks and were smaller in build than the Zaporoghians. One wore the leather apron of a smith, and another, seated by the fire, was making a pair of shoes out of a strip of horsehide.

"Give me corn brandy—food—anything," he cried, and, seeing a bucket of water standing near the door, emptied it over his head. Wiping his eyes clear with his sleeve he moved toward the fire, noticing that a young fellow in a white *svitka* rose to make way for him.

When he had emptied the last bowl of gruel and had downed his fourth cup, he stretched his arms, rubbed his head and spread his legs out to the fire.

"Well, forgive me. God be with you, brothers, Cossacks! I had a little rap on the dome up there at the castle—but who are you and what the —— are you doing in this place?"

To this the tavern-keeper, a dour man, and heavily bearded, made answer slowly.

"We saw that you had met with misfortune, good sir, but that is nothing strange in this country. Are you a Zaporoghian?"

Ayub wrung the water out of his mustaches, and from the long scalp lock that hung down one shoulder.

"Don't you know a Zaporoghian when you see one? Then you must have been born in a Jew's back-yard—that's certain."

The tavern-keeper fingered his beard, and the others nodded understandingly.

"Aye, it's true that this fine knight is a Zaporoghian. That's the way the warriors talk, on the border."

"We are town Cossacks," explained one. "From up Moscow way, —— knows how far. We built cottages there and worked at trades, near the castles of the great lords."

"*Shapoval*," thought Ayub, "workmen who take their hats off to everybody." Aloud he asked, with growing curiosity—

"What are you doing here?"

The tavern-keeper, who was called Kukubenko by the others, sat down on a log and spat into the flames.

"We're here along of Prince Vladimir, noble knight. It happened like this: The illustrious prince was in disgrace at court because he angered the emperor himself in some way or other. So said the priest who is with us here. That is why the prince has let his hair grow long, to show he is in disgrace. Such is the custom up there. But Vladimir fears no man and even his wolf pack—for that is how he calls his *boyars*—take pains not to taunt him to his face."

"But what has that to do with you?"

"*Ekh*—the *boyars* up there and the emperor said that villages must be sent to settle on the border. Out on the plain here there are not enough villages, nor men to tend cattle and raise wheat. So the priest told us. And sure enough, we were ordered out into the steppe —all of our village. And His Illustriousness, the Prince, was ordered by the emperor, because of the crime he committed, to take his *boyars* and his vassals and go and protect us. Aye, to go into exile and not to show himself again until our village was settled."

"It angered him," spoke up another. "It's God's truth that he has been severe with us. We lost half the cattle on the way and the wolves took many of the sheep."

Ayub had heard of these colonists who were being sent out by the Muscovites to claim the new lands along the rivers, and had no great love for them. They turned the open steppe of the Cossacks into tilled land and grazing ground for their cattle.

"Do you know where you are?" he asked.

"Nay," responded Kukubenko. "This river is the Dnieper, isn't it?"

"Who told you that?"

"Durak, good sir."

"May the foul fiend fly away with Durak!" growled Ayub, clenching his hands on his knees.

Kukubenko glanced at the door in alarm, and hastened to talk of something else.

"This youth who crossed the river a little while ago says it is the Donetz. But after all, what does it matter. We are here."

"What youth?" demanded Ayub, and saw at once who they meant.

In the far corner was the boy who had given up his place at the fire to the warrior. He sat against the wall, Tatar fashion, a *bandura* —a three-stringed guitar—across his knees.

His white *svitka* was clean camel's hair, and his slender chest was covered with an embroidered vest. A wide, black velvet sash bound his middle from loins to upper ribs. But what drew Ayub's scrutiny was the boy's pantaloons, tucked into high slippers of soft leather. They were green.

Now green, among the Moslems, was a color only to be worn by the *hadjis*. A Christian having any green upon his person would, if he were captured by the Moslems on the border, be immediately tortured in a peculiarly unpleasant way. Ayub knew of one Cossack who had flaunted the forbidden color until he fell into the hands of the Tatars, who stripped the skin from his legs and feet and turned him loose on the steppe.

And Ayub thought that this stripling had donned green either because he was ignorant and reckless, or because he was at heart a

Moslem, and if so, he was here for no good. Certainly the boy did not belong to the village. Even the Cossack maidens, who loved bright colors, did not wear green.

"You minstrel," he cried, "you with the guitar, what's your name?"

"Kirdy," the youth answered at once, without ceasing to run his fingers over the strings of the *bandura*.

"You speak like a Tcherkessian—no, like something else, I don't know what," growled the warrior. "Do you mean to say that you swam the Donetz in flood?"

"Aye, uncle, and the Volga too. But my horse is a good one."

Ayub was silent, thinking of his own horse, and wondering whence the young minstrel had come. Beyond the Volga were the plains and deserts of the Tatar khans. Beyond that, he vaguely imagined vast mountains barring the way to Cathay and Ind—a part of the earth where no Cossack, save one, had ever set foot. This one was an old ataman, Khlit by name, who had taken it into his head to wander into the world under the rising sun, and had never been heard from again.

"I, too," he said reflectively, "once swam a great river. It was the Dneiper, and such a flood you never saw because your mother had not brought you into the world then. At night, too, and no one could see the other bank. My Kabarda jumped in when I lifted the reins, and when we were out in mid-stream a new wall of water as high as this tavern came rushing down."

The villagers who harkened attentively to every word of the Zaporoghian, now gazed at him, open-mouthed.

"It was impossible to get across, impossible to go back," continued Ayub, emptying his glass and stroking his mustaches. "But my Kabarda was a fine nag. He turned and began to swim down stream, and after I had said a prayer to Saint Nikolas, I sat back and waited for what was to come. *Ekh*, my brothers, it was a fearful night—trees rushing past us, torn up by the flood, and boulders rumbling down underfoot. But my horse did not go down, and after a long, long while he brought me to safety."

"How?" demanded Kukubenko. "I thought you couldn't get out."

"No more we could," the warrior assented. "The stallion swam to something I couldn't see at all. It was a galley, anchored in the river.

You see, before then, he had gone out to attack the galleys of the accursed Turks with me, and now he brought me to this one. As I live, good sirs, it was a Turkish craft."

"Then you were gone, sure enough," remarked the cobbler.

"Nay," Ayub assured him gravely, "it is well known, if you had come to the Dnieper, now, instead of this devil-infested place, you would have heard yourself, that I once brought a captured Turkish galley up the river. I and my horse."

The simple-minded villagers shook their heads in admiration, and Kirdy with half-closed eyes, swept his hand across the strings of the *bandura*.

> "They, who made me bow my head—
> Their heads have I laid low with my sword."

So he sang under his breath, and Ayub, looking at him grimly, was not sure whether he jested or not.

"But, noble sir," objected Kukubenko, "were you not blown out of the water with a cannon?"

"Not then, uncle. Another time, when the knights of the Siech were boarding a ship of the sultan, that was my lot. The ship had been firing off cannon like mad. *Pouf-bong!* For hours they had burned powder until they had not a shot or even a bit of chain left. The accursed Turks had fired off all their belt buckles and iron armor, and so they took the rings from their fingers and emptied their wallets of all sorts of spoil—gold crosses and fine jewels."

Ayub considered while Kukubenko filled his glass. Then he sighed and shook his head.

"For, look you, good sirs! Jewels and such-like would have been no use to those Turks after they had lost their heads. So they loaded one great cannon as I have said. And the cannon went off right in front of me. It blew me out of the skiff and I would have drowned if a brave Cossack—Demid, it was—had not fished me out by the scalp lock and put mud and powder on my wounds. The cuts closed up, but whenever I have needed a bit of coin or a jewel to give to a maid, I have taken a knife and cut them open again and taken out some of the charge of that Turkish cannon."

He ceased his boasting and grunted in astonishment. A girl had slipped into the tavern from the dark regions behind the stove.

"Galka!" cried Kukubenko, frowning because she had presumed to show herself to strange warriors.

"Nay, father—" the maiden seized his arm and whispered to him, her bright head with its tinsel circlet, and straw-hued curls pressed against his dark, shaggy locks. Ayub did not finish his story, and Kirdy ceased stroking his guitar, his fingers poised in mid-air. The dark eyes of the youth glowed for an instant and then he paid no attention to Galka as if fair-faced girls did not interest him in the least.

"Hmm!" said the Zaporoghian to himself. "The young minstrel has not seen a lass like this before. That's strange, because girls always crowd around the *bandura* folk like ravens in a corn field."

But Galka was not like the dark-browed, warm blooded maidens of the southland. She was too slender, as if wasted by illness or brooding—only lips and eyes vivid in a bloodless face. Nearly all the color had gone from her once-bright 'kerchief, what with many washings, and her neat *beshmet,* the long smock that all girls wore, was ornamented with many cross-stitchings where it had been torn. And her boots, instead of soft red or green leather, were of stiff horsehide—evidently the work of the cobbler in the corner.

Nevertheless, Ayub watched her, and a pleasant glow went through him. Ten years ago he would have had a lass like Galka out on the clear sand between the benches, dancing. He would have had Kirdy playing a gay tune, and Kukubenko drawing off all the mead in the place. He would have been gloriously drunk.

"—— fly away with you, Kukubenko!" he bellowed, the wooden bench creaking under his weight suddenly. "You don't laugh at a story; you hide your women like a Turk.* What kind of a dog-kennel is this? Strike up, minstrel! Fill up the cups! We can't live forever."

Kirdy's white teeth flashed under his dark mustache and his fingers struck out the first, swift notes of a Gypsy song. And then they all heard the shuffling of steps outside, the clank of steel, and the spluttering of a torch. The door was thrust open and Durak entered, bending his head to clear the lintel. Behind him could be seen the steel caps of half a dozen men-at-arms.

* Cossacks did not seclude their women, who were high-spirited and well able to take care of themselves; the Muscovites of the sixteenth and seventeenth centuries did not allow their wives and daughters to be seen by any one outside the household, as a rule.

Ayub rose, towering against the chimney piece, taking in his right hand the heavy scabbard that he had unshipped while he was drinking. To a man, the villagers bowed low and fastened their eyes on the giant Muscovite who strode over to the tavern-keeper.

One of the *boyars*, the same who had bandied words with Ayub about the river, followed Durak, accompanied by the servant with the torch.

"Ah, *moi batyushka*—little father mine—you have hidden your bright jewel all this weary way!"

So said the *boyar*, and Kukubenko fell to his knees, his head lowered between his hulking shoulders.

"Don't you know, you dolt," went on the *boyar*, "that it's a crime to hide things from your prince? If he had not seen her himself the other day, driving in the cattle—you kept her well hidden on the road in one of your wagons, old fox."

Kukubenko bent his head and managed to say hoarsely—

"If it please His Illustriousness—"

"Well, it does please His Illustriousness, your master," interrupted the noble, "and so you'll get off with a whole back this time. Only make haste and send the girl up to the castle."

On his knees the tavern-keeper edged toward the *boyar* and caught in his scarred hands the folds of the soiled purple kaftan. Bending still lower, he kissed the other's muddy shoes. The noble stared down, his red eyelids twitching with the sting of the liquor in him, steam rising from his round crimson face.

"Pardon," said Kukubenko slowly, "it was no fault of mine that the lass was not seen by Your Excellencies. She was ill—you know young girls fall ill on a long journey like that. She's my daughter."

Perhaps the sight of his own rags made the stout Muscovite angry. His good-nature vanished, and he shouted to Durak to take Galka along and have done.

"It's no fault of yours, you say, *moujik!* You peasants think you're landowners—when a cow drops a fine calf you hide it, and show a skeleton instead! I'll eat with the dogs if your old woman hasn't pieces of gold and silver tucked away in her stocking this minute. No, it isn't your fault at all! When we send for wine, you take a cask of mead up to the castle and save the *gorilka* to pour down your own stems."

Going over to the table, he lifted Ayub's half filled mug of corn brandy, sniffed at it, and drank it.

"It's as I said, you dog! And now— —— save us!"

Galka had remained perfectly quiet, her gray eyes fastened on her father, while the *boyar* was pronouncing judgment. But when Durak put his hand on her arm she wrenched free and darted at the sleepy servant with the torch. Snatching the blazing brand from him, she beat the stout *boyar* over the head with it, sending sparks and hot coals showering all over him.

With a barbed oath he jumped back, clawing at neck and shoulders. Running up to Durak, the girl struck at him, but the captain of the guards thrust out his shield and the brand was knocked from her hand.

Durak held her fast while he unbuckled his belt and proceeded to lash her wrists together behind her back. This was too much for Ayub who had never before played the part of a spectator when a broil was in progress. A strong belief that the *boyar* would order him cut down or trussed up had kept him in the deep shadow by the chimney, where the wandering gaze of the Muscovite had not identified him. Now he was beginning to fidget and snort.

"Look here, brother," he lifted one of the kneeling villagers, "take up the benches, shout your war cry and we'll make crow's meat of these chaps."

The man twisted up a face pallid with fear.

"Oh, as you love Christ, do not lift a hand. The prince is our lord."

"How, your lord?"

"It would be sin to lift hand. Besides, he would take the cattle and hang some of us up. Then the old folks and the brats would starve."

"Well, your mother bore you once, you can't live forever," grumbled the Cossack who could not understand the other's fear, but realized now that these men would not take up weapons against Vladimir. He glanced at the minstrel, and then a second time, thoughtfully.

Kirdy had shouldered his guitar and was pouring water on the smoking head of the *boyar*. This accomplished, the boy put a hand on his hip, smiling.

"Good sir, is the noble prince out of humor? Does he toss on his bed, sleepless? I can sing of the deeds of the old heroes—aye, of the falcon ship that sailed without a wind, or of Rurik the Fair who slew in his day a host of Moslem knights. I can relate the wonders of the court of the Moghul, or Prester John who lives in a gold tent beyond the roof of the world—"

The *boyar* grunted and chewed his lip.

"Vladimir can not sleep that is true. Are you a *koldun*—a conjurer, to know that."

"Nay, the *bandura* man must know all things."

"Come along then—put the prince to sleep. You'll wish yourself in purgatory if you cross him."

They filed out into the darkness, lacking a torch. Kukubenko did not rise. His shoulders heaved in a sigh, and presently he went to stir up the fire. His task half finished, he sat down heavily, his chin propped in his mighty fists. The cobbler put away his wooden last and his knife.

Ayub's merry-making had come to a sorry end. His broad, good-natured face was troubled as he watched the men who sat in the tavern without so much as a word between them. So might one of the massive *ovtchai*, the gray wolf hound, have sat on his haunches among sheep dogs, puzzled by the sights and smells around him, eager to be off on the trail again.

Such a fine little one, Galka was. Fire enough in her veins! How she had basted the *boyar* on the noodle with the torch! Ayub chuckled aloud and then sighed. Like a heavy mantle, the silence of the northern men enveloped and oppressed him.

A woman entered the room from behind the stove—a bent form, lean with the stoic strength of age and toil, her head hidden in a black 'kerchief. She crept over to Kukubenko and stooped to whisper to him, brushing back a gray lock of hair from her eyes. Then, kneeling by the tavern-keeper, she began to rock back and forth, groaning shrilly and clasping her hands against her wasted breast.

From time to time her bony fingers went up to her face, as if to claw it. The helpless bleating of this mother, aged before her time, was too much for the Zaporoghian to endure.

"I can't stay here," he muttered to himself. "I'll go out on the plain, by ——, and sleep."

Rising, he sought the kegs of spirits in the corner by the cobbler, sniffing them until his experienced nose identified the best *gorilka*. From this cask of corn brandy he filled a stone jug. Then he ripped the purse from his belt, tossing it into the lap of Kukubenko, who did not look up or cease stirring the dead ashes of the fire.

"God keep you, good folk," he said and drew a sigh of relief when the tavern lights were left behind.

He did not take the trail that led back to the castle, but struck out past the cattle-pens to the open steppe, going toward the moon that was sinking into the mist. Like an orange lantern, it hung in front of his eyes, lighting up the stems of tall grass, glinting on the surface of a hidden pool. When he stopped for a moment to choose his path, the myriad sounds of the night swelled louder in his ears— the pulsating rasp of grasshoppers, the buzzing of gnats and the distant crying of wild geese, startled by something or other.

A thousand glow-worms beaded the grass and the scent of the river with its forest of rushes filled his nostrils. Hearing and seeing all this, the warrior nodded to himself gravely.

"A good place, the steppe."

Then he drew in his breath sharply and rubbed his eyes. The moon, half full, was sinking behind a mound on the plain. The high grass was clearly to be seen, and, rising from it, the black outline of a man.

Ayub could not tell how far away the figure was. It loomed gigantic one instant and looked small as a dwarf the next, in that elusive glow from the sky. The figure wore no hat, but the orange rays gleamed on its head as if it had been polished steel. A long cloak concealed its limbs.

Its head was bent forward as if looking into the gloom or listening to the multitudinous sounds of the night. To Ayub's fancy it might have been the spirit of the steppe, incarnate—lord of waste places, ruler of darkness.

Or, he reasoned, it might be the spirit of some Tatar khan, arising from its age-old bed in the burial mound.

"Perhaps it is the arch-fiend himself," he muttered between his teeth, without feeling any fear.

He had had quite a bit of spirits down his throat, and after the dark deeds he had beheld in the settlement, what was more to be expected than that Satan should have come to look at his own?

"In the name of the Father and Son!" he shouted. "Away with you! Devil, you can't terrify the soul of a Cossack."

At once the figure vanished from the mound, and the moon was once more to be seen, glowing over the grass. Ayub uncorked the jug, and, following a custom of which he himself knew not the meaning or origin, lifted it to the four quarters of the earth.

"To the Faith—to all the sir brothers, Cossacks—wherever they may be in the world."

Then he stroked down his long mustaches, lifted the jug in both hands, and threw back his head. After a long moment he sighed and tossed the jug away, empty. Stretching himself out full length in the grass, he spread his coat over his chest, pushed his lambskin hat under his head and began to snore almost at once, oblivious of the evil wrought by a prince who was not at peace in his own soul, of the loss of his horse, and of the presence of a village in the wilderness where no village should be.

Nevertheless, his sleep was broken. Voices penetrated his hearing. The voices belonged to two good Zaporoghians and were close to him and quiet. He turned over and was sure that he heard a Tatar war-cry—*ghar—ghar—ghar!*

III

Distance tries the horse's strength—Time the strength of man.

Kirghiz proverb.

The cry echoed in Ayub's ears until he roused himself, certain that Tatars were rushing on him. Instead, he beheld Kirdy squatting beside him, the rein of a piebald pony over his arm. It was the hour before dawn and the whole eastern sky was alight.

"The Tatars—"

"I am the Tatar. It was the only way to wake you, Uncle Ayub. I tried everything. Now you must listen to me because I have far to ride."

The high grass, waving under the fresh breeze that comes with sunrise, hemmed them in. The young minstrel's face was flushed, and his coat and *kalpak* glistened with dew. Ayub saw that his eyes were coal black and slanted at the corners—the eyes of a man with Mongol blood in him.

Another thing he noticed was that the glow in the sky flickered, and shot up as if the reeds by the river were afire.

"Did you sing the prince to sleep?" he yawned.

"Vladimir did not sleep last night. The Tatars came."

Ayub's jaws clicked together, and his drowsiness vanished.

"— burn this Muscovite drink! Then there was a fight—"

"Nay, there was only a little fight."

Getting up to his knees Ayub beheld dark clouds of smoke rising over the trees where the hamlet of Sirog was—or had been. The glare of flames beat into his eyes, and he heard now a far-off crackling that he had taken to be the wind in the reeds.

"We were near the river gate of the castle," went on the minstrel, "when a *chambul* of Tatars swept on us. They speared the *boyar* and three men, but Durak broke through with his ax and gained the gate. We heard other Tatars at work in the village—"

"And you—what were you doing?" growled the warrior.

Kirdy smiled and shook his dark head.

"I tried to carry off the maiden, when the Muscovites were cut down. What availed it? A lance raked my ribs and my sword blade snapped. They bore her off and I ran to seek my horse."

His green *sharivar* were stained with blood, but Ayub drew a long breath when he looked at the boy's side. A leather scabbard had been thrust through the black sash, a scabbard stamped with strange lettering and strengthened with bronze. From it projected a hilt, not of horn or of iron, but ivory inlaid with gold. It curved, Moslem-fashion. Such a weapon might be worn by the khan of the Golden Horde.[*]

Without a word the Cossack reached out and drew the sword from the scabbard. The blade was whole—an arc of blue steel, unstained and sharpened to a razor edge. The flicker of the distant flames ran along its length, illumining a line of writing, worked in gold. This writing was not Turkish, nor was it any Christian tongue.

Ayub thought that it was an uncommon youth who could take his horse from the stables and ride out of a Tatar raid.

"Your sword was—broken," he said slowly.

[*] The Tatars of the Golden Horde were a branch of the Mongol-Tatars who conquered Russia in the time of Kublai Khan. Their chief was called the Altyn Khan or Golden Khan, and their descendants today are the Kiptchaks, or "desert people."

"This—" Kirdy hesitated a little—"was given me."

"Hmm. Who was the Tatar?"

"Ghirei Khan, of the Nogais, made the raid. I saw his white horse when the tavern was burning."

An old foe of the Siech was Ghirei Khan, and a valiant man. Ayub knew that the Tatar was shrewd as a steppe fox. And he thought that the boy had a wise head on him to see so much when swords were out and flames were roaring.

"Did the prince beat him off?" he asked.

Kirdy was silent for the time that water takes to boil. When he spoke, his accent was so marked that the Cossack barely understood him.

"*In'shalum bak Allah.* God forbid I should judge where I have little wisdom. I did not see the prince or his men. It may be they were too late, or Ghirei-ka hemmed them in. But the Tatars cut down the villagers who took weapons in their hands. They slew many, taking some for captives—the young lads and maidens for slaves. They drove off all the cattle and sheep."

Ayub eyed the piebald pony attentively. It was, as the minstrel had said, a good horse.

"And whither do you ride?"

The youth looked up quickly.

"After the maiden, Galka. I will bring her back from the Tatars."

All this while Ayub had been revolving things in his mind. Kirdy was not like the *bandura* players he had known—too young for one thing. The boy had come from beyond the frontier; his speech was strange. Stranger still, he had emerged from a Tatar raid with almost a whole skin, with a horse and a sword worth a noble's ransom. Now he proposed to cross the river in the path of the Tatars, which was a good way to die immediately, unless he was known to the raiders.

Was he a spy? Had he come to Sirog to measure the strength of Prince Vladimir? Yet, if he were a foeman, why should he linger to talk to Ayub?

"Look here, my lad," said Ayub bluntly. "We shared bread and salt at the tavern, that's a fact. But when you say Prince Vladimir turned his back and picked his nose while a Tatar *chambul* raided his villagers, I believe you're lying like a dog. The prince may be half a devil, but he's an orthodox Christian like myself, and no coward. So I think you're a spy, and that's the long and short of it."

Kirdy's dark head went up and he drew a breath between clenched teeth. Both men reached for their swords, the youth more swiftly than the big warrior. Both were on their knees, their movements hampered by the dense growth around them.

The minstrel did not raise his weapon. No sooner had his hand closed on the hilt than the curved blade sprang from the scabbard. His arm darted forward and to the right, and the scimitar gleamed under Ayub's chin.

Death's scent was in Ayub's nostrils as he flung himself to the left, crashing full length on his back. The razor edge of the scimitar did no more than touch his *kalpak*.

Lying so, he saw Kirdy bending over him, saw the boy's face, pale and twitching, the black eyes burning. In the brush behind him a horse stamped and some one growled a word of reproof. Kirdy, as if struck by an arrow, remained motionless while the big Cossack tried doggedly to free the broad-sword upon which he was lying.

Then, to Ayub's astonishment, the boy thrust the curved sword back in its scabbard and put his foot on the pommel of the Cossack's weapon. He cried out something in a language Ayub did not understand, and added under his breath, "Nay, between us must be peace!"

"You give me life?" Ayub scowled up at him. "By the five wounds, I'll take naught from the hand of a Moslem."

The boy's set lips smiled, though the veins still stood out on his forehead.

"I am no Moslem."

Sitting up, Ayub beheld his cap lying on the ground, cut in two. "Well, you are no minstrel either. Who taught you that cross-stroke with the blade? What are you, then?"

The blood flowed back into Kirdy's lean cheeks and he withdrew his foot from Ayub's sword, standing a moment in silence while the anger of the two men cooled.

"Sir brother, it is true I am no *bandura* player. I have come from afar through many enemies, and a minstrel may go where a warrior would meet only sword strokes.

"I was born in the tents of the Golden Horde, in the sands of the Gobi, beyond the mountains that you call the roof of the world. My mother was a princess, of the line of Kublai Khan. She had the right to bear with her wherever she might go the gold *yarligh* and to sit on the white horse skin. Before I had backed a horse she and my father were slain by tribesmen who raided down from the mountains. A servant hid me in a cart and so I was not carried off a slave.

"My grandsire was a *bogatyr*, a hero. Alone among men he entered the tomb of Tchingis Khan in the pine forest where the Kerulon flows, in the land of the Five Rivers. He carried hence the yak-tail Standard of the Mongol Horde, and with it in his hand, he made war against the emperors of Cathay. But my grandfather was old, and the Horde was no more than a scabbard from which the blade has been drawn. He took me into his tent and taught me how to handle a sword.

"He taught me many things, but not by words. When the Cathayans searched for us, we drew our reins toward the passes in the southern mountains,* and these we crossed in regions where the snow lay and the winds were very strong. A good swordsman, Chauna Singh, of the tribe called Rájputs gave us aid. He had a fine beard and knew a horse when he saw one. He served Jahangir, the Moghul of Ind.

"So we also took service with the Moghul, and crossed swords more than once with the Moslems. Yet there was one Moslem who was a *bogatyr*. He was Abdul Dost, and he taught me how to steal horses and lie in wait for a caravan. I was old enough to follow him in battle, but not old enough to have men to my command.

"Once I think we saved the life of the Moghul of Ind in a war against the Usbeks, and many were slain. But my grandfather tired of the Moghul's court, because there he made many enemies who were always close at hand, and not in a distant camp that could be watched. There were women who plotted against him, smiling at him because he had found favor with the Moghul, but whispering and stirring up the *mansabdars* of the throne against him.

"I, and others with me, begged my grandfather to go before Jahangir, the Lord of the World, the Moghul, and justify himself. But he would not go. He said that once a man might justify himself with

* The Himalayas.

words, but not a second time. Besides, he was very weary of the court.

"So we went at night and led out the best of our horses, taking no more than that with us, for we could not. Aye, many fine pieces of armor and hangings of silk and coralwork and weapons we left behind in the palace grounds of Balkh where the Moghul lay.

"Again we drew our reins toward the mountain passes to the north. We carried grain for our horses in saddle bags, because snow had put an end to grazing. On the other side of the mountains we found a land of rolling, green valleys where the people did not live in tents, but in clay houses, and had a great deal of cattle. The horses, too, were good. When we reached a wide river with ships that bore masts and sails, my grandfather said that he had been in this place before. He called it Khorosan.* It was not a good place for us, because the people were turbaned folk—Moslems.

"Though the grazing was good we had to press on, my grandfather pretending that he was blind, and I saying that I was a cup-companion, a teller of tales from the court of the Moghul. We followed the river and it led us to a city on a sea where all the shore was gray with salt. Aye, we crossed a desert of gray salt where we found no grazing at all, and the caravan beasts were camels.

"In the city my grandfather talked with men who had thin beards and wore dirty caps and seemed always to be afraid. When they heard what my grandfather wanted they feared the more, but they took from us the last of our gold. They were called Jews. When a Jew passed a Turkish grandee in the street, the Moslem would snatch off the Jew's cap and spit in it and put it back on again.

"My grandfather, the *bogatyr*, wanted to be placed on a ship with the horses, to go across the sea. He had begun to feel his age, and his joints were stiff. At that time he would sit against the wall of a house and talk to me about his home. He had never done this before.

"So I learned that his people were all knights who cared not about trade, but fought the Turks and the Tatars. My grandfather's people were the Kazaki—Cossacks of your tribe.

"He said that the brotherhood of Cossacks never left the war camps, but when they had taken gold or fine jewels in plunder, they would give it all to the musicians, to play and the girls to dance, and hold revelry. Now, when he felt death standing near him, he desired

---

* Now northern Persia.

above all things to see the Cossack steppe again, and to greet the warriors, his brothers, so that the minstrels would know of his deeds and his name would not be lost to fame, but would be sung from camp to camp in the steppe.

"And the Jews, greatly fearing, put us on a ship. For a month we sailed across that sea toward the *Jitti-karachi,* the Great Bear in the sky.* Then the shores closed in on us, and we passed up a river, where only reeds and the wagon-tents of the Tatars were to be seen.

"When we set foot on land again the bellies of our horses were drawn up into their ribs. But the eyes of the *bogatyr,* my grandfather, were bright and he shouted and plied his whip. For days we sped on through the tall grass, avoiding the Tatar *auls* and swimming the freshets. We swam the Donetz, and my grandfather began to quiver all over, like an eager horse, when he saw the roofs of the village of Sirog and the men going in and out of the castle.

"But after we had come up to the gate he said to me that these were not Cossacks, because the Cossacks were free men without masters, and he had seen the banner of the prince. So we kept our saddles.

"We stopped after a while, and my grandfather sat down because he was weary, and because he was grieved at finding strangers where he had looked for the sir brothers, Cossacks. I went back to the tavern for meat and wine, and there I met you, sir brother."

So spoke the young Mongol prince, and Ayub meditated upon his tale with lowered eyes, finding in it truth and not falsehood. The Cossack warrior remembered the man he had seen outlined against the moon the night before, and remembered too the Cossack voices that he had heard when he was stretched out drunk. And he was deeply ashamed that an elder Cossack, a *bogatyr,* whose renown had traveled over all the steppe from the Black Sea to Moscow, should have seen him drunk when Tatars were burning and pillaging near at hand.

"*Ekh,*" he said at length, "you are mistaken, Kirdy. The fame of your grandsire has not been unvoiced, his deeds have not been forgotten. The gray-haired *bandura* players have sung of him and chil-

---

* This must have been the Caspian, and the river the Volga.

dren have heard his name. It is in my mind that your grandsire is the *koshevoi ataman* of the Zaporoghian Cossacks, who was called the Wolf. Khlit of the Curved Saber, so his enemies named him."

"That is true," assented Kirdy. "And this is his sword. He gave it to me last night when mine was broken. A Tatar or Mongol would have known it at once for the blade of Kaidu, the rider of the white horse."

Ayub nodded soberly. He had heard of such a sword, but had never set eyes on it before.

"Take me to the *koshevoi,* so that I may hold him in my arms. Eh, he was a hero, and there are not such in the Siech today."

Kirdy glanced up at the sun and shook his head.

"Nay, he is far away by now. Come, there is much to be done—if you trust me."

Rising to his full height, Ayub stretched himself until his bones cracked, then shouldered his sword, and flung an arm around Kirdy.

"Nay, youngling, when you are older you will know that it is ill work rousing one who has been fighting the bear—drunk."

Instead of mounting his horse, Kirdy walked beside the older man, his courtesy forebearing to sit in the saddle while Ayub was afoot. As for the Zaporoghian, he eyed the youth sidewise, taking account of the dark brows, the clear, quick moving eyes and the stalwart neck.

"He's a swordsman, no doubt of that," he thought with pleasure. "He's tall and plain-spoken, and he led a horse out under the spears of a Tatar *chambul.* — take me if we don't make a good Cossack out of him. Only I hope Khlit put this plan in his head—the lad's unfledged yet, for making a plan, and —— knows my head isn't suited for such things."

IV

Prince Vladimir had not slept that night. When his sentinels had brought word of the Tatar attack, he had left the massive chests of gold-and-silver plate where he had been making a tally of his possessions with the aid of a sleepy clerk and had himself given the alarm. For hours his retainers had stood under arms while Vladimir, in a tower of the blockhouse, watched the sacking and burning of the village a musket shot away.

Not until dawn, when the last of the riders had disappeared toward the river, did the prince give command to open the gate in the palisade and sally forth. His arqubusiers went out, carrying lighted matches, and the *boyars* went with a strong guard of pikemen, but Vladimir was attended only by Durak, the clerk, and the priest who had come with him from Moscow.

He merely glanced at the smoldering and charred walls of the tavern, the demolished huts and the broken cattle-pens. He did not go out to the fields where horses had trodden down the tender barley and wheat. Instead, he went from one body to another commanding Durak to turn each one over and identify it.

There were many bodies and few living souls in the hamlet of Sirog. Old women, who had flocked together, dry-eyed and voiceless, kneeled as he went by, mounted on the black Kabarda. Boys, who had run out into the steppe and so had escaped the Tatar lances, took off their caps. To all these Vladimir spoke, asking the names of the slain. He even bade Durak's men-at-arms rake over the débris of the larger buildings to see if any bodies had been buried in the ruins.

The *boyars* soon went back to the castle because the penetrating odor of hot ashes and blood was distasteful to them, but Vladimir kept at his task with feverish eagerness, watching to see that the clerk marked down all the names of the dead on a long roll of paper.

An hour later they came across the forms of the cobbler, and his sons in the trail well on toward the river.

"Mark down Ivashko, and his sons," Durak growled to the clerk. "See, they took cudgels in their hands, and so they were spitted."

"*Deus eos accipe*," murmured Vladimir. "God receive their souls."

The captain of the men-at-arms glanced up at his lord bleakly, as if wondering why His Illustriousness bothered his head about so many peasants.

"The tally is complete, Serene Highness," vouchsafed the clerk.

"How many?"

"Fifty-three, please you, my lord."

Vladimir motioned him to give the list of names to the priest. "Here, father—these names must be prayed for, *per diem*, in perpetuity. As a whole and by individuals, by Mother Church. At

Easter candles must be burned." He considered a moment. "Will five hundred and thirty gold ducats be a sum sufficient?"

The priest, with down-cast eyes, took the list and bowed.

"Yet there is no altar and, save for the *ikona* at the castle—"

"Tomorrow we begin the march to Moscow. There the sum will be paid down." Again Vladimir hesitated, fingering his lip.

"Nay, I doubt me that it suffices. Ten garments of cloth-of-gold, with pearls sewn therein will I give the holy images in the Kremyl."

He glanced at the haze of smoke that still hung over Sirog.

"It is manifest, is it not, father, that I am now relieved of my oath to abide by and protect the dogs of serfs on the border?"

Durak, the voiceless, uttered a croaking sound that might have been a laugh.

"Cattle gone, wenches gone, brats gone—only *kolduns*, only magicians, could rebuild the village."

"Aye, my lord prince," acknowledged the priest to whom exile in the steppe was as abhorrent as to Vladimir, "it is manifest. Will you return to bend the knee at court?"

Vladimir, hands crossed on the saddle pommel, bade the clerk read over the list again, and when he had done, remarked:

"Kukubenko's Galka is not set down. What became of her?"

Durak pointed up the trail.

"There are twain who can give my lord some word of the lass."

The two Cossacks had appeared. They were on foot, Kirdy limping to favor his injured side, Ayub flushed and breathing heavily. At sight of him the stallion had neighed and started forward, only to be restrained by a dig of the spurs. The Zaporoghian stifled a groan, because he had never used spurs on the horse, and he could see plainly that the Kabarda had not been rubbed down or fed that morning. The silver cross on the chest strap that all Cossack horses wore had been taken off, and now the reins had been ornamented with rows of tiny gold crosses in the Muscovite fashion.

When the warriors doffed their caps at his stirrup, Vladimir studied them from under bent brows, his head craned forward from his shoulders. Some slight deformity of the back made it impossible for him to hold it upright, and this painful poise of the head may have made its mark on the man's mind, for the young prince had a restless spirit, beset by black moods that were like evil demons tormenting him with the pangs of conscience.

"Can you lead me back to the Dnieper?" he asked.

"If God wills," responded Ayub, thinking that the prince must have changed his mind about the river. Even a Muscovite could see now that this was no place for a settlement.

"Well, take service with me. Only see that you obey orders."

Prince Vladimir was new to the frontier; he had heard that the Cossacks were vagabonds—masterless men, sprung from fugitives, soldiers, Tatars, Gypsies and whatnot. Since they acknowledged no masters, they were in his eyes no better than the slaves that deserted the estates of the *boyars* in Muscovy. He did not know that in these plainsmen there ran sometimes the blood of nobles.

"We serve a Cossack *ataman*," said Kirdy gravely.

"I'll pay you for your horse, tall ruffian."

Ayub shook his head.

Now Prince Vladimir was not the man to take a refusal from two wanderers. Yet he needed them to guide him into settled country, and it fell in with his mood to humor them a bit. He bade them follow him to the castle, and this they did—Ayub's eye ever on the stallion, Kirdy occupied with thoughts of his own. Near the end of the trail where the ground sloped up sharply the Cossacks halted in surprize.

All the space at one side of the palisade had been dug up. The black earth lay in heaps as high as a man's head and between the mounds were great pits. Ayub thought first that the Muscovites had been making a ditch around the wooden wall, then he wondered if they were burying their dead.

But the bones that littered the ground were dry, and here and there he saw the skull of a horse. The rotting shaft of a spear had been flung aside carelessly and rusted iron arrowheads lay among the stones. The knoll was nothing but a great cemetery, except where the palisade had been built.

"In other days," explained the prince, "a battle was fought in this place. Merchants up the river told me of it, and I have dug out enough gold to line the walls of a palace."

Ayub thought of the goblets and plate he had seen on the *boyars'* tables, and the chests that had been standing in the corner by Vladimir's bed.

"You twain shall have your share, and you shall not lack thereby
—I pledge my word."

Covertly the big Zaporoghian reached up and touched the cross
on his sword. It was ill doing, to his mind, to meddle with bodies
under the earth. Kirdy, who had seen the digging in progress the
day before, made no comment, and there fell a silence that was
broken by the prince, who still sought to win the warriors to his
service.

"What was the fate of the tavern girl—she who fared with you to
my gate?"

"Since she is fair of face, my lord," responded Kirdy, "the Tatars
would not take her life, but would sell her to the Turks for a slave."

A gesture as of tossing something lightly from his fingers, and
Vladimir sighed.

"I would have given a hundred silver crowns for her."

"Sir prince," said the youth earnestly, "I will free her and bring
her to this place unharmed."

"Now by all the saints," Vladimir smiled at Durak, "here is a
minstrel of deeds as well as words. But surely that is a mad thought.
The raiders will be fifty versts away—see, the sun is at the zenith."

"Not with sheep, lord prince," spoke up Ayub. "They were driving
cattle, too. When a Tatar raids, it is like this: They ride at night,
two horses to each man in the horde. They go far into Christian
lands, molesting no village, like ghosts riding to the Devil's summons.
At dawn they turn, spreading out on each wing, making a long net
that closes around the *stanitzas*. You have seen what they do to the
fold of a village. They put the children in hampers and mount the
captives on the led horses. Before you can say a prayer to the Father
and Son, they are across the river again."

Pointing through the haze of smoke at the gray ribbon of the
Donetz, he added:

"But Ghirei Khan knows that you haven't horses, and he will
take his time. Only God knows how he got the sheep across—maybe
in carts, maybe he just drove them in to drown—still, he's not more
than a dozen versts away."

There was bitterness in his voice and harsh accusation in his
bleared eyes. Ayub had looked over Vladimir's forces as only an experienced soldier can, and he saw that the prince had a score of
arquebusiers with good weapons, thirty pikemen, and as many un-

der Durak, besides the *boyars* and the servitors—nearly a hundred and fifty in all, with two brass cannon. Enough to have driven the Tatars out of the village, had the prince advanced at once to the aid of his peasants.

"Give me a horse, my lord," put in Kirdy quickly, "and I will bring back the maiden."

For a moment the prince considered, staring into the dark eyes of the wanderer. He would give much to have Galka again—

"You will return here, minstrel?"

"Aye. Only remember that we serve the *ataman*."

Vladimir shrugged. "Serve the devil if you will—but come back. You are young for the embrace of Mother Death."

Some minutes later Kirdy was leading a sorrel pony toward the thicket near the river bank where he had tethered the piebald—his own horse. Here they were out of sight of those who watched from the castle, and they mounted in silence, urging their beasts into the gray flood of the Donetz, kneeling in their saddles to keep dry above the waist.

"That is an ill place," grumbled the Zaporoghian. "No good ever came of meddling with graveyards, that's a fact. Only, now, it will be worse for us with the Tatars. You ought to take off those trousers, by the saints. If Ghirei Khan gets the upper hand, he'll crucify you and make dog collars out of your hide, and as for me—"

Shaking his head gloomily, Ayub meditated on what the tribesmen might do to him.

"Stratagems are all very well," he went on, "as long as your enemy's at a distance. Trick him all you like as long as your sword point's in between, but don't put your head in the bear's mouth and then kick him in the belly by way of a stratagem."

Kirdy, humming a saddle song under his breath, let the piebald out on the level plain of grass, and Ayub, still grumbling, hastened after him.

V

When the sun is high the lion roars unheeded: when night covers the earth men harken to the howling of a wolf.

Tatar proverb.

Ghirei Khan could not count above a hundred, and when, after some calculation, he decided that he was the richer by half a hundred captives and a good many more than a hundred cows, he was not altogether satisfied. He could not get a good price for the peasants from the Turkish slave traders and he did not want them himself. Not so much as a fistful of gold or silver had come out of the raid, and he began to think he had ridden away from Sirog too quickly. His spies had told him that Muscovite warriors were camped near at hand—and the Tatar always kept his distance from the ruined castle.

While his men made ready to feast on the sheep they had slaughtered and carried along in the peasants' carts, Ghirei Khan sat on a horse skin in a grassy valley by a stream and meditated.

He had a round head, a stub of a nose and eyes that were like black beads. They gleamed angrily when he looked at the groups of Christians who sat wearily in the sun, their hands hanging over their knees. Mounted Tatars paced around them—short-legged riders in polished mail—holding long lances with tufts of painted hair under the steel points.

Ghirei Khan had put aside his armor, and his thick body was resplendent in an orange *khalat* with sleeves too long for his stumpy arms. But either arm could wield with fury and skill the scimitar that lay across his knees. His men feared his anger, his enemies his craftiness. For the Nogai chieftain had lived long on the border, and the sparse red hairs under his chin that did duty for a beard were turning gray.

While the mutton was cooking in the pots he ate sunflower seeds, taking them from the hand of a warrior kneeling beside him—and counted over the prisoners again.

His slant eyes rested momentarily on Galka, who had covered her face and huddled up against gaunt Kukubenko. Then, at the tread of approaching horses, he looked up and resumed his chewing. Six Nogais were bringing in two Cossacks—one as big as an ox, the other slender, a born horseman. The weapons of the Cossacks were in the hands of the Nogais, but Ghirei Khan saw at once there had been no struggle.

"Exalted of Allah, lord of lances, lord of the plain and the river, bearer of the sword of Islam—" one of the Tatar riders began the usual salutation.

"Who are these sons of dogs?" exclaimed the khan.

"They are envoys, they say."

"From the Muscovite pigs?"

"Nay," put in Kirdy, who had understood the remarks, "we come from a *koshevoi ataman* of the Cossacks, from the one called Khlit, of the Curved Saber."

Ghirei Khan stopped chewing and the red hairs on his chin bristled. His memory was good and not so long ago this same Khlit had brought fire and sword against the Nogais. "How many men has he? From what quarter does he ride?"

Kirdy seated himself by the fire and stared into it while the tribesmen watched his face attentively.

"He will come, Ghirei Khan, to your *kibitka* when the shadows grow long. And he will come alone. He has no weapon but there are words that must pass between you twain. You can see we are not mounted for war, otherwise we would not have given up our arms."

Outwardly impassive, Ayub held his breath until his lungs burned in his chest, while he waited to see what the khan would do. Their lives hung in the balance, and he was afraid that Kirdy might grow anxious and urge again that they were envoys and so, according to the custom of the steppe, inviolate from harm.

"What message do you bring?"

"The *ataman* demands that you do not ill-treat the captives, for they are to be freed."

When the Nogai said nothing more, Ayub sighed with relief and stared about him with interest. Never before had he been in the camp of Tatars and his experienced eye took in the horse lines, the orderly groups around the fires—the riders who came as near as they dared to the chieftain to inspect the Cossacks. After a while the khan gave an order and warriors trotted out of the ravine—to double the guards, Ayub reflected, because none came in again. Also, the men at the fires did not eat their fill, but sat or walked about with bows strung and lances in hand.

Nevertheless, Khlit came in without being seen by the guards. He walked his horse down the bed of the stream, and Ayub knew it was he because he wore no sword and because he was older than any Cossack in the Siech.

Ghirei Khan put one stumpy hand on the hilt of his scimitar, and the other on the leather sheath, and his black eyes were no longer beads, but pin points of fire. His voice rumbled in his chest.

"What word have you, who have not an hour to live, to speak to me, O *Kazak?*"

Khlit dismounted and loosened the girth on his pony before coming to the fire and squatting down a spear's length from the Tatar, apparently not noticing that a warrior led his horse away and others crowded in behind him.

"You have mare's milk, Ghirei Khan," he said. "Give me some."

The unblinking gaze of the Tatar was fixed on his old foe. He decided at once that Khlit was unarmed. No knife was in the black girdle around the Cossack's lean waist, and no pistol sagged the pockets of the sheepskin coat that was thrown loosely over his bowed shoulders. Age had thinned the once massive body of the veteran *ataman,* hollowing the flesh under the cheekbones.

Ghirei Khan grunted with satisfaction. Not for the best pony in his herds would he have exchanged this Cossack who had come, afflicted perhaps with the madness that besets the very old, under his hand, to be tortured or slain as he saw fit.

He bent forward to scrutinize his guest, and grunted again. Khlit's attire had changed—under the sheepskin he wore no more than a red shirt, once brilliant but now faded by the sun. He had no tall Cossack *kalpak*. But the gray mustaches that fell to his bare chest, and the somber eyes that peered out under grizzled brows were the same.

With a quick movement of the wrist Ghirei Khan unsheathed his scimitar.

"Many winters have covered the steppe since we have spoken together, O *Kazak,* and is this the only word you have for me?"

Khlit nodded, and Ayub, who could already feel in imagination the lances of the Tatars between his ribs, glanced at Kirdy. The young warrior was apparently not listening at all—he lay on his side, drawing lines and circles in the sandy soil with a stick. Outside the ring of tribesmen, the village Cossacks, who had started up hopefully at sight of the Zaporoghian, returned to their seats by the stream.

"Then hear my word!" The lips of the Nogai drew back from his white teeth. "Your grave will be dug here. Infidel—dog—I will drive my horses over you, and jackals will litter over your bones."

"Eh, I'll have better burial than your fathers."

Blood darkened the Nogai's forehead and his hand quivered on the sword.

"I have seen their graves dug up, Ghirei Khan. Their bodies are no longer covered—nay, their bodies are kicked about."

"*Bak Allah!*" cried the Nogai involuntarily. "God forbid! But that is surely a lie."

When Khlit remained silent, curiosity began to temper his rage.

"What grave have you seen?"

"At Sirog the Muscovites have uncovered the burial-place."

Ghirei Khan took time to consider this. In reality, the Nogai tribes-men knew little of Sirog. But tradition persisted among them that their ancestors had been masters of the steppe and that the dead in the mound by the river were of their race. In any event the act of the Muscovites was an everlasting insult to a devout Muhammadan, and he considered this also, drawing a conclusion from it that brought small comfort to Ayub.

"*Insh'allah*—as God wills. Then I will crucify the three of you, setting the posts where the unbelieving swine, your kindred, can see them."

Khlit glanced at him fleetingly and his mustaches twitched into a smile.

"Do you want the women of the Nogai to point their fingers at you, and the children to shout after you?"

The Tatar was becoming more and more surprized, and he thought again that the *ataman* must have lost his senses.

"What words are these words?"

"Truth, Ghirei Khan. The women would mock you, saying that when the bodies of Sirog were uncovered, you turned your back and fled like a wolf, because the Muscovites had cannon."

Meanwhile Kirdy, who had been weighing the moods of the chief-tain, spoke quickly:

"Many a gold goblet and an ivory sword hilt—many a chain of silver did the Muscovites take from the mound of Sirog."

"How much gold?"

"One horse could not carry the load of it—two horses could not carry the silver."

Ghirei Khan began to calculate on his fingers and this took him some time. When he had finished his eyes were open and he no longer clutched the sword.

"It is clear to me, O *caphar*," he said reflectively, "that you would like to set a trap for me. You are trying to lead me back across the river."

At this Khlit chuckled, deep in his throat.

"I have known the time, Ghirei Khan, when you did not fear a *chambul* of the Moskyas."

"By the ninety-and-nine holy names, I do not fear them. O Khlit, you have seen me drive the folk of the villages like sheep—even Cossacks."

Ayub stirred uneasily, but seeing that his companions were silent, suppressed a hot retort. It was true that Ghirei Khan was a daring raider, wily and experienced, and the Cossacks of the Siech respected him for these qualities.

"But," the Tatar added, "there are more than a hundred Moskyas and I have not a hundred. *Hei-a*, they are behind walls with cannon. I would break my teeth on that place. I grow old, Khlit, and it is more pleasant to sit in the smoke of my *yurt* fire than to carry a torch."

"No need," said Khlit bluntly. "Take back these captives, and exchange them with the khan of the Moskyas for gold and silver. Ghirei Khan, you would redeem the lives of your men with gold—is the Moskya prince less than you? The way is open, without pitfalls. I have spoken."

As if dismissing the others from his mind, he dug a short clay pipe from the pouch at his girdle, and fished in the fire for a glowing ember.

For a long time Ghirei Khan considered matters, and it became apparent to him that he was master of the situation. Riders had come in from scouring the steppe and reported that the three Cossacks had travelled without companions to his *kibitka*. He knew that Vladimir and the foot soldiers could never catch his Tatars, and the Cossacks were unarmed—hostages. The prisoners were in his hands, and he could make his own terms with the Muscovites.

He thought of slaying the three warriors before going back to Sirog. When in doubt Ghirei Khan always took up the sword, and for this reason he was still alive on the steppe where few of his race lived to count their grandchildren on the fingers of both hands. But years had taught him caution. True, he could not understand why the three Cossacks had given themselves up, unless it was to set free the village Cossacks who were their kindred in a way. Without them he could not speak with the Muscovite prince, and if he did not strike a bargain with Vladimir, how could he claim the gold?

"The gold belongs to the Nogai!" he muttered, fingering the strands of his thin beard.

Not for the treasure of the Golden Horde, not for the standard of Tchingis Khan, his ancestor, would he have uncovered the bodies of Sirog. Now that the Muscovites had dug up the gold that had been buried with the bodies, Ghirei Khan saw no reason why he should not take it. This done, he could cover the bodies again, so that the spirits of the slain warriors would not ride upon the steppe, a thing of terror.

"God is one," he said finally. "I will go back to Sirog with the captives. Remember, O youth, the *bogatyr*, your grandsire, has sworn that the prisoners will be paid for with gold."

"He has sworn it," assented Kirdy.

"If matters fall out otherwise," said Ghirei Khan grimly, "you will bow your head to this."

And he touched the scimitar on his knees.

Kirdy laughed.

"Aforetime, O lord of lances, my grandsire was the White Khan of the Golden Horde. Alone among men he stood within the tomb of Tchingis by the shores of the Kerulon in the land of the Five Rivers. His word is not smoke."

"Then let him keep it," responded the chieftain impassively, but with something like wonder in his tiny eyes as he looked at Khlit. The old Cossack's pipe had gone out, and his head was sunk on his chest. Sleep smoothed the hard lines from his brow and lips, and Ghirei Khan thought that here was a man like himself, desiring peace rather than the path of war, and the cup by the fire more than the back of a horse.

Not without reason was Vladimir called the Fortunate. He had been in many scrapes, but a quick wit and a ready sword had brought him out unharmed. Even his disgrace at court was little more than a shadow, and he knew it to be thus. He had slain in a duel a noble whose wife was a woman comely beyond others. When he returned to the emperor's presence he would be pardoned because his sword and the slaves of his many estates were needed in the wars.

His failings were two—pride of person and birth, and superstition. These qualities among the Muscovite *boyars* were common enough, yet in Vladimir they wrought strange fancies. He had gilded the doors of a great church in memory of the noble who had fallen to his sword, and to the woman who had caused the quarrel he sent a pilgrim's staff upon his departure into exile.

From a hint given him by merchants who dared not take the risk themselves, he had shaped his course to Sirog, and its graves had yielded a treasure.

And now, out of the steppe itself—that wilderness of grass and reeds and sandy black earth that he had cursed when he first saw it—had appeared Cossacks who could guide him back to the frontier posts.

"Yet, my lord," suggested the priest, "the young warrior may not return alive from across the river."

Vladimir thrust the last of the sturgeon-roe into his mouth and wiped his plate clean with a morsel of bread.

"Well, little old woman, the youth may not come to Sirog but the tall rogue, his companion, will do so."

The dark priest lifted his eyes inquiringly, and Vladimir rubbed the grease from his fingers on the coat of a shaggy wolf hound.

"He will come to try to steal his horse—that much I read in his face."

"You were ever fortunate, my lord. All men say it."

"Then all men lie, my father. What is fortune, save luck, good or ill? Now the wind blows fair, now foul—who can win mastery by chance?"

The *boyars* at his table shook their heads, for such words were beyond their understanding. More than one glanced over the rim of his wine cup at the chests ranged beside Vladimir's bed. The chests told a story clearly. Yonder was gold, and they would all have a share in it.

"The wind rises," said one. "Hark to it!"

"Chance?" Vladimir pursued the thread of his thought. "'Tis a foul mistress, that—a wench with a heart for any comer. Nay, I am only fortunate in this: I have seen through the tricks of my enemies and they have not seen through mine."

"Still, lord prince," remarked a noble, "you are fortunate. You have never been wounded."

"Nay," growled another who had caught the gist of his leader's remarks, "skill, not luck, brought that about. Who among living men could touch Vladimir the Red with a sword's edge?"

Now the young prince smiled, because mastery with weapons was his pride.

"Drink, my wolves," he cried. "We have found the hunting good. And you, *batko*—old gabbler—what ghost do you see, that your eyes are cast down?"

Mustering an uneasy smile, the priest drew his robe closer about him.

"My lord, the wind blows cold from the river."

In fact, savage gusts beat at the high walls of the blockhouse and whistled through the gaps in the towers. The canopy over the prince's bed flapped, and the fires, fed by great piles of wood, since this was their last night in Sirog, roared, while eddies of sparks shot up against the stars. A vagrant puff of air swept the table and extinguished all the candles on it.

"Saint Piotr guard us!" cried Vladimir, pushing back his chair.

The priest crossed himself thrice, for the darkening of the candles was an evil omen.

"A torch!" commanded the prince, whose mood had changed. Motioning his sword-bearer to follow him, he made his way from the blockhouse into the outer enclosure, his sable cloak whipping about his broad, stooped shoulders. At sight of him the servitors and warriors bowed to the girdle, and he flung harsh words at them, for they labored slowly at greasing the carts and mending the ox chains for the morrow's journey.

Making his rounds, Vladimir hardly glanced at the men who were his slaves; his keen gray eyes rested more often on the cattle, on the few horses, on the weapons of the pikemen, stacked by their quarters in what had been the stables of Sirog, and the firelocks of the arquebusiers who paced their beats along the palisade. Others stood at the two brass cannon, placed a few paces within the gate that now stood open.

The moon gleamed on mail and spear points, and on the ruffled waters of the distant river, save when clouds, racing across it, darkened the faces of those who stood about the young lord of Novgorod.

"Where is Durak?" he asked, when all was arranged to his satisfaction.

"So please you, my lord," spoke up Barnetski, the captain of the arquebusiers, "the sentries on the village trail thought they heard horses."

"It was the wind in the rushes," muttered another, "or else the goblins of this place are riding to the devil's mass."

"By the Saints," laughed Vladimir, "'tis my vagabond, with the maiden!"

His quick eye had picked out three figures advancing between the mounds of earth in the burial ground. A sentry challenged sharply and Durak answered, striding forward with Kirdy and Galka, the daughter of Kukubenko.

"How now, youngling," demanded the prince, "do you take service with me?"

Taking his *kalpak* in his left hand, Kirdy bowed in greeting, and Galka, disturbed by the eager glances of the followers of the prince, bent her head and stepped back beyond the feeble light of the spluttering torch.

"Noble lord," said the young warrior gravely, "I have brought the maiden from the Tatar *aul* as I promised. By the wisdom of the *koshevoi ataman*, my grandfather, was this done. Yet in only one way could it be done. We were too few to make an onset with swords, so we made a bargain with Ghirei Khan."

"What matter? You are here, even if you left your sword behind—and the wench is here. Tomorrow you will show us the road that leads to the Dnieper."

"Perhaps—it rests with you, my lord. Ghirei Khan has brought back all the captives, and they are waiting now under guard across the river."

"I perceive," smiled the prince, "that you have an old head on young shoulders. You are not only a warrior, but a statesman."

"The bargain was this: for your Muscovites you must give over to Ghirei Khan all that you have taken from the graves of Sirog. He has kept the cattle, but your people are unharmed."

For a moment Vladimir considered this, frowning, while Durak and the sentries watched him expectantly.

"And where," he asked, "is the big Cossack, your comrade?"

"The Tatars, my lord, are holding him fast with lariats, against our return. If we should not go back they would tie him and begin torture immediately."

"Will you go back?"

"Lord prince, if Ayub were here in my place, he would go back. No Cossack would forsake a brother in captivity. It was by order of the *koshevoi ataman* that I came in Ayub's stead."

Kirdy did not add that Khlit, who had quaffed more than one stirrup cup before setting out from the camp of the khan, had been drowsy. The old wanderer had been swaying in the saddle and talking to himself, and bade Kirdy go to the castle to consult with the prince, saying that he would follow in a moment. But Kirdy had seen him head for a goatskin of wine as soon as the river was crossed.

"Nay," responded Vladimir, "I see that you are a fool. I will pay down no ransom for two-legged cattle—or four-legged."

The young warrior started, and his hand caught at his belt where his sword had been.

"My lord, do you jest? What was your answer?"

"Ghirei Khan will have no gold from me."

Kirdy looked at the Muscovite in silence, the veins throbbing in his forehead. It had not entered his mind that the prince would not redeem the captives, and he thought with something like dismay of what would follow when he brought such an answer to Ghirei Khan. Like as not, the wild Tatar would massacre the captives out of hand, or even throw his tribesmen against the castle. There was no doubt whatever about the fate of the three Cossacks.

"The khan is not to be trifled with, *Pany*—noble lord," he said. "If you do not alter your decision the waters of the river will be red at sunrise."

With uplifted hand the prince checked his words and peered from the gate within which they were standing. Durak had seen something moving in the moonlight and challenged sharply.

"*Stoi!* What is there?"

It was Khlit, stumbling out of one of the grave pits. He had left his coat somewhere, and he smelled strongly of wet leather and mare's milk. When they saw that he was unarmed and palpably drunk, the sentries let him pass, and he bowed solemnly to Vladimir.

"*Tchelom vam, Kunak*—the forehead to you, brother. And to you, brothers, warriors. And to you, headsman, I give greetings."

Blinking at Durak's great ax, he merely shook his scalp-lock, when they asked his name.

"I tell you, I am a falcon in from the steppe. I fly high—I see far."

Sighting a cask of mead around which several pikemen stood, waiting for the prince to depart so that they could drink, he shambled over to it and, grasping the rim with both hands, thrust in his head. So long did he remain buried in the cask that the Muscovites edged over to look into it, and no man could say for sure how much he drank, although the level of the mead was much lower than before.

A slight figure darted from behind Kirdy and flung itself down before the Muscovite.

"Do not send us away, little father. We have done no harm. Did we not pay the head-tax and the hoof-tax to the noble lords? If Your Illustriousness had come to the tavern you would have seen that we harmed no one—"

"*Par dex*," cried Vladimir, "no hurt shall come to you, Galka. As for the others—" he shrugged and waved a muscular hand at the priest. "That is more his affair than mine."

With a girl's quick intuition Galka saw that Vladimir would yield to no pleading and that the little dark priest was afraid to say anything at all. Catching her breath, she turned to Khlit, who was supporting himself against one of the cannon. But then the torch died down to a glowing stump and the shadows rushed in on them, so that only the pallid face of the Cossack maiden and the vague gleam of armor on the warriors was to be seen.

"God have mercy on us!" she cried suddenly and, hearing a whispered command from the prince, sprang up and fled like a goat down the road before Durak and his men who had been moving toward her could seize her.

Clouds veiled the moon, and Vladimir called back his followers from pursuing the swift-footed maiden. A new torch was brought and Khlit, steadying himself with a hand on either cannon, managed to walk to Kirdy's side.

"Let the brat go—she was a wild one," the prince was saying, "but to you, *koshevoi ataman* of vagabonds, and warrior without a sword, I again offer service. No need to go to the Tatars and be hacked into bits."

Khlit sucked his mustache and passed a quivering hand across his brow, and Kirdy, seeing that he could not manage an answer, lifted his head and spoke for the veteran warrior.

"I say what the *ataman* would say in a better moment. How could Cossacks face life when that maiden has set her foot on the way to death? How could we greet a brother if we broke the law of comradeship and left Ayub to be flayed by the Tatars? We could not!"

The deep voice of the young warrior echoed strongly, because his spirit was moved. Now that Khlit would take no hand in affairs, the responsibility was his to say the right thing. He lifted a hand but did not take off his *kalpak* this time in farewell.

"Vladimir! We will save our lives as best we may, and make what bargain we can with the khan. Only remember this, Ghirei Khan will rage, and it may be that he will come up against you. So guard yourself and do not take off your armor this night."

He had spoken as if to an equal, and Vladimir gazed after the two, frowning, as they made their way down the road to escape the pits. Long after they were lost to sight he heard Khlit singing a saddle song:

> "*Ov vy moi—tchoboty schovi—*"
> My riding boots, my riding boots—
> You are nice and new,
> But to —— with you!"

Then Vladimir shrugged again. He had been mistaken when he thought there was pride in these men.

"*Kasaki**—vagabonds!" he exclaimed.

VI

"A fool or a money-lender may gird on a good sword, but only the hand that uses it may hold a scepter."

Arab proverb.

As the hair of a jackal entering the den of a lion, or of a dog that has come suddenly upon a wolf, the hair on the head of Ghirei Khan

---

* *Kasaki*—Cossacks. The real name of the word is "vagabonds" or "masterless men."

stood up, and his small eyes became fiery sparks that smoldered when he heard the answer Vladimir had given the Cossacks.

"You spoke well at the castle gate—by —— you spoke well there!" Khlit whispered to Kirdy. "Now choose your words with care. Tell this Tatar if he would have his gold he must attack the gate. He has seen his graves uncovered and there is blood in his nostrils. If you do not choose the right words, my fledgling, you will wish you were drunk like me—"

Indeed the anger of the Nogai, squatting in the moonlight like some slant-eyed, armored idol, was enough to inspire fear.

"What did you promise?" cried Ghirei Khan, gnashing his teeth. "Where is my gold?"

"Your gold is in the castle of the Muscovite, O Khan," responded Kirdy calmly.

"Dog of an unbeliever! I will put the torch to the castle. I will spread a carpet of the slain."

"Aye, Ghirei Khan. But without us you will not have your gold."

The Tatar grunted and beat his knees with his fists. "You can not bring me the gold. You said it."

"When we asked the Muscovites for it we had no swords in our hands. Give us our swords and we will take it."

"Allah! Am I a blind man to fall twice in the same pit?"

Nevertheless, he began to ponder. Even in his rage the Nogai chieftain was far from being a fool. In the past he had raided more than one walled town, and while the Cossacks had been within the gate he had visited the outskirts of the cemetery, and the blood was hot in his forehead. He had seen the desecrated graves, and the battle lust was beginning to take hold of him. No longer did he think of returning peacefully to his *yurt* fire. A few guttural commands brought his leading warriors about him, and when he had spoken with them he turned to Kirdy who still stood before him with folded arms.

It occurred to the savage Tatar that the young warrior might have saved his skin if he had stayed in the castle instead of coming back. Ghirei Khan could appreciate daring, as well as loyalty to a comrade.

"My falcons have been flying about the castle. I have no more than seven tens, and they say that the Muscovites have more than a hundred—many with firelocks. I myself saw two cannon. The wooden wall of the castle is stout; our arrows can not pierce it nor our ponies leap over. You say that you can lead my men to the gold. Has your grandfather, the *bogatyr,* a plan? What is it?"

Kirdy glanced at Khlit anxiously, but instead of helping him with a word, the old Cossack was still chanting hoarsely the saddle song, his legs spread wide before him.

"Aforetime," he said boldly, "the *bogatyr* took by stratagem Alamut, the Eagle's Nest of Islam, and a walled city of Cathay. To him, a wooden castle in the steppe is a small matter, and he bade me attend to it."

"Allah!"

The khan, no little astonished, scrutinized Khlit keenly and what he saw seemed to enlighten him. He did not know how to smile but his black eyes snapped.

"And what is your plan, puppy?"

Kirdy himself did not know this, but to hesitate would have been disastrous.

"You also made a promise, O Khan, that the captives should be spared and permitted to go with us in safety from Sirog."

"My word is not smoke."

A powerful voice from the darkness near at hand interrupted them.

"And a horse, Kirdy. Do not forget my Kabarda—black with a white star on the forehead."

"And Ayub is to take out his Kabarda stallion."

"So be it. And what will you do, O my colt?"

Kirdy considered and made his choice—

"We will draw our swords against the Muscovites."

The aid of three such men was worth twenty Tatars, and Ghirei Khan nodded grimly. He understood well enough that the Cossacks' only chance of life was to prevail against the Muscovites and this was well.

"What is your plan?" he demanded.

Having gained a moment for reflection, Kirdy answered without hesitation:

"Divide your forces, half on the steppe side, half by the river gate. Light a fire here—send men to gather dry reeds, and tie bunches to your arrows. Set the reeds afire and shoot your shafts into the blockhouse."

"*Shim!*" cried Ghirei Khan, rising. "Go! Send an arrow through the gate so the dogs will know their fate."

While a warrior mounted and sped up the roadway, wheeling his horse on its haunches after he had loosed an arrow that quivered in the wall of the blockhouse, the Nogais began to flit about in the darkness. Soon the howl of a wolf was heard from the far side of the castle, but the wolf was a Tatar calling to his companions. Ghirei Khan's slant eyes glowed in the murk of moonlight like a cat's and from every quarter came the soft thudding of hoofs, the creaking of saddles. Only a man who knew the warfare of the steppe as Kirdy did could have told what was going on.

The preparations roused Khlit. He rose to his feet, stretching and sniffing the air, and when Ayub came up bearing the two swords of the Cossacks, the *ataman* grasped Kirdy roughly by the shoulder.

"Hi, what kind of a plan is this? If these Nogais dismount to climb the wall they'll be beaten off like flies. Don't go on foot, only dogs do that! Stay in your saddles. Let a dozen Nogais fire the burning arrows from the far side and raise a tumult—and gallop up the road with the rest. The gate is open."

Kirdy shook his head.

"I thought of that, but Vladimir has placed his cannon to bear on the gate. They would wipe us out. You've been licking the cup, *bogatyr*."

Planting his legs wide, though a little unsteadily, Khlit surveyed his grandson from under shaggy brows.

"*Tchoupek-shaitan!* Dog of the devil! What if I had a glass or two? My head's sound. I'll ride up alone if you hang back."

"Well said!" laughed the reckless Ayub, swinging his great blade around his head. "Only Ghirei Khan doesn't love those cannon. He'll make us three lead."

The pulse began to beat in Kirdy's forehead and his thin lips tightened. His had been the responsibility and he had tried to quit himself of it—to save Galka and the captives while Khlit was drinking and Ayub exchanging taunts with his Nogai guards. But now his quick temper flamed up and he cast all cautions aside.

"Aye," he cried, "we'll ride at the gate. Alive or dead, I'll be through it before you twain."

Khlit's eyes gleamed and he turned away to seek his horse, while

Ayub, whose spirits had risen at the prospect of action, leaned on the crosspiece of his broadsword and boasted.

"Eh, *ouchár*—eh, young warrior! No one will take away your bib or spill your milk. But as for me, I've had cannon go off under my nose too often, to cry about it."

Kirdy had gone off to find his horse and tell Ghirei Khan what they meant to do, and Ayub finished his recital to himself.

"Well, it's not exactly all sugar and cream, charging two guns loaded with grape. The balls will go through us as a sickle through grass, but God knows it's better so than lying stretched out for these last hours with a Nogai lariat fast on every wrist and ankle and the ends of the lariats tied to the saddle peaks of their ponies."

The Cossacks were too experienced to try to escape in the darkness now that they had their weapons. The Nogais would have run them down within a mile.

It was noticed in the castle that after the first arrow struck in the wall the howling of wolves was heard on every quarter. The Muscovites climbed the towers but could see nothing in the elusive moonlight. When the first flaming arrows quivered in the palisade on the steppe side, Vladimir's captains roused the sleepers and formed their men in the enclosure, and the prince himself who had been through more than one siege gave command to extinguish all fires.

"Gentlemen," he said to his *boyars*, "the glow-worms of the steppe are showing themselves. We must put our heels on them."

The arquebusiers, slow-match in hand, were told off, half to the menaced quarter and half to take station behind the cannon. They were phlegmatic Moldavians, veterans of the emperor's wars. Under Durak the thirty pikemen were placed in reserve at the door of the blockhouse itself, while the sixty-odd retainers of the *boyars*, armed with sword and spear, were sent to the defense of the palisade.

Watchmen were dispatched to the towers, and reported that the burning arrows were doing little damage. Sometimes the blazing reeds fell off in mid-air, and when a shaft, fanned by the gusts of wind, began to kindle flames in the heavy logs a sack of water or a wet cloak put them out.

More deadly were the unseen arrows of the tribesmen, which hissed through the air whenever a head was shown on the steppe

side. Here, too, resounded the shouts of the Tatars and the trampling of horses through brush.

Vladimir listened, his head out-thrust as if he were looking into
the darkness beyond the walls.

"They make too much ado yonder. The attack will come here,
through the gate. Barnetski, are the cannon primed? Then set your
firelocks in the rests, and Durak, you send a dozen stout fellows to
each side the gate. Keep them out of sight."

The captain of the Moldavians, Barnetski, bent over to look at
the priming of the two pieces, where black grains had been spilled
over the touch-holes. The holes were properly covered, and so he
made announcement to Vladimir, swinging the slow-match gently to
keep the glowing spark at the end of it bright. Like his master,
Barnetski believed in leaving nothing to chance.

Glancing back from where he stood between the two cannon, the
veteran captain observed that the arquebusiers had laid their heavy
firelocks in the pronged rests.

At either side the door Durak's men waited, some with their hands
on the wings of the gate that Vladimir had left open on purpose.

Shining dully in the moonlight, clad in bronzed armor even to
shoulder pieces, brassarts and crested morion, Barnetski looked like
some black Vulcan tending a tiny spark of light. But it was Vladimir
who first heard the thudding of hoofs down by the river.

"They come, Barnetski! Wait for my word to touch off the cannon."

His level voice, amused and eager, as if he were about to watch
some new antics of mountebanks or dwarfs grimacing to pleasure
him, carried to the pikemen by the gate.

"When the artillery has blasted them, close the gate, my fine fellows. If some few ride through alive so much the better. My iron
wolves will pull them down."

Sure of what would happen, having left no slightest alternative
to the whim of that fickle lady, Fortune, Vladimir narrowed his eyes
to stare down the strip of moonlight. By holding his fire he made
certain of havoc, knowing that the tribesmen would never ride to a
second attack, once the gate was shut. So he watched a dark blur of
horses race up the roadway until he could see flying manes and
the flicker of lance points. When he made out the white *svitka* of
Kirdy, the black bulk of Ayub and the gray head of Khlit within
stone's throw of the entrance, he laughed. The Cossacks were stand-

ing in their stirrups, whipping on their ponies, racing with death.

"Touch off both cannon, Barnetski. May the Lord have mercy on their souls!"

The captain lowered the point of flame in his hand to one breech, shifted it to the other and pressed it down in the priming. Then, shouting out an oath, he dropped on one knee, calling over his shoulder—

"Fire with the arquebuses!"

Both cannon had failed to go off.

Behind Barnetski the firelocks roared, covering everything with white, swirling smoke. But an instant before the volley every rider dropped in the saddle. Some, gripping the long manes of the ponies, swung down, crouched upon one stirrup. Some leaped to the ground and sprang into saddle again when smoke rolled over them. Others bent close to the necks of the racing horses.

Kirdy's horse was shot from under him, and he cleared the stirrups in time to run out of the way of the pack behind him, plunging among the arquebusiers who were drawing their rapiers. Ayub's leg was pierced by a ball and he lost his seat in the saddle, rolling to one side and limping to his feet.

"Down pikes!" roared Vladimir. "To me, Durak, you dog!"

Shaggy ponies were catapulting through the portal—only a pair of horses and riders had gone down at the hasty volley from the fire-locks—and the prince saw at once that the gates could not now be closed. The entrance was jammed with Tatars barking their war-cry: *ghar—ghar—ghar!*

Meanwhile the armored *boyars* and their henchmen were running up from all sides.

Khlit had slid from the saddle and had run beside his horse until he was past the cannon. Regaining his seat with a leap he reined off to one side and peered through the smoke. The moon was bright in a clear sky, and one of the wind-whipped towers was breaking into flames. The figures that darted and stumbled through the haze were easily to be seen.

The first Tatars, urged on by Ghirei Khan, had not checked their ponies, but were circling the enclosure around the blockhouse at full speed, brandishing their round shields and thrusting with their lances. So they made room for others to come after, and now seventy or more were wheeling and plunging in the enclosure.

Ranged in clusters, the *boyars* were hacking with their long, straight swords, trying to unite with other groups. The arquebusiers of Barnetski had been separated, knocked asunder by the rush of horses, and the Moldavian captain was down with a broken lance point under his chin. Ayub was nowhere to be seen and Khlit looked anxiously for Kirdy.

He saw the white *svitka* at once, on the far side of the scattered Moldavians. Kirdy had heard Vladimir's shout and made toward him as a hawk stoops. He had lost his hat, and ran bent low, his bare right arm swinging by his left hip—at the end of it a glittering arc of blue steel.

"Cut down the horses!" Vladimir's clear shout rose above the shouting and the clashing of blades. "We are the stronger."

A Muscovite with a pike stepped in front of Kirdy and the young warrior thrust up the man's weapon, drawing the edge of the curved sword under his ribs. The Muscovite lifted the pike as if for another blow, when his knees gave way and he fell on his back.

"Guard yourself, lord prince," Kirdy cried.

Although Vladimir turned eagerly, he was not permitted to cross swords with the young warrior. Durak had brought up the dozen remaining arquebusiers. Neither time nor space served for them to set up their clumsy matchlocks on the rests and their bullets went wild for the most part. Plucking out their rapiers, they advanced in a body toward the prince, coming between him and Kirdy who raged at them, his sword striking sparks from the massive armor that had been cast to turn bullets. And Durak's great ax swept up and down, slaying a dismounted Nogai and splitting open the chest of a rearing pony.

This did not escape the keen eye of Ghirei Khan who had been circling around the heart of the struggle.

"Take your lariats!" the chieftain called to his men. "Pull the iron warriors apart."

His words ended in a grunt, and the *zvuk* of a bullet striking into flesh. He barely swayed in the saddle, but one gnarled hand gripped the horn and he rested his scimitar across his knee. The Nogais swept before him, swinging their long ropes with running nooses at the end.

Then began a strange struggle, the Moldavians thrusting at the elusive tribesmen and the Nogais wheeling away from them. But the heavy iron plates, the gussets at the shoulders and the hip pieces slowed up the movements of the armored men, and first one, then another, was caught by a noose about the neck and jerked from the rank. As the Nogais whipped up their ponies, the arquebusiers were pulled from their feet and dragged, clattering about the wide enclosure until they strangled. Durak and those who escaped the flying nooses ran back to the blockhouse entrance, where the *boyars* had formed at last.

"Will you end your life on a rope, Vladimir?" laughed Kirdy.

"You will not see it!" cried the prince, springing forward. His scimitar grated against the curved saber and such was the power of his long arm that Kirdy gave ground at once.

The Tatars had suffered as severely as the Muscovites, pent in by the palisade, and there fell at this moment a quiet in the merciless conflict. The Muscovites who still kept their feet were backed against the blockhouse, the tribesmen circling about Ghirei Khan, swaying in his saddle.

Over their heads the flames were devouring the tower and burning brands fell thick among the warriors.

Khlit, sitting his horse apart from them, shaded his eyes against the glare of the fire and watched the sword duel, his muscular hands clasping and unclasping.

The two blades, now flashing silver in the moonlight, now gleaming red from reflected flames, coiled together—down and up. They parted and engaged again, and parted when Vladimir slashed wide and left himself open to a cut.

Kirdy darted in and his curved blade grated against the mail under the Muscovite's kaftan. Vladimir, who had foreseen this, hacked down, his arm only moving from the elbow—a swift cut, impossible to parry.

Nor had Kirdy the fraction of a second to leap back. Instead he dropped to his knees, the prince's scimitar flashing in front of his eyes. Then, when Vladimir recovered and thrust swiftly, the young warrior leaped up as a wolf springs back. The two blades struck and sparks flew.

The flames crackled above them, lighting up the pallid, smiling face of the noble, the wild countenance of the boy. Their boots thudding through the smoking ashes of a fire, they changed ground, and Vladimir mustered his strength to attack for the last time, being certain now that his skill was greater than the warrior's.

Kirdy gave ground, but he threw aside all caution as well. Sweat dripped into his eyes and instead of parrying, he slashed with all the strength of his arm in each cut. A groaning shout came from his tense throat—

"*Ou-haa—ou-haa!*"

Vladimir now sought to engage the blades and lock hilts; his breath whistled from his lungs, and his teeth gleamed between his lips. The whirlwind of steel was about his head and he stepped back to gain a second's respite. Again—and he tossed up his scimitar.

The boy's heavy blade whistled in the air and struck full against his side. The keen edge snapped the links of the iron mail and the watchers saw Vladimir drop to one knee when Kirdy jerked his sword free. A rush of blood stained the girdle of the prince, and Vladimir raised his head slowly.

"Better," he gasped, "than rope—or flames."

The curved saber had penetrated far under his heart and the color was already draining from his lips.

Dazed with weariness the young warrior stood before him, scarcely hearing the *ghar—ghar—ghar* of the tribesmen who were beginning to shoot arrows at the Muscovites. Nor did he hear Khlit's shout—

"Well done, little *bogatyr*—by —— that was well done."

Ayub, on one good leg, had hobbled steadily toward the stables, beating down with his broadsword any Muscovite who rushed at him, but never swerving from his course. More than once he fell, and he had been cut with a pike over one ear and down one arm before he reached the carts and began to haul himself around toward the horses of the Muscovites.

For some time he sought among the oxen and the ponies of the *boyars* before he saw the small, black head and loose mane of the Kabarda tossing restlessly.

It was almost dark in the stable and he edged his way toward his horse, stumbling over packs and harness, heedless of what went on outside. When he laid hand on the stallion's sleek flank at last he breathed a sigh of relief. Then he bellowed with anger.

On the other side of the horse a man was quietly putting on a saddle. Reaching for the cinch, he had not seen Ayub. The light was behind him, and the astonished Zaporoghian recognized the square shoulders and steel cap of Durak.

"Turtle-egg!" he shouted, fumbling for the hilt of his broadsword which he was dragging, sheathed, in his right hand to save his injured leg. "A dog fathered you, but now you disgrace your sire by horse stealing."

Durak reared up silently, and even in his blind rage Ayub remembered the great battle-ax. The Cossack leaned back and poised his massive sword as if it had been a javelin. Grunting he heaved it at Durak's head, putting all the strength of his ox-like shoulders into the cast. He heard the round silver ball of the pommel strike something with a dull thud.

Then he flung his arms over the stallion's back, praying that the ax of the Muscovite would not drop on the horse. The Kabarda, recognizing his master, did not kick out, but jerked its head, quivering with excitement.

For a moment Ayub held his breath, listening with all his ears. He heard only the muffled tumult outside, and judged that Durak lay where he had fallen, whether dead or nor he did not know.

Reaching under the horse he felt around in the straw until he grasped his scabbard with the sword in it. The silver ball on the hilt felt damp. Ayub strapped it on his back and satisfied himself that the snorting stallion had the bridle on, and the bit between his teeth.

"You little devilkin," he muttered when the bony muzzle smote his cheek. "Ghirei Khan won't change his mind about you now. I saw him swallow a bullet the wrong way. As for that turtle-egg, it wasn't a knightly blow I struck him, but the son of a dog laid me down with a log. Now we must go and have a look at the battle. I didn't see Khlit or that bit of forked lightning, Kirdy—"

Mounting from the wrong side, to the utter astonishment of the stallion, he pushed his wounded leg into the stirrup with a grimace and wheeled out of the stable.

His first glance was at the tower, up which the flames were roaring, and he shook his head when he beheld the bodies heaped about the gate. No Muscovites were visible, but the Tatars were trotting about the blockhouse, bows in hand, sending arrows into every aperture. Only a few pistols answered them. The *boyars* had taken refuge in the blockhouse and the tribesmen held the palisade and the outer ground.

"If they don't sally out, they'll be smoked like hams in the penthouse," Ayub thought, "and if they do, they'll be cut open like fish in a boat. *Hi*, the *ataman* has a sober head at last."

Khlit had reined his pony in front of the closed gate of the blockhouse, holding up his hand without a weapon in it.

"Ho, within there!" His deep shout was heard above the roar of the flames in the towers. "Lay down your arms and come out. Your game is played."

There was silence for a time, while no pistols barked, and the tribesmen held their arrows on the string.

"Who speaks?" demanded a voice from the log castle.

"A *koshevoi ataman* of the Cossacks."

Other voices began to argue. The Muscovites had lost their leader; Barnetski and Durak were gone. Flight was impossible, and they could not hold the flames in check for long.

"What terms?" asked the first voice, not so arrogantly.

"Fair ransom for the *boyars*—slavery for their slaves," responded Khlit briefly.

"At your hands?"

"Nay, the Tatars."

"But you are taking the villagers safe across the frontier."

"No fault of yours. Open the door or that gold will be lost, and the Tatars will give you only their sword edges."

Almost at once the door was pulled back and some forty men including a half-dozen nobles walked out, weaponless, many of them trying to bind up their wounds. When the last was out, the Nogais ran into the castle, seeking the bed of the prince and the chests that stood beside it.

Ayub trotted over to where Kirdy was kneeling by the dying lord of the Muscovites. Vladimir, propped up on one elbow, was trying to speak to the little priest who was shivering, his cope wrapped close about him.

"*Batko*," the hoarse voice of the prince forced out the words by an effort of will, "do not forget—the fifty-three souls to be prayed for. My estates—money will be given—and for the others, slain back there. For the *boyars* whose wife—ah, *batko* pray that God's mercy be not denied me. I sinned in leading my men here—stood by when the

Tatars came the first time. They came back—the scourge of God."

In spite of himself, looking into the haggard gray eyes, Ayub was moved.

"Faith, 'tis a sad thing to have a black spirit like that. Fall to your work, priest! Nay, Kirdy, don't sigh—you'll get used to things like this. Give him a sip of brandy and make the sign of the cross over him. If he lived like a devil, at least he turned up his toes like a man."

And the boy, rising from his knees, took the curved saber still stained with blood and swept it down and across the dying Muscovite.

By now the Tatars who had been guarding the captive villagers had hurried up, eager to take part in the pillaging, bringing with them Kukubenko and his people. The tavern keeper, standing outside the gate with pale Galka beside him, stared dully at the flames devouring the castle. The events of the last hours were past his understanding, but his daughter was more quick-witted. She watched the Tatars herding the Muscovites down toward the river, and stripping the bodies of armor and weapons. When she saw Ghirei Khan carried by, in a horse litter escorted by a dozen tribesmen, she knew that the Tatars were leaving and that the villagers had been exchanged for the Muscovites.

She tripped up to Ayub, caught his hand and pressed her fresh lips against it.

"Zaporoghian, our hearts thank you. May the Father and Son bless you for this night's work!"

"Well, it was a small affair," responded Ayub, pleased. "You could hardly call it a battle, lass. Still, it was warm for us, for a moment."

He glanced at the spear points of the retreating Tatars, and was silent until they reached the river.

"I thought the Nogais would rub us out after everything was over. Then you'd have been no better off than before. But Ghirei Khan had a bullet in his throat—can't speak for a while—and Khlit, the *ataman* yonder, had got over his drinking bout. He ordered them around in their own language, and when they looked at him they thought his eye was like a basilisk. So they kept their word and went off like lambs."

Only half understanding this, Galka smiled. She was scarcely a woman grown but she knew that she could persuade big Ayub to do what she wanted.

"And now, Zaporoghian, out of your kindness you will take us back to the border where we can find Christians?"

"Aye, why not? This is no place for the likes of you. But first you'll have to bury your former masters. Can't leave them lying around like this."

"The men will see to it, noble knight. I'll tell Kukubenko at once, and he will get the priest. Indeed, you think of everything and I am sure that you are the finest *bogatyr* of all the Zaporoghians."

Ayub stroked up his mustaches and glanced down at the slip of a girl feelingly, but he saw that she was watching Kirdy who sat on a log, his head in his hands, the curved sword still across his knees.

"Nay," he said honestly, "there's the *bogatyr*. At least he'll be one if he keeps on like this. He won't look at you now, lass, because the fever of sword-strokes is still in his veins and his knightly spirit is intent on Cossack glory. Tomorrow he'll strike up with the *bandura* and have you dance."

He stroked her head while the gray eyes looked up at him inscrutably, glowing with the thoughts that come to the young, and the veteran warrior could not read the message in them. Besides, his throat was dry and he had been hunting high and low for *gorilka* to drink.

Abandoning Galka, he continued his search until he halted by the two cannon in the entrance of the palisade. Sniffing strongly he peered to right and left and finally bent over the breech of one of the brass guns.

Thrusting an exploring finger into the tiny heap of powder over the touch-hole, he held it up to the light, then put it to his tongue. Without doubt the priming smelled strongly of corn brandy, and he wondered why. Picking up a blazing stick that had blown from one of the towers he laid it on the breech of the other cannon, to the consternation of the villagers who were in the gate.

"It's quite true," he muttered, "that the priming has been dampened and the guns won't go off."

Waxing curious, he called Kirdy over and explained what he had discovered. The young warrior considered a moment with bent head, and uttered an exclamation.

"When we came to the gate to arrange the ransom with Vladimir, Khlit drank deep from the *gorilka* cask. When all eyes were on the maiden Galka and the torch burned low I saw my grandfather stoop over each cannon. It is in my mind that he was not drunk at that time."

Ayub would have spoken, but then he sighted Khlit approaching. The old *ataman* swaggered in his walk, the silver heels of his boots striking the earth powerfully.

"Hey, Zaporoghian," he cried, "I am too feeble to ride with the brotherhood again. I will not gird on the sword. But I have brought you an *ouchár*—a fledgling grandson who will lead men and whose name will yet be a terror among the Tatars and the Turks. This night he faced Ghirei Khan boldly and cut down the Muscovite prince. Without aid from us he made a good plan."

"The sir brothers will bid him welcome," assented Ayub earnestly. "But when you say he did it without aid you lie, old dog. Was it not you who spat on the breeches of the Muscovite guns? The angels themselves must have put a turnip on Barnetski's face instead of a nose, that he did not smell the corn brandy when he examined the priming."

Khlit looked at him gravely from under shaggy brows.

"Not corn brandy," he growled. "In my day we had corn brandy. If you poured it on the breech of a cannon and put a match to it the powder would go off like mad. More than one cannon did we burst that way."

Ayub put both hands on his massive sides, and bowed to the girdle.

"Prince of liars and father of battles, I bid you welcome. Nay, you are Khlit."